SHARPE'S TRIUMPH

Bernard Cornwell was born in London, raised in Essex and now lives in the USA. In addition to the Sharpe series, he is the author of the Arthurian series, the Warlord Chronicles; the Starbuck Chronicles on the American Civil War; *Stonehenge*; *Gallows Thief*; the Grail Quest series; and his new series, set during the reign of King Alfred.

For more information about Bernard Cornwell and his books, please visit his official website: www.bernardcornwell.net.

To receive exclusive updates about Bernard Cornwell, visit: www.AuthorTracker.co.uk.

D1331695

BERNARD CORNWELL

Sharpe's Triumph

Richard Sharpe and
the Battle of Assaye,
September 1803

HARPER

This edition produced for The Book People Ltd,
Hall Wood Avenue, Haydock, St Helens. WA11 9UL

Harper
An imprint of HarperCollins*Publishers*
77–85 Fulham Palace Road,
Hammersmith, London w6 8jb

www.harpercollins.co.uk

This paperback edition 2007
1

First published in Great Britain by
HarperCollins*Publishers* 1998

A catalogue record for this book
is available from the British Library

ISBN 978-0-00-787070-7

Map by Ken Lewis

Set in Postscript Monotype Baskerville by
Rowland Phototypesetting Ltd,
Bury St Edmunds, Suffolk

Printed and bound in Great Britain by
Clays Ltd, St Ives plc

Sharpe's Triumph is for
Joel Gardner,
who walked Ahmednuggur
and Assaye with me

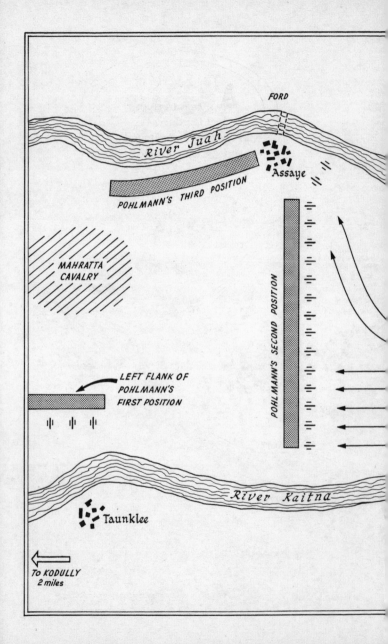

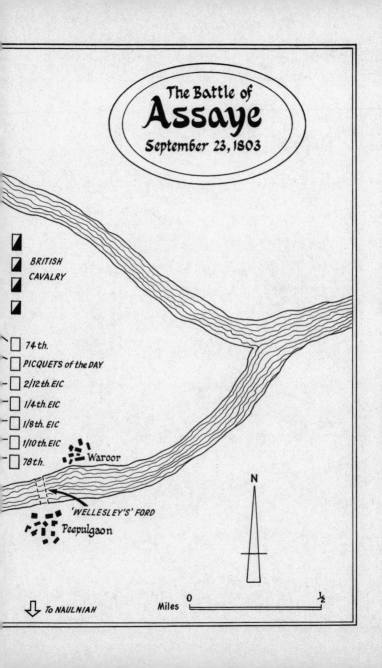

The Battle of
Assaye
September 23, 1803

BRITISH
CAVALRY

74th.
PICQUETS of the DAY
2/12th. EIC
1/4th. EIC
1/8th. EIC
1/10th. EIC
78th.

Waroor

'WELLESLEY'S' FORD

Peepulgaon

N

To NAULNIAH

Miles   0   ½

CHAPTER 1

It was not Sergeant Richard Sharpe's fault. He was not in charge. He was junior to at least a dozen men, including a major, a captain, a subadar and two jemadars, yet he still felt responsible. He felt responsible, angry, hot, bitter and scared. Blood crusted on his face where a thousand flies crawled. There were even flies in his open mouth.

But he dared not move.

The humid air stank of blood and of the rotted egg smell made by powder smoke. The very last thing he remembered doing was thrusting his pack, haversack and cartridge box into the glowing ashes of a fire, and now the ammunition from the cartridge box exploded. Each blast of powder fountained sparks and ashes into the hot air. A couple of men laughed at the sight. They stopped to watch it for a few seconds, poked at the nearby bodies with their muskets, then walked on.

Sharpe lay still. A fly crawled on his eyeball and he forced himself to stay absolutely motionless. There was blood on his face and more blood had puddled in his right ear, though it was drying now. He blinked, fearing that the small motion would attract one of the killers, but no one noticed.

Chasalgaon. That's where he was. Chasalgaon: a miserable, thorn-walled fort on the frontier of Hyderabad, and because the Rajah of Hyderabad was a British ally the fort had been garrisoned by a hundred sepoys of the East India

9

Company and fifty mercenary horsemen from Mysore, only when Sharpe arrived half the sepoys and all of the horsemen had been out on patrol.

Sharpe had come from Seringapatam, leading a detail of six privates and carrying a leather bag stuffed with rupees, and he had been greeted by Major Crosby who commanded at Chasalgaon. The Major proved to be a plump, red-faced, bilious man who disliked the heat and hated Chasalgaon, and he had slumped in his canvas chair as he unfolded Sharpe's orders. He read them, grunted, then read them again. 'Why the hell did they send you?' he finally asked.

'No one else to send, sir.'

Crosby frowned at the order. 'Why not an officer?'

'No officers to spare, sir.'

'Bloody responsible job for a sergeant, wouldn't you say?'

'Won't let you down, sir,' Sharpe said woodenly, staring at the leprous yellow of the tent's canvas a few inches above the Major's head.

'You'd bloody well better not let me down,' Crosby said, pushing the orders into a pile of damp papers on his camp table. 'And you look bloody young to be a sergeant.'

'I was born late, sir,' Sharpe said. He was twenty-six, or thought he was, and most sergeants were much older.

Crosby, suspecting he was being mocked, stared up at Sharpe, but there was nothing insolent on the Sergeant's face. A good-looking man, Crosby thought sourly. Probably had the *bibbis* of Seringapatam falling out of their saris, and Crosby, whose wife had died of the fever ten years before and who consoled himself with a two-rupee village whore every Thursday night, felt a pang of jealousy. 'And how the devil do you expect to get the ammunition back to Seringapatam?' he demanded.

'Hire ox carts, sir.' Sharpe had long perfected the way to address unhelpful officers. He gave them precise answers, added nothing unnecessary and always sounded confident.

'With what? Promises?'

'Money, sir.' Sharpe tapped his haversack where he had the bag of rupees.

'Christ, they trust you with money?'

Sharpe decided not to respond to that question, but just stared impassively at the canvas. Chasalgaon, he decided, was not a happy place. It was a small fort built on a bluff above a river that should have been overflowing its banks, but the monsoon had failed and the land was cruelly dry. The fort had no ditch, merely a wall made of cactus thorn with a dozen wooden fighting platforms spaced about its perimeter. Inside the wall was a beaten-earth parade ground where a stripped tree served as a flagpole, and the parade ground was surrounded by three mud-walled barracks thatched with palm, a cookhouse, tents for the officers and a stone-walled magazine to store the garrison's ammunition. The sepoys had their families with them, so the fort was overrun with women and children, but Sharpe had noted how sullen they were. Crosby, he thought, was one of those crabbed officers who were only happy when all about them were miserable.

'I suppose you expect me to arrange the ox carts?' Crosby said indignantly.

'I'll do it myself, sir.'

'Speak the language, do you?' Crosby sneered. 'A sergeant, banker and interpreter, are you?'

'Brought an interpreter with me, sir,' Sharpe said. Which was over-egging the pudding a bit, because Davi Lal was only thirteen, an urchin off the streets of Seringapatam. He was a smart, mischievous child whom Sharpe had found stealing from the armoury cookhouse and, after giving the starving boy a clout around both ears to teach him respect for His Britannic Majesty's property, Sharpe had taken him to Lali's house and given him a proper meal, and Lali had talked to the boy and learned that his parents were dead, that he had no relatives he knew of, and that he lived by his wits. He was also covered in lice. 'Get rid of him,' she had advised Sharpe, but Sharpe had seen something of his own childhood in Davi Lal and so he had dragged him down to the River Cauvery and given him a decent scrubbing. After that Davi Lal had become Sharpe's errand boy. He learned to pipeclay belts, blackball boots and speak his own version of English which, because it came from the lower ranks, was liable to shock the gentler born.

'You'll need three carts,' Crosby said.

'Yes, sir,' Sharpe said. 'Thank you, sir.' He had known exactly how many carts he would need, but he also knew it was stupid to pretend to knowledge in the face of officers like Crosby.

'Find your damn carts,' Crosby snapped, 'then let me know when you're ready to load up.'

'Very good, sir. Thank you, sir.' Sharpe stiffened to attention, about-turned and marched from the tent to find Davi Lal and the six privates waiting in the shade of one of the barracks. 'We'll have dinner,' Sharpe told them, 'then sort out some carts this afternoon.'

'What's for dinner?' Private Atkins asked.

'Whatever Davi can filch from the cookhouse,' Sharpe said, 'but be nippy about it, all right? I want to be out of this damn place tomorrow morning.'

Their job was to fetch eighty thousand rounds of prime musket cartridges that had been stolen from the East India Company armoury in Madras. The cartridges were the best quality in India, and the thieves who stole them knew exactly who would pay the highest price for the ammunition. The princedoms of the Mahratta Confederation were forever at war with each other or else raiding the neighbouring states, but now, in the summer of 1803, they faced an imminent invasion by British forces. The threatened invasion had brought two of the biggest Mahratta rulers into an alliance that now gathered its forces to repel the British, and those rulers had promised the thieves a king's ransom in gold for the cartridges, but one of the thieves who had helped break into the Madras armoury had refused to let his brother join the band and share in the profit, and so the aggrieved brother had betrayed the thieves to the Company's spies and, two weeks later, the caravan carrying the cartridges across India had been ambushed by sepoys not far from Chasalgaon. The thieves had died or fled, and the recaptured ammunition had been brought back to the fort's small magazine for safekeeping. Now the eighty thousand cartridges were to be taken to the armoury at Seringapatam, three days to the south, from where they would be issued to the British troops who were readying themselves for the war against the Mahrattas. A simple job, and Sharpe, who had spent the last four years as a sergeant in the Seringapatam armoury, had been given the responsibility.

Spoilage, Sharpe was thinking while his men boiled a cauldron of river water on a bullock-dung fire. That was the key to the next few days, spoilage. Say seven thousand cartridges lost to damp? No one in Seringapatam would argue with that, and Sharpe reckoned he could sell the seven thousand cartridges on to Vakil Hussein, so long, of course, as there were eighty thousand cartridges to begin with. Still, Major Crosby had not quibbled with the figure, but just as Sharpe was thinking that, so Major Crosby appeared from his tent with a cocked hat on his head and a sword at his side. 'On your feet!' Sharpe snapped at his lads as the Major headed towards them.

'Thought you were finding ox carts?' Crosby snarled at Sharpe.

'Dinner first, sir.'

'Your food, I hope, and not ours? We don't get rations to feed King's troops here, Sergeant.' Major Crosby was in the service of the East India Company and, though he wore a red coat like the King's army, there was little love lost between the two forces.

'Our food, sir,' Sharpe said, gesturing at the cauldron in which rice and kid meat, both stolen from Crosby's stores, boiled. 'Carried it with us, sir.'

A havildar shouted from the fort gate, demanding Crosby's attention, but the Major ignored the shout. 'I forgot to mention one thing, Sergeant.'

'Sir?'

Crosby looked sheepish for a moment, then remembered he was talking to a mere sergeant. 'Some of the cartridges were spoiled. Damp got to them.'

'I'm sorry to hear that, sir,' Sharpe said straight-faced.

'So I had to destroy them,' Crosby said. 'Six or seven thousand as I remember.'

'Spoilage, sir,' Sharpe said. 'Happens all the time, sir.'

'Exactly so,' Crosby said, unable to hide his relief at Sharpe's easy acceptance of his tale, 'exactly so,' then he turned towards the gate. 'Havildar?'

'Company troops approaching, sahib!'

'Where's Captain Leonard? Isn't he officer of the day?' Crosby demanded.

'Here, sir, I'm here.' A tall, gangling captain hurried from a tent, tripped on a guy rope, recovered his hat, then headed for the gate.

Sharpe ran to catch up with Crosby who was also walking towards the gate. 'You'll give me a note, sir?'

'A note? Why the devil should I give you a note?'

'Spoilage, sir,' Sharpe said respectfully. 'I'll have to account for the cartridges, sir.'

'Later,' Crosby said, 'later.'

'Yes, sir,' Sharpe said. 'And sod you backwards, you miserable bastard,' he added, though too softly for Crosby to hear.

Captain Leonard clambered up to the platform beside the gate where Crosby joined him. The Major took a telescope from his tail pocket and slid the tubes open. The platform overlooked the small river that should have been swollen by the seasonal rains into a flood, but the failure of the monsoon had left only a trickle of water between the flat grey rocks. Beyond the shrunken river, up on the skyline behind a grove of trees, Crosby could see red-coated troops led by a European officer mounted on a black horse, and his first thought was that it must be Captain Roberts returning from patrol, but Roberts had a piebald horse and, besides, he had only taken fifty sepoys whereas this horseman led a company almost twice that size. 'Open the gate,' Crosby ordered, and wondered who the devil it was. He decided it was probably Captain Sullivan from the Company's post at Milladar, another frontier fort like Chasalgaon, but what the hell was Sullivan doing here? Maybe he was marching some new recruits to toughen the bastards, not that the skinny little brutes needed any toughening, but it was uncivil of Sullivan not to warn Crosby of his coming. 'Jemadar,' Crosby shouted, 'turn out the guard!'

'Sahib!' The Jemadar acknowledged the order. Other sepoys were dragging the thorn gates open.

He'll want dinner, Crosby thought sourly, and wondered what his servants were cooking for the midday meal. Kid, probably, in boiled rice. Well, Sullivan would just have to endure the stringy meat as a price for not sending any warning, and damn the man if he expected Crosby to feed his sepoys as well. Chasalgaon's cooks had not expected visitors and would not have enough rations for a hundred more hungry sepoys. 'Is that Sullivan?' he asked Leonard, handing the Captain the telescope.

Leonard stared for a long time at the approaching horseman. 'I've never met Sullivan,' he finally said, 'so I couldn't say.'

Crosby snatched back the telescope. 'Give the bastard a salute when he arrives,' Crosby ordered Leonard, 'then tell him he can join me for dinner.' He paused. 'You too,' he added grudgingly.

Crosby went back to his tent. It was better, he decided, to let Leonard welcome the stranger, rather than look too eager himself. Damn Sullivan, he thought, for not sending warning, though there was a bright side, inasmuch as Sullivan might have brought news. The tall, good-looking Sergeant from Seringapatam doubtless could have told Crosby the latest rumours from Mysore, but it would be a chill day in hell before Crosby sought news from a sergeant. But undoubtedly something was changing in the wider world, for it had been nine weeks since Crosby last saw a Mahratta raider, and that was decidedly odd. The purpose of the fort at Chasalgaon was to keep the Mahratta horse raiders out of the Rajah of Hyderabad's wealthy territory, and Crosby fancied he had done his job well, but even so he found the absence of any enemy marauders oddly worrying. What were the bastards up to? He sat behind his table and shouted for his clerk. He would write the damned armoury Sergeant a note explaining that the loss of seven thousand cartridges was due to a leak in the stone roof of Chasalgaon's magazine. He certainly could not admit that he had sold the ammunition to a merchant.

'What the bastard did,' Sharpe was saying to his men, 'was sell the bloody stuff to some heathen bastard.'

'That's what you were going to do, Sergeant,' Private Phillips said.

'Never you bleeding mind what I was going to do,' Sharpe said. 'Ain't that food ready?'

'Five minutes,' Davi Lal promised.

'A bloody camel could do it faster,' Sharpe grumbled, then hoisted his pack and haversack. 'I'm going for a piss.'

'He never goes anywhere without his bleeding pack,' Atkins commented.

'Doesn't want you thieving his spare shirt,' Phillips answered.

'He's got more than a shirt in that pack. Hiding something he is.' Atkins twisted round. 'Hey, Hedgehog!' They all called Davi Lal 'Hedgehog' because his hair stuck up in spikes; no matter how greasy it was or how short it was cut, it still stuck up in unruly spikes. 'What does Sharpie keep in the pack?'

Davi Lal rolled his eyes. 'Jewels! Gold. Rubies, diamonds, emeralds, sapphires and pearls.'

'Like sod he does.'

Davi Lal laughed, then turned back to the cauldron. Out by the fort's gate Captain Leonard was greeting the visitors. The guard presented arms as the officer leading the sepoys rode through the gate. The visitor returned the salute by touching a riding crop to the brim of his cocked hat which, worn fore and aft, shadowed his face. He was a tall man, uncommonly tall, and he wore his stirrups long so that he looked much too big for his horse, which was a sorry, sway-backed beast with a mangy hide, though there was nothing odd in that. Good horses were a luxury in India, and most Company officers rode decrepit nags. 'Welcome to Chasal-gaon, sir,' Leonard said. He was not certain he ought to call the stranger 'sir', for the man wore no visible badge of rank on his red coat, but he carried himself like a senior officer and he reacted to Leonard's greeting with a lordly nonchalance. 'You're invited to dine with us, sir,' Leonard added, hurrying after the horseman who, having tucked his riding crop under his belt, now led his sepoys straight onto the parade ground. He stopped his horse under the flagpole from which the

British flag drooped in the windless air, then waited as his company of red-coated sepoys divided into two units of two ranks each that marched either side of the flagpole. Crosby watched from inside his tent. It was a flamboyant entrance, the Major decided.

'Halt!' the strange officer shouted when his company was in the very centre of the fort. The sepoys halted. 'Outwards turn! Ground firelocks! Good morning!' He at last looked down at Captain Leonard. 'Are you Crosby?'

'No, sir. I'm Captain Leonard, sir. And you, sir?' The tall man ignored the question. He scowled about Chasalgaon's fort as though he disapproved of everything he saw. What the hell was this? Leonard wondered. A surprise inspection? 'Shall I have your horse watered, sir?' Leonard offered.

'In good time, Captain, all in good time,' the mysterious officer said, then he twisted in his saddle and growled an order to his company. 'Fix bayonets!' The sepoys pulled out their seventeen-inch blades and slotted them onto the muzzles of their muskets. 'I like to offer a proper salute to a fellow Englishman,' the tall man explained to Leonard. 'You are English, aren't you?'

'Yes, sir.'

'Too many damned Scots in the Company,' the tall man grumbled. 'Have you ever noticed that, Leonard? Too many Scots and Irish. Glib sorts of fellow, they are, but they ain't English. Not English at all.' The visitor drew his sword, then took a deep breath. 'Company!' he shouted. 'Level arms!'

The sepoys brought their muskets to their shoulders and Leonard saw, much too late, that the guns were aimed at the troops of the garrison. 'No!' he said, but not loudly, for he still did not believe what he saw.

'Fire!' the officer shouted, and the parade ground air was murdered by the double ripple of musket shots, heavy coughing explosions that blossomed smoke across the sun-crazed mud and slammed lead balls into the unsuspecting garrison.

'Hunt them now!' the tall officer called. 'Hunt them! Fast, fast, fast!' He spurred his horse close to Captain Leonard and, almost casually, slashed down with his sword, ripping the blade hard back once it had bitten into the Captain's neck so that its edge sawed fast and deep through the sinew, muscle and flesh. 'Hunt them! Hunt them!' the officer shouted as Leonard fell. He drew a pistol from his saddle holster and rode towards the officers' tents. His men were screaming their war cries as they spread through the small fort to chase down every last sepoy of Chasalgaon's garrison. They had been ordered to leave the women and children to the last and hunt down the men first.

Crosby had been staring in horror and disbelief, and now, with shaking hands, he started to load one of his pistols, but suddenly the door of his tent darkened and he saw that the tall officer had dismounted from his horse. 'Are you Crosby?' the officer demanded.

Crosby found he could not speak. His hands quivered. Sweat was pouring down his face.

'Are you Crosby?' the man asked again in an irritated voice.

'Yes,' Crosby managed to say. 'And who the devil are you?'

'Dodd,' the tall man said, 'Major William Dodd, at your service.' And Dodd raised his big pistol so that it pointed at Crosby's face.

'No!' Crosby shouted.

Dodd smiled. 'I assume you're surrendering the fort to me, Crosby?'

'Damn you,' Crosby riposted feebly.

'You drink too much, Major,' Dodd said. 'The whole Company knows you're a sot. Didn't put up much of a fight, did you?' He pulled the trigger and Crosby's head was snatched back in a mist of blood that spattered onto the canvas. 'Pity you're English,' Dodd said. 'I'd much rather shoot a Scotsman.' The dying Major made a terrible gurgling sound, then his body jerked uncontrollably and was finally still. 'Praise the Lord, pull down the flag and find the pay chest,' Dodd said to himself, then he stepped over the Major's corpse to see that the pay chest was where he expected it to be, under the bed. 'Subadar!'

'Sahib?'

'Two men here to guard the pay chest.'

'Sahib!'

Major Dodd hurried back onto the parade ground where a small group of redcoats, British redcoats, were offering defiance, and he wanted to make sure that his sepoys took care of them, but a havildar had anticipated Dodd's orders and was leading a squad of men against the half-dozen soldiers. 'Put the blades in!' Dodd encouraged them. 'Hard in! Twist them in! That's the way! Watch your left! Left!' His voice was urgent, for a tall sergeant had suddenly appeared from behind the cookhouse, a white man with a musket and bayonet in his hands, but one of the sepoys still had a loaded musket of his own and he twisted, aimed and fired and Dodd saw another mist of bright blood sparkle in the sunlight. The sergeant had been hit in the head. He stopped, looked surprised as the musket fell from his hands and as blood streamed down his face, then he fell backwards and was still.

'Search for the rest of the bastards!' Dodd ordered, knowing that there must still be a score of the garrison hidden in the barracks. Some of the men had escaped over the thorn wall, but they would be hunted down by the Mahratta horsemen who were Dodd's allies and who should by now have spread either side of the fort. 'Search hard!' He himself went to look at the horses of the garrison's officers and decided that one of them was marginally better than his own. He moved his saddle to the better horse, then led it into the sunlight and picketed it to the flagpole. A woman ran past him, screaming as she fled from the red-coated killers, but a sepoy caught and tripped her and another pulled the sari off her shoulder. Dodd was about to order them away from the woman, then he reckoned that the enemy was well beaten and so his men could take their pleasure in safety. 'Subadar?' he shouted.

'Sahib?'

'One squad to make sure everyone's dead. Another to open the armoury. And there are a couple of horses in the stable. Pick one for yourself, and we'll take the other back to Pohlmann. And well done, Gopal.'

'Thank you, sahib,' Subadar Gopal said.

Dodd wiped the blood from his sword, then reloaded his pistol. One of the fallen redcoats was trying to turn himself over, so Dodd crossed to the wounded man, watched his feeble efforts for a moment, then put a bullet into the man's head. The man jerked in spasm, then was still. Major Dodd scowled at the blood that had sprayed his boots, but he spat, stooped and wiped the blood away. Sharpe watched the tall officer from the corner of his eye. He felt responsible, angry, hot, bitter and scared. The blood had poured from the wound in his scalp. He was dizzy, his head throbbed, but he was alive. There were flies in his mouth. And then his ammunition began to explode and the tall officer whipped round, thinking it was trouble, and a couple of men laughed at the sight of the ashes bursting into the air with each small crack of powder.

Sharpe dared not move. He listened to women screaming and children crying, then heard hooves and he waited until some horsemen came into view. They were Indians, of course, and all wild-looking men with sabres, matchlocks, spears, lances and even bows and arrows. They slid out of their saddles and joined the hunt for loot.

Sharpe lay like the dead. The crusting blood was thick on

his face. The blow of the musket ball had stunned him, so that he did not remember dropping his own musket or falling to the ground, but he sensed that the blow was not deadly. Not even deep. He had a headache, and the skin of his face felt taut with the crusted blood, but he knew head wounds always bled profusely. He tried to make his breathing shallow, left his mouth open and did not even gag when a fly crawled down to the root of his tongue, and then he could smell tobacco, arrack, leather and sweat and a horseman was bending over him with a horrid-looking curved knife with a rusty blade and Sharpe feared his throat was about to be cut, but instead the horseman began slashing at the pockets of Sharpe's uniform. He found the big key that opened Seringapatam's main magazine, a key that Sharpe had ordered cut in the bazaar so that he would not always have to fill in the form in the armoury guardhouse. The man tossed the key away, slit another pocket, found nothing valuable and so moved on to another body. Sharpe stared up at the sun.

Somewhere nearby a garrison sepoy groaned, and almost immediately he was bayoneted and Sharpe heard the hoarse exhalation of breath as the man died and the sucking sound as the murderer dragged the blade back from the constricting flesh. It had all happened so fast! And Sharpe blamed himself, though he knew it was not his fault. He had not let the killers into the fort, but he had hesitated for a few seconds to throw his pack, pouches and cartridge box onto the fire, and now he chided himself because maybe he could have used those few seconds to save his six men. Except most of them had already been dead or dying when Sharpe had first realized there was a fight. He had been pissing against the back wall of the cookhouse store hut when a musket ball ripped through the reed-mat wall and for a second or two he had just stood there, incredulous, hardly believing the shots and screams his ears registered, and he had not bothered to button his trousers, but just turned and saw the dying campfire and had thrown his pack onto it, and by the time he had cocked the musket and run back to where his men had been expecting dinner the fight was almost over. The musket ball had jerked his head back and there had been a stabbing pain either side of his eyes, and the next he knew he was lying with blood crusting on his face and flies crawling down his gullet.

But maybe he could have snatched his men back. He tortured himself with the thought that he could have saved Davi Lal and a couple of the privates, maybe he could have crossed the cactus-thorn wall and run into the trees, but Davi Lal was dead and all six privates were dead and Sharpe could hear the killers laughing as they carried the ammunition out of the small magazine.

'Subadar!' the tall officer shouted. 'Fetch that bloody flag down! I wanted it done an hour ago!'

Sharpe blinked again because he could not help himself, but no one noticed, and then he closed his eyes because the sun was blinding him, and he wanted to weep out of anger and frustration and hatred. Six men dead, and Davi Lal dead, and Sharpe had not been able to do a damned thing to help them, and he wondered who the tall officer was, and then a voice provided the answer.

'Major Dodd, sahib?'

'Subadar?'

'Everything's loaded, sahib.'

'Then let's go before their patrols get back. Well done, Subadar! Tell the men there'll be a reward.'

Sharpe listened as the raiders left the fort. Who the hell were they? Major Dodd had been in East India Company uniform, and so had all his men for that matter, but they sure as hell were not Company troops. They were bastards, that's what they were, bastards from hell and they had done a thorough piece of wicked work in Chasalgaon. Sharpe doubted they had lost a single man in their treacherous attack, and still he lay silent as the sounds faded away. A baby cried somewhere, a woman sobbed, and still Sharpe waited until at last he was certain that Major Dodd and his men were gone, and only then did Sharpe roll onto his side. The fort stank of blood and buzzed with flies. He groaned and got to his knees. The cauldron of rice and kid had boiled dry and so he stood and kicked it off its tripod. 'Bastards,' he said, and he saw the surprised look on Davi Lal's face and he wanted to weep for the boy.

A half-naked woman, bleeding from the mouth, saw Sharpe stand from among the bloodied heap of the dead and she screamed before snatching her child back into a barracks hut. Sharpe ignored her. His musket was gone. Every damn weapon was gone. 'Bastards!' he shouted into the hot air, then he kicked at a dog that was sniffing at Phillips's corpse. The smell of blood and powder and burned rice was thick in his throat. He gagged as he walked into the cookhouse and there found a jar of water. He drank deep, then splashed the water onto his face and rubbed away the clotted blood. He wet a rag and flinched as he cleaned the shallow wound in his scalp, then suddenly he was overcome with horror and pity and he fell onto his knees and half sobbed. He swore instead. 'Bastards!' He said the word again and again, helplessly and furiously, then he remembered his pack and so he stood again and went into the sunlight.

The ashes of the fire were still hot and the charred canvas remnants of his pack and pouches glowed red as he found a stick and raked through the embers. One by one he found what he had hidden in the fire. The rupees that had been for hiring the carts, then the rubies and emeralds, diamonds and pearls, sapphires and gold. He fetched a sack of rice from the cookhouse and he emptied the grains onto the ground and filled the sack with his treasure. A king's ransom, it was, and it had been taken from a king four years before in the Water Gate at Seringapatam where Sharpe had trapped the Tippoo Sultan and shot him down before looting his corpse.

Then, with the treasure clutched to his midriff, he knelt in the stench of Chasalgaon and felt guilty. He had survived a massacre. Anger mingled with his guilt, then he knew he had duties to do. He must find any others who had survived, he must help them, and he must work out how he could take his revenge.

On a man called Dodd.

Major John Stokes was an engineer, and if ever a man was happy with his avocation, it was Major John Stokes. There was nothing he enjoyed so much as making things, whether it was a better gun carriage, a garden or, as he was doing now, improvements to a clock that belonged to the Rajah of Mysore. The Rajah was a young man, scarcely more than a boy indeed, and he owed his throne to the British troops who had ejected the usurping Tippoo Sultan and, as a result, relations between the palace and Seringapatam's small British garrison were good. Major Stokes had found the clock in one of the palace's antechambers and noted its appalling accuracy, which is why he had brought it back to the armoury where he was happily taking it apart. 'It isn't signed,' he told his visitor, 'and I suspect it's local work. But a Frenchman had his hand in it, I can tell that. See the escapement? Typical French work, that.'

The visitor peered at the tangle of cogwheels. 'Didn't know the Frogs had it in them to make clocks, sir,' he said.

'Oh, indeed they do!' Stokes said reprovingly. 'And very fine clocks they make! Very fine. Think of Lépine! Think of Berthoud! How can you ignore Montandon? And Breguet!' The Major shook his head in mute tribute to such great craftsmen, then peered at the Rajah's sorry timepiece. 'Some rust on the mainspring, I see. That don't help. Soft metal, I suspect. It's catch as catch can over here. I've noticed that. Marvellous decorative work, but Indians make shoddy mechanics. Look at that mainspring! A disgrace.'

'Shocking, sir, shocking.' Sergeant Obadiah Hakeswill did not know a mainspring from a pendulum, and could not have cared less about either, but he needed information from Major Stokes so it was politic to show an interest.

'It was striking nine when it should have struck eight,' the Major said, poking a finger into the clock's entrails, 'or perhaps it was striking eight when it ought to have sounded nine. I don't recall. One to seven it copes with admirably, but somewhere about eight it becomes wayward.' The Major, who was in charge of Seringapatam's armoury, was a plump, cheerful fellow with prematurely white hair. 'Do you understand clocks, Sergeant?'

'Can't say as I does, sir. A simple soldier, me, sir, who has the sun as his clock.' The Sergeant's face twitched horribly. It was an uncontrollable spasm that racked his face every few seconds.

'You were asking about Sharpe,' Major Stokes said, peering into the clock. 'Well, I never! This fellow has made the bearings out of wood! Good Lord above. Wood! No wonder she's wayward! Harrison once made a wooden clock, did you know? Even the gearings! All from timber.'

'Harrison, sir? Is he in the army, sir?'

'He's a clockmaker, Sergeant, a clockmaker. A very fine clockmaker too.'

'Not a Frog, sir?'

'With a name like Harrison? Good Lord, no! He's English, and he makes a good honest clock.'

'Glad to hear it, sir,' Hakeswill said, then reminded the Major of the purpose of his visit to the armoury. 'Sergeant Sharpe, sir, my good friend, sir, is he here?'

'He is here,' Stokes said, at last looking up from the clock, 'or rather he was here. I saw him an hour ago. But he went to his quarters. He's been away, you see. Involved in that dreadful business in Chasalgaon.'

'Chiseldown, sir?'

'Terrible business, terrible! So I told Sharpe to clean himself up. Poor fellow was covered in blood! Looked like a pirate. Now that is interesting.'

'Blood, sir?' Hakeswill asked.

'A six-toothed scapewheel! With a bifurcated locking piece! Well, I never! That is enriching the pudding with currants. Rather like putting an Egg lock on a common pistol! I'm sure if you wait, Sergeant, Sharpe will be back soon. He's a marvellous fellow. Never lets me down.'

Hakeswill forced a smile, for he hated Sharpe with a rare and single-minded venom. 'He's one of the best, sir,' he said, his face twitching. 'And will he be leaving Seringapatam soon, sir? Off on an errand again, would he be?'

'Oh no!' Stokes said, picking up a magnifying glass to look more closely into the clock. 'I need him here, Sergeant. That's it, you see! There's a pin missing from the strike wheel. It engages the cogs here, do you see, and the gearing does the rest. Simple, I suppose.' The Major looked up, but saw that the strange Sergeant with the twitching face was gone. Never mind, the clock was far more interesting.

Sergeant Hakeswill left the armoury and turned left towards the barracks where he had temporary accommodation. The King's 33rd was quartered now in Hurryhur, a hundred and fifty miles to the north, and their job was to keep the roads of western Mysore clear of bandits and so the regiment ranged up and down the country and, finding themselves close to Seringapatam where the main armoury was located, Colonel Gore had sent a detachment for replacement ammunition. Captain Morris of the Light Company had drawn the duty, and he had brought half his men and Sergeant Obadiah Hakeswill to protect the shipment which would leave the city next morning and be carried on ox carts to Arrakerry where the regiment was currently camped. An easy task, but one that had offered Sergeant Hakeswill an opportunity he had long sought.

The Sergeant stopped in one of the grog shops and demanded arrack. The shop was empty, all but for himself, the owner and a legless beggar who heaved himself towards the Sergeant and received a kick in the rump for his trouble. 'Get out of here, you scabby bastard!' Hakeswill shouted. 'Bringing the flies in, you are. Go on! Piss off.' The shop thus emptied to his satisfaction, Hakeswill sat in a dark corner contemplating life. 'I chide myself,' he muttered aloud, worrying the shop's owner who feared the look of the twitching man in the red coat. 'Your own fault, Obadiah,' Hakeswill said. 'You should have seen it years ago! Years! Rich as a Jew, he is. Are you listening to me, you heathen darkie bastard?' The shop's owner, thus challenged, fled into the back room, leaving Hakeswill grumbling at the table. 'Rich as a Jew, Sharpie is, only he thinks he hides it, which he don't, on account of me having tumbled to him. He don't even live in barracks! Got himself some rooms over by the Mysore Gate. Got a bleeding servant boy. Always got cash on him, always! Buys drinks.' Hakeswill shook his head at the injustice of it all. The 33rd had spent the last four years patrolling Mysore's roads and Sharpe, all that while, had been living in Seringapatam's comforts. It was not right, not fair, not just. Hakeswill had worried about it, wondering why Sharpe was so rich. At first he had assumed that Sharpe had been fiddling the armoury stores, but that could not explain Sharpe's apparent wealth. 'Only so much milk in a cow,' Hakeswill muttered, 'no matter how hard you squeeze the teats.' Now he knew why Sharpe was rich, or he thought he knew, and what he had learned had filled Obadiah Hakeswill with a desperate jealousy. He scratched at a mosquito bite on his neck, revealing the old dark scar where the hangman's rope had burned and abraded his skin. Obadiah Hakeswill had survived that hanging, and as a result he fervently believed that he could not be killed. Touched by God, he claimed he was, touched by God.

But he was not rich. Not rich at all, and Richard Sharpe was rich. Rumour had it that Richard Sharpe used Lali's house, and that was an officers-only brothel, so why was Sergeant Sharpe allowed inside? Because he was rich, that was why, and Hakeswill had at last discovered Sharpe's secret. 'It was the Tippoo!' he said aloud, then thumped the table with his tin mug to demand more drink. 'And hurry up about it, you black-faced bastard!'

It had to be the Tippoo. Had not Hakeswill seen Sharpe lurking about the area where the Tippoo had been killed? And no soldier had ever claimed the credit for killing the Tippoo. It was widely thought that one of those Suffolk bastards from the 12th had caught the King in the chaos at the siege's end, but Hakeswill had finally worked it out. It had been Sharpe, and the reason Sharpe had kept quiet about the killing was because he had stripped the Tippoo of all his gems and he did not want anyone, least of all the army's senior officers, to know that he possessed the jewels. 'Bloody Sharpe!' Hakeswill said aloud.

So all that was needed now was an excuse to have Sharpe brought back to the regiment. No more clean and easy duty for Sharpie! No more merry rides in Lali's house for him. It would be Obadiah Hakeswill's turn to live in luxury, and all because of a dead king's treasure. 'Rubies,' Hakeswill said aloud, lingering over the word, 'and emeralds and sapphires, and diamonds like stars, and gold thick as butter.' He chuckled. And all it would need, he reckoned, was a little cunning. A little cunning, a confident lie and an arrest. 'And that will be your end, Sharpie, that will be your end,' Hakeswill said, and he could feel the beauty of his scheme unfold like a lotus blossoming in Seringapatam's moat. It would work! His visit to Major Stokes had established that Sharpe was in the town, which meant that the lie could be told and then, just like Major Stokes's clockwork, everything would go right. Every cog and gear and wheel and spike would slot and click and tick and tock, and Sergeant Hakeswill's face twitched and his hands contracted as though the tin mug in his grip were a man's throat. He would be rich.

It took Major William Dodd three days to carry the ammunition back to Pohlmann's *compoo* which was camped just outside the Mahratta city of Ahmednuggur. The *compoo* was an infantry brigade of eight battalions, each of them recruited from among the finest mercenary warriors of north India and all trained and commanded by European officers. Dowlut Rao Scindia, the Maharajah of Gwalior, whose land stretched from the fortress of Baroda in the north to the fastness of Gawilghur in the east and down to Ahmednuggur in the south, boasted that he led a hundred thousand men and that his army could blacken the land like a plague, yet this *compoo*, with its seven thousand men, was the hard heart of his army.

One of the *compoo*'s eight battalions was paraded a mile outside the encampment to greet Dodd. The cavalry that had accompanied the sepoys to Chasalgaon had ridden ahead to warn Pohlmann of Dodd's return and Pohlmann had organized a triumphant reception. The battalion stood in white coats, their black belts and weapons gleaming, but Dodd, riding at the head of his small column, had eyes only for the tall elephant that stood beside a yellow-and-white-striped marquee. The huge beast glittered in the sunlight, for its body and head were armoured with a vast leather cape onto which squares of silver had been sewn in intricate patterns. The silver covered the elephant's body, continued across its face and then, all but for two circles that had been cut for its eyes, cascaded on down the length of its trunk. Gems gleamed between the silver plates while ribbons of purple silk fluttered from the crown of the animal's head. The last few inches of the animal's big curved tusks were sheathed in silver, though the actual points of the tusks were tipped with needle-sharp points of steel. The elephant driver, the mahout, sweated in a coat of old-fashioned chain mail that had been burnished to the same gleaming polish as his animal's silver armour, while behind him was a howdah made of cedarwood on which gold panels had been nailed and above which fluttered a fringed canopy of yellow silk. Long files of purple-jacketed infantrymen stood to attention on either flank of the elephant. Some of the men carried muskets, while others had long pikes with their broad blades polished to resemble silver.

The elephant knelt when Dodd came within twenty paces and the occupant of the howdah stepped carefully down onto a set of silver-plated steps placed there by one of his purple-coated bodyguards then strolled into the shade of the striped marquee. He was a European, a tall man and big, not fat, and though a casual glance might think him overweight, a second glance would see that most of that weight was solid muscle. He had a round sun-reddened face, big black moustaches and eyes that seemed to take delight in everything he saw. His uniform was of his own devising: white silk breeches tucked into English riding boots, a green coat festooned with gold lace and aiguillettes and, on the coat's broad shoulders, thick white silk cushions hung with short golden chains. The coat had scarlet facings and loops of scarlet braid about its turned-back cuffs and gilded buttons. The big man's hat was a bicorne crested with purple-dyed feathers held in place by a badge showing the white horse of Hanover; his sword's hilt was made of gold fashioned into the shape of an elephant's head, and gold rings glinted on his big fingers. Once in the shade of the open-sided marquee he settled himself on a divan where his aides gathered about him. This was Colonel Anthony Pohlmann and he commanded the *compoo*, together with five hundred cavalry and twenty-six field guns. Ten years before, when Scindia's army had been nothing but a horde of ragged troopers on half-starved horses, Anthony Pohlmann had been a sergeant in a Hanoverian regiment of the East India Company; now he rode an elephant and needed two other beasts to carry the chests of gold coin that travelled everywhere with him.

Pohlmann stood as Dodd climbed down from his horse. 'Well done, Major!' the Colonel called in his German-accented English. 'Exceedingly well done!' Pohlmann's aides, half of them European and half Indian, joined their commander in applauding the returning hero, while the body-guard made a double line through which Dodd could advance to meet the resplendent Colonel. 'Eighty thousand cartridges,' Pohlmann exulted, 'snatched from our enemies!'

'Seventy-three thousand, sir,' Dodd said, beating dust off his breeches.

Pohlmann grinned. 'Seven thousand spoiled, eh? Nothing changes.'

'Not spoiled by me, sir,' Dodd growled.

'I never supposed so,' Pohlmann said. 'Did you have any difficulties?'

'None,' Dodd answered confidently. 'We lost no one, sir, not even a scratch, while not a single enemy soldier survived.' He smiled, cracking the dust on his cheeks. 'Not one.'

'A victory!' Pohlmann said, then gestured Dodd into the tent. 'We have wine, of sorts. There is rum, arrack, even water! Come, Major.'

Dodd did not move. 'My men are tired, sir,' he pointed out.

'Then dismiss them, Major. They can take refreshment at my cook tent.'

Dodd went to dismiss his men. He was a gangling English-man with a long sallow face and a sullen expression. He was also that rarest of things, an officer who had deserted from the East India Company, and deserted moreover with one hundred and thirty of his own sepoy troops. He had come to Pohlmann just three weeks before and some of Pohlmann's European officers had been convinced that Lieutenant Dodd was a spy sent by the British whose army was readying to attack the Mahratta Confederation, but Pohlmann had not been so sure. It was true that no other British officer had ever deserted like Dodd, but few had reasons like Dodd, and Pohlmann had also recognized Dodd's hunger, his awkward-ness, his anger and his ability. Lieutenant Dodd's record showed he was no mean soldier, his sepoys liked him, and he had a raging ambition, and Pohlmann had believed the Lieutenant's defection to be both wholehearted and real. He had made Dodd into a major, then given him a test. He had sent him to Chasalgaon. If Dodd proved capable of killing his old comrades then he was no spy, and Dodd had passed the test triumphantly and Scindia's army was now better off by seventy-three thousand cartridges.

Dodd came back to the marquee and was given the chair of honour on the right side of Pohlmann's divan. The chair on the left was occupied by a woman, a European, and Dodd could scarcely keep his eyes from her, and no wonder, for she was a rare-looking woman to discover in India. She was young, scarce more than eighteen or nineteen, with a pale face and very fair hair. Her lips were maybe a trifle too thin and her forehead perhaps a half inch too wide, yet there was something oddly attractive about her. She had a face, Dodd decided, in which the imperfections added up to attractiveness, and her appeal was augmented by a timid air of vulnerability. At first Dodd assumed the woman was Pohlmann's mistress, but then he saw that her white linen dress was frayed at the hem and some of the lace at its modest collar was crudely darned, and he decided that Pohlmann would never allow his mistress to appear so shabbily.

'Let me introduce Madame Joubert to you,' Pohlmann said, who had noticed how hungrily Dodd had stared at the woman. 'This is Major William Dodd.'

'Madame Joubert?' Dodd stressed the 'Madame', half rising and bowing from his chair as he acknowledged her.

'Major,' she said in a low voice, then smiled nervously before looking down at the table that was spread with dishes of almonds.

Pohlmann snapped his fingers for a servant, then smiled at Major Dodd. 'Simone is married to Captain Joubert, and that is Captain Joubert.' He pointed into the sunlight where a short captain stood to attention in front of the paraded battalion that stood so stiff and still in the biting sun.

'Joubert commands the battalion, sir?' Dodd asked.

'No one commands the battalion,' Pohlmann answered. 'But until three weeks ago it was led by Colonel Mathers. Back then it had five European officers; now it has Captain Joubert and Lieutenant Sillière.' He pointed to a second European, a tall thin young man, and Dodd, who was observant, saw Simone Joubert blush at the mention of Sillière's name. Dodd was amused. Joubert looked at least twenty years older than his wife, while Sillière was only a year or two her senior. 'And we must have Europeans,' Pohlmann went on, stretching back on the divan that creaked under his weight. 'The Indians are fine soldiers, but we need Europeans who understand European tactics.'

'How many European officers have you lost, sir?' Dodd asked.

'From this *compoo*? Eighteen,' Pohlmann said. 'Too many.' The men who had gone were the British officers, and all had possessed contracts with Scindia that excused them from fighting against their own countrymen, and to make matters worse the East India Company had offered a bribe to any British officer who deserted the Mahrattas and, as a result, some of Pohlmann's best men were gone. It was true that he still had some good officers left, most of them French, with a handful of Dutchmen, Swiss and Germans, but Pohlmann knew he could ill afford the loss of eighteen European officers. At least none of his artillerymen had deserted and Pohlmann put great faith in the battle-winning capacity of his guns. Those cannon were served by Portuguese, or by half-breed Indians from the Portuguese colonies in India, and those professionals had stayed loyal and were awesomely proficient.

Pohlmann drained a glass of rum and poured himself another. He had an extraordinary capacity for alcohol, a capacity Dodd did not share, and the Englishman, knowing his propensity for getting drunk, restrained himself to sips of watered wine. 'I promised you a reward, Major, if you succeeded in rescuing the cartridges,' Pohlmann said genially.

'Knowing I've done my duty is reward enough,' Dodd said. He felt shabby and ill-uniformed among Pohlmann's gaudy aides and had decided that it was best to play the bluff soldier, a role he thought would appeal to a former sergeant. It was said that Pohlmann kept his old East India Company uniform as a reminder of just how far he had risen.

'Men do not join Scindia's army merely for the pleasures of doing their duty,' Pohlmann said, 'but for the rewards such service offers. We are here to become rich, are we not?' He unhooked the elephant-hilted sword from his belt. The scabbard was made of soft red leather and was studded with small emeralds. 'Here.' Pohlmann offered the sword to Dodd.

'I can't take your sword!' Dodd protested.

'I have many, Major, and many finer. I insist.'

Dodd took the sword. He drew the blade from the scabbard and saw that it was finely made, much better than the drab sword he had worn as a lieutenant these last twenty years. Many Indian swords were made of soft steel and broke easily in combat, but Dodd guessed this blade had been forged in France or Britain, then given its beautiful elephant hilt in India. That hilt was of gold, the elephant's head made the pommel, while the handguard was the beast's curved trunk. The grip was of black leather bound with gold wire. 'Thank you, sir,' he said feelingly.

'It is the first of many rewards,' Pohlmann said airily, 'and those rewards will shower on us when we beat the British. Which we shall, though not here.' He paused to drink rum. 'The British will attack any day now,' he went on, 'and they doubtless hope I'll stay and fight them here, but I don't have a mind to oblige them. Better to make the bastards march after us, eh? The rains may come while they pursue us and the rivers will hold them up. Disease will weaken them. And once they are weak and tired, we shall be strong. All Scindia's *compoos* will join together and the Rajah of Berar has promised his army, and once we are all gathered we shall crush the British. But that means I have to give up Ahmednuggur.'

'Not an important city,' Dodd commented. He noticed that Simone Joubert was sipping wine. She kept her eyes lowered, only occasionally glancing up at her husband or at Lieutenant Sillière. She took no notice of Dodd, but she would, he promised himself, she would. Her nose was too small, he decided, but even so she was a thing of pale and fragile wonder in this hot, dark-skinned land. Her blonde hair, which was hung with ringlets in a fashion that had prevailed ten years before in Europe, was held in place by small mother-of-pearl clips.

'Ahmednuggur is not important,' Pohlmann agreed, 'but

Scindia hates losing any of his cities and he stuffed Ahmednuggur full of supplies and insisted I post one regiment inside the city.' He nodded towards the white-coated troops. 'That regiment, Major. It's probably my best regiment, but I am forced to quarter it in Ahmednuggur.'

Dodd understood Pohlmann's predicament. 'You can't take them out of the city without upsetting Scindia,' he said, 'but you don't want to lose the regiment when the city falls.'

'I can't lose it!' Pohlmann said indignantly. 'A good regiment like that? Mathers trained it well, very well. Now he's gone to join our enemies, but I can't lose his regiment as well, so whoever takes over from Mathers must know how to extricate his men from trouble.'

Dodd felt a surge of excitement. He liked to think that it was not just for the money that he had deserted the Company, nor because of his legal troubles, but for the long overdue chance of leading his own regiment. He could do it well, he knew that, and he knew what Pohlmann was leading up to.

Pohlmann smiled. 'Suppose I give you Mathers's regiment, Major? Can you pull it out of the fire for me?'

'Yes, sir,' Dodd said simply. Simone Joubert, for the first time since she had been introduced to Dodd, looked up at him, but without any friendliness.

'All of it?' Pohlmann asked. 'With its cannon?'

'All of it,' Dodd said firmly, 'and with every damned gun.'

'Then from now it is Dodd's regiment,' Pohlmann said, 'and if you lead it well, Major, I shall make you a colonel and give you a second regiment to command.'

Dodd celebrated by draining his cup of wine. He was so overcome with emotion that he hardly dared speak, though the look on his face said it all. His own regiment at last! He had waited so long for this moment and now, by God, he would show the Company how well their despised officers could fight.

37

Pohlmann snapped his fingers so that a servant girl brought him more rum. 'How many men will Wellesley bring?' he asked Dodd.

'No more than fifteen thousand infantry,' the new commander of Dodd's regiment answered confidently. 'Probably fewer, and they'll be split into two armies. Boy Wellesley will command one, Colonel Stevenson the other.'

'Stevenson's old, yes?'

'Ancient and cautious,' Dodd said dismissively.

'Cavalry?'

'Five or six thousand? Mostly Indians.'

'Guns?'

'Twenty-six at most. Nothing bigger than a twelve-pounder.'

'And Scindia can field eighty guns,' Pohlmann said, 'some of them twenty-eight-pounders. And once the Rajah of Berar's forces join us, we'll have forty thousand infantry and at least fifty more guns.' The Hanoverian smiled. 'But battles aren't just numbers. They're also won by generals. Tell me about this Major General Sir Arthur Wellesley.'

'Boy Wellesley?' Dodd responded scathingly. The British General was younger than Dodd, but that was not the cause of the derisory nickname. Rather it was envy, for Wellesley had connections and wealth, while Dodd had neither. 'He's young,' Dodd said, 'only thirty-four.'

'Youth is no barrier to good soldiering,' Pohlmann said chidingly, though he well understood Dodd's resentment. For years Dodd had watched younger men rise up through the ranks of the King's army while he had been stuck in the Company's hidebound ranks. A man could not buy promotion in the Company, nor were promotions given by merit, but only by seniority, and so forty-year-old men like Dodd were still lieutenants while, in the King's army, mere boys were captains or majors. 'Is Wellesley good?' Pohlmann asked.

'He's never fought a battle,' Dodd said bitterly, 'not unless you count Malavelly.'

'One volley?' Pohlmann asked, half recalling stories of the skirmish.

'One volley and a bayonet charge,' Dodd said, 'not a proper battle.'

'He defeated Dhoondiah.'

'A cavalry charge against a bandit,' Dodd said scornfully. 'My point, sir, is that Boy Wellesley has never faced artillery and infantry on a real battlefield. He was jumped up to major general solely because his brother is Governor General. If his name had been Dodd instead of Wellesley he'd be lucky to command a company, let alone an army.'

'He's an aristocrat?' Pohlmann enquired.

'Of course. What else?' Dodd asked. 'His father was an earl.'

'So . . .' Pohlmann put a handful of almonds in his mouth and paused to chew them. 'So,' he went on, 'he's the younger son of a nobleman, sent into the army because he wasn't good for anything else, and his family purchased him up the ranks?'

'Exactly, sir, exactly.'

'But I hear he is efficient?'

'Efficient?' Dodd thought about it. 'He's efficient, sir, because his brother gives him the cash. He can afford a big bullock train. He carries his supplies with him, so his men are well fed. But he still ain't ever seen a cannon's muzzle, not facing him, not alongside a score of others and backed by steady infantry.'

'He did well as Governor of Mysore,' Pohlmann observed mildly.

'So he's an efficient governor? Does that make him a general?'

'A disciplinarian, I hear,' Pohlmann said.

39

'He sets a lovely parade ground,' Dodd agreed sarcastically. 'But he isn't a fool?'

'No,' Dodd admitted, 'not a fool, but not a general either. He's been promoted too fast and too young, sir. He's beaten bandits, but he took a beating himself outside Seringapatam.'

'Ah, yes. The night attack.' Pohlmann had heard of that skirmish, how Arthur Wellesley had attacked a wood outside Seringapatam and there been roundly thrashed by the Tippoo's troops. 'Even so,' he said, 'it never serves to underestimate an enemy.'

'Overestimate him as much as you like, sir,' Dodd said stoutly, 'but the fact remains that Boy Wellesley has never fought a proper battle, not with more than a thousand men under his command, and he's never faced a real army, not a trained field army with gunners and disciplined infantry, and my guess is that he won't stand. He'll run back to his brother and demand more men. He's a careful man.'

Pohlmann smiled. 'So let us lure this careful man deep into our territory where he can't retreat, eh? Then beat him.' He smiled, then hauled a watch from his fob and snapped open the lid. 'I have to be going soon,' he said, 'but some business first.' He took an envelope from his gaudy coat's pocket and handed the sealed paper to Dodd. 'That is your authority to command Mathers's regiment, Major,' he said, 'but remember, I want you to bring it safely out of Ahmednuggur. You can help the defence for a time, but don't be trapped there. Young Wellesley can't invest the whole city, he doesn't have enough men, so you should be able to escape easily enough. Bloody his nose, Dodd, but keep your regiment safe. Do you understand?'

Dodd understood well enough. Pohlmann was setting Dodd a difficult and ignoble task, that of retreating from a fight with his command intact. There was little glory in such a manoeuvre, but it would still be a difficult piece of soldiering and Dodd knew he was being tested a second time. The first test had been Chasalgaon, the second would be Ahmednuggur. 'I can manage it,' he said dourly.

'Good!' Pohlmann said. 'I shall make things easier for you by taking your regiment's families northwards. You might march soldiers safely from the city's fall, but I doubt you can manage a horde of women and children too. And what about you, Madame?' He turned and laid a meaty hand on Simone Joubert's knee. 'Will you come with me?' He talked to her as though she were a child. 'Or stay with Major Dodd?'

Simone seemed startled by the question. She blushed and looked up at Lieutenant Sillière. 'I shall stay here, Colonel,' she answered in English.

'Make sure you bring her safe home, Major,' Pohlmann said to Dodd.

'I shall, sir.'

Pohlmann stood. His purple-coated bodyguards, who had been standing in front of the tent, hurried to take their places on the elephant's flanks while the mahout, who had been resting in the animal's capacious shade, now mounted the somnolent beast by gripping its tail and clambering up its backside like a sailor swarming up a rope. He edged past the gilded howdah, took his seat on the elephant's neck and turned the beast towards Pohlmann's tent. 'Are you sure' – Pohlmann turned back to Simone Joubert – 'that you would not prefer to travel with me? The howdah is so comfortable, as long as you do not suffer from seasickness.'

'I shall stay with my husband,' Simone said. She had stood and proved to be much taller than Dodd had supposed. Tall and somewhat gawky, he thought, but she still possessed an odd attraction.

'A good woman should stay with her husband,' Pohlmann said, 'or someone's husband, anyway.' He turned to Dodd.

41

'I shall see you in a few days, Major, with your new regiment. Don't let me down.'

'I won't, sir, I won't,' Dodd promised as, holding his new sword, he watched his new commander climb the silver steps to the howdah. He had a regiment to save and a reputation to make, and by God, Dodd thought, he would do both things well.

CHAPTER 2

Sharpe sat in the open shed where the armoury stored its gun carriages. It had started to rain, though it was not the sheeting downpour of the monsoon, just a miserable steady grey drizzle that turned the mud in the yard into a slippery coating of red slime. Major Stokes, beginning the afternoon in a clean red coat, white silk stock and polished boots, paced obsessively about a newly made carriage. 'It really wasn't your fault, Sharpe,' he said.

'Feels like it, sir.'

'It would, it would!' Stokes said. 'Reflects well on you, Sharpe, 'pon my soul, it does. But it weren't your fault, not in any manner.'

'Lost all six men, sir. And young Davi.'

'Poor Hedgehog,' Stokes said, squatting to peer along the trail of the carriage. 'You reckon that timber's straight, Sharpe? Bit hog-backed, maybe?'

'Looks straight to me, sir.'

'Ain't tight-grained, this oak, ain't tight-grained,' the Major said, and he began to unbuckle his sword belt. Every morning and afternoon his servant sent him to the armoury in carefully laundered and pressed clothes, and within an hour Major Stokes would be stripped down to breeches and shirtsleeves and have his hands full of spokeshaves or saws or awls or adzes. 'Like to see a straight trail,' he said. 'There's a number four spokeshave on the wall, Sharpe, be a good fellow.'

'You want me to sharpen it, sir?'

'I did it last night, Sharpe. I put a lovely edge on her.' Stokes unpeeled his red jacket and rolled up his sleeves. 'Timber don't season here properly, that's the trouble.' He stooped to the new carriage and began running the spoke-shave along the trail, leaving curls of new white wood to fall away. 'I'm mending a clock,' he told Sharpe while he worked, 'a lovely-made piece, all but for some crude local gearing. Have a look at it. It's in my office.'

'I will, sir.'

'And I've found some new timber for axletrees, Sharpe. It's really quite exciting!'

'They'll still break, sir,' Sharpe said gloomily, then scooped up one of the many cats that lived in the armoury. He put the tabby on his lap and stroked her into a contented purr.

'Don't be so doom-laden, Sharpe! We'll solve the axletree problem yet. It's only a question of timber, nothing but timber. There, that looks better.' The Major stepped back from his work and gave it a critical look. There were plenty of Indian craftsmen employed in the armoury, but Major Stokes liked to do things himself, and besides, most of the Indians were busy preparing for the feast of Dusshera which involved manufacturing three giant-sized figures that would be paraded to the Hindu temple and there burned. Those Indians were busy in another open-sided shed where they had glue bubbling on a fire, and some of the men were pasting lengths of pale cloth onto a wicker basket that would form one of the giants' heads. Stokes was fascinated by their activity and Sharpe knew it would not be long before the Major joined them. 'Did I tell you a sergeant was here looking for you this morning?' Stokes asked.

'No, sir.'

'Came just before dinner,' Stokes said, 'a strange sort of

fellow.' The Major stooped to the trail and attacked another section of wood. 'He twitched, he did.'

'Obadiah Hakeswill,' Sharpe said.

'I think that was his name. Didn't seem very important,' Stokes said. 'Said he was just visiting town and looking up old companions. D'you know what I was thinking?'

'Tell me, sir,' Sharpe said, wondering why in holy hell Obadiah Hakeswill had been looking for him. For nothing good, that was certain.

'Those teak beams in the Tippoo's old throne room,' Stokes said, 'they'll be seasoned well enough. We could break out a half-dozen of the things and make a batch of axletrees from them!'

'The gilded beams, sir?' Sharpe asked.

'Soon have the gilding off them, Sharpe. Plane them down in two shakes!'

'The Rajah may not like it, sir,' Sharpe said.

Stokes's face fell. 'There is that, there is that. A fellow don't usually like his ceilings being pulled down to make gun carriages. Still, the Rajah's usually most obliging if you can get past his damned courtiers. The clock is his. Strikes eight when it should ring nine, or perhaps it's the other way round. You reckon that quoin's true?'

Sharpe glanced at the wedge which lowered and raised the cannon barrel. 'Looks good, sir.'

'I might just plane her down a shade. I wonder if our templates are out of true? We might check that. Isn't this rain splendid? The flowers were wilting, wilting! But I'll have a fine show this year with a spot of rain. You must come and see them.'

'You still want me to stay here, sir?' Sharpe asked.

'Stay here?' Stokes, who was placing the quoin in a vice, turned to look at Sharpe. 'Of course I want you to stay here, Sergeant. Best man I've got!'

'I lost six men, sir.'

'And it wasn't your fault, not your fault at all. I'll get you another six.'

Sharpe wished it was that easy, but he could not chase the guilt of Chasalgaon out of his mind. When the massacre was finished he had wandered about the fort in a half-daze. Most of the women and children still lived, but they had been frightened and had shrunk away from him. Captain Roberts, the second in command of the fort, had returned from patrol that afternoon and he had vomited when he saw the horror inside the cactus-thorn wall.

Sharpe had made his report to Roberts who had sent it by messenger to Hurryhur, the army's headquarters, then dismissed Sharpe. 'There'll be an enquiry, I suppose,' Roberts had told Sharpe, 'so doubtless your evidence will be needed, but you might as well wait in Seringapatam.' And so Sharpe, with no other orders, had walked home. He had returned the bag of rupees to Major Stokes, and now, obscurely, he wanted some punishment from the Major, but Stokes was far more concerned about the angle of the quoin. 'I've seen screws shatter because the angle was too steep, and it ain't no good having broken screws in battle. I've seen Frog guns with metalled quoins, but they only rust. Can't trust a Frog to keep them greased, you see. You're brooding, Sharpe.'

'Can't help it, sir.'

'Doesn't do to brood. Leave brooding to poets and priests, eh? Those sorts of fellows are paid to brood. You have to get on with life. What could you have done?'

'Killed one of the bastards, sir.'

'And they'd have killed you, and you wouldn't have liked that and nor would I. Look at that angle! Look at that! I do like a fine angle, I declare I do. We must check it against the templates. How's your head?'

'Mending, sir.' Sharpe touched the bandage that wrapped his forehead. 'No pain now, sir.'

'Providence, Sharpe, that's what it is, providence. The good Lord in His ineffable mercy wanted you to live.' Stokes released the vice and restored the quoin to the carriage. 'A touch of paint on that trail and it'll be ready. You think the Rajah might give me one roof beam?'

'No harm in asking him, sir.'

'I will, I will. Ah, a visitor.' Stokes straightened as a horseman, swathed against the rain in an oilcloth cape and with an oilcloth cover on his cocked hat, rode into the armoury courtyard leading a second horse by the reins. The visitor kicked his feet from the stirrups, swung down from the saddle, then tied both horses' reins to one of the shed's pillars. Major Stokes, his clothes just in their beginning stage of becoming dirty and dishevelled, smiled at the tall newcomer whose cocked hat and sword betrayed he was an officer. 'Come to inspect us, have you?' the Major demanded cheerfully. 'You'll discover chaos! Nothing in the right place, records all muddled, woodworm in the timber stacks, damp in the magazines and the paint completely addled.'

'Better that paint is addled than wits,' the newcomer said, then took off his cocked hat to reveal a head of white hair.

Sharpe, who had been sitting on one of the finished gun carriages, shot to his feet, tipping the surprised cat into the Major's wood shavings. 'Colonel McCandless, sir!'

'Sergeant Sharpe!' McCandless responded. The Colonel shook water from his cocked hat and turned to Stokes. 'And you, sir?'

'Major Stokes, sir, at your service, sir. John Stokes, commander of the armoury and, as you see, carpenter to His Majesty.'

'You will forgive me, Major Stokes, if I talk to Sergeant Sharpe?' McCandless shed his oilskin cape to reveal his East

India Company uniform. 'Sergeant Sharpe and I are old friends.'

'My pleasure, Colonel,' Stokes said. 'I have business in the foundry. They're pouring too fast. I tell them all the time! Fast pouring just bubbles the metal, and bubbled metal leads to disaster, but they won't listen. Ain't like making temple bells, I tell them, but I might as well save my breath.' He glanced wistfully towards the happy men making the giant's head for the Dusshera festival. 'And I have other things to do,' he added.

'I'd rather you didn't leave, Major,' McCandless said very formally. 'I suspect what I have to say concerns you. It is good to see you, Sharpe.'

'You too, sir,' Sharpe said, and it was true. He had been locked in the Tippoo's dungeons with Colonel Hector McCandless and if it was possible for a sergeant and a colonel to be friends, then a friendship existed between the two men. McCandless, tall, vigorous and in his sixties, was the East India Company's head of intelligence for all southern and western India, and in the last four years he and Sharpe had talked a few times whenever the Colonel passed through Seringapatam, but those had been social conversations and the Colonel's grim face suggested that this meeting was anything but social.

'You were at Chasalgaon?' McCandless demanded.

'I was, sir, yes.'

'So you saw Lieutenant Dodd?'

Sharpe nodded. 'Won't ever forget the bastard. Sorry, sir.' He apologized because McCandless was a fervent Christian who abhorred all foul language. The Scotsman was a stern man, honest as a saint, and Sharpe sometimes wondered why he liked him so much. Maybe it was because McCandless was always fair, always truthful and could talk to any man, rajah or sergeant, with the same honest directness.

'I never met Lieutenant Dodd,' McCandless said, 'so describe him to me.'

'Tall, sir, and thin like you or me.'

'Not like me,' Major Stokes put in.

'Sort of yellow-faced,' Sharpe went on, 'as if he'd had the fever once. Long face, like he ate something bitter.' He thought for a second. He had only caught a few glimpses of Dodd, and those had been sideways. 'He's got lank hair, sir, when he took off his hat. Brown hair. Long nose on him, like Sir Arthur's, and a bony chin. He's calling himself Major Dodd now, sir, not Lieutenant. I heard one of his men call him Major.'

'And he killed every man in the garrison?' McCandless asked.

'He did, sir. Except me. I was lucky.'

'Nonsense, Sharpe!' McCandless said. 'The hand of the Lord was upon you.'

'Amen,' Major Stokes intervened.

McCandless stared broodingly at Sharpe. The Colonel had a hard-planed face with oddly blue eyes. He was forever claiming that he wanted to retire to his native Scotland, but he always found some reason to stay on in India. He had spent much of his life riding the states that bordered the land administered by the Company, for his job was to explore those lands and report their threats and weaknesses to his masters. Little happened in India that escaped McCandless, but Dodd had escaped him, and Dodd was now McCandless's concern. 'We have placed a price on his head,' the Colonel said, 'of five hundred guineas.'

'Bless me!' Major Stokes said in astonishment.

'He's a murderer,' McCandless went on. 'He killed a gold-smith in Seedesegur, and he should be facing trial, but he ran instead and I want you, Sharpe, to help me catch him. And I'm not pursuing the rogue because I want the reward money; in fact I'll refuse it. But I do want him, and I want your help.'

Major Stokes began to protest, saying that Sharpe was his best man and that the armoury would go to the dogs if the Sergeant was taken away, but McCandless shot the amiable Major a harsh look that was sufficient to silence him.

'I want Lieutenant Dodd captured,' McCandless said implacably, 'and I want him tried, and I want him executed, and I need someone who will know him by sight.'

Major Stokes summoned the courage to continue his objections. 'But I need Sergeant Sharpe,' he protested. 'He organizes everything! The duty rosters, the stores, the pay chest, everything!'

'I need him more,' McCandless snarled, turning on the hapless Major. 'Do you know how many Britons are in India, Major? Maybe twelve thousand, and less than half of those are soldiers. Our power does not rest on the shoulders of white men, Major, but on the muskets of our sepoys. Nine men out of every ten who invade the Mahratta states will be sepoys, and Lieutenant Dodd persuaded over a hundred of those men to desert! To desert! Can you imagine our fate if the other sepoys follow them? Scindia will shower Dodd's men with gold, Major, with lucre and with spoil, in the hope that others will follow them. I have to stop that, and I need Sharpe.'

Major Stokes recognized the inevitable. 'You will bring him back, sir?'

'If it is the Lord's will, yes. Well, Sergeant? Will you come with me?'

Sharpe glanced at Major Stokes who shrugged, smiled, then nodded his permission. 'I'll come, sir,' Sharpe said to the Scotsman.

'How soon can you be ready?'

'Ready now, sir.' Sharpe indicated the newly issued pack and musket that lay at his feet.

'You can ride a horse?'

Sharpe frowned. 'I can sit on one, sir.'

'Good enough,' the Scotsman said. He pulled on his oil-cloth cape, then untied the two reins and gave one set to Sharpe. 'She's a docile thing, Sharpe, so don't saw on her bit.'

'We're going right now, sir?' Sharpe asked, surprised by the suddenness of it all.

'Right now,' McCandless said. 'Time waits for no man, Sharpe, and we have a traitor and a murderer to catch.' He pulled himself into his saddle and watched as Sharpe clumsily mounted the second horse.

'So where are you going?' Stokes asked McCandless.

'Ahmednuggur first, and after that God will decide.' The Colonel touched his horse's flanks with his spurs and Sharpe, his pack hanging from one shoulder and his musket slung on the other, followed.

He would redeem himself for the failure at Chasalgaon. Not with punishment, but with something better: with vengeance.

Major William Dodd ran a white-gloved finger down the spoke of a gunwheel. He inspected his fingertip and nearly nine hundred men, or at least as many of the nine hundred on parade who could see the Major, inspected him in return.

No mud or dust on the glove. Dodd straightened his back and glowered at the gun crews, daring any man to show pleasure in having achieved a near perfect turn-out. It had been hard work, too, for it had rained earlier in the day and the regiment's five guns had been dragged through the muddy streets to the parade ground just inside Ahmednuggur's southern gate, but the gunners had still managed to clean their weapons meticulously. They had removed every scrap of mud, washed the mahogany trails, then polished the barrels until their alloy of copper and tin gleamed like brass.

Impressive, Dodd thought, as he peeled off the glove. Pohlmann had left Ahmednuggur, retreating north to join his *compoo* to Scindia's gathering army, and Dodd had ordered this surprise inspection of his new command. He had given the regiment just one hour's notice, but so far he had found nothing amiss. They were impressive indeed; standing in four long white-coated ranks with their four cannon and single howitzer paraded at the right flank. The guns themselves, despite their gleam, were pitiful things. The four field guns were mere four-pounders, while the fifth was a five-inch howitzer, and not one of the pieces fired a ball of real weight. Not a killing ball. 'Peashooters!' Dodd said disparagingly.

'Monsieur?' Captain Joubert, the Frenchman who had desperately hoped to be given command of the regiment himself, asked.

'You heard me, Monsewer. Peashooters!' Dodd said as he lifted a limber's lid and hoisted out one of the four-pounder shots. It was half the size of a cricket ball. 'You might as well spit at them, Monsewer!'

Joubert, a small man, shrugged. 'At close range, Monsieur . . .' he began to defend the guns.

'At close range, Monsewer, close range!' Dodd tossed the shot to Joubert who fumbled the catch. 'That's no use at close range! No more use than a musket ball, and the gun's ten times more cumbersome than a musket.' He rummaged through the limber. 'No canister? No grape?'

'Canister isn't issued for four-pounder guns,' Joubert said. 'It isn't even made for them.'

'Then we make our own,' Dodd said. 'Bags of scrap metal, Monsewer, strapped to a sabot and a charge. One and a half pounds of powder per round. Find a dozen women in the town and have them sew up the bags. Maybe your wife

52

can help, Monsewer?' He leered at Joubert who showed no reaction. Dodd could smell a man's weakness, and the oddly attractive Simone Joubert was undoubtedly her husband's weakness, for she clearly despised him and he, just as clearly, feared losing her. 'I want thirty bags of grape for each gun by this time tomorrow,' Dodd ordered.

'But the barrels, Major!' Joubert protested.

'You mean they'll be scratched?' Dodd jeered. 'What do you want, Monsewer? A scratched bore and a live regiment? Or a clean gun and a row of dead men? By tomorrow, thirty rounds of canister per gun, and if there ain't room in the limbers then throw out that bloody round shot. Might as well spit cherrystones as fire those pebbles.' Dodd slammed down the limber's lid. Even if the guns fired makeshift grapeshot he was not certain that they were worth keeping. Every battalion in India had such close-support artillery, but in Dodd's opinion the guns only served to slow down a regiment's manoeuvres. The weapons themselves were cumbersome, and the livestock needed to haul them was a nuisance, and if he were ever given his own *compoo* he would strip the regiments of field guns, for if a battalion of infantry could not defend itself with firelocks, what use was it? But he was stuck with the five guns, so he would use them as giant shotguns and open fire at three hundred yards. The gunners would moan about the damage to their barrels, but damn the gunners.

Dodd inspected the howitzer, found it as clean as the other guns, and nodded to the gunner-subadar. He offered no compliment, for Dodd did not believe in praising men for merely doing their duty. Praise was due to those who exceeded their duty, punishment for those who fell short, and silence must serve the rest.

Once the five guns had been inspected Dodd walked slowly down the white-jacketed infantry ranks where he looked every man in the eye and did not change his grim expression once, even though the soldiers had taken particular care to be well turned out for their new commanding officer. Captain Joubert followed a pace behind Dodd and there was something ludicrous about the conjunction of the tall, long-legged Dodd and the diminutive Joubert who needed to scurry to keep up with the Englishman. Once in a while the Frenchman would make a comment. 'He's a good man, sir,' he might say as they passed a soldier, but Dodd ignored all the praise and, after a while, Joubert fell silent and just scowled at Dodd's back. Dodd sensed the Frenchman's dislike, but did not care.

Dodd showed no reaction to the regiment's appearance, though all the same he was impressed. These men were smart and their weapons were as clean as those of his own sepoys who, reissued with white jackets, now paraded as an extra company at the regiment's left flank where, in British regiments, the skirmishers paraded. East India Company battalions had no skirmishers, for it was believed that sepoys were no good at the task, but Dodd had decided to make his loyal sepoys into the finest skirmishers in India. Let them prove the Company wrong, and in the proving they could help destroy the Company.

Most of the men looked up into Dodd's eyes as he walked by, although few of them looked at him for long, but instead glanced quickly away. Joubert saw the reaction, and sympathized with it, for there was something distinctly unpleasant about the Englishman's long sour face that edged on the frightening. Probably, Joubert decided, this Englishman was a flogger. The English were notorious for using the whip on their own men, reducing redcoats' backs to welters of broken flesh and gleaming blood, but Joubert was quite wrong about Dodd. Major Dodd had never flogged a man in his life, and that was not just because the Company forbade it in their army, but because William Dodd disliked the lash and hated to see a soldier flogged. Major Dodd liked soldiers. He hated most officers, especially those senior to him, but he liked soldiers. Good soldiers won battles, and victories made officers famous, so to be successful an officer needed soldiers who liked him and who would follow him. Dodd's sepoys were proof of that. He had looked after them, made sure they were fed and paid, and he had given them victory. Now he would make them wealthy in the service of the Mahratta princes who were famous for their generosity.

He broke away from the regiment and marched back to its colours, a pair of bright-green flags marked with crossed *tulwars*. The flags had been the choice of Colonel Mathers, the Englishman who had commanded the regiment for five years until he resigned rather than fight against his own countrymen, and now the regiment would be known as Dodd's regiment. Or perhaps he should call it something else. The Tigers? The Eagles? The Warriors of Scindia? Not that the name mattered now. What mattered now was to save these nine hundred well-trained men and their five gleaming guns and take them safely back to the Mahratta army that was gathering in the north. Dodd turned beneath the colours. 'My name is Dodd!' he shouted, then paused to let one of his Indian officers translate his words into Marathi, a language Dodd did not speak. Few of the soldiers spoke Marathi either, for most were mercenaries from the north, but men in the ranks murmured their own translation and so Dodd's message was relayed up and down the files. 'I am a soldier! Nothing but a soldier! Always a soldier!' He paused again. The parade was being held in the open space inside the gate and a crowd of townsfolk had gathered to gape at the troops, and among the crowd was a scatter of the robed Arab mercenaries who were reputed to be the fiercest of all the Mahratta troops. They were wild-looking men, armed with every conceivable weapon, but Dodd doubted they had the discipline of his regiment. 'Together,' he shouted at his men, 'you and I shall fight and we shall win.' He kept his words simple, for soldiers always liked simple things. Loot was simple, winning and losing were simple ideas, and even death, despite the way the damned preachers tried to tie it up in superstitious knots, was a simple concept. 'It is my intent,' he shouted, then waited for the translation to ripple up and down the ranks, 'for this regiment to be the finest in Scindia's service! Do your job well and I shall reward you. Do it badly, and I shall let your fellow soldiers decide on your punishment.' They liked that, as Dodd had known they would.

'Yesterday,' Dodd declaimed, 'the British crossed our frontier! Tomorrow their army will be here at Ahmednuggur, and soon we shall fight them in a great battle!' He had decided not to say that the battle would be fought well north of the city, for that might discourage the listening civilians. 'We shall drive them back to Mysore. We shall teach them that the army of Scindia is greater than any of their armies. We shall win!' The soldiers smiled at his confidence. 'We shall take their treasures, their weapons, their land and their women, and those things will be your reward if you fight well. But if you fight badly, you will die.' That phrase sent a shudder through the four white-coated ranks. 'And if any of you prove to be cowards,' Dodd finished, 'I shall kill you myself.'

He let that threat sink in, then abruptly ordered the regiment back to its duties before summoning Joubert to follow him up the red stone steps of the city wall to where Arab guards stood behind the merlons ranged along the firestep. Far to the south, beyond the horizon, a dusky cloud was just visible. It could have been mistaken for a distant rain cloud, but Dodd guessed it was the smear of smoke from the British campfires. 'How long do you think the city will last?' Dodd asked Joubert.

The Frenchman considered the question. 'A month?' he guessed.

'Don't be a fool,' Dodd snarled. He might want the loyalty of his men, but he did not give a fig for the good opinion of its two European officers. Both were Frenchmen and Dodd had the usual Englishman's opinion of the Frogs. Good dancing masters, and experts in tying a stock or arranging lace to fall prettily on a uniform, but about as much use in a fight as spavined lapdogs. Lieutenant Sillière, who had followed Joubert to the firestep, was tall and looked strong, but Dodd mistrusted a man who took such care with his uniform and he could have sworn he detected a whiff of lavender water coming from the young Lieutenant's carefully brushed hair. 'How long are the city walls?' he asked Joubert.

The Captain thought for a moment. 'Two miles?'

'At least, and how many men in the garrison?'

'Two thousand.'

'So work it out, Monsewer,' Dodd said. 'One man every two yards? We'll be lucky if the city holds for three days.' Dodd climbed to one of the bastions from where he could stare between the crenellations at the great fort which stood close to the city. That two-hundred-year-old fortress was an altogether more formidable stronghold than the city, though its very size made it vulnerable, for the fort's garrison, like the city's, was much too small. But the fort's high wall was faced by a big ditch, its embrasures were crammed with cannon and its bastions were high and strong, although the fort was worth nothing without the city. The city was the prize, not the fort, and Dodd doubted that General Wellesley would waste men against the fort's garrison. Boy Wellesley would attack the city, breach the walls, storm the gap and send his men to slaughter the defenders in the rat's tangle of alleys and courtyards, and once the city had fallen the red-coats would hunt for supplies that would help feed the British army. Only then, with the city in his possession, would Wellesley turn his guns against the fort, and it was possible that the fort would hold the British advance for two or three weeks and thus give Scindia more time to assemble his army, and the longer the fort held the better, for the overdue rains might come and hamper the British advance. But of one thing Dodd was quite certain: as Pohlmann had said, the war would not be won here, and to William Dodd the most important thing was to extricate his men so that they could share that victory. 'You will take the regiment's guns and three hundred men and garrison the north gate,' Dodd ordered Joubert.

The Frenchman frowned. 'You think the British will attack in the north?'

'I think, Monsewer, that the British will attack here, in the south. Our orders are to kill as many as we can, then escape to join Colonel Pohlmann. We shall make that escape through the north gate, but even an idiot can see that half the city's inhabitants will also try to escape through the north gate and your job, Joubert, is to keep the bastards from blocking our way. I intend to save the regiment, not lose it with the city. That means you open fire on any civilian who tries to leave the city, do you understand?' Joubert wanted to argue, but one look at Dodd's face persuaded him into hasty agreement. 'I shall be at the north gate in one hour,' Dodd said, 'and God help you, Monsewer, if your three hundred men are not in position.'

Joubert ran off. Dodd watched him go, then turned to Sillière. 'When were the men last paid?'

'Four months ago, sir.'

'Where did you learn English, Lieutenant?'

'Colonel Mathers insisted we speak it, sir.'

'And where did Madame Joubert learn it?'

Sillière gave Dodd a suspicious glance. 'I would not know, sir.'

Dodd sniffed. 'Are you wearing perfume, Monsewer?'

'No!' Sillière blushed.

'Make sure you never do, Lieutenant. And in the meantime take your company, find the Killadar, and tell him to break open the city treasury. If you have any trouble, break the damn thing open yourself with one of our guns. Give every man three months' pay and load the rest of the money on pack animals. We'll take it with us.'

Sillière looked astonished at the order. 'But the Killadar, Monsieur . . .' he began.

'The Killadar, Monsewer, is a wretched little man with the balls of a mouse! You are a soldier. If we don't take the money, the British will get it. Now go!' Dodd shook his head in exasperation as the Lieutenant went. Four months without pay! There was nothing unusual in such a lapse, but Dodd disapproved of it. A soldier risked his life for his country, and the least his country could do in return was pay him promptly.

He walked eastwards along the firestep, trying to anticipate where the British would site their batteries and where they would make a breach. There was always a chance that Wellesley would pass by Ahmednuggur and simply march north towards Scindia's army, but Dodd doubted the enemy would choose that course, for then the city and fort would lie athwart the British supply lines and the garrison could play havoc with the convoys carrying ammunition, shot and food to the redcoats.

A small crowd was gathered on the southernmost ramparts to gaze towards the distant cloud that betrayed the presence of the enemy army. Simone Joubert was among them, sheltering her face from the westering sun with a frayed parasol. Dodd took off his cocked hat. He always felt oddly awkward with women, at least white women, but his new rank gave him an unaccustomed confidence. 'I see you have come to observe the enemy, Ma'am,' he said.

'I like to walk about the walls, Major,' Simone answered,

59

'but today, as you see, the way is blocked with people.'

'I can clear a path for you, Ma'am,' Dodd offered, touching the gold hilt of his new sword.

'It is not necessary, Major,' Simone said.

'You speak good English, Ma'am.'

'I was taught it as a child. We had a Welsh governess.'

'In France, Ma'am?'

'In the Île de France, Monsieur,' Simone said. She was not looking at Dodd as she spoke, but staring into the heat-hazed south.

'Mauritius,' Dodd said, giving the island the name used by the British.

'The Île de France, Monsieur, as I said.'

'A remote place, Ma'am.'

Simone shrugged. In truth she agreed with Dodd. Mauritius was remote, an island four hundred miles east of Africa and the only decent French naval base in the Indian Ocean. There she had been raised as the daughter of the port's captain, and it was there, at sixteen, that she had been wooed by Captain Joubert who was on passage to India where he had been posted as an adviser to Scindia. Joubert had dazzled Simone with tales of the riches that a man could make for himself in India, and Simone, bored with the small petty society of her island, had allowed herself to be swept away, only to discover that Captain Joubert was a timid man at heart, and that his impoverished family in Lyons had first claim on his earnings, and whatever was left was assiduously saved so that the Captain could retire to France in comfort. Simone had expected a life of parties and jewels, of dancing and silks, and instead she scrimped, she sewed and she suffered. Colonel Pohlmann had offered her a way out of poverty, and now she sensed that the lanky Englishman was clumsily attempting to make the same offer, but Simone was not minded to become a man's mistress just because she was bored. She might for love, and in the absence of any love in her life she was fighting an attraction for Lieutenant Sillière, although she knew that the Lieutenant was almost as worthless as her husband and the dilemma was making her think that she was going mad. She wept about it, and the tears only added to her self-diagnosis of insanity. 'When will the British come, Major?' she asked Dodd.

'Tomorrow, Ma'am. They'll establish batteries the next day, knock at the wall for two or three days, make their hole and then come in.'

She looked at Dodd beneath the hem of her parasol. Although he was a tall man, Simone could still look him in the eye. 'They'll take the city that quickly?' she asked, showing a hint of worry.

'Nothing to hold them, Ma'am. Not enough men, too much wall, not enough guns.'

'So how will we escape?'

'By trusting me, Ma'am,' Dodd said, offering Simone a leering smile. 'What you must do, my dear, is pack your luggage, as much as can be carried on whatever packhorses your husband might possess, and be ready to leave. I shall send you warning before the attack, and at that time you go to the north gate where you'll find your husband. It would help, of course, Ma'am, if I knew where you were lodged?'

'My husband knows, Monsieur,' Simone said coldly. 'So once the *rosbifs* arrive I need do nothing for three days except pack?'

Dodd noted her use of the French term of contempt for the English, but chose to make nothing of it. 'Exactly, Ma'am.'

'Thank you, Major,' Simone said, and made a gesture so that two servants, whom Dodd had not noticed in the press of people, came to escort her back to her house.

'Cold bitch,' Dodd said to himself when she was gone, 'but she'll thaw, she'll thaw.'

The dark fell swiftly. Torches flared on the city ramparts, lighting the ghostly robes of the Arab mercenaries who patrolled the bastions. Small offerings of food and flowers were piled in front of the garish gods and goddesses in their candlelit temples. The inhabitants of the city were praying to be spared, while to the south a faint glow in the sky betrayed where a red-coated army had come to bring Ahmednuggur death.

Lieutenant-Colonel Albert Gore had taken command of the King's 33rd in succession to Sir Arthur Wellesley and it had not been a happy battalion when Gore arrived. That unhappiness was not Sir Arthur's fault for he had long left the battalion for higher responsibilities, but in his absence the 33rd had been commanded by Major John Shee who was an incompetent drunk. Shee had died, Gore had received command, and now he was slowly mending the damage. That mending could have been a great deal swifter if Gore had been able to rid himself of some of the battalion's officers, and of all those officers it was the lazy and dishonest Captain Morris of the Light Company whom he would have most liked to dismiss, but Gore was helpless in the matter. Morris had purchased his commission, he was guilty of no offences against the King's regulations and thus he had to stay. And with him stayed the malevolent, unsettling, yellow-faced and perpetually twitching Sergeant Obadiah Hakeswill.

'Sharpe was always a bad man, sir. A disgrace to the army, sir,' Hakeswill told the Colonel. 'He should never have been made into a sergeant, sir, 'cos he ain't the material of what sergeants are made, sir. He's nothing but a scrap of filth, sir, what shouldn't be a corporal, let alone a sergeant. It says so in the scriptures, sir.' The Sergeant stood rigidly at attention, his right foot behind his left, his hands at his sides and his elbows straining towards the small of his back. His voice boomed in the small room, drowning out the sound of the pelting rain. Gore wondered whether the rain was the late beginning of the monsoon. He hoped so, for if the monsoon failed utterly then there would be a lot of hungry people in India the following year.

Gore watched a spider crawl across the table. The house belonged to a leather dealer who had rented it to the 33rd while they were based in Arrakerry and the place seethed with insects that crawled, flew, slunk and stung, and Gore, who was a fastidious and elegant man, rather wished he had used his tents. 'Tell me what happened,' Gore said to Morris, 'again. If you would be so kind.'

Morris, slouching in a chair in front of Gore's table with a thick bandage on his head, seemed surprised to be asked, but he straightened himself and offered the Colonel a feeble shrug. 'I don't really recall, sir. It was two nights ago, in Seringapatam, and I was hit, sir.'

Gore brushed the spider aside and made a note. 'Hit,' he said as he wrote the word in his fine copperplate hand. 'Where exactly?'

'On the head, sir,' Morris answered.

Gore sighed. 'I see that, Captain. I meant where in Seringapatam?'

'By the armoury, sir.'

'And this was at night?'

Morris nodded.

'Black night, sir,' Hakeswill put in helpfully, 'black as a blackamoor's backside, sir.'

The Colonel frowned at the Sergeant's indelicacy. Gore was resisting the urge to push a hand inside his coat and scratch his belly. He feared he had caught the Malabar Itch, a foul complaint that would condemn him to weeks of living with a salve of lard on his skin, and if the lard failed he would be reduced to taking baths in a solution of nitric acid. 'If it

63

was dark,' he said patiently, 'then surely you had no chance to see your assailant?'

'I didn't, sir,' Morris replied truthfully.

'But I did, sir,' Hakeswill said, 'and it was Sharpie. Saw him clear as daylight, sir.'

'At night?' Gore asked sceptically.

'He was working late, sir,' Hakeswill said, 'on account of him not having done his proper work in the daylight like a Christian should, sir, and he opened the door, sir, and the lantern was lit, sir, and he came out and hit the Captain, sir.'

'And you saw that?'

'Clear as I can see you now, sir,' Hakeswill said, his face racked with a series of violent twitches.

Gore's hand strayed to his coat buttons, but he resisted the urge. 'If you saw it, Sergeant, why didn't you have Sharpe arrested? There were sentries present, surely?'

'More important to save the Captain's life, sir. That's what I deemed, sir. Get him back here, sir, into Mister Mickle-white's care. Don't trust other surgeons, sir. And I had to clean up Mister Morris, sir, I did.'

'The blood, you mean?'

Hakeswill shook his head. 'The substances, sir.' He stared woodenly over Colonel Gore's head as he spoke.

'Substances?'

Hakeswill's face twitched. 'Begging your pardon, sir, as you being a gentleman as won't want to hear it, sir, but Sergeant Sharpe hit Captain Morris with a jakes pot, sir. A full jakes pot, sir, liquid and solids.'

'Oh, God,' Gore said, laying down his pen and trying to ignore the fiery itch across his belly. 'I still don't understand why you did nothing in Seringapatam,' the Colonel said. 'The Town Major should have been told, surely?'

'That's just it, sir,' Hakeswill said enthusiastically, 'on account of there not being a Town Major, not proper, seeing as Major Stokes does the duties, sir, and the rest is up to the Rajah's Killadar and I don't like seeing a redcoat being arrested by a darkie, sir, not even Sharpe. It ain't right, that. And Major Stokes, he won't help, sir. He likes Sharpe, see? He lets him live comfortable, sir. Off the fat of the land, sir, like it says in the scriptures. Got himself a set of rooms and a *bibbi*, he has, and a servant, too. Ain't right, sir. Too comfortable, sir, whiles the rest of us sweats like the soldiers we swore to be.'

The explanation made some sort of sense, or at least Gore appreciated that it might convince Sergeant Hakeswill, yet there was still something odd about the whole tale. 'What were you doing at the armoury after dark, Captain?'

'Making certain the full complement of wagons was there, sir,' Morris answered. 'Sergeant Hakeswill informed me that one was missing.'

'And was it?'

'No, sir,' Morris said.

'Miscounted, sir,' Hakeswill said, 'on account of it being dark, sir.' Hakeswill had indeed summoned Morris to the armoury after dark, and there he had hit the Captain with a baulk of timber and, for good measure, had added the contents of a chamber pot that Major Stokes had left outside his office. The sentries had been sheltering from the rain in the guardhouse and none had questioned the sight of Hakeswill dragging the recumbent Morris back to his quarters, for the sight of drunken officers being taken home by sergeants or privates was too common to be remarkable. The important thing was that Morris had not seen who assaulted him and was quite prepared to believe Hakeswill's version, for Morris relied utterly on Hakeswill in everything. 'I blames myself, sir,' Hakeswill went on, 'on account of not chasing Sharpie, but I thought my duty was to look after my Captain, sir, on account of him being drenched by a slop pot.'

'Enough, Sergeant!' Gore said.

'It ain't a Christian act, sir,' Hakeswill muttered resentfully. 'Not with a jakes pot, sir. Says so in the scriptures.'

Gore rubbed his face. The rain had taken the edge off the damp heat, but not by much, and he found the atmosphere horribly oppressive. Maybe the itch was just a reaction to the heat. He rubbed his hand across his belly, but it did not help. 'Why would Sergeant Sharpe assault you without warning, Captain?' he asked.

Morris shrugged. 'He's a disagreeable sort, sir,' he offered weakly.

'He never liked the Captain, sir, Sharpie didn't,' Hakeswill said, 'and it's my belief, sir, that he thought the Captain had come to summon him back to the battalion, where he ought to be soldiering instead of living off the fat of the land, but he don't want to come back, sir, on account of being comfortable, sir, like he's got no right to be. He never did know his place, sir, not Sharpe, sir. Got above himself, sir, he has, and he's got cash in his breeches. On the fiddle, I dare say.'

Gore ignored the last accusation. 'How badly are you hurt?' he asked Morris.

'Only cuts and bruises, sir.' Morris straightened in the chair. 'But it's still a court-martial offence, sir.'

'A capital offence, sir,' Hakeswill said. 'Up against the wall, sir, and God have mercy on his black soul, which I very much doubts God will, God having better things to worry about than a sorry piece of scum like Sharpie.'

Gore sighed. He suspected there was a great deal more to the story than he was hearing, but whatever the real facts Captain Morris was still right. All that mattered was that Sergeant Sharpe was alleged to have struck an officer, and no excuse in the world could explain away such an offence. Which meant Sergeant Sharpe would have to be tried and very probably shot, and Gore would regret that for he had heard some very good things of the young Sergeant Sharpe. 'I had great hopes of Sergeant Sharpe,' the Colonel said sadly.

'Got above himself, sir,' Hakeswill snapped. 'Just 'cos he blew the mine at Seringapatam, sir, he thinks he's got wings and can fly. Needs to have his feathers clipped, sir, says so in the scriptures.'

Gore looked scornfully at the twitching Sergeant. 'And what did you do at the assault of the city, Sergeant?' he asked.

'My duty, sir, my duty,' Hakeswill answered. 'What is all I ever expects any other man to do, sir.'

Gore shook his head regretfully. There really was no way out of this dilemma. If Sharpe had struck an officer, then Sharpe must be punished. 'I suppose he'll have to be fetched back here,' Gore admitted.

'Of course,' Morris agreed.

Gore frowned in irritation. This was all such a damned nuisance! Gore had desperately hoped that the 33rd would be attached to Wellesley's army, which was about to plunge into Mahratta territory, but instead the battalion had been ordered to stay behind and guard Mysore against the bandits who still plagued the roads and hills. Now, it seemed, over-stretched as the battalion was, Gore would have to detach a party to arrest Sergeant Sharpe. 'Captain Lawford could go for him,' he suggested.

'Hardly a job for an officer, sir,' Morris said. 'A sergeant could do the thing just as well.'

Gore considered the matter. Sending a sergeant would certainly be less disruptive to the battalion than losing an officer, and a sergeant could surely do the job as well as anyone. 'How many men would he need?' Gore asked.

'Six men, sir,' Hakeswill snapped. 'I could do the job with six men.'

'And Sergeant Hakeswill's the best man for the job,' Morris

urged. He had no particular wish to lose Hakeswill's services for the few days that it would take to fetch Sharpe, but Hakeswill had hinted that there was money in this business. Morris was not sure how much money, but he was in debt and Hakeswill had been persuasive. 'By far the best man,' he added.

'On account of me knowing the little bugger's cunning ways, sir,' Hakeswill explained, 'if you'll excuse my Hindi.'

Gore nodded. He would like nothing more than to rid himself of Hakeswill for a while, for the man was a baleful influence on the battalion. Hakeswill was hated, that much Gore had learned, but he was also feared, for the Sergeant declared that he could not be killed. He had survived a hanging once, indeed the scar of the rope was still concealed beneath the stiff leather stock, and the men believed that Hakeswill was somehow under the protection of an evil angel. The Colonel knew that was a nonsense, but even so the very presence of the Sergeant made him feel distinctly uncomfortable. 'I'll have my clerk write the orders for you, Sergeant,' the Colonel said.

'Thank you, sir!' Hakeswill said. 'You won't regret it, sir. Obadiah Hakeswill has never shirked his duty, sir, not like some as I could name.'

Gore dismissed Hakeswill who waited for Captain Morris under the building's porch and watched the rain pelt onto the street. The Sergeant's face twitched and his eyes held a peculiar malevolence that made the single sentry edge away. But in truth Sergeant Obadiah Hakeswill was a happy man. God had put Richard Sharpe into his grasp and he would pay Sharpe back for all the insults of the last few years and especially for the ghastly moment when Sharpe had hurled Hakeswill among the Tippoo Sultan's tigers. Hakeswill had thought the beasts would savage him, but his luck had held and the tigers had ignored him. It seemed they had been fed not an hour before and thus the guardian angel who preserved Hakeswill had once again come to his rescue.

So now Obadiah Hakeswill would have his revenge. He would choose six men, six bitter men who could be trusted, and they would take Sergeant Sharpe, and afterwards, somewhere on the road home from Seringapatam where there were no witnesses, they would find Sharpe's money and then finish him. Shot while attempting to escape, that would be the explanation, and good riddance too. Hakeswill was happy and Sharpe was condemned.

Colonel McCandless led Sharpe north towards the wild country where the frontiers of Hyderabad, Mysore and the Mahratta states met. 'Till I hear otherwise,' McCandless told Sharpe, 'I'm assuming our traitor is in Ahmednuggur.'

'What's that, sir? A city?'

'A city and a fort next to each other,' the Colonel said. McCandless's big gelding seemed to eat up the miles, but Sharpe's smaller mare offered a lumpy ride. Within an hour of leaving Seringapatam Sharpe's muscles were sore, within two he felt as though the backs of his thighs were burning, and by late afternoon the stirrup leathers had abraded through his cotton trousers to grind his calves into bloody patches. 'It's one of Scindia's frontier strongholds,' the Colonel went on, 'but I doubt it can hold out long. Wellesley plans to capture it, then strike on north.'

'So we're going to war, sir?'

'Of course.' McCandless frowned. 'Does that worry you?'

'No, sir,' Sharpe said, nor did it. He had a good life in Seringapatam, maybe as good a life as any soldier had ever had anywhere, but in the four years between the fall of Seringapatam and the massacre at Chasalgaon Sharpe had not heard a shot fired in anger, and a part of him was envious of his old colleagues in the 33rd who fought brisk skirmishes against the bandits and rogues who plagued western Mysore.

'We're going to fight the Mahrattas,' McCandless said. 'You know who they are?'

'I hear they're bastards, sir.'

McCandless frowned at Sharpe's foul language. 'They are a confederation of independent states, Sharpe,' he said primly, 'that dominate much of western India. They are also warlike, piratical and untrustworthy, except, of course, for those which are our allies, who are romantic, gallant and heroic.'

'Some are on our side, sir?'

'A few. The Peshwa, for one, and he's their titular leader, but small notice they take of him. Others are staying aloof from this war, but two of the biggest princes have decided to make a fight of it. One's called Scindia, and he's the Maharajah of Gwalior, and the other's called Bhonsla, and he's the Rajah of Berar.'

Sharpe tried standing in the stirrups to ease the pain in his seat, but it only made the chafing of his calves worse. 'And what's our quarrel with those two, sir?'

'They've been much given to raiding into Hyderabad and Mysore lately, so now it's time to settle them once and for all.'

'And Lieutenant Dodd's joined their army, sir?'

'From what we hear, he's joined Scindia's army. But I haven't heard much.' The Colonel had already explained to Sharpe how he had been keeping his ears open for news of Dodd ever since the Lieutenant had persuaded his sepoys to defect, but then had come the terrible news of Chasalgaon, and McCandless, who had been travelling north to join Wellesley's army, had seen Sharpe's name in the report and so had turned around and hurried south to Seringapatam. At the same time he had sent some of his own Mahratta agents north to discover Dodd's whereabouts. 'We should meet those fellows today,' the Colonel said, 'or tomorrow at the latest.'

The rain had not stopped, but nor was it heavy. Mud spattered up the horses' flanks and onto Sharpe's boots and white trousers. He tried sitting half sideways, he tried leaning forward or tipping himself back, but the pain did not stop. He had never much liked horses, but now decided he hated them. 'I'd like to meet Lieutenant Dodd again, sir,' he told McCandless as the two men rode under dripping trees.

'Be careful of him, Sharpe,' McCandless warned. 'He has a reputation.'

'For what, sir?'

'A fighter, of course. He's no mean soldier. I've not met him, of course, but I've heard tales. He's been up north, in Calcutta mostly, and made a name for himself there. He was first over the *pettah* wall at Panhapur. Not much of a wall, Sharpe, just a thicket of cactus thorn really, but it took his sepoys five minutes to follow him, and by the time they reached him he'd killed a dozen of the enemy. He's a tall man who can use a sword and is a fine pistol shot too. He is, in brief, a killer.'

'If he's so good, sir, why is he still a lieutenant?'

The Colonel sighed. 'I fear that is the way of the Company's army, Sharpe. A man can't buy his way up the ladder as he can in the King's army, and there's no promotion for good service. It all goes by seniority. Dead men's shoes, Sharpe. A fellow must wait his turn in the Company, and there's no way round it.'

'So Dodd has been waiting, sir?'

'A long time. He's forty now, and I doubt he'd have got his captaincy much before he was fifty.'

'Is that why he ran, sir?'

'He ran because of the murder. He claimed a goldsmith cheated him of money and had his men beat the poor fellow

71

so badly that he died. He was court-martialled, of course, but the only sentence he got was six months without pay. Six months without pay! That's sanctioning murder, Sharpe! But Wellesley insisted the Company discharge him, and he planned to have Dodd tried before a civilian court and condemned to death, so Dodd ran.' The Colonel paused. 'I wish I could say we're pursuing him because of the murder, Sharpe,' he went on, 'but that isn't so. We're pursuing him because he persuaded his men to defect. Once that rot starts, it might never stop, and we have to show the other sepoys that desertion will always be punished.'

Just before nightfall, when the rain had stopped and Sharpe thought his sore muscles and bleeding calves would make him moan aloud in agony, a group of horsemen came cantering towards them. To Sharpe they looked like *silladars*, the mercenary horsemen who hired themselves, their weapons and their horses to the British army, and he pulled his mare over to the left side of the road to give the heavily armed men room to pass, but their leader slowed as he approached, then raised a hand in greeting. 'Colonel!' he shouted.

'Sevajee!' McCandless cried and spurred his horse towards the oncoming Indian. He held out his hand and Sevajee clasped it.

'You have news?' McCandless asked.

Sevajee nodded. 'Your fellow is inside Ahmednuggur, Colonel. He's been given Mathers's regiment.' He was pleased with his news, grinning broadly to reveal red-stained teeth. He was a young man dressed in the remnants of a green uniform Sharpe did not recognize. The jacket had European epaulettes hung with silver chains, and over it was strapped a sword sling and a sash, both of white silk and both stained brown with dried blood.

'Sergeant Sharpe,' McCandless made the introductions, 'this is Syud Sevajee.'

Sharpe nodded a wary greeting. 'Sahib,' he said, for there was something about Syud Sevajee that suggested he was a man of rank.

'The Sergeant has seen Lieutenant Dodd,' McCandless explained. 'He'll make sure we capture the right man.'

'Kill all the Europeans,' Sevajee suggested, 'and you'll be sure.' The suggestion, it seemed to Sharpe, was not entirely flippant.

'I want him captured alive,' McCandless said irritably. 'Justice must be seen to be done. Or would you rather that your people believe a British officer can beat a man to death without any punishment?'

'They believe that anyway,' Sevajee said carelessly, 'but if you wish to be scrupulous, McCandless, then we shall capture Mister Dodd.' Sevajee's men, a dozen wild-looking warriors armed with everything from bows and arrows to lances, had fallen in behind McCandless.

'Syud Sevajee is a Mahratta, Sharpe,' McCandless explained.

'One of the romantic ones, sir?'

'Romantic?' Sevajee repeated the word in surprise.

'He's on our side, if that's what you mean,' McCandless said.

'No,' Sevajee hurried to correct the Colonel. 'I am opposed to Beny Singh, and so long as he lives I help the enemies of my enemy.'

'Why's this fellow your enemy, sir, if you don't mind me asking?' Sharpe asked.

Sevajee touched the hilt of his *tulwar* as if it was a fetish. 'Because he killed my father, Sergeant.'

'Then I hope you get the bastard, sir.'

'Sharpe!' McCandless said in reprimand.

Sevajee laughed. 'My father,' he explained to Sharpe, 'led one of the Rajah of Berar's *compoos*. He was a great warrior,

73

Sergeant, and Beny Singh was his rival. He invited my father to a feast and served him poison. That was three years ago. My mother killed herself, but my younger brother serves Beny Singh and my sister is one of his concubines. They too will die.'

'And you escaped, sir?' Sharpe asked.

'I was serving in the East India Company cavalry, Sergeant,' Sevajee answered. 'My father believed a man should know his enemy, so sent me to Madras.'

'Where we met,' McCandless said brusquely, 'and now Sevajee serves me.'

'Because in return,' Sevajee explained, 'your British bayonets will hand Beny Singh to my revenge. And with him, of course, the reward for Dodd. Four thousand, two hundred rupees, is it not?'

'So long as he's taken alive,' McCandless said dourly, 'and it might be increased once the Court of Directors hears what he did at Chasalgaon.'

'And to think I almost caught him,' Sevajee said, and described how he and his few men had visited Ahmednuggur posing as *brindarrie*s who were loyal to Scindia.

'*Brindarrie*?' Sharpe asked.

'Like *silladars*,' McCandless told him. 'Freelance horsemen. And you saw Dodd?' he asked Sevajee.

'I heard him, Colonel, though I never got close. He was lecturing his regiment, telling them how they would chase you British out of India.'

McCandless scoffed. 'He'll be lucky to escape from Ahmednuggur! Why has he stayed there?'

'To give Pohlmann a chance to attack?' Sevajee suggested. 'His *compoo* was still close to Ahmednuggur a few days ago.'

'Just one *compoo*, sir?' Sharpe suggested. 'One *compoo* won't beat Wellesley.'

Sevajee gave him a long, speculative look. 'Pohlmann,

Sergeant,' he said, 'is the best infantry leader in Indian service. He has never lost a battle, and his *compoo* is probably the finest infantry army in India. It already outnumbers Wellesley's army, but if Scindia releases his other *compoos*, then together they will outnumber your Wellesley three to one. And if Scindia waits until Berar's troops are with him, he'll outnumber you ten to one.'

'So why are we attacking, sir?'

'Because we're going to win,' McCandless said firmly. 'God's will.'

'Because, Sergeant,' Sevajee said, 'you British think that you are invincible. You believe you cannot be defeated, but you have not fought the Mahrattas. Your little army marches north full of confidence, but you are like mice waking an elephant.'

'Some mice,' McCandless snorted.

'Some elephant,' Sevajee said gently. 'We are the Mahrattas, and if we did not fight amongst ourselves we would rule all India.'

'You've not faced Scottish infantry yet,' McCandless said confidently, 'and Wellesley has two Scottish regiments with him. Besides, you forget that Stevenson has an army too, and he's not so very far away.' Two armies, both small, were invading the Mahratta Confederation, though Wellesley, as the senior officer, had control of both. 'I reckon the mice will startle you yet,' McCandless said.

They spent that night in a village. To the north, just beyond the horizon, the sky glowed red from the reflection of flames on the smoke of thousands of campfires, the sign that the British army was just a short march away. McCandless bargained with the headman for food and shelter, then frowned when Sevajee purchased a jar of fierce local arrack. Sevajee ignored the Scotsman's disapproval, then went to join his men who were gaming in the village's tavern. McCandless

75

shook his head. 'He fights for mercenary reasons, Sharpe, nothing else.'

'That and vengeance, sir.'

'Aye, he wants vengeance, I'll grant him that, but once he's got it he'll turn on us like a snake.' The Colonel rubbed his eyes. 'He's a useful man, all the same, but I wish I felt more confident about this whole business.'

'The war, sir?'

McCandless shook his head. 'We'll win that. It doesn't matter by how many they outnumber us, they won't outfight us. No, Sharpe, I'm worried about Dodd.'

'We'll get him, sir,' Sharpe said.

The Colonel said nothing for a while. An oil lamp flickered on the table, attracting huge winged moths, and in its dull light the Colonel's thin face looked more cadaverous than ever. McCandless finally grimaced. 'I've never been one for believing in the supernatural, Sharpe, other than the providences of Almighty God. Some of my countrymen claim they see and hear signs. They tell of foxes howling about the house when a death is imminent, or seals coming ashore when a man's to be lost at sea, but I never credited such things. It's mere superstition, Sharpe, pagan superstition, but I can't chase away my dread about Dodd.' He shook his head slowly. 'Maybe it's age.'

'You're not old, sir.'

McCandless smiled. 'I'm sixty-three, Sharpe, and I should have retired ten years ago, except that the good Lord has seen fit to make me useful, but the Company isn't so sure of my worth now. They'd like to give me a pension, and I can't blame them. A full colonel's salary is a heavy item on the Company's accounts.' McCandless offered Sharpe a rueful look. 'You fight for King and country, Sharpe, but I fight and die for the shareholders.'

'They'd never replace you, sir!' Sharpe said loyally.

'They already have,' McCandless admitted softly, 'or Wellesley has. He has his own head of intelligence now, and the Company knows it, so they tell me I am a "supernumerary upon the establishment".' He shrugged. 'They want to put me out to pasture, Sharpe, but they did give me this one last errand, and that's the apprehension of Lieutenant William Dodd, though I rather think he's going to be the death of me.'

'He won't, sir, not while I'm here.'

'That's why you are here, Sharpe,' McCandless said seriously. 'He's younger than I am, he's fitter than I am and he's a better swordsman than I am, and that's why I thought of you. I saw you fight at Seringapatam and I doubt Dodd can stand up to you.'

'He won't, sir, he won't,' Sharpe said grimly. 'And I'll keep you alive, sir.'

'If God wills it.'

Sharpe smiled. 'Don't they say God helps those who help themselves, sir? We'll do the job, sir.'

'I pray you're right, Sharpe,' McCandless said, 'I pray you're right.' And they would start at Ahmednuggur, where Dodd waited and where Sharpe's new war would begin.

CHAPTER 3

Colonel McCandless led his small force into Sir Arthur Wellesley's encampment late the following afternoon. For most of the morning they had been shadowed by a band of enemy horsemen who sometimes galloped close as if inviting Sevajee's men to ride out and fight, but McCandless kept Sevajee on a tight leash and at midday a patrol of horsemen in blue coats with yellow facings had chased the enemy away. The blue-coated cavalry were from the 19th Light Dragoons and the Captain leading the troop gave McCandless a cheerful wave as he cantered after the enemy who had been prowling the road in hope of finding a laggard supply wagon. Four hours later McCandless topped a gentle rise to see the army's lines spread across the countryside while, four miles farther north, the red walls of Ahmednuggur stood in the westering sun. From this angle the fort and the city appeared as one continuous building, a vast red rampart studded with bastions. Sharpe cuffed sweat from his face. 'Looks like a brute, sir,' he said, nodding at the walls.

'The wall's big enough,' the Colonel said, 'but there's no ditch, no glacis and no outworks. It'll take us no more than three days to punch a hole.'

'Then pity the poor souls who must go through the hole,' Sevajee commented.

'It's what they're paid to do,' McCandless said brusquely.

The area about the camp seethed with men and animals.

Every cavalry horse in the army needed two lascars to gather forage, and those men were busy with sickles, while nearer to the camp's centre was a vast muddy expanse where the draught bullocks and pack oxen were picketed. *Puckalees*, the men who carried water for the troops and the animals, were filling their buckets from a tank scummed with green. A thorn hedge surrounded six elephants that belonged to the gunners, while next to the great beasts was the artillery park with its twenty-six cannon, and after that came the sepoys' lines where children shrieked, dogs yapped and women carried patties of bullock dung on their heads to build the evening fires. The last part of the journey took them through the lines of the 78th, a kilted Highland regiment, and the soldiers saluted McCandless and then looked at the red facings on Sharpe's coat and called out the inevitable insults. 'Come to see how a real man fights, Sergeant?'

'You ever done any proper fighting?' Sharpe retorted.

'What's a Havercake doing here?'

'Come to teach you boys a lesson.'

'What in? Cooking?'

'Where I come from,' Sharpe said, 'it's the ones in skirts what does the cooking.'

'Enough, Sharpe,' McCandless snapped. The Colonel liked to wear a kilt himself, claiming it was a more suitable garment for India's heat than trousers. 'We must pay our respects to the General,' McCandless said, and turned towards the larger tents in the centre of the encampment.

It had been two years since Sharpe had last seen his old Colonel and he doubted that Major-General Sir Arthur Wellesley would prove any friendlier now than he ever had. Sir Arthur had always been a cold fish, sparing with approval and frightening in his disapproval, and his most casual glance somehow managed to make Sharpe feel both insignificant and inadequate, and so, when McCandless dismounted

79

outside the General's tent, Sharpe deliberately hung back. The General, still a young man, was standing beside a line of six picketed horses and was evidently in a blazing temper. An orderly, in the blue-and-yellow coat of the 19th Dragoons, was holding a big grey stallion by its bridle and Wellesley was alternately patting the horse and snapping at the half-dozen aides who cowered nearby. A group of senior officers, majors and colonels, stood beside the General's tent, suggesting that a council of war had been interrupted by the horse's distress. The grey stallion was certainly suffering. It was shivering, its eyes were rolling white and sweat or spittle was dripping from its drooping head.

Wellesley turned as McCandless and Sevajee approached. 'Can you bleed a horse, McCandless?'

'I can put a knife in it, sir, if it helps,' the Scotsman answered.

'It does not help, damn it!' Wellesley retorted savagely. 'I don't want him butchered, I want him bled. Where is the farrier?'

'We're looking for him, sir,' an aide replied.

'Then find him, damn it! Easy, boy, easy!' These last three words were spoken in a soothing tone to the horse which had let out a feeble whinny. 'He's fevered,' Wellesley explained to McCandless, 'and if he ain't bled, he'll die.'

A groom hurried to the General's side carrying a fleam and a blood stick, both of which he mutely offered to Wellesley. 'No good giving them to me,' the General snapped, 'I can't bleed a horse.' He looked at his aides, then at the senior officers by the tent. 'Someone must know how to do it,' Wellesley pleaded. They were all men who lived with horses and professed to love them, though none knew how to bleed a horse, for that was a job left to servants, but finally a Scottish major averred that he had a shrewd idea of how the thing was done, and so he was given the fleam and its hammer. He took off his red coat, chose a fleam blade at random and stepped up to the shivering stallion. He placed the blade on the horse's neck and drew back the hammer with his right hand.

'Not like that!' Sharpe blurted out. 'You'll kill him!' A score of men stared at him while the Scottish Major, the blade unhit, looked rather relieved. 'You've got the blade the wrong way round, sir,' Sharpe explained. 'You have to line it up along the vein, sir, not across it.' He was blushing for having spoken out in front of the General and all the army's senior officers.

Wellesley scowled at Sharpe. 'Can you bleed a horse?'

'I can't ride the things, sir, but I do know how to bleed them. I worked in an inn yard,' Sharpe added as though that was explanation enough.

'Have you actually bled a horse?' Wellesley demanded. He showed not the slightest surprise at seeing a man from his old battalion in the camp, but in truth he was far too distracted by his stallion's distress to worry about mere men.

'I've bled dozens, sir,' Sharpe said, which was true, but those horses had been big heavy carriage beasts, and this white stallion was plainly a thoroughbred.

'Then do it, damn it,' the General said. 'Don't just stand there, do it!'

Sharpe took the fleam and the blood stick from the Major. The fleam looked like a mis-shapen penknife, and inside its brass case were folded a dozen blades. Two of the blades were shaped as hooks, while the rest were spoon-shaped. He selected a middle-sized spoon, checked that its edge was keen, folded the other blades away and then approached the horse. 'You'll have to hold him hard,' he told the dragoon orderly.

'He can be lively, Sergeant,' the orderly warned in a low voice, anxious not to provoke another outburst from Wellesley.

'Then hang on hard,' Sharpe said to the orderly, then he stroked the horse's neck, feeling for the jugular.

'How much are you going to let out?' Wellesley asked.

'Much as it takes, sir,' Sharpe said, who really had no idea how much blood he should spill. Enough to make it look good, he reckoned. The horse was nervous and tried to pull away from the orderly. 'Give him a stroke, sir,' Sharpe said to the General. 'Let him know it ain't the end of the world.'

Wellesley took the stallion's head from the orderly and gave the beast's nose a fondling. 'It's all right, Diomed,' he said, 'we're going to make you better. Get on with it, Sharpe.'

Sharpe had found the jugular and now placed the sharp curve of the spoon-blade over the vein. He held the knife in his left hand and the blood stick in his right. The stick was a small wooden club that was needed to drive the fleam's blade through a horse's thick skin. 'All right, boy,' he murmured to the horse, 'just a prick, nothing bad,' and then he struck the blade hard with the stick's blunt head.

The fleam sliced through hair and skin and flesh straight into the vein, and the horse reared up, but Sharpe, expecting the reaction, held the fleam in place as warm blood spurted out over his shako. 'Hold him!' he snapped at Wellesley, and the General seemed to find nothing odd in being ordered about by a sergeant and he obediently hauled Diomed's head down. 'That's good,' Sharpe said, 'that's good, just keep him there, sir, keep him there,' and he skewed the blade slightly to open the slit in the vein and so let the blood pulse out. It ran red down the white horse's flank, it soaked Sharpe's red coat and puddled at his feet.

The horse shivered, but Sharpe sensed that the stallion was calming. By relaxing the pressure on the fleam he could lessen the blood flow and after a while he slowed it to a trickle and then, when the horse had stopped shivering, Sharpe pulled the blade free. His right hand and arm were drenched in blood.

He spat on his clean left hand, then wiped the small wound. 'I reckon he'll live, sir,' he told the General, 'but a bit of ginger in his feed might help.' That was another trick he had learned at the coaching tavern.

Wellesley stroked Diomed's nose and the horse, suddenly unconcerned by the fuss all about him, lowered his head and cropped at a miserable tuft of grass. The General smiled, his bad mood gone. 'I'm greatly obliged to you, Sharpe,' Wellesley said, relinquishing the bridle into the orderly's grasp. ''Pon my soul, I'm greatly obliged to you,' he repeated enthusiastically. 'As neat a blood-letting as ever I did see.' He put a hand into his pocket and brought out a *haideri* that he offered to Sharpe. 'Well done, Sergeant.'

'Thank you, sir,' Sharpe said, taking the gold coin. It was a generous reward.

'Good as new, eh?' Wellesley said, admiring the horse. 'He was a gift.'

'An expensive one,' McCandless observed drily.

'A valued one,' Wellesley said. 'Poor Ashton left him to me in his will. You knew Ashton, McCandless?'

'Of course, sir.' Henry Ashton had been Colonel of the 12th, a Suffolk regiment posted to India, and he had died after taking a bullet in the liver during a duel.

'A damned shame,' Wellesley said, 'but a fine gift. Pure Arab blood, McCandless.'

Most of the pure Arab blood seemed to be on Sharpe, but the General was delighted with the horse's sudden improvement. Indeed, Sharpe had never seen Wellesley so animated. He grinned as he watched the horse, then he told the orderly to walk Diomed up and down, and he grinned even more widely as he watched the horse move. Then, suddenly aware that the men about him were taking an amused pleasure from his own delight, his face drew back into its accustomed cold mask. 'Obliged to you, Sharpe,' he said yet again, then he turned and walked towards his tent. 'McCandless! Come and give me your news!'

McCandless and Sevajee followed the General and his aides into the tent, leaving Sharpe trying to wipe the blood from his hands. The dragoon orderly grinned at him. 'That's a six-hundred-guinea horse you just bled, Sergeant,' he said.

'Bloody hell!' Sharpe said, staring in disbelief at the dragoon. 'Six hundred!'

'Must be worth that. Best horse in India, Diomed is.'

'And you look after him?' Sharpe asked.

The orderly shook his head. 'He's got grooms to look after his horses, and the farrier to bleed and shoe them. My job is to follow him into battle, see? And when one horse gets tired I give him another.'

'You drag all those six horses around?' Sharpe asked, astonished.

'Not all six of them,' the dragoon said, 'only two or three. But he shouldn't have six horses anyway. He only wants five, but he can't find anyone to buy the spare. You don't know anyone who wants to buy a horse, do you?'

'Hundreds of the buggers,' Sharpe said, gesturing at the encampment. 'Every bleeding infantryman over there for a start.'

'It's theirs if they've got four hundred guineas,' the orderly said. 'It's that bay gelding, see?' He pointed. 'Six years old and good as gold.'

'No use looking at me,' Sharpe said. 'I hate the bloody things.'

'You do?'

'Lumpy, smelly beasts. I'm happier on my feet.'

'You see the world from a horse's back,' the dragoon said, 'and catch women's eyes.'

'So they're not entirely useless,' Sharpe said and the orderly grinned. He was a happy, round-faced young man with tousled brown hair and a ready smile. 'How come you're the General's orderly?' Sharpe asked him.

The dragoon shrugged. 'He asked my Colonel to give him someone and I was chosen.'

'You don't mind?'

'He's all right,' the orderly said, jerking his head towards Wellesley's tent. 'Don't crack a smile often, leastwise not with the likes of you and me, but he's a fair man.'

'Good for him.' Sharpe stuck out his bloodied hand. 'My name's Dick Sharpe.'

'Daniel Fletcher,' the orderly said, 'from Stoke Poges.'

'Never heard of it,' Sharpe said. 'Where can I get a scrub?'

'Cook tent, Sergeant.'

'And riding boots?' Sharpe asked.

'Find a dead man in Ahmednuggur,' Fletcher said. 'It'll be cheaper than buying them off me.'

'That's true,' Sharpe said, then he limped to the cook tent. The limp was caused by the sore muscles from long hours in the saddle. He had purchased a length of cotton cloth in the village where they had spent the night, then torn the cloth into strips that he had wrapped about his calves to protect them from the stirrup leathers, but his calves still hurt. God, he thought, but he hated bloody horses.

He washed the worst of Diomed's blood from his hands and face, diluted what was on his uniform, then went back to wait for McCandless. Sevajee's men still sat on their horses and stared at the distant city that was topped by a smear of smoke. Sharpe could hear the murmur of voices inside the General's tent, but he paid no attention. It wasn't his business. He wondered if he could scrounge a tent for his own use, for it had already rained earlier in the day and Sharpe suspected it might rain again, but Colonel McCandless was not a man much given to tents. He derided them as women's luxuries, preferring to seek shelter with local villagers or, if no peasant house or cattle byre was available, happily sleeping beneath the stars or in the rain. A pint of rum, Sharpe thought, would not go amiss either.

'Sergeant Sharpe!' Wellesley's familiar voice broke into his thoughts and Sharpe turned to see his old commanding officer coming from the big tent.

'Sir!' Sharpe stiffened to attention.

'So Colonel McCandless has borrowed you from Major Stokes?' Wellesley asked.

'Yes, sir,' Sharpe said. The General was bareheaded and Sharpe saw that his temples had turned prematurely grey. He seemed to have forgotten Sharpe's handiwork with his horse, for his long-nosed face was as unfriendly as ever.

'And you saw this man Dodd at Chasalgaon?'

'I did, sir.'

'Repugnant business,' Wellesley said, 'repugnant. Did he kill the wounded?'

'All of them, sir. All but me.'

'And why not you?' Wellesley asked coldly.

'I was covered in blood, sir. Fair drenched in it.'

'You seem to be in that condition much of the time, Sergeant,' Wellesley said with just a hint of a smile, then he turned back to McCandless. 'I wish you joy of the hunt, Colonel. I'll do my best to help you, but I'm short of men, woefully short.'

'Thank you, sir,' the Scotsman said, then watched as the General went back into his big tent which was crammed with red-coated officers. 'It seems,' McCandless said to Sharpe when the General was gone, 'that we're not invited to supper.'

'Were you expecting to be, sir?'

'No,' McCandless said, 'and I've no business in that tent tonight either. They're planning an assault for first light tomorrow.'

Sharpe thought for a moment that he must have misheard. He looked northwards at the big city wall. 'Tomorrow, sir? An assault? But they only got here today and there isn't a breach!'

'You don't need a breach for an escalade, Sergeant,' McCandless said. 'An escalade is nothing but ladders and murder.'

Sharpe frowned. 'Escalade?' He had heard the word, but was not really sure he knew what it meant.

'March straight up to the wall, Sharpe, throw your ladders against the ramparts and climb.' McCandless shook his head. 'No artillery to help you, no breach, no trenches to get you close, so you must accept the casualties and fight your way through the defenders. It isn't pretty, Sharpe, but it can work.' The Scotsman still sounded disapproving. He was leading Sharpe away from the General's tent, seeking a place to spread his blanket. Sevajee and his men were following, and Sevajee was walking close enough to listen to McCandless's words. 'Escalades can work well against an unsteady enemy,' the Colonel went on, 'but I'm not at all convinced the Mahrattas are shaky. I doubt they're shaky at all, Sharpe. They're dangerous as snakes and they usually have Arab mercenaries in their ranks.'

'Arabs, sir? From Arabia?'

'That's where they usually come from,' McCandless confirmed. 'Nasty fighters, Sharpe.'

'Good fighters,' Sevajee intervened. 'We hire hundreds of them every year. Hungry men, Sergeant, who come from their bare land with sharp swords and long muskets.'

'Doesn't serve to underestimate an Arab,' McCandless agreed. 'They fight like demons, but Wellesley's an impatient man and he wants the business over. He insists they won't be expecting an escalade and thus won't be ready for one, and I pray to God he's right.'

'So what do we do, sir?' Sharpe asked.

'We go in behind the assault, Sharpe, and beseech Almighty God that our ladder parties do get into the city. And once we're inside we hunt for Dodd. That's our job.'

'Yes, sir,' Sharpe said.

'And once we have the traitor we take him to Madras, put him on trial and have him hanged,' McCandless said with satisfaction, as though the job was as good as done. His gloomy forebodings of the previous night seemed to have vanished. He had stopped at a bare patch of ground. 'This looks like a fair billet. No more rain in the offing, I think, so we should be comfortable.'

Like hell, Sharpe thought. A bare bed, no rum, a fight in the morning, and God only knew what kind of devils waiting across the wall, but he slept anyway.

And woke when it was still dark to see shadowy men straggling past with long ladders across their shoulders. Dawn was near and it was time for an escalade. Time for ladders and murder.

Sanjit Pandee was Killadar of the city, which meant that he commanded Ahmednuggur's garrison in the name of his master, Dowlut Rao Scindia, Maharajah of Gwalior, and in principle every soldier in the city, though not in the adjacent fortress, was under Pandee's command. So why had Major Dodd ejected Pandee's troops from the northern gatehouse and substituted his own men? Pandee had sent no orders, but the deed had been done anyway and no one could explain why, and when Sanjit Pandee sent a message to Major Dodd and demanded an answer, the messenger was told to wait and, so far as the Killadar knew, was still waiting.

Sanjit Pandee finally summoned the courage to confront the Major himself. It was dawn, a time when the Killadar was not usually stirring, and he discovered Dodd and a group of his white-coated officers on the southern wall from where the Major was watching the British camp through a heavy telescope mounted on a tripod. Sanjit Pandee did not like to disturb the tall Dodd who was being forced to stoop awkwardly because the tripod was incapable of raising the glass to the level of his eye. The Killadar cleared his throat, but that had no effect, and then he scraped a foot on the firestep, and still Dodd did not even glance at him, so finally the Killadar demanded his explanation, though in very flowery terms just in case he gave the Englishman offence. Sanjit Pandee had already lost the battle over the city treasury which Dodd had simply commandeered without so much as a by-your-leave, and the Killadar was nervous of the scowling foreigner.

'Tell the bloody man,' Dodd told his interpreter without taking his eye from the telescope, 'that he's wasting my bloody time. Tell him to go and boil his backside.'

Dodd's interpreter, who was one of his younger Indian officers, courteously suggested to the Killadar that Major Dodd's attention was wholly consumed by the approaching enemy, but that as soon as he had a moment of leisure, the Major would be delighted to hold a conversation with the honoured Killadar.

The Killadar gazed southwards. Horsemen, British and Indian, were ranging far ahead of the approaching enemy column. Not that Sanjit Pandee could see the column properly, only a dark smudge among the distant green that he supposed was the enemy. Their feet kicked up no dust, but that was because of the rain that had fallen the day before. 'Are the enemy truly coming?' he enquired politely.

'Of course they're not bloody coming,' Dodd said, standing

upright and massaging the small of his back. 'They're running away in terror.'

'The enemy are indeed approaching, sahib,' the interpreter said deferentially.

The Killadar glanced along his defences and was reassured to see the bulk of Dodd's regiment on the firestep, and alongside them the robed figures of his Arab mercenaries. 'Your regiment's guns,' he said to the interpreter, 'they are not here?'

'Tell the interfering little bugger that I've sold all the bloody cannon to the enemy,' Dodd growled.

'The guns are placed where they will prove most useful, sahib,' the interpreter assured the Killadar with a dazzling smile, and the Killadar, who knew that the five small guns were at the north gate where they were pointing in towards the city rather than out towards the plain, sighed in frustration. Europeans could be so very difficult.

'And the three hundred men the Major has placed at the north gate?' Sanjit Pandee said. 'Is it because he expects an attack there?'

'Ask the idiot why else they would be there,' Dodd instructed the interpreter, but there was no time to tell the Killadar anything further because shouts from the ramparts announced the approach of three enemy horsemen. The emissaries rode beneath a white flag, but some of the Arabs were aiming their long-barrelled matchlocks at the approaching horsemen and the Killadar quickly sent some aides to tell the mercenaries to hold their fire. 'They've come to offer us *cowle*,' the Killadar said as he hurried towards the south gate. *Cowle* was an offer of terms, a chance for the defenders to surrender rather than face the horrors of assault, and the Killadar hoped he could prolong the negotiations long enough to persuade Major Dodd to bring the three hundred men back from the north gate.

The Killadar could see that the three horsemen were riding towards the south gate which was topped by a squat tower from which flew Scindia's gaudy green and scarlet flag. To reach the tower the Killadar had to run down some stone steps because the stretch of wall just west of the gate possessed no firestep, but was simply a high, blank wall of red stone. He hurried along the foot of the wall, then climbed more steps to reach the gate tower just as the three horsemen reined in beneath.

Two of the horsemen were Indians while the third was a British officer, and the three men had indeed come to offer the city *cowle*. If the Killadar surrendered, one of the Indians shouted, the city's defenders would be permitted to march from Ahmednuggur with all their hand weapons and whatever personal belongings they could carry. General Wellesley would guarantee the garrison safe passage as far as the River Godavery, beyond which Pohlmann's *compoo* had withdrawn. The officer finished by demanding an immediate answer.

Sanjit Pandee hesitated. The *cowle* was generous, surprisingly generous, and he was tempted to accept because no man would die if he took the terms. He could see the approaching column clearly now, and it looked to him like a red stain smothering the plain. There would be guns there, and the gods alone knew how many muskets. Then he glanced to his left and right and he saw the reassuring height of his walls, and he saw the white robes of his fearsome Arabs, and he contemplated what Dowlut Rao Scindia would say if he meekly surrendered Ahmednuggur. Scindia would be angry, and an angry Scindia was liable to put whoever had angered him beneath the elephant's foot. The Killadar's task was to delay the British in front of Ahmednuggur while Scindia gathered his allies and so prepared the vast army that would crush the invader. Sanjit Pandee sighed. 'There can be no *cowle*,' he called down to Wellesley's three messengers, and the horsemen did not try to change his mind. They just tugged on their reins, spurred their horses and rode away. 'They want battle,' the Killadar said sadly, 'they want loot.'

'That's why they come here,' an aide replied. 'Their own land is barren.'

'I hear it is green,' Sanjit Pandee said.

'No, sahib, barren and dry. Why else would they be here?'

News spread along the walls that *cowle* had been refused. No one had expected otherwise, but the Killadar's reluctant defiance cheered the defenders whose ranks thickened as townsfolk climbed to the firestep to see the approaching enemy.

Dodd scowled when he saw that women and children were thronging the ramparts to view the enemy. 'Clear them away!' he ordered his interpreter. 'I want only the duty companies up here.' He watched as his orders were obeyed. 'Nothing's going to happen for three days now,' he assured his officers. 'They'll send skirmishers to harass us, but skirmishers can't hurt us if we don't show our heads above the wall. So tell the men to keep their heads down. And no one's to fire at the skirmishers, you understand? No point in wasting good balls on skirmishers. We'll open fire after three days.'

'In three days, sahib?' a young Indian officer asked.

'It will take the bastards one day to establish batteries and two to make a breach,' Dodd forecast confidently. 'And on the fourth day the buggers will come, so there's nothing to get excited about now.' The Major decided to set an example of insouciance in the face of the enemy. 'I'm going for breakfast,' he told his officers. 'I'll be back when the bastards start digging their breaching batteries.'

The tall Major ran down the steps and disappeared into the city's alleys. The interpreter looked back at the approaching column, then put his eye to the telescope. He was looking for guns, but at first he could see only a mass of men in red coats with the odd horseman among their ranks, and then he saw something odd. Something he did not comprehend.

Some of the men in the front ranks were carrying ladders. He frowned, then saw something more familiar beyond the red ranks and tilted the glass so that he could see the enemy's cannon. There were only five guns, one being hauled by men and the four larger by elephants, and behind the artillery were more redcoats. Those redcoats wore patterned skirts and had high black hats, and the interpreter was glad that he was behind the wall, for somehow the men in skirts looked fearsome.

He looked back at the ladders and did not really understand what he saw. There were only four ladders, so plainly they did not mean to lean them against the wall. Maybe, he thought, the British planned to make an observation tower so that they could see over the defences, and that explanation made sense and so he did not comprehend that there was to be no siege at all, but an escalade. The enemy was not planning to knock a hole in the wall, but to swarm straight over it. There would be no waiting, no digging, no saps, no batteries and no breach. There would just be a charge, a scream, a torrent of fire, and then death in the morning sun.

'The thing is, Sharpe,' McCandless said, 'not to get yourself killed.'

'Wasn't planning on it, sir.'

'No heroics, Sharpe. It's not your job. We just follow the heroes into the city, look for Mister Dodd, then go back home.'

'Yes, sir.'

'So stay close to me, and I'm staying close to Colonel Wallace's party, so if you lose me, look for him. That's Wallace there, see him?' McCandless indicated a tall, bareheaded officer riding at the front of the 74th.

'I see him, sir,' Sharpe said. He was mounted on McCandless's spare horse and the extra height allowed him to see over the heads of the King's 74th who marched in front of him. Beyond the Highlanders the city wall looked dark red in the early sun, and on its summit he could see the occasional glint of a musket showing between the dome-shaped merlons that topped the wall. Big round bastions stood every hundred yards and those bastions had black embrasures which Sharpe assumed hid the defenders' cannon. The brightly coloured statues of a temple's tower showed above the rampart while a slew of flags drooped over the gate. No one fired yet. The British were within cannon range, but the defenders were keeping their guns quiet.

Most of the British force now checked a half-mile from the walls while the three assault parties organized themselves. Two of the attacking groups would escalade the wall, one to the left of the gate and the other to the right, and both would be led by Scottish soldiers with sepoys in support. The King's 78th, the kilted regiment, would attack the wall to the left while their fellow Highlanders of the 74th would assault to the right. The third attack was in the centre and would be led by the 74th's Colonel, William Wallace, who was also commander of one of the two infantry brigades and evidently an old friend of McCandless for, seeing his fellow Scot, Wallace rode back through his regiment's ranks to greet him with a warm familiarity. Wallace would be leading men of the 74th in an assault against the gate itself and his plan was to run a six-pounder cannon hard up against the big timber gates then fire the gun to blast the entrance open. 'None of our gunners have ever done it before,' Wallace told McCandless, 'and they've insisted on putting a round shot down the gun, but I swear my mother told me you should never load shot to open gates. A double powder charge, she instructed me, and nothing else.'

'Your mother told you that, Wallace?' McCandless asked.

'Her father was an artilleryman, you see, and he brought her up properly. But I can't persuade our gunners to leave out the ball. Stubborn fellows, they are. English to a man, of course. Can't teach them anything.' Wallace offered McCandless his canteen. 'It's cold tea, McCandless, nothing that will send your soul to perdition.'

McCandless took a swig of the tea, then introduced Sharpe. 'He was the fellow who blew the Tippoo's mine in Seringapatam,' he told Wallace.

'I heard about you, Sharpe!' Wallace said. 'A damn fine day's work, Sergeant, well done.' And the Scotsman leaned across to give Sharpe his hand. He was a middle-aged man, balding, with a pleasant face and a quick smile. 'I can tempt you to some cold tea, Sharpe?'

'I've got water, sir, thank you,' Sharpe said, patting his canteen which was filled with rum, a gift from Daniel Fletcher, the General's orderly.

'You'll forgive me if I'm about my business,' Wallace said to McCandless, retrieving his canteen. 'I'll see you inside the city, McCandless. Joy of the day to you both.' Wallace spurred back to the head of his column.

'A very good man,' McCandless said warmly, 'a very good man indeed.'

Sevajee and his dozen men cantered up to join McCandless. They all wore red jackets, for they planned to ride into the city with McCandless and none wanted to be mistaken for the enemy, yet somehow the unbuttoned jackets, which had been borrowed from a sepoy battalion, made them look more piratical than ever. They all carried naked *tulwars*, curved sabres that they had honed to a razor's edge at dawn. Sevajee reckoned there would be no time for aiming firelocks once they were inside Ahmednuggur. Ride in, charge whoever still put up a fight and cut down hard.

The two escalade parties started forward. Each had a pair of ladders, and each party was led by those men who had volunteered to be first up the rungs. The sun was fully above the horizon now and Sharpe could see the wall more plainly. He reckoned it was twenty foot high, give or take a few inches, and the glint of guns in every embrasure and loophole showed that it would be heavily defended. 'Ever seen an escalade, Sharpe?' McCandless asked.

'No, sir.'

'Risky business. Frail things, ladders. Nasty being first up.'

'Very nasty, sir.'

'And if it fails it gives the enemy confidence.'

'So why do it, sir?'

'Because if it succeeds, Sharpe, it lowers the enemy's spirits. It will make us seem invincible. *Veni, vidi, vici.*'

'I don't speak any Indian, sir, not proper.'

'Latin, Sharpe, Latin. I came, I saw, I conquered. How's your reading these days?'

'It's good, sir, very good,' Sharpe answered enthusiastically, though in truth he had not read very much in the last four years other than lists of stores and duty rosters and Major Stokes's repair orders. But it had been Colonel McCandless and his nephew, Lieutenant Lawford, who had first taught Sharpe to read when they shared a cell in the Tippoo Sultan's prison. That was four years ago now.

'I shall give you a Bible, Sharpe,' McCandless said, watching the escalade parties march steadily forward. 'It's the one book worth reading.'

'I'd like that, sir,' Sharpe said straight-faced, then saw that the picquets of the day were running ahead to make a skirmish line that would pepper the wall with musket fire. Still no one fired from the city wall, though by now both the picquets and the two ladder parties were well inside musket range. 'If you don't mind me asking, sir,' Sharpe said to McCandless, 'what's to stop that bugger – sorry, sir – what's to stop Mister Dodd from escaping out the other side of the city, sir?'

'They are, Sharpe,' McCandless said, indicating the cavalry that now galloped off on both sides of the city. The British 19th Dragoons rode in a tight squadron, but the other horsemen were Mahratta allies or else *silladars* from Hyderabad or Mysore, and they rode in a loose swarm. 'Their job is to harass anyone leaving the city,' McCandless went on. 'Not the civilians, of course, but any troops.'

'But Dodd's got a whole regiment, sir.'

McCandless dismissed the problem. 'I doubt that two whole regiments will serve him. In a minute or two there'll be sheer panic inside Ahmednuggur, and how's Dodd to get away? He'll have to fight his way through a crowd of terrified civilians. No, we'll find him inside the place if he's still there.'

'He is,' Sevajee put in. He was staring at the wall through a small telescope. 'I can see the uniforms of his men on the firestep. White jackets.' He pointed westwards, beyond the stretch of wall that would be attacked by the 78th.

The picquets suddenly opened fire. They were scattered along the southern edge of the city, and their musketry was sporadic and, to Sharpe, futile. Men firing at a city? The musket balls smacked into the red stone of the wall which echoed back the crackle of the gunfire, but the defenders ignored the threat. Not a musket replied, not a cannon fired. The wall was silent. Shreds of smoke drifted from the skirmish line which went on chipping the big red stones with lead.

Colonel Wallace's assault party was late in starting, while the kilted men of the 78th, who were assaulting the wall to the left of the gate, were now far in advance of the other attackers. They were running across open ground, their two ladders in plain sight of the enemy, but still the defenders ignored them. A regiment of sepoys was wheeling left, going to add their musket fire to the picquet line. A bagpiper was playing, but he must have been running for his instrument kept giving small ignominious hiccups. In truth it all seemed ignominious to Sharpe. The battle, if it could even be called a battle, had begun so casually, and the enemy was not even appearing to regard it as a threat. The skirmishers' fire was scattered, the assault parties looked under strength and there seemed to be no urgency and no ceremony. There ought to be ceremony, Sharpe considered. A band should be playing, flags should be flying, and the enemy should be visible and threatening, but instead it was ramshackle and almost unreal.

'This way, Sharpe,' McCandless said, and swerved away to where Colonel Wallace was chivvying his men into formation. A dozen blue-coated gunners were clustered about a six-pounder cannon, evidently the gun that would be rammed against the city gate, while just beyond them was a battery of four twelve-pounder cannon drawn by elephants and, as Sharpe and McCandless urged their horses towards Wallace, the four mahouts halted their elephants and the gunners hurried to unharness the four guns. Sharpe guessed the battery would spray the wall with canister, though the silence of the defenders seemed to suggest that they had nothing to fear from these impudent attackers. Sir Arthur Wellesley, mounted on Diomed who seemed no worse for his blood-letting, rode up behind the guns and called some instruction to the battery commander who raised a hand in acknowledgement. The General was accompanied by three scarlet-coated aides and two Indians who, from the richness of their robes, had to be commanders of the allied horsemen who had ridden to stop the flight of fugitives from the city's northern gate.

The attackers from the 78th were just a hundred paces from the wall now. They had no packs, only their weapons. And still the enemy treated them with lordly disdain. Not a gun fired, not a musket flamed, not a single rocket slashed out from the wall.

'Looks like it will be easy, McCandless!' Wallace called.

'I pray as much!' McCandless said.

'The enemy has been praying too,' Sevajee said, but McCandless ignored the remark.

Then, suddenly and appallingly, the silence ended.

The enemy was not ignoring the attack. Instead, from serried loopholes in the wall and from the bastions' high embrasures and from the merlons along the parapet, a storm of gunfire erupted. One moment the wall had been clear in the morning sun, now it was fogged by a thick screen of powder smoke. A whole city was rimmed white, and the ground about the attacking troops was pitted and churned by the strike of bullets. 'Ten minutes of seven,' McCandless shouted over the noise, as though the time was important. Rockets, like those Sharpe had seen at Seringapatam, seared out from the walls to stitch their smoke trails in crazy tangles above the assaulting parties' heads, yet, despite the volume of fire, the defenders' opening volley appeared to do little harm. One redcoat was staggering, but the assault parties still went forward, and then a pain-filled squeal made Sharpe look to his right to see that an elephant had been struck by a cannonball. The beast's mahout was dragging on its tether, but the elephant broke free and, maddened by its wound, charged straight towards Wallace's men. The Highlanders scattered. The gunners had begun to drag their loaded six-pounder forward, but they were right in the injured beast's path and now sensibly abandoned the gun to flee from the crazed animal's charge. The wrinkled skin of the elephant's left flank was sheeted in red. Wallace shouted incoherently, then spurred his horse out of the way. The elephant, trunk raised and eyes white, thumped past McCandless and Sharpe. 'Poor girl,' McCandless said.

'It's a she?' Sharpe asked.

'All draught animals are female, Sharpe. More docile.'

'She ain't docile, sir,' Sharpe said, watching the elephant burst free of the army's rear and trample through a field of stubble pursued by her mahout and an excited crowd of small skinny children who had followed the attacking troops from the encampment and now whooped shrilly as they enjoyed the chase. Sharpe watched them, then involuntarily ducked as a musket ball whipped just over his shako and another ricocheted off the six-pounder's barrel with a surprisingly musical note.

'Not too close now, Sharpe,' McCandless warned, and Sharpe obediently reined in his mare.

Colonel Wallace was calling his men back into formation. 'Damned animals!' he snarled at McCandless.

'Your mother had no advice on elephants, Wallace?'

'None I'd repeat to a godly man, McCandless,' Wallace said, then spurred his horse towards the six-pounder's disordered gunners. 'Pick up the traces, you rogues. Hurry!'

The 78th had reached the wall to the left of the gate. They rammed the foot of their two ladders into the soil, then swung the tops up and over onto the wall's parapet. 'Good boys,' McCandless shouted warmly, though he was far too distant for the attackers to hear his encouragement. 'Good boys!' The first kilted Highlanders were already scrambling up the rungs, but then a man was hit by a bullet from the flanking bastion and he stopped, clung to the ladder, then slowly toppled sideways. A crowd of Highlanders jostled at the bottom of the ladders to be the next up the rungs. Poor bastards, Sharpe thought, so eager to climb to death, and he saw that the leading men on both ladders were officers. They had swords. The men climbed with their bayonet-tipped muskets slung over their shoulders, but the officers climbed sword in hand. One of them was struck and the man behind unceremoniously shoved him off the ladder and hurried up to the parapet and there, inexplicably, he stopped.

His comrades shouted at him to get a bloody move on and scramble over the wall, but the man did nothing except to unsling his musket, and then he was hurled backwards in a misting spray of blood. Another man took his place, and the same happened to him. The officer at the top of the second ladder was crouching on the top rung, occasionally peering over the coping of the wall between two of the dome-shaped merlons, but he was making no attempt to cross the parapet. 'They should have more than two ladders, sir,' Sharpe grumbled.

'Wasn't time, laddie, wasn't time,' McCandless said. 'What's holding them?' he asked as he stared with an agonized expression at the stalled men. The Arab defenders in the nearest bastion were being given a fine target and their musketry was having a terrible effect on the crowded ladders. The noise of the defenders' fire was continuous; a staccato crackle of musketry, the hiss of rockets and the thunderous crash of cannon. Men were blasted off the ladders, and their place was immediately taken by others, but still the men at the top of the rungs did not try to cross the wall, and still the defenders fired and the dead and injured heaped up at the foot of the ladders and the living pushed them aside to reach the rungs and so offer themselves as targets to the unending gunfire. One man at last heaved himself onto the wall and straddled the coping where he unslung his musket and fired a shot down into the city, but almost immediately he was hit by a blast of musket fire. He swayed for a second, his musket clattered down the wall's red face, then he followed it to the ground. The new man at the top of the ladder heaved himself up, then, just like the rest, he checked and ducked back.

'What's holding them?' McCandless cried in frustration. 'In God's name! Go!'

'There's no bloody firestep,' Sharpe said grimly.

McCandless glanced at him. 'What?'

'Sorry, sir. Forgot not to curse, sir.'

But McCandless was not worried about Sharpe's language. 'What did you say, man?' he insisted.

'There's no firestep there, sir.' Sharpe pointed at the wall where the Scotsmen were dying. 'There's no musket smoke on the parapet, sir.'

McCandless looked back. 'By God, you're right.'

The wall had merlons and embrasures, but not a single patch of musket smoke showed in those defences, which meant that the castellation was false and there was no firestep on the wall's far side where defenders could stand. From the outside the stretch of wall looked like any other part of the city's defences, but Sharpe guessed that once the Highlanders reached the wall's summit they were faced with a sheer drop on the far side, and doubtless there was a crowd of enemies waiting at the foot of that inner wall to massacre any man who survived the fall. The 78th were attacking into thin air and being bloodied mercilessly by the jubilant defenders.

The two ladders emptied as the officers at last realized their predicament and shouted at their men to come down. The defenders cheered the repulse and kept firing as the two ladders were carried back from the ramparts.

'Dear God,' McCandless said, 'dear God.'

'I warned you,' Sevajee said, unable to conceal his pride in the fighting qualities of the Mahratta defenders.

'You're on our side!' McCandless snarled, and the Indian just shrugged.

'It ain't over yet, sir,' Sharpe tried to cheer up the Scotsman.

'Escalades work by speed, Sharpe,' McCandless said, 'and we've lost surprise now.'

'It will have to be done properly,' Sevajee remarked smugly, 'with guns and a breach.'

But the escalade was not defeated yet. The assault party

of the 74th had now reached the wall to the right of the gate and their two ladders were swung up against the high red stones, but this stretch of wall did possess a firestep and it was crowded with eager defenders who rained a savage fire down onto the attackers. The British twelve-pounders had opened fire, and their canister was savaging the defenders, but the dead and wounded were dragged away to be replaced by reinforcements who quickly learned that if they let the attackers come up the two ladders then the cannon would cease fire, and so they let the Scots climb the rungs and then hurled down baulks of wood that could scrape a ladder clear in seconds. Then a cannon in one of the flanking bastions hammered a barrel load of stones and scrap iron into the men crowding about the foot of the ladders. 'Oh, dear God,' McCandless prayed again, 'dear God.' More men began to climb the ladders while the wounded crawled and limped back from the walls, pursued by the musket fire of the defenders. A Scottish officer, claymore in hand, ran up one of the ladders with the facility of a sailor swarming up rigging. He cut the claymore at a lunging bayonet, somehow survived a musket blast, put a hand on the coping, but then a spear took him in the throat and he seemed to shake like a gaffed fish before tumbling backwards and carrying two men down to the ground with him. The sound of the defenders' musketry was punctuated by the deeper crash of the small cannon that were mounted in the hidden galleries of the bastions. One of those cannon now struck a ladder in the flank and Sharpe watched appalled as the whole flimsy thing buckled and broke, carrying seven men down to the ground in its wreckage. The 78th had been repulsed and the 74th had lost one of their two ladders. 'This is not good,' McCandless said grimly, 'not good at all.'

'Fighting Mahrattas,' Sevajee said smugly, 'is not like fighting men from Mysore.'

Colonel Wallace's party was still a good hundred yards from the gate, slowed by the weight of their six-pounder cannon. It seemed to Sharpe that Wallace needed more men to handle the cumbersome gun and the enemy's musket fire was taking its toll of the few men he did have shoving at the wheels or dragging at the traces. Wellesley was not far behind Wallace, and just behind the General, mounted on one of his spare horses and with a second on a leading rein, was Daniel Fletcher. The musket fire spurted scraps of dried mud all around Wellesley and his aides, but the General seemed to have a charmed life.

The 78th returned to the attack on the left, only this time they ran their two ladders directly at the bastion which flanked the wall where their first attempt had failed. The threatened bastion reacted with an angry explosion of musket fire. One of the ladders fell, its carriers hard hit by the volley, but the other swung on up and as soon as its top struck the bastion's summit a kilted officer climbed the rungs. 'No!' McCandless cried, as the officer was hit and fell. Other men took his place, but the defenders tipped a basket of stones over the parapet and the tumbling rocks scoured the ladder clear. A volley of musketry made the defenders duck and when the smoke cleared Sharpe saw that the kilted officer was again ascending the ladder, this time without his tall hat. He carried his claymore in his right hand and the big sword hampered him. An Arab fleetingly appeared at the top of the ladder with a lump of timber that he hurled down at the attacker, and the officer was thrown back a second time. 'No!' McCandless lamented again, but then the same officer appeared a third time. He was determined to have the honour of being first into the city, and this time he had tied his red waist-sash to his wrist and let his claymore hang by its hilt from a loop of the silk, thus leaving both hands free and allowing him to climb much faster. He kept climbing, and his men crowded behind him in their big bearskin hats, and the loopholes in the bastion's galleries spat flame and smoke as they scrambled past the bastion's storeys, but magically the officer survived the fusillade and Sharpe had his heart in his mouth as the man drew nearer and nearer to the top. He expected to see a defender appear at any moment, but the attackers who were not queuing at the foot of the ladder were now hammering the bastion's summit with musket fire and under its cover the bare-headed officer scrambled up the last few rungs, paused to take hold of his claymore's hilt, then leaped over the top of the wall. Someone cheered, and Sharpe caught a distinct view of the officer's claymore rising and falling above the red wall's coping. More Highlanders were clambering up the ladder and though some were blasted off by musket fire from the bastion's loopholes, others were at last reaching the high parapet and following their officer onto the defences. The second ladder was swung into place and the trickle of attackers became a stream. 'Thank God,' McCandless said fervently, 'thank God indeed.'

The 78th were in the bastion, and now the 74th, which had been reduced to just one ladder, also made their lodgement. An officer had organized two companies to give the parapet a blast of musketry just as a sergeant reached the top of the ladder, and the fusillade cleared the embrasures as the sergeant clambered over the wall. His bayonet stabbed down, then he reeled backwards as a defender slashed at him with a *tulwar*, but a lieutenant was behind him and he hacked down with his claymore and then kicked the defender in the face. A third man crossed, the fourth was killed, and then another man was on the wall and the Scotsmen screamed their war cries as they began the grim job of clearing the defenders off the firestep. Sharpe could hear the clash of blades on the wall, and see a cloud of powder smoke above the crenellations where the Scots of the 74th were fighting their way along the parapet, but he could see nothing on the bastion where the kilted 78th were fighting. He guessed they were clearing the bastion floor by floor, charging down the steep stone steps and carrying their bayonets to the gunners and infantrymen who manned the lower galleries.

The Scots at last reached the bastion's ground floor where they killed one last defender and then burst out of the tower's inner doorway to be faced by a horde of Arabs who poured a volley of matchlock fire into the attackers' ranks. 'Charge the bastards! Charge them!' The same young officer who had led the assault now rallied his men and led them against the robed defenders who were reloading their long-barrelled muskets. The Highlanders attacked with bayonets and a ferocity born of desperation.

The Scots were inside the city, but so far the only route to reinforce them was up the three remaining ladders, and one of those was bending dangerously after being struck by a small round shot. Wellesley was shouting at Wallace to get the gate open, and Colonel Wallace was bellowing at his gunners to get their damned weapon into place. The defenders above the gate did their best to stop the advancing cannon, but Wallace ordered a company of infantry to help the gunners roll the cannon forward and those men cheered as they bounced and rattled the heavy gun towards the gate. 'Give them fire,' Wallace shouted, 'give them fire!' and his remaining infantrymen blasted a ragged volley up at the gate's defenders. The flags above the rampart twitched as the balls snatched at the silk. The six-pounder rumbled forward, thumping over the uneven road surface that was being pocked by musket balls spat from the gatehouse loopholes. A bagpipe was playing and the savage music made a fine accompaniment to the gun's wild charge. 'Keep firing,' Wallace shouted at his infantry, 'keep firing!' His men's musket balls struck tiny puffs of dust and flakes of stone from the gate that was wreathed in smoke, smoke so thick that the gun seemed to disappear in fog as it rolled the last few yards, but then Sharpe heard the resounding thump as the gun's muzzle was rammed hard against the big wooden gate. 'Get back,' the gun commander shouted, 'get back!' and the men who had hauled the gun scrambled clear.

'Make ready!' Wallace shouted, and his men stopped their firing and dragged out bayonets that they slotted over their blackened musket muzzles. 'Fire the gun!' Wallace shouted. 'Fire it! For God's sake, fire!' A rocket seethed out of the smoke, trailing sparks, and for a second Sharpe thought it would plunge into the heart of Wallace's waiting men, but then it arced up into the clear blue sky and blazed safely away.

Inside the city the Arabs who had tried to defend the bastion now retreated in front of the battle-maddened Scots who swarmed out of the bastion's inner door. The Arabs might come from a hard, warlike country, but so did the kilted men who came snarling into the city. Sepoys were climbing the ladders now and they joined the Highlanders. Their instinct was to charge across the cleared space inside the wall and so reach the cover of the city's alleyways, but the young officer who led the attack knew that the defenders could still rally if he did not open the gate and so let in a flood of attackers. 'To the gate!' he shouted, and led his men along the inner face of the wall to reach the south gate. The Arabs waiting just inside the arch turned and fired as the Scots approached, but the young officer seemed invincible. He screamed as he charged, then his reddened claymore slashed down, and his men's bayonets lunged forward. Two sepoys joined them, stabbing and screaming, and the outnumbered Arabs died or fled. 'Open the gate!' the young officer shouted, and one of the sepoys ran forward to lift the heavy locking bar out of its iron brackets.

'Fire!' Colonel Wallace shouted on the gate's far side.

The gun captain touched his portfire to the priming reed. There was a fizz of spark, a wisp of smoke and then the double-charged gun leaped back and the sound of its massive discharge was magnified by the echo that bounced deafeningly off the gate's high archway. The doors splintered, and the sepoy who had been lifting the bar was cut in two by the six-pound ball and by the wicked-edged scraps of shattered timber that exploded into the city. The other attackers on the inner side of the gate reeled away from the smoke and flame of the blast, but the bar was lifted and the cannon's discharge swung the gates open.

'Charge!' Wallace shouted, and his men screamed as they ran into the smoke-shrouded arch and pushed past the gun and trampled over the bloody halves of the slaughtered sepoy.

'Come on, Sharpe, come on!' McCandless had his own claymore drawn and the old man's face was alight with excitement as he spurred his horse towards the doomed city. The assault troops who had been waiting to climb the ladders now joined the surge of men running towards the broken gates.

For Ahmednuggur had fallen, and from the first shot until the opening of the gate it had taken just twenty minutes. And now the redcoats went for their reward and the suffering inside the city could begin.

Major William Dodd had never reached his breakfast. Instead he had hurried back to the walls the moment he heard the first muskets fire and, once on the firestep, he had stared appalled at the ladder parties, for he had never once anticipated that the British would attempt an escalade. Of all the methods of taking a city, an escalade was the riskiest, but Dodd realized he should have foreseen it. Ahmednuggur had no ditch, nor any glacis, indeed the city had no obstacle outside its ramparts and that made it a prime candidate for escalade, though Dodd had never believed that Boy Wellesley would dare try such a stratagem. He thought Wellesley too cautious.

None of the assaults was aimed at the stretch of wall where Dodd's men were positioned, so all they could do was fire their muskets obliquely at the advancing British, but the distance was too great for their fire to be effective and the thick powder smoke of their muskets soon obscured their aim and so Dodd ordered them to cease fire. 'I can only see four ladders,' his interpreter said.

'Must have more than four,' Dodd remarked. 'Can't do it with just four.'

For a time it seemed the Major must be right for the defence was making a mockery of the attack, while Dodd's men were troubled by nothing more threatening than a scatter of sepoy skirmishers who fired ineffectually at his stretch of the wall. He showed his derision of the skirmishers' fire by standing openly in an embrasure from where he could watch the enemy's cavalry ride about the city's flank to cut off any escape from the northern gate. He could deal with a few cavalrymen, he decided. A scrap of stone was driven from the coping beside him by a musket ball. The stone flake rapped against the leather swordbelt that was buckled round Dodd's new white coat. He did not like wearing white. It showed the dirt, but worse, it made any wound look much worse than it really was. Blood on a red coat hardly showed, but even a small amount of blood on a white coat could make a nervous man terrified. He wondered if Pohlmann or Scindia would agree to the cost of new jackets. Brown, maybe, or dark blue.

The interpreter came to where the Major stood in the embrasure. 'The Killadar requests that we form up behind the gate, sir.'

'Noted,' Dodd said curtly.

'He says the enemy are approaching the gate with a gun, sahib.'

'Sensible of them,' Dodd said, but otherwise ignored the request. Instead he stared eastwards and saw a Scottish officer suddenly appear at the summit of a bastion. Kill him, he silently urged the Arabs in the bastion, but the young officer jumped down and began laying about him with his claymore, and suddenly there were more kilted Scotsmen crossing the wall. 'I do hate the bloody Scots,' he said.

'Sahib?' The interpreter asked.

'Priggish bastards, they are,' Dodd said, but the priggish bastards looked as if they had just captured the city and Dodd knew it would be madness to get involved in a doomed fight to save it. That way he would lose his regiment.

'Sahib?' the interpreter interrupted Dodd nervously. 'The Killadar was insistent, sir.'

'Bugger the Killadar,' Dodd said, jumping down from the embrasure. 'I want the men off the wall,' he ordered, 'and formed in companies on the inner esplanade.' He pointed down to the wide space just inside the wall. 'Now,' he added and, with one last glance at the attackers, he ran down the steps. 'Jemadar!' he shouted to Gopal, whom he had promoted as a reward for loyalty.

'Sahib!'

'Form up! March by companies to the north gate! If any civilians block your path, open fire!'

'Kill them?' the Jemadar asked.

'I don't want you to bloody tickle them, Gopal. Slaughter them!'

The interpreter had listened to this exchange and stared appalled at the tall Englishman. 'But, sir . . .' he began to plead.

'The city's lost,' Dodd growled, 'and the second rule of war is not to reinforce failure.'

The interpreter wondered what the first rule was, but knew this was not the time to ask. 'But the Killadar, sir . . .'

'Is a lily-livered mouse and we are men. Our orders are to save the regiment so it can fight again. Now, go!'

Dodd saw the first redcoats burst out of the inner door of the bastion, heard the Arab volley that threw some of the attackers down into the bloodied dust, but then he turned away from the fight and followed his men into the city's streets. It went against the grain to abandon a fight, but Dodd knew his duty. The city might die, but the regiment must live. Captain Joubert should be holding the north gate safe where Dodd's guns waited, and where his own saddle horses and pack mule were ready, and so he called for his other French officer, the young Lieutenant Sillière, and told him to take a dozen men to rescue Simone Joubert from the panic that he knew was about to engulf the city. Dodd had rather hoped he could fetch Simone himself, posing as her protector, but he knew that the fall of the city was imminent and there would be no time for such gallantries. 'Bring her safe, Lieutenant.'

'Of course, sir,' Sillière said and, glad to be given such a duty, he ordered a dozen men to follow him into the alleys.

Dodd gave one backward glance towards the south, then marched away from the fight. There was nothing for him here but failure. It was time to go north, for it was there, Dodd knew, beyond the wide rivers and among the far hills and a long way from their supplies, that the British would be lured to their deaths.

But Ahmednuggur, and everything inside it, was doomed.

CHAPTER 4

Sharpe followed McCandless into the gatehouse's high archway, using the weight of his mare to push through the sepoys
and Highlanders who jostled in the narrow roadway that was
still half blocked by the six-pounder cannon. The mare shied
from the thick powder smoke that hung in the air between
the scorched and smoking remnants of the two gates and
Sharpe, gripping the mane to keep in the saddle, kicked his
heels back so that the horse shot forward and trampled
through the fly-blown intestines of the sepoy who had been
struck in the belly by the six-pound shot. He hauled on the
reins, checking the mare's fright among the sprawled bodies
of the Arabs who had died trying to defend the gate. The
fight here had been short and brutal, but there was no resistance left in the city by the time Sharpe caught up with
McCandless who was staring in disapproval at the victorious
redcoats who hurried into Ahmednuggur's alleyways. The
first screams were sounding. 'Women and drink,' McCandless
said disapprovingly. 'That's all they'll be thinking of, women
and drink.'

'Loot too, sir,' Sharpe corrected the Scotsman. 'It's a
wicked world, sir,' he added hastily, wishing he could be let
off the leash himself to join the plunderers. Sevajee and his
men were through the gate now, wheeling their horses behind
Sharpe, who glanced up at the walls to see, with some surprise,
that many of the city's defenders were still on the firestep,

though they were making no effort to fire at the red-coated enemy who flooded through the broken gate. 'So what do we do, sir?' he asked.

McCandless, usually so sure of himself, seemed at a momentary loss, but then he saw a wounded Mahratta crawling across the cleared space inside the wall and, throwing his reins to Sharpe, he dismounted and crossed to the casualty. He helped the wounded man into the shelter of a doorway and there propped him against a wall and gave him a drink from his canteen. He spoke to the wounded man for a few seconds. Sevajee, his *tulwar* still drawn, came alongside Sharpe. 'First we kill them, then we give them water,' the Indian said.

'Funny business, war, sir,' Sharpe said.

'Do you enjoy it?' Sevajee asked.

'Don't rightly know, sir. Haven't seen much.' A short skirmish in Flanders, the swift victory of Malavelly, the chaos at the fall of Seringapatam, the horror of Chasalgaon and today's fierce escalade: that was Sharpe's full experience of war and he harboured all the memories and tried to work out from them some pattern that would tell him how he would react when the next violence erupted in his life. He thought he enjoyed it, but he was dimly aware that perhaps he ought not to enjoy it. 'You, sir?' he asked Sevajee.

'I love it, Sergeant,' the Indian said simply.

'You've never been wounded?' Sharpe guessed.

'Twice. But a gambler does not stop throwing dice because he loses.'

McCandless came running back from the wounded man. 'Dodd's heading for the north gate!'

'This way,' Sevajee said, sawing his reins and leading his cut-throats off to the right where he reckoned they would avoid the press of panicked people crowding the centre of the city.

'That wounded man was the Killadar,' McCandless said as he fiddled his left boot into the stirrup, then hauled himself into the saddle. 'Dying, poor fellow. Took a bullet in the stomach.'

'Their chief man, eh?' Sharpe said, looking up at the gate-house where a Highlander was ripping down Scindia's flags.

'And he was bitterly unhappy with our Lieutenant Dodd,' McCandless said as he spurred his horse after Sevajee. 'It seems he deserted the defences.'

'He's in a hurry to get away, sir,' Sharpe suggested.

'Then let us hurry to stop him,' McCandless said, quickening his horse so that he could push through Sevajee's men to reach the front ranks of the pursuers. Sevajee was using the alleyways beneath the eastern walls and for a time the narrow streets were comparatively empty, but then the crowds increased and their troubles began. A dog yapped at the heels of McCandless's horse, making it rear, then a holy cow with blue painted horns wandered into their path and Sevajee insisted they wait for the beast, but McCandless angrily banged the cow's bony rump with the flat of his claymore to drive it aside, then his horse shied again as a blast of musketry sounded just around the corner. A group of sepoys were shooting open a locked door, but McCandless could not spare the time to stop their depredations. 'Wellesley will have to hang some of them,' he said, spurring on. Refugees were fleeing into the alleys, hammering on locked doors or scaling mud walls to find safety. A woman, carrying a vast bundle on her head, was knocked to the ground by a sepoy who began slashing at the bundle's ropes with his bayonet. Two Arabs, both armed with massive matchlock guns with pearl-studded stocks, appeared ahead of them and Sharpe unslung his musket, but the two men were not disposed to continue a lost fight and so vanished into a gateway. The street was littered with discarded uniform jackets, some green, some blue, some brown, all thrown off by panicking defenders who now tried to pass themselves off as civilians. The crowds thickened as they neared the city's northern edge and the air of panic here was palpable. Muskets sounded constantly in the city and every shot, like every scream, sent a shudder through the crowds that eddied in hopeless search of an escape.

McCandless was shouting at the crowds, and using the threat of his sword to make a passage. There were plenty of men in the streets who might have opposed the Colonel's party, and some of those men still had weapons, but none made any threatening move. Ahmednuggur's surviving defenders only wanted to live, while the civilians had been plunged into terror. A crowd had invaded a Hindu temple where the women swayed and wailed in front of their garlanded idols. A child carrying a birdcage scurried across the road and McCandless wrenched his horse aside to avoid trampling the toddler, and then a loud volley of musketry sounded close ahead. There was a pause, and Sharpe imagined the men tearing open new cartridges and ramming the bullets into their muzzles, and then, exactly at the moment he expected it, the second volley sounded. This was not the ragged noise of plundering men blasting open locked doors, but a disciplined infantry fight. 'I warrant that fight's at the north gate!' McCandless called back excitedly.

'Sounds heavy, sir,' Sharpe said.

'It'll be panic, man, panic! We'll just ride in and snatch the fellow!' McCandless, so close to his quarry, was elated. A third volley sounded, and this time Sharpe heard the musket balls smacking against mud walls or ripping through the thatched roofs. The crowds were suddenly thinner and McCandless drove back his spurs to urge his big gelding closer to the firefight. Sevajee was alongside him, *tulwar* shining, and his men just behind. The city walls were close to their right-hand side, and ahead, over a jumble of thatched and slate roofs, Sharpe could see a blue-and-green-striped flag flying over the ramparts of a square tower like the bastion that crowned the south gate. The tower had to be above the north gate, and he kicked his horse on and hauled back the cock of his musket.

The horsemen cleared the last buildings and the gate was now only thirty yards ahead on the far side of an open, paved space, but the moment McCandless saw the gate he wrenched his reins to swerve his horse aside. Sevajee did the same, but the men behind, Sharpe included, were too late. Sharpe had thought that the disciplined volleys must be being fired by redcoats or sepoys, but instead two companies of white-jacketed soldiers were barring the way to the gate and it was those men who were firing to keep the space around the gate clear for other white-coated companies who were marching in double-quick time to escape the city. The volleys were being fired indiscriminately at civilians, redcoats and fugitive defenders alike, their aim solely to keep the gate free for the white-coated companies that were under the command of an unnaturally tall man mounted on a gaunt black horse. And just as Sharpe saw the man, and recognized him, so the left-hand company aimed at the horsemen and fired.

A horse screamed. Blood spurted fast and warm over the cobbles as the beast fell, trapping its rider and breaking his leg. Another of Sevajee's men was down, his *tulwar* ringing as it skittered across the stones. Sharpe heard the whistle of musket balls all about him and he tugged on the reins, wrenching the mare back towards the alley, but she protested his violence and turned back towards the enemy. He kicked her. 'Move, you bitch!' he shouted. 'Move!' He could hear ramrods rattling in barrels and he knew it would only be seconds before another volley came his way, but then McCandless was beside him and the Scotsman leaned over, seized Sharpe's bridle and hauled him safely into the shelter of an alley.

'Thank you, sir,' Sharpe said. He had lost control of his horse and felt ashamed. The mare was quivering and he patted her neck just as Dodd's next volley hammered its huge noise through the city. The balls thumped into the mud-brick walls, shattered tiles and tore handfuls out of the palm thatch. McCandless had dismounted, so Sharpe now kicked his feet from the stirrups, dropped from the saddle and ran to join the Colonel at the mouth of the alley. Once there, he looked for Dodd through the clearing smoke, found him and aimed the musket.

McCandless hurriedly pushed the musket down. 'What are you doing, man?'

'Killing the bugger, sir,' Sharpe snarled, remembering the stench of blood at Chasalgaon.

'You'll do no such thing, Sergeant,' McCandless growled. 'I want him alive!'

Sharpe cursed, but did not shoot. Dodd, he saw, was very calm. He had caused another massacre here, but this time he had been killing Ahmednuggur's civilians to prevent them from crowding the gateway, and his killers, the two white-coated companies, still stood guard on the gate even though the remaining companies had all vanished into the sunlit country beyond the archway's long dark tunnel. So why were those two companies lingering? Why did Dodd not extricate them before the rampaging sepoys and Highlanders caught up with him? The ground ahead of the two rearguard companies was littered with dead and dying fugitives and a horrid number of those corpses and casualties were women and children, while more weeping and shrieking people, terrified by the volley fire and equally frightened of the invaders spreading into the city behind them, were crammed into every street or alley that opened onto the cleared space by the gate.

'Why doesn't he leave?' McCandless wondered aloud.

'He's waiting for something, sir,' Sharpe said.

'We need men,' McCandless said. 'Go and fetch some. I'll keep an eye on Dodd.'

'Me, sir? Fetch men?'

'You're a sergeant, aren't you?' McCandless snapped. 'So behave like one. Get me an infantry company. Highlanders, preferably. Now go!'

Sharpe cursed under his breath, then sprinted back into the city. How the hell was he expected to find men? There were plenty of redcoats in sight, but none was under discipline, and demanding that looters abandon their plunder to go into another fight would like as not prove a waste of time if not downright suicidal. Sharpe needed to find an officer, and so he bullied his way through the terrified crowd in hope of discovering a company of Highlanders that was still obeying orders.

A splintering crash directly above his head made him duck into a doorway just seconds before a flimsy balcony collapsed under the weight of three sepoys and a dark wooden trunk they had dragged from a bedroom. The trunk split apart when it hit the street, spilling out a trickle of coins, and the three injured sepoys screamed as they were trampled by a rush of soldiers and civilians who plunged in to collect the loot. A tall Scottish sergeant used his musket butt to clear a space about the broken trunk, then knelt and began scooping the coins into his upturned bearskin. He snarled at Sharpe, thinking him a rival for the plunder, but Sharpe stepped over the Sergeant, tripped on the broken leg of one of the sepoys, and shoved on. Bloody chaos!

A half-naked girl ran out of a potter's shop, then suddenly stopped as her unwinding sari jerked her to a halt. Two redcoats hauled her back towards the shop. The girl's father, blood on his temple, was slumped just outside the doorway amidst the litter of his wares. The girl stared into Sharpe's eyes and he saw her mute appeal, then the door of the shop was slammed shut and he heard the bar dropping into place. Whooping Highlanders had discovered a tavern and were setting up shop, while another Highlander was calmly reading his Bible while sitting on a brass-bound trunk he had pulled from a goldsmith's shop. 'It's a fine day, Sergeant,' he said equably, though he took care to keep his hand on his musket until Sharpe had safely gone past.

Another woman screamed in an alley, and Sharpe instinctively headed towards the terrible sound. He discovered a riotous mob of sepoys fighting with a small squad of white-jacketed soldiers who had to be among the very last of the city's defenders still in recognizable uniforms. They were led by a very young European officer who flailed a slender sword from his saddle, but just as Sharpe caught sight of him, the officer was caught from behind by a bayonet. He arched his back, and his mouth opened in a silent scream as his sword faltered, then a mass of dark hands reached up and hauled him down from his white-eyed horse. Bayonets plunged down, then the officer's blood-soaked uniform was being rifled for money.

Beyond the dead officer, and also on horseback, was a woman. She was wearing European clothes and had a white net veil hanging from the brim of her straw hat, and it was her scream that Sharpe had heard. Her horse had been trapped against a wall and she was clinging to a roof beam that jutted just above her head. She was sitting side-saddle, facing the street and screaming as excited sepoys clawed at her. Other sepoys were looting a pack mule that had been following her horse, and she turned and shouted at them to stop, then gasped as two men caught her legs. 'No!' she shouted. A small riding whip hung from a loop about her right wrist and she tried letting go of the roof beam and slashing down with the leather thong, but the defiance only made her predicament worse.

Sharpe used his musket butt to hammer his way through the sepoys. He was a good six inches taller than any of them, and much stronger, and he used his anger as a weapon to drive them aside. He kicked a man away from the slaughtered officer, stepped over the body, and swung the musket butt into the skull of one of the men trying to pull the woman from her horse. That man went down and Sharpe turned the musket and drove its muzzle into the belly of the second sepoy. That man doubled over and staggered backwards, but just then a third man seized the horse's bridle and yanked it out from the wall so fast that the woman fell back onto the roadway. The sepoys, seeing her upended with her long legs in the air, shouted in triumph and surged forward and Sharpe whirled the musket like a club to drive them backwards. One of them aimed his musket at Sharpe who stared him in the eyes. 'Go on, you bastard,' Sharpe said, 'I dare you.'

The sepoys decided not to make a fight of it. There were other women in the city and so they backed away. A few paused to plunder the dead European officer, while others finished looting the woman's pack mule which had been stripped of its load and grinning sepoys now tore apart her linen dresses, stockings and shawls. The woman was kneeling behind Sharpe, shaking and sobbing, and so he turned and took her by the elbow. 'Come on, love,' he said, 'you're all right now. Safe now.'

She stood. Her hat had come off when she fell from her horse and her dishevelled golden hair hung about her pale face. Sharpe saw she was tall, had an impression that she was pretty even though her blue eyes were wide with shock and she was still shaking. He stooped for her hat. 'You look like you've been dragged through a hedge backwards, you do,' he said, then shook the dust off her hat and held it out to her. Her horse was standing free in the street, so he grabbed the beast's bridle then led woman and animal to a nearby gateway that opened into a courtyard. 'Have to look after your horse,' he said, 'valuable things, horses. You know how a trooper gets a replacement mount?' He was not entirely sure why he was talking so much and he did not even know if the woman understood him, but he sensed that if he stopped talking she would burst into tears again and so he kept up his chatter. 'If a trooper loses his horse he has to prove it's died, see? To show he hasn't sold it. So he chops off a hoof. They carry little axes for that, some of them do. Can't sell a three-footed horse, see? He shows the hoof to his officers and they issue a new horse.'

There was a rope bed in the courtyard and he led the woman to it. She sat and cuffed at her face. 'They said you wouldn't come for three more days,' she said bitterly in a strong accent.

'We were in a hurry, love,' Sharpe said. She had still not taken the hat so he crouched and held it close to her. 'Are you French?'

She nodded. She had begun to cry again and tears were running down her cheeks. 'It's all right,' he said, 'you're safe now.' Then he saw the wedding ring on her finger and a terrible thought struck him. Had the white-coated officer been her husband? And had she watched him hacked down in front of her? 'That officer,' he said, jerking his head towards the street where sepoys were kicking at doors and forcing shuttered windows with their firelocks, 'was he your husband, love?'

She shook her head. 'Oh, no,' she said, 'no. He was a lieutenant. My husband is a captain.' She at last took the hat, then sniffed. 'I'm sorry.'

'Nothing to be sorry about,' Sharpe said, 'except you had a nasty fright. It's all right now.'

She took a deep breath, then wiped her eyes. 'I seem to be crying always.' She looked into Sharpe's eyes. 'Life is always tears, isn't it?'

'Not for me, love, no. Haven't had a weep since I was a kid, not that I can remember.'

She shrugged. 'Thank you,' she said, gesturing towards the street where she had been assailed by the sepoys. 'Thank you.'

Sharpe smiled. 'I didn't do anything, love, 'cept drive the buggers off. A dog could have done that as well as me. Are you all right? You weren't hurt?'

'No.'

He patted her hand. 'Your husband went without you, did he?'

'He sent Lieutenant Sillière to fetch me. No, he didn't. Major Dodd sent Sillière.'

'Dodd?' Sharpe asked.

The woman heard the interest in Sharpe's voice. 'You know him?' she asked.

'I know of him,' Sharpe said carefully. 'Ain't met him, not properly.'

She studied Sharpe's face. 'You don't like him?'

'I hate him, Ma'am.'

'I hate him too.' She shrugged. 'I am called Simone. Simone Joubert.'

'It's a pretty name, Ma'am. Simone? Very pretty.'

She smiled at his clumsy gallantry. 'You have a name?'

'Richard Sharpe, Ma'am, Sergeant Richard Sharpe, King's 33rd.'

'Richard,' she said, trying it out, 'it suits you. Richard the Lion-Heart, yes?'

'He was a great one for fighting, Ma'am.'

'For fighting the French, Sergeant,' she said reprovingly.

'Someone has to,' Sharpe said with a grin, and Simone

Joubert laughed and at that moment Sharpe thought she was the prettiest girl he had seen in years. Maybe not really pretty, but vivacious and blue-eyed and golden-haired and smiling. But an officer's woman, Sharpe told himself, an officer's woman.

'You must not fight the French, Sergeant,' Simone said. 'I won't let you.'

'If it looks like it's going to happen, Ma'am, then I'll let you know and you'll have to hold me down.'

She laughed again, then sighed. A fire had broken out not far away and scraps of burning thatch were floating in the warm air. One of the smuts landed on Simone's white dress and she brushed at it, smearing the black ash into the weave. 'They have taken everything,' she said sadly. 'I had little enough, but it is gone. All my clothes! All!'

'Then you get more,' Sharpe said.

'What with? This?' She showed him a tiny purse hanging from her waist. 'What will happen to me, Sergeant?'

'You'll be all right, Ma'am. You'll be looked after. You're an officer's wife, aren't you? So our officers will make sure you're all right. They'll probably send you back to your husband.'

Simone gave him a dutiful smile and Sharpe wondered why she was not overjoyed at the thought of being reunited with her captain, then he forgot the question as a ragged volley of shots sounded in the street and he turned to see an Arab staggering in the gateway, his robes bright with blood, and an instant later a half-dozen Highlanders leaped onto the twitching body and began to tear its clothing apart. One of them slit the victim's robes with his bayonet and Sharpe saw that the dying man had a fine pair of riding boots.

'There's a woman!' one of the looters shouted, seeing Simone in the courtyard, but then he saw Sharpe's levelled musket and he raised a placatory hand. 'All yours, eh? No trouble, Sergeant, no trouble.' Then the man twisted to look down the street and shouted a warning to his comrades and the six men took to their heels. A moment later a file of sepoys showed in the gateway under the command of a mounted officer. They were the first disciplined troops Sharpe had seen in the city and they were restoring order. The officer peered into the courtyard, saw nothing amiss, and so ordered his men onwards. A half company of kilted redcoats followed the sepoys and Sharpe assumed that Wellesley had ordered the picquets of the day into the city. The picquets, who provided the sentries for the army, were made up of half companies from every battalion.

There was a well in the corner of the yard and Sharpe hauled up its leather bucket to give himself and Simone a drink. He brought up more water for the Frenchwoman's horse, and just then heard McCandless shouting his name through the streets. 'Here, sir!' he called back. 'Here!'

It took a moment or two for McCandless to find him, and when he did the Scotsman was furious. 'Where were you, man?' the Colonel demanded querulously. 'He got away! Clean away! Marched away like a toy soldier!' He had remounted his gelding and stared imperiously down on Sharpe from his saddle. 'Got clean away!'

'Couldn't find men, sir, sorry, sir,' Sharpe said.

'Just one company! That's all we needed!' McCandless said angrily, then he noticed Simone Joubert and snatched off his hat. 'Ma'am,' he said, nodding his head.

'This is Colonel McCandless, Ma'am,' Sharpe made the introduction. 'And this is Simone, sir.' He could not recall her surname.

'Madame Joubert,' Simone introduced herself.

McCandless scowled at her. He had ever been awkward in the presence of women, and he had nothing to say to this young woman so he just glowered at Sharpe instead. 'All I needed was one company, Sharpe. One company!'

'He was rescuing me, Colonel,' Simone said.

'So I surmised, Madame, so I surmised,' the Colonel said unhappily, implying that Sharpe had been wasting his time. More smuts swirled in the smoke down to the yard, while in the street beyond the gateway the picquets were hauling looters from the shops and houses. McCandless stared irritably at Simone who gazed placidly back. The Scotsman was a gentleman and knew the woman was now his responsibility, but he resented the duty. He cleared his throat, then found he still had nothing to say.

'Madame Joubert's husband, sir,' Sharpe said, 'serves in Dodd's regiment.'

'He does, does he?' McCandless asked, showing sudden interest.

'My husband hoped to take command of the regiment when Colonel Mathers left,' Simone explained, 'but, alas, Major Dodd arrived.' She shrugged.

The Colonel frowned. 'Why didn't you leave with your husband?' he demanded sternly.

'That is what I was trying to do, Colonel.'

'And you were caught, eh?' The Colonel patted his horse which had been distracted by one of the burning scraps of straw. 'Tell me, Ma'am, do you have quarters in the city?'

'I did, Colonel, I did. Though if anything is left now . . . ?' Simone shrugged again, implying that she expected to find the quarters ransacked.

'You have servants?'

'The landlord had servants and we used them. My husband has a groom, of course.'

'But you have somewhere to stay, Ma'am,' McCandless demanded.

'I suppose so, yes.' Simone paused. 'But I am alone, Colonel.'

'Sergeant Sharpe will look after you, Ma'am,' McCandless

said, then a thought struck him forcibly. 'You don't mind doing that, do you, Sharpe?' he enquired anxiously.

'I'll manage, sir,' Sharpe said.

'And I am just to stay here?' Simone demanded fiercely. 'Nothing else? That is all you propose, Colonel?'

'I propose, Ma'am, to reunite you with your husband,' McCandless said, 'but it will take time. A day or two. You must be patient.'

'I am sorry, Colonel,' Simone said, regretting the tone of the questions she had shot at McCandless.

'I'm sorry to give you so unfortunate a duty, Sharpe,' McCandless said, 'but keep the lady safe till we can arrange things. Send word to me where you are, and I'll come and find you when everything's arranged.'

'Yes, sir.'

The Colonel turned and spurred out of the courtyard. His spirits, which had collapsed when Dodd had marched out of the city's northern gate, were reviving again, for he saw in Simone Joubert a God-sent opportunity to ride into the heart of his enemy's army. Restoring the woman to her husband might do nothing to visit the vengeance of the Company on Dodd, but it would surely be an unparalleled opportunity to scout Scindia's forces and so McCandless rode to fetch Wellesley's permission for such an excursion, while Simone led Sharpe through the exhausted streets to find her house. On their way they passed an ox cart that had been tipped backwards and weighted down with stones so that its single shaft pointed skywards. A sepoy hung from the shaft's tip by his neck. The man was not quite dead yet and so made small spasmodic motions, and officers, both Scottish and Indian, were forcing sheepish and half-drunken men to stare at the dying sepoy as a reminder of the fate that awaited plunderers. Simone shuddered and Sharpe hurried her past, her horse's reins in his left hand.

'Here, Sergeant,' she said, leading him into an alley that was littered with discarded plunder. Above them smoke drifted across a city where women wept and redcoats patrolled the walls. Ahmednuggur had fallen.

Major Dodd had misjudged Wellesley, and that misjudgement shook him. An escalade seemed too intrepid, too head-strong, for the man Dodd derided as Boy Wellesley. It was neither what Dodd had expected nor what he had wanted from Wellesley. Dodd had wanted caution, for a cautious enemy is more easily defeated, but instead Wellesley had shown a scathing contempt for Ahmednuggur's defenders and launched an assault that should have been easily beaten back. If Dodd's men had been on the ramparts directly in the path of the assault then the attack would have been defeated, of that Dodd had no doubt, for there had only been four ladders deployed and that small number made the ease and swiftness of the British victory even more humiliating. It suggested that General Sir Arthur Wellesley possessed a confidence that neither his age nor experience should have provided, and it also suggested that Dodd might have underestimated Wellesley, and that worried him. Dodd's decision to desert to Pohlmann's army had been forced on him by circumstance, but he had not regretted the decision, for European officers who served the Mahratta chiefs were notorious for the riches they made, and the Mahratta armies far outnumbered their British opponents and were thus likely to be the winners of this war, but if the British were suddenly to prove invincible there would be no riches and no victory. There would only be defeat and ignominious flight.

And so, as he rode away from the fallen city, Dodd was inclined to ascribe Wellesley's sudden success to beginner's luck. Dodd persuaded himself that the escalade must have been a foolish gamble that had been unfairly rewarded with victory. It had been a rash strategy, Dodd told himself, and though it had succeeded, it could well tempt Wellesley into rashness again, and next time the rashness would surely be punished. Thus Dodd attempted to discover good news within the bad.

Captain Joubert could find no good news. He rode just behind Dodd and continually turned in his saddle for a glimpse of Simone's white dress among the fugitives that streamed from the northern gate, but there was no sign of her, nor of Lieutenant Sillière, and each disappointment made Pierre Joubert's loss harder to bear. He felt a tear prickle at the corner of his eye, and then the thought that his young Simone might be raped made the tear run down his cheek.

'What the hell are you blubbing about?' Dodd demanded.

'Something in my eye,' Joubert answered. He wished he could be more defiant, but he felt belittled by the Englishman and unable to stand up to his bullying. In truth Pierre Joubert had felt belittled for most of his life. His small stature and timid nature made him a target, and he had been the obvious choice when his regiment in France had been ordered to find one officer who could be sent as an adviser to Scindia, the Maharajah of Gwalior. They had chosen Joubert, the one officer no one would miss, but the unpopular posting had brought Joubert the one stroke of good fortune that had ever come his way when the ship bringing him to India had stopped at the Île de France. He had met Simone, he had wooed her, he had won her, and he was proud of her, intensely proud, for he knew other men found her attractive and Joubert might have enjoyed that subtle flattery had he not known how desperately unhappy she was. He put her unhappiness down to the vagaries of a newly married woman's temperament and to the heat of India. He consoled himself with the thought that in a year or two he would be summoned back to France and there Simone would learn contentment in the company of his huge family. She would become a mother, learn to keep house and so accept her comfortable fate. So long, that was, as she had survived Ahmednuggur's fall. He spurred his horse alongside Dodd's. 'You were right, Colonel,' the Frenchman said grudgingly. 'There was nothing to be gained by fighting.' He was making conversation in order to keep his mind away from his fears for Simone.

Dodd acknowledged the compliment with a grunt. 'I'm sorry about Madame Joubert,' he forced himself to say.

'The British will send news, I'm sure,' Joubert said, clinging to a hope that Simone would have been rescued by some gallant officer.

'But a soldier's best off without a woman,' Dodd said, then twisted in his saddle to look at the rearguard. 'Sikal's company is lagging,' he told Joubert. 'Tell the buggers to hurry up!' He watched Joubert ride away, then spurred to the head of the column where his vanguard marched with fixed bayonets and charged muskets.

The regiment might have escaped from Ahmednuggur, but it was not yet clear of all danger. British and Mahratta cavalry had ridden around the city to harass any of the garrison who might succeed in escaping, and those horsemen now threatened both flanks of Dodd's column, but their threat was small. Scores of other men were fleeing the city, and those fugitives, because they were not marching in disciplined formations, made much easier targets for the horsemen who gleefully swooped and circled about the refugees. Dodd watched as lances and sabres slashed into the scattered fugitives, but if any of the horsemen came too close to his own white-jacketed ranks he called a company to halt, turned it outwards and made them level their muskets. The threat of a volley was usually enough to drive the horsemen to search for easier pickings, and not one of the enemy came within pistol shot of Dodd's ranks. Once, when the column was some two miles north of the city, a determined squadron of British dragoons tried to head off the regiment's march, but Dodd ordered two of his small cannon to be unlimbered and their paltry round shots, bouncing across the flat, dry ground, were sufficient to make the blue-coated horsemen veer away to find another angle of attack. Dodd reinforced the threat by having his lead company fire one volley of musketry which, even though it was at long range, succeeded in unhorsing one dragoon. Dodd watched the defeated horsemen ride away and felt a surge of pride in his new regiment. This was the first time he had observed them in action, and though the excited cavalry was hardly a worthy foe, the men's calmness and efficiency were entirely praiseworthy. None of them hurried, none shot a ramrod out in panic, none seemed unsettled by the sudden, savage fall of the city and none had shown any reluctance to fire on the civilians who had threatened to obstruct their escape through the north gate. Instead they had bitten the enemy like a cobra defending itself, and that gave Dodd an idea. The Cobras! That was what he would call his regiment, the Cobras! He reckoned the name would inspire his men and put fear into an enemy. Dodd's Cobras. He liked the thought.

Dodd soon left his pursuers far behind. At least four hundred other men, most of them Arabs, had attached themselves to his regiment and he welcomed them, for the more men he brought from the disaster, the higher his reputation would stand with Colonel Pohlmann. By early afternoon his Cobras had reached the crest of the escarpment that looked across the vast Deccan plain to where, far in the hazy distance, he could see the brown River Godavery snaking through the dry land. Beyond that river was safety. Behind him the road was empty, but he knew it would not be long before the pursuing cavalry reappeared. The regiment had paused on the escarpment's edge and Dodd let them rest for a while. Some of the fugitive Arabs were horsemen and Dodd sent those men ahead to find a village that would yield food for his regiment. He guessed he would need to camp short of the Godavery, but tomorrow he would find a way to cross, and a day or so later he would march with flying colours into Pohlmann's camp. Ahmednuggur might have fallen like a rotted tree, but Dodd had brought his regiment out for the loss of only a dozen men. He regretted those twelve men, though not the loss of Sillière, but he particularly regretted that Simone Joubert had failed to escape from the city. Dodd had sensed her dislike of him, and he had taken a piquant delight in the thought of cuckolding her despised husband in spite of that dislike, but it seemed that pleasure must be forgotten or at least postponed. Not that it mattered. He had saved his regiment and saved his guns and the future promised plenty of profitable employment for both.

So William Dodd marched north a happy man.

Simone led Sharpe to three small rooms on an upper floor of a house that smelt as though it belonged to a tanner. One room had a table and four mismatched chairs, two of which had been casually broken by looters, the second had been given over to a huge hip bath, while the third held nothing but a straw mattress that had been slit open and its stuffing scattered over the floorboards. 'I thought men joined Scindia to become rich,' Sharpe said in wonderment at the cramped, ill-furnished rooms.

Simone sat on one of the undamaged chairs and looked close to tears. 'Pierre is not a mercenary,' she said, 'but an adviser. His salary is paid by France, not by Scindia, and what money he makes, he saves.'

'He certainly doesn't spend it, does he?' Sharpe asked,

looking about the small grubby rooms. 'Where are the servants?'

'Downstairs. They work for the house owner.'

Sharpe had spotted a broom in the stable where they had put Simone's horse, so now he went and fetched it. He drew a pail of water from the well and climbed the steps that ran up the side of the house to discover that Simone had not moved, except to hide her face in her hands, and so he set about cleaning up the mess himself. Whichever men had searched the rooms for loot had decided to use the bath as a lavatory, so he began by dragging it to the window, throwing open the shutters and pouring the contents into the alley. Then he sloshed the bath with water and scrubbed it with a dirty towel.

'The landlord is very proud of the bath' – Simone had come to the door and was watching him – 'and makes us pay extra.'

'I've never had a proper bath.' Sharpe gave the zinc tub a slap. He assumed it must have been brought to India by a European, for the outside was painted with square-rigged ships. 'How do you fill it?'

'The servants do it. It takes a long time, and even then it's usually cold.'

'I'll have them fill it for you, if you want.'

Simone shrugged. 'We need food first.'

'Who cooks? Don't tell me, the servants downstairs?'

'But we have to buy the food.' She touched the purse at her waist.

'Don't worry about money, love,' Sharpe said. 'Can you sew?'

'My needles were on the packhorse.'

'I've got a sewing kit,' Sharpe said, and he took the broom through to the bedroom and swept up the straw and stuffed it into the slit mattress. Then he took the sewing kit from his pack, gave it to Simone, and told her to sew the mattress together. 'I'll find some food while you do that,' he said, and went out with his pack. The city was silent now, its survivors cowering from their conquerors, but he managed to barter a handful of cartridges for some bread, some lentil paste and some mangoes. He was stopped twice by patrolling redcoats and sepoys, but his sergeant's stripes and Colonel McCandless's name convinced the officers he was not up to mischief. He found the body of the Arab who had been shot just outside the courtyard where he had sheltered Simone and dragged the riding boots off the corpse. They were fine boots of red leather with hawk-claw steel spurs, and Sharpe hoped they would fit. Nearby, in an alley, he discovered a pile of silk saris evidently dropped by a looter and he gathered up the whole bundle before hurrying back to Simone's rooms.

He pushed open the door. 'Even got you some sheets,' he called, then dropped the bundle of silks because Simone had screamed from the bedroom. Sharpe ran to the door to see her facing three Indians who now turned to confront him. One was an older man dressed in a dark tunic richly embroidered with flowers, while the younger two were in simple white robes. 'You got trouble?' Sharpe asked Simone.

The older man snarled at Sharpe, letting loose a stream of words in Marathi.

'Shut your face,' Sharpe said, 'I was talking to the lady.'

'It is the house owner,' Simone said, gesturing to the man in the embroidered tunic.

'He wants you out?' Sharpe guessed, and Simone nodded. 'Reckons he can get a better rent from a British officer, is that it?' Sharpe asked. He put his food on the floor, then walked to the landlord. 'You want more rent? Is that it?'

The landlord stepped back from Sharpe and said something to his two servants who closed in on either side of the redcoat. Sharpe slammed his right elbow into the belly of one and stamped his left foot onto the instep of the other, then grabbed both men's heads and brought them together with a crack. He let go of them and they staggered away in a daze as Sharpe pulled the bayonet from its sheath and smiled at the landlord. 'She wants a bath, you understand? Bath.' He pointed at the room where the bath stood. 'And she wants it hot, you greedy bastard, hot and steaming. And she needs food.' He pointed at the miserable pile of food. 'You cook it, we eat it, and if you want to make any other changes, you bastard, you talk to me first. Understand?'

One of the servants had recovered enough to intervene and was unwise enough to try to tug Sharpe away from his master. The servant was a big and young man, but he had none of Sharpe's ferocity. Sharpe hit him hard, hit him again, kneed him in the crotch, and by then the servant was halfway across the living-room floor and Sharpe pursued him, hauled him upright, hit him again and that last blow took the servant onto the small balcony at the top of the outside stairs. 'Go and break a leg, you sod,' Sharpe said, and tipped the man over the balustrade. He heard the man cry out as he fell into the alley, but Sharpe had already turned back towards the bedroom. 'Have we still got a problem?' he demanded of the landlord.

The man did not understand a word of English, but he understood Sharpe by now. There was no problem. He backed out of the rooms, followed by his remaining servant, and Sharpe went with them to the stairs. 'Food,' he said, pushing the bread, lentils and fruit into the hands of the cowed landlord. 'And Madame's horse needs cleaning and watering. And feeding. Horse, there, see?' He pointed into the courtyard. 'Feed the bugger,' he ordered. The servant he had pushed over the balcony had propped himself against the alley's far wall where he was gingerly touching his bleeding nose. Sharpe spat on him for good measure, then went back inside. 'I never did like landlords,' he said mildly.

Simone was half laughing and half afraid that the landlord would exact a terrible vengeance. 'Pierre was afraid of him,' she explained, 'and he knows we are poor.'

'You're not poor, love, you're with me,' Sharpe said.

'Rich Richard?' Simone said, pleased to have made a joke in a foreign language.

'Richer then you know, love. How much thread is left?'

'Thread? Ah, for the needle. You have plenty, why?'

'Because, my love, you can do me a favour,' he said, and he stripped off his pack, his belt and his jacket. 'I'm not that handy with a needle,' he explained. 'I can patch and darn, of course, but what I need now is some fine needlework. Real fine.' He sat, and Simone, intrigued, sat opposite and watched as he tipped out the contents of his pack. There were two spare shirts, his spare foot cloths, a blacking ball, a brush and the tin of flour he was supposed to use on his clubbed hair, though ever since he had ridden from Seringapatam with McCandless he had let his hair go unpowdered. He took out his stock, which he had similarly abandoned, then the copy of *Gulliver's Travels* that Mister Lawford had given him so he could practise his reading. He had neglected that lately, and the book was damp and had lost some of its pages. 'You can read?' Simone asked, touching the book with a tentative finger.

'I'm not very good.'

'I like to read.'

'Then you can help me get better, eh?' Sharpe said, and he pulled out the folded piece of leather that was for repairing his shoes, and beneath that was a layer of sacking. He took that out, then tipped the rest of the pack's contents onto the table. Simone gasped. There were rubies and emeralds and pearls, there was gold and more emeralds and sapphires and diamonds and one great ruby half the size of a hen's egg.

'The thing is,' Sharpe said, 'that there's bound to be a battle before this Scindia fellow learns his lesson, and as like as not we won't wear packs in a battle, on account of them being too heavy, see? So I don't want to leave this lot in my pack to be looted by some bastard of a baggage guard.'

Simone touched one of the stones, then looked up at Sharpe with wonderment in her eyes. He was not sure that it was wise to show her the treasure, for such things were best kept very secret, but he knew he was trying to impress her, and it was evident that he had. 'Yours?' she asked.

'All mine,' he said.

Simone shook her blonde head in amazement, then began arranging the stones into ranks and files. She formed platoons of emeralds, platoons of rubies and another of pearls, there was a company of sapphires and a skirmish line of diamonds, and all of them were commanded by the great ruby. 'That belonged to the Tippoo Sultan,' Sharpe said, touching the ruby. 'He wore it in his hat.'

'The Tippoo? He's dead, isn't he?' Simone asked.

'And me it was who killed him,' Sharpe said proudly. 'It wasn't really a hat, it was a cloth helmet, see? And the ruby was right in the middle, and he reckoned he couldn't die because the hat had been dipped in the fountain of Zum-Zum.'

Simone smiled. 'Zum-Zum?'

'It's in Mecca. Wherever the hell Mecca is. Didn't work, though. I put a bullet in his skull, right through the bloody hat. Might as well have dunked it in the Thames for all the good it did him.'

'You are rich!' Simone said.

The problem was how to stay rich. Sharpe had not had time to make false compartments in the new pack and pouch that had replaced those he had burned at Chasalgaon, and so he had kept the stones loose in his pack. He had a layer of emeralds at the bottom of his new cartridge pouch, where they would be safe enough, but he needed secure hiding places for the other jewels. He gave a file of diamonds to Simone and she tried to refuse, then shyly accepted the stones and held one against the side of her nose where fashionable Indian women often wore just such a jewel. 'How does it look?' she asked.

'Like a piece of expensive snot.'

She stuck her tongue out at him. 'It's beautiful,' she said. She peered at the diamond that still had its black velvet backing so that the stone would shine more brightly, then she opened her purse. 'Are you sure?'

'Go on, girl, take them.'

'How do I explain them to Pierre?'

'You say you found them on a dead body after the fight. He'll believe that.' He watched her put the diamonds in the purse. 'I have to hide the rest,' he explained to her. He reckoned some of the stones could go in his canteen, where they would rattle a bit when it was dry, and he would have to take care when drinking in case he swallowed a fortune, but that still left a mound of gems unhidden. He used his knife to slit open a seam of his red coat and began feeding the small rubies into the slot, but the stones bunched along the bottom hem and the bulge was an advertisement to every soldier that he was carrying plunder. 'See what I mean?' He showed Simone the bulging seam.

She took the coat, fetched Sharpe's sewing kit from the bedroom, and then began to trap each gem in its own small pouch of the opened seam. The job took her all afternoon, and when she was finished the red coat was twice as heavy. The most difficult stone to hide was the huge ruby, but Sharpe solved that by unwinding his long hair from the shot-weighted bag that clubbed it, then slitting open the bag and emptying the shot. He filled the bag with the ruby and with whatever small stones were left, then Simone rewound his hair about the bag. By nightfall the jewels had vanished.

They ate by lamplight. The bath had never been filled, but Simone said she had taken one a week before so it did not matter. Sharpe had made a brief excursion in the dusk and had returned with two clay bottles filled with arrack, and they drank the liquor in the gloom. They talked, they laughed, and at last the oil in the lamp ran dry and the flame flickered out to leave the room lit by shafts of moonlight coming through the filigree shutters. Simone had fallen silent and Sharpe knew she was thinking of bed. 'I brought you some sheets.' He pointed to the saris.

She looked up at him from under her fringe. 'And where will you sleep, Sergeant Sharpe?'

'I'll find a place, love.'

It was the first time he had slept in silk, not that he noticed, so showing her the gems had not been such a bad idea after all.

He woke to the crowing of cockerels and the bang of a twelve-pounder gun, a reminder that the world and the war went on.

Major Stokes had decided that the real problem with the Rajah's clock was its wooden bearings. They swelled in damp weather, and he was happily contemplating the problem of making a new set of bearings out of brass when the twitching Sergeant reappeared in his office. 'You again,' the Major greeted him. 'Can't remember your name.'

'Hakeswill, sir. Sergeant Obadiah Hakeswill.'

'Punishment on Edom, eh?' the Major said, wondering whether to cast or drill the brass.

'Edom, sir? Edom?'

'The prophet Obadiah, Sergeant, foretells punishment on Edom,' the Major said. 'He threatened it with fire and captivity, as I recall.'

'He doubtless had his reasons, sir,' Hakeswill said, his face jerking in its uncontrollable spasms, 'like I have mine. It's Sergeant Sharpe I'm after, sir.'

'Not here, Sergeant, alas. The place falls apart!'

'He's gone, sir?' Hakeswill demanded.

'Summoned away, Sergeant, by higher authority. Not my doing, not my doing at all. If it was up to me I'd keep Sharpe here for ever, but a Colonel McCandless demanded him and when colonels demand, mere majors comply. So far as I know, which isn't much, they went to join General Wellesley's forces.' The Major was now rummaging through a wooden chest. 'We had some fine augers, I know. Same ones we use on touch-holes. Not that we ever did. Haven't had to rebore a touch-hole yet.'

'McCandless, sir?'

'A Company colonel, but still a colonel. I'll need a round-file too, I suspect.'

'I knows Colonel McCandless, sir,' Hakeswill said gloomily. He had shared the Tippoo's dungeons with McCandless and Sharpe, and he knew the Scotsman disliked him. Which did not matter by itself, for Hakeswill did not like McCandless either, but the Scotsman was a colonel and, as Major Stokes had intimated, when colonels demand, other men obey. Colonel McCandless, Hakeswill decided, could be a problem. But a problem that could wait. The urgent need was to catch up with Sharpe. 'Do you have any convoys going north, sir? To the army, sir?'

'One leaves tomorrow,' Stokes said helpfully, 'carrying ammunition. But have you authority to travel?'

'I have authority, sir, I have authority.' Hakeswill touched the pouch where he kept the precious warrant. He was angry that Sharpe had gone, but knew there was little point in displaying the anger. The thing was to catch up with the quarry, and then God would smile on Obadiah Hakeswill's fortunes.

He explained as much to his detail of six men as they drank in one of Seringapatam's soldiers' taverns. So far the six men only knew that they were ordered to arrest Sergeant Sharpe, but Hakeswill had long worked out that he needed to share more information with his chosen men if they were to follow him enthusiastically, especially if they were to follow him northwards to where Wellesley was fighting the Mahrattas. Hakeswill considered them all good men, by which he meant that they were all cunning, violent and biddable, but he still had to make sure of their loyalty. 'Sharpie's rich,' he told them. 'Drinks when he likes, whores when he likes. He's rich.'

'He works in the stores,' Private Kendrick explained. 'Always on the fiddle, the stores.'

'And he never gets caught? He can't be fiddling that much,' Hakeswill said, his face twitching. 'You want to know the truth of Dick Sharpe? I'll tell you. He was the lucky bugger what caught the Tippoo at Seringapatam.'

''Course he weren't!' Flaherty said.

'So who was it?' Hakeswill challenged them. 'And why was Sharpie made up into a sergeant after the battle? He shouldn't be a sergeant! He ain't experienced.'

'He fought well. That's what Mister Lawford says.'

'Mister bloody Lawford,' Hakeswill said scathingly. 'Sharpie didn't get noticed for fighting well! Bleeding hell, boys, I'd be a major-general if that's all it took! No, it's my belief he paid his way up to the stripes.'

'Paid?' The privates stared at Hakeswill.

'Stands to reason. No other way. Says so in the scriptures! Bribes, boys, bribes, and I knows where he got the money. I know 'cos I followed him once. Here in Seringapatam. Down to the goldsmiths' street he went, and he did his business and after he done it I went to see the fellow he did it with. He didn't want to tell me what the business was, but I thumped him a bit, friendly like, and he showed me a ruby. Like this it was!' The Sergeant held a finger and thumb a quarter-inch apart. 'Sharpie was selling it, see? And where does Sharpie get a prime bit of glitter?'

'Off the Tippoo?' Kendrick said wonderingly.

'And do you know how much loot the Tippoo had? Weighed down with it, he was! Had more stones on him than a Christmas whore, and you know where those stones are?'

'Sharpe,' Flaherty breathed.

'Right, Private Flaherty,' Hakeswill said. 'Sewn into his uniform seams, in his boots, hidden in his pouches, tucked away in his hat. A bloody fortune, lads, which is why when we gets him, we don't want him to get back to the battalion, do we?'

The six men stared at Hakeswill. They knew they were his favourites, and all of them were in his debt, but now they realized he was giving them even more reason to be grateful. 'Equal shares, Sergeant?' Private Lowry asked.

'Equal shares?' Hakeswill exclaimed. 'Equal? Listen, you horrid toad, you wouldn't have no chance of any share, not one, if it wasn't for my loving kindness. Who chose you to come on this parish outing?'

'You did, Sergeant.'

'I did. I did. Kindness of my heart, and you repays it by wanting equal shares?' Hakeswill's face shuddered. 'I've half a mind to send you back, Lowry.' He looked aggrieved and the privates were silent. 'Ingratitude,' Hakeswill said in a hurt voice, 'sharp as a serpent's tooth, it is. Equal shares! Never heard the like! But I'll see you right, don't you worry.' He took out the precious orders for Sharpe's arrest and smoothed the paper on the table, carefully avoiding the spills of arrack. 'Look at that, boys,' he breathed, 'a fortune. Half for me, and you leprous toads get to share the other half. Equally.' He paused to prod Lowry in the chest. 'Equally. But I gets one half, like it says in the scriptures.' He folded the paper and put it carefully in his pouch. 'Shot while escaping,' Hakeswill said, and grinned. 'I've waited four years for this chance, lads, four bloody years.' He brooded for a few seconds. 'Put me in among the tigers, he did! Me! In a tigers' den!' His face contorted in a rictus at the memory. 'But they spared me, they spared me. And you know why? Because I can't die, lads! Touched by God, I am! Says so in the scriptures.'

The six privates were silent. Mad, he was, mad as a twitching hatter, and no one knew why hatters were mad either, but they were. Even the army was reluctant to recruit a hatter because they dribbled and twitched and talked to themselves, but they had taken on Hakeswill and he had survived; malevolent, powerful and apparently indestructible. Sharpe had put him among the Tippoo's tigers, yet the tigers were dead and Hakeswill still breathed. He was a bad man to have as an enemy, and now the piece of paper in Hakeswill's pouch put Sharpe into his power and Obadiah could taste the money already. A fortune. All that was needed was to travel north, join the army, produce the warrant and skin the victim. Obadiah shuddered. The money was so near he could almost spend it already. 'Got him,' he said to himself, 'got him. And I'll piss on his rotten corpse, I will. Piss on it good. That'll learn him.'

The seven men left Seringapatam in the morning, travelling north.

CHAPTER 5

Sharpe was curiously relieved when Colonel McCandless found him next morning, for the mood in the small upper rooms was awkward. Simone seemed ashamed by what had happened in the night and, when Sharpe tried to speak to her, she shook her head abruptly and would not meet his eye. She did try to explain to him, mumbling about the arrack and the jewels, and about her disappointment in marriage, but she could not frame her words in adequate English, though no language was needed to show that she regretted what had happened, which was why Sharpe was glad to hear McCandless's voice in the alley beyond the staircase. 'I thought I told you to let me know where you were!' McCandless complained when Sharpe appeared at the top of the steps.

'I did, sir,' Sharpe lied. 'I told an ensign of the 78th to find you, sir.'

'He never arrived!' McCandless said as he climbed the outside stairs. 'Are you telling me you spent the night alone with this woman, Sergeant?'

'You told me to protect her, sir.'

'I didn't tell you to risk her honour! You should have sought me out.'

'Didn't want to bother you, sir.'

'Duty is never a bother, Sharpe,' McCandless said when he reached the small balcony at the stair head. 'The General expressed a wish to dine with Madame Joubert and I had to

143

explain she was indisposed. I lied, Sharpe!' The Colonel thrust an indignant finger at Sharpe's chest. 'But what else could I do? I could hardly admit I'd left her alone with a sergeant!'

'I'm sorry, sir.'

'There's no harm done, I suppose,' McCandless said grudgingly, then took off his hat as he followed Sharpe into the living room where Simone sat at the table. 'Good morning, Madame,' the Colonel boomed cheerfully. 'I trust you slept well?'

'Indeed, Colonel,' Simone said, blushing, but McCandless was far too obtuse to see or to interpret the blush.

'I have good news, Madame,' the Scotsman went on. 'General Wellesley is agreeable that you should rejoin your husband. There is, however, a difficulty.' It was McCandless's turn to blush. 'I can provide no chaperone, Madame, and you do not possess a maid. I assure you that you may rely utterly upon my honour, but your husband might object if you lack a female companion on the journey.'

'Pierre will have no objection, Colonel,' Simone said meekly.

'And I warrant Sergeant Sharpe will behave like a gentleman,' McCandless said with a fierce look at Sharpe.

'He does, Colonel, he does,' Simone said, offering Sharpe a very shy glance.

'Good!' McCandless said, relieved to be done with such a delicate topic. He slapped his cocked hat against his leg. 'No rain again,' he declared, 'and I dare say it'll be a hot day. You can be ready to ride in an hour, Madame?'

'In less, Colonel.'

'One hour will suffice, Madame. You will do me the honour, perhaps, of meeting me by the north gate? I'll have your horse ready, Sharpe.'

They left promptly, riding northwards past the battery that had been dug to hammer the fort's big walls. The battery's four guns were mere twelve-pounders, scarce big enough to dent the fort's wall, let alone break it down, but General Wellesley reckoned the garrison would be so disheartened by the city's swift defeat that even a few twelve-pound shots might persuade them into surrender. The four guns had opened fire at dawn, but their firing was sporadic until McCandless led his party out of the city when they suddenly all fired at once and Simone's horse, startled by the unexpected noise, skittered sideways. Simone rode side-saddle just behind the Colonel, while Sevajee and his men brought up the rear. Sharpe was wearing boots at last; the tall red leather boots with steel spurs that he had dragged from the body of an Arab.

He glanced back as they rode away. He saw the huge jet of smoke burst from a twelve-pounder's muzzle and a second later heard the percussive thump of the exploding charge and, just as that sound faded, a crack as the ball struck the wall of the fort. Then the other three guns fired and he imagined the steam hissing into the air as the gunners poured water on the overheated barrels. The fort's red walls blossomed with smoke as the defenders' cannon replied, but the pioneers had dug the gunners a deep battery and protected it with a thick wall of red earth, and the enemy's fire wasted itself in those defences. Then Sharpe rode past a grove of trees and the distant fight was hidden and the sound of the guns grew fainter and fainter as they rode farther north until, at last, the sound of the cannonade was a mere grumbling on the horizon. Then they dropped down the escarpment and the noise of the guns faded away altogether.

It was a disconsolate expedition. Colonel McCandless had nothing to say to Simone who was still withdrawn. Sharpe tried to cheer her up, but his clumsy attempts only made her more miserable and after a time he too fell silent. Women were a mystery, he thought. During the night Simone had clung to him as though she were drowning, but since the dawn it had seemed as if she would prefer to be drowned.

'Horsemen on our right, Sergeant!' McCandless said, his tone a reproof that Sharpe had not spotted the cavalry first. 'Probably ours, but they could be enemy.'

Sharpe stared eastwards. 'They're ours, sir,' he called, kicking his horse to catch up with McCandless. One of the distant horsemen carried the new Union flag and Sharpe's good eyes had spotted the banner. The flag was easier to recognize at a distance these days, for since the incorporation of Ireland into the United Kingdom a new red diagonal cross had been added to the flag, and though the new-fangled design looked odd and unfamiliar, it did make the banner stand out.

The cavalry left a plume of dust as they rode to intercept McCandless's party. Sevajee and his men cantered to meet them and Sharpe saw the two groups of horsemen greet each other warmly. The strangers turned out to be *brindarries* from the Mahratta states who, like Sevajee, had sided with the British against Scindia. These mercenaries were under the command of a British officer and, like Sevajee's men, they carried lances, *tulwars*, matchlock guns, flintlocks, pistols and bows and arrows. They wore no uniform, but a handful of the sixty men possessed breastplates and most had metal helmets that were crested with feathers or horsehair plumes. Their officer, a dragoon captain, fell in alongside McCandless and reported seeing a white-coated battalion on the far side of the River Godavery. 'I didn't try and cross, sir,' the Captain said, 'for they weren't exactly friendly.'

'But you're sure they had white coats?'

'No doubts at all, sir,' the Captain said, thus confirming that Dodd must have crossed the river already. He added that he had questioned some grain merchants who had travelled south across the Godavery and those men had told him that Pohlmann's *compoo* was camped close to Aurungabad.

That city belonged to Hyderabad, but the merchants had seen no evidence that the Mahrattas were preparing to besiege the city walls. The Captain tugged his reins, turning his horse southwards so he could carry his news to Wellesley. 'Bid you good day, Colonel. Your servant, Ma'am.' The dragoon officer touched his hat to Simone, then led his brigands away.

McCandless decreed that they would camp that night on the south bank of the River Godavery where Sharpe rigged two horse blankets as a tent for Simone. Sevajee and his men made their beds on the bluff above the river, a score of yards from the tent, and McCandless and Sharpe spread their blankets alongside. The river was high, but it had still not filled the steep-sided ravine that successive monsoons had scarred into the flat earth and Sharpe guessed that the river was only at half flood. If the belated monsoon did arrive the Godavery would swell into a swirling torrent a full quarter-mile wide, but even half full the river looked a formidable obstacle as it surged westwards with its burden of flotsam. 'Too deep to wade,' McCandless said as the sun fell.

'Current looks strong, sir.'

'It'll sweep you to your death, man.'

'So how's the army to cross it, sir?'

'With difficulty, Sharpe, with difficulty, but discipline always overcomes difficulty. Dodd got across, so we surely can.' McCandless had been reading his Bible, but the falling dark now obscured the pages and so he closed the book. Simone had eaten with them, but she had been uncommunicative and McCandless was glad when she withdrew behind her blankets. 'Women upset matters,' the Scotsman said unhappily.

'They do, sir?'

'Perturbations,' McCandless said mysteriously, 'perturbations.' The small flames of the campfire made his already gaunt face seem skeletal. He shook his head. 'It's the heat, Sharpe, I'm convinced of it. The further south you travel, the more sin is provoked among womankind. It makes sense, of course. Hell is a hot place, and hell is sin's destination.'

'So you think that heaven's cold, sir?'

'I like to think it's bracing,' the Colonel answered seriously. 'Something like Scotland, I imagine. Certainly not as hot as India, and the heat here has a very bad effect on some women. It releases things in them.' He paused, evidently deciding he risked saying too much. 'I'm not at all convinced India is a place for European women,' the Colonel went on, 'and I shall be very glad when we're rid of Madame Joubert. Still, I can't deny that her predicament is propitious. It enables us to take a look at Lieutenant Dodd.'

Sharpe poked a half-burned scrap of driftwood into the hottest part of the fire, provoking an updraught of sparks. 'Are you hoping to capture Lieutenant Dodd, sir? Is that why we're taking Madame back to her husband?'

McCandless shook his head. 'I doubt we'll get the chance, Sharpe. No, we're using a heaven-sent opportunity to take a look at our enemy. Our armies are marching into dangerous territory, for no place in India can raise armies the size of the Mahratta forces, and we are precious few in number. We need intelligence, Sharpe, so when we reach them, watch and pray! Keep your eyes skinned. How many battalions? How many guns? What's the state of the guns? How many limbers? Look hard at the infantry. Matchlocks or firelocks? In a month or so we'll be fighting these rogues, so the more we know of them the better.' The Colonel scuffed earth onto the fire, dousing the last small flames that Sharpe had just provoked. 'Now sleep, man. You'll be needing all your strength and wits in the morning.'

Next morning they rode downstream until they found a village next to a vast empty Hindu temple, and in the village were small basket boats that resembled Welsh coracles and McCandless hired a half-dozen of these as ferries. The unsaddled horses were made to swim behind the boats. It was a perilous crossing, for the brown current snatched at the light vessels and whirled them downstream. The horses, white-eyed, swam desperately behind the reed boats that Sharpe noted had no caulking of any kind, but depended on skilful close weaving to keep the water out, and the tug of the horses' leading reins strained the light wooden frames and stretched the weave so that the boats let in water alarmingly. Sharpe used his shako to bail out his coracle, but the boatmen just grinned at his futile efforts and dug their paddles in harder. Once a half-submerged tree almost speared Sharpe's boat, and if the trunk had struck them the boat must surely have been tipped over, but the two boatmen skilfully spun the coracle away, let the tree pass, then paddled on.

It took half an hour to land and saddle the horses. Simone had shared a coracle with McCandless and the brief voyage had soaked the bottom half of her thin linen dress so that the damp weave clung to her legs. McCandless was embarrassed, and offered her a horse blanket for modesty's sake, but Simone shook her head. 'Where do we go now, Colonel?' she asked.

'Towards Aurungabad, Ma'am,' McCandless said gruffly, keeping his eyes averted from her beguiling figure, 'but doubtless we shall be intercepted long before we reach that city. You'll be with your husband by tomorrow night, I don't doubt.'

Sevajee's men rode far ahead now, spread into a picquet line to give warning of any enemy. This land all belonged to the Rajah of Hyderabad, an ally of the British, but it was frontier land and the only friendly troops now north of the Godavery were the garrisons of Hyderabad's isolated fortresses. The rest were all Mahrattas, though Sharpe saw no enemies that day. The only people he saw were peasants cleaning out the irrigation channels in their stubble fields or tending the huge brick kilns that smoked in the sunlight. The brick-workers were all women and children, greasy and sweaty, who gave the travellers scarcely a glance. 'It's a hard life,' Simone said to Sharpe as they passed one half-built kiln where an overseer lazed under a woven canopy and shouted at the children to work faster.

'All life's hard unless you've got money,' Sharpe said, grateful that Simone had at last broken her silence. They were riding a few paces behind the Colonel and kept their voices low so he could not hear them.

'Money and rank,' Simone said.

'Rank?' Sharpe asked.

'They're usually the same thing,' Simone said. 'Colonels are richer than captains, are they not?' And captains are generally richer than sergeants, Sharpe thought, but he said nothing. Simone touched the pouch at her waist. 'I should give you back your diamonds.'

'Why?'

'Because . . .' she said, but then fell silent for a while. 'I do not want you to think . . .' she tried again, but the words would not come.

Sharpe smiled at her. 'Nothing happened, love,' he told her. 'That's what you say to your husband. Nothing happened, and you found the diamonds on a dead body.'

'He will want me to give them to him. For his family.'

'Then don't tell him.'

'He is saving money,' Simone explained, 'so his family can live without work.'

'We all want that. Dream of life without work, we do. That's why we all want to be officers.'

'And I think to myself,' she went on as if Sharpe had not spoken, 'what shall I do? I cannot stay here in India. I must go to France. We are like ships, Sergeant, who look for a safe harbour.'

'And Pierre is safe?'

'He is safe,' Simone said bleakly, and Sharpe understood what she had been thinking for the last two days. He could offer her no security, while her husband could, and although she found Pierre's world stultifying, she was terrified by the alternative. She had dared taste that alternative for one night, but now shied away from it. 'You do not think badly of me?' she asked Sharpe anxiously.

'I'm probably half in love with you,' Sharpe told her, 'so how can I think badly of you?'

She seemed relieved, and for the rest of that day she chattered happily enough. McCandless questioned her closely about Dodd's regiment, how it had been trained and how it was equipped, and though she had taken scant interest in such things, her replies satisfied the Colonel who pencilled notes in a small black book.

They slept that night in a village, and next day rode even more warily. 'When we meet the enemy, Sharpe,' McCandless advised him, 'keep your hands away from your weapon.'

'Yes, sir.'

'Give a Mahratta one excuse to think you're hostile,' the Colonel said cheerfully, 'and he'll use you as an archery butt. They don't make decent heavy horsemen, but as raiders they're unsurpassed. They attack in swarms, Sharpe. A horde of horsemen. Like watching a storm approach. Nothing but dust and the shine of swords. Magnificent!'

'You like them, sir?' Sharpe asked.

'I like the wild, Sharpe,' McCandless said fiercely. 'We've tamed ourselves at home, but out here a man still lives by his weapon and his wits. I shall miss that when we've imposed order.'

'So why tame it, sir?'

'Because it is our duty, Sharpe. God's duty. Trade, order, law, and Christian decency, that's our business.' McCandless was gazing ahead to where a patch of misty white hung just above the northern horizon. It was dust kicked into the air, and maybe it was nothing more than a herd of cattle or a flock of sheep, but the dust smear grew and suddenly Sevajee's men veered sharply away to the west and galloped out of sight.

'Are they running out on us, sir?' Sharpe asked.

'The enemy will likely enough treat you and me with respect, Sharpe,' McCandless said, 'but Sevajee cannot expect courtesy from them. They'd regard him as a traitor and execute him on the spot. We'll meet up with him when we've delivered Madame Joubert to her husband. He and I have arranged a rendezvous.'

The dust cloud drew nearer and Sharpe saw a sliver of reflected sunlight glint in the whiteness and he knew he was seeing the first sign of McCandless's magnificent wild horsemen. The storm was coming.

The Mahratta cavalrymen had spread into a long line as they approached McCandless's small party. There were, Sharpe guessed, two hundred or more of the horsemen and, as they drew nearer, the flanks of their line quickened to form a pair of horns that would encircle their prey. McCandless feigned not to notice the threat, but kept riding gently ahead while the wild horns streamed past in a flurry of dust and noise.

They were, Sharpe noticed, small men on small horses. British cavalry were bigger and their horses were heavier, but these nimble horsemen still looked effective enough. The curved blades of their drawn *tulwars* glittered like their plumed helmets which rose to a sharp point decorated with a crest. Some of the crests were horse-tails, some vultures' feathers and some just brightly coloured ribbons. More ribbons were woven into their horses' plaited manes or were tied to the horn tips of the archers' bows. The horsemen pounded past McCandless, then turned with a swerve, a slew of choking dust, a skid of hooves, a jangle of curb chains and the thump of scabbarded weapons.

The Mahratta leader confronted McCandless who pretended to be surprised to find his path blocked, but nevertheless greeted the enemy with an elaborate and confident courtesy. The cavalry commander was a wildly bearded man with a scarred cheek, a wall eye and lank hair that hung far below his helmet's cloth-rimmed edge. He held his *tulwar* menacingly, but McCandless ignored the blade's threat, indeed he ignored most of what the enemy commander said, and instead boomed his own demands in a voice that showed not the least nervousness. The Scotsman towered over the smaller horsemen and, because he seemed to regard his presence among them as entirely natural, they meekly accepted his version of what was happening. 'I have demanded that they escort us to Pohlmann,' the Scotsman informed Sharpe.

'They probably planned on doing that anyway, sir.'

'Of course they did, but it's far better that I should demand it than that they should impose it,' McCandless said and then, with a lordly gesture, he gave permission for the Mahratta chief to lead the way and the enemy dutifully formed themselves into an escort either side of the three Europeans. 'Fine-looking beggars, are they not?' McCandless asked.

'Wicked, sir.'

'But sadly out of date.'

'They could fool me, sir,' Sharpe said, for though many of the Mahratta horsemen carried weapons that might have been more usefully employed at Agincourt or Crécy than in modern India, all had firelocks in their saddle holsters and all had savagely curved *tulwars*.

McCandless shook his head. 'They may be the finest light

horsemen in the world, but they won't press a charge home and they can't stand volley fire. There's rarely any need to form square against men like these, Sharpe. They're fine for picquet work, unrivalled at pursuit, but chary of dying in front of the guns.'

'Can you blame them?' Simone asked.

'I don't blame them, Madame,' McCandless said, 'but if a horse can't stand fire, then it's of scant use in battle. You don't gain victories by rattling across country like a pack of hunters, but by enduring the enemy's fire and overcoming it. That's where a soldier earns his pay, hard under the enemy muzzles.'

And that, Sharpe thought, was something he had never really done. He had faced the French in Flanders years before, but those battles had been fleeting and rain-obscured, and the lines had never closed on each other. He had not stared at the whites of the enemy's eyes, heard his volleys and returned them. He had fought at Malavelly, but that battle had been one volley and a charge, and the enemy had not contested the day, but fled, while at Seringapatam Sharpe had been spared the horror of going through the breach. One day, he realized, he would have to stand in a battle line and endure the volleys, and he wondered whether he would stand or instead break in terror. Or whether he would even live to see a battle, for, despite McCandless's blithe confidence, there was no assurance that he would survive this visit to the enemy's encampment.

They reached Pohlmann's army that evening. The camp was a short march south of Aurungabad and it was visible from miles away because of the great smear of smoke that hung in the sky. Most of the campfires were burning dried cakes of bullock dung and the acrid smoke caught in Sharpe's throat as he trotted through the lines of infantry shelters. It all looked much like a British camp, except that most of the tents were made from reed matting rather than canvas, but the lines were still neatly arrayed, muskets were carefully stacked in threes and a disciplined ring of picquets guarded the camp's perimeter. They passed some European officers exercising their horses, and one of those men spurred to intercept the newcomers. He ignored McCandless and Sharpe, raising his plumed hat to Simone instead. '*Bonsoir, Madame.*'

Simone did not look at the man, but just tapped her horse's rump with her riding crop. 'That fellow's French, sir,' Sharpe said to McCandless.

'I do speak the language, Sergeant,' the Colonel said.

'So what's a Frog doing here, sir?'

'The same as Lieutenant Dodd, Sharpe. Teaching Scindia's infantry how to fight.'

'Don't they know how to fight, sir? Thought it came natural.'

'They don't fight as we do,' McCandless said, watching the rebuffed Frenchman canter away.

'How's that, sir?'

'The European, Sergeant, has learned to close the gap fast. The closer you are to a man, the more likely you are to kill him; however, the closer you get, the more likely you are to be killed, but it's no use entertaining that fear in battle. Get up close, hold your ranks and start killing, that's the trick of it. But given a chance an Indian will hold back and try to kill at long range, and fellows like Dodd are teaching them how to close the gap hard and fast. You need discipline for that, discipline and tight ranks and good sergeants. And no doubt he's teaching them how to use cannon as well.' The Colonel spoke sourly, for they were trotting beside an artillery park that was crammed with heavy cannon. The guns looked odd to Sharpe, for many of them had been cast with ornate patterns on their barrels, and some were even painted in

gaudy colours, but they were neatly parked and all had limbers and full sets of equipment; rammers and wormscrews
and handspikes and buckets. The axles gleamed with grease
and there was not a spot of rust to be seen on the long barrels.
Someone knew how to maintain guns, and that suggested
they also knew how to use them. 'Counting them, Sharpe?'
McCandless asked abruptly.

'No, sir.'

'Seventeen in that park, mostly nine-pounders, but there
are some much heavier brutes at the back. Keep your eyes
open, man. That's why we're here.'

'Yes, sir, of course, sir.'

They passed a line of tethered camels, then a compound
where a dozen elephants were being brought their supper of
palm leaves and butter-soaked rice. Children followed the
men carrying the rice to scavenge what slopped from the
pails. Some of the Mahratta escort had spurred ahead to
spread news of the visitors and curious crowds gathered to
watch as McCandless and his two companions rode still
deeper into the huge encampment. Those crowds became
thicker as they drew close to the camp's centre which was
marked by a spread of large tents. One of the tents was made
of blue-and-yellow-striped canvas, and in front of it were twin
flagpoles, though the wind was slack and the brightly coloured
banners just hung from their tall poles. 'Leave the talking to
me,' McCandless ordered Sharpe.

'Of course, sir.'

Simone suddenly gasped. Sharpe turned and saw she was
staring across the heads of the curious crowd towards a group
of European officers. She looked at Sharpe suddenly and he
saw the sadness in her eyes. She gave him a half-smile.
'Pierre,' she offered in brief explanation, then she shrugged
and tapped her horse with her crop so that it hurried away
from Sharpe. Her husband, a small man in a white coat,

gazed in disbelief, then ran to meet her with a look of pleasure on his face. Sharpe felt oddly jealous of him.

'That's our main duty discharged,' McCandless said happily. 'A disobliging woman, I thought.'

'Unhappy, sir.'

'Doesn't have enough to keep her busy, that's why. The devil likes idle hands, Sharpe.'

'Then he must hate me, sir, most of the time.' He stared after Simone, watching as she slid down from the saddle and was embraced by her shorter husband. Then the crowds hid the couple from him. Someone shouted an insult at the two British horsemen and the other spectators jeered or laughed, but Sharpe, despite their hostility, took some consolation from McCandless's confidence. The Scotsman, indeed, was in a happier mood than he had shown for days, for he revelled being in his enemy's lines.

A group of men emerged from the big striped tent. They were almost all Europeans, and in their forefront was a tall muscled man in shirtsleeves who was attended by a bodyguard of Indian soldiers wearing purple coats. 'That's Colonel Pohlmann,' McCandless said, nodding towards the big red-faced man.

'The fellow who used to be a sergeant, sir?'

'That's him.'

'You've met him, sir?'

'Once, a couple of years back. He's an affable sort of man, Sharpe, but I doubt he's trustworthy.'

If Pohlmann was surprised to see a British officer in his camp, he did not show it. Instead he spread his arms in an expansive gesture of welcome. 'Are you new recruits?' he shouted in greeting.

McCandless did not bother to answer the mocking question, but just slid from his horse. 'You don't remember me, Colonel?'

'Of course I remember you,' Pohlmann said with a smile. 'Colonel Hector McCandless, once of His Majesty's Scotch Brigade, and now in the service of the East India Company. How could I forget you, Colonel? You tried to make me read the Bible.' Pohlmann grinned, displaying tobacco-stained teeth. 'But you haven't answered my question, Colonel. Have you come to join our army?'

'I am the merest emissary, Colonel,' McCandless said, beating dust from the kilt that he had insisted on wearing in honour of meeting the enemy. The garment was causing some amusement to Pohlmann's companions, though they took care not to let their smiles show if McCandless glanced their way. 'I brought you a woman,' McCandless added in explanation.

'How do you say in England, Colonel,' Pohlmann asked with a puzzled frown, 'coals to Newcastle?'

'I offered safe conduct to Madame Joubert,' the Scotsman said stiffly.

'So that was Simone I saw riding past,' Pohlmann said. 'I did wonder. And she'll be welcome, I dare say. We have enough of everything in this army: cannon, muskets, horses, ammunition, men, but there can never really be enough women in any army, can there?' He laughed, then summoned two of his purple-coated bodyguards to take charge of the horses. 'You've ridden a long way, Colonel,' Pohlmann said to McCandless, 'so let me offer you refreshment. You too, Sergeant,' he included Sharpe in his invitation. 'You must be tired.'

'I'm sore after that ride, sir,' Sharpe said, dropping clumsily and gratefully from the saddle.

'You're not used to horses, eh?' Pohlmann crossed to Sharpe and draped a genial arm about his shoulders. 'You're an infantryman, which means you've got hard feet and a soft bum. Me, I never like being on a horse. You know how I go to battle? On an elephant. That's the way to do it, Sergeant. What's your name?'

'Sharpe, sir.'

'Then welcome to my headquarters, Sergeant Sharpe. You're just in time for supper.' He steered Sharpe into the tent, then stopped to let his guests stare at the lavish interior which was carpeted with soft rugs, hung with silk drapes, lit with ornate brass chandeliers and furnished with intricately carved tables and couches. McCandless scowled at such luxury, but Sharpe was impressed. 'Not bad, eh?' Pohlmann squeezed Sharpe's shoulders. 'For a former sergeant.'

'You, sir?' Sharpe asked, pretending not to know Pohlmann's history.

'I was a sergeant in the East India Company's Hanoverian Regiment,' Pohlmann boasted, 'quartered in a rathole in Madras. Now I command a king's army and have all these powdered fops to serve me.' He gestured at his attendant officers who, accustomed to Pohlmann's insults, smiled tolerantly. 'Need a piss, Sergeant?' Pohlmann asked, taking his arm from Sharpe's shoulders. 'A wash?'

'Wouldn't mind both, sir.'

'Out the back.' He pointed the way. 'Then come back and drink with me.'

McCandless had watched this bonhomie with suspicion. He had also smelt the reek of strong liquor on Pohlmann's breath and suspected he was doomed to an evening of hard drinking in which, even though McCandless himself would refuse all alcohol, he would have to endure the drunken badinage of others. It was a grim prospect, and one he did not intend to endure alone. 'Not you, Sharpe,' he hissed when Sharpe returned to the tent.

'Not me what, sir?'

'You're to stay sober, you hear me? I'm not mollycoddling your sore head all the way back to the army.'

'Of course not, sir,' Sharpe said, and for a time he tried to obey McCandless, but Pohlmann insisted Sharpe join him in a toast before supper.

'You're not an abstainer, are you?' Pohlmann demanded of Sharpe in feigned horror when the Sergeant tried to refuse a beaker of brandy. 'You're not a Bible-reading abstainer, are you? Don't tell me the British army is becoming moral!'

'No, sir, not me, sir.'

'Then drink with me to King George of Hanover and of England!'

Sharpe obediently drank to the health of their joint sovereign, then to Queen Charlotte, and those twin courtesies emptied his beaker of brandy and a serving girl was summoned to fill it so that he could toast His Royal Highness George, Prince of Wales.

'You like the girl?' Pohlmann asked, gesturing at the serving girl who swerved lithely away from a French major who was trying to seize her sari.

'She's pretty, sir,' Sharpe said.

'They're all pretty, Sergeant. I keep a dozen of them as wives, another dozen as servants, and God knows how many others who merely aspire to those positions. You look shocked, Colonel McCandless.'

'A man who dwells among the tents of the ungodly,' McCandless said, 'will soon pick up ungodly ways.'

'And thank God for it,' Pohlmann retorted, then clapped his hands to summon the supper dishes.

A score of officers ate in the tent. Half a dozen were Mahrattas, the rest Europeans, and just after the bowls and platters had been placed on the tables, Major Dodd arrived. Night was falling and candles illuminated the tent's shadowed interior, but Sharpe recognized Dodd's face instantly. The sight of the long jaw, sallow skin and bitter eyes brought back sharp memories of Chasalgaon, of flies crawling on Sharpe's eyes and in his gullet, and of the staccato bangs as men stepped over the dead to shoot the wounded. Dodd, oblivious of Sharpe's glare, nodded to Pohlmann. 'I apologize, Colonel Pohlmann, for being late,' he announced with stiff formality.

'I expected Captain Joubert to be late,' Pohlmann said, 'for a man newly reunited with his wife has better things to do than hurry to his supper, if indeed he takes his supper at all. Were you also welcoming Simone, Major?'

'I was not, sir. I was attending to the picquets.'

'Major Dodd's attention to his duty puts us all to shame,' Pohlmann said. 'Do you have the pleasure of knowing Major Dodd, Colonel?' he asked McCandless.

'I know the Company will pay five hundred guineas for Lieutenant Dodd's capture,' McCandless growled, 'and more now, I dare say, after his bestiality at Chasalgaon.'

Dodd showed no reaction to the Colonel's hostility, but Pohlmann smiled. 'You've come for the reward money, Colonel, is that it?'

'I wouldn't touch the money,' McCandless said, 'for it's tainted by association. Tainted by murder, Colonel, and by disloyalty and dishonour.'

The words were spoken to Pohlmann, but addressed to Dodd whose face seemed to tighten as he listened. He had taken a place at the end of the table and was helping himself to the food. The other guests were silent, intrigued by the tension between McCandless and Dodd. Pohlmann was enjoying the confrontation. 'You say Major Dodd is a murderer, Colonel?'

'A murderer and a traitor.'

Pohlmann looked down the table. 'Major Dodd? You have nothing to say?'

Dodd reached for a loaf of flat bread that he tore in half. 'When I had the misfortune to serve in the Company, Colonel,' he said to Pohlmann, 'Colonel McCandless was well known as the head of intelligence. He did the dishonour-able job of spying on the Company's enemies, and I've no doubt that is his purpose here. He can spit all he likes, but he's here to spy, Colonel.'

Pohlmann smiled. 'Is that true, McCandless?'

'I returned Madame Joubert to her husband, Pohlmann, nothing more,' McCandless insisted.

'Of course it's more,' Pohlmann said. 'Major Dodd is right! You're head of the Company's intelligence service, are you not? Which means that you saw in dear Simone's predicament a chance to inspect our army.'

'You infer too much,' McCandless said.

'Nonsense, Colonel. Do try the lamb. It's seethed in milk curds. So what do you wish to see?'

'My bed,' McCandless said curtly, waving away the lamb dish. He never touched meat. 'Just my bed,' he added.

'And see it you shall,' Pohlmann said genially. The Han-overian paused, wondering whether to re-ignite the hostility between McCandless and Dodd, but he must have decided that each had insulted the other sufficiently. 'But tomorrow, Colonel, I will provide a tour of inspection for you. You may see whatever you like, McCandless. You can watch our gunners at work, you may inspect our infantry, you may go wherever you wish and talk to whoever you desire. We have nothing to hide.' He smiled at the astonished McCandless. 'You are my guest, Colonel, so I must show you a proper hospitality.'

He was as good as his word, and next morning McCandless was invited to inspect all of Pohlmann's *compoo*. 'I wish there were more troops here,' Pohlmann said, 'but Scindia is a few miles northwards with Saleur's and Dupont's *compoos*. I like to think they're not as able as mine, but in truth they're both very good units. Both have European officers, of course, and both are properly trained. I can't say as much for the

Rajah of Berar's infantry, but his gunners are the equal of ours.'

McCandless said very little all morning, and Sharpe, who had learned to read the Scotsman's moods, saw that he was severely discomfited. And no wonder, for Pohlmann's troops looked as fine as any in the Company's service. The Hanoverian commanded six and a half thousand infantry, five hundred cavalry and as many pioneers who served as engineers, and possessed thirty-eight guns. This *compoo* alone outnumbered the infantry of Wellesley's army, and was much stronger in guns, and there were two similar *compoos* in Scindia's service, let alone his horde of cavalry. It was no surprise, Sharpe thought, that McCandless's spirits were falling, and they fell even further when Pohlmann arranged for a demonstration of his artillery and the Scotsman, feigning gratitude to his host, was forced to watch as teams of gunners served a battery of big eighteen-pounder guns with all the alacrity and efficiency of the British army.

'Well-made pieces, too,' Pohlmann boasted, leading McCandless up to the hot guns that stood behind the swathes of burnt grass caused by their muzzle fire. 'A little gaudy, perhaps, for European tastes, but none the worse for that.' The guns were all painted in bright colours and some had names written in a curly script on their breeches. '*Megawati*,' Pohlmann read aloud, 'the goddess of clouds. Inspect them, Colonel! They're well made. Our axletrees don't break, I can assure you.'

Pohlmann was willing to show McCandless even more, but after dinner the Scotsman elected to spend the afternoon in his borrowed tent. He claimed he wished to rest, but Sharpe suspected the Scotsman had endured enough humiliation and wanted some quiet in which to make notes on all he had seen. 'We'll leave tonight, Sharpe,' the Colonel said. 'You can occupy yourself till then?'

'Colonel Pohlmann wants me to ride with him on his elephant, sir.'

The Colonel scowled. 'He likes to show off.' For a moment he seemed about to order Sharpe to refuse the invitation, then he shrugged. 'Don't get seasick.'

The motion of the elephant's howdah was indeed something like a ship, for it swayed from side to side as the beast plodded northwards and at first Sharpe had to grip onto the edge of the basket, but once he had accustomed himself to the motion he relaxed and leaned back on the cushioned seat. The howdah had two seats, one in front of the other, and Sharpe had the rearmost, but after a while Pohlmann twisted in his seat and showed how he could raise his own backrest and lay it flat so that the whole howdah became one cushioned bed that could be concealed by the curtains that hung from the wicker-framed canopy. 'It's a fine place to bring a woman, Sergeant,' Pohlmann said as he restored the backrest to its upright position, 'but the girth straps broke once and the whole thing fell off! It fell slowly, luckily, and I still had my breeches on so not too much dignity was lost.'

'You don't look like a man who worries much about dignity, sir.'

'I worry about reputation,' Pohlmann said, 'which isn't the same thing. I keep my reputation by winning victories and giving away gold. Those men' – he gestured at his purple-coated bodyguards who marched on either flank of the elephant – 'are each paid as much as a lieutenant in British service. And as for my European officers!' He laughed. 'They're all making more money than they dreamed possible. Look at 'em!' He jerked his head at the score of European officers who followed the elephant. Dodd was among them, but riding apart from the others and with a morose expression on his long face as though he resented having to pay court to his commanding officer. His horse was a sway-backed, hard-mouthed mare, a poor beast as ungainly and sullen as her master. 'Greed, Sharpe, greed, that's the best motive for a soldier,' Pohlmann said. 'Greed will make them fight like demons, if our lord and master ever allows us to fight.'

'You think he won't, sir?'

Pohlmann grinned. 'Scindia listens to his astrologers rather more than he listens to his Europeans, but I'll slip the bastards some gold when the time comes, and they'll tell him the stars are propitious and he'll give me the whole army and let me loose.'

'How big is the whole army, sir?'

Pohlmann smiled, recognizing that Sharpe was asking questions on behalf of Colonel McCandless. 'By the time you face us, Sergeant, we should have over a hundred thousand men. And of those, fifteen thousand infantry are first class, thirty thousand infantry are reliable, and the rest are horsemen who are only good for plundering the wounded. We'll also have a hundred guns, all of them as good as any in Europe. And how big will your army be?'

'Don't know, sir,' Sharpe said woodenly.

Pohlmann smiled. 'Wellesley has, maybe, seven and a half thousand men, infantry and cavalry, while Colonel Stevenson has perhaps another seven thousand so together you'll number, what? Fourteen and a half thousand? With forty guns? You think fourteen thousand men can beat a hundred thousand? And what happens, Sergeant Sharpe, if I manage to catch one of your little armies before the other can support it?' Sharpe said nothing, and Pohlmann smiled. 'You should think about selling me your skills, Sharpe.'

'Me, sir?' Sharpe answered lightly.

'You, Sergeant Sharpe,' Pohlmann said forcibly, and the Hanoverian twisted in his seat to stare at Sharpe. 'That's why I invited you this afternoon. I need European officers, Sharpe, and any man as young as you who becomes a sergeant must have a rare ability. I am offering you rank and riches, Sharpe. Look at me! Ten years ago I was a sergeant like you. Now I ride to war on an elephant, need two more to carry my gold and have three dozen women competing to sharpen my sword. Have you ever heard of George Thomas?'

'No, sir.'

'An Irishman, Sergeant, and not even a soldier! George was an illiterate seaman out of the gutters of Dublin, and before he drank himself to death, poor man, he'd become the Begum Somroo's general. I think he was her lover too, though that ain't any distinction with that particular lady, but before he died George needed a whole herd of elephants to haul his gold about. And why? Because the Indian princes, Sergeant, need our skills. Equip yourself with a good European and you win your wars. I captured seventy-two guns at the battle of Malpura and I demanded the weight of one of those guns in pure gold as my reward. I got it, too. In ten years you could be as rich as you want, rich as Benoît de Boigne. You must have heard of him?'

'No, sir.'

'He was a Savoyard, Sergeant, and in just four years he made a hundred thousand pounds and then he went off home and married a seventeen-year-old girl fresh from her father's castle. In only four years! From being a captain in Savoy's army to being governor of half Scindia's territory. There's a fortune to be made here and rank and birth don't come into it. Only ability counts. Nothing but ability.' Pohlmann paused, his eyes on Sharpe. 'I'll make you a lieutenant tomorrow, Sergeant, and you can fight in my *compoo*, and if you're any damn good then you'll be a captain by month's end.' Sharpe looked at the Hanoverian, but said nothing. Pohlmann smiled. 'What are your chances of getting a commission in the British army?'

Sharpe grinned. 'No chance, sir.'

'So? I offer you rank, wealth and as many *bibbis* as you can handle.'

'Is that why Mister Dodd deserted, sir?'

Pohlmann smiled. 'Major Dodd deserted, Sharpe, because he faces execution for murder, and because he's sensible, and because he wants my job. Not that he'll admit to that.' The Hanoverian twisted in the howdah. 'Major Dodd!' he shouted.

The Major urged his awkward horse to the elephant's side and looked up into the howdah. 'Sir?'

'Sergeant Sharpe wants to know why you joined us.'

Dodd gave Sharpe a suspicious look, but then shrugged. 'I ran because there's no future in the Company,' he said. 'I was a lieutenant for twenty-two years, Sergeant, twenty-two years! It don't matter to the Company how good a soldier you are, you have to wait your turn, and all the while I watched wealthy young fools buying themselves majorities in the King's ranks and I had to bow and scrape to the useless bastards. Yes, sir, no, sir, three bloody bags full, sir, and can I carry your bags, sir, and wipe your arse, sir.' Dodd had been getting angrier and angrier as he spoke, but now made an effort to control himself. 'I couldn't join the King's army, Sergeant, because my father runs a grist mill in Suffolk and there ain't no money to buy a King's commission. That meant I was only fit for the Company, and King's officers treat Company men like dirt. I can outfight twenty of the bastards, but ability don't count in the Company. Keep your nose clean, wait your turn, then die for the shareholders when the Court of Directors tells you.' He was becoming angry again. 'That's why,' he finished curtly.

'And you, Sergeant?' Pohlmann asked. 'What opportunities will the army offer you?'

'Don't know, sir.'

'You do know,' Pohlmann said, 'you do know.' The

167

elephant had stopped and the Hanoverian now pointed ahead and Sharpe saw that they had come to the edge of a wood, and a half-mile away was a great city with walls like those the Scots had climbed at Ahmednuggur. The city walls were bright with flags, while its embrasures glinted with the reflection of sunlight from gun barrels. 'That's Aurungabad,' Pohlmann said, 'and everyone inside those walls is pissing themselves in fear that I'm about to start a siege.'

'But you're not?'

'I'm looking for Wellesley,' Pohlmann said, 'and you know why? Because I've never lost a battle, Sharpe, and I'm going to add a British major-general's sword to my trophies. Then I'll build myself a palace, a bloody great marble palace, and I'll line the halls with British guns and hang British colours to shield my bedroom from the sun and I'll bounce my *bibbis* on a mattress stuffed with the hair of British horses.' Pohlmann luxuriated in that dream for a while and then, with a last glance at the city, ordered the mahout to turn the elephant about. 'When is McCandless leaving?' he asked Sharpe.

'Tonight, sir.'

'After dark?'

'Around midnight, sir, I think.'

'That gives you plenty of time to think, Sergeant. To think of your future. To contemplate what the red coat offers you, and what I offer you. And when you have thought about those things, come to me.'

'I'm thinking on it, sir,' Sharpe said, 'I'm thinking on it.' And he was.

CHAPTER 6

Colonel McCandless excused himself from Pohlmann's supper, but did not forbid Sharpe to attend. 'But don't get drunk,' he warned the Sergeant, 'and be at my tent at midnight. I want to be back at the River Godavery by dawn.'

'Yes, sir,' Sharpe said dutifully, then went to Pohlmann's tent where most of the *compoo*'s officers had gathered. Dodd was there, and so were a half-dozen wives of Pohlmann's European officers and among them was Simone Joubert, though there was no sign of her husband. 'He is in charge of the army picquets tonight,' Simone explained when Sharpe asked her, 'and Colonel Pohlmann invited me to eat.'

'He invited me to join his army,' Sharpe told her.

'He did?' Her eyes widened as she stared up from her chair. 'And will you?'

'It would mean I'd be close to you, Ma'am,' Sharpe said, 'and that's an inducement.'

Simone half smiled at the clumsy gallantry. 'I think you would not be a good soldier if you changed your loyalty for a woman, Sergeant.'

'He says I'll be an officer,' Sharpe said.

'And is that what you want?'

Sharpe squatted on his heels so that he could be closer to her. The other European wives saw him crouch and pursed their mouths with a disapproval born of envy, but Sharpe was oblivious of their gaze. 'I think I'd like to be an officer,

169

yes. And I can think of one very good reason to be an officer in this army.'

Simone blushed. 'I am a married woman, Sergeant. You know that.'

'But even married women need friends,' Sharpe said, and just then a large hand took unceremonious hold of his clubbed hair and hauled him to his feet.

Sharpe turned belligerently on whoever had manhandled him, then saw that it was a smiling Major Dodd. 'Can't have you stooping to women, Sharpe,' Dodd said before offering an ungainly bow to Simone. 'Good evening, Madame.'

'Major,' Simone acknowledged him coldly.

'You will forgive me, Madame, if I steal Sergeant Sharpe from you?' Dodd asked. 'I want a word with him. Come on, Sharpe.' He plucked Sharpe's arm, guiding him across the tent. The Major was very slightly drunk and evidently intent on becoming more drunk, for he snatched a whole jug of arrack from a servant, then scooped up two beakers from a table. 'Fancy Madame Joubert, do you?' he asked Sharpe.

'I like her well enough, sir.'

'She's spoken for, Sergeant. Remember that if you join us, she's spoken for.'

'You mean she's married, sir?'

'Married?' Dodd laughed, then poured the arrack and gave one beaker to Sharpe. 'How many European officers can you see here? And how many European women? And how many of them are young and pretty like Madame Joubert? Work it out, lad. And you're not jumping the queue.' Dodd smiled as he spoke, evidently meaning his tone to be jocular. 'But you are joining us, aren't you?'

'I'm thinking about it, sir.'

'You'll be in my regiment, Sharpe,' Dodd said. 'I need European officers. I've only got Joubert and he's no damn use, so I've spoken with Pohlmann and he says you can join my Cobras. I'll give you three companies of your own to look after, and God help you if they're not kept in prime condition. I like to look after the men, because come battle they look after you, but God help any officer who lets me down.' He paused to drink half his arrack and pour some more. 'I'll work you hard, Sharpe, I'll work you damned hard, but there'll be plenty of gold washing round this army once we've thrashed Boy Wellesley. Money's your reward, lad, money.'

'Is that why you're here, sir?'

'It's why we're all here, you fool. All except Joubert, who was posted here by his government and is too damned timid to help himself to Scindia's gold. So report to me in the morning. We're marching north tomorrow night, which means you'll have one day to learn my ropes and after that you're Mister Sharpe, gentleman. Come to me tomorrow morning, Sharpe, at dawn, and get rid of that damned red coat.' He poked Sharpe's chest hard. 'I see a red coat,' he went on, 'and I want to start killing.' He grinned, showing yellow teeth.

'Is that what happened at Chasalgaon, sir?' Sharpe asked.

Dodd's grin vanished. 'Why the hell do you ask that?' he growled.

Sharpe had asked because he had been remembering the massacre, and wondering if he could ever serve under a man who had ordered such a killing, but he said none of that. He shrugged instead. 'I heard tales, sir, but no one ever tells us anything proper. You know that, sir, so I just wondered what happened there.'

Dodd considered that answer for a moment, then shrugged. 'I didn't take prisoners, Sharpe, that's what happened. Killed the bastards to the last man.'

And to the last boy, Sharpe thought, remembering Davi Lal. He remained impassive, not letting a hint of memory or hate show. 'Why not take prisoners, sir?'

'Because it's war!' Dodd said vehemently. 'When men fight me, Sergeant, I want them to fear me, because that way the battle's half won before it's started. It ain't kind, I'm sure, but who ever said war was kind? And in this war, Sergeant' – he waved his hand towards the officers clustering about Colonel Pohlmann – 'it's dog eat dog. We're all in competition, and you know who'll win? The most ruthless, that's who. So what did I do at Chasalgaon? I made sure of a reputation, Sharpe. Made a name for myself. That's the first rule of war, Sergeant. Make the bastards fear you. And you know what the second rule is?'

'Don't ask questions, sir?'

Dodd grinned. 'No, lad, the second rule is never to reinforce failure, and the third, lad, is to look after your men. You know why I had that goldsmith thrashed? You've heard of that, haven't you? I'll tell you. It wasn't because he'd cheated me, which he did, but because he cheated some of my men. So I looked after them and let them give him a solid kicking, and the bastard died. Which he deserved to do, rich fat bastard that he was.' The Major turned and scowled at the servants bringing dishes from Pohlmann's cook tent. 'And they're just as bad here, Sharpe. Look at all that food! Enough to feed two regiments there, Sharpe, and the men are going hungry. No proper supply system, see? It costs money, that's why. You don't get issued food in this army, you go out and steal it.' He plainly disapproved. 'I've told Pohlmann, I have. Lay on a commissary, I said, but he won't, because it costs money. Scindia hoards food in his fortresses, but he won't issue it, not unless he's paid, and Pohlmann won't give up a penny of profit, so no food ever comes. It just rots in the warehouses while we have to keep moving, because after a week we've stripped one set of fields bare and have to go on to the next. It's no bloody way to run an army.'

'Maybe one day you'll change the system, sir,' Sharpe said.

'I will!' Dodd said vigorously. 'I bloody will! And if you've any sense, lad, you'll be here helping me. You learn one thing as a miller's son, Sergeant, and that's not just how to grind corn, but that a fool and his money are easily parted. And Scindia's a fool, but given a chance I'll make the bugger into the Emperor of India.' He turned as a servant beat a gong with a muffled stick. 'Time for our vittles.'

It was a strangely subdued supper, though Pohlmann did his best to amuse his company. Sharpe had tried to manoeuvre himself into a seat beside Simone, but Dodd and a Swedish captain beat him to it and Sharpe found himself next to a small Swiss doctor who spent the whole meal quizzing Sharpe about the religious arrangements in British regiments. 'Your chaplains are godly men, yes?'

'Drunken bastards, sir, most of them.'

'Surely not!'

'I hauled two of them out of a whorehouse not a month ago, sir. They didn't want to pay, see?'

'You are not telling me the truth!'

'God's honour, sir. The Reverend Mister Cooper was one of them, and it's a rare Sunday that he's sober. He preached a Christmas sermon at Easter, he was that puzzled.'

Most of the guests left early, Dodd among them, though a few diehards stayed on to give the Colonel a game of cards. Pohlmann grinned at Sharpe. 'You wager, Sharpe?'

'I'm not rich enough, sir.'

Pohlmann shook his head in mock exasperation at the answer. 'I will make you rich, Sharpe. You believe me?'

'I do, sir.'

'So you've made up your mind? You're joining me?'

'I still want to think a bit, sir.'

Pohlmann shrugged. 'You have nothing to think about. You either become a rich man or you die for King George.'

Sharpe left the remaining officers at their cards and walked away into the encampment. He really was thinking, or trying to think, and he sought a quiet place, but a crowd of soldiers were wagering on dog fights, and their cheers, as well as the yelps and snarls of the dogs, carried far through the darkness. Sharpe settled on an empty stretch of ground close to the picketed camels that carried Pohlmann's supply of rockets, and there he lay and stared up at the stars through the mist of smoke. A million stars. He had always thought there was an answer to all life's mysteries in the stars, yet whenever he stared at them the answer slipped out of his grasp. He had been whipped in the foundling home for staring at a clear night's sky through the workshop skylight. 'You ain't here to gawp at the dark, boy,' the overseer had snapped, 'you're here to labour,' and the whip had slashed down across his shoulders and he had dutifully looked down at the great tarry lump of hemp rope that had to be picked apart. The old ropes had been twisted and tightened and tarred into vast knots bigger than Sharpe himself, and they had been used as fenders on the London docks, but when the grinding and thumping of the big ships had almost worn the old fenders through they were sent to the foundling home to be picked apart so that the strands could be sold as furniture stuffing or to be mixed into wall plaster. 'Got to learn a trade, boy,' the master had told him again and again, and so Sharpe had learned a trade, but it was not hemp-picking. He learned the killing trade. Load a musket, ram a musket, fire a musket. And he had not done much of it, not yet, but he liked doing it. He remembered Malavelly, remembered firing the volley at the approaching enemy, and he remembered the sheer exultation as all his unhappiness and anger had been concentrated into his musket's barrel and been gouted out in one explosive rush of flame, smoke and lead.

He did not think of himself as unhappy. Not now. The army had been good to him in these last years, but there was still something wrong in his soul. What that was, he did not know, because Sharpe did not reckon he was any good at thinking. He was good at action, for whenever there was a problem to be solved Sergeant Sharpe could usually find the solution, but he was not much use at simply thinking. But he had to think now, and he stared at the smoke-dimmed stars in the hope that they would help him, but all they did was go on shining. Lieutenant Sharpe, he thought, and was surprised to realize that he saw nothing very odd in that idea. It was ridiculous, of course. Richard Sharpe, an officer? But somehow he could not shake the idea loose. It was a laughable idea, he tried to convince himself; at least in the British army it was, but not here. Not in Pohlmann's army, and Pohlmann had once been a sergeant. 'Bloody hell,' he said aloud, and a camel belched in answer.

The cheers of the spectators greeted the death of a dog, and, nearer, a soldier was playing one of the strange Indian instruments, plucking its long strings to make a sad, plangent music. In the British camp, Sharpe thought, they would be singing, but no one was singing here. They were too hungry, though hunger did not stop a man from fighting. It had never stopped Sharpe. So these hungry men could fight, and they needed officers, and all he had to do was stand up, brush the dirt away and stroll across to Pohlmann's tent and become Lieutenant Sharpe. Mister Sharpe. And he would do a good job. He knew that. Better than Morris, better than most of the army's junior officers. He was a good sergeant, a bloody good sergeant, and he enjoyed being a sergeant. He got respect, not just because of the stripes on his red sleeves, and not just because he had been the man who blew the mine at Seringapatam, but because he was good and tough. He wasn't frightened of making a decision, and that was the key to it, he reckoned. And he enjoyed making decisions, and he enjoyed the respect that decisiveness brought him, and he realized he had been seeking respect all his life. Christ, he thought, but would it not be a joy to walk back into the foundling home with braid on his coat, gold on his shoulders and a sword at his side? That was the respect he wanted, from the bastards in Brewhouse Lane who had said he would never amount to anything and who had whipped him bloody because he was a bastard off the streets. By Christ, he thought, but going back there would make life perfect! Brewhouse Lane, him in a braided coat and a sword, and with Simone on his arm and a dead king's jewels about her neck, and them all touching their hats and bobbing like ducks in a pond. Perfect, he thought, just perfect, and as he indulged himself in that dream an angry shout came from the tents close to Pohlmann's marquee and an instant later a gun sounded.

There was a moment's pause after the gunshot, as if its violence had checked a drunken fight, then Sharpe heard men laughing and the sound of hoofbeats. He was standing now, staring towards the big marquee. The horses went by quite close to him, then the noise of their hooves receded into the dark. 'Come back!' a man shouted in English, and Sharpe recognized McCandless's voice.

Sharpe began running.

'Come back!' McCandless shouted again, and then there was another gunshot and Sharpe heard the Colonel yelp like a whipped dog. A score of men were shouting now. The officers who had been playing cards were running towards McCandless's tent and Pohlmann's bodyguards were following them. Sharpe dodged round a fire, leaped a sleeping man, then saw a figure hurrying away from the commotion. The man had a musket in his hand and he was half crouching as if he did not want to be seen, and Sharpe did not hesitate, but just swerved and ran at the man.

When the fugitive heard Sharpe coming, he quickened his pace, then realized he would be caught and so he turned on his pursuer. The man whipped out a bayonet and screwed it onto the muzzle of his musket. Sharpe saw the glint of moonlight on the long blade, saw the man's teeth white in the dark, then the bayonet lunged at him, but Sharpe had dropped to the ground and was sliding forward in the dust beneath the blade. He wrapped his arms around the man's legs, heaved once and the man fell backwards. Sharpe cuffed the musket aside with his left hand, then hammered his right hand down onto the moon-whitened teeth. The man tried to kick Sharpe's crotch, then clawed at his eyes, but Sharpe caught one of the hooked fingers in his mouth and bit hard. The man screamed in pain, Sharpe kept biting and kept hitting, then he spat the severed fingertip into the man's face and gave him one last thump with his fist. 'Bastard,' Sharpe said, and hauled the man to his feet. Two of Pohlmann's officers had arrived now, one still with a fan of cards in his hand. 'Get his bloody musket,' Sharpe ordered them. The man struggled in Sharpe's hands, but he was much smaller than Sharpe and a good kick between his legs brought him to order. 'Come on, you bastard,' Sharpe said.

One of the officers had picked up the fallen musket and Sharpe reached over and felt the muzzle. It was hot, showing that the weapon had just been fired. 'If you killed my Colonel, you bastard, I'll kill you,' Sharpe said and dragged the man through the campfires to the knot of officers who had gathered about the Colonel's tent.

McCandless's two horses were gone. Both the mare and the gelding had been stolen, and Sharpe realized it was their hoofbeats he had heard go past him. McCandless, woken by the noise of the horse thieves, had come from the tent and fired his pistol at the men, and one of them had fired back and the bullet had buried itself in the Colonel's left thigh. He was lying on the ground now, looking horribly pale, and Pohlmann was bellowing for his doctor to come quickly.

'Who's that?' he demanded of Sharpe, and nodding at the prisoner.

'The bastard who fired at Colonel McCandless, sir. Musket's still hot.'

The man proved to be one of Major Dodd's sepoys, one of the men who had deserted with Dodd from the Company, and he was put into the charge of Pohlmann's bodyguard. Sharpe knelt beside McCandless who was trying not to cry aloud as the newly arrived doctor, the Swiss man who had sat beside Sharpe at dinner, examined his leg. 'I was sleeping!' the Colonel complained. 'Thieves, Sharpe, thieves!'

'We'll find your horses,' Pohlmann reassured the Scotsman, 'and we'll find the thieves.'

'You promised me safety!' McCandless complained.

'The men will be punished,' Pohlmann promised, then he helped Sharpe and two other men lift the wounded Colonel and carry him into the tent where they laid him on the rope cot. The doctor said the bullet had missed the bone, and no major artery was cut, but he still wanted to fetch his probes, forceps and scalpels and try to pull the ball out. 'You want some brandy, McCandless?' Pohlmann asked.

'Of course not. Tell him to get on with it.'

The doctor called for more lanterns, for water and for his instruments, and then he spent ten excruciating minutes looking for the bullet deep inside McCandless's upper thigh. The Scotsman uttered not a sound as the probe slid into his lacerated flesh, nor as the long-necked forceps were pushed down to find a purchase on the bullet. The Swiss doctor was sweating, but McCandless just lay with eyes tight shut and teeth clenched. 'It comes now,' the doctor said and began to pull, but the flesh had closed on the forceps and he had to use almost all his strength to drag the bullet up from the wound. It came free at last, releasing a spill of bright blood, and McCandless groaned.

'All done now, sir,' Sharpe told him.

'Thank God,' McCandless whispered, 'thank God.' The Scotsman opened his eyes. The doctor was bandaging the thigh and McCandless looked past him to Pohlmann. 'This is treachery, Colonel, treachery! I was your guest!'

'Your horses will be found, Colonel, I promise you,' Pohlmann said, but though his men made a search of the camp, and though they searched until morning, the two horses were not found. Sharpe was the only man who could identify them, for Colonel McCandless was in no state to walk, but Sharpe saw no horses that resembled the stolen pair, but nor did he expect to, for any competent horse thief knew a dozen tricks to disguise his catch. The beast would be clipped, its coat would be dyed with blackball, it would be force-fed an enema so that its head drooped, then it would as likely as not be put among the cavalry mounts where one horse looked much like another. Both McCandless's horses had been European bred and were larger and of finer quality than most in Pohlmann's camp, yet even so Sharpe saw no sign of the two animals.

Colonel Pohlmann went to McCandless's tent and confessed that the horses had vanished. 'I shall pay you their value, of course,' he added.

'I won't take it!' McCandless snapped back. The Colonel was still pale, and shivering despite the heat. His wound was bandaged, and the doctor reckoned it should heal swiftly enough, but there was a danger that the Colonel's recurrent fever might return. 'I won't take my enemy's gold,' McCandless explained, and Sharpe reckoned it must be the pain speaking for he knew the two missing horses must have cost the Colonel dearly.

'I shall leave you the money,' Pohlmann insisted anyway, 'and this afternoon we shall execute the prisoner.'

'Do what you must,' McCandless grumbled.

'Then we shall carry you northwards,' the Hanoverian promised, 'for you must stay under Doctor Viedler's care.'

McCandless levered himself into a sitting position. 'You'll not take me anywhere!' he insisted angrily. 'You leave me here, Pohlmann. I'll not depend on your care, but on God's mercy.' He let himself drop back onto the bed and hissed with pain. 'And Sergeant Sharpe can tend me.'

Pohlmann glanced at Sharpe. The Hanoverian seemed about to say that Sharpe might not wish to stay with McCandless, but then he just nodded his acceptance of McCandless's decision. 'If you wish to be abandoned, McCandless, so be it.'

'I have more faith in God than in a faithless mercenary like you, Pohlmann.'

'As you wish, Colonel,' Pohlmann said gently, then backed from the tent and gestured for Sharpe to follow. 'He's a stubborn fellow, isn't he?' The Hanoverian turned and looked at Sharpe. 'So, Sergeant? Are you coming with us?'

'No, sir,' Sharpe said. Last night, he reflected, he had very nearly decided to accept the Hanoverian's offer, but the theft of the horses and the single shot fired by the sepoy had served to change Sharpe's mind. He could not leave McCandless to suffer and, to his surprise, he felt no great disappointment in thus having the decision forced on him. Duty dictated he should stay, but so did sentiment, and he had no regret. 'Someone has to look after Colonel McCandless, sir,' Sharpe explained, 'and he's looked after me in the past, so it's my turn now.'

'I'm sorry,' Pohlmann said, 'truly I am. The execution will be in one hour. I think you should see it, so you can assure your Colonel that justice was done.'

'Justice, sir?' Sharpe asked scornfully. 'It ain't justice, shooting that fellow. He was put up to it by Major Dodd.' Sharpe had no proof of that, but he suspected it strongly. Dodd, he reckoned, had been hurt by McCandless's insults and must have decided to add horse-thieving to his catalogue of crimes. 'You have questioned your prisoner, haven't you, sir?' Sharpe asked. 'Because he must know that Dodd was up to his neck in the business.'

Pohlmann smiled wearily. 'The prisoner told us everything, Sergeant, or I assume he did, but what use is that? Major Dodd denies the man's story, and a score of sepoys swear the Major was nowhere near McCandless's tent when the shots were fired. And who would the British army believe? A desperate man or an officer?' Pohlmann shook his head. 'So you must be content with the death of one man, Sergeant.'

Sharpe expected that the captured sepoy would be shot, but there was no sign of any firing squad when the moment arrived for the man's death. Two companies from each of Pohlmann's eight battalions were paraded, the sixteen companies making three sides of a hollow square with Pohlmann's striped marquee forming the fourth side. Most of the other tents had already been struck ready for the move northwards, but the marquee remained and one of its canvas walls had been brailed up so that the *compoo*'s officers could witness the execution from chairs set in the tent's shade. Dodd was not there, nor were any of the regiment's wives, but a score of officers took their places and were served sweetmeats and drink by Pohlmann's servants.

The prisoner was fetched onto the makeshift execution ground by four of Pohlmann's bodyguards. None of the four carried a musket, instead they were equipped with tent pegs, mallets and short lengths of rope. The prisoner, who wore nothing but a strip of cloth around his loins, glanced from side to side as if trying to find an escape route, but, on a nod from Pohlmann, the bodyguards kicked his feet out from beneath him and then knelt beside his sprawling body and pinioned it to the ground by tying the ropes to his wrists and ankles, then fastening the bonds to the tent pegs. The condemned man lay there, spread-eagled, gazing up at the cloudless sky as the mallets banged the eight pegs home.

Sharpe stood to one side. No one spoke to him, no one even looked at him, and no wonder, he thought, for this was a farce. All the officers must have known that Dodd was the guilty man, yet the sepoy must die. The paraded troops seemed to agree with Sharpe, for there was a sullenness in the ranks. Pohlmann's *compoo* might be well armed and superbly trained, but it was not happy.

The four bodyguards finished tying the prisoner down, then walked away to leave him alone in the centre of the execution ground. An Indian officer, resplendent in silk robes and with a lavishly curved *tulwar* hanging from his belt, made a speech. Sharpe did not understand a word, but he guessed that the watching soldiers were being harangued about the fate which awaited any thief. The officer finished, glanced once at the prisoner, then walked back to the tent and, just as he entered its shade, so Pohlmann's great elephant with its silver-encased tusks and cascading metal coat was led out from behind the marquee. The mahout guided the beast by tugging on one of its ears, but as soon as the elephant saw the prisoner it needed no guidance, but just plodded across to the spread-eagled man. The victim shouted for mercy, but Pohlmann was deaf to the pleas.

The Colonel twisted round. 'You're watching, Sharpe?'

'You've got the wrong man, sir. You should have Dodd there.'

'Justice must be done,' the Colonel said, and turned back to the elephant that was standing quietly beside the victim who twisted in his bonds, thrashed, and even managed to free one hand, but instead of using that free hand to tug at the other three ropes that held him, he flailed uselessly at the elephant's trunk. A murmur ran through the watching sixteen companies, but the jemadars and havildars shouted and the sullen murmur ceased. Pohlmann watched the prisoner struggle for a few more seconds, then took a deep breath. '*Haddah*!' he shouted. '*Haddah*!'

The prisoner screamed in anticipation as, very slowly, the elephant lifted one ponderous forefoot and moved its body slightly forward. The great foot came down on the prisoner's chest and seemed to rest there. The man tried to push the foot away, but he might as well have attempted to shove a mountain aside. Pohlmann leaned forward, his mouth open, as, slowly, very slowly, the elephant transferred its weight onto the man's chest. There was another scream, then the man could not draw breath to scream again, but still he jerked and twitched and still the weight pressed on him, and Sharpe saw his legs try to contract against the bonds at his ankles, and saw his head jerk up, and then he heard the splinter of ribs and saw the blood spill and bubble at the victim's mouth. He winced, trying to imagine the pain as the elephant pressed on down, crushing bone and lung and spine. The prisoner gave one last jerk, his hair flapping, then his head fell back and a great wash of blood brimmed from his open mouth and puddled beside his corpse.

There was a last crunching sound, then the elephant stepped back and a sigh sounded gently through the watching ranks. Pohlmann applauded, and the officers joined in. Sharpe turned away. Bastards, he thought, bastards.

And that night Pohlmann marched north.

Sergeant Obadiah Hakeswill was not an educated man, and he was not even particularly clever unless slyness passed for wits, but he did understand one thing very well, and that was the impression he made on other men. They feared him. It did not matter whether the other man was a raw private, fresh from the recruiting sergeant, or a general whose coat was bright with gold lace and heavy with braid. They all feared him, all but two, and those two frightened Obadiah Hakeswill. One was Sergeant Richard Sharpe, in whom Hakeswill sensed a violence that was equal to his own, while the other was Major General Sir Arthur Wellesley who, when he had been colonel of the 33rd, had always been serenely impervious to Hakeswill's threats.

So Sergeant Hakeswill would have much preferred not to confront General Wellesley, but when his convoy reached Ahmednuggur his enquiries established that Colonel McCandless had ridden north and had taken Sharpe with him, and the Sergeant had known he could do nothing further without Wellesley's permission and so he had gone to the General's tent where he announced himself to an orderly, who had informed an aide, who had commanded the Sergeant to wait in the shade of a banyan tree.

He waited the best part of a morning while the army readied itself to leave Ahmednuggur. Guns were being attached to limbers, oxen harnessed to carts and tents being struck by lascars. The fortress of Ahmednuggur, fearing the same fate as the city, had meekly surrendered after a few cannon shots and, with both the city and its fort safe in his hands, Wellesley was now planning to march north, cross the Godavery and seek out the enemy army. Sergeant Hakeswill had no great wish to take part in that adventure, but he could see no other way of catching up with Sharpe and so he was resigned to his fate.

'Sergeant Hakeswill?' An aide came from the General's big tent.

'Sir!' Hakeswill scrambled to his feet and stiffened to attention.

'Sir Arthur will see you now, Sergeant.'

Hakeswill marched into the tent, snatched off his shako,

184

turned smartly to the left, quick-marched three short paces, then slammed to a halt in front of the camp table where the General was doing paperwork. Hakeswill stood quivering at attention. His face shuddered.

'At ease, Sergeant,' Wellesley, bare-headed, had barely glanced up from his papers as the Sergeant entered.

'Sir!' Hakeswill allowed his muscles to relax slightly. 'Papers for you, sir!' He pulled the warrant for Sharpe's arrest from his pouch and offered it to the General.

Wellesley made no move to accept the warrant. Instead he leaned back in his chair and examined Hakeswill as though he had never seen the Sergeant before. Hakeswill stood rigid, his eyes staring at the tent's brown wall above the General's head. Wellesley sighed and leaned forward again, still ignoring the warrant. 'Just tell me, Sergeant,' he said, his attention already returned to the documents on his desk. An aide was taking whatever sheets the General signed, sprinkling sand on the signatures, then placing more papers on the table.

'I'm ordered here by Lieutenant Colonel Gore, sir. To apprehend Sergeant Sharpe, sir.'

Wellesley looked up again and Hakeswill almost quailed before the cold eyes. He sensed that Wellesley could see right through him, and the sensation made his face quiver in a series of uncontrollable twitches. Wellesley waited for the spasms to end. 'On your own, are you, Sergeant?' the General asked casually.

'Detail of six men, sir.'

'Seven of you! To arrest one man?'

'Dangerous man, sir. I'm ordered to take him back to Hurryhur, sir, so he can . . .'

'Spare me the details,' Wellesley said, looking back to the next paper needing his signature. He tallied up a list of figures. 'Since when did four twelves and eighteen yield a sum of sixty-eight?' he asked no one in particular, then corrected the calculation before signing the paper. 'And since when did Captain Lampert dispose of the artillery train?'

The aide wielding the sand-sprinkler blushed. 'Colonel Eldredge, sir, is indisposed.' Drunk, if the truth was known, which it was, but it was impolitic to say that a colonel was drunk in front of a sergeant.

'Then invite Captain Lampert to supper. We must feed him some arithmetic along with a measure of common sense,' Sir Arthur said. He signed another paper, then rested his pen on a small silver stand before leaning back and looking at Hakeswill. He resented the Sergeant's presence, not because he disliked Sergeant Hakeswill, though he did, but rather because Wellesley had long ago left behind the cares of being the commander of the 33rd and he did not want to be reminded of those duties now. Nor did he want to be in a position to approve or disapprove of his successor's orders, for that would be an impertinence. 'Sergeant Sharpe is not here,' he said coldly.

'So I hear, sir. But he was, sir?'

'Nor am I the person you should be troubling with this matter, Sergeant,' Wellesley went on, ignoring Hakeswill's question. He took up the pen again, dipped it in ink, and crossed a name from a list before adding his signature. 'In a few days,' he continued, 'Colonel McCandless will return to the army and you will report to him with your warrant and I've no doubt he will give the matter its due attention. Till then I shall employ you usefully. I won't have seven men idling while the rest of the army works.' Wellesley turned to the aide. 'Where do we lack men, Barclay?'

The aide considered for a moment. 'Captain Mackay could certainly use some assistance, sir.'

'Very well.' Wellesley pointed the pen's steel nib at Hakeswill. 'You'll attach yourself to Captain Mackay. Captain Mackay commands our bullock train and you will do whatever he desires until Colonel McCandless relieves you of that duty. Dismissed.'

'Sir!' Hakeswill said dutifully, but inwardly he was furious that the General had not shared his indignation about Sharpe. He about-turned, stamped from the tent, and went to find his men. 'Going to the dogs,' he said bitterly.

'Sergeant?' Flaherty asked.

'The dogs. Time was in this army when even a general officer respected sergeants. Now we're to be bullock guards. Pick up your bleeding firelocks!'

'Sharpe ain't here, Sergeant?'

'Of course he ain't here! If he was here we wouldn't be ordered to wipe bullocks' arses, would we? But he's coming back. General's word on it. Just a few days, lads, just a few days and he'll be back with all his glittering stones hidden away.' Hakeswill's fury was abating. At least he had not been ordered to attach himself to a fighting battalion, and he was beginning to realize that any duty attached to the baggage animals would give him a fine chance to fillet the army stores. Pickings were to be made there, and more than just the pickings of stores, for the baggage always travelled with the army's tail of women and that meant more opportunity. It could be worse, Hakeswill thought, so long as this Captain Mackay was no martinet. 'You know what the trouble is with this army?' Hakeswill demanded.

'What?' Lowry asked.

'Full of bleeding Scotchmen.' Hakeswill glowered. 'I hates Scotchmen. Not English, are they? Peasant bleeding Scotchmen. Sawney creatures, they are, sawney! Should have killed them all when we had the chance, but we takes pity on them instead. Scorpions in our bosoms, that's what they are. Says so in the scriptures. Now get a bleeding move on!'

But it would only be a few days, the Sergeant consoled himself, only a few days, and Sharpe would be finished.

* * *

Colonel Pohlmann's bodyguard carried McCandless to a small house that lay at the edge of the encampment. A widow and three children lived there, and the woman shrank away from the Mahratta soldiers who had raped her, stolen all her food and fouled her well with their sewage. The Swiss doctor left Sharpe with strict instructions that the dressing on the Colonel's leg was to be kept damp. 'I'd give you some medicine for his fever, but I have none,' the doctor said, 'so if the fever gets worse just keep him warm and make him sweat.' The doctor shrugged. 'It might help.'

Pohlmann left food and a leather bag of silver coins. 'Tell McCandless that's for his horses,' he told Sharpe.

'Yes, sir.'

'The widow will look after you,' Pohlmann said, 'and when the Colonel's well enough you can move him to Aurungabad. And if you change your mind, Sharpe, you know I'll welcome you.' The Colonel shook Sharpe's hand, then mounted the silver steps to his howdah. A horseman unfurled his banner of the white horse of Hanover. 'I'll spread word that you're not to be molested,' Pohlmann called back, then his mahout tapped the elephant's skull and the great beast set off northwards.

Simone Joubert was the last to say farewell. 'I wish you were staying with us,' she said unhappily.

'I can't.'

'I know, and maybe it's for the best.' She looked left and right to make certain no one was watching, then leaned swiftly forward and kissed Sharpe on the cheek. '*Au revoir*, Richard.'

He watched her ride away, then went back into the hovel which was nothing but a palm thatch roof set above walls made of decayed reed mats. The interior of the hut was blackened by years of smoke, and its only furniture was the rope cot on which McCandless lay. 'She's an outcast,' the Colonel told Sharpe, indicating the woman. 'She refused to jump onto her husband's funeral fire, so her family sent her away.' The Colonel flinched as a stab of pain scythed through his thigh. 'Give her the food, Sergeant, and some cash out of that bag. How much did Pohlmann leave us?'

The coins in Pohlmann's bag were of silver and copper, and Sharpe sorted and counted each different denomination, and McCandless then translated their rough worth into pounds. 'Sixty!' He announced the total bitterly. 'That might just buy one cavalry hack, but it won't buy a horse that can stay over country for days on end.'

'How much did your gelding cost, sir?' Sharpe asked.

'Five hundred and twenty guineas,' McCandless said ruefully. 'I bought him four years ago, when you and I were released from Seringapatam, and I prayed he'd be the last horse I'd ever buy. Except for the mare, of course, but she was just a remount. Even so she cost me a hundred and forty guineas. A bargain, too! I bought her in Madras, fresh off the boat and she was just skin and bones then, but two months of pasture put some muscle on her.'

The figures were almost incomprehensible to Sharpe. Five hundred and twenty guineas for a horse? A man could live his whole life on five hundred and forty-six pounds, and live well. Ale every day. 'Won't the Company replace the horses, sir?' he asked.

McCandless smiled sadly. 'They might, Sharpe, but I doubt it. I doubt it very much.'

'Why not, sir?'

'I'm an old man,' the Scotsman said, 'and my salary is a heavy impost on the Company's debit column. I told you they'd like me to retire, Sharpe, and if I indent for the value of two horses they might well insist on my retirement.' He sighed. 'I knew this pursuit of Dodd was doomed. I felt it in my bones.'

'We'll get you another horse, sir,' Sharpe said.

McCandless grimaced. 'How, pray?'

'We can't have you walking, sir. Not a full colonel. Besides, it was my fault, really.'

'Your fault? Don't be absurd, Sharpe.'

'I should have been with you, sir. But I wasn't. I was off thinking.'

The Colonel looked at him steadily for what seemed a long while. 'I should imagine, Sergeant,' he said at last, 'that you had a lot to think about. How was your elephant ride with Colonel Pohlmann?'

'He showed me Aurungabad, sir.'

'I think he took you to the mountain top and showed you the kingdoms of this world,' the Colonel said. 'What did he offer you? A lieutenancy?'

'Yes, sir.' Sharpe blushed to admit as much, but it was dark inside the widow's hovel and the Colonel did not see.

'He told you of Benoît de Boigne,' McCandless asked, 'and of that rogue George Thomas? And he said you could be a rich man in two or three years, aren't I right?'

'Something like that, sir.'

McCandless shrugged. 'I won't deceive you, Sharpe, he's right. Everything he told you is true. Out there' – he waved towards the setting sun which glinted through the chinks in the reed-mat walls – 'is a lawless society that for years has rewarded the soldier with gold. The soldier, mark me, not the honest farmer or the hard-working merchant. The prince-doms grow fat, Sharpe, and the people grow lean, but there is nothing to stop you serving those princes. Nothing but the oath you took to serve your King.'

'I'm still here, sir, aren't I?' Sharpe said indignantly.

'Yes, Sharpe, you are,' McCandless said, then he closed his eyes and groaned. 'I fear the fever is going to come. Maybe not.'

'So what do we do, sir?'

'Do? Nothing. Nothing helps the fever except a week of shivering in the heat.'

'I meant about getting you back to the army, sir. I could go to Aurungabad and see if I can find someone to take a message.'

'Not unless you speak their language, you won't,' McCandless said, then he lay for a while in silence. 'Sevajee will find us,' he went on eventually. 'News carries far in this countryside, and Sevajee will smell us out in the end.' Again he fell silent, and Sharpe thought he had fallen asleep, but then he saw the Colonel shake his head. 'Doomed,' the Colonel said. 'Lieutenant Dodd is going to be the end of me.'

'We'll capture Dodd, sir, I promise.'

'I pray so, I pray so.' The Colonel pointed to his saddlebags in the corner of the hut. 'Would you find my Bible, Sharpe? And perhaps you'd read to me while there's still a little light? Something from the Book of Job, I think.'

McCandless fell into days of fever and Sharpe into days of isolation. For all he knew the war might have been won or lost, for he saw no one and no news came to the thatched hovel under its thin-leaved trees. To keep himself busy he cleared out an old irrigation ditch that ran northwards across the woman's land, and he hacked at the brush, killed snakes and shovelled earth until he was rewarded by a trickle of water. That done, he tackled the hovel's roof, laying new palm thatch on the old and binding it in place with twists of frond. He went hungry, for the woman had little food other than the grain Pohlmann had left and some dried beans. Sharpe stripped to the waist when he worked and his skin went as brown as the stock of his musket. In the evenings he played with the woman's three children, making forts out of the red soil that they bombarded with stones and, in one memorable twilight, when a toy rampart proved impregnable to thrown pebbles, Sharpe laid a fuse of powder and blew a breach with three of his musket cartridges.

He did his best to tend McCandless, washing the Colonel's face, reading him the scriptures and feeding him spoonfuls of bitter gunpowder diluted in water. He was not sure that the powder helped, but every soldier swore that it was the best medicine for the fever, and so Sharpe forced spoonfuls of the salty mixture down the Colonel's throat. He worried about the bullet wound in McCandless's thigh, for the widow had shyly pushed him aside one day when he was dampening the dressing and had insisted on untying the bandage and putting a poultice of her own making onto the raw wound. There were moss and cobwebs in the poultice, and Sharpe wondered if he had done the right thing by letting her apply the mixture, but as the first week passed the wound did not seem to worsen and, in his more lucid moments, the Colonel claimed the pain was lessening.

Once the irrigation ditch was cleared Sharpe tackled the widow's well. He devised a dredge out of a broken wooden bucket and used it to scoop out handfuls of foul-smelling mud from the base of the well, and all the while he thought about his future. He knew Major Stokes would welcome him back to the Seringapatam armoury, but after a time the regiment would surely remember his existence and want him back and that would mean rejoining the Light Company with Captain Morris and Sergeant Hakeswill, and Sharpe shuddered at that thought. Maybe Colonel Gore would transfer him? The lads said that Gore was a decent fellow, not as chilling as Wellesley, and that was good news, yet even so Sharpe often wondered whether he should have accepted Pohlmann's offer. Lieutenant Sharpe, he muttered it aloud, Lieutenant Sharpe. Why not? And in those moments he would daydream of the joy of going back to the foundling home in Brewhouse Lane. He would wear a sword and a cocked hat, have braid on his jacket and spurs at his heels, and for every lash the bastards had ever laid on small Richard Sharpe he would pay them back tenfold. He felt a terrible anger when he remembered those beatings and he would haul at his makeshift dredge as if he could slake the anger with hard work.

But in all those daydreams he never once returned to Brewhouse Lane in a white coat, or in a purple coat, or in any other coat except a red one. No one in Britain had ever heard of Anthony Pohlmann, and why should they care that a child had gone from the gutters of Wapping to a commission in the Maharajah of Gwalior's army? A man might as well claim to be Colonel of the Moon for all anyone would care. Unless it was a red coat, they would condemn him as a flash bastard, and be done with him, but if he walked back in Britain's scarlet coat then they would take him seriously and that meant he had to become an officer in his own army.

So one night, when the rain was beating on the widow's repaired thatch and the Colonel was sitting on the rope bed declaring that his fever was abating, Sharpe asked McCandless how a man became an officer in Britain's army. 'I mean I know it can be done, sir,' he said awkwardly, 'because we had a Mister Devlin back in England and he came up from the ranks. He'd been a shepherd's boy on the dales before he took the shilling, but he was Lieutenant Devlin when I knew him.'

And was most likely to die as an old and embittered Lieutenant Devlin, McCandless thought, but he did not say as much. Instead he paused before saying anything. He was even tempted to evade the question altogether by pretending that his fever had suddenly taken a turn for the worse, for he understood only too well what lay behind Sharpe's question. Most officers would have mocked the ambition, but Hector McCandless was not a mocker. But he also knew that for a man to aspire to rise from the ranks to the officers' mess was to risk two disappointments: the disappointments of both failure and success. The most likely outcome was failure, for such promotions were as scarce as hens' teeth, but a few men did make the leap and their success inevitably led to unhappiness. They lacked the education of the other officers, they lacked their manners and they lacked their confidence. They were generally disdained by the other officers, and set to work as quartermasters in the belief that they could not be trusted to lead men in battle. And there was even some truth to that belief, for the men themselves did not like their officers to have come from the ranks, but McCandless decided Sharpe knew all that for himself and so he spared him the need to listen to it all over again. 'There are two ways, Sharpe,' McCandless said. 'First you can buy a commission. The rank of ensign will cost you four hundred pounds, but you'll need another hundred and fifty to equip yourself, and even that will only buy a barely adequate horse, a four-guinea sword and a serviceable uniform, and you'll still need a private income to cover your mess bills. An ensign earns close to ninety-five pounds a year, but the army stops some of that for expenses and more for the income tax. Have you heard of that new tax, Sharpe?'

'No, sir.'

'A pernicious thing. Taking from a man what he has honestly earned! It's thievery, Sharpe, disguised as government.' The Colonel scowled. 'So an ensign is lucky to see seventy pounds out of his salary, and even if he lives frugal that won't cover his mess bills. Most regiments charge an officer two shillings for dinner every day, a shilling for wine, though of course you could go without wine well enough and water's free, but there's sixpence a day for the mess servant, another sixpence for breakfast and sixpence for washing and mending. You can't live as an officer without at least a hundred pounds a year on top of your salary. Have you got the money?'

'No, sir,' Sharpe lied. In truth he had enough jewels sewn into his red coat to buy himself a majority, but he did not want McCandless to know that.

'Good,' McCandless said, 'because that isn't the best way. Most regiments won't look at a man buying himself out of the ranks. Why should they? They've got plenty of young hopefuls coming from the shires with their parents' cash hot in their purses, so the last thing they need is some half-educated ranker who can't meet his mess bills. I'm not saying it's impossible. Any regiment posted to the West Indies will sell you an ensign's post cheap, but that's because they can't get anyone else on account of the yellow fever. A posting to the West Indies is a death sentence. But if a man wants to get into anything other than a West-Indies-bound regiment, Sharpe, then he must hope for the second route. He must be a sergeant and he must be able to read and write, but there's a third requirement too. The fellow must perform a quite impossibly gallant act. Leading a Forlorn Hope will do the trick, but any act, so long as it's suicidal, will serve, though of course he must do it under the General's eye or else it's all a waste of time.'

Sharpe sat in silence for a while, daunted by the obstacles that lay in the way of his daydream's fulfilment. 'Do they give him a test, sir?' he asked. 'In reading?' That thought worried him for, although his reading was improving night by night, he still stumbled over quite simple words. He claimed that the Bible's print was too small, and McCandless was kind enough to believe the excuse.

'A test in reading? Good Lord, no! For an officer!' McCandless smiled tiredly. 'They take his word, of course.' The Colonel paused for a second. 'But I've often wondered, Sharpe,' he went on, 'why a man from the ranks would want to be an officer?'

So he could go back to Brewhouse Lane, Sharpe thought,

and kick some teeth in. 'I was just wondering about it, sir,' he said instead. 'Just thinking, sir.'

'Because in many ways,' McCandless said, 'sergeants have more influence with the men. Less formal prestige, perhaps, but certainly more influence than any junior officer. Ensigns and lieutenants, Sharpe, are very insignificant creatures. They're really of very little use most of the time. It's not till a man reaches his captaincy that he begins to be valuable.'

'I'm sure you're right, sir,' Sharpe said lamely. 'I was just thinking.'

That night the Colonel relapsed into fever, and Sharpe sat in the hut doorway and listened to the rain beat on the land. He could not shake the daydream, could not drive away the picture of him ducking through the gate in Brewhouse Lane and seeing the faces he hated. He wanted it, he wanted it terribly, and so he dreamed on, dreaming the impossible, but unable to check the dream. He did not know how, but he would somehow make the leap. Or else die in the attempt.

CHAPTER 7

Dodd called his new gelding Peter. 'Because it's got no balls, Monsewer,' he informed Pierre Joubert, and he repeated the poor joke a dozen times in the next two days just to make certain that its insult was understood. Joubert smiled and said nothing, and the Major would launch himself into a panegyric on Peter's merits. His old horse had whistling lungs, while this one could be ridden all day and still had its head up and a spring in its long stride. 'A thoroughbred, Captain,' he told Joubert, 'an English thoroughbred. Not some screw-backed old French nag, but a proper horse.'

The men in Dodd's Cobras liked to see their Major on his fine big horse. It was true that one man had died in the beast's acquisition, yet the theft had still been a fine piece of banditry, and the men had laughed to see the English Sergeant searching the camp while all the while Major Dodd's Jemadar, Gopal, was hiding the horses a long way to the north.

Colonel Pohlmann was less amused. 'I promised McCandless safe conduct, Major,' he growled at Dodd the first time he saw the Englishman on his new gelding.

'Quite right, sir.'

'And you've added horse-thieving to your catalogue of crimes?'

'I can't think what you mean, sir,' Dodd protested in mock innocence. 'I purchased this beast off a horse trader yesterday, sir. Gypsy-looking fellow from Korpalgaon. Took the last of my savings.'

'And your Jemadar's new horse?' Pohlmann asked, pointing to Gopal who was riding Colonel McCandless's mare.

'He bought her from the same fellow,' Dodd said.

'Of course he did, Major,' Pohlmann said wearily. The Colonel knew it was pointless to chide a man for theft in an army that was encouraged to steal for its very existence, yet he was offended by Dodd's abuse of the hospitality that had been extended to McCandless. The Scotsman was right, Pohlmann thought, Dodd was a man without honour, yet the Hanoverian knew that if Scindia employed none but saints then he would have no European officers.

The theft of McCandless's horses only added more reason for Pohlmann to dislike William Dodd. He found the Englishman too dour, too jealous and too humourless, yet still, despite his dislike, he recognized that the Major was a fine soldier. His rescue of his regiment from Ahmednuggur had been an inglorious operation executed superbly, and Pohlmann, at least, understood the achievement, just as he appreciated that Dodd's men liked their new commanding officer. The Hanoverian was not certain why Dodd was popular, for he was not an easy man; he had no small talk, he smiled rarely, and he was punctilious about details that other officers might let pass, yet still the men liked him. Maybe they sensed that he was on their side, wholly on their side, recognizing that nothing is achieved in war by officers without men, and a good deal by men without officers, and for that reason, if no other, they were glad he was their commanding officer. And men who like their commanding officer are more likely to fight well than men who do not, and so Pohlmann was glad that he had William Dodd as a regimental commander even if he did disdain him as little better than a common thief.

Pohlmann's *compoo* had now joined the rest of Scindia's army, which had already been swollen by the troops of the Rajah of Berar, so that over a hundred thousand men and all their animals now wandered the Deccan Plain in search of grazing, forage and grain. The vast army hugely outnumbered its enemy, but Scindia made no attempt to bring Wellesley to battle. Instead he led his horde in an apparently aimless fashion. They went south towards the enemy, then withdrew north, they made a lumbering surge to the east and then retraced their steps to the west, and everywhere they marched they stripped the farms, slashed down crops, broke into granaries, slaughtered livestock and rifled humble homes in search of rice, wheat or lentils. Every day a score of cavalry patrols rode south to find the enemy armies, but the Mahratta horsemen rarely came close to the redcoats, for the British cavalry counter-patrolled aggressively and each day left dead horses on the plain while Scindia's great host wandered mindlessly on.

'Now that you have such a fine horse,' Pohlmann said to Dodd a week after the Major's theft, 'perhaps you can lead a cavalry patrol?'

'Gladly, sir.'

'Someone has to find out what the British are doing,' Pohlmann grumbled.

Dodd rode south with some of Pohlmann's own cavalry and his patrol succeeded where so many others had failed, but only because the Major donned his old red coat so that it would appear as if his score of horsemen were under the command of a British officer, and the ruse worked, for Dodd came across a much smaller force of Mysore cavalry who rode unsuspecting into the trap. Six enemy escaped, eight died, and their leader yielded a mass of information before Dodd shot him through the head.

'You might have brought him back to us,' Pohlmann remonstrated gently when Dodd returned. 'I could have talked with him myself,' the Colonel added, peering down from his green-curtained howdah. The elephant plodded behind a purple-coated horseman who carried Pohlmann's red flag emblazoned with the white horse of Hanover. There was a girl with Pohlmann, but all Dodd could see of her was a dark languid hand bright with gems hanging over the howdah's edge. 'So tell me what you learned, Major,' Pohlmann ordered.

'The British are back close to the Godavery, sir, but they're still split into two forces and neither has more than six thousand infantry. Wellesley's nearest to us while Stevenson's moving off to the west. I've made a map, sir, with their dispositions.' Dodd held the paper up towards the swaying howdah.

'Hoping to pincer us, are they?' Pohlmann asked, reaching down to pluck the map from the Major's hand. 'Not now, *Liebchen,*' he added, though not to Dodd.

'I imagine they're staying divided because of the roads, sir,' Dodd said.

'Of course,' Pohlmann said, wondering why Dodd was teaching him to suck eggs. The British need for decent roads was much greater than the Mahrattas', for the British carried all their foodstuffs in ox wagons and the cumbersome vehicles could not manage any country other than the smoothest grass plains. Which meant that the two enemy armies could only advance where the ground was smooth or the roads adequate. It made their movements clumsy, and it made any attempt to pincer Scindia's army doubly difficult, though by now, Pohlmann reflected, the British commander must be thoroughly confused about Scindia's intentions. So was Scindia, for that matter, for the Maharajah was taking his tactical advice from astrologers rather than from his European officers which meant that the great horde was impelled to its wanderings by the glimmer of stars, the import of dreams and the entrails of goats.

200

'If we marched south now,' Dodd urged Pohlmann, 'we could trap Wellesley's men south of Aurungabad. Stevenson's too far away to support him.'

'It does sound a good idea,' Pohlmann agreed genially, pocketing Dodd's map.

'There must be some plan,' Dodd suggested irritably.

'Must there?' Pohlmann asked airily. 'Higher up, *Liebchen*, just there! That's good!' The bejewelled hand had vanished inside the howdah. Pohlmann closed his eyes for an instant, then opened them and smiled down on Dodd. 'The plan,' the Hanoverian said grandly, 'is to wait and see whether Holkar will join us.' Holkar was the most powerful of all the Mahratta chieftains, but he was biding his time, uncertain whether to join Scindia and the Rajah of Berar or whether to sit out the war with his huge forces intact. 'And the next part of the plan,' Pohlmann went on, 'is to hold a durbar. Have you ever attended a durbar, Dodd?'

'No, sir.'

'It is a council, a committee of the old and the wise, or rather of the senile and the talkative. The war will be discussed, as will the position of the stars and the mood of the gods and the failure of the monsoon and, once the durbar is over, if indeed it ever ends, we shall commence our wandering once again, but perhaps a decision of sorts will have been made, though whether that decision will be to retire on Nagpoor, or to advance on Hyderabad, or to choose a battlefield and allow the British to attack us, or simply to march from now until the Day of Judgment, I cannot yet tell you. I shall offer advice, of course, but if Scindia dreams of monkeys on the night before the durbar then not even Alexander the Great could persuade him to fight.'

'But Scindia must know better than to let the two British forces unite, sir?' Dodd said.

'He does, he does, indeed he does. Our lord and master

is no fool, but he is inscrutable. We are waiting for the omens to be propitious.'

'They're propitious now,' Dodd protested.

'That is not for you or me to decide. We Europeans can be relied upon to fight, but not to read the messages of the stars or to understand the meaning of dreams. But when it comes to the battle, Major, you can be sure that the stars and the dreams will be ignored and that Scindia will leave all the decisions to me.' Pohlmann smiled benignly at Dodd, then gazed out at the horde of cavalry that covered the plain. There must have been fifty thousand horsemen in view, but Pohlmann would happily have marched with only a thousand. Most of the Mahratta horsemen were only present for the loot they hoped to steal after victory and, though they were all fine riders and brave fighters, they had no conception of picquet duty and none was willing to charge into the face of an infantry unit. They did not understand that a cavalry troop needed to take horrific casualties if it was to break infantry; instead they reckoned Scindia's great guns and his mercenary infantry would do the shattering and they would then pursue the broken enemy like hornets, and until that happy moment they were just so many useless mouths to feed. If they all went away tomorrow it would make no difference to the war's outcome, for the victory would still be won by the artillery and the infantry. Pohlmann knew that and he imagined lining his guns wheel to wheel in batteries, with his infantry formed just behind and then watching the redcoats walk into a tumult of fire and iron and death. A flail of fire! A storm of metal whipping the air into a gale of bloody ruin amongst which the British would be chopped into butcher's scraps.

'You're hurting me,' the girl said.

'*Liebchen*, I'm so sorry,' Pohlmann said, releasing his grip. 'I was thinking.'

'Sir?' Dodd asked, thinking the Hanoverian was speaking to him.

'I was thinking, Dodd, that it is no bad thing that we wander so aimlessly.'

'It isn't?' Dodd retorted with astonishment.

'Because if we do not know where we are going, then nor will the British, so one day they will march a few miles too far and then we shall pounce on them. Someone will blunder, Dodd, because in war someone always does blunder. It is an immutable rule of war: someone will blunder. We must just have patience.' In truth Pohlmann was just as impatient as Dodd, but the Colonel knew it would not serve any purpose to betray that impatience. In India, he had learned, matters moved at their own pace, as imponderable and unstoppable as an elephant. But soon, Pohlmann reckoned, one of the British forces would make a march too far and find itself so close to the vast Mahratta army that even Scindia could not refuse battle. And even if the two enemy armies joined, what did that matter? Their combined forces were small, the Mahratta horde was vast, and the outcome of their meeting as certain as anything could be in war. And Pohlmann was confident that Scindia would eventually give him command of the army, and Pohlmann would then roll over the enemy like the great Juggernaut of Hindu legend and with that happy prospect he was content.

Dodd looked up to say something more, but the howdah's green curtains had been drawn shut. The girl giggled, while the mahout, seated just in front of the closed howdah, stared impassively ahead. The Mahrattas were on the march, covering the earth like a swarm, just waiting for their enemies to blunder.

Sharpe was tired of being hungry so one day he took his musket and walked in search of game. He reckoned anything would do, even a tiger, but he hoped to find beef. India seemed full of beeves, but that day he saw none, though after four miles he found a herd of goats grazing in a small wood. He drew his bayonet, reckoning it would be easier to cut one of the beast's throats than shoot it and so attract the attention of the herd's vengeful owner, but when he came close to the animals a dog burst out of the trees and attacked him.

He clubbed the dog down with his musket butt, and the brief commotion put the goats to flight and it took him the best part of an hour to find the animals again and by then he could not have cared if he attracted half the population of India and so he aimed and fired, and all he succeeded in doing was wounding one poor beast that started bleating pitifully. He ran to it, cut its throat, which was harder than he had thought, then hoisted the carcass onto his shoulder.

The widow boiled the stringy flesh which tasted foul, but it was still meat and Sharpe wolfed it down as though he had not eaten in months. The smell of the meat roused Colonel McCandless who sat up in his bed and frowned at the pot. 'I could almost eat that,' he said.

'You want some, sir?'

'I haven't eaten meat in eighteen years, Sharpe. I won't start now.' He ran a hand through his lank white hair. 'I do declare I'm feeling better, God be praised.'

The Colonel swung his feet onto the floor and tried to stand. 'But I'm weak as a kitten,' he said.

'Plate of meat will put some strength in you, sir.'

' "Get thee behind me, Satan," ' the Colonel said, then put a hand on one of the posts which held up the roof and hauled himself to his feet. 'I might take a walk tomorrow.'

'How's the leg, sir?'

'Mending, Sharpe, mending.' The Colonel put some

weight on his left leg and seemed pleasantly surprised that it did not buckle. 'God has preserved me again.'

'Thank God for that, sir.'

'I do, Sharpe, I do.'

Next morning the Colonel felt better still. He ducked out of the hut and blinked in the bright sunlight. 'Have you seen any soldiers these last two weeks?'

'Not a one, sir. Nothing but farmers.'

The Colonel scraped a hand across the white bristles on his chin. 'A shave, I think. Would you be so kind as to fetch my box of razors? And perhaps you could heat some water?'

Sharpe dutifully put a pot of water on the fire, then stropped one of the Colonel's razors on a saddle's girth strap. He was just perfecting the edge when McCandless called him from outside the house. 'Sharpe!'

Something in McCandless's voice made Sharpe snatch up his musket, then he heard the beat of hooves as he ducked under the low doorway and he hauled back the musket's cock in expectation of enemies, but McCandless waved the weapon down. 'I said Sevajee would find us!' the Colonel said happily. 'Nothing stays secret in this countryside, Sharpe.'

Sharpe lowered the musket's flint as he watched Sevajee lead his men towards the widow's house. The young Indian grinned at McCandless's dishevelled condition. 'I heard there was a white devil near here, and I knew it would be you.'

'I wish you'd come sooner,' McCandless grumbled.

'Why? You were ill. The folk I spoke to said you would die.' Sevajee slid out of the saddle and led his horse to the well. 'Besides, we've been too busy.'

'Following Scindia, I trust?' the Colonel asked.

'Here, there and everywhere.' Sevajee hauled up a skin of water and held it under his horse's nose. 'They've been south, east, back north again. But now they're going to hold a durbar, Colonel.'

'A durbar!' McCandless brightened, and Sharpe wondered what on earth a durbar was.

'They've gone to Borkardan,' Sevajee announced happily. 'All of them! Scindia, the Rajah of Berar, the whole lot! A sea of enemies.'

'Borkardan,' McCandless said, summoning a mental map in his head. 'Where's that? Two days' march north?'

'One for a horseman, two on foot,' Sevajee agreed.

McCandless, his shave forgotten, stared northwards. 'But how long will they stay there?'

'Long enough,' Sevajee said gleefully, 'and first they have to make a place fit for a prince's durbar and that will take them two or three days, and then they'll talk for another two or three days. And they need to rest their animals too, and in Borkardan they've found plenty of forage.'

'How do you know?' McCandless asked.

'Because we met some *brindarries*,' Sevajee said with a smile, and turned at the same time to indicate four small, lean and riderless horses that were the trophies of that meeting. 'We had a talk with them,' Sevajee said airily, and Sharpe wondered how brutal that talk had been. 'Forty thousand infantry, sixty thousand cavalry,' Sevajee said, 'and over a hundred guns.'

McCandless limped back into the house to fetch paper and ink from his saddlebag. Then, back in the sunlight, he wrote a despatch and Sevajee detailed six of his horsemen to take the precious news south as fast as they could. They would need to search for Wellesley's army and Sevajee told them to whip their horses bloody because, if the British moved fast, there was a chance to catch the Mahrattas while they were encamped for their durbar and then to attack them before they could form their battle array. 'That would even things up,' McCandless announced happily. 'A surprise attack!'

'They're not fools,' Sevajee warned, 'they'll have a host of picquets.'

'But it takes time to organize a hundred thousand men, Sevajee, a lot of time! They'll be milling about like sheep while we march into battle!'

The six horsemen rode away with the precious despatch and McCandless, tired again, let Sharpe shave him. 'All we can do now is wait,' the Colonel said.

'Wait?' Sharpe asked indignantly, believing that McCandless was implying that they would do nothing while the battle was being fought.

'If Scindia's at Borkardan,' the Colonel said, 'then our armies will have to march this way to reach him. So we might as well wait for them to come to us. Then we can join up again.'

It was time to stop dreaming. It was time to fight.

Wellesley's army had crossed the Godavery and marched towards Aurungabad, then heard that Scindia's forces had gone far to the east before lunging south towards the heartland of Hyderabad, and the report made sense, for the old Nizam had just died and left a young son on the throne and a young ruler's state could make for rich pickings, and so Wellesley had turned his small army and hurried back to the Godavery. They laboriously recrossed the river, swimming the horses, bullocks and elephants to the southern bank, and floating the guns, limbers and wagons across on rafts. The men used boats made from inflated bladders, and it took two whole days to make the crossing and then, after a day's march south towards threatened Hyderabad, more news came that the enemy had turned about and gone back northwards.

'Don't know what they're bleeding doing,' Hakeswill declared.

'Captain Mackay says we're looking for the enemy,' Private Lowry suggested helpfully.

'Looking for his arse, more like. Bloody Wellesley.' Hakeswill was sitting beside the river, watching the bullocks being goaded back into the water to cross once again to the north bank. 'In the water, out the water, up one road, down the next, walk in bleeding circles, then back through the bleeding river again.' His blue eyes opened wide in indignation and his face twitched. 'Arthur Wellesley should never be a general.'

'Why not, Sarge?' Private Kendrick asked, knowing that Hakeswill wanted the opportunity to explain.

'Stands to reason, lad, stands to reason.' Hakeswill paused to light a clay pipe. 'No bleeding experience. You remember that wood outside Seringapatam? Bloody chaos, that's what it was, bloody chaos and who caused it? He did, that's who.' He gestured at Wellesley who, mounted on a tall white horse, had come to the bluff above the river. 'He's a general,' Hakeswill explained, 'because his father's an earl and because his elder brother's the Governor General, that's why. If my father had been a bleeding earl, then I'd be a bleeding general, says so in the scriptures. Lord Obadiah Hakeswill, I'd be, and you wouldn't see me buggering about like a dog chasing fleas up its arse. I'd bleeding well get the job done. On your feet, lads, look smart now!'

The General, with nothing to do except wait while his army crossed the river, had turned his horse up the bank and his path brought him close to where Hakeswill had been seated. Wellesley looked across, recognized the Sergeant and seemed about to turn away, but then an innate courtesy overcame his distaste for speaking with the lower ranks. 'Still here, Sergeant?' he asked awkwardly.

'Still here, sir,' Hakeswill said. He was quivering at attention, his clay pipe thrust into a pocket and his firelock by his side. 'Doing my duty, sir, like a soldier.'

'Your duty?' Wellesley asked. 'You came to arrest Sergeant Sharpe, isn't that right?'

'Sir!' Hakeswill affirmed.

The General grimaced. 'Let me know if you see him. He's with Colonel McCandless, and they both seem to be missing. Dead, probably.' And on that cheerful note the General tugged on his reins and spurred away.

Hakeswill watched him go, then retrieved his clay pipe and sucked the tobacco back to glowing life. Then he spat onto the bank. 'Sharpie ain't dead,' he said malevolently. 'I'm the one who's going to kill Sharpie. Says so in the scriptures.'

Then Captain Mackay arrived and insisted that Hakeswill and his six men help organize the transfer of the bullocks across the river. The animals carried packs loaded with spare round shot for the artillery, and the Captain had been provided with two rafts for that precious ammunition. 'They're to transfer the shot to the rafts, understand? Then swim the beasts over. I don't want chaos, Sergeant. Make them line up decently. And make sure they don't roll the shot into the river to save themselves the bother of reloading it.'

'It isn't a soldier's job,' Hakeswill complained when the Captain was gone. 'Chivvying bullocks? I ain't a bleeding Scotchman. That's all they're good for, chivvying bullocks. Do it all the time, they do, down the green roads to London, but it ain't a job for an Englishman.' But he nevertheless did an effective job, using his bayonet to prod men and animals into the queue which slowly snaked its way down to the water. By nightfall the whole army was over, and next morning, long before dawn, they marched north again. They camped before midday, thus avoiding the worst of the heat, and by mid-afternoon the first enemy cavalry patrols showed in the distance and the army's own cavalry rode out to drive the horsemen away.

They did not move at all for the next two days. Cavalry

scouts tried to discover the enemy's intentions, while Company spies spread gold throughout the north country in search of news, but the gold was wasted, for every scrap of intelligence was contradicted by another. One said Holkar had joined Scindia, another said Holkar was declaring war on Scindia, then the Mahrattas were said to be marching west, or east, or perhaps north, until Wellesley felt he was playing a slow version of blind man's buff.

Then, at last, some reliable news arrived. Six Mahratta horsemen in the service of Syud Sevajee came to Wellesley's camp with a hastily written despatch from Colonel McCandless. The Colonel regretted his absence and explained that he had taken a wound that had been slow to heal, but he could assure Sir Arthur that he had not abandoned his duty and could thus report, with a fair degree of certainty, that the forces of Dowlut Rao Scindia and the Rajah of Berar had finally ceased their wanderings at Borkardan. They planned to stay there, McCandless wrote, to hold a durbar and to let their animals recover their strength, and he estimated those intentions implied a stay in Borkardan of five or six days. The enemy numbered, he reported, at least eighty thousand men and possessed around a hundred pieces of field artillery, many of inferior calibre, but an appreciable number throwing much heavier shot. He reckoned, from his own earlier observations in Pohlmann's camp, that only fifteen thousand of the enemy's infantry were trained to Company standards, while the rest were makeweights, but the guns, he added ominously, were well served and well maintained. The despatch had been written in a hurry, and in a shaky hand, but it was concise, confident and comprehensive.

The Colonel's despatch drove the General to his maps and then to a flurry of orders. The army was readied to march that night, and a galloper went to Colonel Stevenson's force, west of Wellesley's, with orders to march north on a parallel course. The two small armies should combine at Borkardan in four days' time. 'That will give us, what?' Wellesley thought for a second or two. 'Eleven thousand prime infantry and forty-eight guns.' He jotted the figures on the map, then absent-mindedly tapped the numbers with a pencil. 'Eleven thousand against eighty,' he said dubiously, then grimaced. 'It will serve,' he concluded, 'it will serve very well.'

'Eleven against eighty will serve, sir?' Captain Campbell asked with astonishment. Campbell was the young Scottish officer who had thrice climbed the ladder to be the first man into Ahmednuggur and his reward had been a promotion and an appointment as Wellesley's aide. Now he stared at the General, a man Campbell considered as sensible as any he had ever met, yet the odds that Wellesley was welcoming seemed insane.

'I'd rather have more men,' Wellesley admitted, 'but we can probably do the job with eleven thousand. You can forget Scindia's cavalry, Campbell, because it won't manage a thing on a battlefield, and the Rajah of Berar's infantry will simply get in everyone else's way, which means we'll be fighting against fifteen thousand good infantry and rather too many well-served guns. The rest don't matter. If we beat the guns and the infantry, the rest of them will run. Depend on it, they'll run.'

'Suppose they adopt a defensive position, sir?' Campbell felt impelled to insert a note of caution into the General's hopes. 'Suppose they're behind a river, sir? Or behind walls?'

'We can suppose what we like, Campbell, but supposing is only fancy, and if we take fright at fancies then we might as well abandon soldiering. We'll decide how to deal with the rogues once we find them, but the first thing to do is find them.' Wellesley rolled up the map. 'Can't kill your fox till you've run him down. So let's be about our business.'

The army marched that night. Six thousand cavalry, nearly

all of them Indian, led the way, and behind them were twenty-two pieces of artillery, four thousand sepoys of the East India Company and two battalions of Scots, while the great clumsy tail of bullocks, wives, children, wagons and merchants brought up the rear. They marched hard, and if any man was daunted by the size of the enemy's army, they showed no sign of it. They were as well trained as any men that had ever worn the red coat in India, they had been promised victory by their long-nosed General, and now they were going for the kill. And, whatever the odds, they believed they would win. So long as no one blundered.

Borkardan was a mere village with no building fit for a prince, and so the great durbar of the Mahratta chiefs was held in an enormous tent that was hastily made by sewing a score of smaller tents together, then lining the canvas with swathes of brightly coloured silk, and it would have made a marvellously impressive structure had the heavens not opened when the durbar began so that the sound of men's voices was half drowned by the beat of rain on stretched canvas and if the hastily made seams had not opened to let the water pour through in streams.

'It's all a waste of time,' Pohlmann grumbled to Dodd, 'but we have to attend.' The Colonel was fixing his newly tied stock with a diamond-studded pin. 'And it isn't a time for any European opinion except mine, understand?'

'Yours?' Dodd, who had rather hoped to make a case for boldness, asked dourly.

'Mine,' Pohlmann said forcibly. 'I want to twist their tails, and I need every European officer nodding like a demented monkey in agreement with me.'

A hundred men had gathered under the dripping silk. Scindia, the Maharajah of Gwalior, and Bhonsla, the Rajah of Berar, sat on *musnuds*, elegant raised platform-thrones that were draped in brocade and sheltered from the intrusive rain by silk parasols. Their Highnesses were cooled by men waving long-handled fans while the rest of the durbar sweltered in the close, damp heat. The high-class brahmins, all in baggy trousers cut from gold brocade, white tunics and tall white turbans, sat closest to the two thrones, while behind them stood the military officers, Indian and European, who were perspiring in their finest uniforms. Servants moved unobtrusively through the crowd offering silver dishes of almonds, sweetmeats or raisins soaked in arrack. The three senior European officers stood together. Pohlmann, in a purple coat hung with golden braid and loops of chain, towered over Colonel Dupont, a wiry Dutchman who commanded Scindia's second *compoo*, and over Colonel Saleur, a Frenchman, who led the infantry of the Begum Somroo. Dodd lingered just behind the trio and listened to their private durbar. The three men agreed that their troops would have to take the brunt of the British attack, and that one of them must exercise overall command. It could not be Saleur, for the Begum Somroo was a client ruler of Scindia's, so her commander could hardly take precedence over her feudal overlord's officers, which meant that it had to be either Dupont or Pohlmann, but the Dutchman generously ceded the honour to the Hanoverian. 'Scindia would have chosen you anyway,' Dupont said.

'Wisely,' Pohlmann said cheerfully, 'very wisely. You're content, Saleur?'

'Indeed,' the Frenchman said. He was a tall, dour man with a badly scarred face and a formidable reputation as a disciplinarian. He was also reputed to be the Begum Somroo's lover, a post that evidently accompanied the command of that lady's infantry. 'What are the bastards talking about now?' he asked in English.

Pohlmann listened for a few seconds. 'Discussing whether to retreat to Gawilghur,' he said. Gawilghur was a hill fort that lay north and east of Borkardan and a group of brahmins were urging the army to retire there and let the British break their skulls against its cliffs and high walls. 'Goddamn brahmins,' Pohlmann said in disgust. 'Don't know a damn thing about soldiering. Know how to talk, but not how to fight.'

But then an older brahmin, his white beard reaching to his waist, stood up and declared that the omens were more suitable for battle. 'You have assembled a great army, dread Lord,' he addressed Scindia, 'and you would lock it away in a citadel?'

'Where did they find him?' Pohlmann muttered. 'He's actually talking sense!'

Scindia said little, preferring to let Surjee Rao, his chief minister, do the talking, while he himself sat plump and inscrutable on his throne. He was wearing a rich gown of yellow silk that had emeralds and pearls sewn into patterns of flowers, while a great yellow diamond gleamed from his pale-blue turban.

Another brahmin pleaded for the army to march south on Seringapatam, but he was ignored. The Rajah of Berar, darker-skinned than the pale Scindia, frowned at the durbar in an attempt to look warlike, but said very little. 'He'll run away,' Colonel Saleur growled, 'as soon as the first gun is fired. He always does.'

Beny Singh, the Rajah's warlord, argued for battle. 'I have five hundred camels laden with rockets, I have guns fresh from Agra, I have infantry hungry for enemy blood. Let them loose!'

'God help us if we do,' Dupont growled. 'Bastards don't have any discipline.'

'Is it always like this?' Dodd asked Pohlmann.

'Good God, no!' the Hanoverian said. 'This durbar is positively decisive! Usually it's three days of talk and a final decision to delay any decision until the next time.'

'You think they'll come to a decision today?' Saleur asked cynically.

'They'll have to,' Pohlmann said. 'They can't keep this army together for much longer. We're running out of forage! We're stripping the country bare.' The soldiers were still receiving just enough to eat, and the cavalrymen made certain their horses were fed, but the camp followers were near starvation and in a few days the suffering of the women and children would cause the army's morale to plummet. Only that morning Pohlmann had seen a woman sawing at what he had assumed was brown bread, then realized that no Indian would bake a European loaf and that the great lump was actually a piece of elephant dung and that the woman was crumbling it apart in search of undigested grains. They must fight now.

'So if we fight,' Saleur asked, 'how will you win?'

Pohlmann smiled. 'I think we can give young Wellesley a problem or two,' he said cheerfully. 'We'll put the Rajah's men behind some strong walls where they can't do any damage, and we three will line our guns wheel to wheel, hammer them hard for their whole approach, then finish them off with some smart volleys. After that we'll let the cavalry loose on their remnants.'

'But when?' Dupont asked.

'Soon,' Pohlmann said, 'soon. Has to be soon. Buggers are eating dung for breakfast these days.' There was a sudden silence in the tent and Pohlmann realized a question had been addressed to him. Surjee Rao, a sinister man whose reputation for cruelty was as widespread as it was deserved, raised an eyebrow to the Hanoverian. 'The rain, Your Serene Excellency,' Pohlmann explained, 'the rain deafened me so I could not hear your question.'

'What my Lord wishes to know,' the minister said, 'is whether we can destroy the British?'

'Oh, utterly,' Pohlmann said as though it was risible to even ask the question.

'They fight hard,' Beny Singh pointed out.

'And they die like other men when fought hard in return,' Pohlmann said dismissively.

Scindia leaned forward and whispered in Surjee Rao's ear. 'What the Lord of our land and the conqueror of our enemy's lands wishes to know,' the minister said, 'is how you will beat the British?'

'In the way that His Royal Highness suggested, Excellency, when he gave me his wise advice yesterday,' Pohlmann said, and it was true that he had enjoyed a private talk with Scindia the day before, though the advice had all been given by Pohlmann, but if he was to sway this durbar then he knew he must let them think that he was simply repeating Scindia's suggestions.

'Tell us, please,' Surjee Rao, who knew full well that his master had no ideas except how to increase the tax yields, asked suavely.

'As we all know,' Pohlmann said, 'the British have divided their forces into two parts. By now both those small armies will know that we are here at Borkardan and, because they are fools eager for death, they will both be marching towards us. Both armies lie to our south, but they are separated by some miles. They nevertheless hope to join together, then attack us, but yesterday, in his unparalleled wisdom, His Royal Highness suggested that if we move eastwards we shall draw the enemy's easternmost column towards us and so make them march away from their allies. We can then fight the two armies in turn, defeat them in turn, and then let our dogs chew the flesh from their carcasses. And when the last enemy is dead, Excellency, I shall bring their General to our ruler's tents in chains and send their women to be his slaves.' More to the point, Pohlmann thought, he would capture

Wellesley's food supplies, but he dared not say that in case Scindia took the words as a criticism. But Pohlmann's bravado was rewarded by a scatter of applause that was unfortunately spoiled as a whole section of the tent roof collapsed to let in a deluge of rain.

'If the British are doomed,' Surjee Rao asked when the commotion had subsided, 'why do they advance on us?'

It was a good question, and one that had worried Pohlmann slightly, though he believed he had found an answer. 'Because, Excellency,' he said, 'they have the confidence of fools. Because they believe that their combined armies will prove sufficient. Because they do not truly understand that our army has been trained to the same level as their own, and because their General is young and inexperienced and too eager for a reputation.'

'And you believe, Colonel, that we can keep their two armies apart?'

'If we march tomorrow, yes.'

'How big is the British General's army?'

Pohlmann smiled. 'Wellesley has five thousand infantry-men, Excellency, and six thousand cavalry. We could lose as many men as that and not even notice they were gone! He has eleven thousand men, but the only ones he relies on are his five thousand infantry. Five thousand men! Five thousand!' He paused, making sure that everyone in the tent had heard the figure. 'And we have eighty thousand men. Five against eighty!'

'He has guns,' the minister observed sourly.

'We have five guns for every one of his. Five against one. And our guns are bigger and they are served just as well as his.'

Scindia whispered to Surjee Rao who then demanded that the other European officers give their advice, but all had been forewarned by Pohlmann to sing his tune. March east, they said, draw one British army into battle, then turn on the other. The minister thanked the foreign officers for their advice, then pointedly turned back to the brahmins for their comments. Some advised that emissaries should be sent to Holkar, begging his help, but Pohlmann's confidence had worked its magic and another man indignantly demanded to know why Holkar should be offered a share in the glory of victory. The tide of the durbar was turning in Pohlmann's favour, and he said nothing more, but nor did he need to.

The durbar talked all day and no course of action was formally agreed, but at dusk Scindia and the Rajah of Berar conferred briefly, then Scindia took his leave between rows of brahmins who bowed as their ruler passed. He paused in the huge tent's doorway while his servants brought the palanquin that would preserve him from the rain. Only when the palanquin was ready did he turn and speak loudly enough for all the durbar to hear. 'We march east tomorrow,' he said, 'then we shall ponder another decision. Colonel Pohlmann will make the arrangements.' He stood for a second, looking up at the rain, then ducked under the palanquin's canopy.

'Praise God,' Pohlmann said, for he reckoned that the decision to march eastwards was sufficient to bring on battle. The enemy was closing all the time, and so long as the Mahrattas did not run northwards, the two sides must eventually meet. And if Scindia's men went eastwards then they would meet on Pohlmann's terms. He rammed on his cocked hat and stalked from the tent, followed by all the European officers. 'We'll march east along the Kaitna!' he said excitedly. 'That's where we'll march tomorrow, and the river bank will be our killing ground.' He whooped like an excited child. 'One short march, gentlemen, and we shall be close to Wellesley's men, and in two or three days we'll fight whether our lords and masters want it or not.'

The army marched early next morning. It covered the earth like a dark swarm that flowed beneath the clearing clouds alongside the muddy River Kaitna which slowly deepened and widened as the army followed it eastwards. Pohlmann gave them a very short march, a mere six miles, so that the leading horsemen had reached Pohlmann's chosen campsite long before dawn and by nightfall the slowest of the Mahratta infantry had reached a small, mud-walled village that lay just two miles north of the Kaitna. Scindia and the Rajah of Berar pitched their lavish tents just outside the village, while the Rajah's infantry was ordered to barricade the streets and make loopholes in the thick mud walls of the outermost houses.

The village lay on the southern bank of the River Juah, a tributary of the Kaitna, and south of the village stretched two miles of open farmland that ended at the steep bank of the River Kaitna. Pohlmann placed his best infantry, his three *compoos* of superbly trained killers, south of the village on the high bluff of the Kaitna's northern bank, and in front of them he ranged his eighty best guns. Wellesley, if he wished to reach Borkardan, must come to the Kaitna and he would find his path blocked by a river, by a fearsome line of heavy guns, by an array of infantry and, behind them, like a fortress, a village crammed with the Rajah of Berar's troops. The trap was laid.

In the fields of a village called Assaye.

The two British armies were close to each other now, close enough for General Wellesley to ride across country to see Colonel Stevenson, the commander of the second army. The General rode with his aides and an escort of Indian cavalry, but they saw no enemy on their way westwards across a long flat plain greened by the previous day's rain. Colonel Stevenson, old enough to be Wellesley's father, was alarmed by his General's high spirits. He had seen such elation in young officers before, and seen it crushed by humiliating defeats brought on by over-confidence. 'Are you sure you're not hurrying too much?' he asked.

'We must hurry, Stevenson, must.' Wellesley unrolled a map onto the Colonel's table and pointed to Borkardan. 'We hear they're likely to stay there, but they won't stay for ever. If we don't close on them now, they'll slip away.'

'If the bastards are that close,' Stevenson said, peering at the map, 'then maybe we should join forces now?'

'And if we do,' the General said, 'it will take us twice as long to reach Borkardan.' The two roads on which the armies advanced were narrow and, a few miles south of the River Kaitna, those roads followed passes through a small but steep range of hills. Every wheeled vehicle in both armies would have to be fed through those defiles in the hills, and if the two small armies combined, the cumbersome business of negotiating the pass would take a whole day, a day in which the Mahrattas might escape northwards.

Instead the two armies would advance separately and meet at Borkardan. 'Tomorrow night,' Wellesley ordered, 'you camp here' – he made a cross on the map at a village called Hussainabad – 'and we'll be here.' The pencil made another cross at a village called Naulniah which lay four miles south of the River Kaitna. The villages were ten miles apart, and both about the same distance south of Borkardan. 'On the twenty-fourth,' Wellesley said, 'we march and join here.' He dashed a circle about the village of Borkardan. 'There!' he added, jabbing the pencil down and breaking its point.

Stevenson hesitated. He was a good soldier with a long experience of India, but he was cautious by nature and it seemed to him that Wellesley was being headstrong and fool-ish. The Mahratta army was vast, the British armies small, yet Wellesley was rushing into battle. There was a dangerous excitement in the usually cool-headed Wellesley, and Stevenson now tried to rein it in. 'We could meet at Naulniah,' he suggested, thinking it better if the armies combined the day before the battle rather than attempt to make their junction under fire.

'We have no time,' Wellesley declared, 'no time!' He swept aside the weights holding down the map's corners so that the big sheet rolled up with a snap. 'Providence has put their army within striking distance, so let us strike!' He tossed the map to his aide, Campbell, then ducked out of the tent into the day's late sunlight and there found himself staring at Colonel McCandless who was mounted on a small, bony horse. 'You!' Wellesley said with surprise. 'I thought you were wounded, McCandless?'

'I am, sir, but it's healing.' The Scotsman patted his left thigh.

'So what are you doing here?'

'Seeking you, sir,' McCandless answered, though in truth he had come to Stevenson's army by mistake. One of Sevajee's men, scouting the area, had seen the redcoats and McCandless had thought it must be Wellesley's men.

'And what on earth are you riding?' Wellesley asked, pulling himself onto Diomed's back. 'Looks like a gypsy nag, McCandless. I've seen ponies that are bigger.'

McCandless patted the captured Mahratta horse. 'She's the best I can do, sir. I lost my own gelding.'

'For four hundred guineas you can have my spare. Give me a note, McCandless, and he's all yours. Aeolus, he's called, a six-year-old gelding out of County Meath. Good lungs, got a capped hock, but it don't stop him. I'll see you in two days, Colonel,' Wellesley now addressed Stevenson. 'Two days! We'll test our Mahrattas, eh? See if their vaunted infantry can stand some pounding. Good day, Stevenson! Are you coming, McCandless?'

'I am, sir, I am.'

Sharpe fell in beside Daniel Fletcher, the General's orderly. 'I've never seen the General so happy,' Sharpe said to Fletcher.

'Got the bit between his teeth,' Fletcher said. 'He reckons we're going to surprise the enemy.'

'He ain't worried? There are thousands of the buggers.'

'He ain't showing nothing if he is frightened,' Fletcher said. 'Up and at them, that's his mood.'

'Then God help the rest of us,' Sharpe said.

The General talked with McCandless on his way back, but nothing the Scotsman said diminished Wellesley's eagerness, even though McCandless warned him of the effectiveness of the Mahratta artillery and the efficiency of the infantry. 'We knew all that when we declared war,' Wellesley said testily, 'and if it didn't deter us then, why should it now?'

'Don't underestimate them, sir,' McCandless said grimly.

'I rather hope they'll underestimate me!' Wellesley said. 'You want that gelding of mine?'

'I don't have the money, sir.'

'Oh come, McCandless! You on a Company colonel's salary! You must have a fortune stacked away!'

'I've some savings, sir, for my retirement, which is not far off.'

'I'll make it three hundred and eighty guineas, seeing as it's you, and in a couple of years you can sell him for four hundred. You can't go into battle on that thing.' He gestured at the Mahratta horse.

'I'll think on it, sir, I'll think on it,' McCandless said gloomily. He prayed that the good Lord would restore his own horse to him, along with Lieutenant Dodd, but if that did not happen soon then he knew he would have to buy a decent horse, though the prospect of spending such a vast sum grieved him.

'You'll take supper with me tonight, McCandless?' Wellesley asked. 'We have a fine leg of mutton. A rare leg!'

'I eschew meat, sir,' the Scotsman answered.

'You eschew meat? And chew vegetables?' The General decided this was a splendid joke and frightened his horse by uttering a fierce neigh of a laugh. 'That's droll! Very. You eschew meat to chew vegetables. Never mind, McCandless, we shall find you some chewable shrubs.'

McCandless chewed his vegetables that night, and afterwards, excusing himself, went to the tent that Wellesley had lent to him. He was tired, his leg was throbbing, but there had been no sign of the fever all day and for that he was grateful. He read his Bible, knelt in prayer beside the cot, then blew out the lantern to sleep. An hour later he was woken by the thump of hooves, the sound of suppressed voices, a giggle, and the brush of someone half falling against the tent. 'Who is it?' McCandless demanded angrily.

'Colonel?' Sharpe's voice answered. 'Me, sir. Sorry, sir. Lost my footing, sir.'

'I was sleeping, man.'

'Didn't mean to wake you, sir, sorry, sir. Stand still, you bugger! Not you, sir, sorry, sir.'

McCandless, dressed in shirt and breeches, snatched the tent flap open. 'Are you drunk?' he demanded, then fell silent as he gazed at the horse Sharpe was holding. The horse was a gelding, a splendid bay gelding with pricked ears and a quick, nervous energy.

'He's six years old, sir,' Sharpe said. Daniel Fletcher was trying to hammer in the picket and doing a very bad job because of the drink inside him. 'He's got a capped hock, sir, whatever that is, but nothing that'll stop him. Comes from Ireland, he does. All that green grass, sir, makes a good horse. Aeolus, he's called.'

'Aeolus,' McCandless said, 'the god of the wind.'

'Is he one of those Indian idols, sir? All arms and snake heads?'

'No, Sharpe, Aeolus is Greek.' McCandless took the reins from Sharpe and stroked the gelding's nose. 'Is Wellesley lending him to me?'

'Oh no, sir.' Sharpe had taken the mallet from the half-drunk Fletcher and now banged the picket firmly into the soil. 'He's yours, sir, all yours.'

'But . . .' McCandless said, then stopped, not understanding the situation at all.

'He's paid for, sir,' Sharpe said.

'Paid for by whom?' McCandless demanded sternly.

'Just paid for, sir.'

'You're blithering, Sharpe!'

'Sorry, sir.'

'Explain yourself!' the Colonel demanded.

General Wellesley had said much the same thing when, just forty minutes before, an aide had told him that Sergeant Sharpe was begging to see him and the General, who was just bidding goodnight to the last of his supper guests, had reluctantly agreed. 'Make it quick, Sergeant,' he had said, his fine mood disguised by his usual coldness.

'It's Colonel McCandless, sir,' Sharpe said woodenly. 'He's decided to buy your horse, sir, and he sent me with the money.' He stepped forward and tipped a bag of gold onto the General's map table. The gold was Indian, from every state and princedom, but it was real gold and it lay shining like butter in the candle flames.

Wellesley gazed in astonishment at the treasure. 'He said he didn't have the money!'

'He's a Scotsman, sir, the Colonel,' Sharpe had said, as though that explained everything, 'and he's sorry it ain't real money, sir. Guineas. But it's the full price, sir. Four hundred.'

'Three hundred and eighty,' Wellesley said. 'Tell the

Colonel I'll return some to him. But a note would have done just as well! I'm supposed to carry gold on me?'

'Sorry, sir,' Sharpe had said lamely, but he could never have provided a note for the General, so instead he had sought out one of the *bhinjarries* who followed the army, and that merchant had exchanged emeralds for gold. Sharpe suspected he had been cheated, but he had wanted to give the Colonel the pleasure of owning a fine horse and so he had accepted the *bhinjarrie*'s price. 'Is it all right, sir?' he had asked Wellesley anxiously.

'Extraordinary way to do business,' Wellesley had said, but he had nodded his agreement. 'A fair sale, Sergeant,' he said, and he had almost held out his hand to shake Sharpe's as a man always shook hands on the sale of a horse, then he remembered that Sharpe was a sergeant and so he had hastily converted his gesture into a vague wave. And after Sharpe had gone and while he was scooping the coins into their bag, the General also remembered Sergeant Hakeswill. Not that it was any of his business, so perhaps it had been sensible not to mention the Sergeant's presence to Sharpe.

McCandless now admired the gelding. 'Who paid for it?'

'Good-looking horse, ain't he, sir?' Sharpe said. 'Good as your other, I'd say.'

'Sharpe! You're blithering again. Who paid for it?'

Sharpe hesitated, but knew he was not going to be spared the interrogation. 'In a manner of speaking, sir,' he said, 'the Tippoo did.'

'The Tippoo? Are you mad?'

Sharpe blushed. 'The fellow that killed the Tippoo, sir, he took some jewels off him.'

'A king's ransom, I should imagine,' McCandless snorted.

'So I persuaded the fellow to buy the horse, sir. As a gift for you, sir.'

McCandless stared at Sharpe. 'It was you.'

'It was me who did what, sir?'

'You killed the Tippoo.' It was almost an accusation.

'Me, sir?' Sharpe asked innocently. 'No, sir.'

McCandless stared at the gelding. 'I can't possibly accept, Sergeant.'

'He's no good to me, sir. A sergeant can't own a horse. Not a proper horse from Ireland, sir. And if I hadn't been daydreaming in Pohlmann's camp, sir, I might have stopped those thieves, so it's only fair that you should let me get you another.'

'You can't do this, Sharpe!' McCandless protested, embarrassed by the generosity of the gift. 'Besides, in a day or two I hope to get my own horse back along with Mister Dodd.'

Sharpe had not thought of that, and for a second he cursed himself for throwing away his money. Then he shrugged. 'It's done anyway, sir. General's got the money and you've got the horse. Besides, sir, you've always been fair to me, so I wanted to do something for you.'

'It's intolerable!' McCandless protested. 'Uncalled for. I shall have to repay you.'

'Four hundred guineas?' Sharpe asked. 'That's the price of an ensign's commission, sir.'

'So?' McCandless stared fiercely at Sharpe.

'So we're going into battle, sir. You on that horse, and me on a Mahratta pony. It's a chance, sir, a chance, but if I do well, sir, real well, I'll need you to talk to the General.' Sharpe blushed as he spoke, amazed at his own temerity. 'That's how you repay me, sir, but that's not why I bought him. I just wanted you to have a proper horse, sir. Colonel like you shouldn't be sitting on a scabby native pony, sir.'

McCandless, appalled at Sharpe's ambition, did not know what to say. He stroked the gelding, felt tears in his eyes and could not tell whether they were for Sharpe's impossible dreams or because he had been so touched by the Sergeant's gift. 'If you do well, Sharpe,' he promised, 'I'll talk to Colonel Wallace. He's a good friend. It's possible he'll have a vacant ensign's post, but don't raise your hopes too high!' He paused, wondering if emotion had driven him to promise far too much. 'How did the Tippoo die?' he asked after a while. 'And don't lie to me, Sharpe, it must have been you who killed him.'

'Like a man, sir. Bravely. Facing front, he was. Never gave up.'

'He was a good soldier,' McCandless said, reflecting that the Tippoo had been beaten by a better one. 'I trust you've still got some of his jewels?'

'Jewels, sir?' Sharpe asked. 'I don't know about jewels, sir.'

'Of course not,' McCandless said. If the Company ever heard that Sharpe was carrying the Tippoo's gems their prize agents would descend on the Sergeant like locusts. 'Thank you, Sharpe,' McCandless said fulsomely, 'thank you very much. I shall repay you, of course, but you've touched me. 'Pon my soul, you have touched me.' He insisted upon shaking Sharpe's hand, then watched the Sergeant walk away with the General's orderly. So much sin there, McCandless thought, and so much goodness. But why had Pohlmann ever put the idea of a commission into Sharpe's head? It was an impossible dream, doomed to disappointment.

Another man also watched Sharpe walk away. It was Private Lowry, of the King's 33rd, who now hurried back to the baggage camp. 'It was him, Sergeant,' he told Hakeswill.

'You sure?'

'Large as life.'

'God bless you, Lowry, God bless you.' And God, Hakeswill thought, had certainly blessed him. He had feared that he would have to endure a battle, but now Sharpe had come and Hakeswill could produce his precious warrant and be on his way south. Let the army fight its battle, and let it win or lose, Hakeswill did not care, for Sergeant Hakeswill had what he wanted and he would be rich.

CHAPTER 8

General Wellesley was like a gambler who had emptied his purse onto the table and now had to wait for the cards to fall. There was still time to scoop the money back and walk away from the game, but if he ever felt that temptation, he did not betray it to his aides, nor to any of the army's senior officers. The colonels in his army were all older than Wellesley, some much older, and Wellesley courteously sought their advice, though he largely ignored it. Orrock, a Company colonel and commander of the 8th Madras Infantry, recommended an extravagant outflanking march to the east, though so far as Wellesley could determine the only ambition of such a manoeuvre was to remove the army as far as possible from the enemy horde. The General was forced to pay more attention to his two Williams, Wallace and Harness, the commanding officers of his two Scottish battalions who were also his brigade leaders. 'If we join Stevenson, sir, we might manage the business,' Wallace opined, his tone making it clear that, even combined, the two British armies would be dangerously outnumbered. 'I've no doubt Harness will agree with me, sir,' Wallace added, though William Harness, the commander of the 78th, seemed surprised to have his opinion sought. 'Your business how you fight them, Wellesley,' he growled. 'Point my men and I warrant they'll fight. The bastards had better fight. I'll flog the scum witless if they don't.'

Wellesley forbore to point out that if the 78th refused to fight then there would be no one left to flog, for there would be no army. Harness would not have listened anyway, for he had taken the opportunity to lecture the General on the ameliorative effects of a flogging. 'My first colonel liked to see one well-scourged back a week, Wellesley,' he said. 'He reckoned it kept the men to their duty. He once flogged a sergeant's wife, I recall. He wanted to know if a woman could take the pain, you see, and she couldn't. The lass was fair wriggling.' Harness sighed, recalling happier days. 'D'you dream, Wellesley?'

'Dream, Harness?'

'When you sleep.'

'At times.'

'A flogging will stop it. Nothing to bring on a good night's sleep like a well-whipped back.' Harness, a tall black-browed man who seemed to wear a constant expression of wide-eyed disapproval, shook his head sadly. 'A dreamless sleep, that's what I dream of! Loosens the bowels too, y'know?'

'Sleep?'

'A flogging!' Harness snapped angrily. 'Stimulates the blood, y'see?'

Wellesley disliked making enquiries about senior officers, but he took care to ride alongside his new aide, Colin Campbell. 'Was there much flogging in the 78th?' he asked the aide who, until the siege of Ahmednuggur, had served under Harness.

'There's been much recent talk of it, sir, but not in practice.'

'Your Colonel seems much enamoured of the practice.'

'His enthusiasms come and go,' Campbell said blandly. 'But until a few weeks ago, sir, he was not a man for enthusiasms. Now, suddenly, he is. He encouraged us to eat snakes in July, though he didn't insist on it. I gather he tried some cobra seethed in milk, but it didn't agree with him.'

'Ah!' the General said, understanding the carefully phrased message. So Harness was going out of his wits? Wellesley chided himself for not guessing as much from the Colonel's fixed glare. 'The battalion has a doctor?'

'You can take a horse to water, sir,' Campbell said carefully.

'Indeed, indeed.' Not that the General could do anything about Harness's incipient madness now, nor had the Colonel done anything that deserved dismissal. Indeed, mad or not, he led a fine battalion and Wellesley would need the Scotsmen when he came to Borkardan.

He thought constantly of Borkardan, though what that place was other than a mark on the map, he did not know. He simply imagined the village as swirls of dust and bellowing noise, a place of galloping horses where big guns would flatten the air with their hot thumps and the sky would be ripped apart with shrieking metal and murderous volleys. It would be Wellesley's first field battle. He had fought skirmishes enough, and led a cavalry charge that rode a bandit army into bloody oblivion, but he had never commanded guns and horse and infantry together, and he had never tried to impose his own will on an enemy general. He did not doubt his ability, nor did he doubt that he would stay calm amidst the dust and smoke and flame and blood, but he did fear that some unlucky shot would kill or maim him and the army would then be in the hands of a man without a vision of victory. Stevenson or Wallace would be competent enough, though Wellesley privately thought them both too cautious, but God help an army guided by Harness's enthusiasms.

The other colonels, all Company men, echoed Wallace's advice to make sure of the junction with Stevenson before battle was joined, and Wellesley recognized the wisdom of that opinion, even while he refused to deflect his army to join Stevenson before they both reached Borkardan. There was no time for such a nicety, so instead whichever army first came to the enemy must engage him first, and the other must join the battle, to which end Wellesley knew he must keep his left flank open, for that was where Stevenson's men would join his own. The General reckoned he must put the bulk of his cavalry on the left and station one of his two Highland regiments to serve as a bulwark on that flank, but beyond that he did not know what he would do once he reached Borkardan except attack, attack and attack again. He reasoned that when a small army faced a great horde then the small army had better keep moving and so destroy the enemy piece by piece, but if the small army stayed still then it risked being surrounded and pulverized into surrender.

Borkardan on the twenty-fourth day of September, that was the goal, and Wellesley marched his men hard. The cavalry vanguard and the infantry picquets of the day were roused at midnight and, an hour later, just as the rest of the army was being stirred into sullen wakefulness, those men would start the northwards march. By two o'clock the whole army was moving. Dogs barked as the cavalry vanguard clattered through the villages, and after the horsemen came heavy guns hauled by oxen, marching Highlanders and long ranks of sepoys under their leather-cased colours. Ten miles to the west Stevenson's army marched parallel to Wellesley's, but ten miles was a half-day's march and if either force was confronted by the enemy then the other could do nothing to help. Everything hinged on their meeting at Borkardan.

Most of the men had little idea of what waited for them. They sensed the sudden urgency and guessed it presaged battle, but though the rumours spoke of the enemy as a numberless horde, they marched confidently. They grumbled, of course, for all soldiers grumble. They complained about being hungry, they swore at being made to tramp through the cavalry's manure, and they cursed the oppressive heat that seemed scarcely alleviated by marching at night. Each march finished by midday when the men would rig their tents and sprawl in the shade while the picquets set guards, the cavalry watered horses and the commissary butchered bullocks to provide ration meat.

The cavalry were the busiest men. Their job was to ride ahead and to the flanks of the army to drive any enemy scouts far away so that Scindia would not know that the two red-coated armies marched to trap him, but each morning, as the eastern horizon turned grey, then flushed with pink, then glowed gold and red before finally exploding into light, the patrols searched in vain for any enemies. The Mahratta horse seemed to be staying home, and some of the cavalry officers feared that their enemy might have slipped away again.

As they were nearing Naulniah which would be Wellesley's last resting place before he marched through the night to Borkardan, the General called his patrols closer to the army, ordering them to ride just a mile or two in front of his column. If the enemy was asleep, he explained to his aides, then it was best to do nothing to wake him. It was Sunday, and if the enemy was still engaged in its durbar, then the next day would bring battle. One day to let fears harass hope, though Wellesley's aides seemed careless enough as they marched the last few miles to Naulniah. Major John Blackiston, an engineer on Wellesley's staff, was needling Captain Campbell by saying that the Scots had no harvest to speak of. 'Oats alone, isn't that it, Captain?'

'You've not seen barley, Major, till you've been to Scotland,' Campbell declared. 'You could hide a regiment in a field of Scottish barley.'

'Can't think why you'd want to do such a thing, but doubtless you have your reasons. But as I understand it, Campbell, you heathen Scots have no order of service to give thanks to God for a harvest?'

'You've not heard of the kirn, Major? The mell feast?'

'Kirn?'

'Harvest-home, you call it, when you scavenge those few weeds in England, then beg us generous Scots to send you food. Which we do, being Christian folk who take pity on those less fortunate than ourselves. And talking of the less fortunate, Major, here's the sick list.' Campbell handed Blackiston a piece of paper on which was tallied the number of men from each regiment who were too sick to march. Those men were now being carried on the ox carts of the baggage train and, routinely, those who were unlikely to recover quickly were sent southwards on returning convoys, but Blackiston knew the General would not want to detach any cavalry to protect a convoy just before a battle.

'Tell Sears the sick can all wait in Naulniah,' Blackiston ordered, 'and warn Captain Mackay to have at least a score of empty wagons ready.' He did not specify why Mackay should prepare empty wagons, but nor did he need to do so. The wagons would carry the men wounded in battle, and Blackiston fervently prayed that no more than a score of ox carts would be needed.

Captain Mackay had anticipated the need for empty wagons and had already put chalk marks on those whose burdens were light and could be transferred to other carts. Once at Naulniah he would have the cargoes rearranged, and he sought out Sergeant Hakeswill to supervise the business, but Obadiah Hakeswill had other plans. 'My criminal's back with the army, sir.'

'And you haven't arrested him already?' Mackay asked in surprise.

'Can't march a man in irons, sir, not at this pace. But if you're establishing a camp, sir, at Naulniah, sir, I can hold my prisoner under guard like my duties say I should.'

'So I shall be losing your services, Sergeant?'

'It ain't what I want, sir,' Hakeswill lied, 'but I has my responsibilities, sir, and if we're leaving baggage at Naulniah, sir, then I shall have to stay there with my prisoner. Colonel Gore's orders, sir. Is that Naulniah up ahead, sir?'

'It seems to be,' Mackay said, for the distant village was busy with men laying out the lines for the regiments' tents.

'Then, if you'll forgive, sir, I have to be about my duties.'

Hakeswill had deliberately waited for this moment, reckoning that it would be far too great a bother to keep marching northwards with Sharpe under escort. It would be better to wait until the army had established the baggage camp where Hakeswill could keep Sharpe while the battle was fought, and if one more redcoat died that day, who would miss him? So now, freed from Mackay's baggage guard, the Sergeant hurried his six men up the column to find Colonel McCandless.

McCandless's leg was still throbbing, and the fever had left him weak, but his spirits had recovered, because riding Aeolus had convinced him that no finer horse had ever stepped on earth. The gelding was tireless, McCandless declared, and better schooled than any horse he had ever ridden. Sevajee was amused by the Colonel's enthusiasm. 'You sound like a man with a new woman, McCandless.'

'If you say so, Sevajee, if you say so,' McCandless said, not rising to the Indian's bait. 'But isn't he a beauty?'

'Magnificent.'

'County Meath,' the Colonel said. 'They breed good hunters in County Meath. They have big hedges! Like jumping a haystack.'

'County Meath is in Ireland?' Sevajee asked.

'It is, it is.'

'Another country beneath Britain's heel?'

'For a man beneath my heel, Sevajee,' the Colonel said, 'you look in remarkably fine fettle. Can we talk about tomorrow? Sharpe! I want you to listen.'

Sharpe urged his small Mahratta horse alongside the Colonel's big gelding. Like Wellesley, Colonel McCandless was planning what he would do at Borkardan and, though the Colonel's task was much smaller than the General's, it was no less important to him. 'Let us assume, gentlemen, that we shall win this battle at Borkardan tomorrow,' he said, and waited for the invariable riposte from Sevajee, but the tall Indian said nothing. 'Our task, then,' the Colonel went on, 'is to hunt Dodd among the fugitives. Hunt him and capture him.'

'If he still lives,' Sevajee remarked.

'Which I pray God he does. He must face British justice before he goes to God's condemnation. So when the battle is joined, gentlemen, our task is not to get involved with the fighting, but to search for Dodd's men. It won't be difficult. So far as I know they're the only regiment in white jackets, and once we have them, we stay close. Stay close till they break, then we pursue.'

'And if they don't break?' Sevajee asked.

'Then we march again and fight again,' the Colonel answered grimly. 'But by God's grace, Sevajee, we shall find this man even if we have to hunt him into the deserts of Persia. Britain has more than a heavy heel, Sevajee, it has a long arm.'

'Long arms are easily cut off,' Sevajee said.

Sharpe had stopped listening. He had heard a commotion behind as a group of army wives were thrust off the road and had turned to see who had barged the women aside and, at first, all he had seen was a group of redcoats. Then he had recognized the red facings on the jackets and he had wondered what on earth men of the 33rd were doing here, and then he had recognized Sergeant Hakeswill.

Obadiah Hakeswill! Of all people, Hakeswill! Sharpe stared in horror at his long-time enemy and Obadiah Hakeswill caught his eye and grinned maliciously and Sharpe knew that his appearance boded no good. Hakeswill broke into a lumbering run so that his haversack, pouches, bayonet and musket thumped against his body. 'Sir!' he called up to Colonel McCandless. 'Colonel McCandless, sir!'

McCandless turned and frowned at the interruption, then, like Sharpe, he stared at the Sergeant as though he did not believe his eyes. McCandless knew Hakeswill, for Hakeswill had been imprisoned in the Tippoo Sultan's dungeons at the same time as Sharpe and the Colonel, and what McCandless knew he did not like. The Scotsman scowled. 'Sergeant Hakeswill? You're far from home.'

'As are we all, sir, doing our duties to King and country in an 'eathen land, sir.' Hakeswill slowed to a march, keeping pace with the Scotsman's horse. 'I'm ordered to see you, sir, by the General himself, sir. By Sir Arthur Wellesley, sir, God bless him, sir.'

'I know who the General is, Sergeant,' McCandless said coldly.

'Glad to hear it, sir. Got a paper for you, sir. Urgent paper, sir, what needs your urgent attention, sir.' Hakeswill gave a venomous glance at Sharpe, then held the warrant up to McCandless. 'This paper, sir, what I've been carrying in my pouch, sir, on Colonel Gore's orders, sir.'

McCandless unfolded the warrant. Sevajee had hurried ahead, going to find somewhere to billet his men in the village and, while McCandless read the orders for Sharpe's arrest, Hakeswill fell back so that he was walking beside Sharpe. 'We'll have you off that horse in a quick minute, Sharpie,' he said.

'Go and boil your head, Obadiah.'

'You always did have ideas above your station, Sharpie. Won't do! Not in this army. We ain't the Frogs. We don't wear pretty long red boots like yours, we don't, 'cos we don't

237

have airs and graces, not in this army. Says so in the scriptures.'

Sharpe tugged on his rein so that his small horse swerved into Hakeswill's path. The Sergeant skipped aside. 'Under arrest, you are, Sharpie!' Hakeswill crowed. 'Under arrest! Court-martial offence. Be a shooting job, I dare say.' Hakeswill grinned, showing his yellow teeth. 'Bang bang, you're dead. Taken me a long time, Sharpie, but I'm going to be evens with you. All over for you, it is. Says so in the scriptures.'

'It says nothing of the sort, Sergeant!' McCandless snapped, turning in his saddle and glaring at the Sergeant. 'I've had occasion to speak to you before about the scriptures, and if I hear you cite their authority one more time I shall break you, Sergeant Hakeswill, I shall break you!'

'Sir!' Hakeswill acknowledged. He doubted that McCandless, a Company officer, could break anyone in the King's army, at least not without a deal of effort, but he did not let his scepticism show, for Obadiah Hakeswill believed in showing complete subservience to all officers. 'Never meant to upset you, sir,' he said, 'apologize, sir. No offence meant, sir.'

McCandless read the warrant a third time. Something about the wording worried him, but he could not quite place his concern. 'It says here, Sharpe,' McCandless said, 'that you struck an officer on August the fifth this year.'

'I did what, sir?' Sharpe asked, horrified.

'Assaulted Captain Morris. Here.' And McCandless thrust the warrant towards Sharpe. 'Take it, man. Read it.'

Sharpe took the paper and while he read Sergeant Hakeswill embellished the charge to Colonel McCandless. 'An assault, sir, with a jakes pot, sir. A full one, sir. Liquids and solids, sir, both. Right on the Captain's head, sir.'

'And you were the only witness?' McCandless asked.

'Me and Captain Morris, sir.'

'I don't believe a word of it,' McCandless growled.

'Up to a court to decide, sir, begging your pardon. Your job, sir, is to deliver the prisoner to my keeping.'

'You do not instruct me in my duties, Sergeant!' McCandless said angrily.

'I just knows you will do your duty, sir, like we all does. Except for some as I could mention.' Hakeswill smiled at Sharpe. 'Finding the long words difficult, are we, Sharpie?'

McCandless reached over and took the warrant back from Sharpe, who had, indeed, been finding some of the longer words difficult. The Colonel had expressed his disbelief in the charge, but that was more out of loyalty to Sharpe than from any conviction, though there was still something out of kilter in the warrant. 'Is it true, Sharpe?' McCandless now asked.

'No, sir!' Sharpe said indignantly.

'He was always a good liar, sir,' Hakeswill said helpfully. 'Lies like a rug, sir, he does. Famous for it.' The Sergeant was becoming breathless as he hurried to keep pace with the Scotsman's horse.

'So what do you intend to do with Sergeant Sharpe?' McCandless asked.

'Do, sir? Do my duty, of course, sir. Escort the prisoner back to battalion, sir, as is ordered.' Hakeswill gestured at his six men who marched a few paces behind. 'We'll guard him nice and proper, sir, all the way home and then have him stand trial for his filthy crime.'

McCandless bit his right thumb and shook his head. He rode in silence for a few paces, and when Sharpe protested he ignored the indignant words. He put the warrant in his right hand again and seemed to read it yet another time. Far off to the east, at least a mile away, there was a sudden flurry of dust and the sparkle of sword blades catching the sun. Some enemy horsemen had been waiting in a grove of trees from where they had been watching the British march, but now they were flushed out by a troop of Mysore horsemen who pursued them northwards. McCandless glanced at the distant action. 'So they'll know we're here now, more's the pity. How do you spell your name, Sharpe? With or without an "e"?'

'With, sir.'

'You will correct me if I'm wrong,' McCandless said, 'but it seems to me that this is not your name.' He handed the warrant back to Sharpe who saw that the 'e' at the end of his name had been smeared out. There was a smudge of black ink there, and beneath it the impression of the 'e' made by the steel nib in the paper, but the ink had been diluted and nearly erased.

Sharpe hid his astonishment that McCandless, a stickler for honesty and straight-dealing, had resorted to such a subterfuge. 'Not my name, sir,' Sharpe said woodenly.

Hakeswill looked from Sharpe to McCandless, then back to Sharpe and finally at McCandless again. 'Sir!' The word exploded from him.

'You're out of breath, Sergeant,' McCandless said, taking the warrant back from Sharpe. 'But you will see here that you are expressly ordered to arrest a sergeant whose name is Richard Sharp. No "e", Sergeant. This Sergeant Sharpe uses an "e" on his name so he cannot be the man you want, and I certainly cannot release him to your custody on the authority of this piece of paper. Here.' McCandless held the warrant out, letting it drop a heartbeat before Hakeswill could take it. The paper fluttered down to the dusty road.

Hakeswill snatched the warrant up and peered at the writing. 'Ink's run, sir!' he protested. 'Sir?' He ran after McCandless's horse, stumbling on the uneven road. 'Look, sir! Ink's run, sir.'

McCandless ignored the offered warrant. 'It is clear, Sergeant Hakeswill, that the spelling of the name has been corrected. In all conscience I cannot act upon that warrant. What you must do, Sergeant, is send a message to Lieutenant Colonel Gore asking him to clear up the confusion. A new warrant, I think, would be best, and until such time as I see such a warrant, legibly written, I cannot release Sergeant Sharpe from his present duties. Good day, Hakeswill.'

'You can't do this, sir!' Hakeswill protested.

McCandless smiled. 'You fundamentally misunderstand the hierarchy of the army, Sergeant. It is I, a colonel, who define your duties, not you, a sergeant, who define mine. "I say to a man, go, and he goeth." It says so in the scriptures. I bid you good day.' And with that the Scotsman touched his spurs to the gelding's flanks.

Hakeswill's face twitched as he turned on Sharpe. 'I'll have you, Sharpie, I will have you. I ain't forgotten nothing.'

'You ain't learned nothing either,' Sharpe said, then spurred after the Colonel. He lifted two fingers as he passed Hakeswill, then left him behind in the dust.

He was, for the moment, free.

Simone Joubert placed the eight diamonds on the window ledge of the tiny house where the wives of Scindia's European officers had been quartered. She was alone for the moment, for the other women had gone to visit the three *compoos* that were stationed on the Kaitna's northern bank, but Simone had not wanted their company and so she had pleaded a turbulent stomach, though she supposed she ought to visit Pierre before the battle, if indeed there was to be a fight. Not that Simone cared much. Let them have their battle, she thought, and at the end of it, when the river was dark with British blood, her life would be no better. She gazed at the diamonds again, thinking about the man who had given them to her. Pierre would be angry if he learned she was concealing such wealth, but once his anger had passed he would sell the stones and send the money back to his rapacious family in France.

'Madame Joubert!' A voice hailed her from outside the window and Simone guiltily swept the diamonds into her small purse, though, because she was on an upper floor, no one could see the gems. She peered down from the window and saw a cheerful Colonel Pohlmann in shirtsleeves and braces standing among the straw in the courtyard of the neighbouring house.

'Colonel,' she responded dutifully.

'I am hiding my elephants,' the Colonel said, gesturing at the three beasts which were being led into the courtyard. The tallest carried Pohlmann's howdah, while the other two were burdened with the wooden chests in which the Colonel was reputed to keep his gold. 'Might I leave you to guard my menagerie?' the Colonel asked.

'From what?' Simone asked.

'From thieves,' the Colonel said happily.

'Not the British?'

'They will never reach this far, Madame,' Pohlmann said, 'except as prisoners.' And Simone had a sudden vision of Sergeant Richard Sharpe again. She had been raised to believe that the British were a piratical race, a nation without a conscience who mindlessly impeded the spread of French enlightenment, but perhaps, she thought, she liked pirates.

'I will guard your elephants, Colonel,' she called down.

'And have some dinner with me?' Pohlmann asked. 'I have some cold chicken and warm wine.'

'I have promised to join Pierre,' Simone said, dreading the two-mile ride across the drab fields to where Dodd's Cobras waited beside the Kaitna.

'Then I shall escort you to his side, Madame,' Pohlmann said courteously. Once the battle was over he reckoned he might mount an assault on Madame Joubert's virtue. It would be an amusing diversion, but not, he thought, an especially difficult campaign. Unhappy women yielded to patience and sympathy, and there would be plenty of time for both once Wellesley and Stevenson had been destroyed. And there would be a pleasure, too, in beating Major Dodd to the prize of Simone's virtue.

Pohlmann detailed twenty of his bodyguard to guard the three elephants. He never rode one of the beasts in battle, for an elephant became the target of every enemy gunner, but he looked forward to mounting the howdah for a great victory parade after the campaign. And victory would leave Pohlmann rich, rich enough to start building his great marble palace in which he planned to hang the captured banners of his enemy. From sergeant to princeling in ten years, and the key to that princedom was the gold that he was storing in Assaye. He ordered his bodyguard that no one, not even the Rajah of Berar whose troops were garrisoning the village, should be allowed into the courtyard, then he instructed his servants to detach the golden panels from the howdah and add them to the boxes of treasure. 'If the worst should happen,' he told the subadar who was in charge of the men guarding the treasure, 'I'll join you here. Not that it will,' he added cheerfully.

A clatter of hooves in the alley outside the courtyard announced the arrival of a patrol of horsemen returning from a foray south of the Kaitna. For three days Pohlmann had kept his cavalry on a tight rein, not wanting to alarm Wellesley as the British General marched north towards the trap, but that morning he had released a few patrols southwards and one of those now returned with the welcome news that the enemy was only four miles south of the Kaitna. Pohlmann already knew that the second British army, that of Colonel Stevenson, was still ten miles off to the west, and that meant that the British had blundered. Wellesley, in his eagerness to reach Borkardan, had brought his men to the waiting arms of the whole Mahratta army.

The Colonel thought about waiting for Madame Joubert, then decided he could not afford the time and so he mounted the horse he rode in battle and, with those of his bodyguard not deputed to guard his gold, and with a string of aides surrounding him, he galloped south from Assaye to the Kaitna's bank where his trap was set. He passed the news to Dupont and Saleur, then rode to prepare his own troops. He spoke with his officers, finishing with Major William Dodd. 'I hear the British are making camp in Naulniah,' Pohlmann said, 'so what we should do is march south and hammer him. It's one thing to have Wellesley so close, but it's quite another to bring him to battle.'

'So why don't we march?' Dodd asked.

'Because Scindia won't have it, that's why. Scindia insists we fight on the defensive. He's nervous.' Dodd spat, but made no other comment on his employer's timidity. 'So there's a nasty danger,' Pohlmann went on, 'that Wellesley won't attack us at all, but will retreat towards Stevenson.'

'So we beat them both at once,' Dodd said confidently.

'As we shall, if we must,' Pohlmann agreed drily, 'but I'd rather fight them separately.' He was confident of victory, no soldier could be more confident, but he was no fool and given the chance to defeat two small armies instead of one medium-sized force, he would prefer the former. 'If you have a god, Major,' he said, 'pray that Wellesley is over-confident. Pray that he attacks us.'

It was a fervent prayer, for if Wellesley did attack he would be forced to send his men across the Kaitna which was some sixty or seventy paces broad and flowing brown between high banks that were over a hundred paces apart. If the monsoon had come the river would have filled its bed and been twelve or fifteen feet deep, while now it was only six or seven, though that was quite deep enough to stop an army crossing, but right in front of Pohlmann's position there was a series of fords, and Pohlmann's prayer was that the British would try to cross the fords and attack straight up the road to Assaye. Wellesley would have no other choice, not if he wanted a battle, for Pohlmann had summoned farmers from every village in the vicinity, from Assaye and Waroor, from Kodully, Taunklee and Peepulgaon, and asked them where a man could drive a herd of cattle through the river. He had used the example of a herd of oxen because where such a herd could go so could oxen drawing guns, and every man had agreed that in this season the only crossing places were the fords between Kodully and Taunklee. A man could drive his herds upriver to Borkardan, they told Pohlmann's interpreter, and cross there, but that was a half-day's walk away and why would a man be that foolish when the river provided eight safe fords between the two villages?

'Are there any crossing places downstream?' Pohlmann asked.

A score of dark faces shook in unison. 'No, sahib, not in the wet season.'

'This season isn't wet.'

'There are still no fords, sahib.' They were sure, as sure as only local men who had lived all their lives bounded by the same water and trees and soil could be sure.

Pohlmann had still been unconvinced. 'And if a man does not want to drive a herd, but just wants to cross himself, where would he cross?'

The villagers provided the same answer. 'Between Kodully and Taunklee, sahib.'

'Nowhere else?'

Nowhere else, they assured him, and that meant Wellesley would be forced to cross the river in the face of Pohlmann's waiting army. The British infantry and guns would have to slither down the steep southern bank of the Kaitna, cross a wide expanse of mud, wade through the river, then climb the steep northern bank, and all the while they would be under fire from the Mahratta guns until, when they reached the green fields on the northern shore, they would re-form their ranks and march forward into a double storm of musketry and artillery. Wherever the British crossed the Kaitna, anywhere between Kodully and Taunklee, they would find the same murderous reception waiting, for Pohlmann's three prime *compoos* were arrayed in one long line that fronted that whole stretch of the river. There were eighty guns in that line, and though some threw nothing but a five- or six-pound ball, at least half were heavy artillery and all were manned by Goanese gunners who knew their business. The cannon were grouped in eight batteries, one for each ford, and there was not an inch of ground between the batteries that could not be flailed by canister or beaten by round shot or scorched by shells. Pohlmann's well-trained infantry waited to pour a devastating weight of volley fire into red-coated regiments already deafened and demoralized by the cannon fire that would have torn their ranks into shreds as they struggled across the bloody fords. The numberless Mahratta cavalry were off to the west, strung along the bank towards Borkardan, and there it would wait until the British were defeated and Pohlmann released the horsemen to the joys of pursuit and slaughter.

The Hanoverian reckoned that his battle line waiting at the fords would decimate the enemy and the horsemen would turn the British defeat into a bloody rout, but there was always a small chance that the enemy might survive the river crossing and succeed in gaining the Kaitna's northern bank in good order. He doubted the British could force his three *compoos* back, but in case they did Pohlmann planned to retreat two miles to the village of Assaye and invite the British to waste more men in an assault on what was now a miniature fortress. Assaye, like every other village on the plain, lived in fear of bandit raids and so the outermost houses had high, windowless walls made of thick mud, and the houses were joined so that their walls formed a continous rampart as high as the wall at Ahmednuggur. Pohlmann had blocked the village's streets with ox carts, he had ordered loopholes hacked in the outer wall, he had placed all his smaller guns, a score of two- and three-pounder cannon, at the foot of the wall and then he had garrisoned the houses with the Rajah of Berar's twenty thousand infantrymen. Pohlmann doubted that any of those twenty thousand men would need to fight, but he had the luxury of knowing they were in reserve should anything go wrong at the Kaitna.

He had just one problem left and to solve it he asked Dodd to accompany him eastwards along the river bank. 'If you were Wellesley,' he asked Dodd, 'how would you attack?'

Dodd considered the question, then shrugged as if to suggest that the answer was obvious. 'Concentrate all my best troops at one end of the line and hammer my way through.'

'Which end?'

Dodd thought for a few seconds. He had been tempted to say that Wellesley would attack in the west, at the fords by Kodully, for that would keep him closest to Stevenson's army, but Stevenson was a long way away and Pohlmann was deliberately riding eastwards. 'The eastern end?' Dodd suggested diffidently.

Pohlmann nodded. 'Because if he drives our left flank back he can place his army between us and Assaye. He divides us.'

'And we surround him,' Dodd observed.

'I'd rather we weren't divided,' Pohlmann said, for if Wellesley did succeed in driving back the left flank he might well succeed in capturing Assaye, and while that would still leave Pohlmann's *compoos* on the field, it would mean that the Colonel would lose his gold. So the Colonel needed a good hard anchor at the eastern end of his line to prevent his left flank being turned, and of all the regiments under his command he reckoned Dodd's Cobras were the best. The left flank was now being held by one of Dupont's regiments, a good one, but not as good as Dodd's.

Pohlmann gestured at the Dutchman's brown-coated troops who looked across the river towards the small village of Taunklee. 'Good men,' he said, 'but not as good as yours.'

'Few of them are.'

'But we'd best pray those fellows hold,' Pohlmann said, 'because if I was Wellesley that's where I'd put my sharpest attack. Straight up, turn our flank, cut us off from Assaye. It worries me, it does.'

Dodd could not see that it was overmuch cause for worry, for he doubted that the best troops in the world could survive the river crossing under the massed fire of Pohlmann's batteries, but he did see the left flank's importance. 'So reinforce Dupont,' he suggested carelessly.

Pohlmann looked surprised, as though the idea had not already occurred to him. 'Reinforce him? Why not? Would you care to hold the left, Major?'

'The left?' Dodd said suspiciously. Traditionally the right of the line was the station of honour on a battlefield and, while most of Pohlmann's troops neither cared nor knew about such courtesies, William Dodd certainly knew, which was why Pohlmann had let the Major suggest that the left should be reinforced rather than simply order the touchy Dodd to move his precious Cobras.

'You would not be under Dupont's orders, of course not,' Pohlmann reassured Dodd. 'You'll be your own master, Major, answerable to me, only to me.' Pohlmann paused. 'Of course, if you'd rather not take post on the left I'd entirely understand, and some other fellows can have the honour of defeating the British right.'

'My fellows can do it!' Dodd said belligerently.

'It is a very responsible post,' Pohlmann said diffidently.

'We can do it, sir!' Dodd insisted.

Pohlmann smiled his gratitude. 'I was hoping you'd say so. Every other regiment is commanded by a Frog or a Dutchman, Major, and I need an Englishman to fight the hardest battle.'

'And you've found one, sir,' Dodd said.

I've found an idiot, Pohlmann thought as he rode back to the line's centre, but Dodd was a reliable idiot and a hard-fighting man. He watched as Dodd's men left the line, and as the line closed up to fill the gap, and then as the Cobras took their place on the left flank. The line was complete now, it was deadly, it was anchored firmly, and it was ready. All it needed was the enemy to compound their blunder by trying to attack, and then Pohlmann would crown his career by filling the Kaitna with British blood. Let them attack, he prayed, just let them attack, and the day, with all its glory, would be his.

The British camp spread around Naulniah. Lines of tents sheltered infantry, quartermasters sought out the village head-man and arranged that the women of the village would bake bread in return for rupees, while the cavalry led their horses down to drink from the River Purna which flowed just to the north of the village. One squadron of the 19th Dragoons was ordered to cross the river and ride a couple of miles north in search of enemy patrols and those troopers dropped their bags of forage in the village, watered their horses, washed the dust from their faces, then remounted and rode on out of sight.

Colonel McCandless picked a broad tree as his tent. He

had no servant, nor wanted one, so he brushed down Aeolus with handfuls of straw while Sharpe fetched a pail of water from the river. The Colonel, in his shirtsleeves, straightened as Sharpe came back. 'You do realize, Sergeant, that I am guilty of some dishonesty in the matter of that warrant?'

'I wanted to thank you, sir.'

'I doubt I deserve any thanks, except that my deception might have staved off a greater evil.' The Colonel crossed to his saddlebags and brought out his Bible which he gave to Sharpe. 'Put your right hand on the scriptures, Sergeant, and swear to me you are innocent of the charge.'

Sharpe placed his right palm on the Bible's worn cover. He felt foolish, but McCandless's face was stern and Sharpe made his own face solemn. 'I do swear it, sir. I never touched the man that night, didn't even see him.' His voice proclaimed both his indignation and his innocence, but that was small consolation. The warrant might be defeated for the moment, but Sharpe knew such things did not go away. 'What will happen now, sir?'

'We'll just have to make certain the truth prevails,' McCandless said vaguely. He was still trying to decide what had been wrong with the warrant, but he could not identify what had troubled him. He took the Bible, stowed it away, then put his hands in the small of his back and arched his spine. 'How far have we come today? Fourteen miles? Fifteen?'

'Thereabouts, sir.'

'I'm feeling my age, Sharpe, feeling my age. The leg's mending well enough, but now my back aches. Not good. But just a short march tomorrow, God be thanked, no more than ten miles, then battle.' He pulled a watch from his fob pocket and snapped open the lid. 'We have fifteen minutes, Sergeant, so it might be wise to prepare our weapons.'

'Fifteen minutes, sir?'

'It's Sunday, Sharpe! The Lord's day. Colonel Wallace's chaplain will be holding divine service on the hour, and I expect you to come with me. He preaches a fine sermon. But there's still time for you to clean your musket first.'

The musket was cleaned with boiling water which Sharpe poured down the barrel, then sloshed about so that the very last remnants of powder residue were washed free. He doubted the musket needed cleaning, but he dutifully did it, then oiled the lock and put a new flint into the doghead. He borrowed a sharpening stone from one of Sevajee's men and honed the bayonet's point so that the tip shone white and deadly, then he dabbed some oil on the blade before sliding it home into its scabbard. There was nothing else to do now except listen to the sermon, sleep and do the mundane tasks. There would be a meal to cook and the horses to water again, but those commonplace jobs were overshadowed by the knowledge that the enemy was just a short march away at Borkardan. Sharpe felt a shudder of nerves. What would battle be like? Would he stand? Or would he turn out like that corporal at Boxtel who had started to rave about angels and then had run like a spring hare through the Flanders rain?

A half-mile behind Sharpe the baggage train began to trudge into a wide field where the oxen were hobbled, the camels picketed and the elephants tethered to trees. Grass-cutters spread out into the countryside to find forage for the animals which were watered from a muddy irrigation channel. The elephants were fed piles of palm leaves and buckets of rice soaked in butter, while Captain Mackay scurried through the chaos on his small bay horse, making sure that the ammunition was being properly stowed and the animals suitably fed. He suddenly caught sight of a disconsolate Sergeant Hakeswill and his six men. 'Sergeant! You're still here? I thought you'd have your rogue safely pinioned by now?'

'Problems, sir,' Hakeswill said, standing rigidly to attention.

'Easy, Sergeant, stand easy. No rogue?'

'Not yet, sir.'

'So you're back in my command, are you? That's splendid, just splendid.' Mackay was an eager young officer who did his best to see the good in everybody, and though he found the Sergeant from the 33rd somewhat daunting, he did his best to communicate his own enthusiasm. '*Puckalees*, Sergeant,' he said brightly, '*puckalees*.'

Hakeswill's face wrenched in a series of spasms. '*Puckalees*, sir?'

'Water carriers, Sergeant.'

'I knows what a *puckalee* is, sir, on account of having lived in this heathen land more years than I can count, but begging your pardon, sir, what has a *puckalee* to do with me?'

'We have to establish a collecting point for them,' Mackay said. The *puckalees* were all on the strengths of the individual regiments and in battle their job was to keep the fighting men supplied with water. 'I need a man to watch over them,' Mackay said. 'They're good fellows, all of them, but oddly frightened of bullets! They need chivvying along. I'll be busy enough with the ammunition wagons tomorrow, so can I rely on you to make sure the *puckalees* do their job like the stout fellows they are?' The 'stout fellows' were boys, grandfathers, cripples, the half-blind and the halfwitted. 'Excellent! Excellent!' the young Captain said. 'A problem solved! Make sure you get some rest, Sergeant. We'll all need to be sprightly tomorrow. And if you feel the need for some spiritual refreshment you'll find the 74th are holding divine service any moment now.' Mackay smiled at Hakeswill, then set off in pursuit of an errant group of bullock carts. 'You! You! You with the tents! Not there! Come here!'

'*Puckalees*,' Hakeswill said, spitting, '*puckalees*.' None of his men responded for they knew well enough to leave Sergeant

Hakeswill alone when he was in a more than usually foul mood. 'Could be worse, though,' he said.

'Worse?' Private Flaherty ventured.

Hakeswill's face twitched. 'We has a problem, boys,' he said dourly, 'and the problem is one Scottish Colonel who is attempting to bugger up the good order of our regiment. I won't abide it, I won't. Regimental honour is at stake, it is. He's been wool-pulling, ain't he? And he thinks he's pulled it clean over our eyes, but he ain't, because I've seen through him, I have, I've seen through his Scotch soul and it's as rotten as rotten eggs. Sharpie's paying him off, ain't he? Stands to reason! Corruption, boys, nothing but corruption.' Hakeswill blinked, his mind racing. 'If we're flogging *puckalees* halfway across bleeding India tomorrow, lads, then we will have our moment and the regiment would want us to seize it.'

'Seize it?' Lowry asked.

'Kill the bugger, you blockheaded toad.'

'Kill Sharpie?'

'God help me for leading halfwits,' Hakeswill said. 'Not Sharpie! We wants him private like, where we can fillet him fair and square. You kills the Scotchman! Once Mister bleeding McCandless is gone, Sharpie's ours.'

'You can't kill a colonel!' Kendrick said aghast.

'You points your firelock, Private Kendrick,' Hakeswill said, ramming his own musket's muzzle hard into Kendrick's midriff. 'You cocks your musket, Private Kendrick' – Hakeswill pulled back the doghead and the heavy lock clicked into place – 'and then you shoots the bugger clear through.' Hakeswill pulled his trigger. The powder in the pan exploded with a small crackle and fizz, and Kendrick leaped back as the smoke drifted away from the lock, but the musket had not been charged. Hakeswill laughed. 'Got you, didn't I? You thought I was putting a *goolie* in your belly! But that's what you do to McCandless. A *goolie* in his belly or in his brain or in any other part what kills him. And you do it tomorrow.' The six men looked dubious, and Hakeswill grinned. 'Extra shares for you all if it happens, boys, extra shares. You'll be paying the officers' whores when you get home, and all it will take is one *goolie*.' He smiled wolfishly. 'Tomorrow, boys, tomorrow.'

But across the river, where the blue-coated patrol of the 19th Dragoons was exploring the countryside south of the Kaitna, everything was changing.

Wellesley had dismounted, stripped off his jacket and was washing his face from a basin of water held on a tripod. Lieutenant Colonel Orrock, the Company officer who commanded the picquets that day, was complaining about the two galloper guns that were supposedly attached to his small command. 'They wouldn't keep up, sir. Laggards, sir. I found myself four hundred yards ahead of them! Four hundred yards!'

'I asked you to set a brisk pace, Orrock,' the General said, wishing the fool would go away. He reached for a towel and vigorously scrubbed his face dry.

'But if we'd been challenged!' Orrock protested.

'Gallopers can move briskly when they must,' the General said, then sighed as he realized the prickly Orrock needed placating. 'Who commanded the guns?'

'Barlow, sir.'

'I'll speak to him,' the General promised, then turned as the patrol of 19th Dragoons that had crossed the River Purna to reconnoitre the ground on the far bank came threading through the rising tents towards him. Wellesley had not expected the patrol back this soon and their return puzzled him, then he saw they were escorting a group of *bhinjarries*, the black-cloaked merchants who traversed India buying and selling food. 'You'll excuse me, Orrock,' the General said, plucking his coat from a stool.

'You will talk with Barlow, sir?' Orrock asked.

'I said so, didn't I?' Wellesley called as he walked towards the horsemen.

The patrol leader, a captain, slid off his horse and gestured at the *bhinjarries'* leader. 'We found these fellows a half-mile north of the river, sir. They've got eighteen pack oxen loaded with grain and they reckon the enemy ain't in Borkardan at all. They were planning to sell the grain in Assaye.'

'Assaye?' The General frowned at the unfamiliar name.

'It's a village four or five miles north of here, sir. He says it's thick with the enemy.'

'Four or five miles?' Wellesley asked in astonishment. 'Four or five?'

The cavalry captain shrugged. 'That's what they say, sir.' He gestured at the grain merchants who stood impassively among the mounted troopers.

Dear God, Wellesley thought, four or five miles? He had been humbugged! The enemy had stolen a march on him, and at any moment that enemy might appear to the north and launch an attack on the British encampment and there was no chance for Stevenson to come to his help. The 74th were singing hymns and the enemy was five miles away, maybe less? The General spun round. 'Barclay! Campbell! Horses! Quick now!'

The flurry of activity at the General's tent sent a rumour whipping through the camp, and the rumour was fanned into alarm when the whole of the 19th Dragoons and the 4th Native Cavalry trotted through the river on the heels of the General and his two aides. Colonel McCandless had been walking with Sharpe towards the 74th's lines, but seeing the sudden excitement, he turned and hurried back towards his horse. 'Come on, Sharpe!'

'Where to, sir?'

'We'll find out. Sevajee?'

'We're ready.'

McCandless's party left the camp five minutes after the General. They could see the dust left by the cavalry ahead and McCandless hurried to catch up. They rode through a landscape of small fields cut by deep dry gulches and cactus-thorn hedges. Wellesley had been following the earth road northwards, but after a while the General swerved westwards onto a field of stubble and McCandless did not follow, but kept straight on up the road. 'No point in tiring the horses unnecessarily,' he explained, though Sharpe suspected the Colonel was merely impatient to go north and see whatever had caused the excitement. The two British cavalry regiments were in sight to the east, but there was no enemy visible.

Sevajee and his men had ridden ahead, but when they reached a crest some two hundred yards in front of McCandless they suddenly wrenched on their reins and swerved back. Sharpe expected to see a horde of Mahratta cavalry come boiling over the crest, but the skyline stayed empty as Sevajee and his men halted a few yards short of the ridge and there dismounted.

'You'll not want them to see you, Colonel,' Sevajee said drily when McCandless caught up.

'Them?'

Sevajee gestured at the crest. 'Take a look. You'll want to dismount.'

McCandless and Sharpe both slid from their saddles, then walked to the skyline where a cactus hedge offered conceal-ment and from where they could stare at the country to the north and Sharpe, who had never seen such a sight before, simply gazed in amazement.

It was not an army. It was a horde, a whole people, a

nation. Thousands upon thousands of the enemy, all in line, mile after mile of them. Men and women and children and guns and camels and bullocks and rocket batteries and horses and tents and still more men until there seemed to be no end to them. 'Jesus!' Sharpe said, the imprecation torn from him.

'Sharpe!'

'Sorry, sir.' But no wonder he had sworn, for Sharpe had never imagined that an army could look so vast. The nearest men were no more than half a mile away, beyond a discoloured river that flowed between steep mud banks. A village lay on the nearer bank, but on the northern side, just beyond the mud bluff, there was a line of guns. Big guns, the same painted and sculpted cannon that Sharpe had seen in Pohlmann's camp. Beyond the guns was the infantry and behind the infantry, and spreading far out of sight to the east, was a mass of cavalry and beyond them the myriad of camp followers. More infantry were posted about a distant village where Sharpe could just see a cluster of bright flags. 'How many are there?' he asked.

'At least a hundred thousand men?' McCandless ventured.

'At least,' Sevajee agreed, 'but most are adventurers come for loot.' The Indian was peering through a long ivory-clad telescope. 'And the cavalry won't help in a battle.'

'It'll be down to these fellows,' McCandless said, indicating the infantry just behind the gun line. 'Fifteen thousand?'

'Fourteen or fifteen,' Sevajee said. 'Too many.'

'Too many guns,' McCandless said gloomily. 'It'll be a retreat.'

'I thought we came here to fight!' Sharpe said belligerently.

'We came here expecting to rest, then march on Borkardan tomorrow,' McCandless said testily. 'We didn't come here to take on the whole enemy army with just five thousand infantry. They know we're coming, they're ready for us and they simply want us to walk into their fire. Wellesley's not a fool, Sharpe. He'll march us back, link up with Stevenson, then find them again.'

Sharpe felt a pang of relief that he would not discover the realities of battle, but the relief was tempered by a tinge of disappointment. The disappointment surprised him, and the relief made him fear he might be a coward.

'If we retreat,' Sevajee warned, 'those horsemen will harry us all the way.'

'We'll just have to fight them off,' McCandless said confidently, then let out a long satisfied breath. 'Got him! There, the left flank!' He pointed and Sharpe saw, far away at the very end of the enemy gunline, a scatter of white uniforms. 'Not that it helps us,' McCandless said wryly, 'but at least we're on his heels.'

'Or he's on ours,' Sevajee said, then he offered his telescope to Sharpe. 'See for yourself, Sergeant.'

Sharpe rested the glass's long barrel on a thick cactus leaf. He moved the lens slowly along the line of infantry. Men slept in the shade, some were in their small tents and others sat in groups and he could have sworn a few were gambling. Officers, Indian and European, strolled behind their men, while in front of them the massive line of guns waited with their ammunition limbers. He moved the glass to the very far left of the enemy line and saw the white jackets of Dodd's men, and saw something else. Two huge guns, much bigger than anything he had seen before. 'They've got their siege guns in the line, sir,' he told McCandless, who trained his own telescope.

'Eighteen-pounders,' McCandless guessed, 'maybe bigger?' The Colonel collapsed his glass. 'Why aren't they patrolling this side of the river?'

'Because they don't want to frighten us away,' Sevajee said. 'They want us to stroll up to their guns and die in the river, but they'll still have some horsemen hidden on this bank, waiting to tell them when we retreat.'

The sound of hooves made Sharpe whip round in expectation of those enemy cavalry, but it was only General Wellesley and his two aides who cantered along the lower ground beneath the crest. 'They're all there, McCandless,' the General shouted happily.

'So it seems, sir.'

The General reined in, waiting for McCandless to come down from the skyline and join him. 'They seem to presume we'll make a frontal attack,' Wellesley said wryly, as though he found the idea amusing.

'They're certainly formed for it, sir.'

'They must assume we're blockheads. What time is it?'

One of his aides consulted a watch. 'Ten minutes of noon, sir.'

'Plenty of time,' the General murmured. 'Onwards, gentlemen, stay below the skyline. We don't want to frighten them away!'

'Frighten them away?' Sevajee asked with a smile, but Wellesley ignored the comment as he spurred on eastwards, parallel with the river. Some troops of Company cavalry were scouring the fields and at first Sharpe thought they were looking for concealed enemy picquets, then he saw they were hunting down local farmers and harrying them along in the General's wake.

Wellesley rode two miles eastwards, a string of horsemen behind him. The farmers were breathless by the time they reached the place where his horse was picketed just beneath a low hill. The General was kneeling on the crest, staring east through a glass. 'Ask those fellows if there are any fords east of here!' he shouted down to his aides.

A hurried consultation followed, but the farmers were quite sure there was no ford. The only crossing places, they insisted, were directly in front of Scindia's army. 'Find a clever one,' Wellesley ordered, 'and bring him up here. Colonel? Maybe you'd translate?'

McCandless picked one of the farmers and led him up the hill. Sharpe, without being asked, followed and Wellesley did not order him back, but just muttered that they should all keep their heads low. 'There' – the General pointed eastwards to a village on the Kaitna's southern bank – 'that village, what's it called?'

'Peepulgaon,' the farmer said, and added that his mother and two sisters lived in the huddle of mud-walled houses with their thatched roofs.

Peepulgaon lay only a half-mile from the low hill, but it was all of two miles east of Taunklee, the village that was opposite the eastern extremity of the Mahratta line. Both villages were on the river's southern bank while the enemy waited on the Kaitna's northern side, and Sharpe did not understand Wellesley's interest. 'Ask him if he has any relatives north of the river,' the General ordered McCandless.

'He has a brother and several cousins, sir,' McCandless translated.

'So how does his mother visit her son north of the river?' Wellesley asked.

The farmer launched himself into a long explanation. In the dry season, he said, she walked across the river bed, but in the wet season, when the waters rose, she was forced to come upstream and cross at Taunklee. Wellesley listened, then grunted in apparent disbelief. He was staring intently through the glass. 'Campbell?' he called, but his aide had gone to another low rise a hundred yards westwards that offered a better view of the enemy ranks. 'Campbell?' Wellesley called again and, getting no answer, turned. 'Sharpe, you'll do. Come here.'

'Sir?'

'You've got young eyes. Come here, and keep low.'

Sharpe joined the General on the crest where, to his surprise, he was handed the telescope. 'Look at the village,' Wellesley ordered, 'then look at the opposite bank and tell me what you see.'

It took Sharpe a moment to find Peepulgaon in the lens, but suddenly its mud walls filled the glass. He moved the telescope slowly, sliding its view past oxen, goats and chickens, past clothes set to dry on bushes by the river bank, and then the lens slid across the brown water of the River Kaitna and up its opposite bank where he saw a muddy bluff topped by trees and, just beyond the trees, a fold of land. And in the fold of land were roofs, straw roofs. 'There's another village there, sir,' Sharpe said.

'You're sure?' Wellesley asked urgently.

'Pretty sure, sir. Might just be cattle sheds.'

'You don't keep cattle sheds apart from a village,' the General said scathingly, 'not in a country infested by bandits.' Wellesley twisted round. 'McCandless? Ask your fellow if there's a village on the other side of the river from Peepulgaon.'

The farmer listened to the question, then nodded. 'Waroor,' he said, then helpfully informed the General that his cousin was the village headman, the *naique*.

'How far apart are those villages, Sharpe?' Wellesley asked.

Sharpe judged the distance for a couple of seconds. 'Three hundred yards, sir?'

Wellesley took the telescope back and moved away from the crest. 'Never in my life,' he said, 'have I seen two villages on opposite banks of a river that weren't connected by a ford.'

'He insists not, sir,' McCandless said, indicating the farmer.

'Then he's a rogue, a liar or a blockhead,' Wellesley said cheerfully. 'The latter, probably.' He frowned in thought, his

261

right hand drumming a tattoo on the telescope's barrel. 'I'll warrant there is a ford,' he said to himself.

'Sir?' Captain Campbell had run back from the western knoll. 'Enemy's breaking camp, sir.'

'Are they, by God!' Wellesley returned to the crest and stared through the glass again. The infantry immediately on the Kaitna's north bank were not moving, but far away, close to the fortified village, tents were being struck. 'Preparing to run away, I daresay,' Wellesley muttered.

'Or readying to cross the river and attack us,' McCandless said grimly.

'And they're sending cavalry across the river,' Campbell added ominously.

'Nothing to worry us,' Wellesley said, then turned back to stare at the opposing villages of Peepulgaon and Waroor. 'There has to be a ford,' he said to himself again, so quietly that only Sharpe could hear him. 'Stands to reason,' he said, then he went silent for a long time.

'That enemy cavalry, sir,' Campbell prompted him.

Wellesley seemed startled. 'What?'

'There, sir.' Campbell pointed westwards to a large group of enemy horsemen who had appeared from a grove of trees, but who seemed content to watch Wellesley's group from a half-mile away.

'Time we were away,' Wellesley said. 'Give that lying block-head a rupee, McCandless, then let's be off.'

'You plan to retreat, sir?' McCandless asked.

Wellesley had been hurrying down the slope, but now stopped and stared in surprise at the Scotsman. 'Retreat?'

McCandless blinked. 'You surely don't intend to fight, sir, do you?'

'How else are we to do His Majesty's business? Of course we'll fight! There's a ford there.' Wellesley flung his arm east towards Peepulgaon. 'That wretched farmer might deny it, but he's a blockhead! There has to be a ford. We'll cross it, turn their left flank and pound them into scraps! But we must hurry! Noon already. Three hours, gentlemen, three hours to bring on battle. Three hours to turn his flank.' He ran on down the hill to where Diomed, his white Arab horse, waited.

'Good God,' McCandless said. 'Good God.' For five thousand infantry would now cross the Kaitna at a place where men said the river was uncrossable, then fight an enemy horde at least ten times their number. 'Good God,' the Colonel said again, then hurried to follow Wellesley south. The enemy had stolen a march, the redcoats had journeyed all night and were bone tired, but Wellesley would have his battle.

CHAPTER 9

'There!' Dodd said, pointing.

'I can't see,' Simone Joubert complained.

'Drop the telescope, use your naked eye, Madame. There! It's flashing.'

'Where?'

'There!' Dodd pointed again. 'Across the river. Three trees, low hill.'

'Ah!' Simone at last saw the flash of reflected sunlight from the lens of a telescope that was being used on the far bank of the river and well downstream from where Dodd's Cobras held the left of Pohlmann's line.

Simone and her husband had dined with the Major who was grimly happy in anticipation of a British attack which, he claimed, must inevitably fall hardest on his Cobras. 'It will be slaughter, Ma'am,' Dodd said wolfishly, 'sheer slaughter!' He and Captain Joubert had walked Simone to the edge of the bluff above the Kaitna and shown her the fords, and demonstrated how any men crossing the fords must be caught in the mangling crossfire of the Mahratta cannon, then maintained that the British had no option but to walk forward into that weltering onslaught of canister, round shot and shell. 'If you wish to stay and watch, Madame,' Dodd had offered, 'I can find a place of safety for you.' He gestured towards a low rise of ground just behind the regiment. 'You could watch from there, and I credit no British soldier will come near you.'

'I could not bear to watch a slaughter, Major,' Simone had said feelingly.

'Your squeamishness does you credit, Ma'am,' Dodd had answered. 'War is man's work.' It was then that Dodd had spotted the British soldiers on the opposite bank and had trained his telescope on the distant men. Simone, knowing now where to look, rested the glass on her husband's shoulder and trained its lens on the far hill. She could see two men there, one in a cocked hat and the other in a shako. Both were keeping low. 'Why are they so far down the river?' she asked.

'They're looking for a way round our flank,' Dodd said.

'Is there one?'

'No. They must cross here, Ma'am, or else they don't cross at all.' Dodd gestured at the fords in front of the *compoo*. A band of cavalrymen was galloping through the shallow water, spraying silver from their horses' hooves as they crossed to the Kaitna's south bank. 'And those horsemen,' Dodd explained, 'are going to see whether they will cross or not.'

Simone collapsed the telescope and handed it back to the Major. 'They might not attack?'

'They won't,' her husband answered in English for Dodd's benefit. 'They have too much sense.'

'Boy Wellesley don't have sense,' Dodd said scathingly. 'Look how he attacked at Ahmednuggur? Straight at the wall! A hundred rupees says he will attack.'

Captain Joubert shook his head. 'I do not gamble, Major.'

'A soldier should relish risk,' Dodd said.

'And if they don't cross,' Simone asked, 'there is no battle?'

'There'll be a battle, Ma'am,' Dodd said grimly. 'Pohlmann's gone to fetch Scindia's permission for us to cross the river. If they won't come to us, we'll go to them.'

Pohlmann had indeed gone to find Scindia. The Hanoverian had dressed for battle, donning his finest coat, which was a blue silk jacket, trimmed in scarlet and decorated with loops of gold braid and black aiguillettes. He wore a white silk sash on which was blazoned a star of diamonds and from which hung a gold-hilted sword, though Dupont, the Dutchman, who accompanied Pohlmann to meet Scindia, noted that the Colonel's breeches and boots were old and shabby. 'I wear them for luck,' Pohlmann said, noting Dupont's puzzled glance at his decrepit breeches. 'They're from my old East India Company uniform.' The Hanoverian was in a fine mood. His short march eastwards had achieved all he had desired, for it had brought one of the two small British armies into his lap while it was still far away from the other. All he needed to do now was snap it up like a minnow, then march on Stevenson's force, but Scindia had been insistent that no infantry were to cross the Kaitna's fords without his permission and Pohlmann now needed that permission. The Hanoverian did not plan to cross immediately, for first he wanted to be certain that the British were retreating, but nor did he wish to wait for permission once he heard news of the enemy's withdrawal.

'Our lord and master will be scared at the thought of attacking,' Pohlmann told Dupont, 'so we'll flatter the bugger. Slap on the *ghee* with a shovel, Dupont. Tell him he'll be lord of all India if he lets us loose.'

'Tell him there are a hundred white women in Wellesley's camp and he'll lead the attack himself,' Dupont observed drily.

'Then that is what we shall tell him,' Pohlmann said, 'and promise him that every little darling will be his concubine.'

Except that when Pohlmann and Dupont reached the tree-shaded stretch of ground above the River Juah where the Maharajah of Gwalior had been awaiting his army's victory, there was no sign of his lavish tents. They had been struck, all of them, together with the striped tents of the Rajah of

Berar, and all that remained were the cook tents that even now were being collapsed and folded onto the beds of a dozen ox carts. All the elephants but one were gone, the horses of the royal bodyguards were gone, the concubines were gone and the two princes were gone.

The one remaining elephant belonged to Surjee Rao and that minister, ensconced in his howdah where he was being fanned by a servant, smiled benevolently down on the two sweating and red-faced Europeans. 'His Serene Majesty deemed it safer to withdraw westwards,' he explained airily, 'and the Rajah of Berar agreed with him.'

'They did what?' Pohlmann snarled.

'The omens,' Surjee Rao said vaguely, waving a bejewelled hand to indicate that the subtleties of such supernatural messages would be beyond Pohlmann's comprehension.

'The bloody omens are propitious!' Pohlmann insisted. 'We've got the buggers by the balls! What more omens can you want?'

Surjee Rao smiled. 'His Majesty has sublime confidence in your skill, Colonel.'

'To do what?' the Hanoverian demanded.

'Whatever is necessary,' Surjee Rao said, then smiled. 'We shall wait in Borkardan for news of your triumph, Colonel, and eagerly anticipate seeing the banners of our enemies heaped in triumph at the foot of His Serene Majesty's throne.' And with that hope expressed he snapped his fingers and the mahout prodded the elephant which lumbered away westwards.

'Bastards,' Pohlmann said to Dupont, loudly enough for the retreating minister to hear. 'Lily-livered bastards! Cowards!' Not that he cared whether Scindia and the Rajah of Berar were present at the battle; indeed, given the choice, he would much prefer to fight without them, but that was not true of his men who, like all soldiers, fought better when their rulers were watching, and so Pohlmann was angry for his men. Yet, he consoled himself as he returned southwards, they would still fight well. Pride would see to that, and confidence, and the promise of plunder.

And Surjee Rao's final words, Pohlmann decided, had been more than enough to give him permission to cross the River Kaitna. He had been told to do whatever was necessary, and Pohlmann reckoned that gave him a free hand, so he would give Scindia a victory even if the yellow bastard did not deserve it.

Pohlmann and Dupont cantered back to the left of the line where they saw that Major Dodd had called his men out from the shade of the trees and into their ranks. The sight suggested that the enemy was approaching the Kaitna and Pohlmann spurred his horse into a gallop, clamping one hand onto his extravagantly plumed hat to stop it falling off. He slewed to a stop just short of Dodd's regiment and stared above their heads across the river.

The enemy had come, except this enemy was merely a long line of cavalrymen with two small horse-drawn galloper guns. It was a screen, of course. A screen of British and Indian horsemen intended to stop his own patrols from discovering what was happening in the hidden country beyond. 'Any sign of their infantry?' he called to Dodd.

'None, sir.'

'The buggers are running!' Pohlmann exulted. 'That's why they've put up a screen.' He suddenly noticed Simone Joubert and hastily took off his feathered hat. 'My apologies for my language, Madame.' He put his hat back on and twisted his horse about. 'Harness the guns!' he shouted.

'What is happening?' Simone asked anxiously.

'We're crossing the river,' her husband said quietly, 'and you must go back to Assaye.'

Simone knew she must say something loving to him, for

was that not expected of a wife at a moment such as this? 'I shall pray for you,' she said shyly.

'Go back to Assaye,' her husband said again, noting that she had not given him any love, 'and stay there till it is all over.'

It would not take long. The guns needed to be attached to their limbers, but the infantry were ready to march and the cavalry were eager to begin their pursuit. The existence of the British cavalry screen suggested that Wellesley must be withdrawing, so all Pohlmann needed to do was cross the river and then crush the enemy. Dodd drew his elephant-hilted sword, felt its newly honed edge and waited for the orders to begin the slaughter.

The Mahratta cavalry pursued Wellesley's party the moment they saw that the General was retreating from his observation post above the river. 'We must look to ourselves, gentlemen!' Wellesley had called and driven back his heels so that Diomed had sprung ahead. The other horsemen matched his pace, but Sharpe, on his small captured Mahratta horse, could not keep up. He had mounted in a hurry, and in his haste he could not fit his right boot into the stirrup and the horse's jolting motion made it all the more difficult, but he dared not curb the beast for he could hear the enemy's shouts and the beat of their hooves not far behind. For a few moments he was in a panic. The thud of the pursuing hooves grew louder, he could see his companions drawing ever farther ahead of him and his horse was blowing hard and trying to resist the frantic kicks he gave, and each kick threatened to unseat him so that he clung to the saddle's pommel and still his right boot would not find the stirrup. Sevajee, racing free on the right flank, saw his predicament and curved back towards him. 'You're not a horseman, Sergeant.'

'Never bloody was, sir. Hate the bloody things.'

'A warrior and his horse, Sergeant, are like a man and a woman,' Sevajee said, leaning over and pushing the stirrup iron onto Sharpe's boot. He did it without once checking his own horse's furious pace, then he slapped Sharpe's small mare on the rump and she took off like one of the enemy's rockets, almost tipping Sharpe backwards.

Sharpe clung on to the pommel, while his musket, which was hanging by its sling from his left elbow, banged and thumped his thigh. His shako blew off and he had no time to rescue it, but then a trumpet sounded off to his right and he saw a stream of British cavalrymen riding to head off the pursuit. Still more cavalrymen were spurring north from Naulniah and Wellesley, as he passed them, urged them on towards the Kaitna.

'Thank you, sir,' Sharpe said to Sevajee.

'You should learn horsemanship.'

'I'll stay a foot soldier, sir. Safer. Don't like sitting on things with hooves and teeth.'

Sevajee laughed. Wellesley had slowed now and was patting the neck of his horse, but the brief pursuit had only increased his high spirits. He turned Diomed to watch the Mahratta cavalry spur away. 'A good omen!' he said happily.

'For what, sir?' Sevajee asked.

Wellesley heard the Indian's sceptical tone. 'You don't think we should give battle?'

Sevajee shrugged, seeking some tactful way of expressing his disagreement with Wellesley's decision. 'The battle isn't always to the largest army, sir.'

'Always, no,' Wellesley said, 'but usually, yes? You think I am being impetuous?' Sevajee refused to be drawn and simply shrugged again in answer. 'We shall see, we shall see,' the General said. 'Their army looks fine, I grant you, but once we break the regular *compoos*, the others will run.'

'I do hope so, sir.'

'Depend on it,' Wellesley said, then spurred on.

Sharpe looked at Sevajee. 'Are we mad to fight, sir?'

'Quite mad,' Sevajee said, 'completely mad. But maybe there's no choice.'

'No choice?'

'We blundered, Sergeant. We marched too far and came too close to the enemy, so either we attack him or run away from him, and either way we have to fight. By attacking him we just make the fight shorter.' He twisted in the saddle and pointed towards the now hidden Kaitna. 'Do you know what's beyond that river?'

'No, sir.'

'Another river, Sharpe, and they meet just a couple of miles downstream' – he pointed eastwards towards the place where the waters met – 'and if we cross that ford we shall find ourselves on a tongue of land and the only way out is forward, through a hundred thousand Mahrattas. Death on one side and water on the other.' Sevajee laughed. 'Blundering, Sergeant, blundering!'

But if Wellesley had blundered he was still in high spirits. Once back at Naulniah he ordered Diomed unsaddled and rubbed down, then began issuing commands. The army's baggage would stay at Naulniah, dragged into the village's alleyways which were to be barricaded so that no marauding Mahratta cavalry could plunder the wagons which would be guarded by the smallest battalion of sepoys. McCandless heard that order given, understood its necessity, but groaned aloud when he realized that almost five hundred infantrymen were thus being shorn from the attacking army.

The cavalry that remained in Naulniah were ordered to saddle their horses and ride to the Kaitna, there to form a screen on the southern bank, while the tired infantry, who had marched all morning, were now rousted from their tents and chivvied into ranks. 'No packs!' the sergeants called.

'Firelocks and cartridge boxes only. No packs! Off to a Sunday battle, lads! Save your bleeding prayers and hurry up! Come on, Johnny, boots on, lad! There's a horde of heathens to kill. Look lively, now! Wake yourselves up! On your feet!'

The picquets of the day, composed of a half company from each of the army's seven battalions, marched first. They splashed through the small river north of Naulniah and were met on its far bank by one of the General's aides who guided them onto the farm track that led to Peepulgaon. The picquets were followed by the King's 74th accompanied by their battalion artillery, while behind them came the second battalion of the 12th Madras Regiment, the first battalion of the 4th Madras, the first of the 8th Madras and the first of the 10th Madras, and lastly the kilted Highlanders of the King's 78th. Six battalions crossed the river and followed the beaten-earth track between fields of millet beneath the furnace of an Indian sun. No enemy was visible as they marched, though rumour said the whole of the Mahratta army was not far away.

Two guns fired around one o'clock. The sound was flat and hard, echoing across the heat-shimmering land, but the infantry could see nothing. The sound came from their left, and the battalion officers said there was cavalry somewhere out there, and that doubtless meant that the cavalry's light galloper guns had engaged the enemy, or else the enemy had brought cannon to face the British cavalry, but the fighting did not seem to be ominous, for there was silence after the two shots. McCandless, his nerves strung by the disaster he feared was imminent, galloped Aeolus a few yards westwards as if wanting to find an explanation for the two gunshots, but then he thought better of it and turned his horse back to the road.

More cannon fire sounded a few moments later, but there was nothing urgent in the distant shots which were monotonous, flat and sporadic. If battle had been brewing to the boil the gunshots would have sounded hard and fast, but these shots were almost lackadaisical, as though the gunners were merely practising on Aldershot Heath on a lazy summer's day. 'Their guns or ours, sir?' Sharpe asked McCandless.

'Ours, I suspect,' the Scotsman said. 'Cavalry galloper guns keeping the enemy horse on their toes.' He tugged on Aeolus's rein, moving the gelding out of the path of sixty sepoy pioneers who were doubling down the road's left verge with pick-axes and shovels on their shoulders. The pioneers' task was to reach the Kaitna and make certain that its banks were not too steep for the ox-drawn artillery. Wellesley cantered after the pioneers, riding to the head of the column and trailing a succession of aides. McCandless joined the General's party and Sharpe kicked his horse alongside Daniel Fletcher who was mounted on a big roan mare and leading an unsaddled Diomed by a long rein. 'He'll want him when the bay's tired,' Fletcher told Sharpe, nodding ahead at Wellesley who was now riding a tall bay stallion. 'And the mare's in case both horses get shot,' he added, slapping the rump of the horse he rode.

'So what do you do?' Sharpe asked the dragoon.

'Just stay close until he wants to change horses and keep him from getting thirsty,' Fletcher said. He carried no less than five water canteens on his belt, bulked over a heavy sabre in a metal scabbard, the first time Sharpe had ever seen the orderly carrying a weapon. 'Vicious thing, that,' Fletcher said when he saw Sharpe glance at the weapon, 'a good wide blade, perfect for slicing.'

'Ever used it?' Sharpe asked.

'Against Dhoondiah,' Fletcher answered. Dhoondiah had been a bandit chieftain whose depredations in Mysore had finally persuaded Wellesley to pursue him with cavalry. The resultant battle had been a short clash of horsemen that had been won in moments by the British. 'And I killed a goat with it for the General's supper a week ago,' Fletcher continued, drawing the heavy curved blade, 'and I think the poor bugger died of fright when it saw the blade coming. Took its head clean off, it did. Look at this, Sergeant.' He handed the blade to Sharpe. 'See what it says there? Just above the hilt?'

Sharpe tipped the sabre to the sun. ' "Warranted Never to Fail",' he read aloud. He grinned, for the boast seemed oddly out of place on a thing designed to kill or maim.

'Made in Sheffield,' Fletcher said, taking the blade back, 'and guaranteed never to fail! Good slicer this is, real good. You can cut a man in half with one of these if you get the stroke right.'

Sharpe grinned. 'I'll stick with a musket.'

'Not on horseback, you won't, Sergeant,' Fletcher said. 'A firelock's no good on horseback. You want a blade.'

'Never learned to use one,' Sharpe said.

'It ain't difficult,' Fletcher said with the scorn of a man who had mastered a difficult trade. 'Keep your arm straight and use the point when you're fighting cavalry, because if you bend the elbow the bastards will chop through your wrist as sure as eggs, and slash away like a haymaker at infantry because there ain't bugger all they can do back to you, not once they're on the run. Not that you could use any kind of sword off the back of that horse.' He nodded at Sharpe's small native beast. 'It's more like an overgrown dog, that is. Does it fetch?'

The road reached the high point between the two rivers and Fletcher, mounted high on the General's mare, caught his first glimpse of the enemy army on the distant northern bank of the Kaitna. He whistled softly. 'Millions of the buggers!'

'We're going to turn their flank,' Sharpe said, repeating what he had heard the General say. So far as Sharpe understood, the idea was to cross the river at the ford which no one except Wellesley believed existed, then make an attack on the left flank of the waiting infantry. The idea made sense to Sharpe, for the enemy line was facing south and, by coming at them from the east, the British could well plunge the *compoos* into confusion.

'Millions of the buggers!' Fletcher said again in wonderment, but then the road dropped and took the enemy out of their view. The dragoon orderly sheathed his sabre. 'But he's confident,' he said, nodding ahead at Wellesley who was dressed in his old uniform coat of the 33rd. The General wore a slim straight sword, but had no other weapon, not even a pistol.

'He was always confident,' Sharpe said. 'Cool as you like.'

'He's a good fellow,' Fletcher said loyally. 'Proper officer. He ain't friendly, of course, but he's always fair.' He touched his spurs to the mare's flanks because Wellesley and his aides had hurried ahead into the village of Peepulgaon where the villagers gaped at the foreigners in their red coats and black cocked hats. Wellesley scattered chickens from his path as he cantered down the dusty village street to where the road dropped down a precipitous bluff into the half-dry bed of the Kaitna. The pioneers arrived a moment later and began attacking the bluff to smooth its steep slope. On the river's far bank Sharpe could see the road twist up into the trees that half obscured the village of Waroor. The General was right, he reckoned, and there had to be a ford, for why else would the road show on both banks? But whether the ford was shallow enough for the army to cross no one yet knew.

Wellesley stood his horse at the top of the bluff and drummed the fingers of his right hand on his thigh. It was the only sign of nerves. He was staring across the river, thinking. No enemy was in sight, but nor should they have been for the Mahratta line was now two miles to the west, which

275

meant that Scindia's army was now between him and Stevenson. Wellesley grimaced, realizing that he had already abandoned his first principle for fighting this battle, which had been to secure his left flank so Stevenson could join. Doubtless, the moment the guns began their proper, concentrated work, the sound of their cannonade would bring Stevenson hurrying across country, but now the older man would simply have to join the fight as best he could. But Wellesley had no regrets at posing such difficulties for Stevenson, for the chance to turn the enemy's flank was heaven-sent. So long, that is, as the ford was practicable.

The pioneer Captain led a dozen of his sepoys down towards the river. 'I'll just see to that far bank, sir,' the Captain called up to the General, startling Wellesley out of his reverie.

'Come back!' Wellesley shouted angrily. 'Back!'

The Captain had almost reached the water, but now turned and stared at Wellesley in puzzlement. 'Have to grade that bluff, sir,' he shouted, pointing to where the road climbed steeply to the screen of trees on the Kaitna's northern bank. 'Too steep for guns, sir.'

'Come back!' Wellesley called again, then waited as the dozen men trudged back to the southern bank. 'The enemy can see the river, Captain,' the General explained, 'and I have no wish that they should see us yet. I do not want them knowing our intentions, so you will wait until the first infantry make the crossing, then do your work.'

But the enemy had already seen the pioneers. The dozen men had only been visible in the river's open bed for a few seconds, but someone in the Mahratta gun line was wide awake and there was a sudden and violent plume of water in the river and, almost simultaneously, the sky-battering sound of a heavy gun.

'Good shooting,' McCandless said quietly when the fifteen-foot-high fountain had subsided to leave nothing but a whirling eddy in the river's brown water. The range must have been almost two miles, yet the Mahrattas had turned a gun, trained and fired it in seconds, and their aim had been almost perfect. A second gun fired and its heavy ball ploughed a furrow in the dry, crazed mud beside the river and bounced up to scatter bucket-loads of dry earth from the bluff's face. 'Eighteen-pounders,' McCandless guessed aloud, thinking of the two heavy siege guns that he had seen in front of Dodd's men.

'Damn,' Wellesley said quietly. 'But no real harm done, I suppose.' The first of the infantry were now marching down Peepulgaon's steep street. Lieutenant Colonel Orrock led the picquets of the day, while behind them Sharpe could see the grenadier company of the 74th. The Scottish drums were beating a march rhythm and the sound of the flurries made Sharpe's blood race. The sound presaged battle. It seemed like a dream, but there would be a battle this Sunday afternoon and a bloody one too.

'Afternoon, Orrock,' Wellesley spurred his horse to meet the infantry vanguard. 'Straight across, I think.'

'Has the ford been sounded?' Colonel Orrock, a lugubrious and worried-looking man, asked nervously.

'Our task, I think,' Wellesley said cheerfully. 'Gentlemen?' This last invitation was to his aides and orderly. 'Shall we open proceedings?'

'Come on, Sharpe,' McCandless said.

'You can cross after us, Captain!' Wellesley called to the eager pioneer Captain, then he put his big bay stallion down the slope of the bluff and trotted towards the river. Daniel Fletcher followed close behind with Diomed's leading rein in his hand, while the aides and McCandless and Sevajee and Sharpe all followed. Forty horsemen would be the first men across the Kaitna and the General would be the first of all, and Sharpe watched as Wellesley's stallion trotted into the river. He wanted to see how deep the water was, and he was determined to watch the General all the way through, but suddenly the bang of an eighteen-pounder gun bullied the sky and Sharpe glanced upstream to see a puff of gunsmoke smear the horizon, then he heard a horse screaming and he looked back to see that Daniel Fletcher's mount was rearing at the water's edge. Fletcher was still in the saddle, but the orderly had no head left, only a pulsing spurt of blood from his ragged neck. Diomed's rein was still in the dead man's hand, but somehow the body would not fall from the mare's saddle and she was screaming in fear as her rider's blood splashed across her face.

A second gun fired, but high, and the shot crashed low overhead to tear into the trees on the southern bank. A third ball smashed into the water, drenching McCandless. Fletcher's mare bolted upstream, but was checked by a fallen tree and so she stood, quivering, and still the trooper's decapitated body was in the saddle and Diomed's rein in his dead hand. The grey horse's left flank was reddened with Fletcher's blood. The trooper had slumped now, his headless trunk leaning eerily to drip blood into the river.

To Sharpe it seemed as if time had stopped. He was aware of someone shouting, aware of the blood dripping from the dragoon's collar, aware of his small horse shivering, but the sudden violence had immobilized him. Another gun fired, this one of smaller calibre, and the ball struck the water a hundred yards upstream, ricocheted once, then vanished in a plume of white spray.

'Sharpe!' a voice snapped. Horsemen were wheeling in the river's shallows and reaching for the dead man's bridle. 'Sharpe!' It was Wellesley who shouted. The General was in the middle of the river where the water did not even reach his stirrups, so there was a ford after all and the river could be crossed, but the enemy was hardly going to be taken by surprise now. 'Take over as orderly, Sharpe!' Wellesley shouted. 'Hurry, man!' There was no one else to replace Fletcher, not unless one of Wellesley's aides took over his duties, and Sharpe was the nearest man.

'Go on, Sharpe!' McCandless said. 'Hurry, man!'

Captain Campbell had secured Fletcher's mare. 'Ride her, Sharpe!' the Captain called. 'That little horse won't keep up with us. Just let her go. Let her go.'

Sharpe dismounted and ran to the mare. Campbell was trying to dislodge Fletcher's blood-soaked body, but the trooper's feet were caught in the stirrups. Sharpe heaved Fletcher's left boot free, then gave the booted leg a tug and the corpse slid towards him. He jumped back as the bloody remnants of the neck, all sinew and flesh and tattered scraps, slapped at his face. The corpse fell into the edge of the river and Sharpe stepped over it to mount the General's mare. 'Get the General's canteens,' Campbell ordered him, and an instant later another eighteen-pounder shot hammered low overhead like a clap of thunder. 'The canteens, man, hurry!' Campbell urged Sharpe, but Sharpe was having trouble untying the water bottles from Fletcher's belt, so instead he heaved the body over so that a gush of blood spurted from the neck to be instantly diluted in the shallow water. He tugged at the trooper's belt buckle, unfastened it, then hauled the belt free with its pouches, canteens and the heavy sabre. He wrapped the belt over his own, hastily buckled it, then clambered up into the mare's saddle and fiddled his right foot into the stirrup. Campbell was holding out Diomed's rein.

Sharpe took the rein. 'Sorry, sir.' He apologized for making the aide wait.

'Stay close to the General,' Campbell ordered him, then leaned over and patted Sharpe's arm. 'Stay close, be alert, enjoy the day, Sergeant,' he said with a grin. 'It looks as if it's going to be a lively afternoon!'

'Thank you, sir,' Sharpe said. The first infantry were in the ford now and Sharpe turned the mare, kicked back his heels and tugged Diomed through the water. Campbell was spurring ahead to catch up with Wellesley and Sharpe clumsily kicked the mare into a canter and was almost thrown as she stumbled on the riverbed, but he somehow clung to her mane as she recovered. A round shot thrashed the water white to his left, drenching him with spray. The musket had fallen off his shoulder and was dangling awkwardly from his elbow and he could not manage both it and Diomed's rein, so he let the firelock drop into the river, then wrenched the sword and the heavy canteens into a more comfortable position. Bugger this, he thought. Lost a hat, a horse and a gun in less than an hour!

The pioneers were hacking at the bluff on the northern bank to make the slope less steep, but the first galloper guns, those that accompanied the picquets of the day, were already in the Kaitna. Galloper guns were drawn by horses and the gunners shouted at the pioneers to clear out of their way. The pioneers scattered as the horses came up from the river with water streaming from the leading gun's spinning wheels; a whip cracked over the leader's head and the team galloped up the bluff with the gun and limber bouncing erratically behind. A gunner was thrown off the limber, but he picked himself up and ran after the cannon. Sharpe kicked his horse up the bluff once the second gun was safely past and suddenly he was in low ground, protected from the enemy's cannonade by the rising land to his left.

But where the hell was Wellesley? He could see no one on the high ground that led towards the enemy, and the only men on the road straight ahead were the leading companies of the picquets of the day who continued to march north-

280

wards. A slapping sound came from the river and he twisted
in his saddle to see that a round shot had whipped through
a file of infantry. A body floated downstream in eddies of
blood, then the sergeants shouted at the ranks to close up
and the infantry kept on coming. But where the hell was
Sharpe to go? To his right was the village of Waroor, half
hidden behind its trees and for a second Sharpe thought the
General must have gone there, but then he saw Lieutenant
Colonel Orrock riding up onto the higher ground to the left
and Sharpe guessed the Colonel was following Wellesley and
so he tugged the mare that way.

The land climbed to a gentle crest across stubble fields
dotted by a few trees. Colonel Orrock was the only man in
sight and he was forcing his horse up the slope towards the
skyline and so Sharpe followed him. He could hear the enemy
guns firing, presumably still bombarding the ford that had
not been supposed to exist, but as he kicked the mare up
through the growing crop the guns suddenly ceased and all
he could hear was the thump of hooves, the banging of the
sabre's metal scabbard against his boot and the dull sound
of the Scottish drums behind.

Orrock had turned north along the skyline and Sharpe,
following him, saw that the General and his aides were clustered under a group of trees from where they were gazing
westwards through their telescopes. He joined them in the
shade, and felt awkward to be in such exalted company without McCandless, but Campbell turned in his saddle and
grinned. 'Well done, Sergeant. Still with us, eh?'

'Managing, sir,' Sharpe said, rearranging the canteens that
had tangled themselves into a lump.

'Oh, dear God,' Colonel Orrock said a moment later. He
was gazing through his own telescope, and whatever he
saw made him shake his head before peering through the
glass again. 'Dear me,' he said, and Sharpe stood in his

stirrups to see what had so upset the East India Company Colonel.

The enemy was redeploying. Wellesley had crossed the ford to bring his small army onto the enemy's left flank, but the Mahratta commander had seen his purpose and was now denying him the advantage. The enemy line was marching towards the Peepulgaon ford, then wheeling left to make a new defence line that stretched clean across the land between the two rivers; a line that would now face head on towards Wellesley's army. Instead of attacking a vulnerable flank, Wellesley would be forced to make a head-on assault. Nor were the Mahrattas making their manoeuvre in a panicked hurry, but were marching calmly in disciplined ranks. The guns were moving with them, drawn by bullocks or elephants. The enemy was less than a mile away now and their steady unhurried redeployment was obvious to the watching officers.

'They anticipate us, sir!' Orrock informed Wellesley, as though the General might not have understood the purpose of the enemy's manoeuvre.

'They do,' Wellesley agreed calmly, 'they do indeed.' He collapsed his telescope and patted his horse's neck. 'And they manoeuvre very well!' he added admiringly, as though he was engaged in nothing more ominous than watching a brigade go through its paces in Hyde Park. 'Your men are through the ford?' he asked Orrock.

'They are, sir, they are,' Orrock said. The Colonel had a nervous habit of jutting his head forward every few seconds as if his collar was too tight. 'And they can reverse themselves,' he added meaningfully.

Wellesley ignored the defeatist sentiment. 'Take them one half-mile up the road,' he ordered Orrock, 'then deploy on the high ground this side of the road. I shall see you before we advance.'

Orrock gazed goggle-eyed at the General. 'Deploy?'

'On this side of the road, if you please, Colonel. You will form the right of our line, Colonel, and have Wallace's brigade on your left. Let us do it now, Colonel, if you would so oblige me?'

'Oblige you . . .' Orrock said, his head darting forward like a turtle. 'Of course,' he added nervously, then turned his horse and spurred it back towards the road.

'Barclay?' the General addressed one of his aides. 'My compliments to Colonel Maxwell and he will bring all Company and King's cavalry to take post to Orrock's right. Native horse will stay south of the river.' There was still enemy cavalry south of the Kaitna and the horsemen from Britain's Indian allies would stay on that bank to keep those enemies at bay. 'Then stay at the ford,' Wellesley went on addressing Barclay, 'and tell the rest of the infantry to form on Orrock's picquets. Two lines, Barclay, two lines, and the 78th will form the left flank here.' The General, who had been gazing at the enemy's calm redeployment, now turned to Barclay who was scribbling in pencil on a scrap of paper. 'First line, from the left. The 78th, Dallas's 10th, Corben's 8th, Orrock's picquets. Second line, from the left. Hill's 4th, Macleod's 12th, then the 74th. They are to form their lines and wait for my orders. You understand? They are to wait.' Barclay nodded, then tugged on his reins and spurred his horse back towards the ford as the General turned again to watch the enemy's redeployment. 'Very fine work,' he said approvingly. 'I doubt we could have manoeuvred any more smartly than that. You think they were readying to cross the river and attack us?'

Major Blackiston, his engineer aide, nodded. 'It would explain why they were ready to move, sir.'

'We shall just have to discover whether they fight as well as they manoeuvre,' Wellesley said, collapsing his telescope, then he sent Blackiston north to explore the ground up to the River Juah. 'Come on, Campbell,' Wellesley said when

Blackiston was gone and, to Sharpe's surprise, instead of riding back to where the army was crossing the ford, the General spurred his horse still further west towards the enemy. Campbell followed and Sharpe decided he had better go as well.

The three men rode into a steep-sided valley that was thick with trees and brush, then up its far side to another stretch of open farmland. They cantered through a field of unharvested millet, then across pastureland, always inclining north towards another low hill crest. 'I'll oblige you for a canteen, Sergeant,' Wellesley called as they neared the crest and Sharpe thumped his heels on the mare's flanks to catch up with the General, then fumbled a canteen free and held it out, but that meant taking his left hand off the reins while his right was still holding Diomed's tether and the mare, freed of the rein, swerved away from the General. Wellesley caught up with Sharpe and took the canteen. 'You might tie Diomed's rein to your belt, Sergeant,' he said. 'It will provide you with another hand.'

A man needed three hands to do Sharpe's job, but once they reached the low crest the General halted again and so gave Sharpe time to fasten the Arab's rein to Fletcher's belt. The General was staring at the enemy who was now only a quarter-mile away, well inside cannon shot, but either the enemy guns were not ready to fire or else they were under orders not to waste powder on a mere three horsemen. Sharpe took the opportunity to explore what was in Fletcher's pouch. There was a piece of mouldy bread that had been soaked when the trooper's body fell into the river, a piece of salted meat that Sharpe suspected was dried goat, and a sharpening stone. That made him half draw the sabre to feel its edge. It was keen.

'A nasty little settlement!' Wellesley said cheerfully.

'Aye, it is, sir!' Campbell agreed enthusiastically.

'That must be Assaye,' Wellesley remarked. 'You think we're about to make it famous?'

'I trust so, sir,' Campbell said.

'Not infamous, I hope,' Wellesley said, and gave his short, high-pitched laugh.

Sharpe saw they were both staring towards a village that lay to the north of the enemy's new line. Like every village in this part of India it was provided with a rampart made of the outermost houses' mud walls. Such walls could be five or six feet in thickness, and though they might crumble to the touch of an artillery bombardment, they still made a formidable obstacle to infantry. Enemy soldiers stood on every rooftop, while outside the wall, in an array as thick as a hedgehog's quills, was an assortment of cannon. 'A very nasty little place,' the General said. 'We must avoid it. I see your fellows are there, Sharpe!'

'My fellows, sir?' Sharpe asked in puzzlement.

'White coats, Sergeant.'

So Dodd's regiment had taken their place just to the south of Assaye. They were still on the left of Pohlmann's line, but now that line stretched southwards from the bristling defences about the village to the bank of the River Kaitna. The infantry were already in place and the last of the guns were now being hauled into their positions in front of the enemy line, and Sharpe remembered Syud Sevajee's grim words about the rivers meeting, and he knew that the only way out of this narrowing neck of land was either back through the fords or else straight ahead through the enemy's army. 'I see we shall have to earn our pay today,' the General said to no one in particular. 'How far ahead of the infantry is their gun line, Campbell?'

'A hundred yards, sir?' the young Scotsman guessed after gazing through his spyglass for a while.

'A hundred and fifty, I think,' Wellesley said.

Sharpe was watching the village. A lane led from its eastern wall and a file of cavalry was riding out from the houses towards some trees.

'They think to allow us to take the guns,' Wellesley guessed, 'reckoning we'll be so pounded by round shot and peppered by canister that their infantry can then administer the *coup de grâce*. They wish to treat us to a double dose! Guns and firelocks.'

The trees where the cavalry had disappeared dropped into a steep gully that twisted towards the higher ground from where Wellesley was observing the enemy. Sharpe, watching the tree-filled gully, saw birds fly out of the branches as the cavalry advanced beneath the thick leaves. 'Horsemen, sir,' Sharpe warned.

'Where, man, where?' Wellesley asked.

Sharpe pointed towards the gully. 'It's full of the bastards, sir. They came out of the village a couple of moments ago. You can't see them, sir, but I think there might be a hundred men hidden there.'

Wellesley did not dispute Sharpe. 'They want to put us in the bag,' he said in seeming amusement. 'Keep an eye out for them, Sharpe. I have no wish to watch the battle from the comfort of Scindia's tent.' He looked back to the enemy's line where the last of the heavy guns were being lugged into place. Those last two guns were the big eighteen-pounder siege guns that had done the damage as the British army crossed the ford, and now the huge pieces were being emplaced in front of Dodd's regiment. Elephants pulled the guns into position, then were led away towards the baggage park beyond the village. 'How many guns do you reckon, Campbell?' the General asked.

'Eighty-two, sir, not counting the ones by Assaye.'

'Around twenty there, I think. We shall be earning our pay! And their line's longer than I thought. We shall have to extend.' He was not so much speaking to Campbell as to himself, but now he glanced at the young Scots officer. 'Did you count their infantry?'

'Fifteen thousand in the line, sir?' Campbell hazarded.

'And at least as many again in the village,' Wellesley said, snapping his telescope shut, 'not to mention a horde of horsemen behind them, but they'll only count if we meet disaster. It's the fifteen thousand in front who concern us. Beat them and we beat all.' He made a pencilled note in a small black book, then stared again at the enemy line beneath its bright flags. 'They did manoeuvre well! A creditable performance. But do they fight, eh? That's the nub of it. Do they fight?'

'Sir!' Sharpe called urgently, for, not two hundred paces away, the first enemy horsemen had emerged from the gully with their *tulwars* and lances bright in the afternoon sun, and now were spurring towards Wellesley.

'Back the way we came,' the General said, 'and fairly briskly, I think.'

This was the second time in one day that Sharpe had been pursued by Mahratta cavalry, but the first time he had been mounted on a small native horse and now he was on one of the General's own chargers and the difference was night and day. The Mahrattas were at a full gallop, but Wellesley and his two companions never went above a canter and still their big horses easily outstripped the frantic pursuit. Sharpe, clinging for dear life to the mare's pommel, glanced behind after two minutes and saw the enemy horsemen pulling up. So that, he thought, was why officers were willing to pay a small fortune for British and Irish horses.

The three men dropped into the valley, climbed its farther side and Sharpe saw that the British infantry had now advanced from the road to form its line of attack along the low ridge that lay parallel to the road, and the redcoat array looked pitifully small compared to the great enemy host less than a mile to the west. Instead of a line of heavy guns, there was only a scatter of light six-pounder cannon and a single battery of fourteen bigger guns, and to face Pohlmann's three *compoos* of fifteen thousand men there were scarcely five thousand red-coated infantry, but Wellesley seemed unworried by the odds. Sharpe did not see how the battle was to be won, indeed he wondered why it was being fought at all, but whenever the doubt made his fears surge he only had to look at Wellesley and take comfort from the General's serene confidence.

Wellesley rode first to the left of his line where the kilted Highlanders of the 78th waited in line. 'You'll advance in a moment or two, Harness,' he told their Colonel. 'Straight ahead! I fancy you'll find bayonets will be useful. Tell your skirmishers that there are cavalry about, though I doubt you'll meet them at this end of the line.'

Harness appeared not to hear the General. He sat on a big horse as black as his towering bearskin hat and carried a huge claymore that looked as if it had been killing the enemies of Scotland for a century or more. 'It's the Sabbath, Wellesley,' he finally spoke, though without looking at the General. '"Remember the Sabbath day, to keep it holy. Six days shalt thou labour, and do all thy work, but the seventh is the Sabbath of the Lord thy God. In it thou shalt not do any work."' The Colonel glowered at Wellesley. 'Are you sure, man, that you want to fight today?'

'Quite sure, Colonel,' Wellesley answered very equably.

Harness grimaced. 'Won't be the first commandment I've broken, so to hell and away with it.' He gave his huge claymore a flourish. 'You'll not need to worry about my rogues, Wellesley, they can kill as well as any man, even if it is a Sunday.'

'I never doubted it.'

'Straight ahead, eh? And I'll lay the lash on any dog who falters. You hear that, you bastards! I'll flog you red!'

'I wish you joy of the afternoon, Colonel,' Wellesley said to Harness, then he rode north to speak with his other five battalion commanders. He gave them much the same instructions as he had given Colonel Harness, though because the Madrassi sepoys deployed no skirmishers, he simply warned them that they had one chance of victory and that was to march straight into the enemy fire and, by enduring it, carry their bayonets into the Mahratta ranks. He told the commanding officers of the two sepoy battalions in the second line that they would now need to join the front line. 'You'll incline right,' he told them, 'forming between Corben's 8th and Colonel Orrock's picquets.' He had hoped to attack in two lines, so that the men behind could reinforce those in front, but the enemy array was too wide and so he would need to throw every infantryman forward in one line. There would be no reserves. The General rode to meet Colonel Wallace who today would command a brigade of his own 74th Highlanders and two sepoy battalions which, with Orrock's picquets, would form the right side of the attacking force. He warned Wallace of the line's extension. 'I'll have Orrock incline right to give your sepoys room,' he promised Wallace, 'and I'm putting your own regiment on Orrock's right flank.' Wallace, because he was commanding the brigade, would not lead his own Highlanders who would be under the command of his deputy, Major Swinton. Colonel McCandless had joined his friend Wallace, and Wellesley greeted him. 'I see your man holds their left, McCandless.'

'So I've seen, sir.'

'But I don't wish to tangle with him early on. He's hard by the village and they've made it a stronghold, so we'll take the right of their line, then swing north and pin the rest against the Juah. You'll get your chance, McCandless, get your chance.'

'I'm depending on it, sir,' McCandless answered. The

Colonel nodded a mute greeting to Sharpe, who then had to follow Wellesley to the ranks of the 74th. 'You'll oblige me, Swinton,' Wellesley said, 'by doubling your fellows to the right and taking station beyond Colonel Orrock's picquets. You're to form the new right flank. I've told Colonel Orrock to move somewhat to his right, so you'll have a good way to go to make your new position. You understand?'

'Perfectly, sir,' Swinton said. 'Orrock will incline right and we double round behind him to form the new flank and sepoys replace us here.'

'Good man!' Wellesley said, then rode on to Colonel Orrock. Sharpe guessed that the General had ordered the 74th to move outside Orrock because he did not trust the nervous Colonel to hold the right flank. Orrock's contingent of half companies was a small but potent force, but it lacked the cohesion of the men's parent battalions. 'You're to lead them rightwards,' Wellesley told the red-faced Colonel, 'but not too far. You comprehend? Not too far right! Because you'll find a defended village on your front right flank and it's a brute. I don't want any of our men near it until we've sent the enemy infantry packing.'

'I go right?' Orrock asked.

'You incline right,' Wellesley said, 'then straighten up. Two hundred paces should do it. Incline right, Orrock, give the line two hundred paces more width, then straighten and march straight for the enemy. Swinton will be bringing his men onto your right flank. Don't wait for him, let him catch you, and don't hesitate when we attack. Just go straight in with the bayonet.'

Orrock jutted his head, scratched his chin and blinked. 'I go rightwards?'

'Then straight ahead,' Wellesley said patiently.

'Yes, sir,' Orrock said, then jerked nervously as one of his small six-pounder cannon, which had been deployed fifty yards in front of his line, fired.

'What the devil?' Wellesley asked, turning to look at the small gun that had leaped back five or six yards. He could not see what the gun had fired at, for the smoke of the discharge made a thick cloud in front of the muzzle, but a second later an enemy round shot screamed through the smoke, twitching it, to bounce between two of Orrock's half companies. Wellesley cantered to his left to see that the enemy guns had opened fire. For the moment they were merely sending ranging shots, but soon the guns would be pouring their metal at the red ranks.

The General cantered back southwards. It was close to mid afternoon now and the sun was burning the world white. The air was humid, hard to breathe, and every man in the British line was sweating. The enemy round shot bounced on the ground in front of them, and one shot ricocheted up to churn a file of sepoys into blood and bone. The sound of the enemy cannon was harsh, banging over the warm ground in successive punches that came closer and closer together as more guns joined the cannonade. The British guns replied, and the smoke of their discharges betrayed their positions, and the enemy gunners levered their pieces to aim at the British cannon which, hugely outnumbered, were having by far the worst of the exchange. Sharpe saw the earth around one six-pounder struck again and again by enemy round shot, each strike kicking up a barrow-load of soil, and then the small gun seemed to disintegrate as a heavy ball struck it plumb on the front of its carriage. Splinters flew to eviscerate the crew that had been ramming the gun. The barrel reared up, its trunnions tearing out of the carriage, then the heavy metal tube slowly toppled onto a wounded man. Another gunner reeled away, gasping for breath, while a third lay on the ground looking as though he slept.

A piper began to play as the General neared the kilted 78th. 'I thought I ordered all musicians to leave their instruments behind, drummers excepted,' Wellesley said angrily.

'Very hard to go into battle without the pipes, sir,' Campbell said reprovingly.

'Hard to save the wounded without orderlies,' Wellesley complained. In battle the pipers' job was to save the wounded, but Harness had blithely disobeyed the order and brought his bagpipers. However, it was too late to worry about that disobedience now. Another round shot found its mark in a sepoy battalion, flinging men aside like broken dolls, while a high ball struck a tall tree, shaking its topmost leaves and provoking a small green parrot to squawk as it fled the branches.

Wellesley reined in close to the 78th. He glanced to his right, then looked back to the eight or nine hundred yards of country that separated his small force from the enemy. The sound of the guns was constant now, its thunder deafening, and the smoke of their cannonade was hiding the Mahratta infantry that waited for his assault. If the General was nervous he showed no sign of it, unless the fingers drumming softly against his thigh betrayed some worry. This was his first proper battle in the field, gun against gun and infantry against infantry, yet he seemed entirely cool.

Sharpe licked dry lips. His mare fidgeted and Diomed kept pricking his ears at the gunfire. Another British gun was hit, this time losing a wheel to an enemy round shot. The gunners rolled a new wheel forward, while the officer commanding the small battery ran forward with a handspike. The infantry waited beneath their bright silk colours, their long line of two ranks tipped with shining bayonets.

'Time to go,' Wellesley said very quietly. 'Forward, gentlemen,' he said, but still not loudly. He took a breath. 'Forward!'

he shouted and, at the same time, took off his cocked hat and waved it towards the enemy.

The British drums began their beat. Sergeants shouted. Officers drew swords. The men began to march.

And the battle had begun.

CHAPTER 10

The redcoats advanced in a line of two ranks. The troops spread out as they walked and sergeants shouted at the files to keep closed. The infantry first had to pass the British gun line that was suffering badly in an unequal artillery duel with the Goanese gunners. The enemy was firing shell as well as solid shot, and Sharpe flinched as a shell exploded among a team of oxen that was picketed a hundred yards behind their gun. The wounded beasts bellowed, and one broke from its picket to limp with a bleeding and trailing leg towards the 10th Madras infantry. A British officer ran and put the beast out of its misery with his pistol and the sepoys stepped delicately about the shuddering corpse. Colonel Harness, seeing that his two small battalion guns would inevitably be destroyed if they stayed in action, ordered his gunners to limber up and follow the regiment forward. 'Do it fast, you rogues! I want you close behind me.'

The enemy gunners, seeing that they had won the fight between the batteries, turned their pieces on the infantry. They were firing at seven hundred yards now, much too far for canister, but a round shot could whip a file into bloody scraps in the blinking of an eye. The sound of the guns was unending, one shot melding into the next and the whole making a thunderous noise of deafening violence. The enemy line was shrouded in grey-white smoke which was constantly lit by flashes of gunfire deep in the smoke's heart. Sometimes a Mahratta battery would pause to let the smoke thin and Sharpe, riding twenty paces behind the General who was advancing just to the right of the 78th, could watch the enemy gunners heave at their pieces, see them back away as the gun captain swung the linstock over the barrel, then the gun would disappear again in a cloud of powder smoke and, an instant later, a ball would plunge down in front of the infantry. Sometimes it would bounce clean over the men's heads, but too often the heavy shots slammed into the files and men would be broken apart in a spray of blood. Sharpe saw the front half of a shattered musket wheel up out of the Highlanders' ranks. It turned in the air, pursued by its owner's blood, then fell to impale its bayonet into the turf. A gentle north wind blew a patch of gunsmoke away from the centre of the enemy line where the guns were almost axle boss to axle boss. Sharpe watched men ram the barrels, watched them run clear, watched the smoke blossom again and heard the shriek of a round shot just overhead. Sometimes Sharpe could see the tongue of dark-red fire streaking towards him in the cloud's heart, and then the lead-grey stroke of a ball arcing towards him in the sky, and once he saw the madly spiralling wisp of smoke left by the burning fuse of a shell, but every time the shots went wide or else fell short to churn up a dusty patch of earth.

'Close the files!' the sergeants shouted. 'Close up!'

The drummer boys beat the advance. There was low ground ahead, and the sooner the attacking line was in that gentle valley, the sooner they would be out of sight of the gunners. Wellesley looked to his right and saw that Orrock had paused in his advance and that the 74th, who should have been forming to the right of Orrock's men, had stopped as well. 'Tell Orrock to go! Tell him to go!' the General called to Campbell who spurred across the advancing line. His horse galloped through a cloud of shell smoke, leaped a broken limber, then Sharpe lost sight of the aide. Wellesley urged his horse closer to the 78th who were now drawing ahead of the sepoys. The Highlanders were taller than the Madrassi battalions and their stride was longer as they hurried to gain the dead ground where the bombardment could not reach them. A bouncing shell came to rest near the grenadier company that was on the right of the 78th's line and the kilted soldiers skipped aside, all but for one man who dashed out of the front rank as the missile spun crazily on the ground with its fuse spitting out a tangle of smoke. He rammed his right boot on the shell to make it still, then struck hard down with the brass butt of his musket to knock the fuse free. 'Am I spared the punishment now, Sergeant?' he called.

'You get in file, John, get in file,' the sergeant answered.

Wellesley grinned, then shuddered as a ball went perilously close to his hat. He looked round, seeking his aides, and saw Barclay. 'The calm before the storm,' the General remarked.

'Some calm, sir.'

'Some storm,' an Indian answered. He was one of the Mahratta chiefs who were allied to the British and whose horsemen were keeping the cavalry busy south of the river. Three such men rode with Wellesley and one had a badly trained horse that kept skittering sideways whenever a shell exploded.

Major Blackiston, the engineer on Wellesley's staff who had been sent to reconnoitre the land north of the army, now galloped back behind the advancing line. 'Broken ground up by the village, sir, cut by gullies,' he reported, 'no place to advance.'

Wellesley grunted. He had no intention of sending infantry near the village yet, so Blackiston's report was not immediately useful. 'Did you see Orrock?'

'He was worried about his two guns, sir. Can't take them forward because the teams have all been killed, but Campbell's chivvying him on.'

Wellesley stood in his stirrups to look north and saw Orrock's picquets at last moving smartly away. They were marching obliquely, without their two small guns, making space for the two sepoy battalions to come into the line. The 74th was beyond them, vanishing into a fold of ground. 'Not too far, Orrock, not too far,' Wellesley muttered, then he lost sight of Orrock's men as his horse followed the 78th into the lower ground. 'Once we have them pinned against the river,' he asked Blackiston, gesturing to show he meant the River Juah to the north, 'can they get away?'

'Eminently fordable, sir, I'm afraid,' Blackiston answered. 'I doubt they can move more than a handful of the guns down the bank, but a man can escape easily enough.'

Wellesley grunted an acknowledgement and spurred ahead, leaving the engineer behind. 'He didn't even ask if I was chased!' Blackiston said to Barclay with mock indignation.

'Were you, John?'

'Damned sure I was. Two dozen of the bastards on those wiry little ponies. They look like children riding to hounds.'

'But no bullet holes?' Barclay asked.

'Not a one,' Blackiston said regretfully, then saw Sharpe's surprised look. 'It's a wager, Sergeant,' the engineer explained. 'Whichever of the General's family ends up with the most bullet holes wins the pot.'

'Do I count, sir?'

'You replace Fletcher, and he didn't have to pay to get in because he claimed he was penniless. We admitted him from the goodness of our hearts. But no cheating now. We can't have fellows poking their coats with swords to win points.'

'How many points does Fletcher get, sir?' Sharpe asked. 'For having his head blown off?'

'He's disqualified, of course, on grounds of extreme carelessness.'

Sharpe laughed. Blackiston's words were not funny, of

course, but the laughter burst out of him, causing Wellesley to turn in his saddle and give him a scowl. In truth Sharpe was fighting a growing fear. For the moment he was safe enough, for the left flank of the attack was now in dead ground and the enemy bombardment was concentrating on the sepoy battalions who had still not reached the valley, but Sharpe could hear the whip-fast rumble of the round shots tearing up the air, he could hear the cannon fire, and every few seconds a howitzer shell would fall into the valley and explode in a puff of flaming smoke. So far the howitzers had failed to do any damage, but Sharpe could see the small bushes bend away from their blasts and hear the scraps of shell casing rip through leaves. In places the dry brush had caught fire.

He tried to concentrate on the small things. One of the canteens had a broken strap, so he knotted it. He watched his mare's ears flicker at every shell burst and he wondered if horses felt fear. Did they understand this kind of danger? He watched the Scots, stolidly advancing through the shrubs and trees, magnificent in their feathered bearskin hats and their pleated kilts. They were a long way from bloody home, he thought, and was surprised that he did not really feel that for himself, but he did not know where home was. Not London, for sure, though he had grown up there. England? He supposed so, but what was England to him? Not what it was to Major Blackiston, he guessed. He wondered again about Pohlmann's offer, and thought what it would be like to be standing in sash and sword behind that line of Mahratta guns. Safe as houses, he reckoned, just standing there and watching through the smoke as a thin line of redcoat enemies marched into horror. So why had he not accepted? And he knew the real reason was not some half-felt love of country, nor an aversion to Dodd, but because the only sash and sword he wanted were the ones that would let him go back to

England and spit on the men who had made his life miserable. Except there would be no sash and sword. Sergeants did not get made into officers, not often, and he was suddenly ashamed of ever having quizzed McCandless about the matter. But at least the Colonel had not laughed at him.

Wellesley had turned to speak to Colonel Harness. 'We'll give the guns a volley of musketry, Harness, at your discretion. That should give us time to reload, but save the second volley for their infantry.'

'I'd already worked out the same for myself,' Harness answered with a scowl. 'And I'll not use skirmishers, not on a Sunday.' Usually the light company went ahead of the rest of the battalion and scattered into a loose line that would fire at the enemy before the main attack arrived, but Harness must have decided that he would rather reserve the light company's fire for the one volley he planned to unload on the gunners.

'Soon be over,' Wellesley said, not contesting Harness's decision to keep his light company in line, and Sharpe decided the General must be nervous, for those last three words were unusually loquacious. Wellesley himself must have decided he had betrayed his feelings, for he looked blacker than ever. His high spirits had vanished ever since the enemy artillery had started firing.

The Scots were climbing now. They were tramping through stubble and at any minute they would cross the brow of the gentle hill and find themselves back in the gunners' sights. The first the gunners would see would be the two regimental standards, then the officers on horseback, then the line of bearskins, and after that the whole red, white and black array of a battalion in line with the glint of their fixed bayonets showing in the sun. And God help us then, Sharpe thought, because every buggering gun straight ahead must be reloaded by now and just waiting for its target, and suddenly the first round shot banged on the crest just a few paces ahead and ricocheted harmlessly overhead. 'That man fired early,' Barclay said. 'Take his name.'

Sharpe looked to his right. The next four battalions, all sepoys, were safe in the dead ground now, while Orrock's picquets and the 74th had vanished among the trees north of the valley. Harness's Scots would climb into view first and, for a moment or two, would have the gunners' undivided attention. Some of the Highlanders were hurrying, as if to get the ordeal over. 'Hold your dressing!' Harness bellowed at them. 'This ain't a race to the tavern! Damn you!'

Elsie. Sharpe suddenly remembered the name of a girl who had worked in the tavern near Wetherby where he had fled after running away from Brewhouse Lane. Why had he thought of her, he wondered, and he had a sudden vision of the taproom, all steaming on a winter night from men's wet coats, and Elsie and the other girls carrying the ale on trays and the fire sputtering in the hearth and the blind shepherd getting drunk and the dogs sleeping under the tables, and he imagined walking back into that smoke-blackened room with his officer's sash and sword, and then he forgot all about Yorkshire as the 78th, with Wellesley's family on its right, emerged onto the flat land in front of the enemy guns.

Sharpe's first surprised reaction was how close they were. The low ground had brought them within a hundred and fifty paces of the enemy guns, and his second reaction was how splendid the enemy looked, for their guns were lined up as though for inspection, while behind them the Mahratta battalions stood in four closely dressed ranks beneath their flags, and then he thought that this was what death must look like, and just as he thought that, so the whole gorgeous array of the enemy army vanished behind a vast bank of smoke, a roiling bank in which the smoke twisted as though it was tortured, and every few yards there was a spear of flame in the whiteness, while in front of the cloud the crops flattened away from the blast of the exploding powder as the heavy round shots tore through the Highlanders' files.

There seemed to be blood everywhere, and broken men falling or sliding in the carnage. Somewhere a man gasped, but no one was screaming. A piper dropped his instrument and ran to a fallen man whose leg had been torn away. Every few yards there was a tangle of dead and dying men, showing where the round shot had snatched files from the regiment. A young officer tried to calm his horse which was edging sideways in fright, its eyes white and head tossing. Colonel Harness guided his own horse round a disembowelled man without giving the dead man a glance. Sergeants shouted angrily for the files to close up, as though it was the Highlanders' fault that there were gaps in the line. Then everything seemed oddly silent. Wellesley turned and spoke to Barclay, but Sharpe did not hear a thing, then he realized that his ears were ringing from the terrible sound of that discharge of gunnery. Diomed pulled away from him and he tugged the grey horse back. Fletcher's blood had dried to a crust on Diomed's flank. Flies crawled all over the blood. A Highlander was swearing terribly as his comrades marched away from him. He was on his hands and knees, with no obvious wound, but then he looked up at Sharpe, spoke one last obscenity and collapsed forward. More flies congregated on the shining blue spill of the disembowelled man's guts. Another man crawled through stubble, dragging his musket by its whitened sling.

'Steady now!' Harness shouted. 'Damn your haste! Ain't running a race! Think of your mothers!'

'Mothers?' Blackiston asked.

'Close up!' a sergeant shouted. 'Close up!'

The Mahratta gunners would be frantically reloading, but this time with canister. The gunsmoke was dissipating, twisting as the small breeze carried it away, and Sharpe could see the misty shapes of men ramming barrels and carrying charges to muzzles. Other men handspiked gun trails to line the recoiled weapons on the Scots. Wellesley was curbing his stallion lest it get too far ahead of the Highlanders. Nothing showed on the right. The sepoys were still in dead ground and the right flank was lost among the scatter of trees and broken ground to the north, so that for the moment it seemed as if Harness's Highlanders were fighting the battle all on their own, six hundred men against a hundred thousand, but the Scotsmen did not falter. They just left their wounded and dead behind and crossed the open land towards the guns that were loaded with their deaths. The piper began playing again, and the wild music seemed to put a new spring in the High-landers' steps. They were walking to death, but they went in perfect order and in seeming calm. No wonder men made songs about the Scots, Sharpe thought, then turned as hooves sounded behind and he saw it was Captain Campbell returning from his errand. The Captain grinned at Sharpe. 'I thought I'd be too late.'

'You're in time, sir. Just in time, sir,' Sharpe said, but for what? he wondered.

Campbell rode on to Wellesley to make his report. The General listened, nodded, then the guns straight ahead started firing again, only raggedly this time as each enemy gun fired as soon as it was loaded. The sound of each gun was a terrible bang, as deafening as a thump on the ear, and the canister flecked the field in front of the Scots with a myriad puffs of dust before bouncing up to snatch men backwards. Each round was a metal canister, crammed with musket balls or shards of metal and scraps of stone, and as it left the barrel the canister was ripped apart to spread its missiles like a giant blast of duckshot.

Another cannon fired, then another, each gunshot pummelling the land and each taking its share of Scotsmen to eternity, or else making another cripple for the parish or a sufferer for the surgeon. The drummer boys were still playing, though one was limping and another was dripping blood onto his drumskin. The piper began playing a jauntier tune, as though this walk into an enemy horde was something to celebrate, and some of the Highlanders quickened their pace. 'Not so eager!' Harness shouted. 'Not so eager!' His basket-hilted claymore was in his hand and he was close behind his men's two ranks as though he wanted to spur through and carry the dreadful blade against the gunners who were flaying his regiment. A bearskin was blown apart by canister, leaving the man beneath untouched.

'Steady now!' a major called.

'Close up! Close up!' the sergeants shouted. 'Close the files!' Corporals, designated as file-closers, hurried behind the ranks and dragged men left and right to seal the gaps blown by the guns. The gaps were bigger now, for a well-aimed barrel of canister could take four or five files down, while a round shot could only blast away a single file at a time.

Four guns fired, a fifth, then a whole succession of guns exploded together and the air around Sharpe seemed to be filled with a rushing, shrieking wind, and the Highlanders' line seemed to twist in that violent gale, but though it left men behind, men who were bleeding and vomiting and crying and calling for their comrades or their mothers, the others closed their ranks and marched stolidly on. More guns fired, blanketing the enemy with smoke, and Sharpe could hear the canister hitting the regiment. Each blast brought a rattling sound as bullets struck muskets, while the Highlanders, like infantry everywhere, made sure their guns' wide stocks covered their groins. The line was shorter now, much shorter, and it had almost reached the lingering edge of the great bank of smoke pumped out by the enemy's guns.

303

'78th,' Harness shouted in a huge voice, 'halt!'

Wellesley curbed his horse. Sharpe looked to his right and saw the sepoys coming out of the valley in one long red line, a broken line, for there were gaps between the battalions and the passage through the shrub-choked valley had skewed the sepoys' dressing, and then the guns in the northern part of the Mahratta line opened fire and the line of sepoys became even more ragged. Yet still, like the Scots to their left, they pressed on into the gunfire.

'Present!' Harness shouted, a note of anticipation in his voice.

The Scotsmen brought their firelocks to their shoulders. They were only sixty yards from the guns and even a smoothbore musket was accurate enough at that range. 'Don't fire high, you dogs!' Harness warned them. 'I'll flog every man who fires high. Fire!'

The volley sounded feeble compared to the thunder of the big guns, but it was a comfort all the same and Sharpe almost cheered as the Highlanders fired and their crackling volley whipped away across the stubble. The gunners were vanishing. Some must have been killed, but others were merely sheltering behind the big trails of their cannon.

'Reload!' Harness shouted. 'No dallying! Reload!'

This was where the Highlanders' training paid its dividends, for a musket was an awkward brute to reload, and made more cumbersome still by the seventeen-inch bayonet fixed to its muzzle. The triangular blade made it difficult to ram the gun properly, and some of the Highlanders twisted the blades off to make their job easier, but all reloaded swiftly, just as they had been trained to do in hard long weeks at home. They loaded, rammed, primed, then slotted the ramrods back into the barrel hoops. Those who had removed their bayonets refastened them to the lugs, then brought the guns back to the ready.

'You save that volley for the infantry!' Harness warned

them. 'Now, boys, forward, and give the heathen bastards a proper Sabbath killing!'

This was revenge. This was anger let loose. The enemy guns were still not loaded and their crews had been hard hit by the volley, and most of the guns would not have time to charge their barrels before the Scots were on them. Some of the gunners fled. Sharpe saw a mounted Mahratta officer rounding them up and driving them back to their pieces with the flat of his sword, but he also saw one gun, a painted monster directly to his front, being rammed hard by two men who heaved on the rammer, plucked it free then ran aside.

'For what we are about to receive,' Blackiston murmured. The engineer had also seen the gunners charge their barrel.

The gun fired, and its jet of smoke almost engulfed the General's family. For an instant Sharpe saw Wellesley's tall figure outlined against the pale smoke, then he could see nothing but blood and the General falling. The heat and discharge of the gun's gasses rushed past Sharpe just a heart-beat after the scraps of canister had filled the air about him, but he had been directly behind the General and was in his shadow, and it was Wellesley who had taken the gun's blast.

Or rather it was his horse. The stallion had been struck a dozen times while Wellesley, charmed, had not taken a scratch. The big horse toppled, dead before he struck the ground, and Sharpe saw the General kick his feet out from the stirrups and use his hands to push himself up from the saddle as the horse collapsed. Wellesley's right foot touched the ground first and, before the stallion's weight could roll onto his leg, he jumped away, staggering slightly in his hurry. Campbell turned towards him, but the General waved him away. Sharpe kicked the mare on and untied Diomed's reins from his belt. Was he supposed to get the saddle off the dead horse? He supposed so, and thus slid out of his own saddle. But what the hell was he to do with the mare and Diomed while he untangled the saddle from the dead stallion? Then he thought to tie both to the dead horse's bridle.

'Four hundred guineas gone to a penny bullet,' Wellesley said sarcastically, watching as Sharpe unbuckled the girth from the dead stallion. Or near dead, for the beast still twitched and kicked as the flies came to feast on its new blood. 'I'll take Diomed,' Wellesley told Sharpe, then stooped to help, tugging the saddle with its attached bags and holsters free of the dying horse, but then a feral scream made the General turn back to watch as Harness's men charged into the gun line. The scream was the noise they made as they struck home, a scream that was the release of all their fears and a terrible noise presaging their enemies' death. And how they gave it. The Scotsmen found the gunners who had stayed at their posts crouching under the trails and they dragged them out and bayoneted them again and again. 'Bastard,' one man screamed, plunging his blade repeatedly into a dead gunner's belly. 'Heathen black bastard!' He kicked the man's head, then stabbed down with his bayonet again. Colonel Harness backswung his sword to kill a man, then casually wiped the blood off the blade onto his horse's black mane. 'Form line!' he shouted. 'Form line! Hurry, you rogues!'

A scatter of gunners had fled back from the Scots to the safety of the Mahratta infantry who were now little more than a hundred paces away. They should have charged, Sharpe thought. While the Scots were blindly hacking away at the gunners, the infantry should have advanced, but instead they waited for the next stage of the Scots attack. To his right there were still guns firing at the sepoys, but that was a separate battle, unrelated to the scramble as sergeants dragged Highlanders away from the dead and dying gunners and pushed them into their ranks.

'There are still gunners alive, sir!' a lieutenant shouted at Harness.

'Form up!' Harness shouted, ignoring the lieutenant. Sergeants and corporals shoved men into line. 'Forward!' Harness shouted.

'Hurry, man,' Wellesley said to Sharpe, but not angrily. Sharpe had heaved the saddle over Diomed's back and now stooped under the grey horse's belly to gather the girth. 'He doesn't like it too tight,' the General said.

Sharpe buckled the strap and Wellesley took Diomed's reins from him and heaved himself up into the saddle without another word. The General's coat was smeared with blood, but it was horse blood, not his own. 'Well done, Harness!' he called ahead to the Scotsman, then rode away and Sharpe unhitched the mare from the dead horse's bridle, clambered onto her back and followed.

Three pipers played for the 78th now. They were far from home, under a furnace sun in a blinding sky, and they brought the mad music of Scotland's wars to India. And it was madness. The 78th had suffered hard from the gunfire and the line of their advance was littered with dead, dying and broken men, yet the survivors now re-formed to attack the main Mahratta battle line. They were back in two ranks, they held their bloody bayonets in front, and they advanced against Pohlmann's own *compoo* on the right of the enemy line. The Highlanders looked huge, made into giants by their tall bearskin hats with their feather plumes, and they looked terrible, for they were. These were northern warriors from a hard country and not a man spoke as they advanced. To the waiting Mahrattas they must have seemed like creatures from nightmare, as terrible as the gods who writhed on their temple walls. Yet the Mahratta infantry in their blue and yellow coats were just as proud. They were warriors recruited from the martial tribes of northern India, and now they levelled their muskets as the two Scottish ranks approached.

The Scots were terribly outnumbered and it seemed to

Sharpe that they must all die in the coming volley. Sharpe himself was in a half-daze, stunned by the noise yet aware that his mood was swinging between elation at the Scottish bravery and the pure terror of battle. He heard a cheer and looked right to see the sepoys charging into the guns. He watched gunners flee, then saw the Madrassi sepoys tear into the laggards with their bayonets.

'Now we'll see how their infantry fights,' Wellesley said savagely to Campbell, and Sharpe understood that this was the real testing point, for infantry was everything. The infantry was despised for it did not have the cavalry's glamour, nor the killing capacity of the gunners, but it was still the infantry that won battles. Defeat the enemy's infantry and the cavalry and gunners had nowhere to hide.

The Mahrattas waited with levelled muskets. The Highlanders, silent again, marched on. Ninety paces to go, eighty, and then an officer's sword swung down in the Mahratta ranks and the volley came. It seemed ragged to Sharpe, maybe because most men did not fire on the word of command, but instead fired after they heard their neighbour's discharge, and he was not even aware of a bullet going close past his head because he was watching the Scots, terrified for them, but it seemed to him that not a man fell. Some men must have been hit, for he saw ripples where the files opened to step past the fallen, but the 78th, or what was left of the 78th, was intact still and still Harness did not fire, but just kept marching them onward.

'They fired high!' Campbell exulted.

'They drill well, fire badly,' Barclay observed happily.

Seventy paces to go, then sixty. A Highlander staggered from the line and collapsed. Two other men who had been wounded by the canister, but were now recovered, hurried from the rear and pushed their way into the ranks. 'Halt!' Harness suddenly called. 'Present!'

The guns, tipped by their bloodstained steel blades, came up into the Highlanders' shoulders so that the whole line seemed to take a quarter-turn to the right. The Mahratta gunsmoke was clearing and the enemy soldiers could see the Scots' heavy muskets, with hate behind them, and the Highlanders waited a heartbeat so the enemy could also see their death in the levelled muskets.

'You'll fire low, you bastards, or I'll want to know why,' Harness growled, then took a deep breath. 'Fire!' he shouted, and his Highlanders did not fire high. They fired low and their heavy balls ripped into bellies and thighs and groins.

'Now go for them!' Harness shouted. 'Just go for the bastards!' And the Highlanders, unleashed, ran forward with their bayonets and began to utter their shrill war cries, as discordant as the music of the pipes that flayed them onwards. They were killers loosed to the joys of slaughter and the enemy did not wait for its coming, but just turned and fled.

The enemy in the rearward ranks of the *compoo* had room to run, but those in front were impeded by those behind and could not escape. A terrible despairing wail sounded as the 78th struck home and as their bayonets rose and fell in an orgy of killing. An officer led an attack on a knot of standard-bearers who tried desperately to save their flags, but the Scots would not be denied and Sharpe watched as the kilted men stepped over the dead to lunge their blades at the living. The flags fell, then were raised again in Scottish hands. A cheer went up, and just then Sharpe heard another cheer and saw the sepoys charging home at the next section of the enemy line and, just as the first Mahratta troops had run from the Scots, so now the neighbouring battalions fled from the sepoys. The enemy's vaunted infantry had crumpled at the first contact. They had watched the thin line come towards them, and they must have assumed that the red coats would be turned even redder by the heavy fire of the artillery, but the line had taken the guns' punishment and just kept coming, battered and bleeding, and it must have seemed to the Mahrattas that such men were invincible. The huge Scots in their strange kilts had started the rout, but the sepoy battalions from Madras now set about the destruction of all the enemy's centre and right. Only his left still stood its ground.

The sepoys killed, then pursued the fugitives who streamed westwards. 'Hold them!' Wellesley shouted at the nearest battalion commanders. 'Hold them!' But the sepoys would not be held. They wanted to pursue a beaten enemy and they streamed raggedly in his wake, killing as they went. Wellesley wheeled Diomed. 'Colonel Harness!'

'You'll want me to form post here?' the Scotsman asked. Blood dripped from his sword.

'Here,' Wellesley agreed. The enemy infantry might have fled, but there was a maelstrom of cavalry a half-mile away and those horsemen were cantering forward to attack the disordered British pursuers. 'Deploy your guns, Harness.'

'I've given the order already,' Harness said, gesturing towards his two small gun teams that were hurrying six-pounders into position. 'Column of full companies!' Harness shouted. 'Quarter distance!'

The Scots, one minute so savage, now ran back into their ranks and files. The battalion faced no immediate enemy, for there was neither infantry nor artillery within range, but the distant cavalry was a threat and so Harness arranged them in their ten companies, close together, so that they resembled a square. The close formation could defend itself against any cavalry attack, and just as easily shake itself into a line or into a column of assault. Harness's twin six-pounders were unlimbered and now began firing towards the horsemen who, appalled by the wreckage of their infantry, paused rather than attack the redcoats. British and Indian officers were galloping among the pursuing sepoys, ordering them back to their ranks, while Harness's 78th stood like a fortress to which the sepoys could retreat. 'So sanity is not a requisite of soldiering,' Wellesley said quietly.

'Sir?' Sharpe was the only man close enough to hear the General and assumed that the words were addressed to him.

'None of your business, Sharpe, none of your business,' Wellesley said, startled that he had been overheard. 'A canteen, if you please.'

It had been a good start, the General decided, for the right of Pohlmann's army had been destroyed and that destruction had taken only minutes. He watched as the sepoys hurried back to their ranks and as the first *puckalees* appeared from the nearby Kaitna with their huge loads of canteens and waterskins. He would let the men have their drink of water, then the line would be turned to face north and he could finish the job by assaulting Assaye. The General kicked Diomed around to examine the ground over which his infantry must advance and, just as he turned, so all hell erupted at the village.

Wellesley frowned at the dense cloud of gunsmoke that had suddenly appeared close to the mud walls. He heard volley fire, and he could see that it was the surviving Mahratta left wing that did the firing, not his redcoats, and, more ominously, a surge of Mahratta cavalry had broken through on the northern flank and was now riding free in the country behind Wellesley's small army.

Someone had blundered.

The left flank of William Dodd's regiment lay just a hundred paces from the mud walls of Assaye where the twenty guns which defended the village gave that flank an added measure of safety. In front of the Cobras were another six guns, two of them the long-barrelled eighteen-pounders that had bombarded the ford, while Dodd's own small battery of four-pounder guns was bunched in the small gap between his men's right flank and the neighbouring regiment. Pohlmann had chosen to array his guns in front of the infantry, but Dodd expected the British to attack in line and a gun firing straight towards an oncoming line could do much less damage than a gun firing obliquely down the line's length, and so he had placed his cannon wide on the flank where they could work the most havoc.

It was not a bad position, Dodd reckoned. In front of his line were two hundred yards of open killing ground after which the land fell into a steepish gully that angled away eastwards. An enemy could approach in the gully, but to reach Dodd's men they would have to climb onto the flat farmland and there be slaughtered. A cactus-thorn hedge ran across the killing ground, and that would give the enemy some cover, but there were wide gaps in the thorns. If Dodd had been given time he would have sent men to cut down the whole hedge, but the necessary axes were back with the baggage a mile away. Dodd, naturally, blamed Joubert for the missing tools. 'Why are they not here, Monsewer?' he had demanded.

'I did not think. I'm sorry.'

'Sorry! Sorry don't win battles, Monsewer.'

'I shall send for the axes,' Joubert said.

'Not now,' Dodd said. He did not want to send any men back to the baggage camp, for their loss would momentarily weaken his regiment and he expected to be attacked at any moment. He looked forward to that moment, for the enemy would need to expose himself to a withering fire, and Dodd kept standing in his stirrups to search for any sign of an approaching enemy. There were some British and Company cavalry far off to the east, but those horsemen were staying well out of range of the Mahratta guns. Other enemies must have been within the range of Pohlmann's guns, for Dodd could hear them firing and see the billowing clouds of grey-white smoke pumped out by each shot, but that cannonade was well to his south and it did not spread down the line towards him and it slowly dawned on Dodd that Wellesley was deliberately avoiding Assaye. 'God damn him!' he shouted aloud.

'Monsieur?' Captain Joubert asked resignedly, expecting another reprimand.

'We're going to be left out,' Dodd complained.

Captain Joubert thought that was probably a blessing. The Captain had been saving his meagre salary in the hope of retiring to Lyons, and if General Wellesley chose to ignore Captain Joubert then Captain Joubert was entirely happy. And the longer he stayed in India, the more attractive he found Lyons. And Simone would be better off in France, he thought, for the heat of India was not good for her. It had made her restless, and inactivity gave her time to brood and no good ever came from a thinking woman. If Simone was in France she would be kept busy. There would be meals to cook, clothes to mend, a garden to tend, even children to raise. Those things were women's work, in Joubert's opinion, and the sooner he could take his Simone away from India's languorous temptations the better.

Dodd stood in his stirrups again to stare southwards through his cheap glass. 'The 78th,' he grunted.

'Monsieur?' Joubert was startled from his happy reverie about a house near Lyons where his mother could help Simone raise a busy little herd of children.

'The 78th,' Dodd said again, and Joubert stood in his stirrups to gaze at the distant sight of the Scottish regiment emerging from low ground to advance against the Mahratta line. 'And no support for them?' Dodd asked, puzzled, and he had begun to think that Boy Wellesley had blundered very badly, but just then he saw the sepoys coming from the valley.

The attacking line looked very thin and frail, and he could see men being snatched backwards by the artillery fire. 'Why won't they come here?' he asked petulantly.

'They are, Monsieur,' Joubert answered, and pointed eastwards.

Dodd turned and stared. 'Praise God from Whom all blessings flow,' he said softly. 'The fools!' For the enemy was not just coming towards Dodd's position, but approaching in a column of half companies. The enemy infantry had suddenly appeared at the upper edge of the gully, but on Dodd's side of that obstacle, and it was clear that the redcoats must have wandered far out of their position for they were a long way from the rest of the attacking British infantry. Better still, they had not deployed into line. Their commander must have decided that they would make better progress if they advanced in column and doubtless he planned to deploy into line when he launched his attack, but the men showed no sign of deploying yet.

Dodd aimed his telescope and was momentarily puzzled. The leading half company were King's troops in red jackets, black shakoes and white trousers, while the forty or fifty men of the half company behind were in kilts, but the other five half companies were all sepoys of the East India Company. 'It's the picquets of the day,' he said, suddenly understanding the strange formation. He heard a shout as a gun captain ordered his cannon to be levered around to take aim at the approaching men, and he hurriedly shouted to his gunners to hold their fire. 'No one's to fire yet, Joubert,' Dodd ordered, then he spurred his horse northwards to the village.

The infantry and gunners defending the village of Assaye were not under Dodd's command, but he issued them orders anyway. 'You're to hold your fire,' he snapped at them, 'hold your fire. Wait! Wait!' Some of the Goanese gunners spoke a little English, and they understood him and passed the order on. The Rajah's infantry, on the mud walls above the guns, were not so quick and some of those men opened fire on the distant redcoats, but their muskets were far outranged and Dodd ignored them. 'You fire when we fire, understand?' he shouted at the gunners, and some of them understood what he was doing, and they grinned approval of his cunning.

He spurred back to the Cobras. A second British formation had appeared a hundred paces behind the picquets. This second unit was a complete battalion of redcoats advancing in line and, because marching an extended line across country was inevitably slower than advancing in a column of half companies, they had fallen behind the picquets who, in sublime disregard of Assaye's waiting defenders, continued their progress towards the cactus hedge. It seemed to be an isolated attack, far from the clamour in the south that Dodd now ignored. God had given Dodd a chance of victory and he felt the excitement rise in him. It was bliss, pure bliss. He could not lose. He drew the elephant-hilted sword and, as if to give thanks, kissed the steel blade.

The leading half company of picquets had reached the thorn hedge and there they had checked, at last unwilling to continue their suicidal progress towards the waiting Mahrattas. Some artillery from further up the line, which did not lie under Dodd's control, had opened fire on the column, but the white-coated Mahratta forces immediately to the front of the column were silent and the picquets' commanding officer seemed encouraged by that and now urged his men onwards. 'Why doesn't he deploy?' Dodd asked no one, and prayed that they would not deploy, but as soon as the half company of kilted Highlanders had filed through a gap in the cactus thorn they began to spread out and Dodd knew his moment was close. But wait, he told himself, wait for more victims, and sure enough the sepoys pushed through the breaks in the hedge until all the picquets were in front of the cactus and their officers and sergeants began chivvying them forward onto the open pasture where there would be more space for the half companies to deploy into line.

Captain Joubert was worried that Dodd was leaving the command to open fire too late. The second British formation was close to the hedge now, and once they were through the gaps they would add a vast weight of musketry to the attack. But Dodd knew it would take that regiment a long time to manoeuvre through the hedge, and he was concerned solely with the three or four hundred men of the picquets who were now just eighty yards from his gun line and still not properly deployed. His own men were a hundred paces behind the guns, but now he took them forward. 'Regiment will advance,' he ordered, 'at the double!' His interpreter shouted the order and Dodd watched proudly as his men ran smartly forward. They kept their ranks, and checked promptly on his command when they reached the emplaced artillery. 'Thank you, Lord,' he prayed. The picquets, suddenly aware of the horror that awaited them, began to hurry as they spread into line, but still Dodd did not fire. Instead he rode his new horse behind his men's ranks. 'You fire low!' he told his Cobras. 'Make sure you fire low! Aim at their thighs.' Most troops fired high and thus a man who aimed at his enemy's knees would as like as not hit his chest. Dodd paused to watch the picquets who were now advancing in a long double line. Dodd took a deep breath. 'Fire!'

Forty guns and over eight hundred muskets were aimed at the picquets and scarce a gun or a musket missed. One moment the ground in front of the hedge was alive with soldiers, the next it was a charnel house, swept by metal and flayed by fire, and though Dodd could see nothing through the powder smoke, he knew he had virtually annihilated the redcoat line. The volley had been massive. Two of the guns, indeed, had been the eighteen-pounder siege guns and Dodd's only regret was that they had been loaded with round shot instead of canister, but at least they could now reload with canister and so savage the British battalion that had almost reached the cactus hedge.

'Reload!' Dodd called to his men. The smoke was writhing away, thinning as it went, and he could see enemy bodies on the ground. He could see men twitching, men crawling, men dying. Most did not move at all, though miraculously their commanding officer, or at least the only man who had been on horseback, still lived. He was whipping his horse back through the hedge.

'Fire!' Dodd shouted, and a second volley whipped across the killing ground to thrash through the hedge and strike the battalion behind. That battalion was taking even worse punishment from the artillery which was now firing canister, and the blasts of metal were tearing the hedge apart, destroying the redcoats' small cover. The little four-pounder guns, which fired such puny round shot, now served as giant shotguns to spray the redcoats with Dodd's home-made bags of canister. His sepoys loaded and rammed their muskets. The dry grass in front of them flickered with hundreds of small pale flames where the burning wadding had started fires.

'Fire!' Dodd shouted again, and saw, just before the cloud of powder smoke blotted out his view, that the enemy was stepping backwards. The volley crashed out, filling the air with the stench of rotten eggs.

'Reload!' Dodd shouted and admired his men's efficiency. Not one had panicked, not one had fired his ramrod by mistake. Clockwork soldiers, he thought, as soldiers ought to be, while the enemy's return fire was pathetic. One or two of Dodd's men had been killed, and a handful were wounded, but in return they had destroyed the leading British unit and were driving the next one back. 'The regiment will advance!'

he shouted and listened to his interpreter repeat the order.

They marched in line through their own powder smoke and then across the scores of dead and dying enemy picquets. Soldiers stooped to the bodies to filch keepsakes and loot and Dodd shouted at them to keep going. The loot could wait. They reached the remnants of the cactus hedge where Dodd halted them. The British battalion was still going backwards, evidently seeking the safety of the gully. 'Fire!' he shouted, and his men's volley seemed to push the redcoats even further back. 'Reload!'

Ramrods rattled in barrels, dogheads were dragged back to the full. The British line was retreating fast now, but from the north, from the land hard by the river, a mass of Mahratta cavalry was riding south to join the slaughter. Dodd wished the cavalry would stay out of it, for he had an idea that he could have pursued this British battalion clear down the tongue of land to where the rivers met and the last of their men would die in the Kaitna's muddy shallows, but he dared not fire another volley in case he hit the cavalry. 'The regiment will advance!' he told his interpreter. He would let the cavalry have their moment, then go on with the slaughtering himself.

The British battalion commander saw the cavalry and knew his retreat must stop. His men were still in line, a line of only two ranks, and cavalrymen dreamed of encountering infantry in line. 'Form square!' their commanding officer shouted, and the two wings of the line dutifully withdrew towards the centre. The double rank became four, the four ranks wheeled and dressed, and suddenly the cavalry faced a fortress of redcoats, muskets and bayonets. The front rank of the square knelt and braced their muskets on the ground while the other three readied their muskets for the coming horsemen.

The cavalry should have sheered away at the sight of the square, but they had seen the earlier slaughter and thought to add to it, and so they dipped their pennanted lances, raised their *tulwars* and screamed their war cries as they galloped straight towards the redcoats. And the redcoats let them come, let them come perilously close before the order was shouted and the face of the square nearest the cavalry exploded in flame and smoke and the horses screamed as they were hit and died. The surviving horsemen swerved aside and received another killing volley as they swept past the sides of the square. More horses tumbled, dust spewing from their sliding bodies. A *tulwar* spun along the ground, its owner shrieking as his trapped leg was ground into bloody ruin by the weight of his dying horse.

'Reload!' a Scots voice shouted from inside the square and the redcoats recharged their muskets.

The cavalry charged on into open country and there wheeled about. Some of the horses were riderless now, others were bloody, but all came back towards the square.

'Let them come close!' a mounted British officer shouted inside the square. 'Let them come close. Wait for it! Fire!'

More horses tumbled, their legs cracking as the bones shattered, and this time the cavalry did not sheer away to ride down the square's lethal flanks, but instead wheeled clean about and spurred out of range. Two lessons were sufficient to teach them caution, but they did not go far away, just far enough to be out of range of the redcoats' muskets. The cavalry's leaders had seen Dodd's regiment come through the cactus hedge and they knew that their own infantry, attacking in line, must overwhelm the square with musketry and, when the square shattered, as it must under the infantry's assault, the horsemen could sweep back to pick off the survivors and pluck the great gaudy banners as trophies to lay before Scindia.

Dodd could scarcely believe his luck. At first he had resented the cavalry's intrusion, believing that they were about to steal his victory, but their two impotent charges had forced the enemy battalion to form square and mathematics alone dictated that a battalion in square could only use one quarter of its muskets against an attack from any one side. And the British battalion, which Dodd now recognized from its white facings as the 74th, was much smaller than Dodd's Cobras, probably having only half the numbers Dodd possessed. And, in addition to Dodd's men, a ragged regiment of the Rajah of Berar's infantry had poured out of Assaye to join the slaughter while a battalion from Dupont's *compoo*, which had been posted immediately on Dodd's right, had also come to join the killing. Dodd resented the presence of those men whom he feared might dilute the glory of his victory, but he could scarcely order them away. The important thing was to slaughter the Highlanders. 'We're going to kill the bastards with volley fire,' he told his men, then waited for his translator to interpret. 'And then we'll finish them off with bayonets. And I want those two colours! I want those flags hanging in Scindia's tent tonight.'

The Scots were not waiting idly for the attack. Dodd could see small groups of men dashing out of the square and at first he thought they were plundering the dead cavalrymen, and then he saw they were dragging the bodies of men and horses back to make a low rampart. The few survivors of the picquets were among the Scots, who were now caught in a terrible dilemma. By staying in square they would keep themselves safe from any attack by the cavalry which still hovered to the south, though the square made them into an easy target for the enemy's muskets, but if they deployed into line, so that they could use all their muskets against the enemy's infantry line, they made themselves into cavalry bait. Their commanding officer decided to stay in square. Dodd reckoned he would do the same if he was ever so foolish as to be trapped like these fools were trapped. They still had to be finished off, and that promised to be grim work, for the 74th was a notoriously tough regiment, but Dodd had the advantage of numbers and the advantage of position and he knew he must win.

Except that the Scotsmen did not agree with him. They crouched behind their barricade of dead men and horses and poured a blistering fire of musketry at the white-coated Cobras. A lone piper, who had disobeyed the order to leave his instrument at Naulniah, played in the square's centre. Dodd could hear the sound, but he could not see the piper, nor, indeed, the square itself, which was hidden by a churning fog of dark powder smoke. The smoke was illuminated by the flashes of musket fire, and Dodd could hear the heavy balls thumping into his men. The Cobras were no longer advancing, for the closer they got to the deadly smoke the greater their casualties and so they had paused fifty yards from the square to let their own muskets do the work. They were reloading as fast as their enemies, but too many of their bullets were being wasted on the barricade of corpses. All four faces of the square were firing now, for the 74th was surrounded. To the west they fired at Dodd's attacking line, to the north they fired at the Rajah's infantry, while to the east and south they kept the cavalry at bay. The Mahratta horsemen, scenting the Scottish regiment's death, were prowling ever closer in the hope that they could dash in and take the colours before the infantry.

Dodd's Cobras, together with the battalion from Dupont's *compoo*, began to curl about the southern flank of the trapped regiment. It should take only three or four volleys, Dodd thought, to end the business, after which his men could go in with the bayonet. Not that his men were firing volleys any longer; instead they were firing as soon as their muskets were charged and Dodd felt their excitement and sought to curb it. 'Don't waste your fire!' he shouted. 'Aim low!' William

Dodd had no desire to lead a charge through the stinking smoke to find an unbroken formation of vengeful Highlanders waiting with bayonets. Dodd might dislike the Scots, but he had a healthy fear of fighting them with cold steel. Thin the bastards first, he thought, batter them, bleed them, then massacre them, but his men were too excited at the prospect of imminent victory and far too much of their fire was either going high or else being wasted on the barricade of the dead. 'Aim low!' he shouted again. 'Aim low!'

'They won't last,' Joubert said. Indeed the Frenchman was amazed that the Scots still survived.

'Awkward things to kill, Scotsmen,' Dodd said. He took a drink from his canteen. 'I do hate the bastards. All preachers or thieves. Stealing Englishmen's jobs. Aim low!' A man was thrown back near Dodd, blood bright on his white coat. 'Joubert?' Dodd called back to the Frenchman.

'Monsieur?'

'Bring up two of the regiment's guns. Load with canister.' That would end the bastards. Two gouts of canister from the four-pounders would blow great gaps in the Scottish square and Dodd could then lead his men into those gaps and fillet the dying regiment from its inside out. He would be damned if the cavalry would take the flags. They were his! It was Dodd who had fought these Highlanders to a standstill and Dodd who planned to carry the silk banners to Scindia's tent and there fetch his proper reward. 'Hurry, Joubert!' he called.

Dodd drew his pistol and fired over his men's ranks into the smoke that hid the dying square. 'Aim low!' he shouted. 'Don't waste your fire!' But it would not be long now. Two blasts of canister, he reckoned, and then the bayonets would bring him victory.

Major Samuel Swinton stood just behind the western face of the square which looked towards the white-coated infantry.

He could hear an English voice shouting orders and encouragement in the enemy lines and, though Swinton himself was an Englishman, the accent angered him. No English bastard was going to destroy the 74th, not while Major Swinton commanded, and he told his men that a Sassenach was their enemy and that seemed to add zest to their efforts. 'Keep low!' he told them. 'Keep firing!' By staying low the Scots kept behind the protection of their makeshift barricade, but it also made their muskets much more difficult to reload and some men took the risk of standing after each shot. Their only protection then was the mask of smoke that hid the regiment from its enemies. And thank God, Swinton thought, that the enemy had brought no artillery forward.

The square was swept by musket fire. Much of it, especially from the north, flew high, but the white-coated regiment was better trained and their musketry was having an effect, so much so that Swinton took the inside rank of the eastern face and added it to the west. The sergeants and corporals closed the ranks as the enemy bullets hurled men back into the bloody interior of the shrinking square where the Major stepped among the Scottish dead and wounded. Swinton's horse had died, struck by three musket balls and put out of its misery by the Major's own pistol. Colonel Orrock, who had first led the picquets to disaster, had also lost his horse. 'It wasn't my fault,' he kept telling Swinton, and Swinton wanted to hit the bastard every time he spoke. 'I obeyed Wellesley's orders!' Orrock insisted.

Swinton ignored the fool. Right from the beginning of the advance Swinton had sensed that the picquets were going too far to the right. Orrock's orders had been clear enough. He was to incline right, thus making space for the two sepoy battalions to come into the line, then attack straight ahead, but the fool had led his men ever more northwards and Swinton, who had been trying to loop about the picquets to come up on their right, never had a chance to get into position. He had sent the 74th's adjutant to speak with Orrock, pleading with the East India Company Colonel to turn ahead, but Orrock had arrogantly brushed the man off and kept marching towards Assaye.

Swinton had a choice then. He could have ignored Orrock and straightened his own attack to form the right of the line that Wellesley had taken forward, but the leading half company of Orrock's picquets were fifty men from Swinton's own regiment and the Major was not willing to see those fifty men sacrificed by a fool and so he had followed the picquets on their errant course in the hope that his men's fire could rescue Orrock. It had failed. Only four of the fifty men of the half company had rejoined the regiment, the rest were dead and dying, and now the whole 74th seemed to be doomed. They were encompassed by noise and smoke, surrounded by enemies, dying in their square, but the piper was still playing and the men were still fighting and the regiment still lived, and the two flags were still lifted high, though by now the fringed squares of silk were ripped and tattered by the blast of bullets.

An ensign in the colour party took a musket ball in his left eye and fell backwards without a sound. A sergeant gripped the staff in one hand and in his other was a halberd with a wicked blade. In a moment, the sergeant knew, he might have to fight with the halberd. The square would end with a huddle of bloodied men around the colours and the enemy would fall on them and for a few moments it would be steel against steel, and the sergeant reckoned he would give the flag to a wounded man and do what harm he could with the heavy, long-shafted axe. It was a pity to die, but he was a soldier, and no one had yet devised a way a man could live for ever, not even those clever bastards in Edinburgh. He thought of his wife in Dundee, and of his woman in the camp at Naulniah, and he regretted his many sins, for it was not good for a man to go to his God with a bad conscience, but it was too late now and so he gripped the halberd and hid his fear and determined he would die like a man and take a few other men with him.

The muskets banged into Highlanders' shoulders. They bit the tips from new cartridges and every bite added salty gunpowder to their mouths so that they had no spittle, only bone-dry throats that breathed filthy smoke, and the regiment's *puckalees* were far away, lost somewhere in the country behind. The Scots went on firing, and the powder sparks from the pan burned their cheeks, and they loaded and rammed and knelt and fired again, and somewhere beyond the smoke the enemy's fire came flashing in to shudder the corpses of the barricade or else to snatch a man back in a spray of blood. Wounded men fought alongside the living, their faces blackened by powder, their mouths parched, their shoulders bruised, and the white facings and cuffs of their red coats were spattered with the blood of men now dead or dying.

'Close up!' the sergeants shouted and the square shrank another few feet as dying men were hauled back to the square's centre and the living closed the files. Men who had started the day five or six files apart were neighbours now.

'It wasn't my fault!' Orrock insisted.

Swinton had nothing to say. There was nothing to say, and nothing more to do except die, and so he picked up the musket of a dead man, took the cartridge box from the corpse's pouch, and pushed into the square's western face. The man to his right was drunk, but Swinton did not care, for the man was fighting. 'Come to do some proper work, Major?' the drunken man greeted Swinton, with a toothless grin.

'Come to do some proper work, Tam,' Swinton agreed.

He bit the end from a cartridge, charged the musket, primed the lock and fired into the smoke. He reloaded, fired again, and prayed he would die bravely.

Fifty yards away William Dodd watched the cloud of smoke made by the Scottish muskets. The cloud was getting smaller, he thought. Men were dying there and the square was shrinking, but it was still spitting flame and lead. Then he heard the jingle of chains and turned to see the two four-pounder guns being hauled towards him. He would let the guns fire one blast of canister each, then he would have his men fix bayonets and he would lead them across the rampart of corpses into the heart of the smoke.

And then the trumpet called.

CHAPTER 11

Colonel McCandless had stayed close to his friend Colonel Wallace, the commander of the brigade which formed the right of Wellesley's line. Wallace had seen the picquets and his own regiment, the 74th, vanish somewhere to the north, but he had been too busy bringing his two sepoy battalions into the attacking line to worry about Orrock or Swinton. He did charge an aide to keep watching for Orrock's men, expecting to see them veering back towards him at any moment, then he forgot the errant picquets as his men climbed from the low ground into the fire of the Mahratta gun line. Canister shredded Wallace's ranks, it beat like hail on his men's muskets and it swept the leaves from the scattered trees through which the Madrassi battalions marched, but, just like the 78th, the sepoys did not turn. They walked doggedly on like men pushing into a storm, and at sixty paces Wallace halted them to pour a vengeful volley into the gunners and McCandless could hear the musket balls clanging off the painted gun barrels. Sevajee was with McCandless and he stared in awe as the sepoys reloaded and went forward again, this time carrying their bayonets to the gunners. For a moment there was chaotic slaughter as Madrassi sepoys chased Goanese gunners around limbers and guns, but Wallace was already looking ahead and could see that the vaunted enemy infantry was wavering, evidently shaken by the easy victory of the 78th, and so the Colonel shouted at his sepoys to ignore the gunners and re-form and push on to attack the infantry. It took a moment to re-form the line, then it advanced from the guns. Wallace gave the enemy infantry one volley, then charged, and all along the line the vaunted Mahratta foot fled from the sepoy attack.

McCandless was busy for the next few moments. He knew that the assault had gone nowhere near Dodd's regiment, but nor had he expected it to, and he was anticipating riding northwards with Wallace to find the 74th, the regiment McCandless knew was nearest to his prey, but when the sepoys lost their self-control and broke ranks to pursue the beaten enemy infantry, McCandless helped the other officers round them up and herd them back. Sevajee and his horsemen stayed behind, for there was a possibility that they would be mistaken for enemy cavalry. For a moment or two there was a real danger that the scattered sepoys would be charged and slaughtered by the mass of enemy cavalry to the west, but its own fleeing infantry was in the cavalry's way, the 78th stood like a fortress on the left flank, and the Scottish guns were skipping balls along the cavalry's face, and the Mahratta horsemen, after a tentative move forward, thought better of the charge. The sepoys took their ranks again, grinning because of their victory. McCandless, his small chore done, rejoined Sevajee. 'So that's how Mahrattas fight.' The Colonel could not resist the provocation.

'Mercenaries, Colonel, mercenaries,' Sevajee said, 'not Mahrattas.'

Five victorious redcoat regiments now stood in ranks on the southern half of the battlefield. To the west the enemy infantry was still disordered, though officers were trying to re-form them, while to the east there was a horror of bodies and blood left on the ground across which the redcoats had advanced. The five regiments had swept through the gun line and chased away the infantry and now formed their ranks some two hundred paces west of where the Mahratta infantry had made their line so that they could look back on the trail of carnage they had caused. Riderless horses galloped through the thinning skeins of powder smoke where dogs were already gnawing at the dead and birds with monstrous black wings were flapping down to feast on corpses. Beyond the corpses, on the distant ground where the Scots and sepoys had started their advance, there were now Mahratta cavalrymen, and McCandless, gazing through his telescope, saw some of those cavalrymen harnessing British artillery that had been abandoned when its ox teams had been killed by the bombardment that had opened the battle.

'Where's Wellesley?' Colonel Wallace asked McCandless.

'He went northwards.' McCandless was now staring towards the village where a dreadful battle was being fought, but he could see no details, for there were just enough trees to obscure the fight, though the mass of powder smoke rising above the leaves was as eloquent as the unending crackle of musketry. McCandless knew his business was to be where that battle was being fought, for Dodd was surely close to the fight if not involved, but in McCandless's path was the stub of the Mahratta defence line, that part of the line which had not been attacked by the Scots or the sepoys, and those men were turning to face southwards. To reach that southern battle McCandless would have to loop wide to the east, but that stretch of country was full of marauding bands of enemy cavalry. 'I should have advanced with Swinton,' he said ruefully.

'We'll catch up with him soon enough,' Wallace said, though without conviction. It was clear to both men that Wallace's regiment, the 74th, had marched too far to the north and had become entangled in the thicket of Mahratta defences about Assaye and their commanding officer, removed from them to lead the brigade, was plainly worried.

'Time to turn north, I think,' Wallace said, and he shouted at his two sepoy battalions to wheel right. He had no authority over the remaining two sepoy battalions, nor over the 78th, for those were in Harness's brigade, but he was ready to march his two remaining battalions towards the distant village in the hope of rescuing his own regiment.

McCandless watched as Wallace organized the two battalions. This part of the battlefield, which minutes before had been so loud with screaming canister and the hammer of volleys, was now strangely quiet. Wellesley's attack had been astonishingly successful, and the enemy was regrouping while the attackers, left victorious on the Kaitna's northern bank, drew their breath and looked for the next target. McCandless thought of using Sevajee's handful of horsemen as an escort to take him safely towards the village, but another rush of Mahratta cavalry galloped up from the low ground. Wellesley and his aides had ridden northwards and they seemed to have survived the milling enemy horsemen, but the General's passing had attracted more horsemen to the area and McCandless had no mind to run the gauntlet of their venom and so he abandoned the idea of a galloping dash northwards. It was just then that he noticed Sergeant Hakeswill, crouching by a dead enemy with the reins of a riderless horse in one hand. A group of redcoats was with him, all from his own regiment, the 33rd. And just as McCandless saw the Sergeant, so Hakeswill looked up and offered the Scotsman a glance of such malevolence that McCandless almost turned away in horror. Instead he spurred his horse across the few yards that separated them. 'What are you doing here, Sergeant?' he asked harshly.

'My duty, sir, as is incumbent on me,' Hakeswill said. As ever, when addressed by an officer, he had straightened to attention, his right foot tucked behind his left, his elbows back and his chest thrust out.

'And what are your duties?' McCandless asked.

'*Puckalees*, sir. In charge of *puckalees*, sir, making sure the scavenging little brutes does their duty, sir, and nothing else, sir. Which they does, sir, on account of me looking after them like a father.' He unbent sufficiently to give a swift nod in the direction of the 78th where, sure enough, a group of *puckalees* was distributing heavy skins of water they had brought from the river.

'Have you written to Colonel Gore yet?' McCandless asked.

'Have I written to Colonel Gore yet, sir?' Hakeswill repeated the question, his face twitching horribly under the shako's peak. He had forgotten that he was supposed to have the warrant reissued, for he was relying instead on McCandless's death to clear the way to Sharpe's arrest. Not that this was the place to murder McCandless, for there were a thousand witnesses within view. 'I've done everything what ought to be done, sir, like a soldier should,' Hakeswill answered evasively.

'I shall write to Colonel Gore myself,' McCandless now told Hakeswill, 'because I've been thinking about that warrant. You have it?'

'I do, sir.'

'Then let me see it again,' the Colonel demanded.

Hakeswill unwillingly pulled the grubby paper from his pouch and offered it to the Colonel. McCandless unfolded the warrant, quickly scanned the lines, and suddenly the falsity in the words leaped out at him. 'It says here that Captain Morris was assaulted on the night of August the fifth.'

'So he was, sir. Foully assaulted, sir.'

'Then it could not have been Sharpe who committed the assault, Sergeant, for on the night of the fifth he was with me. That was the day I collected Sergeant Sharpe from Seringapatam's armoury.' McCandless's face twisted with dis-

331

taste as he looked down at the Sergeant. 'You say you were a witness to the assault?' he asked Hakeswill.

Hakeswill knew when he was beaten. 'Dark night, sir,' the Sergeant said woodenly.

'You're lying, Sergeant,' McCandless said icily, 'and I know you are lying, and my letter to Colonel Gore will attest to your lying. You have no business here, and I shall so inform Major General Wellesley. If it was up to me then your punishment would take place here, but that is for the General to decide. You will give me that horse.'

'This horse, sir? I found it, sir. Wandering, sir.'

'Give it here!' McCandless snapped. Sergeants had no business having horses without permission. He snatched the reins from Hakeswill. 'And if you do have duties with the *puckalees*, Sergeant, I suggest you attend to them rather than plunder the dead. As for this warrant . . .' The Colonel, before Hakeswill's appalled gaze, tore the paper in two. 'Good day, Sergeant,' McCandless said and, his small victory complete, turned his horse and spurred away.

Hakeswill watched the Colonel ride away, then stooped and picked up the two halves of the warrant which he carefully stowed in his pouch. 'Scotchman,' he spat.

Private Lowry shifted uncomfortably. 'If he's right, Sergeant, and Sharpie wasn't there, then we shouldn't be here.'

Hakeswill turned savagely on the private. 'And since when, Private Lowry, did you dispose of soldiery? The Duke of York has made you an officer, has he? His Grace put braid on your coat without telling me, did he? What Sharpie did is no business of yours, Lowry.' The Sergeant was in trouble, and he knew it, but he was not broken yet. He turned and stared at McCandless who had given the horse to a dismounted officer and was now in deep conversation with Colonel Wallace. The two men glanced towards Hakeswill and the Sergeant guessed they were discussing him. 'We follows that

Scotchman,' Hakeswill said, 'and this is for the man who puts him under the sod.' He fished a gold coin from his pocket and showed it to his six privates.

The privates stared solemnly at the coin, then, all at once, they ducked as a cannonball screamed low over their heads. Hakeswill swore and dropped flat. Another gun sounded, and this time a barrelful of canister flecked the grass just south of Hakeswill.

Colonel Wallace had been listening to McCandless, but now turned eastwards. Not all the gunners in the Mahratta line had been killed and those who survived, together with the cavalry which had been looking for employment, were now manning their guns again. They had turned the guns to face west instead of east and were now firing at the five regiments who were waiting for the battle to begin again. Except the gunners had surprised them, and the captured British guns, fetched from the east, now joined the battery to pour their shot, shell and canister into the red-coated infantry. They fired at three hundred paces, point-blank range, and their missiles tore bloodily through the ranks.

For the Mahrattas, it seemed, were not beaten yet.

William Dodd could smell victory. He could almost feel the sheen of the captured silk colours in his hands, and all it would take was two blasts of canister, a mucky slaughter with bayonets, and then the 74th would be destroyed. Horse Guards in London could cross the first battalion of the regiment off the army list, all of it, and mark down that it had been sacrificed to William Dodd's talent. He snarled at his gunners to load their home-made canister, watched as the loaders rammed the missiles home, and then the trumpet sounded.

The British and Company cavalry had been posted in the northern half of the battlefield to guard against enemy horsemen sweeping about the infantry's rear, but now they came to the 74th's rescue. The 19th Dragoons emerged from the gully behind the Highlanders and their charge curved northwards out of the low ground towards the 74th and the village beyond. The troopers were mostly recruits from the English shires, young men brought up to know horses and made strong by farm work, and they all carried the new light cavalry sabre that was warranted never to fail. Nor did it.

They struck the Mahratta horse first. The English riders were outnumbered, but they rode bigger horses and their blades were better made, and they cut through the cavalry with a maniacal savagery. It was hacking work, brutal work, screaming and fast work, and the Mahrattas turned their lighter horses away from the bloody sabres and fled northwards, and once the enemy horsemen were killed or fleeing, the British cavalry raked back their spurs and charged at the Mahratta infantry.

They struck the battalion from Dupont's *compoo* first, and because those men were not prepared for cavalry, but were still in line, it was more an execution than a fight. The cavalry were mounted on tall horses, and every man had spent hours of sabre drill learning how to cut, thrust and parry, but all they had to do now was slash with their heavy, wide-bladed weapons that were designed for just such butchery. Slash and hack, scream and spur, then push on through panicking men whose only thought was flight. The sabres made dreadful injuries, the weight of the blade gave the weapons a deep bite and the curve of the steel dragged the newly sharpened edges back through flesh and muscle and bone to lengthen the wound.

Some Mahratta cavalry bravely tried to stem the charge, but their light *tulwars* were no match for Sheffield steel. The 74th were standing and cheering as they watched the English horsemen carve into the enemy who had come so terribly close, and behind the Englishmen rode Company cavalry, Indians on smaller horses, some carrying lances, who spread the attack wider to drive the broken Mahratta horsemen northwards.

Dodd did not panic. He knew he had lost this skirmish, but the helpless mass of Dupont's battalion was protecting his right flank and those doomed men gave Dodd the few seconds he needed. 'Back,' he shouted, 'back!' and he needed no interpreter now. The Cobras hurried back towards the cactus-thorn hedge. They did not run, they did not break ranks, but stepped swiftly backwards to leave the enemy's horse room to sweep across their front, and, as the horsemen passed, those of Dodd's men who still had loaded muskets fired. Horses stumbled and fell, riders sprawled, and still the Cobras went backwards.

But the regiment was still in line and Dupont's panicked infantry were now pushing their way into Dodd's right-hand companies, and the second rank of dragoons rode in among that chaos to slash their sabres down onto the white-coated men. Dodd shouted at his men to form square, and they obeyed, but the two right-hand companies had been reduced to ragged ruin and their survivors never joined the square which was so hastily made that it was more of a huddle than an ordered formation. Some of the fugitives from the two doomed companies tried to join their comrades in the square, but the horsemen were among them and Dodd shouted at the square to fire. The volley cut down his own men with the enemy, but it served to drive the horsemen away and so gave Dodd time to send his men back through the hedge and still further back to where they had first waited for the British attack. The Rajah of Berar's infantry, who had been on Dodd's left, had escaped more lightly, but none had stayed to fight. Instead they ran back to Assaye's mud walls. The gunners by the village saw the cavalry coming and fired canister, killing more of their own fugitives than enemy cavalry, but the brief cannonade at least signalled to the dragoons that the village was defended and dangerous.

The storm of cavalry passed northwards, leaving misery in its wake. The two four-pounder cannon that Joubert had taken forward were abandoned now, their teams killed by the horsemen, and where the 74th had been there was now nothing but an empty enclosure of dead men and horses that had formed the barricade. The survivors of the beleaguered square had withdrawn eastwards, carrying their wounded with them, and it seemed to Dodd that a sudden silence had wrapped about the Cobras. It was not a true silence, for the guns had started firing again on the southern half of the battlefield, the distant sound of hooves was neverending and the moaning of the nearby wounded was loud, but it did seem quiet.

Dodd spurred his horse southwards in an attempt to make some sense of the battle. Dupont's *compoo* next to him had lost one regiment to the sabres, but the next three regiments were intact and the Dutchman was now turning those units to face southwards. Dodd could see Pohlmann riding along the back of those wheeling regiments and he suspected that the Hanoverian would now turn his whole line to face south. The British had broken the far end of the line, but they had still not broken the army.

Yet the possibility of annihilation existed. Dodd fidgeted with the elephant hilt of his sword and contemplated what less than an hour before had seemed an impossibility: defeat. God damn Wellesley, he thought, but this was no time for anger, just for calculation. Dodd could not afford to be captured and he had no mind to die for Scindia and so he must secure his line of retreat. He would fight to the end, he decided, then run like the wind. 'Captain Joubert?'

The long-suffering Joubert trotted his horse to Dodd's side. 'Monsieur?'

Dodd did not speak at once, for he was watching Pohlmann come nearer. It was clear now that the Hanoverian was making a new battle line, and one, moreover, that would lie to the west of Assaye with its back against the river. The regiments to Dodd's right, which had yet to be attacked, were now pulling back and the guns were going with them. The whole line was being redeployed, and Dodd guessed the Cobras would move from the east side of the mud walls to the west, but that was no matter. The best ford across the Juah ran out of the village itself, and it was that ford Dodd wanted. 'Take two companies, Joubert,' he ordered, 'and march them into the village to guard this side of the ford.'

Joubert frowned. 'The Rajah's troops, surely . . .' he began to protest.

'The Rajah of Berar's troops are useless!' Dodd snapped. 'If we need to use the ford, then I want it secured by our men. You secure it.' He jabbed at the Frenchman with a finger. 'Is your wife in the village?'

'*Oui, Monsieur.*'

'Then now's your chance to impress her, Monsewer. Go and protect her. And make sure the damn ford isn't captured or clogged up with fugitives.'

Joubert was not unhappy to be sent away from the fighting, but he was dismayed by Dodd's evident defeatism. Nevertheless he took two companies, marched into the village, and posted his men to guard the ford so that if all was lost, there would still be a way out.

Wellesley had ridden north to investigate the furious fighting that had erupted close to the village of Assaye. He rode with a half-dozen aides and with Sharpe trailing behind on the last of the General's horses, the roan mare. It was a furious ride, for the area east of the infantry was infested with Mahratta horsemen, but the General had faith in the size and speed of his big English and Irish horses and the enemy was easily outgalloped. Wellesley came within sight of the beleaguered 74th just as the dragoons crashed in on their besiegers from the south. 'Well done, Maxwell!' Wellesley shouted aloud, though he was far out of earshot of the cavalry's leader, and then he curbed his horse to watch the dragoons at work.

The mass of the Mahratta horsemen who had been waiting for the 74th's square to collapse, now fled northwards and the British cavalry, having hacked the best part of an enemy infantry regiment into ruin, pursued them. The cavalry's good order was gone now, for the blue-coated troopers were spurring their horses to chase their broken enemy across country. Men whooped like fox hunters, closed on their quarry, slashed with sabre, then spurred on to the next victim. The Mahratta horsemen were not even checked by the River Juah, but just plunged in and spurred their horses through the water and up the northern bank. The British and Indian cavalry followed so that the pursuit vanished in the north. The 74th, who had fought so hard to stay alive, now marched out of range of the cannon by the village and Wellesley, who had smelt disaster just a few minutes before, breathed a great sigh of relief. 'I told them to stay clear of the village, did I not?' he demanded of his aides, but before anyone could answer, new cannon fire sounded from the south. 'What the devil?' Wellesley said, turning to see what the gunfire meant.

The remaining infantry of the Mahratta line were pulling back, taking their guns with them, but the artillery which had stood in front of the enemy's defeated right wing, the same guns that had been overrun by the red-coated infantry, were now coming alive again. The weapons had been turned and were crashing back on their trails and jetting smoke from their muzzles, and behind the guns was a mass of enemy cavalry ready to protect the gunners who were flaying the five battalions that had defeated the enemy infantry. 'Barclay?' Wellesley called.

'Sir?' The aide spurred forward.

'Can you reach Colonel Harness?'

The aide looked at the southern part of the battlefield. A moment before it had been thick with Mahratta horsemen, but those men had now withdrawn behind the revived guns and there was a space in front of those guns, a horribly narrow space, but the only area of the battlefield that was now free of enemy cavalry. If Barclay was to reach Harness then he would have to risk that narrow passage and, if he was very lucky, he might even survive the canister. And dead or alive, Barclay thought, he would win the lottery of bullet holes in his coat. The aide took a deep breath. 'Yes, sir.'

'My compliments to Colonel Harness, and ask him to retake the guns with his Highlanders. The rest of his brigade will stay where they are to keep the cavalry at bay.' The General was referring to the mass of cavalry that still threatened from the west, none of which had yet entered the battle. 'And my compliments to Colonel Wallace,' the General went on, 'and his sepoy battalions are to move northwards, but are not to engage the enemy until I reach them. Go!' He waved Barclay away, then twisted in his saddle. 'Campbell?'

'Sir?'

'Who's that?' The General pointed eastwards to where one single cavalry unit had been left out of the charge that had rescued the 74th, presumably in case the dragoons had galloped into disaster and needed a rescue.

Campbell peered at the distant unit. '7th Native Cavalry, sir.'

'Fetch them. Quick now!' The General drew his sword as Campbell galloped away. 'Well, gentlemen,' he said to his remaining aides, 'time to earn our keep, I think. Harness can drive the wretches away from the southernmost guns, but we shall have to take care of the nearer ones.' For a moment Sharpe thought the General planned to charge the guns with just the handful of men who remained with him, then he realized Wellesley was waiting for the 7th Native Cavalry to arrive. For a few seconds Wellesley had considered summoning the survivors of the 74th, but those men, who had retreated back across the gully, were still recovering from their ordeal. They were collecting their wounded, taking the roll call and reorganizing ten broken companies into six. The 7th Native Cavalry would have to beat down the guns and Campbell brought them across the battlefield, then led their commanding officer, a red-faced major with a bristling moustache, to Wellesley's side. 'I need to reach our infantry, Major,' the General explained, 'and you're going to escort me to them, and the quickest way is through their gun line.'

The Major gaped at the guns with their crowd of attendant cavalry. 'Yes, sir,' he said nervously.

'Two lines, if you please,' the General ordered brusquely. 'You will command the first line and drive off the cavalry. I shall ride in the second and kill the gunners.'

'You'll kill the gunners, sir?' the Major asked, as though he found that idea novel, then he realized his question was dangerously close to insubordination. 'Yes, sir,' he said hurriedly, 'of course, sir.' The Major stared at the gun line again. He would be charging the line's flank, so at least no gun would be pointing at his men. The greater danger was the mass of Mahratta cavalry that had gathered behind the guns and which far outnumbered his troopers, but then, sensing Wellesley's impatience, he spurred his horse back to his men and shouted at his troopers. 'Two lines by the right!' The Major commanded a hundred and eighty men and Sharpe saw them grin as they drew their sabres and spurred their horses into formation.

'Ever been in a cavalry charge, Sergeant?' Campbell asked Sharpe.

'No, sir. Never wanted to be, sir.'

'Nor me. Should be interesting.' Campbell had his claymore drawn and he gave the huge sword a cut in the air which almost took his horse's ears off. 'You might find it more enjoyable, Sergeant,' he said helpfully, 'if you drew your sabre.'

'Of course, sir,' Sharpe said, feeling foolish. He had somehow imagined that his first battle would be spent in an infantry battalion, firing and reloading as he had been trained to do, but instead it seemed that he was to fight as a cavalry trooper. He drew the heavy weapon which felt unnatural in his hand, but then this whole battle seemed unnatural. It swung from moments of bowel-loosening terror to sudden calm, then back to terror again. It also ebbed and flowed, flaring in one part of the field, then dying down as the tide of killing passed to another patch of dun-coloured farmland.

'And our job is to kill the gunners,' Campbell explained, 'to make sure they don't fire at us again. We'll let the experts look after their cavalry and we just slaughter whatever they leave us. Simple.'

Simple? All Sharpe could see was a mass of enemy horsemen behind the huge guns that were bucking and rearing as they crashed out smoke, flame and death, and Campbell thought it was easy? Then he realized that the young Scots officer was just trying to reassure him, and he felt grateful. Campbell was watching Captain Barclay ride through the artillery barrage. It seemed the Captain must be killed, for he went so close to the Mahratta guns that at one point his horse vanished in a cloud of powder smoke, but a moment later he reappeared, low in his saddle, his horse galloping, and Campbell cheered when he saw Barclay swerve away towards Harness's brigade.

'A canteen, Sergeant, if you please?' Wellesley demanded, and Sharpe, who had been watching Barclay, fumbled to loosen one of the canteen straps. He gave the water to the General, then opened his own canteen and drank from it. Sweat was pouring down his face and soaking his shirt. Wellesley drank half the water, stoppered it and gave the canteen back, then trotted his horse into a gap in the right-hand side of the second line of the cavalry. The General drew his slim sword. The other aides also found places in the line, but there seemed no space for Sharpe and so he positioned himself a few yards behind the General. 'Go!' Wellesley shouted to the Major.

'Forward line, by the centre,' the Major shouted. 'Walk! March!'

It seemed an odd order, for Sharpe had expected the two lines to start at the gallop, but instead the leading line of horsemen set off at a walk and the second line just waited. Leaving the wide gap made sense to Sharpe, for if the second line was too close to the first then it could get entangled with whatever carnage the leading line made, whereas if there was a good distance between the two lines then there was space for the second to swerve around obstacles, but even so, walking a horse into battle seemed idiocy to Sharpe. He licked his lips, already dry again, then wiped his sweaty hand on his trousers before regripping the sabre's hilt.

'Now, gentlemen!' Wellesley said and the second line started forward at the same sedate pace as the first. Curb chains jingled and empty scabbards flapped. After a few seconds the Major in the first line called out an order and the two lines went into the trot. Dust swirled away from the hooves. The troopers' black hats had tall scarlet plumes that tossed prettily, while their curved sabres flashed with reflected sunlight. Wellesley spoke to Blackiston beside him and Sharpe saw the Major laugh, then the trumpeter beside the Major blew a call and the twin lines went into the canter. Sharpe tried to keep up, but he was a bad rider and the mare kept swerving aside and tossing her head. 'Keep going!' Sharpe snarled at her. The Mahrattas had seen the attack coming now and the gunners were desperately trying to lever the northernmost gun about to face the threat while a mass of enemy cavalrymen was spurring forward to confront the charge.

'Go!' the Major shouted and his trumpeter sounded the full charge and Sharpe saw the sabres of the leading line drop so that their points were jutting forward like spears. This was more like it, he thought, for the horses were galloping now, their hooves making a furious thunder as they swept on to the enemy.

The leading line crashed into the oncoming enemy cavalry. Sharpe expected to see the line stop, but it hardly seemed to check. Instead there was the flash of blades, an impression of a man and horse falling and then the Major's line was through the cavalry and riding over the first gun. Sabres rose and fell. The second line was swerving to avoid the fallen horses, then they too were among the enemy and closing on the first line which was at last being slowed by the enemy's resistance.

'Keep going!' Wellesley shouted at the foremost riders. 'Keep going! Get me to the infantry!'

The cavalry had charged so that their right flank would overrun the guns, while the rest of the attack would face the cavalry to the east of the gun line. Those easternmost men were making good progress, but the right-flank troopers were being held up by the big ammunition limbers that were parked behind the guns. The Indian troopers slashed at the Goanese gunners who dived beneath their cannon for shelter. One gunner swung a rammer and swept a trooper off a horse. Muskets banged, a horse screamed and fell in a tangle of flailing hooves. An arrow flicked towards Sharpe, missing him by a hair's breadth. Sabres slashed and bit. Sharpe saw one tall trooper standing in his stirrups to give his swing more room. The man screamed as he hacked down, then wrenched his blade free from his victim and spurred on to find another. Sharpe clung desperately to the saddle as the mare swerved to avoid a wounded horse, then he was among the guns himself. Two lines of cavalry had ridden over these weapons, but still some of the gunners lived and Sharpe swung at one man with the sabre, but at the last moment the mare's motion unbalanced him and the blade went far above the enemy's head. It was all bloody chaos now. The cavalry was fighting its way up the line, but some of the enemy horsemen were galloping around the first line's flank to attack the second line, and groups of gunners were fighting back like infantry. The gunners were armed with muskets and pikes, and Sharpe, kicking his horse behind Wellesley, saw a group of them appear from the shelter of a painted eighteen-pounder gun and run towards the General. He tried to shout a warning, but the sound that emerged was more like a scream for help.

Wellesley was isolated. Major Blackiston had wheeled left to chop down at a tall Arab wielding a massive blade, while Campbell was loose on the right where he was racing in pursuit of a fugitive horseman. The Indian troopers were all in front of the General, sabring gunners as they spurred ahead, while Sharpe was ten paces behind. Six men attacked the General, and one of them wielded a long, narrow-bladed pike that he thrust up at Wellesley's horse. The General sawed on Diomed's reins to wheel him out of the man's path, but the big horse was going too fast and ran straight onto the levelled pike.

Sharpe saw the man holding the pike twist aside as the horse's weight wrenched the staff out of his hands. He saw the white stallion falling and sliding, and he saw Wellesley thrown forward onto the horse's neck. He saw the half-dozen enemy closing in for the kill and suddenly the chaos and terror of the day all vanished. Sharpe knew what he had to do, and knew it as clearly as though his whole life had been spent waiting for just this moment.

He kicked the roan mare straight at the enemy. He could not reach the General, for Wellesley was still in the saddle of the wounded Diomed who was sliding on the ground and trailing the pikestaff from his bleeding chest, and the threat of the horse's weight had driven the enemy aside, three to the left and three to the right. One fired his musket at Wellesley, but the ball flew wide, and then, as Diomed slowed, the Mahrattas closed in and it was then that Sharpe struck them. He used the mare as a battering ram, taking her perilously close to where the General had fallen from the saddle, and he drove her into the three gunners on the right, scattering them, and at the same time he kicked his feet from the stirrups and swung himself off the horse so that he fell just beside the dazed Wellesley. Sharpe stumbled as he fell, but he came up from the ground snarling with the sabre sweeping wide at the three men he had charged, but they had been driven back by the mare's impact, and so Sharpe whipped back to see a gunner standing right over the General with a bayonet raised, ready to strike, and he lunged at the man, screaming at him, and felt the sabre's tip tear through the muscles of the gunner's belly. Sharpe pushed the sabre, toppling the gunner back onto Diomed's blood-flecked flank.

The sabre stuck in the wound. The gunner was thrashing, his musket fallen, and one of his comrades was climbing over Diomed with a *tulwar* in his hand. Sharpe heaved on the sabre, jerking the dying man, but the blade would not free itself of the flesh's suction and so he stepped over Wellesley, who was still dizzied and on his back, put his left boot on the gunner's groin and heaved again. The man with the *tulwar*

345

struck down, and Sharpe felt a blow on his left shoulder, but then his own sabre came free and he swung it clumsily at his new attacker. The man stepped back to avoid the blade and tripped on one of Diomed's rear legs. He fell. Sharpe turned, his sabre sweeping blindly wide with drops of blood flicking from its tip as he sought to drive back any enemies coming from his right. There were none. The General said something, but he was still scarcely conscious of what was happening, and Sharpe knew that he and the General were both going to die here if he did not find some shelter fast.

The big painted eighteen-pounder gun offered some small safety, and so Sharpe stooped, took hold of Wellesley's collar, and unceremoniously dragged the General towards the cannon. The General was not unconscious, for he clung to his slim straight sword, but he was half stunned and helpless. Two men ran to cut Sharpe off from the gun's sanctuary and he let go of the General's stiff collar and attacked the pair. 'Bastards,' he screamed as he fought them. Bugger the advice about straight arm and parrying, this was a time to kill in sheer rage and he went for the two gunners in a berserk fury. The sabre was a clumsy weapon, but it was sharp and heavy and he almost severed the first man's neck and the subsequent backswing opened the second man's arm to the bone, and Sharpe turned back to Wellesley, who was still not recovered from the impact of his fall, and he saw an Arab lancer spurring his horse straight at the fallen General. Sharpe bellowed an obscenity at the man, then leaped forward and slashed the sabre's heavy blade across the face of the lancer's horse and saw the beast swerve aside. The lance blade jerked up into the air as the Arab tried to control his pain-maddened horse, and Sharpe stooped, took Wellesley's collar again, and hauled the General into the space between the gun's gaudy barrel and one of its gigantic wheels. 'Stay there!' Sharpe snapped to Wellesley, then turned around to see that the Arab had been thrown from his horse, but was now leading a charge of gunners. Sharpe went to meet them. He swept the lance aside with the sabre's blade, then rammed the weapon's bar hilt into the Arab's face. He felt the man's nose break, kicked him in the balls, shoved him back, hacked down with the sabre, then turned to his left and sliced the blade within an inch of a gunner's eyes.

The attackers backed away, leaving Sharpe panting. Wellesley at last stood, steadying himself with one hand on the gunwheel. 'Sergeant Sharpe?' Wellesley asked in puzzlement.

'Stay there, sir,' Sharpe said, without turning round. He had four men in front of him now, four men with bared teeth and bright weapons. Their eyes flicked from Sharpe to Wellesley and back to Sharpe. The Mahrattas did not know they had the British General trapped, but they knew the man beside the gun must be a senior officer, for his red coat was bright with braid and lace, and they came to capture him, but to reach him they first needed to pass Sharpe. Two men came from the gun's far side, and Wellesley parried a pike blade with his sword, then stepped away from the gun to stand beside Sharpe and immediately a rush of enemy came to seize him. 'Get back!' Sharpe shouted at Wellesley, then stepped into the enemy's charge.

He grabbed a pike that was reaching for the General's belly, tugged it towards him, and met the oncoming gunner with the sabre's tip. Straight into the man's throat, and he twisted the blade free and swung it right and felt the steel jar on a man's skull, but there was no time to assess the damage, just to step left and stab at a third man. His shoulder was bleeding, but there was no pain. He was keening a mad noise as he fought and it seemed to Sharpe at that instant as though he could do nothing wrong. It was as if the enemy had been magically slowed to half speed and he had been quickened. He was much taller than any of them, he was much stronger, and he was suddenly much faster. He was even enjoying the fight, had he known anything of what he felt, but he sensed only the madness of battle, the sublime madness that blots out fear, dulls pain and drives a man close to ecstasy. He was screaming obscenities at the enemy, begging them to come and be killed.

He moved to his right and slashed the blade in a huge downward cut that opened a man's face. The enemy had retreated, and Wellesley again came to Sharpe's side and so invited the attackers to close in again, and Sharpe again pushed the General back into the space between the tall gunwheel and the huge painted barrel of the eighteen-pounder. 'Stay there,' he snapped, 'and watch under the barrel!' He turned away to face the attackers. 'Come on, you bastards! Come on! I want you!'

Two men came, and Sharpe stepped towards them and used both his hands to bring the heavy sabre down in a savage cut that bit through the hat and skull of the nearest enemy. Sharpe screamed a curse at the dying man, for his sabre was trapped in his skull, but he wrenched it free and sliced it right, a grey jelly sliding off its edge, to chase the second man back. That man held up his hands as he retreated, as if to suggest that he did not want to fight after all, and Sharpe cursed him as he slashed the blade's tip through his gullet. He spat on the staggering man and spat dry-mouthed again at the enemies who were watching him. 'Come on! Come on!' he taunted them. 'Yellow bastards! Come on!'

There were at last horsemen riding back to help now, but more Mahrattas were closing in on the fight. Two men tried to reach Wellesley across the cannon barrel and the General stabbed one in the face, then slashed at the arm of the other as he reached beneath the gun barrel. Behind him Sharpe was screaming insults at the enemy and one man took up the challenge and ran at Sharpe with a bayonet. Sharpe shouted in what sounded like delight as he parried the lunge and then punched the sabre's hilt into the man's face. Another man was coming from the right and so Sharpe kicked his first assailant's legs out from under him, then slashed at the new-comer. Christ knows how many of the bastards there were, but Sharpe did not care. He had come here to fight and God had given him one screaming hell of a battle. The man parried Sharpe's cut, lunged, and Sharpe stepped past the lunge and hammered the sabre's bar hilt into the man's eye. The man screamed and clutched at Sharpe, who tried to throw him off by punching the hilt into his face again. The other attackers were vanishing now, fleeing from the horsemen who spurred back towards Wellesley.

But one Mahratta officer had been stalking Sharpe and he now saw his opportunity as Sharpe was held by the half-blinded man. The officer came from behind Sharpe and he swung his *tulwar* at the back of the redcoat's neck.

The stroke was beautifully aimed. It hit Sharpe plumb on the nape of his neck, and it should have cut through his spine and dropped him dead to the bloody ground in an instant, but there was a dead king's ruby hidden in the leather bag around which Sharpe's hair was clubbed and the big ruby stopped the blade dead. The jolt of the blow jerked Sharpe forward, but he kept his feet and the man who had been clutching him at last released his grip and Sharpe could turn. The officer swung again and Sharpe parried so hard that the Sheffield steel slashed clean through the *tulwar's* light blade and the next stroke cut through the blade's owner. 'Bastard!' Sharpe shouted as he tugged the blade free and he whirled around to kill the next man who came near, but instead it was Captain Campbell who was there, and behind him were a dozen troopers who spurred their horses into the enemy and hacked down with their sabres.

For a second or two Sharpe could scarcely believe that he was alive. Nor could he believe that the fight was over. He wanted to kill again. His blood was up, the rage was seething in him, and there was no more enemy and so he contented himself by slashing the sabre down onto the Mahratta officer's head. 'Bastard!' he shouted, then booted the man's face to jolt the blade free. Then, suddenly, he was shaking. He turned and saw that Wellesley was staring at him aghast and Sharpe was certain he must have done something wrong. Then he remembered what it was. 'Sorry, sir,' he said.

'You're sorry?' Wellesley said, though he seemed scarcely able to speak. The General's face was pale.

'For pushing you, sir,' Sharpe said. 'Sorry, sir. Didn't mean to, sir.'

'I hope you damn well did mean to,' Wellesley said forcibly, and Sharpe saw that the General, usually so calm, was shaking too.

Sharpe felt he ought to say something more, but he could not think what it was. 'Lost your last horse, sir,' he said instead. 'Sorry, sir.'

Wellesley gazed at him. In all his life he had never seen a man fight like Sergeant Sharpe, though in truth the General could not remember everything that had happened in the last two minutes. He remembered Diomed falling and he remembered trying to loosen his feet from the stirrups, and he remembered a blow on the head that was probably one of Diomed's flailing hooves, and he thought he remembered seeing a bayonet bright in the sky above him and he had known that he must be killed at that moment, and then everything was a dizzy confusion. He recalled Sharpe's voice, using language that shocked even the General, who was not easily offended, and he remembered being thrust back against the gun so that the Sergeant could face the enemy alone, and Wellesley had approved of that decision, not because it spared him the need to fight, but because he had recognized that Sharpe would be hampered by his presence.

Then he had watched Sharpe kill, and he had been astonished by the ferocity, enthusiasm and skill of that killing, and Wellesley knew that his life had been saved, and he knew he must thank Sharpe, but for some reason he could not find the words and so he just stared at the embarrassed Sergeant whose face was spattered with blood and whose long hair had come loose so that he looked like a fiend from the pit. Wellesley tried to frame the words that would express his gratitude, yet the syllables choked in his throat, but just then a trooper came trotting to the gun with the reins of the roan mare in his hand. The mare had survived unhurt, and now the trooper offered the reins towards Wellesley who, as if in a dream, walked out of the sheltered space inside the gun's tall wheel to step across the bodies Sharpe had put onto the ground. The General suddenly stooped and picked up a stone. 'This is yours, Sergeant,' he said to Sharpe, holding out the ruby. 'I saw it fall.'

'Thank you, sir. Thank you.' Sharpe took the ruby.

The General frowned at the ruby. It seemed wrong for a sergeant to have a stone that size, but once Sharpe had closed his fingers about the stone, the General decided it must have been a blood-soaked piece of rock. It surely was not a ruby? 'Are you all right, sir?' Major Blackiston asked anxiously.

'Yes, yes, thank you, Blackiston.' The General seemed to shake off his torpor and went to stand beside Campbell who had dismounted to kneel beside Diomed. The horse was shaking and neighing softly. 'Can he be saved?' Wellesley asked.

'Don't know, sir,' Campbell said. 'The pike blade's deep in his lung, poor thing.'

'Pull it out, Campbell. Gently. Maybe he'll live.' Wellesley looked around him to see that the 7th Native Cavalry had scoured the gunners away and driven the remaining Mahratta horsemen off, while Harness's 78th had again marched into canister and round shot to capture the southern part of the Mahratta artillery. Harness's adjutant now cantered through the bodies scattered around the guns. 'We've nails and mauls if you want us to spike the guns, sir,' he said to Wellesley.

'No, no. I think the gunners have learned their lesson, and we might take some of the cannon into our own service,' Wellesley said, then saw that he was still holding his sword. He sheathed it. 'Pity to spike good guns,' he added. It could take hours of hard work to drill a driven nail out of a touch-hole, and so long as the enemy gunners were defeated then the guns would no longer be a danger. The General turned to an Indian trooper who had joined Campbell beside Diomed. 'Can you save him?' he asked anxiously.

The Indian very gently pulled at the pike, but it would not move. 'Harder, man, harder,' Campbell urged him, and laid his own hands on the pike's bloodied shaft.

The two men tugged at the pike and the fallen horse screamed with pain. 'Careful!' Wellesley snapped.

'You want the pike in or out, sir?' Campbell asked.

'Try and save him,' the General said, and Campbell shrugged, took hold of the shaft again, put his boot on the horse's red wet chest, and gave a swift, hard heave. The horse screamed again as the blade left his hide and as a new rush of blood welled down to soak his white hair.

'Nothing more we can do now, sir,' Campbell said.

'Look after him,' Wellesley ordered the Indian trooper, then he frowned when he saw that his last horse, the roan mare, still had her trooper's saddle and that no one had thought to take his own saddle off Diomed. That was the orderly's job and Wellesley looked for Sharpe, then remembered he had to express his thanks to the Sergeant, but again the words would not come and so Wellesley asked Campbell to change the saddles, and once that was done he climbed onto the mare's back. Captain Barclay, who had survived his dash across the field, reined in beside the General. 'Wallace's brigade is ready to attack, sir.'

'We need to get Harness's fellows into line,' Wellesley said. 'Any news of Maxwell?'

'Not yet, sir,' Barclay said. Colonel Maxwell had led the cavalry in their pursuit across the River Juah.

'Major!' Wellesley shouted at the commander of the 7th Native Cavalry. 'Have your men hunt down the gunners here. Make sure none of them live, then guard the guns so they can't be retaken. Gentlemen?' He spoke to his aides. 'Let's move on.'

Sharpe watched the General ride away into the thinning skein of cannon smoke, then he looked down at the ruby in his hand and saw that it was as red and shiny as the blood that dripped from his sabre tip. He wondered if the ruby had been dipped in the fountain of Zum-Zum along with the Tippoo's helmet. Was that why it had saved his life? It had done bugger all for the Tippoo, but Sharpe was alive when he should have been dead, and so, for that matter, was Major General Sir Arthur Wellesley.

The General had left Sharpe alone by the gun, all but for the dead and dying men and the trooper who was trying to staunch Diomed's wound with a rag. Sharpe laughed suddenly, startling the trooper. 'He didn't even say thank you,' Sharpe said aloud.

'What, sahib?' the trooper asked.

'You don't call me sahib,' Sharpe said. 'I'm just another bloody soldier like you. Good for bloody nothing except fighting other people's battles. And ten to one the buggers won't thank you.' He was thirsty so he opened one of the General's canteens and drank from it greedily. 'Is that horse going to live?'

The Indian did not seem to understand everything Sharpe

said, but the question must have made some sense for he pointed at Diomed's mouth. The stallion's lips were drawn back to reveal yellow teeth through which a pale pink froth seeped. The Indian shook his head sadly.

'I bled that horse,' Sharpe said, 'and the General said he was greatly obliged to me. Those were his very words, "greatly obliged". Gave me a bloody coin, he did. But you save his life and he doesn't even say thank you! I should have bled him, not his bloody horse. I should have bled him to bloody death.' He drank more of the water and wished it were arrack or rum. 'You know what the funny thing is?' he asked the Indian. 'I didn't even do it because he was the General. I did it because I like him. Not personally, but I do like him. In a strange sort of way. I wouldn't have done it for you. I'd have done it for Tom Garrard, but he's a friend, see? And I'd have done it for Colonel McCandless, because he's a proper gentleman, but I wouldn't have done it for too many others.' Sharpe sounded drunk, even to himself, but in truth he was stone cold sober in a battlefield that had suddenly gone silent beneath the westering sun. It was almost evening, but there was still enough daylight left to finish the battle, though whether Sharpe would have anything to do with the finishing seemed debatable, for he had lost his job as the General's orderly, had lost his horse, had lost his musket and was stranded with nothing but a dented sabre. 'That ain't really true,' he confessed to the uncomprehending Indian, 'what I said about liking him. I want him to like me, and that's different, ain't it? I thought the miserable bugger might make me an officer! Sod that for a hope, eh? No sash for me, lad. It's back to being a bloody infantryman.' He used the bloody sabre to cut a strip of cloth from the robes of a dead Arab, and he folded the strip into a pad that he pushed under his jacket to staunch the blood from the *tulwar* wound on his left shoulder. It was not a serious injury, he decided, for he could feel no broken bones and his left arm was unhindered. He tossed the dented sabre away, found a discarded Mahratta musket, tugged the cartridge box and bayonet off the dead owner's belt, then went to find someone to kill.

It took half an hour to form the new line from the five battalions that had marched through the Mahratta gunfire and put Pohlmann's right to flight, but now the five battalions faced north towards Pohlmann's new position which rested its left flank on Assaye's mud walls then stretched along the southern bank of the River Juah. The Mahrattas had forty guns remaining, Pohlmann still commanded eight thousand infantry and innumerable cavalry, and the Rajah of Berar's twenty thousand infantrymen still waited behind the village's makeshift ramparts. Wellesley's infantry numbered fewer than four thousand men, he had only two light guns that were serviceable and scarcely six hundred cavalrymen mounted on horses that were bone weary and parched dry. 'We can hold them!' Pohlmann roared at his men. 'We can hold them and beat them! Hold them and beat them.' He was still on horseback, and still in his gaudy silk coat. He had dreamed of riding his elephant across a field strewn with the enemy's dead and piled with the enemy's captured weapons, but instead he was encouraging his men to a last stand beside the river. 'Hold them,' he shouted, 'hold them and beat them.' The Juah flowed behind his men, while in front of them the shadows stretched long across Assaye's battle-littered farmlands.

Then the pipes sounded again, and Pohlmann turned his horse to look at the right-hand end of his line and he saw the tall black bearskins and the swinging kilts of the damned Scottish regiment coming forward again. The sun caught their white crossbelts and glinted from their bayonets. Beyond them, half hidden by the trees, the British cavalry was threatening, though they seemed to be checked by a battery of cannon on the right of Pohlmann's line. The Hanoverian knew the cavalry was no danger. It was the infantry, the unstoppable red-jacketed infantry, that was going to beat him, and he saw the sepoy battalions starting forward on the Highlanders' flank and he half turned his horse, thinking to ride to where the Scottish regiment would strike his line. It would hit Saleur's *compoo*, and suddenly Pohlmann could not care less any more. Let Saleur fight his battle, because Pohlmann knew it was lost. He stared at the 78th and he reckoned that no force on earth could stop such men. 'The best damned infantry on earth,' he said to one of his aides.

'Sahib?'

'Watch them! You'll not see better fighting men while you live,' Pohlmann said bitterly, then sheathed his sword as he gazed at the Scots who were once again being battered by cannon fire, but still their two lines kept marching forward. Pohlmann knew he should go west to encourage Saleur's men, but instead he was thinking of the gold he had left behind in Assaye. These last ten years had been a fine adventure, but the Mahratta Confederation was dying before his eyes and Anthony Pohlmann did not wish to die with it. The rest of the Mahratta princedoms might fight on, but Pohlmann had decided it was time to take his gold and run.

Saleur's *compoo* was already edging backwards. Some of the men from the rearward ranks were not even waiting for the Scots to arrive, but were running back to the River Juah and wading through its muddy water that came up to their chests. The rest of the regiments began to waver. Pohlmann watched. He had thought these three *compoos* were as fine as any infantry in the world, but they had proved to be brittle. The British fired a volley and Pohlmann heard the heavy balls thump into his infantry and he heard the cheer from the redcoats as they charged forward with the bayonet, and suddenly there was no army opposing them, just a mass of men fleeing to the river.

Pohlmann took off his gaudily plumed hat that would mark him as a prize capture and threw it away, then stripped off his sash and coat and tossed them after the hat as he spurred towards Assaye. He had a few minutes, he reckoned, and those minutes should be enough to secure his money and get away. The battle was lost and, for Pohlmann, the war with it. It was time to retire.

CHAPTER 12

Assaye alone remained in enemy hands, for the rest of Pohlmann's army had simply disintegrated. The great majority of the Mahratta horsemen had spent the afternoon as spectators, but now they turned and spurred west towards Borkardan while to the north, beyond the Juah, the remnants of Pohlmann's three *compoos* fled in panic, pursued by a handful of British and Company cavalry on tired horses. Great banks of gunsmoke lay like fog across the field where men of both armies groaned and died. Diomed gave a great shudder, lifted his head a final time, then rolled his eyes and went still. The sepoy trooper, charged with guarding the horse, stayed at his post and waved the flies away from the dead Diomed's face.

The sun reddened the layers of gunsmoke. There was an hour of daylight left, a few moments of dusk, and then it would be night, and Wellesley used the last of the light to turn his victorious infantry towards the mud walls of Assaye. He summoned gunners and had them haul captured enemy cannon towards the village. 'They won't stand,' he told his aides. 'A handful of round shot and the sight of some bayonets will send them packing.'

The village still held a small army. The Rajah of Berar's twenty thousand men were behind its thick walls, and Major Dodd had succeeded in marching his own regiment into the village. He had seen the remainder of the Mahratta line crumple, he had watched Anthony Pohlmann discard his hat and coat as he fled to the village and, rather than let the panic infect his own men, Dodd had turned them eastwards, ordered the regiment's cumbersome guns to be abandoned, then followed his commanding officer into the tangle of Assaye's narrow alleys. Beny Singh, the Rajah of Berar's warlord and the Killadar of the village's garrison, was glad to see the European. 'What do we do?' he asked Dodd.

'Do? We get out, of course. The battle's lost.'

Beny Singh blinked at him. 'We just go?'

Dodd dismounted from his horse and steered Beny Singh away from his aides. 'Who are your best troops?' he asked.

'The Arabs.'

'Tell them you're going to fetch reinforcements, tell them to defend the village, and promise that if they can hold the place till nightfall then help will come in the morning.'

'But it won't,' Beny Singh protested.

'But if they hold,' Dodd said, 'they cover your escape, sahib.' He smiled ingratiatingly, knowing that men like Beny Singh could yet play a part in his future. 'The British will pounce on any fugitives leaving the village,' Dodd explained, 'but they won't dare attack men who are well drilled and well commanded. I proved that at Ahmednuggur. So you're most welcome to march north with my men, sahib. I promise they won't be broken like the rest.' He climbed back into his saddle and rode back to his Cobras and ordered them to join Captain Joubert at the ford. 'You're to wait for me there,' he told them, then shouted for his own sepoy company to follow him deeper into the village.

The battle might be lost, but Dodd's men had not failed him and he was determined they should have a reward and so he led them to the house where Colonel Pohlmann had stored his treasure. Dodd knew that if he did not give his men gold then they would melt away to find another warlord who would reward them, but if he paid them they would stay under his command while he sought another prince as employer.

He heard the sonorous bang of a great gun being fired beyond the village and he reckoned that the British had begun to pound Assaye's mud wall. Dodd knew that wall could not last long, for every shot would crumble the dried mud bricks and collapse the roof beams of the outermost houses so that in a few minutes there would be a wide breach leading into Assaye's heart. A moment later the redcoats would be ordered into the dusty breach and the village's alleys would be clogged by panic and filled with screams and bayonets.

Dodd reached the alley leading to the courtyard where Pohlmann had placed his elephants and he saw, as he had expected, that the big gate was still shut. Pohlmann was undoubtedly inside the courtyard, readying to escape, but Dodd could not wait for the Hanoverian to throw open the gates, so instead he ordered his men to fight their way through the house. He left a dozen men to block the alley, gave one of those men his horse to hold, then led the rest of the sepoys towards the house. Pohlmann's bodyguard saw them coming and fired, but fired too early and Dodd survived the panicked volley and roared his men on. 'Kill them!' he shouted as, sword in hand, he charged through the musket smoke. He kicked the house door open and plunged into a kitchen crowded with purple-coated men. He lunged with his sword, driving the defenders back, and then his sepoys arrived to carry their bayonets to Pohlmann's men. 'Gopal!' Dodd shouted.

'Sahib?' the Jemadar said, tugging his *tulwar* from the body of a dead man.

'Find the gold! Make sure it's loaded on the elephants, then open the courtyard gate!' Dodd snapped the orders, then went on killing. He was consumed with a huge anger. How could any fool have lost this battle? How could a man, given a hundred thousand troops, be beaten by a handful of redcoats? It was Pohlmann's fault, all Pohlmann, and Dodd knew Pohlmann had to be somewhere in the house or courtyard and so he hunted him and vented his rage on Pohlmann's guards, pursuing them from room to room, slaughtering them mercilessly, and all the while the great guns hammered the sky with their noise and the round shot thumped into the village walls.

Most of the Rajah of Berar's infantry fled. Those on the makeshift ramparts could see the redcoats massing beyond the smoke of the big cannon and they did not wait for that infantry to attack, but instead ran northwards. Only the Arab mercenaries stayed, and some of those men decided caution was better than bravery and so joined the other infantry that splashed through the ford where Captain Joubert waited with Dodd's regiment.

Joubert was nervous. The village's defenders were fleeing, Dodd was missing, and Simone was still somewhere in the village. It was like Ahmednuggur all over again, he thought, only this time he was determined that his wife would not be left behind and so he kicked back his heels and urged his horse towards the house where she had taken refuge.

That house was hard by the courtyard where Dodd was searching for Pohlmann, but the Hanoverian had vanished. His gold was all in its panniers, and Pohlmann's bodyguard had succeeded in strapping the panniers onto the two pack elephants before Dodd's men attacked, but there was no sign of Pohlmann himself. Dodd decided he would let the bastard live, and so, abandoning the hunt, he sheathed his sword then lifted the locking bar from the courtyard gates. 'Where's my horse?' he shouted to the men he had left guarding the alley.

'Dead, sahib!' a man answered.

Dodd ran down the alley to see that his precious new gelding had been struck by a bullet from the one volley fired by Pohlmann's bodyguard. The beast was not yet dead, but it was leaning against the alley wall with its head down, dulled eyes and blood dripping from its mouth. Dodd swore. The big guns were still firing beyond the village, showing that the redcoats were not advancing yet, but suddenly they went silent and Dodd knew he had only minutes left to make his escape, and just then he saw another horse turn into the alley. Captain Joubert was in the saddle, and Dodd ran to him. 'Joubert!'

Joubert ignored Dodd. Instead he cupped his hands and shouted up at the house where the wives had been sheltered during the fighting. 'Simone!'

'Give me your horse, Captain!' Dodd demanded.

Joubert still ignored the Major. 'Simone!' he called again, then spurred his horse on up the alley. Had she already gone? Was she north of the Juah? 'Simone?' he shouted.

'Captain!' Dodd screamed behind him.

Joubert turned, summoned the courage to tell the Englishman to go to hell, but as he turned he saw that Dodd was holding a big pistol.

'No!' Joubert protested.

'Yes, Monsewer,' Dodd said, and fired. The ball snatched Joubert back against the alley wall and he slid down to leave a trail of blood. A woman screamed from a window above the alley as Dodd pulled himself into the Frenchman's saddle. Gopal was already leading the first elephant out of the gate. 'To the ford, Gopal!' Dodd shouted, then he spurred into the courtyard to make certain that the second elephant was ready to leave.

While outside, in the alleys, there was a sudden silence. Most of the village's garrison had fled, the dust drifted from its broken walls, and then the order was given for the redcoats to advance. Assaye was doomed.

Colonel McCandless had watched Dodd's men retreat into the village and he doubted that the traitor was leading his men to reinforce the doomed garrison. 'Sevajee!' McCandless called. 'Take your men to the far side!'

'Across the river?' Sevajee asked.

'Watch to see if he crosses the ford,' McCandless said.

'Where will you be, Colonel?'

'In the village.' McCandless slid from Aeolus's back and limped towards the captured guns that had started to fire at the mud walls. The shadows were long now, the daylight short and the battle ending, but there was still time for Dodd to be trapped. Let him be a hero, McCandless prayed, let him stay in the village just long enough to be caught.

The big guns were only three hundred paces from the village's thick wall and each shot pulverized the mud bricks and started great clouds of red dust that billowed thick as gunsmoke. Wellesley summoned the survivors of the 74th and a Madrassi battalion and lined them both up behind the guns. 'They won't stand, Wallace,' Wellesley said to the 74th's commander. 'We'll give them five minutes of artillery, then your fellows can take the place.'

'Allow me to congratulate you, sir,' Wallace said, taking a hand from his reins and holding it towards the General.

'Congratulate me?' Wellesley asked with a frown.

'On a victory, sir.'

'I suppose it is a victory. 'Pon my soul, so it is. Thank you, Wallace.' The General leaned across and shook the Scotsman's hand.

'A great victory,' Wallace said heartily, then climbed out of his saddle so that he could lead the 74th into the village.

McCandless joined him. 'You don't mind if I come, Wallace?'

'Glad of your company, McCandless. A great day, is it not?'

'The Lord has been merciful to us,' McCandless agreed. 'Praise His name.'

The guns ceased, their smoke drifted northwards and the dying sun shone on the broken walls. There were no defenders visible, nothing but dust and fallen bricks and broken timbers.

'Go, Wallace!' Wellesley called, and the 74th's lone piper hoisted his instrument and played the redcoats and the sepoys forward. The other battalions watched. Those other battalions had fought all afternoon, they had destroyed an army, and now they sprawled beside the Juah and drank its muddy water to slake their powder-induced thirst. None crossed the river, only a handful of cavalry splashed through the water to chase the laggard fugitives on the farther bank.

Major Blackiston brought Wellesley a captured standard, one of a score that had been abandoned by the fleeing Mahrattas. 'They left all their guns too, sir, every last one of them!'

Wellesley acknowledged the standard with a smile. 'I'd rather you brought me some water, Blackiston. Where are my canteens?'

'Sergeant Sharpe still has them, sir,' Campbell answered, holding his own canteen to the General.

'Ah yes, Sharpe.' The General frowned, knowing there was unfinished business there. 'If you see him, bring him to me.'

'I will, sir.'

Sharpe was not far away. He had walked north through the litter of the Mahratta battle line, going to where the guns fired on the village and, just as they stopped, so he saw McCandless walking behind the 74th as it advanced on the village. He hurried to catch up with the Colonel and was rewarded with a warm smile from McCandless. 'Thought I'd lost you, Sharpe.'

'Almost did, sir.'

'The General released you, did he?'

'He did, sir, in a manner of speaking. We ran out of horses, sir. He had two killed.'

'Two! An expensive day for him! It sounds as if you had an eventful time!'

'Not really, sir,' Sharpe said. 'Bit confusing, really.'

The Colonel frowned at the blood staining the light infantry insignia on Sharpe's left shoulder. 'You're wounded, Sharpe.'

'A scratch, sir. Bastard with – sorry, sir – man with a *tulwar* tried to tickle me.'

'But you're all right?' McCandless asked anxiously.

'Fine, sir.' He raised his left arm to show that the wound was not serious.

'The day's not over yet,' McCandless said, then gestured at the village. 'Dodd's there, Sharpe, or he was. I'm glad you're here. He'll doubtless try to escape, but Sevajee's on the far side of the river and between us we might yet trap the rogue.'

Sergeant Obadiah Hakeswill was a hundred paces behind McCandless. He too had seen the Colonel following the 74th and now Hakeswill followed McCandless, for if McCandless wrote his letter, then Hakeswill knew his sergeantcy was imperilled. 'It ain't that I like doing it,' he said to his men as he stalked after the Colonel, 'but he ain't giving me a choice. No choice at all. His own fault. His own fault.' Three of his men were following him, the others had refused to come.

A musket fired from Assaye's rooftops, showing that not all the defenders had fled. The ball fluttered over Wallace's head and the Colonel, not wanting to expose his men to any other fire that might come from the village, shouted at his men to double. 'Just get in among the houses, boys,' he called. 'Get in and hunt them down! Quick now!'

More muskets fired from the houses, but the 74th were running now, and cheering as they ran. The first men scrambled over the makeshift breach blown by the big guns, while others hauled aside a cart that blocked an alleyway and, with that entrance opened, a twin stream of Scotsmen and sepoys hurried into the village. The Arab defenders fired their last shots, then retreated ahead of the redcoat rush. A few were trapped in houses and died under Scottish or Indian bayonets.

'You go ahead, Sharpe,' McCandless said, for his wounded leg was making him limp and he was now far behind the Highlanders. 'See if you can spot the man,' McCandless suggested, though he doubted Sharpe would. Dodd would be long gone by now, but there was always a chance he had waited until the end and, if men of the 74th had trapped Dodd, then Sharpe could at least try and make sure that the wretch was taken alive. 'Go, Sharpe,' the Colonel ordered, 'hurry!'

Sharpe dutifully ran on ahead. He clambered up the dust of the breach and jumped down into the pitiful wreckage of a room. He pushed through the house, stepped over a dead Arab sprawled in the outer door, edged about a dungheap in the courtyard, then plunged into an alleyway. Shots sounded from the river and so he headed that way past houses that were being looted of what little remained after the Mahratta occupation. A sepoy emerged from one house with a broken pot while a Highlander had found a broken brass weighing-scale, but the plunder was nothing like the riches that had been taken in Ahmednuggur. Another volley sounded ahead and Sharpe broke into a run, turned a corner and then stopped above the village's ford.

Dodd's regiment was on the far side of the river where

two white-coated companies had formed a rearguard. It was just like Ahmednuggur, where Dodd had guarded his escape route with volley fire, and now the Major had done it again. He was safely over the river with Pohlmann's two elephants, and his men had been firing at any redcoats who dared show on the ford's southern bank, but then, just as Sharpe arrived at the ford, the rearguard about-turned and marched north.

'He got away,' a man said, 'the bastard got clean away,' and Sharpe looked at the speaker and saw an East India Company sergeant in a doorway a few yards away. The man was smoking a cheroot and appeared to be standing guard over a group of prisoners in the house behind him.

Sharpe turned to watch Dodd's regiment march into the shadow of some trees. 'The bastard,' Sharpe spat. He could see Dodd on his horse just ahead of the two rearguard companies, and he was tempted to raise his musket and try one last shot, but the range was much too great and then Dodd vanished among the shadows. His rearguard followed him. Sharpe could see Sevajee off to the west, but the Indian was helpless. Dodd had five hundred men in ranks and files, and Sevajee had but ten horsemen. 'He bloody got away again,' Sharpe said, and spat towards the river.

'With my gold,' the East India Company sergeant said miserably, and Sharpe looked again at the man.

'Bloody hell,' Sharpe said in astonishment, for he was looking at Anthony Pohlmann who had donned his old sergeant's uniform. Pohlmann's 'prisoners' were a small group of his bodyguard.

'A pity,' Pohlmann said, spitting a scrap of tobacco from between his teeth. 'Ten minutes ago I was one of the richest men in India. Now I suppose I'm your prisoner?'

'I couldn't care less about you, sir,' Sharpe said, slinging the musket on his shoulder.

'You don't want to march me to Wellesley?' the Hanoverian asked. 'It would be a great feather in your cap.'

'That bastard doesn't give feathers,' Sharpe said. 'He's a stuck-up, cold-hearted bastard, he is, and I'd rather fillet him than you.'

Pohlmann grinned. 'So I can go, Sergeant Sharpe?'

'Do what you bloody like,' Sharpe said. 'How many men have you got in there?'

'Five. That's all he left me. He slaughtered the rest.'

'Dodd did?'

'He tried to kill me, but I hid under some straw. A shameful end to my career as a warlord, wouldn't you say?' Pohlmann smiled. 'I think you did well, Sergeant Sharpe, to turn down my commission.'

Sharpe laughed bitterly. 'I know my place, sir. Down in the gutter. Officers don't want men like me joining them. I might scratch my arse on parade or piss in their soup.' He walked to the small house and peered through the open door. 'Better tell your fellows to take their coats off, sir. They'll be shot otherwise.' Then he went very still for, crouching at the back of the small room, was a woman in a shabby linen dress and a straw hat. It was Simone. Sharpe pulled off his shako. 'Madame?'

She stared at him, seeing only his silhouette against the dazzle of the day's last sun.

'Simone?' Sharpe said.

'Richard?'

'It's me, love.' He grinned. 'Don't tell me you got left behind again!'

'He killed Pierre!' Simone cried. 'I watched him. He shot him!'

'Dodd?'

'Who else?' Pohlmann asked behind Sharpe.

Sharpe stepped into the room and held his hand towards

368

Simone. 'You want to stay here,' he asked her, 'or come with me?'

She hesitated a second, then stood and took his hand. Pohlmann sighed. 'I was hoping to console the widow, Sharpe.'

'You lost, sir,' Sharpe said, 'you lost.' And he walked away with Simone, going to find McCandless to give him the bad news. Dodd had escaped.

Colonel McCandless limped up the breach and into Assaye. He sensed that Dodd was gone, for there was no more fighting in the village, though some shots still sounded from the river bank, but even those shots ended as the Scotsman edged past the dead man in the house doorway and through the court-yard into the street.

And perhaps, he thought, it did not really matter any longer, for this day's victory would echo throughout all India. The redcoats had broken two armies, they had ruined the power of two mighty princes, and from this day on Dodd would be hunted from refuge to refuge as the British power spread northwards. And it would spread, McCandless knew. Each new advance was declared to be the last, but each brought new frontiers and new enemies and so the redcoats marched again, and maybe they would never stop marching until they reached the great mountains in the very north. And maybe it was there, McCandless thought, that Dodd would at last be trapped and shot down like a dog.

And suddenly McCandless did not care very much. He felt old. The pain in his leg was terrible. He was still weak from his fever. It was time, he thought, to go home. Back to Scotland. He should sell Aeolus, repay Sharpe, take his pension, and board a ship. Go home, he thought, to Lochaber and to the green slopes of Glen Scaddle. There was work to be done in Britain, useful work, for he was corresponding with men in London and Edinburgh who wished to establish a society to spread Bibles throughout the heathen world and McCandless decided he could find a small house in Lochaber, hire a servant, and spend his days translating God's word into the Indian languages. That, he thought, would be a job worth doing, and he wondered why he had waited so long. A small house, a large fire, a library, a table, a supply of ink and paper and, with God's help, he could do more for India from that one small house than he could ever achieve by hunting down one traitor.

The thought of the great task cheered him, then he turned a corner and saw Pohlmann's great elephant wandering free in an alleyway. 'You're lost, boy,' he said to the elephant and took hold of one of its ears. 'Someone left the gate open, didn't they?'

He turned the elephant which followed him happily enough. They walked past a dead horse, and then McCandless saw a dead European in a white jacket, and for an instant he thought it must be Dodd, then he recognized Captain Joubert lying on his back with a bullet hole in his breast. 'Poor man,' he said, and he guided the elephant through the gate into the courtyard. 'I'll make sure you're brought some food,' he told the beast, then he turned and barred the gate.

He left the courtyard through the house, picking his way across the welter of bodies in the kitchen. He pushed open the outer door and found himself staring into Sergeant Hakeswill's blue eyes.

'I've been looking for you, sir,' Hakeswill said.

'You and I have no business, Sergeant,' McCandless said.

'Oh, but we does, sir,' Hakeswill said, and his three men blocked the alley behind him. 'I wanted to talk to you, sir,' Hakeswill said, 'about that letter you ain't going to write to my Colonel Gore.'

McCandless shook his head. 'I have nothing to say to you, Sergeant.'

'I hates the bleeding Scotch,' Hakeswill said, his face twitching. 'All prayers and morals, ain't you, Colonel? But I ain't cumbered with morals. It's an advantage I have.' He grinned, then drew his bayonet and slotted it onto the muzzle of his musket. 'They hanged me once, Colonel, but I lived 'cos God loves me, He does, and I ain't going to be punished again, not ever. Not by you, Colonel, not by any man. Says so in the scriptures.' He advanced on McCandless with the bayonet. His three men hung back and McCandless reckoned they were nervous, but Hakeswill showed no fear of this confrontation.

'Put up your weapon, Sergeant,' McCandless snapped.

'Oh, I will, sir, I'll put it up inside you unless you promises me on the holy word of God that you won't write no letter.'

'I shall write the letter tonight,' McCandless said, then drew his claymore. 'Now put up your weapon, Sergeant.'

Hakeswill's face twitched. He stopped three paces from McCandless. 'You'd like to strike me down, wouldn't you, sir? 'Cos you don't like me, sir, do you? But God loves me, sir, he does. He looks after me.'

'You're under arrest, Sergeant,' McCandless said, 'for threatening an officer.'

'Let's see who God loves most, sir. Me or you.'

'Put up your weapon!' McCandless roared.

'Bloody Scotch bastard,' Hakeswill said, and pulled his trigger. The bullet caught McCandless in the gullet and blew out through the back of his spine, and the Colonel was dead before his body touched the floor. The elephant in the nearby courtyard, startled by the shot, trumpeted, but Hakeswill ignored the beast. 'Scotch bastard,' he said, then stepped through the doorway and knelt to the body which he searched for gold. 'And if any one of you three says a bleeding word,' he threatened his men, 'you'll join him in heaven. If he's gone there, which I doubt, on account of God not wanting to clutter paradise with Scotchmen. Says so in the scriptures.' He found gold in McCandless's sporran and turned to show the coins to his men. 'You want it?' he asked. 'Then you keeps silent about it.'

They nodded. They wanted gold. Hakeswill tossed them the coins, then led them deeper into the house to see if there was anything worth plundering in its rooms. 'And once we're done,' he said, 'we'll find the General, we will, and have him give us Sharpie. We're almost there, lads. It's been a long road, it has, and hard in places, but we're almost there.'

Sharpe searched the village for Colonel McCandless, but could not find him in any of the alleys. He took Simone with him as he searched some of the larger houses and, from one high window, he found himself staring down into the court-yard where Pohlmann's great elephant was penned, but there was no sign of McCandless and Sharpe decided he was wasting his time. 'I reckon we'll give up, love,' he told Simone. 'He'll look for me, like enough, probably down by the river.' They walked back to the ford. Pohlmann had vanished and Dodd's men had long disappeared. The sun was at the horizon now and the farmlands north of the Juah were stained black by long shadows. The men who had captured the village were filling their canteens from the river, and the first few campfires glittered in the dusk as men boiled water to make themselves tea. Simone clung to him and kept talking of her husband. She felt guilty because she had not loved him, yet he had died because he had gone back into the village to find her, and Sharpe did not know how to console her. 'He was a soldier, love,' he told her, 'and he died in battle.'

'But I killed him!'

'No, you didn't,' Sharpe said, and he heard hooves behind him and he turned, hoping to see Colonel McCandless, but instead it was General Wellesley and Colonel Wallace and a score of aides riding up to the ford. He straightened to attention.

'Sergeant Sharpe,' Wellesley said, sounding embarrassed.

'Sir,' Sharpe said woodenly.

The General slid from his saddle. His face was red, and Sharpe supposed that was the effect of the sun. 'I have been remiss, Sergeant,' the General said awkwardly, 'for I believe I owe you my life.'

Sharpe felt himself blushing and was glad that the sun was low and the roadway where he stood was in deep shadow. 'Just did my best, sir,' he muttered. 'This is Madame Joubert, sir. Her husband was killed, sir, fighting for Colonel Pohlmann.'

The General took off his hat and bowed to Simone. 'My commiserations, Madame,' he said, then looked back to Sharpe whose long black hair still spilled over his collar. 'Do you know where Colonel McCandless is?' he asked.

'No, sir. I've been looking for him, sir.'

Wellesley fidgeted with his hat, paused to take a deep breath, then nodded. 'Colonel McCandless managed to have a long talk with Colonel Wallace this afternoon,' the General said. 'How they found time to have a conversation in battle, I don't know!' This was evidently a jest, for the General smiled, though Sharpe stayed straight-faced, and his lack of reaction disconcerted Wellesley. 'I have to reward you, Sharpe,' Wellesley said curtly.

'For what, sir?'

'For my life,' the General said in a tone of irritation.

'I'm just glad I was there, sir,' Sharpe said, feeling as awkward as Wellesley himself evidently felt.

'I'm rather glad you were there too,' the General said, then

373

took a step forward and held out his hand. 'Thank you, Mister Sharpe.'

Sharpe hesitated, astonished at the gesture, then made himself shake the General's hand. It was only then that he noticed what Wellesley had said. 'Mister, sir?' he asked.

'It is customary in this army, Mister Sharpe, to reward uncommon bravery with uncommon promotion. Wallace tells me you desire a commission, and he has vacancies in the 74th. God knows he has too many vacancies, so if you're agreeable, Sharpe, you can join the Colonel's regiment as an ensign.'

For a second Sharpe did not really comprehend what was being said, then he suddenly did and he smiled. There were tears in his eyes, but he reckoned that must be because of the powder smoke that lingered in the village. 'Thank you, sir,' he said warmly, 'thank you.'

'There, that's done,' Wellesley said with relief. 'My congratulations, Sharpe, and my sincere thanks.' His aides were all smiling at Sharpe, not Sergeant Sharpe any longer, but Ensign Sharpe of the King's 74th. Captain Campbell even climbed down from his saddle and offered his hand to Sharpe who was still smiling as he shook it.

'It'll turn out badly, of course,' Wellesley said to Campbell as he turned away. 'It always does. We promote them beyond their station and they inevitably take to drink.'

'He's a good man, sir,' Campbell said loyally.

'I doubt that too. But he's a good soldier, I'll say that. He's all yours now, Wallace, all yours!' The General pulled himself into his saddle, then turned to Simone. 'Madame? I can offer you very little, but if you care to join me for supper I would be honoured. Captain Campbell will escort you.'

Campbell held his hand out to Simone. She looked at Sharpe, who nodded at her, and she shyly accepted Campbell's arm and followed the General back up the street.

Colonel Wallace paused to lean down from his horse and shake Sharpe's hand. 'I'll give you a few minutes to clean yourself up, Sharpe, and to get those stripes off your arm. You might like to chop off some of that hair, while you're about it. And I hate to suggest it, but if you walk a few paces east of the village you'll find plenty of red sashes on corpses. Pick one, help yourself to a sword, then come and meet your fellow officers. They're few enough now, I fear, so you'll surely be welcome. Even the men might be glad of you, despite your being English.' Wallace smiled.

'I'm very grateful to you, sir,' Sharpe said. He was still scarcely able to believe what had happened. He was Mister Sharpe! Mister!

'And what do you want?' Wallace suddenly asked in an icy tone, and Sharpe saw that his new Colonel was staring at Obadiah Hakeswill.

'Him, sir,' Hakeswill said, pointing at Sharpe. 'Sergeant Sharpe, sir, what is under arrest.'

Wallace smiled. 'You may arrest Sergeant Sharpe, Sergeant, but you will certainly not arrest Ensign Sharpe.'

'Ensign?' Hakeswill said, going pale.

'Mister Sharpe is a commissioned officer, Sergeant,' Wallace said crisply, 'and you will treat him as such. Good day.' Wallace touched his hat to Sharpe, then turned his horse and rode away.

Hakeswill gaped at Sharpe. 'You, Sharpie,' he said, 'an officer?'

Sharpe walked closer to the Sergeant. 'That's not how you address a King's officer, Obadiah, and you know it.'

'You?' Hakeswill's face twitched. 'You?' he asked again in horror and amazement.

Sharpe thumped him in the belly, doubling him over. 'You call me "sir", Obadiah,' he said.

'I won't call you "sir",' Hakeswill said between gasps for

breath. 'Not till hell freezes, Sharpie, and not even then.'

Sharpe hit him again. Hakeswill's three men watched, but did nothing. 'You call me "sir",' Sharpe said.

'You ain't an officer, Sharpie,' Hakeswill said, then yelped because Sharpe had seized his hair and was dragging him up the street. The three men started to follow, but Sharpe snarled at them to stay where they were, and all three obeyed.

'You'll call me "sir", Sergeant,' Sharpe said, 'just you watch.' And he pulled Hakeswill up the street, going back to the house from where he had seen the elephant. He dragged Hakeswill through the door and up the stairs. The Sergeant screamed at him, beat at him, but Hakeswill had never been a match for Sharpe who now snatched the musket from Hakeswill's hand, threw it away, then took him to the window that opened just one floor above the courtyard. 'See that elephant, Obadiah?' he asked, holding the Sergeant's face in the open window. 'I watched it trample a man to death not long ago.'

'You won't dare, Sharpie,' Hakeswill squealed, then yelped as Sharpe took hold of the seat of his pants.

'Call me "sir",' Sharpe said.

'Never! You ain't an officer!'

'But I am, Obadiah, I am. I'm Mister Sharpe. I'll wear a sword and a sash and you'll have to salute me.'

'Never!'

Sharpe heaved Hakeswill onto the window ledge. 'If you ask me to put you down,' he said, 'and if you call me "sir", I'll let you go.'

'You ain't an officer,' Hakeswill protested. 'You can't be!'

'But I am, Obadiah,' Sharpe said, and he heaved the Sergeant over the ledge. The Sergeant screamed as he fell into the straw below, and the elephant, made curious by this strange irruption into this already strange day, plodded over to inspect him. Hakeswill beat feebly at the animal which had him cornered. 'Goodbye, Obadiah,' Sharpe called, then he used the words he remembered Pohlmann shouting when Dodd's sepoy had been trampled to death. '*Haddah!*' Sharpe snapped. '*Haddah!*'

'Get the bastard off me!' Hakeswill screamed as the elephant moved still closer and raised a forefoot.

'That won't do, Obadiah,' Sharpe said.

'Sir!' Hakeswill called. 'Please, sir! Get it off me!'

'What did you say?' Sharpe asked, cupping a hand to his ear.

'Sir! Sir! Please, sir! Mister Sharpe, sir!'

'Rot in hell, Obadiah,' Sharpe called down, and walked away. The sun was gone, the village was stinking with powder smoke, and two armies lay in ragged ruin on the bloody fields outside Assaye, but that great victory was not Sharpe's. It was the voice calling from the courtyard, calling frantically as Sharpe ran down the wooden stairs and walked down the alleyway. 'Sir! Sir!' Hakeswill shouted, and Sharpe listened and smiled, for that, he reckoned, was his real victory. It was Mister Sharpe's triumph.

Historical Note

The background events to *Sharpe's Triumph*, the siege of Ahmednuggur and the battle of Assaye, both happened much as described in the novel, just as many of the characters in the story existed. Not just the obvious characters, like Wellesley, but men like Colin Campbell, who was the first man over the wall at Ahmednuggur, and Anthony Pohlmann who truly was once a sergeant in the East India Company, but who commanded the Mahratta forces at Assaye. What happened to Pohlmann after the battle is something of a mystery, but there is some evidence that he rejoined the East India Company army again, only this time as an officer. Colonel Gore, Colonel Wallace and Colonel Harness all existed, and poor Harness was losing his wits and would need to retire soon after the battle. The massacre at Chasalgaon is a complete invention, though there was a Lieutenant William Dodd who did defect to the Mahrattas just before the campaign rather than face a civilian trial for the death of the goldsmith he had ordered beaten. Dodd had been sentenced to six months' loss of pay and Wellesley, enraged by the leniency of the court martial, persuaded the East India Company to impose a new sentence, that of dismissal from their army, and planned to have Dodd tried for murder in a civilian court. Dodd, hearing of the decision, fled, though I doubt that he took any sepoys with him. Nevertheless desertion was a problem for the Company at that time, for many sepoys knew that the Indian states would pay well for British-trained troops. They would pay even more for competent European (or American) officers, and many such made their fortunes in those years.

The city of Ahmednuggur has grown so much that most traces of its wall have now been swallowed by new building, but the adjacent fortress remains and is still a formidable stronghold. Today the fort is a depot of the Indian Army, and something of a shrine to Indians, for it was within the vast circuit of its red stone ramparts that the leaders of Indian independence were imprisoned by the British during the Second World War. Visitors are welcome to explore the ramparts with their impressive bastions and concealed galleries. The height of the fort's wall was slightly greater than the city's defences, and the fort, unlike the city, had a protective ditch, but the ramparts still offer an idea of the obstacle Wellesley's men faced when they launched their surprise escalade on the morning of 8 August 1803. It was a brave decision, and a calculated one, for Wellesley knew he would be heavily outnumbered in the Mahratta War and must have decided that a display of arrogant confidence would abrade his enemy's morale. The success of the attack certainly impressed some Indians. Goklah, a Mahratta leader who allied himself with the British, said of the capture of Ahmednuggur, 'These English are a strange people, and their General a wonderful man. They came here in the morning, looked at the *pettah* wall, walked over it, killed all the garrison, and returned to breakfast! What can withstand them?' Goklah's tribute was apt, except that it was Scotsmen who 'walked over the wall' and not Englishmen, and the celerity of their victory helped establish Wellesley's reputation for invincibility. Lieutenant Colin Campbell of the 78th was rewarded for his bravery with a promotion and a place on Wellesley's staff. He eventually became Sir Colin Campbell, governor of Ceylon.

The story of Wellesley deducing the presence of the ford at Peepulgaon by observation and common sense is well attested. To use the ford was an enormously brave decision, for no one knew if it truly existed until Wellesley himself spurred into the river. His orderly, from the 19th Dragoons, was killed as he approached the River Kaitna and nowhere is it recorded who took his place, but some soldier must have picked up the dragoon's duties, for Wellesley did have two horses killed beneath him that day and someone was close at hand on both occasions with a remount. Both horses died as described in the novel, the first during the 78th's magnificent assault on Pohlmann's right, and Diomed, Wellesley's favourite charger, during the scrappy fighting to retake the Mahratta gun line. It was during that fight that Wellesley was unhorsed and surrounded momentarily by enemies. He never told the tale in detail, though it is believed he was forced to use his sword to defend himself, and it was probably the closest he ever came to death in his long military career. Was his life saved by some unnamed soldier? Probably not, for Wellesley would surely have given credit for such an act that could well have resulted in a battlefield commission. Wellesley was notorious for disliking such promotions from the ranks ('they always take to drink'), though he did promote two men for conspicuous bravery on the evening of Assaye.

Assaye is not the most famous of Arthur Wellesley's battles, but it was the one of which he was most proud. Years later, long after he had swept the French out of Portugal and Spain, and after he had defeated Napoleon at Waterloo, the Duke of Wellington (as Arthur Wellesley became) was asked what had been his finest battle. He did not hesitate. 'Assaye,' he answered, and so it surely was, for he outmanoeuvred and outfought a much larger enemy, and did it swiftly, brutally and brilliantly. He did it, too, without Colonel Stevenson's help. Stevenson tried to reinforce Wellesley, but his local guide misled him as he hurried towards the sound of the guns, and Stevenson was so upset by the guide's error that he hanged the man.

Assaye was one of the costliest of Wellesley's battles: 'the bloodiest for the numbers that I ever saw,' the Duke recalled in later life. Pohlmann's forces had 1200 killed and about 5000 wounded, while Wellesley suffered 456 dead (200 of them Scottish) and around 1200 wounded. All the enemy guns, 102 of them, were captured and many were discovered to be of such high quality that they were taken into British service, though others, mostly because their calibres did not match the British standard artillery weights, were double-shotted and blown up on the battlefield where some of their remnants still lie.

The battlefield remains virtually unchanged. No roads have been metalled, the fords look as they did, and Assaye itself is scarcely larger now than it was in 1803. The outer walls of the houses are still ramparts of mud bricks, while bones and bullets are constantly ploughed out of the soil ('they were very big men', one farmer told me, indicating the ground where the 74th suffered so much). There is no memorial at Assaye, except for a painted map of the armies' dispositions on one village wall and the grave of a British officer which has had its bronze plate stolen, but the inhabitants know that history was made in their fields, are proud of it and proved remarkably welcoming when we visited. There ought to be some marker on the field, for the Scottish and Indian troops who fought at Assaye gained an astonishing victory. They were all extraordinarily brave men, and their campaign was not yet over, for some of the enemy have escaped and the war will go on as Wellesley and his small army pursue the remaining Mahrattas towards their great hill fastness at Gawilghur. Which means that Mister Sharpe must march again.

EX LIBRIS

VINTAGE CLASSICS

ALDOUS HUXLEY

Aldous Huxley was born on 26 July 1894 near Godalming, Surrey. He began writing poetry and short stories in his early twenties, but it was his first novel, *Crome Yellow* (1921), which established his literary reputation. This was swiftly followed by *Antic Hay* (1923), *Those Barren Leaves* (1925) and *Point Counter Point* (1928) – bright, brilliant satires of contemporary society. For most of the 1920s Huxley lived in Italy but in the 1930s he moved to Sanary, near Toulon.

In the years leading up to the Second World War, Huxley's work took on a more sombre tone in response to the confusion of society which he felt to be spinning dangerously out of control. His great novels of ideas, including his most famous work *Brave New World* (published in 1932 this warned against the dehumanising aspects of scientific and material 'progress') and the pacifist novel *Eyeless in Gaza* (1936) were accompanied by a series of wise and brilliant essays, collected in volume form under titles such as *Music at Night* (1931) and *Ends and Means* (1937).

In 1937, at the height of his fame, Huxley left Europe to live in California, working for a time as a screenwriter in Hollywood. As the West braced itself for war, Huxley came increasingly to believe that the key to solving the world's problems lay in changing the individual through mystical enlightenment. The exploration of the inner life through mysticism and hallucinogenic drugs was to dominate his work for the rest of his life. His beliefs found expression in both fiction (*Time Must Have a Stop*, 1944 and *Island*, 1962) and non-fiction (*The Perennial Philosophy*, 1945, *Grey Eminence*, 1941 and the famous account of his first mescalin experience, *The Doors of Perception*, 1954.)

Huxley died in California on 22 November 1963.

ALSO BY ALDOUS HUXLEY

ALDOUS HUXLEY

After Many a Summer

VINTAGE

1 3 5 7 9 10 8 6 4 2

Vintage
20 Vauxhall Bridge Road,
London SW1V 2SA

Vintage is part of the Penguin Random House group of companies whose
addresses can be found at global.penguinrandomhouse.com

Copyright © Aldous Huxley 1939

Aldous Huxley has asserted his right to be identified as the author of this
Work in accordance with the Copyright, Designs and Patents Act 1988

First published in Great Britain by Chatto & Windus in 1939

www.vintage-books.co.uk

A CIP catalogue record for this book is
available from the British Library

ISBN 9781784870355

Printed and bound by CPI Group (UK) Ltd, Croydon CR0 4YY

Penguin Random House is committed to a sustainable
future for our business, our readers and our planet.
This book is made from Forest Stewardship Council®
certified paper

The woods decay, the woods decay and fall,
The vapours weep their burthen to the ground,
Man comes and tills the field and lies beneath,
And after many a summer dies the swan.

TENNYSON

PART ONE

Chapter One

IT HAD all been arranged by telegram; Jeremy Pordage was to look out for a coloured chauffeur in a grey uniform with a carnation in his button-hole; and the coloured chauffeur was to look out for a middle-aged Englishman carrying the Poetical Works of Wordsworth. In spite of the crowds at the station, they found one another without difficulty.

'Mr. Stoyte's chauffeur?'

'Mr. Pordage, sah?'

Jeremy nodded and, his Wordsworth in one hand, his umbrella in the other, half extended his arms in the gesture of a self-deprecatory mannequin exhibiting, with a full and humorous consciousness of their defects, a deplorable figure accentuated by the most ridiculous clothes. 'A poor thing,' he seemed to be implying, 'but myself.' A defensive and, so to say, prophylactic disparagement had become a habit with him. He resorted to it on every sort of occasion. Suddenly a new idea came into his head. Anxiously he began to wonder whether, in this democratic Far West of theirs, one shook hands with the chauffeur—particularly if he happened to be a blackamoor, just to demonstrate that one wasn't a pukka sahib even if one's country did happen to be bearing the White Man's burden. In the end he decided to do nothing. Or, to be more accurate, the decision was forced upon him—as usual, he said to himself, deriving a curious wry pleasure from the recognition of his own shortcomings. While he was hesitating what to do, the chauffeur took off his cap and, slightly over-acting the part of an old-world negro retainer, bowed, smiled toothily and said, 'Welcome to Los Angeles, Mr. Pordage, sah!' Then, changing the tone of his chanting drawl from the dramatic to the confidential, 'I should have knowed you by your voice, Mr. Pordage,' he went on, 'even without the book.'

Jeremy laughed a little uncomfortably. A week in America had made him self-conscious about that voice of his. A product of Trinity College, Cambridge, ten years before the War, it was a small, fluty voice, suggestive of evensong in an English cathedral. At home, when he used it, nobody paid any particular attention. He had never had to make jokes about it, as he had done, in self-protection, about his appearance for example, or his age. Here, in America, things were different. He had only to order a cup of coffee or ask the way to the lavatory (which anyhow wasn't called the lavatory in this disconcerting country) for people to stare at him with an amused and attentive curiosity, as though he were a freak on show in an amusement park. It had not been at all agreeable.

'Where's my porter?' he said fussily in order to change the subject.

A few minutes later they were on their way. Cradled in the back seat of the car, out of range, he hoped, of the chauffeur's conversation, Jeremy Pordage abandoned himself to the pleasure of merely looking. Southern California rolled past the windows; all he had to do was to keep his eyes open.

The first thing to present itself was a slum of Africans and Filipinos, Japanese and Mexicans. And what permutations and combinations of black, yellow and brown! What complex bastardies! And the girls—how beautiful in their artificial silk! 'And negro ladies in white

muslin gowns.' His favourite line in *The Prelude*. He
smiled to himself. And meanwhile the slum had given
place to the tall buildings of a business district.

The population took on a more Caucasian tinge. At
every corner there was a drug-store. The newspaper
boys were selling headlines about Franco's drive on
Barcelona. Most of the girls, as they walked along,
seemed to be absorbed in silent prayer; but he supposed,
on second thoughts, it was only gum that they were thus
incessantly ruminating. Gum, not God. Then suddenly
the car plunged into a tunnel and emerged into another
world, a vast, untidy, suburban world of filling-stations
and billboards, of low houses in gardens, of vacant lots
and waste-paper, of occasional shops and office buildings
and churches—Primitive Methodist churches built, surprisingly enough, in the style of the Cartuja at Granada,
Catholic churches like Canterbury Cathedral, synagogues
disguised as Hagia Sophia, Christian Science churches
with pillars and pediments, like banks. It was a winter
day and early in the morning; but the sun shone brilliantly, the sky was without a cloud. The car was travelling westwards, and the sunshine, slanting from behind
them as they advanced, lit up each building, each sky-
sign and billboard, as though with a spot-light, as though
on purpose to show the new arrival all the sights.

EATS. COCKTAILS. OPEN NITES.

JUMBO MALTS.

DO THINGS, GO PLACES WITH CONSOL SUPER GAS!
AT BEVERLY PANTHEON FINE FUNERALS ARE *NOT*
EXPENSIVE.

The car sped onwards, and here in the middle of a
vacant lot was a restaurant in the form of a seated bulldog,
the entrance between the front paws, the eyes illuminated.

'Zoomorph,' Jeremy Pordage murmured to himself,

and again, 'zoomorph.' He had the scholar's taste for words. The bulldog shot back into the past.

ASTROLOGY, NUMEROLOGY, PSYCHIC READINGS.

DRIVE IN FOR NUTBERGERS—whatever they were. He resolved at the earliest opportunity to have one. A nutberger and a jumbo malt.

STOP HERE FOR CONSOL SUPER GAS.

Surprisingly, the chauffeur stopped. 'Ten gallons of Super-Super,' he ordered; then, turning back to Jeremy, 'This is our company,' he added. 'Mr. Stoyte, he's the president.' He pointed to a billboard across the street. CASH LOANS IN FIFTEEN MINUTES, Jeremy read; CONSULT COMMUNITY SERVICE FINANCE CORPORATION. 'That's another of ours,' said the chauffeur proudly.

They drove on. The face of a beautiful young woman, distorted, like a Magdalene's, with grief, stared out of a giant billboard. BROKEN ROMANCE, proclaimed the caption. SCIENCE PROVES THAT 73 PER CENT. OF ALL ADULTS HAVE HALITOSIS.

IN TIME OF SORROW LET BEVERLY PANTHEON BE YOUR FRIEND.

FACIALS, PERMANENTS, MANICURES.

BETTY'S BEAUTY SHOPPE.

Next door to the beauty shoppe was a Western Union office. That cable to his mother . . . Heavens, he had almost forgotten! Jeremy leaned forward and, in the apologetic tone he always used when speaking to servants, asked the chauffeur to stop for a moment. The car came to a halt. With a preoccupied expression on his mild, rabbit-like face, Jeremy got out and hurried across the pavement, into the office.

'Mrs. Pordage, The Araucarias, Woking, England,' he wrote, smiling a little as he did so. The exquisite absurdity of that address was a standing source of amusement. 'The

Araucarias, Woking.' His mother, when she bought the house, had wanted to change the name, as being too ingenuously middle-class, too much like a joke by Hilaire Belloc. 'But that's the beauty of it,' he had protested. 'That's the charm.' And he had tried to make her see how utterly right it would be for them to live at such an address. The deliciously comic incongruity between the name of the house and the nature of its occupants! And what a beautiful, topsy-turvy appositeness in the fact that Oscar Wilde's old friend, the witty and cultured Mrs. Pordage, should write her sparkling letters from The Araucarias, and that from these same Araucarias, these Araucarias, mark you, at *Woking*, should come the works of mingled scholarship and curiously rarefied wit for which her son had gained his reputation. Mrs. Pordage had almost instantly seen what he was driving at. No need, thank goodness, to labour your points where she was concerned. You could talk entirely in hints and anacoluthons; she could be relied on to understand. The Araucarias had remained The Araucarias.

Having written the address, Jeremy paused, pensively frowned and initiated the familiar gesture of biting his pencil—only to find, disconcertingly, that this particular pencil was tipped with brass and fastened to a chain. 'Mrs. Pordage, The Araucarias, Woking, England,' he read out aloud, in the hope that the worlds would inspire him to compose the right, the perfect message—the message his mother expected of him, at once tender and witty, charged with a genuine devotion ironically worded, acknowledging her maternal domination, but at the same time making fun of it, so that the old lady could salve her conscience by pretending that her son was entirely free, and herself the least tyrannical of mothers. It wasn't easy—particularly with this pencil on a chain. After several abortive essays he decided, though it was definitely unsatisfactory, on : 'Climate being subtropical shall break vow re underclothes stop Wish you were here my sake not yours as you would scarcely appreciate this unfinished Bournemouth indefinitely magnified stop.'

'Unfinished what ?' questioned the young woman on the further side of the counter.

'B-o-u-r-n-e-m-o-u-t-h,' Jeremy spelled out.   He smiled; behind the bi-focal lenses of his spectacles his blue eyes twinkled, and, with a gesture of which he was quite unconscious, but which he always, automatically, made when he was about to utter one of his little jokes, he stroked the smooth bald spot on the top of his head. '*You* know,' he said, in a particularly fluty tone, 'the bourne to which no traveller goes, if he can possibly help it.'

The girl looked at him blankly; then, inferring from his expression that something funny had been said, and remembering that courteous Service was Western Union's slogan, gave the bright smile for which the poor old chump was evidently asking, and went on reading: 'Hope you have fun at Grasse stop Tendresses Jeremy.'

It was an expensive message; but luckily, he reflected, as he took out his pocket-book, luckily Mr. Stoyte was grossly overpaying him.   Three months' work, six thousand dollars.   So damn the expense.

He returned to the car and they drove on.   Mile after mile they went, and the suburban houses, the gas-stations, the vacant lots, the churches, the shops went along with them, interminably.   To right and left, between palms, or pepper trees, or acacias, the streets of the enormous residential quarter receded to the vanishing point.

CLASSY EATS.   MILE HIGH CONES.
JESUS SAVES.
HAMBURGERS.

Yet once more the traffic lights turned red. A paper-boy came to the window. 'Franco claims gains in Cata-lonia.' Jeremy read, and turned away. The frightfulness of the world had reached a point at which it had become for him merely boring. From the halted car in front of them, two elderly ladies, both with permanently waved white hair and both wearing crimson trousers, descended, each carrying a Yorkshire terrier. The dogs were set down at the foot of the traffic signal. Before the animals could make up their minds to use the convenience, the lights had changed. The negro shifted into first, and the car swerved forward, into the future. Jeremy was think-ing of his mother. Disquietingly enough, she too had a Yorkshire terrier.

Fine Liquors.

Turkey Sandwiches.

Go To Church And Feel Better All The Week.

What Is Good For Business Is Good For *You*.

Another zoomorph presented itself, this time a real estate agent's office in the form of an Egyptian sphinx.

Jesus Is Coming Soon.

You Too Can Have Abiding Youth With Thrill-phorm Brassieres.

Beverly Pantheon, The Cemetery That Is *Differ-ent*.

With the triumphant expression of Puss-in-Boots en-umerating the possessions of the Marquis of Carabas, the negro shot a glance over his shoulder at Jeremy, waved his hand towards the billboard and said, 'That's ours too.'

'You mean, the Beverly Pantheon?'

The man nodded. 'Finest cemetery in the world, I guess,' he said : and added, after a moment's pause, 'Maybe you's like to see it. It wouldn't hardly be out of our way.'

'That would be very nice,' said Jeremy with upper-

class English graciousness. Then, feeling that he ought
to express his acceptance rather more warmly and demo-
cratically, he cleared his throat and, with a conscious
effort to reproduce the local vernacular, added that it
would be *swell*. Pronounced in his Trinity-College-
Cambridge voice, the word sounded so unnatural that
he began to blush with embarrassment. Fortunately, the
chauffeur was too busy with the traffic to notice.

They turned to the right, sped past a Rosicrucian
Temple, past two cat-and-dog hospitals, past a School
for Drum-Majorettes and two more advertisements of
the Beverly Pantheon. As they turned to the left on
Sunset Boulevard, Jeremy had a glimpse of a young
woman who was doing her shopping in a hydrangea-
blue strapless bathing-suit, platinum curls and a black
fur jacket. Then she too was whirled back into the past.

The present was a road at the foot of a line of steep
hills, a road flanked by small, expensive-looking shops,
by restaurants, by night-clubs shuttered against the sunlight, by offices and apartment houses. Then they too
had taken their places in the irrevocable. A sign proclaimed that they were crossing the city limits of Beverly
Hills. The surroundings changed. The road was flanked
by the gardens of a rich residential quarter. Through
trees, Jeremy saw the façades of houses, all new, almost
all in good taste—elegant and witty pastiches of Lutyens
manor houses, of Little Trianons, of Monticellos; light-
hearted parodies of Le Corbusier's solemn machines-for-
living-in; fantastic Mexican adaptations of Mexican
haciendas and New England farms.

They turned to the right. Enormous palm trees lined
the road. In the sunlight, masses of mesembryanthemums
blazed with an intense magenta glare. The houses succeeded one another, like the pavilions at some endless

international exhibition. Gloucestershire followed Anda-
lusia and gave place in turn to Touraine and Oaxaca,
Düsseldorf and Massachusetts.

'That's Harold Lloyd's place,' said the chauffeur, indicating a kind of Boboli. 'And that's Charlie Chaplin's.
And that's Pickfair.'

The road began to mount, vertiginously. The chauffeur
pointed across an intervening gulf of shadow at what
seemed a Tibetan lamasery on the opposite hill, 'That's
where Ginger Rogers lives. Yes, *sir*,' he nodded triumphantly, as he twirled the steering-wheel.

Five or six more turns brought the car to the top of
the hill. Below and behind lay the plain, with the city
like a map extending indefinitely into a pink haze.

Before and to either hand were mountains—ridge after
ridge as far as the eye could reach, a desiccated Scotland,
empty under the blue desert sky.

The car turned a shoulder of orange rock, and there all
at once, on a summit hitherto concealed from view, was
a huge sky sign, with the words, BEVERLY PANTHEON,
THE PERSONALITY CEMETERY, in six-foot neon tubes and,
above it, on the very crest, a full-scale reproduction of the
Leaning Tower of Pisa—only this one didn't lean.

'See that?' said the negro impressively. 'That's the
Tower of Resurrection. Two hundred thousand dollars,
that's what it cost. Yes, *sir*.' He spoke with an emphatic
solemnity. One was made to feel that the money had
all come out of his own pocket.

Chapter Two

An hour later, they were on their way again, having seen everything. Everything. The sloping lawns, like a green oasis in the mountain desolation. The groves of trees. The tombstones in the grass. The Pets' Cemetery, with its marble group after Landseer's 'Dignity and Impudence.' The tiny Church of the Poet—a miniature reproduction of Holy Trinity at Stratford-on-Avon complete with Shakespeare's tomb and a twenty-four-hour service of organ music played automatically by the Perpetual Wurlitzer and broadcast by concealed loud-speakers all over the cemetery.

Then, leading out of the vestry, the Bride's Apartment (for one was married at the Tiny Church as well as buried from it)—the Bride's Apartment that had just been re-decorated, said the chauffeur, in the style of Norma Shearer's boudoir in *Marie Antoinette*. And, next to the Bride's Apartment, the exquisite black marble Vestibule of Ashes, leading to the Crematorium, where three super-modern oil-burning mortuary furnaces were always under heat and ready for any emergency.

Accompanied wherever they went by the tremolos of the Perpetual Wurlitzer, they had driven next to look at the Tower of Resurrection—from the outside only; for it housed the executive offices of the West Coast Cemeteries Corporation. Then the Children's Corner with its statues of Peter Pan and the Infant Jesus, its groups of alabaster babies playing with bronze rabbits, its lily pool and an apparatus labelled The Fountain of Rainbow Music, from which there spouted simultaneously water,

12

coloured lights and the inescapable strains of the Perpetual Wurlitzer. Then, in rapid succession, the Garden of Quiet, the Tiny Taj Mahal, the Old World Mortuary. And, reserved by the chauffeur to the last, as the final and crowning proof of his employer's glory, the Pantheon itself.

Was it possible, Jeremy asked himself, that such an object existed? It was certainly not probable. The Beverly Pantheon lacked all verisimilitude, was something entirely beyond his powers to invent. The fact that the idea of it was now in his mind proved, therefore, that he must really have seen it. He shut his eyes against the landscape and recalled to his memory the details of that incredible reality. The external architecture, modelled on that of Boecklin's 'Toteninsel.' The circular vestibule. The replica of Rodin's 'Le Baiser,' illuminated by concealed pink floodlights. With its flights of black marble stairs. The seven-story columbarium, the endless galleries, its tiers on tiers of slab-sealed tombs. The bronze and silver urns of the cremated, like athletic trophies. The stained-glass windows after Burne-Jones. The texts inscribed on marble scrolls. The Perpetual Wurlitzer crooning on every floor. The sculpture . . .

That was the hardest to believe, Jeremy reflected, behind closed eyelids. Sculpture almost as ubiquitous as the Wurlitzer. Statues wherever you turned your eyes. Hundreds of them, bought wholesale, one would guess, from some monumental masonry concern at Carrara or Pietrasanta. All nudes, all female, all exuberantly nubile. The sort of statues one would expect to see in the reception-room of a high-class brothel in Rio de Janeiro. 'Oh, Death,' demanded a marble scroll at the entrance to every gallery, 'where is thy sting?' Mutely, but eloquently, the statues gave their reassuring reply. Statues of young ladies in nothing but a very tight belt imbedded, with Bernini-like realism, in the Parian flesh. Statues of young ladies crouching; young ladies using both hands to be modest; young ladies stretching, writhing, calli-pygously stooping to tie their sandals, reclining. Young ladies with doves, with panthers, with other young ladies, with upturned eyes expressive of the soul's awakening. 'I am the Resurrection and the Life,' proclaimed the scrolls. 'The Lord is my shepherd; therefore shall I want nothing.' Nothing, not even Wurlitzer, not even girls in tightly buckled belts. 'Death is swallowed up in victory'—the victory no longer of the spirit but of the body, the well-fed body, for ever youthful, immortally athletic, indefatigably sexy. The Moslem paradise had had copulations six centuries long. In this new Christian heaven, progress, no doubt, would have stepped up the period to a millennium and added the joys of everlasting tennis, eternal golf and swimming.

All at once the car began to descend. Jeremy opened his eyes again, and saw that they had reached the further edge of the range of hills, among which the Pantheon was built.

Below lay a great tawny plain, chequered with patches of green and dotted with white houses. On its further side, fifteen or twenty miles away, ranges of pinkish mountains fretted the horizon.

'What's this?' Jeremy asked.

'The San Fernando Valley,' said the chauffeur. He pointed into the middle distance. 'That's where Groucho Marx has his place,' he said. 'Yes, *sir*.'

At the bottom of the hill the car turned to the left along a wide road that ran, a ribbon of concrete and suburban buildings, through the plain. The chauffeur put on speed; sign succeeded sign with bewildering rapidity.

MALTS CABIN DINE AND DANCE AT THE CHATEAU HONO-
LULU SPIRITUAL HEALING AND COLONIC IRRIGATION
BLOCKLONG HOT DOGS BUY YOUR DREAM HOME *NOW*.
And behind the signs the mathematically planted rows of
apricot and walnut trees flicked past—a succession of
glimpsed perspectives preceded and followed every time
by fan-like approaches and retirements.

Dark-green and gold, enormous orange orchards man-
œuvred, each one a mile-square regiment glittering in
the sunlight. Far off, the mountains traced their un-
interpretable graph of boom and slump.

'Tarzana,' said the chauffeur startlingly; there, sure
enough, was the name suspended, in white letters, across
the road. 'There's Tarzana College,' the man went on,
pointing to a group of Spanish-Colonial palaces clustering
round a Romanesque basilica. 'Mr. Stoyte, he's just
given them an auditorium.'

They turned to the right along a less important road.
The orange groves gave place for a few miles to huge
fields of alfalfa and fusty grass, then returned again more
luxuriant than ever. Meanwhile the mountains on the
northern edge of the valley were approaching and, slanting in from the west, another range was looming up to
the left. They drove on. The road took a sudden turn,
aiming, it seemed, at the point where the two ranges must
come together. All at once, through a gap between two
orchards, Jeremy Pordage saw a most surprising sight.
About half a mile from the foot of the mountains, like an
island off a cliff-bound coast, a rocky hill rose abruptly,
in places almost precipitously, from the plain. On the
summit of the bluff and as though growing out of it in
a kind of efflorescence, stood a castle. But what a castle!
The donjon was like a skyscraper, the bastions plunged
headlong with the effortless swoop of concrete dams.

The thing was Gothic, mediaeval, baronial—doubly baronial, Gothic with a Gothicity raised, so to speak, to a higher power, more mediaeval than any building of the thirteenth century. For this . . . this Object, as Jeremy was reduced to calling it, was mediaeval, not out of vulgar historical necessity, like Coucy, say, or Alnwick, but out of pure fun and wantonness, platonically, one might say. It was mediaeval as only a witty and irresponsible modern architect would wish to be mediaeval, as only the most competent modern engineers are technically equipped to be.

Jeremy was startled into speech. 'What on earth is that?' he asked, pointing at the nightmare on the hill-top.

'Why, that's Mr. Stoyte's place,' said the retainer; and smiling yet once more with the pride of vicarious owner-ship, he added: 'It's a pretty fine home, I guess.'

The orange groves closed in again; leaning back in his seat, Jeremy Pordage began to wonder, rather appre-hensively, what he had let himself in for when he accepted Mr. Stoyte's offer. The pay was princely; the work, which was to catalogue the almost legendary Hauberk Papers, would be delightful. But that cemetery, this . . . Object—Jeremy shook his head. He had known, of course, that Mr. Stoyte was rich, collected pictures, owned a show-place in California. But no one had ever led him to expect *this*. The humorous puritanism of his good taste was shocked; he was appalled at the prospect of meeting the person capable of committing such an enor-mity. Between that person and oneself, what contact, what community of thought or feeling could possibly exist? Why had he sent for one? For it was obvious that he couldn't conceivably like one's books. But had he even read one's books? Did he have the faintest idea of what one was like? Would he be capable, for example,

of understanding why one had insisted on the name of
The Araucarias remaining unchanged? Would he
appreciate one's point of view about . . . ?

These anxious questionings were interrupted by the
noise of the horn, which the chauffeur was sounding with
a loud and offensive insistence. Jeremy looked up. Fifty
yards ahead, an ancient Ford was creeping tremulously
along the road. It carried, lashed insecurely to roof and
running-boards and luggage-rack, a squalid cargo of
household goods—rolls of bedding, an old iron stove, a
crate of pots and pans, a folded tent, a tin bath. As they
flashed past, Jeremy had a glimpse of three dull-eyed,
anaemic children, of a woman with a piece of sacking
wrapped around her shoulders, of a haggard, unshaved
man.

'Transients,' the chauffeur explained in a tone of contempt.

'What's that?' Jeremy asked.

'Why, *transients*,' the negro repeated, as though the
emphasis were an explanation. 'Guess that lot's from the
dust bowl. Kansas licence plate. Come to pick our
navels.'

'Come to pick your navels?' Jeremy echoed incredulously.

'Navel oranges,' said the chauffeur. 'It's the season.
Pretty good year for navels, I guess."

They emerged once more into the open, and there once
more was the Object, larger than ever. Jeremy had time
to study the details of its construction. A wall with
towers encircled the base of the hills, and there was a
second line of defence, in the most approved post-
Crusades manner, half-way up. On the summit stood
the square keep, surrounded by subsidiary buildings.

From the donjon, Jeremy's eyes travelled down to a

group of buildings in the plain, not far from the foot of the hill. Across the façade of the largest of them the words, 'Stoyte Home for Sick Children,' were written in gilded letters. Two flags, one the stars and stripes, the other a white banner with the letter S in scarlet, fluttered in the breeze. Then a grove of leafless walnut trees shut out the view once again. Almost at the same moment the chauffeur threw his engine out of gear and put on the brakes. The car came gently to a halt beside a man who was walking at a brisk pace along the grassy verge of the road.

'Want a ride, Mr. Propter?' the negro called.

The stranger turned his head, gave the man a smile of recognition and came to the window of the car. He was a large man, broad-shouldered, but rather stooping, with brown hair turning grey and a face, Jeremy thought, like the face of one of those statues which Gothic sculptors carved for a place high up on a West front—a face of sudden prominences and deeply shadowed folds and hollows, emphatically rough-hewn so as to be expressive even at a distance. But this particular face, he went on to notice, was not merely emphatic, not only for the distance; it was a face also for the near point, also for intimacy, a subtle face, in which there were the signs of sensibility and intelligence as well as of power, of a gentle and humorous serenity no less than of energy and strength.

'Hullo, George,' the stranger said, addressing the chauffeur; 'nice of you to stop for me.'

'Well, I'm sure glad to see you, Mr. Propter,' said the negro cordially. Then he half-turned in his seat, waved a hand towards Jeremy, and with a florid formality of tone and manner said, 'I'd like to have you meet Mr. Pordage of England. Mr. Pordage, this is Mr. Propter.'

The two men shook hands, and, after an exchange of courtesies, Mr. Propter got into the car.

'You're visiting with Mr. Stoyte?' he asked, as the chauffeur drove on.

Jeremy shook his head. He was here on business; had come to look at some manuscripts—the Hauberk Papers, to be precise.

Mr. Propter listened attentively, nodded from time to time and, when Jeremy had finished, sat for a moment in silence.

'Take a decayed Christian,' he said at last in a meditative tone, 'and the remains of a Stoic; mix thoroughly with good manners, a bit of money and an old-fashioned education; simmer for several years in a university. Result: a scholar and a gentleman. Well, there were worse types of human being.' He uttered a little laugh. 'I might almost claim to have been one myself, once, long ago.'

Jeremy looked at him enquiringly. 'You're not *William* Propter, are you?' he asked. 'Not *Short Studies in the Counter Reformation*, by any chance?'

The other inclined his head.

Jeremy looked at him in amazement and delight. Was it possible? he asked himself. Those *Short Studies* had been one of his favourite books—a model, he had always thought, of their kind.

'Well, I'm jiggered!' he said aloud, using the schoolboyish locution deliberately and as though between inverted commas. He had found that, both in writing and in conversation, there were exquisite effects to be obtained by the judicious employment, in a solemn or cultural context, of a phrase of slang, a piece of childish profanity or obscenity. 'I'll be damned!' he exploded again, and his consciousness of the intentional silliness of the words made him stroke his bald head and cough.

There was another moment of silence. Then, instead of talking, as Jeremy had expected, about the *Short Studies*, Mr. Propter merely shook his head and said, 'We mostly are.'

'Mostly are what?' asked Jeremy.

'Jiggered,' Mr. Propter answered. 'Damned. In the psychological sense of the word,' he added.

The walnut trees came to an end, and there once more, on the starboard bow, was the Object. Mr. Propter pointed in its direction. 'Poor Jo Stoyte!' he said. 'Think of having *that* millstone round one's neck. Not to mention, of course, all the other millstones that go with it. What luck we've had, don't you think?—we who've never been given the opportunity of being anything much worse than scholars and gentlemen!' After another little silence, 'Poor Jo,' he went on with a smile, 'he isn't either of them. You'll find him a bit trying. Because of course he'll want to bully you, just because tradition says that your type is superior to his type. Not to mention the fact,' he added, looking into Jeremy's face with an expression of mingled amusement and sympathy, 'that you're probably the sort of person that invites persecution. A bit of a murderee, I'm afraid, as well as a scholar and gentleman.'

Feeling simultaneously annoyed by the man's indiscretion and touched by his friendliness, Jeremy smiled rather nervously and nodded his head.

'Maybe,' Mr. Propter went on, 'maybe it would help you to be less of a murderee towards Jo Stoyte if you knew what gave him the original impulsion to get damned in just *that* way'—and he pointed again towards the Object. 'We were at school together, Jo and I— only nobody called him Jo in those days. We called him Slob, or Jelly-Belly. Because, you see, poor Jo was the local fat-boy, the only fat-boy in the school during those years.' He paused for a moment; then went on in another tone, 'I've often wondered why people have always made fun of fatness. Perhaps there's something intrinsically wrong with fat. For example, there isn't a single fat saint—except, of course, old Thomas Aquinas; and I cannot see any reason to suppose that he was a real saint, a saint in the popular sense of the word, which happens to be the true sense. If Thomas is a saint, then Vincent de Paul isn't. And if Vincent's a saint, which he obviously is, then Thomas isn't. And perhaps that enormous belly of his had something to do with it. Who knows? But anyhow, that's by the way. We're talking about Jo Stoyte. And poor Jo, as I say, was a fat-boy and, being fat, was fair game for the rest of us. God, how we punished him for his glandular deficiencies! And how disastrously he reacted to that punishment! Over-compensation. . . . But here I am at home,' he added, looking out of the window as the car slackened speed and came to a halt in front of a small white bungalow set in the midst of a clump of eucalyptus trees. 'We'll go on with this another time. But remember, if poor Jo gets too offensive, think of what he was at school and be sorry for him—and don't be sorry for yourself.' He got out of the car, closed the door behind him and, waving a hand to the chauffeur, walked quickly up the path and entered the little house.

The car rolled on again. At once bewildered and reassured by his encounter with the author of the *Short Studies*, Jeremy sat, inertly looking out of the window. They were very near the Object now; and suddenly he noticed, for the first time, that the castle hill was surrounded by a moat. Some few hundred yards from the water's edge, the car passed between two pillars, topped

by heraldic lions. Its passage, it was evident, interrupted
a beam of invisible light directed on a photo-electric cell;
for no sooner were they past the lions than a drawbridge
began to descend. Five seconds before they reached the
moat, it was in place; the car rolled smoothly across and
came to a halt in front of the main gateway of the castle's
outer walls. The chauffeur got out and, speaking into a
telephone-receiver concealed in a convenient loophole,
announced his presence. The chromium-plated portcullis rose noiselessly, the double doors of stainless steel
swung back. They drove in. The car began to climb.
The second line of walls was pierced by another gate,
which opened automatically as they approached. Between
the inner side of this second wall and the slope of the hill
a ferro-concrete bridge had been constructed, large enough
to accommodate a tennis-court. In the shadowy space
beneath, Jeremy caught sight of something familiar. An
instant later he had recognized it as a replica of the grotto
of Lourdes.

'Miss Maunciple, she's a Catholic,' remarked the chauffeur, jerking his thumb in the direction of the grotto.
'That's why he had it made for her. We's Presbyterians
in *our* family,' he added.

'And who is Miss Maunciple?'

The chauffeur hesitated for a moment. 'Well, she's a
young lady Mr. Stoyte's kind of friendly with,' he explained at last; then changed the subject.

The car climbed on. Beyond the grotto all the hillside
was a cactus garden. Then the road swung round to the
northern slope of the bluff, and the cactuses gave place to
grass and shrubs. On a little terrace, over-elegant like a
fashion-plate from some mythological *Vogue* for goddesses, a bronze nymph by Giambologna spouted two
streams of water from her deliciously polished breasts.

A little further on, behind wire netting, a group of baboons squatted among the rocks or paraded the obscenity of their hairless rumps.

Still climbing, the car turned again and finally drew up on a circular concrete platform, carried out on cantilevers over a precipice. Once more the old-fashioned retainer, the chauffeur taking off his cap, did a final impersonation of himself welcoming the young master home to the plantation, then set to work to unload the luggage.

Jeremy Pordage walked to the balustrade and looked over. The ground fell almost sheer for about a hundred feet, then sloped steeply to the inner circle of walls and, below them, to the outer fortifications. Beyond lay the moat, and on the further side of the moat stretched the orange orchards. '*Im dunklen Laub die goldn' Orangen glühen*,' he murmured to himself; and then : 'He hangs in shades the orange bright. Like golden lamps in a green night.' Marvell's rendering, he decided, was better than Goethe's. And, meanwhile, the oranges seemed to have become brighter and more significant. For Jeremy, direct, unmediated experience was always hard to take in, always more or less disquieting. Life became safe, things assumed meaning, only when they had been translated into words and confined between the covers of a book. The oranges were beautifully pigeon-holed ; but what about the castle ? He turned round and, leaning back against the parapet, looked up. The Object impended, insolently enormous. Nobody had dealt poetically with *that*. Not Childe Roland, not the King of Thule, not Marmion, not the Lady of Shalott, not Sir Leoline. Sir Leoline, he repeated to himself with a connoisseur's appreciation of romantic absurdity, Sir Leoline, the baron rich who had—what ? A toothless mastiff bitch. But Mr. Stoyte had baboons and a sacred grotto, Mr. Stoyte had a chromium portcullis and the Hauberk Papers, Mr. Stoyte had a cemetery like an amusement park and a donjon like . . .

There was a sudden rumbling sound; the great nail-studded doors of the Early English entrance porch rolled back, and from between them, as though propelled by a hurricane, a small, thick-set man, with a red face and a mass of snow-white hair, darted out on to the terrace and bore down upon Jeremy. His expression, as he advanced, did not change. The face wore that shut, unsmiling mask which American workmen tend to put on in their dealing with strangers—in order to prove, by not making the ingratiating grimaces of courtesy, that theirs is a free country and you're not going to come it over *them*.

Not having been brought up in a free country, Jeremy had automatically begun to smile as this person, whom he guessed to be his host and employer, came hurrying towards him. Confronted by the unwavering grimness of the other's face, he suddenly became conscious of this smile—conscious that it was out of place, that it must be making him look a fool. Profoundly embarrassed, he tried to readjust his face.

'Mr. Pordage?' said the stranger in a harsh, barking voice. 'Pleased to meet you. My name's Stoyte.' As they shook hands, he peered, still unsmiling, into Jeremy's face. 'You're older than I thought,' he added.

For the second time that morning Jeremy made his mannequin's gesture of apologetic self-exhibition.

'The sere and withered leaf,' he said. 'One's sinking into senility. One's . . .'

Mr. Stoyte cut him short. 'What's your age?' he asked in a loud peremptory tone, like that of a police sergeant interrogating a captured thief.

'Fifty-four.'

'Only fifty-four?' Mr. Stoyte shook his head. 'Ought

to be full of pep at fifty-four. How's your sex-life?' he added disconcertingly.

Jeremy tried to laugh off his embarrassment. He twinkled; he patted his bald head. '*Mon beau printemps et mon été ont fait le sault par la fenêtre*,' he quoted.

'What's that?' said Mr. Stoyte, frowning. 'No use talking foreign languages to me. I never had any education.' He broke into sudden braying of laughter. 'I'm head of an oil company here,' he said. 'Got two thousand filling-stations in California alone. And not one man in any of those filling-stations that isn't a college graduate!' He brayed again, triumphantly. 'Go and talk foreign languages to *them*.' He was silent for a moment; then, pursuing an unexplicit association of ideas, 'My agent in London,' he went on, 'the man who picks up things for me there—he gave me your name. Told me you were the right man for those—what do you call them? You know, those papers I bought this summer. Roebuck? Hobuck?'

'Hauberk,' said Jeremy, and with a gloomy satisfaction noted that he had been quite right. The man had never read one's books, never even heard of one's existence. Still, one had to remember that he had been called Jelly-Belly when he was young.

'Hauberk,' Mr. Stoyte repeated with a contemptuous impatience. 'Anyhow, he said you were the man.' Then, without pause or transition, 'What was it you were saying, about your sex-life, when you started that foreign stuff on me?'

Jeremy laughed uncomfortably. 'One was implying that it was normal for one's age.'

'What do *you* know about what's normal at your age?' said Mr. Stoyte. 'Go and talk to Dr. Obispo about it. It won't cost you anything. Obispo's on salary. He's the

house physician.' Abruptly changing the subject, 'Would
you like to see the castle ?' he asked. 'I'll take you round.'

'Oh, that's very kind of you,' said Jeremy effusively.
And, for the sake of making a little polite conversation,
he added : 'I've already seen your burial-ground."

'Seen my burial-ground ?' Mr. Stoyte repeated in a tone
of suspicion : suspicion turned suddenly to anger. 'What
the hell do you mean ?' he shouted.

Quailing before his fury, Jeremy stammered something
about the Beverly Pantheon and that he had understood
from the chauffeur that Mr. Stoyte had a financial interest
in the company.

'I see,' said the other, somewhat mollified, but still
frowning. 'I thought you meant . . .' Stoyte broke off
in the middle of the sentence, leaving the bewildered
Jeremy to guess what he had thought. 'Come on,' he
barked ; and, bursting into movement, he hurried towards the entrance to the house.

Chapter Three

THERE was silence in Ward Sixteen of the Stoyte Home for Sick Children; silence and the luminous twilight of drawn venetian blinds. It was the mid-morning rest period. Three of the five small convalescents were asleep. A fourth lay staring at the ceiling, pensively picking his nose. The fifth, a little girl, was whispering to a doll as curly and Aryan as herself. Seated by one of the windows, a young nurse was absorbed in the latest issue of *True Confessions*.

'His heart gave a lurch,' she read. 'With a strangled cry he pressed me closer. For months we'd been fighting against just this; but the magnet of our passion was too strong for us. The clamorous pressure of his lips had struck an answering spark within my melting body.

'"Germaine," he whispered. "Don't make me wait. Won't you be good to me now, darling?"

'He was so gentle, but so ruthless too—as a girl in love wants a man to be ruthless. I felt myself swept away by the rising tide of . . .'

There was a noise outside in the corridor. The door of the ward flew open, as though before the blast of a hurricane, and someone came rushing into the room.

The nurse looked up with a start of surprise which the completeness of her absorption in 'The Price of a Thrill' rendered positively agonizing. Her almost immediate reaction to the shock was one of anger.

'What's the idea?' she began indignantly; then she recognized the intruder and her expression changed. 'Why, Mr. Stoyte!'

Disturbed by the noise, the young nose-picker dropped his eyes from the ceiling, the little girl turned away from her doll.

'Uncle Jo!' they shouted simultaneously. 'Uncle Jo!' Starting out of sleep, the others took up the cry.

'Uncle Jo!   Uncle Jo!'

Mr. Stoyte was touched by the warmth of his reception. The face which Jeremy had found so disquietingly grim relaxed into a smile. In mock protest he covered his ears with his hands. 'You'll make me deaf,' he cried. Then, in an aside to the nurse, 'Poor kids!' he murmured. 'Makes me feel I'd kind of like to cry.' His voice became husky with sentiment. 'And when one thinks how sick they've been . . .' He shook his head, leaving the sentence unfinished; then, in another tone, 'By the way,' he added, waving a large square hand in the direction of Jeremy Pordage, who had followed him into the ward and was standing near the door, wearing an expression of bewildered embarrassment, 'this is Mr. . . . Mr. . . . Hell! I've forgotten your name.'

'Pordage,' said Jeremy, and reminded himself that Mr. Stoyte's name had once been Slob.

'Pordage, that's it. Ask him about history and literature,' he added derisively to the nurse. 'He knows it all.'

Jeremy was modestly protesting that his period was only from the invention of Ossian to the death of Keats, when Mr. Stoyte turned back to the children and in a voice that drowned the other's faintly fluted disclaimers, shouted: 'Guess what Uncle Jo's brought you!'

They guessed. Candies, bubble gum, balloons, guinea-pigs. Mr. Stoyte continued triumphantly to shake his head. Finally, when the children had exhausted their power of imagination, he dipped into the pocket of his old tweed jacket and produced, first a whistle, then a mouth-organ, then a small musical box, then a trumpet, then a wooden rattle, then an automatic pistol. This, however, he hastily put back.

'Now play,' he said, when he had distributed the instruments. 'All together. One, two, three.' And, beating time with both arms, he began to sing, 'Way down upon the Swanee River.'

At this latest in a long series of shocks and surprises, Jeremy's mild face took on an expression of intenser bewilderment.

What a morning! The arrival at dawn. The negro retainer. The interminable suburb. The Beverly Pantheon. The Object among the orange trees, and his meeting with William Propter and this really dreadful Stoyte. Then, inside the castle, the Rubens and the great El Greco in the hall, the Vermeer in the elevator, the Rembrandt etchings along the corridors, the Winterhalter in the butler's pantry.

Then Miss Maunciple's Louis XV boudoir, with the Watteau and the two Lancrets and the fully equipped soda-fountain in a rococo embrasure, and Miss Maunciple herself, in an orange kimono, drinking a raspberry and peppermint ice-cream soda at her own counter. He had been introduced, had refused the offer of a sundae and been hurried on again, always at top speed, always as though on the wings of a tornado, to see the other sights of the castle. The Rumpus Room, for example, with frescoes of elephants by Sert. The library, with its woodwork by Grinling Gibbons, but with no books, because Mr. Stoyte had not yet brought himself to buy any. The small dining-room, with its Fra Angelico and its furniture from Brighton Pavilion. The large dining-room, modelled on the interior of the mosque at Fatehpur Sikri. The ballroom, with its mirrors and coffered ceiling. The thirteenth-century stained-glass in the eleventh-floor W.C. The morning-room, with Boucher's picture of 'La Petite Morphil' bottom upwards on a pink satin sofa. The chapel, imported in fragments from Goa, with the walnut confessional used by St. François de Sales at Annecy. The functional billiard-room. The indoor swimming-pool. The Second Empire bar, with its nudes by Ingres. The two gymnasiums. The Christian Science Reading Room, dedicated to the memory of the late Mrs. Stoyte. The dentist's office. The Turkish bath. Then down, with Vermeer, into the bowels of the hill, to look at the cellar in which the Hauberk Papers had been stored. Down again yet deeper, to the safe-deposit vaults, the power-house, the air-conditioning plant, the well and pumping-station. Then up once more to ground level and the kitchens, where the Chinese chef had shown Mr. Stoyte the newly arrived consignment of turtles from the Caribbean. Up again to the four-teenth, to the bedroom which Jeremy was to occupy during his stay. Then up another six stories to the busi-ness office, where Mr. Stoyte gave orders to his secretary, dictated a couple of letters and had a long telephone conversation with his brokers in Amsterdam. And when that was finished, it had been time to go to the hospital.

Meanwhile, in Ward Sixteen, a group of nurses had collected and were watching Uncle Jo, his white hair flying like Stokowski's, frantically spurring his orchestra to yet louder crescendos of cacophony.

'He's like a great big kid himself,' said one of them in a tone of almost tender amusement.

Another, evidently with literary leanings, declared that it was like something in Dickens. 'Don't you think so ?' she insisted to Jeremy.

He smiled nervously and nodded a vague and non-committal assent.

More practical, a third wished she had her Kodak with her. 'Candid Camera portrait of the President of Consol Oil, California Land and Minerals Corporation. Bank of the Pacific, West Coast Cemeteries, etc., etc. . . .' She reeled off the names of Mr. Stoyte's chief companies, mock-heroically, indeed, but with admiring gusto, as a convinced legitimist with a sense of humour might enumerate the titles of a grandee of Spain. 'The papers would pay you good money for a snap like that,' she insisted. And to prove that what she was saying was true, she went on to explain that she had a boy friend who worked with an advertising firm, so that he ought to know, and only the week before he had told her that . . .

Mr. Stoyte's knobbed face, as he left the hospital, was still illuminated with benevolence and happiness.

'Makes you feel kind of good, playing with those poor kids,' he kept repeating to Jeremy.

A wide flight of steps led down from the hospital entrance to the roadway. At the foot of these steps Mr. Stoyte's blue Cadillac was waiting. Behind it stood another, smaller car which had not been there when they arrived. A look of suspicion clouded Mr. Stoyte's beaming face as he caught sight of it. Kidnappers, blackmailers—one never knew. His hand went to the pocket of his coat. 'Who's there?' he shouted in a tone of such loud fury that Jeremy thought for a moment that the man must have suddenly gone mad.

Moon-like, a large, snub-featured face appeared at the car window, smiling round the chewed butt of a cigar.

'Oh, it's you, Clancy,' said Mr. Stoyte. 'Why didn't they tell me you were here?' he went on. His face had flushed darkly; he was frowning and a muscle in his

cheek had begun to twitch. 'I don't like having strange
cars around. Do you hear, Peters?' he almost screamed
at his chauffeur—not because it was the man's business, of
course; simply because he happened to be there, available. 'Do you hear, I say?' Then, suddenly, he remembered what Dr. Obispo had said to him that time he had
lost his temper with the fellow. 'Do you really *want* to
shorten your life, Mr. Stoyte?' The doctor's tone had
been one of cool amusement; he had smiled with an
expression of politely sarcastic indulgence. 'Are you
absolutely *bent* on having a stroke? A second stroke,
remember; and you won't get off so lightly next time.
Well, if so, then go on behaving as you're doing now.
Go on.' With an enormous effort of will, Mr. Stoyte
swallowed his anger. 'God is love,' he said to himself.
'There is no death.' The late Prudence McGladdery
Stoyte had been a Christian Scientist. 'God is love,' he
said again, and reflected that if people would only stop
being so exasperating he would never have to lose his
temper. 'God is love.' It was all their fault.

Clancy, meanwhile, had left his car and, grotesquely
pot-bellied over spindly legs, was coming up the steps,
mysteriously smiling and winking as he approached.

'What is it?' Mr. Stoyte enquired, and wished to God
the man wouldn't make those faces. 'Oh, by the way,'
he added, 'this is Mr. . . . Mr. . . .'

'Pordage,' said Jeremy.

Clancy was pleased to meet him. The hand he gave
to Jeremy was disagreeably sweaty.

'I got some news for you,' said Clancy in a hoarse
conspiratorial whisper; and, speaking behind his hand,
so that his words and the smell of cigar should be for Mr.
Stoyte alone, 'You remember Tittelbaum?' he added.

'That chap in the City Engineer's Department?'

Clancy nodded. 'One of the boys,' he affirmed enigmatically and again winked.

'Well, what about him?' asked Mr. Stoyte; and in spite of God's being love, there was a note in his voice of renascent exasperation.

Clancy shot a glance at Jeremy Pordage; then, with the elaborate by-play of Guy Fawkes talking to Catesby on the stage of a provincial theatre, he took Mr. Stoyte by the arm and led him a few feet away, up the steps. 'Do you know what Tittelbaum told me to-day?' he asked rhetorically.

'How the devil should I know?' (But no, God is love. There is no death.)

Undeterred by the signs of Mr. Stoyte's irritation, Clancy went on with his performance. 'He told me what they've decided about . . .' he lowered his voice still further, 'about the San Felipe Valley.'

'Well, what *have* they decided?' Once more Mr. Stoyte was at the limits of his patience.

Before answering, Clancy removed the cigar-butt from his mouth, threw it away, produced another cigar out of his waistcoat pocket, tore off the cellophane wrapping and stuck it, unlighted, in the place occupied by the old one.

'They've decided,' he said very slowly, so as to give each word its full dramatic effect, 'they've decided to pipe the water into it.'

Mr. Stoyte's expression of exasperation gave place at last to one of interest. 'Enough to irrigate the whole valley?' he asked.

'Enough to irrigate the whole valley,' Clancy repeated with solemnity.

Mr. Stoyte was silent for a moment. 'How much time have we got?' he asked at last.

'Tittelbaum thought the news wouldn't break for another six weeks.'

'Six weeks?' Mr. Stoyte hesitated for a moment; then made his decision. 'All right. Get busy at once,' he said with the peremptory manners of one accustomed to command. 'Go down yourself and take a few of the other boys along with you. Independent purchasers—interested in cattle-raising; want to start a Dude Ranch. Buy all you can. What's the price, by the way?'

'Averages twelve dollars an acre.'

'Twelve,' Mr. Stoyte repeated, and reflected that it would go to a hundred as soon as they started laying the pipe. 'How many acres do you figure you can get?' he asked.

'Maybe thirty thousand.'

Mr. Stoyte's face beamed with satisfaction. 'Good,' he said briskly. 'Very good. No mention of my name, of course,' he added, and then, without pause or transition: 'What's Tittelbaum going to cost?'

Clancy smiled contemptuously. 'Oh, I'll give him four or five hundred bucks.'

'That all?'

The other nodded. 'Tittelbaum's in the bargain basement,' he said. 'Can't afford to ask any fancy prices. He needs the money—needs it awful bad.'

'What for?' asked Mr. Stoyte, who had a professional interest in human nature. 'Gambling? Women?'

Clancy shook his head. 'Doctors,' he explained. 'He's got a kid that's paralysed.'

'Paralysed?' Mr. Stoyte echoed in a tone of genuine sympathy. 'That's too bad.' He hesitated for a moment; then, in a sudden burst of generosity, 'Tell him to send the kid here,' he went on, making a large gesture towards the hospital. 'Best place in the State for infantile paralysis, and it won't cost him anything. Not a red cent.'

'Hell, that's kind of you, Mr. Stoyte,' said Clancy admiringly. 'That's real kind.'

'Oh, it's nothing,' said Mr. Stoyte, as he moved towards his car. ' I'm glad to be able to do it. Remember what it says in the Bible about children. You know,' he added, 'I get a real kick out of being with those poor kids in there. Makes you feel kind of warm inside.' He patted the barrel of his chest. 'Tell Tittelbaum to send in an application for the kid. Send it to me personally. I'll see that it goes through at once.' He climbed into the car and shut the door after him; then, catching sight of Jeremy, opened it again without a word. Mumbling apologetically, Jeremy scrambled in. Mr. Stoyte slammed the door once more, lowered the glass and looked out. 'So long,' he said. 'And don't lose any time about that San Felipe business. Make a good job of it, Clancy, and I'll let you have ten per cent. of all the acreage over twenty thousand.' He raised the window and signalled to the chauffeur to start. The car swung out of the drive and headed towards the castle. Leaning back in his seat, Mr. Stoyte thought of those poor kids and the money he would make out of the San Felipe business. 'God is love,' he said yet once more, with momentary conviction and in a whisper that was audible to his companion. 'God is love.' Jeremy felt more uncomfortable than ever.

The drawbridge came down as the blue Cadillac approached, the chromium portcullis went up, the gates of the inner rampart rolled back to let it pass. On the concrete tennis-court the seven children of the Chinese cook were roller-skating. Below, in the sacred grotto, a group of masons were at work. At the sight of them, Mr. Stoyte shouted to the chauffeur to stop.

'They're putting up a tomb for some nuns,' he said to Jeremy as they got out of the car.

'Some nuns?' Jeremy echoed in surprise.

Mr. Stoyte nodded, and explained that his Spanish agents had bought some sculpture and iron-work from the chapel of a convent that had been wrecked by the anarchists at the beginning of the civil war. 'They sent some nuns along too,' he added. 'Embalmed, I guess. Or maybe just sun-dried: I don't know. Anyhow, there they are. Luckily I happened to have something nice to put them in.' He pointed to the monument which the masons were in process of fixing to the south wall of the grotto. On a marble shelf above a large Roman sarcophagus were the statues by some nameless Jacobean stonemason of a gentleman and lady, both in ruffs, kneeling, and behind them, in three rows of three, nine daughters diminishing from adolescence to infancy. '*Hic jacet Carolus Franciscus Beals, Armiger* . . .' Jeremy began to read.

'Bought it in England, two years ago,' said Mr. Stoyte, interrupting him. Then, turning to the workmen, 'When will you boys be through?' he asked.

'To-morrow noon. Maybe to-night.'

'That's all I wanted to know,' said Mr. Stoyte, and turned away. 'I must have those nuns taken out of storage,' he said, as they walked back to the car.

They drove on. Poised on the almost invisible vibration of its wings, a humming-bird was drinking at the jet that spouted from the left nipple of Giambologna's nymph. From the enclosure of the baboons came the shrill noise of battle and copulation. Mr. Stoyte shut his eyes. 'God is love,' he repeated, trying deliberately to prolong the delightful condition of euphoria into which those poor kids and Clancy's good news had plunged him. 'God is love. There is no death.' He waited to feel that sense of inward warmth, like the after-effect of whisky, which had followed his previous utterance of the words. Instead, as though some immanent fiend were playing a practical joke on him, he found himself thinking of the shrunken leathery corpses of those nuns, and of his own corpse, and of judgment and the flames. Prudence McGladdery Stoyte had been a Christian Scientist; but Joseph Budge Stoyte, his father, had been a Sandemanian; and Letitia Morgan, his maternal grandmother, had lived and died a Plymouth Sister. Over his cot in the attic room of the little framehouse in Nashville, Tennessee, had hung the text, in vivid orange on a black background: 'IT IS A TERRIBLE THING TO FALL INTO THE HANDS OF THE LIVING GOD.' 'God is love,' Mr. Stoyte desperately reaffirmed. 'There is no death.' But for sinners, such as himself, it was only the worm that never died.

'If you're always scared of dying,' Obispo had said, 'you'll surely die. Fear's a poison; and not such a slow poison either.'

Making another enormous effort, Mr. Stoyte suddenly began to whistle. The tune was, 'I'm making hay in the moonlight in my Baby's arms,' but the face which Jeremy Pordage saw and, as though from some horrible and indecent secret, immediately averted his eyes from, was the face of a man in a condemned cell.

'Old sour-puss,' the chauffeur muttered to himself as he watched his employer get out of the car and walk away.

Followed by Jeremy, Mr. Stoyte hurried in silence through the Gothic portal, crossed a pillared Romanesque lobby like the Lady Chapel at Durham, and, his hat still pulled down over his eyes, stepped into the cathedral twilight of the great hall.

A hundred feet overhead, the sound of the two men's footsteps echoed in the vaulting. Like iron ghosts, the suits of armour stood immobile round the walls. Above them, sumptuously dim, the fifteenth-century tapestries opened windows upon a leafy world of phantasy. At one end of the cavernous room, lit by a hidden search-light, El Greco's 'Crucifixion of St. Peter' blazed out in the darkness like the beautiful revelation of something incomprehensible and profoundly sinister. At the other, no less brilliantly illuminated, hung a full-length portrait of Hélène Fourment, dressed only in a bearskin cape. Jeremy looked from one to the other—from the ecto-plasm of the inverted saint to the unequivocal skin and fat and muscle which Rubens had so loved to see and touch; from unearthly flesh-tints of green-white ochre and carmine, shadowed with transparent black, to the creams and warm pinks, the nacreous blues and greens of Flemish nudity. Two shining symbols, incomparably powerful and expressive—but of what, of what? That, of course, was the question.

Mr. Stoyte paid attention to none of his treasures, but strode across the hall, inwardly cursing his buried wife for having made him think about death by insisting that there wasn't any.

The door of the elevator was in an embrasure between pillars. Mr. Stoyte opened it, and the light came on, revealing a Dutch lady in blue satin sitting at a harpsi-chord—sitting, Jeremy reflected, at the very heart of an equation, in a world where beauty and logic, painting and analytical geometry, had become one. With what intention? To express, symbolically, what truths about the nature of things? Again, that was the question.

Where art was concerned, Jeremy said to himself, that was always the question.

'Shut the door,' Mr. Stoyte ordered; then when it was done, 'We'll have a swim before lunch,' he added, and pressed the topmost of a long row of buttons.

Chapter Four

MORE than a dozen families of transients were already at work in the orange grove, as the man from Kansas, with his wife and his three children and his yellow dog, hurried down the line towards the trees which the overseer had assigned to him. They walked in silence, for they had nothing to say to one another and no energy to waste on words.

Only half a day, the man was thinking; only four hours till work would be stopped. They'd be lucky if they made as much as seventy-five cents. Seventy-five cents. Seventy-five cents; and that right front tyre wasn't going to last much longer. If they meant to get up to Fresno and then Salinas, they'd just have to get a better one. But even the rottenest old second-hand tyre cost money. And money was food. And did they eat! he thought with sudden resentment. If he were alone, if he didn't have to drag the kids and Minnie around, then he could rent a little place somewhere. Near the highway, so that he could make a bit extra by selling eggs and fruit and things to the people that rode past in their automobiles, sell a lot cheaper than the markets and still make good money. And then, maybe, he'd be able to buy a cow and a couple of hogs; and then he'd find a girl—one of those fat ones, he liked them rather fat: fat and young with . . .

His wife started coughing again; the dream was shattered. Did they eat! More than they were worth. Three kids with no strength in them. And Minnie going sick on you half the time so that you had to do her work as well as yours!

The dog had paused to sniff at a post. With sudden and surprising agility the man from Kansas took two quick steps forward and kicked the animal squarely in the ribs. 'You goddam dog!' he shouted. 'Get out of the way!' It ran off, yelping. The man from Kansas turned his head in the hope of catching in his children's faces an expression of disapproval or commiseration. But the children had learnt better than to give him an excuse for going on from the dog to themselves. Under the tousled hair, the three pale, small faces were entirely blank and vacant. Disappointed, the man turned away, grumbling indistinctly that he'd belt the hell out of them if they weren't careful. The mother did not even turn her head. She was feeling too sick and tired to do anything but walk straight on. Silence settled down again over the party.

Then, suddenly, the youngest of the three children let out a shrill cry. 'Look there!' She pointed. In front of them was the castle. From the summit of its highest tower rose a spidery metal structure, carrying a succession of platforms to a height of twenty or thirty feet above the parapet. On the highest of these platforms, black against the shining sky, stood a tiny human figure. As they looked, the figure spread its arms and plunged head foremost out of sight behind the battlements. The children's shrill outcry of astonishment gave the man from Kansas the pretext which, a moment before, they had denied him. He turned on them furiously. 'Stop that yellin','
he yelled; then rushed at them, hitting out—a slap on the side of the head for each of them. With an enormous effort, the woman lifted herself from the abyss of fatigue into which she had fallen; she halted, she turned, she cried out protestingly, she caught her husband's arm. He pushed her away, so violently that she almost fell.

'You're as bad as the kids,' he shouted at her. 'Just

layin' around and eatin'. Not worth a damn. I tell you,
I'm just sick and tired of the whole lot of you. Sick and
tired,' he repeated. 'So you keep your mouth shut, see!'
He turned away and, feeling a good deal better for his
outburst, walked briskly on, at a rate which he knew his
wife would find exhausting, between the rows of loaded
orange trees.

From that swimming-pool at the top of the donjon the
view was prodigious. Floating on the translucent water,
one had only to turn one's head to see, between the battlement, successive vistas of plain and mountain, of green
and tawny and violet and faint blue. One floated, one
looked, and one thought, that is, if one were Jeremy
Pordage, of that tower in *Epipsychidion*, that tower with
its chambers

> *Looking towards the golden Eastern air*
> *And level with the living winds.*

Not so, however, if one were Miss Virginia Maunciple.
Virginia neither floated, nor looked, nor thought of
Epipsychidion, but took another sip of whisky and soda,
climbed to the highest platform of the diving-tower,
spread her arms, plunged, glided under water and, coming
up immediately beneath the unsuspecting Pordage, caught
him by the belt of his bathing-pants and pulled him under.

'You asked for it,' she said, as he came up again, gasping
and spluttering, to the surface, 'lying there without moving, like a silly old Buddha.' She smiled at him with an
entirely good-natured contempt.

These people that Uncle Jo kept bringing to the castle.
An Englishman with a monocle to look at the armour; a
man with a stammer to clean the pictures; a man who
couldn't speak anything but German to look at some silly
old pots and plates; and to-day this other ridiculous

Englishman with a face like a rabbit's and a voice like
Songs without Words on the saxophone.

Jeremy Pordage blinked the water out of his eyes and,
dimly, since he was presbyopic and without his spectacles,
saw the young laughing face very close to his own, the
body foreshortened and wavering uncertainly through
the water. It was not often that he found himself in such
proximity to such a being. He swallowed his annoyance
and smiled at her.

Miss Maunciple stretched out a hand and patted the bald
patch at the top of Jeremy's head. 'Boy,' she said, 'does
it shine. Talk of billiard-balls. I know what I shall call
you : Ivory. Good-bye, Ivory.' She turned, swam to the
ladder, climbed out, walked to the table on which the
bottles and glasses were standing, drank the rest of her
whisky and soda, then went and sat down on the edge of
the couch on which, in black spectacles and bathing-
drawers, Mr. Stoyte was taking his sun-bath.

'Well, Uncle Jo,' she said in a tone of affectionate
playfulness, 'feeling kind of good ?'

'Feeling fine, Baby,' he answered. It was true ; the sun
had melted away his dismal forebodings ; he was living
again in the present, that delightful present in which one
brought happiness to sick children ; in which there were
Tittelbaums prepared, for five hundred bucks, to give one
information worth at the very least a million ; in which
the sky was blue and the sunshine a caressing warmth
upon the stomach ; in which, finally, one stirred out of a
delicious somnolence to see little Virginia smiling down
at one as though she really cared for her old Uncle Jo,
and cared for him, what was more, not merely as an old
uncle—no, *sir* ; because, when all's said and done, a man
is only as old as he feels and acts ; and where his Baby was
concerned did he feel young ? did he *act* young ? Yes,

sir. Mr. Stoyte smiled to himself, a smile of triumphant self-satisfaction.

'Well, Baby,' he said aloud, and laid a square, thick-fingered hand on the young woman's bare knee.

Through half-closed eyelids Miss Maunciple gave him a secret and somehow indecent look of understanding and complicity; then uttered a little laugh and stretched her arms. 'Doesn't the sun feel good!' she said; and, closing her lids completely, she lowered her raised arms, clasped her hands behind her neck, and threw back her shoulders. It was a pose that lifted the breasts, that emphasized the inward curve of the loins and the contrary swell of the buttocks—the sort of pose that a new arrival in the seraglio would be taught by the eunuchs to assume at her first interview with the sultan; the very pose, Jeremy recognized, as he had chanced to look her way, of that quite particularly unsuitable statue on the third floor of the Beverly Pantheon.

Through his dark glasses, Mr. Stoyte looked up at her with an expression of possessiveness at once gluttonous and paternal. Virginia was his baby, not only figuratively and colloquially, but also in the literal sense of the word. His sentiments were simultaneously those of the purest father-love and the most violent eroticism.

He looked up at her. By contrast with the shiny white satin of her beach clout and brassière the sunburnt skin seemed more richly brown. The planes of the young body flowed in smooth continuous curves, effortlessly solid, three-dimensional, without accent or abrupt transition. Mr. Stoyte's regards travelled up to the auburn hair and came down by way of the rounded forehead, of the wide-set eyes, and small, straight, impudent nose, to the mouth. That mouth—it was her most striking feature. For it was to the mouth's short upper lip that

Virginia's face owed its characteristic expression of child-like innocence—an expression that persisted through all her moods, that was noticeable whatever she might be doing, whether it was telling smutty stories or making conversation with the Bishop, taking tea in Pasadena or getting tight with the boys, enjoying what she called 'a bit of yum-yum' or attending Mass. Chronologically, Miss Maunciple was a young woman of twenty-two; but that abbreviated upper lip gave her, in all circumstances, an air of being hardly adolescent, of not having reached the age of consent. For Mr. Stoyte, at sixty, the curiously perverse contrast between childishness and maturity, between the appearance of innocence and the fact of experience, was intoxicatingly attractive. It was not only so far as he was concerned that Virginia was both kinds of baby; she was also both kinds of baby objectively, in herself.

Delicious creature! The hand that had lain inert, hitherto, upon her knee slowly contracted. Between the broad spatulate thumb and the strong fingers, what smoothness, what a sumptuous and substantial resilience!

'Jinny, he said. 'My Baby!'

The Baby opened her large blue eyes and dropped her arms to her sides. The tense back relaxed, the lifted breasts moved downwards and forwards like soft living creatures sinking to repose. She smiled at him.

'What are you pinching me for, Uncle Jo?'

'I'd like to eat you,' her Uncle Jo replied in a tone of cannibalistic sentimentality.

'I'm tough.'

Mr. Stoyte uttered a maudlin chuckle. 'Little tough kid!' he said.

The tough kid stooped down and kissed him.

Jeremy Pordage, who had been quietly looking at the

panorama and continuing his silent recitation of *Epipsy-chidion*, happened at this moment to turn once more in the direction of the couch, and was so much embarrassed by what he saw that he began to sink and had to strike out violently with arms and legs to prevent himself from going under. Turning round in the water, he swam to the ladder, climbed out and, without waiting to dry himself, hurried to the elevator.

'Really!' he said to himself as he looked at the Vermeer. '*Really!*'

'I did some business this morning,' said Mr. Stoyte when the Baby had straightened herself up again.

'What sort of business?'

'Good business,' he answered. 'Might make a lot of money. *Real* money,' he insisted.

'How much?'

'Maybe half a million,' he said cautiously, understating his hopes; 'maybe a million; maybe even more.'

'Uncle Jo,' she said, 'I think you're wonderful.' Her voice had the ring of complete sincerity. She genuinely did think him wonderful. In the world in which she had lived it was axiomatic that a man who could make a million dollars must be wonderful. Parents, friends, teachers, newspapers, radio, advertisements—explicitly or by implication, all were unanimous in proclaiming his wonderfulness. And besides, Virginia was very fond of her Uncle Jo. He had given her a wonderful time, and she was grateful. Besides, she liked to like people if she possibly could; she liked to please them. Pleasing them made her feel good—even when they were elderly, like Uncle Jo, and when some of the ways in which she was called upon to please them didn't happen to be very appetizing. 'I think you're wonderful,' she repeated.

Her admiration gave him an intense satisfaction. 'Oh,

it's quite easy,' he said with hypocritical modesty, angling for more.

Virginia gave it him. 'Easy, nothing !' she said firmly. 'I say you *are* wonderful. So just keep your mouth shut.'

Enchanted, Mr. Stoyte took another handful of firm flesh and squeezed it affectionately. 'I'll give you a present, if the deal goes through,' he said. 'What would you like, Baby ?'

'What would I like ?' she repeated. 'But I don't want anything.'

Her disinterestedness was not assumed. For it was true ; she never did want things this way, in cold blood. At the moment a want occurred, for an ice-cream soda, for example, for a bit of yum-yum, for a mink coat seen in a shop-window—at such moments she did want things, and wanted them badly, couldn't wait to have them. But as for long-range wants, wants that had to be thought about in advance—no, she never had wanted like that. The best part of Virginia's life was spent in enjoying the successive instants of present contentment of which it was composed ; and if ever circumstances forced her out of this mindless eternity into the world of time, it was a narrow little universe in which she found herself, a world whose furthest boundaries were never more than a week or two away in the future. Even as a show-girl, at eighteen dollars a week, she had found it difficult to bother much about money and security and what would happen if you had an accident and couldn't show your legs any more. Then Uncle Jo had come along, and everything was there, as though it grew on trees—a swimming-pool tree, a cocktail tree, a Schiaparelli tree. You just had to reach out your hand and there it was, like an apple in the orchard back home in Oregon. So where did presents come in ? Why should she want anything ? Besides, it was obvious that Uncle Jo got a tremendous kick out of her not wanting things; and to be able to give Uncle Jo a kick always made her feel good. 'I tell you, Uncle Jo, I don't want *anything*.'

'Don't you?' said a strange voice, startlingly close behind them. 'Well, I do.'

Dark-haired and dapper, glossily Levantine, Dr. Sigmund Obispo stepped briskly up to the side of the couch.

'To be precise,' he went on, 'I want to inject one-point-five cubic centimetres of testosterones into the great man's *gluteus medius*. So off you go, my angel,' he said to Virginia in a tone of derision, but with a smile of unabashed desire. 'Hop!' He gave her a familiar little pat on the shoulder, and another, when she got up to make room for him, on the white satin posterior.

Virginia turned round sharply, with the intention of telling him not to be so fresh; then, as her glance travelled from that barrel of hairy flesh which was Mr. Stoyte to the other's handsome face, so insultingly sarcastic and at the same time so flatteringly concupiscent, she changed her mind and, instead of telling him, loudly, just where he got off, she made a grimace and stuck out her tongue at him. What was begun as a rebuke had ended, before she knew it, as the acquiescence in an impertinence, as an act of complicity with the offender and of disloyalty to Uncle Jo. Poor Uncle Jo! she thought, with a rush of affectionate pity for the old gentleman. For a moment she felt quite ashamed of herself. The trouble, of course, was that Dr. Obispo was so handsome; that he made her laugh; that she liked his admiration; that it was fun to lead him on and see how he'd act. She even enjoyed getting mad at him, when he was rude, which he constantly was.

'I suppose you think you're Douglas Fairbanks Junior,'

she said, making an attempt to be scathing; then walked
away with as much dignity as her two little strips of white
satin would permit her to assume and, leaning against a
battlement, looked down at the plain below. Ant-like
figures moved among the orange trees. She wondered
idly what they were doing; then her mind wandered to
other, more interesting and personal matters. To Sig and
the fact that she couldn't help feeling rather thrilled when
he was around, even when he acted the way he had done
just now. Some day, maybe—some day, just to see what
it was like and if things got a bit dull out here at the
castle . . . Poor Uncle Jo! she reflected. But then what
could he expect—at his age and at hers? The unexpected
thing was that, in all these months, she hadn't yet given
him any reason for being jealous—unless, of course, you
counted Enid and Mary Lou; which she didn't; because
she really wasn't that way at all; and when it did happen,
it was nothing more than a kind of little accident; nice,
but not a bit important. Whereas with Sig, if it ever
happened, the thing would be different; even though it
weren't very serious; which it wouldn't be—not like
with Walt, for example, or even with little Buster back
in Portland. It would be different from the accidents with
Enid and Mary Lou, because, with a man, those things
generally did matter a good deal, even when you didn't
mean them to matter. Which was the only reason for
not doing them, outside of their being sins, of course;
but somehow that never seemed to count very much
when the boy was a real good looker (which one had
to admit Sig was, even though it was rather in the style
of Adolphe Menjou; but, come to think of it, it was
those dark ones with oil on their hair that had always
given her the biggest kick!). And when you'd had a
couple of drinks, maybe, and you felt you'd like some

thrills, why, then it never even occurred to you that it was a sin; and then the one thing led to another, and before you knew what had happened—well, it *had* happened; and really she just couldn't believe it was as bad as Father O'Reilly said it was; and, anyhow, Our Lady would be a lot more understanding and forgiving than he was; and what about the way Father O'Reilly ate his food, whenever he came to dinner?—like a hog, there wasn't any other word for it; and wasn't gluttony just as bad as the other thing? So who was he to talk like that?

'Well, and how's the patient?' Dr. Obispo enquired in the parody of a bedside manner, as he took Virginia's place on the couch. He was in the highest of spirits. His work in the laboratory was coming along unexpectedly well; that new preparation of bile salts had done wonders for his liver; the rearmament boom had sent his aircraft shares up another three points; and it was obvious that Virginia wasn't going to hold out much longer. 'How's the little invalid this morning?' he went on, enriching his parody with the caricature of an English accent; for he had done a year of post-graduate work at Oxford.

Mr. Stoyte growled inarticulately. There was something about Dr. Obispo's facetiousness that always enraged him. In some not easily definable way it had the quality of a deliberate insult. Mr. Stoyte was always made to feel that Obispo's apparently good-natured banter was in reality the expression of a calculated and malignant contempt. The thought of it made Mr. Stoyte's blood boil. But when his blood boiled, his blood-pressure, he knew, went up, his life was shortened. He could not afford to be as angry with Obispo as he would have liked. And what was more, he couldn't afford to get rid of the man. Obispo was an indispensable evil. 'God is love;

there is no death.' But Mr. Stoyte remembered with
terror that he had had a stroke, that he was growing old.
Obispo had put him on his feet again when he was almost
dying, had promised him ten more years of life even if
those researches didn't work out as well as he hoped; and
if they did work out—then more, much more. Twenty
years, thirty, forty. Or it might even be that the loath-
some little kike would find some way of proving that
Mrs. Eddy was right, after all. Perhaps there really and
truly wouldn't be any death—not for Uncle Jo, at any
rate. Glorious prospect! Meanwhile . . . Mr. Stoyte
sighed, resignedly, profoundly. 'We all have our cross
to bear,' he said to himself, echoing, across the intervening
years, the words his grandmother used to repeat when she
made him take castor oil.

Dr. Obispo, meanwhile, had sterilized his needle, filed
the top off a glass ampoule, filled his syringe. His movements, as he worked, were characterized by a certain
studied exquisiteness, by a florid and self-conscious precision. It was as though the man were simultaneously
his own ballet and his own audience—a sophisticated and
highly critical audience, it was true; but then, what a
ballet! Nijinsky, Karsavina, Pavlova, Massine—all on a
single stage. However terrific the applause it was always
merited.

'Ready,' he called at last.

Obediently and in silence, like a trained elephant, Mr.
Stoyte rolled over on to his stomach.

Chapter Five

JEREMY had dressed again and was sitting in the subterranean store-room that was to serve as his study. The dry acrid dust of old documents had gone to his head, like a kind of intoxicating snuff. His face was flushed as he prepared his files and sharpened his pencils; his bald head shone with perspiration; behind their bifocal lenses his eyes were bright with excitement.

There! Everything was ready. He turned round in his swivel-chair and sat for a little while quite still, voluptuously savouring his anticipations. Tied up in innumerable brown-paper parcels, the Hauberk Papers awaited their first reader. Twenty-seven crates of still unravished brides of quietness. He smiled to himself at the thought that he was to be their Bluebeard. Thousands of brides of quietness accumulated through centuries by successive generations of indefatigable Hauberks. Hauberk after Hauberk; barony after knighthood; earldom after barony; and then Earl of Gonister after Earl of Gonister down to the last, the eighth. And, after the eighth, nothing but death-duties and an old house and two old spinster ladies, sinking ever deeper into solitude and eccentricity, into poverty and family pride, but finally, poor pets! more deeply into poverty than pride. They had sworn they would never sell; but in the end they had accepted Mr. Stoyte's offer. The papers had been shipped to California. They would be able, now, to buy themselves a couple of really sumptuous funerals. And that would be the end of the Hauberks. Delicious fragment of English history!

52

Cautionary perhaps, or perhaps, and more probably, merely senseless, merely a tale told by an idiot. A tale of cut-throats and conspirators, of patrons of learning and shady speculators, of bishops and kings' catamites and minor poets, of admirals and pimps, of saints and heroines and nymphomaniacs, of imbeciles and prime ministers, of art collectors and sadists. And here was all that remained of them, in twenty-seven crates, higgledy-piggledy, never catalogued, never even looked at, utterly virgin. Gloating over his treasure, Jeremy forgot the fatigues of the journey, forgot Los Angeles and the chauffeur, forgot the cemetery and the castle, forgot even Mr. Stoyte. He had the Hauberk Papers, had them all to himself. Like a child dipping blindly into a bran pie for a present which he knows will be exciting, Jeremy picked up one of the brown-paper parcels with which the first crate was filled and cut the string. What rich confusion awaited him within! A book of household accounts for the year 1576 and 1577; a narrative by some Hauberk cadet of Sir Kenelm Digby's expedition to Scanderoon; eleven letters in Spanish from Miguel de Molinos to that Lady Ann Hauberk who had scandalized her family by turning papist; a collection, in early eighteenth-century handwriting, of sickroom recipes; a copy of Drelincourt *On Death*; and an odd volume of Andréa de Nerciat's *Félicia, ou Mes Fredaines*. He had just cut the string of the second bundle and was wondering whose was the lock of pale brown hair preserved between the pages of the Third Earl's holograph Reflections on the Late Popish Plot, when there was a knock at the door. He looked up and saw a small, dark man in a white overall advancing towards him. The stranger smiled, said, 'Don't let me disturb you,' but nevertheless disturbed him. 'My name's Obispo,' he went on,

'Dr. Sigmund Obispo : Physician in ordinary to His Majesty King Stoyte the First—and let's hope also the last.'

Evidently delighted by his own joke, he broke into a peal of startlingly loud metallic laughter. Then, with the elegantly fastidious gesture of an aristocrat in a dust-heap, he picked up one of Molinos's letters and started, slowly, and out loud, to decipher the first line of the flowing seventeenth-century calligraphy that met his eyes. '"*Ame a Dios como es en sí y no como se lo dice y forma su imaginación.*"' He looked up at Jeremy with an amused smile. 'Easier said than done, I should think. Why, you can't even love a woman as she is in herself; and after all, there is some sort of objective physical basis for the phenomenon we call a female. A pretty nice basis in some cases. Whereas poor old Dios is only a spirit—in other words, pure imagination. And here's this idiot, whoever he is, telling some other idiot that people mustn't love God as he is in their imagination.' Once again self-consciously the aristocrat, he threw down the letter with a contemptuous flick of the wrist. 'What drivel it all is !' he went on. 'A string of words called religion. Another string of words called philosophy. Half a dozen other strings called political ideals. And all the words either ambiguous or meaningless. And people getting so excited about them they'll murder their neighbours for using a word they don't happen to like. A word that probably doesn't mean as much as a good belch. Just a noise without even the excuse of gas on the stomach. "*Ame a Dios come es en sí,*"' he repeated derisively. 'It's about as sensible as saying "hiccough *a* hiccough *como es en* hiccough." I don't know how you *litterae humaniores* boys manage to stand it. Don't you pine for some sense once in a while ?'

Jeremy smiled with an expression of nervous apology. 'One doesn't bother too much about the meanings,' he said. Then, anticipating further criticism by disparaging himself and the things he loved most dearly, 'One gets a lot of fun, you know,' he went on, 'just scrabbling about in the dust-heaps.'

Dr. Obispo laughed and patted Jeremy encouragingly on the shoulders. 'Good for you!' he said. 'You're frank. I like that. Most of the Ph.D. boys one meets are such damned Pecksniffs. Trying to pull that high-moral culture stuff on you! You know: wisdom rather than knowledge; Sophocles instead of science. "Funny," I always say to them when they try that on me, "funny that the thing you get your income from should happen to be the thing that's going to save humanity." Whereas you don't try to glorify your little racket. You're honest. You admit you're in the thing merely for the fun of it. Well, that's why I'm in *my* little racket. For the fun. Though, of course, if you'd given me any of that Sophocles stuff, I'd just have let you have my piece about science and progress, science and happiness, even science and ultimate truth, if you'd been obstinate.' He showed his white teeth in a happy derision of everybody.

His amusement was infectious. Jeremy also smiled. 'I'm glad I wasn't obstinate,' he said in a tone whose fluty demureness implied how much he objected to dis-quisitions on ultimate truth.

'Mind you,' Dr. Obispo went on, 'I'm not entirely blind to the charms of your racket. I'd draw the line at Sophocles, of course. And I'd be deadly bored with this sort of stuff'—he nodded towards the twenty-seven crates. 'But I must admit,' he concluded handsomely, 'I've had a lot of fun out of old books in my time. Really, a lot of fun.'

Jeremy coughed and caressed his scalp; his eyes twinkled in anticipation of the deliciously dry little joke he was just about to make. But, unfortunately, Dr. Obispo gave him no time. Serenely unaware of Jeremy's preparations he looked at his watch; then rose to his feet. 'I'd like to show you my laboratory,' he said. 'There's plenty of time before lunch.'

'Instead of asking if I'd like to see his bloody laboratory.' Jeremy protested inwardly, as he swallowed his joke; and it had been such a good one! He would have liked, of course, to go on unpacking the Hauberk Papers; but, lacking the courage to say so, he rose obediently and followed Dr. Obispo towards the door.

Longevity, the doctor explained, as they left the room. That was his subject. Had been ever since he left medical school. But, of course, so long as he was in practice he hadn't been able to do any serious work on it. Practice was fatal to serious work, he added parenthetically. How could you do anything sensible, when you had to spend all your time looking after patients? Patients belonged to three classes: those that imagined they were sick, but weren't; those that were sick, but would get well anyhow; those that were sick and would be much better dead. For anybody capable of serious work to waste his time with patients was simply idiotic. And, of course, nothing but economic pressure would ever have driven him to do it. And he might have gone on in that groove for ever. Wasting himself on morons. But then, quite suddenly, his luck had turned. Jo Stoyte had come to consult him. It had been positively providential.

'Most awfully a godsend,' Jeremy murmured, quoting his favourite phrase of Coleridge.

Jo Stoyte, Dr. Obispo repeated, Jo Stoyte on the verge of breaking up completely. Forty pounds overweight

and having had a stroke. Not a bad one, luckily; but
enough to put the old bastard into a sweat. Talk of being
scared to death! (Dr. Obispo's white teeth flashed again
in wolfish good-humour.) In Jo's case it had been a
panic. Out of that panic had come Dr. Obispo's
liberation from his patients; had come his income, his
laboratory for work on the problems of longevity, his
excellent assistant; had come, too, the financing of that
pharmaceutical work at Berkeley, of those experiments
with monkeys in Brazil, of that expedition to study the
tortoises on the Galapagos Islands. Everything a research
worker could ask for, with old Jo himself thrown in as
the perfect guinea-pig—ready to submit to practically
anything short of vivisection without anaesthetics, provided it offered some hope of keeping him above ground
a few years longer.

Not that he was doing anything spectacular with the
old buzzard at the moment. Just keeping his weight
down; and taking care of his kidneys; and pepping him
up with periodical shots of synthetic sex hormone; and
watching out for those arteries. The ordinary, common-
sense treatment for a man of Jo Stoyte's age and medical
history. Meanwhile, however, he was on the track of
something new, something that promised to be important.
In a few months, perhaps in a few weeks, he'd be in a
position to make a definite pronouncement.

'That's very interesting,' said Jeremy with hypocritical politeness.

They were walking along a narrow corridor, whitewashed and bleakly illuminated by a series of electric
bulbs. Through open doors Jeremy had occasional
glimpses of vast cellars crammed with totem poles and
armour, with stuffed orang-utans and marble groups by
Thorwaldsen, with gilded Bodhisattvas and early steam-

engines, with lingams and stage-coaches and Peruvian pottery, with crucifixes and mineralogical specimens.

Dr. Obispo, meanwhile, had begun to talk again about longevity. The subject, he insisted, was still in the pre-scientific stage. A lot of observations without any explanatory hypothesis. A mere chaos of facts. And what odd, what essentially eccentric facts! What was it, for example, that made a cicada live as long as a bull? or a canary outlast three generations of sheep? Why should dogs be senile at fourteen and parrots sprightly at a hundred? Why should female humans become sterile in the forties, while female crocodiles continued to lay eggs into their third century? Why in heaven's name should a pike live to two hundred without showing any signs of senility? Whereas poor old Jo Stoyte . . .

From a side passage two men suddenly emerged carrying between them on a stretcher a couple of mummified nuns. There was a collision.

'Damned fools!' Dr. Obispo shouted angrily.

'Damned fool yourself!'

'Can't you look where you're going?'

'Keep your face shut!'

Dr. Obispo turned contemptuously away and walked on.

'Who the hell do you think you are?' they called after him.

Jeremy meanwhile had been looking with lively curiosity at the mummies. 'Discalced Carmelites,' he said to nobody in particular; and enjoying the flavour of that curious combination of syllables, he repeated them with a certain emphatic relish. 'Discalced Carmelites.'

'Discalced your ass,' said the foremost of the two men, turning fiercely upon this new antagonist.

Jeremy gave one glance at that red and angry face, then, with ignominious haste, hurried after his guide.

Dr. Obispo halted at last. 'Here we are,' he said, opening a door. A smell of mice and absolute alcohol floated out into the corridor. 'Come on in,' he said cordially.

Jeremy entered. There were the mice all right—cage upon cage of them, in tiers along the wall directly in front of him. To the left, three windows, hewn in the rock, gave on to the tennis-court and a distant panorama of orange trees and mountains. Seated at a table in front of one of these windows, a man was looking through a microscope. He raised his fair, tousled head as they approached, and turned towards them a face of almost child-like candour and openness. 'Hullo, doc,' he said with a charming smile.

'My assistant,' Dr. Obispo explained. 'Peter Boone. Pete, this is Mr. Pordage.' Pete rose and revealed himself an athletic young giant.

'Call me Pete,' he said, when Jeremy had called him Mr. Boone. 'Everyone calls me Pete.'

Jeremy wondered whether he ought to invite the young man to call him Jeremy—but wondered, as usual, so long that the appropriate moment for doing so passed, irrevocably.

'Pete's a bright boy,' Dr. Obispo began again in a tone that was affectionate in intention, but a little patronizing in fact. 'Knows his physiology. Good with his hands, too. Best mouse surgeon I ever saw.' He patted the young man on the shoulder.

Pete smiled—a little uncomfortably, it seemed to Jeremy, as though he found it rather difficult to make the right response to the other's cordiality.

'Takes his politics a bit too seriously,' Dr. Obispo went on. 'That's his only defect. I'm trying to cure him of that. Not very successfully so far, I'm afraid. Eh, Pete?'

C

The young man smiled again, more confidently; this time he knew exactly where he stood and what to do.

'*Not* very successfully,' he repeated. Then, turning to Jeremy, 'Did you see the Spanish news this morning?' he asked. The expression on his large, fair, open face changed to one of concern.

Jeremy shook his head.

'It's something awful,' said Pete gloomily. 'When I think of those poor devils without planes or artillery or . . .'

'Well, don't think of them,' Dr. Obispo cheerfully advised. 'You'll feel better.'

The young man looked at him, then looked away again without saying anything. After a moment of silence he pulled out his watch. 'I think I'll go and have a swim before lunch,' he said, and walked towards the door.

Dr. Obispo picked up a cage of mice and held it within a few inches of Jeremy's nose. 'These are the sex-hormone boys,' he said with a jocularity that the other found curiously offensive. The animals squeaked as he shook the cage. 'Lively enough while the effect lasts. The trouble is that the effects are only temporary.'

Not that temporary effects were to be despised, he added, as he replaced the cage. It was always better to feel temporarily good than temporarily bad. That was why he was giving old Jo a course of that testosterone stuff. Not that the old bastard had any great need of it with that Maunciple girl around. . . .

Dr. Obispo suddenly put his hand over his mouth and looked round towards the window. 'Thank God,' he said, 'he's out of the room. Poor old Pete!' A derisive smile appeared on his face. 'Is he in love!' He tapped his forehead. 'Thinks she's like something in the Works

of Tennyson. You know, chemically pure. Last month
he nearly killed a man for suggesting that she and the
old boy . . . Well, you know. God knows what he
figures the girl is doing here. Telling Uncle Jo about the
spiral nebulae, I suppose. Well, if it makes him happy
to think that way, I'm not the one that's going to spoil
his fun.' Dr. Obispo laughed indulgently. 'But to come
back to what I was saying about Uncle Jo. . . .'

Just having that girl around the house was the equivalent of a hormone treatment. But it wouldn't last. It
never did. Brown-Séquard and Voronoff and all the
rest of them—they'd been on the wrong track. They'd
thought that the decay of sexual power was the cause of
senility. Whereas it was only one of the symptoms.
Senescence started somewhere else and involved the sex
mechanism along with the rest of the body. Hormone
treatments were just palliatives and pick-me-ups. Helped
you for a time, but didn't prevent your growing old.

Jeremy stifled a yawn.

For example, Dr. Obispo went on, why should some
animals live much longer than human beings and yet
show no signs of old age? Somehow, somewhere we
had made a biological mistake. Crocodiles had avoided
that mistake; so had tortoises. The same was true of
certain species of fish.

'Look at this,' he said; and, crossing the room, he
drew back a rubber curtain, revealing as he did so the
glass front of a large aquarium recessed into the wall.
Jeremy approached and looked in.

In the green and shadowy translucence, two huge fish
hung suspended, their snouts almost touching, motionless
except for the occasional ripple of a fin and the rhythmic
panting of their gills. A few inches from their staring
eyes a rosary of bubbles streamed ceaselessly up towards

the light, and all around them the water was spasmodically silver with the dartings of smaller fish. Sunk in their mindless ecstasy, the monsters paid no attention.

Carp, Dr. Obispo explained; carp from the fishponds of a castle in Franconia—he had forgotten the name; but it was somewhere near Bamberg. The family was impoverished; but the fish were heirlooms, unpurchasable. Jo Stoyte had had to spend a lot of money to have these two stolen and smuggled out of the country in a specially constructed automobile with a tank under the back seats. Sixty-pounders they were; over four feet long; and those rings in their tails were dated 1761.

'The beginning of my period,' Jeremy murmured in a sudden access of interest. 1761 was the year of *Fingal*. He smiled to himself; the juxtaposition of carp and Ossian, carp and Napoleon's favourite poet, carp and the first premonitions of the Celtic Twilight, gave him a peculiar pleasure. What a delightful subject for one of his little essays! Twenty pages of erudition and absurdity—of sacrilege in lavender—of a scholar's delicately *canaille* irreverence for the illustrious or unillustrious dead.

But Dr. Obispo would not allow him to think his thoughts in peace. Indefatigably riding his own hobby, he began again. There they were, he said, pointing at the huge fish; nearly two hundred years old; perfectly healthy; no symptoms of senility; no apparent reason why they shouldn't go on for another three or four centuries. There they were; and there were you. He turned back accusingly towards Jeremy. Here were you; no more than middle-aged, but already bald, already long-sighted and short-winded; already more or less edentate; incapable of prolonged physical exertion; chronically constipated (could you deny it?); your memory already not so good as it was; your digestion capricious; your potency falling off—if it hadn't, indeed, already disappeared for good.

Jeremy forced himself to smile, and at every fresh item nodded his head in what was meant to look like an amused assent. Inwardly, he was writhing with a mixture of distress at this all too truthful diagnosis and anger against the diagnostician for the ruthlessness of his scientific detachment. Talking with a humorous self-deprecation about one's own advancing senility was very different from being bluntly told about it by someone who took no interest in you except as an animal that happened to be unlike a fish. Nevertheless, he continued to nod and smile.

Here you were, Dr. Obispo repeated at the end of his diagnosis, and there were the carp. How was it that you didn't manage your physiological affairs as well as they did? Just where and how and why did you make the mistake that had already robbed you of your teeth and hair and would bring you in a very few years to the grave?

Old Metchnikoff had asked those questions and made a bold attempt to answer. Everything he said happened to be wrong: phagocytosis didn't occur; intestinal auto-intoxication wasn't the sole cause of senility; neuronophags were mythological monsters; drinking sour milk didn't materially prolong life; whereas the removal of the large gut *did* materially shorten it. Chuckling, he recalled those operations that were so fashionable just before the War! Old ladies and gentlemen with their colons cut out, and in consequence being forced to evacuate every few minutes, like canaries! All to no purpose, needless to say; because of course the operation that was meant to make them live to a hundred killed them all off within a year or two. Dr. Obispo threw back his glossy head and uttered one of those peals of brazen laughter which were his regular response to any tale of human stupidity resulting in misfortune. Poor old Metchnikoff, he went on, wiping the tears of merriment from his eyes. Consistently wrong. And yet almost certainly not nearly so wrong as people had thought. Wrong, yes, in supposing that it was all a matter of intestinal stasis and autointoxication. But probably right in thinking that the secret was somewhere down there, in the gut. Somewhere in the gut, Dr. Obispo repeated; and, what was more, he believed that he was on its track.

He paused and stood for a moment in silence, drumming with his fingers on the glass of the aquarium. Poised between mud and air, the two obese and aged carps hung in their greenish twilight, serenely unaware of him. Dr. Obispo shook his head at them. The worst experimental animals in the world, he said in a tone of resentment mingled with a certain gloomy pride. Nobody had a right to talk about technical difficulties who hadn't tried to work with fish. Take the simplest operation; it was a nightmare. Had you ever tried to keep its gills properly wet while it was anaesthetized on the operating-table? Or, alternatively, to do your surgery under water? Had you ever set out to determine a fish's basal metabolism, or take an electro-cardiograph of its heart action, or measure its blood-pressure? Had you ever wanted to analyse its excreta? And, if so, did you know how hard it was even to collect them? Had you ever attempted to study the chemistry of a fish's digestion and assimilation? To determine its blood-pressure under different conditions? To measure the speed of its nervous reactions?

No, you had not, said Dr. Obispo contemptuously. And until you had, you had no right to complain about anything.

He drew the curtain on his fish, took Jeremy by the arm and led him back to the mice.

'Look at those,' he said, pointing to a batch of cages on an upper shelf.

Jeremy looked. The mice in question were exactly like all other mice. 'What's wrong with them?' he asked.

Dr. Obispo laughed. 'If those animals were human beings,' he said dramatically, 'they'd all be over a hundred years old.'

And he began to talk, very rapidly and excitedly, about fatty alcohols and the intestinal flora of carp. For the secret was there, the key to the whole problem of senility and longevity. There, between the sterols and the peculiar flora of the carp's intestine.

Those sterols! (Dr. Obispo frowned and shook his head over them.) Always linked up with senility. The most obvious case, of course, was cholesterol. A senile animal might be defined as one with an accumulation of cholesterol in the walls of its arteries. Potassium thiocyanate seemed to dissolve those accumulations. Senile rabbits would show signs of rejuvenation under a treatment with potassium thiocyanate. So would senile humans. But, again, not for very long. Cholesterol in the arteries was evidently only one of the troubles. But then cholesterol was only one of the sterols. They were a closely related group, those fatty alcohols. It didn't take much to transform one into another. But if you'd read old Schneeglock's work and the stuff they'd been publishing at Upsala, you'd know that some of the sterols were definitely poisonous—much more than cholesterol, even in large accumulations. Longbotham had even suggested a connection between fatty alcohols and neoplasms. In other words, cancer might be regarded, in a final analysis, as a symptom of sterol-poisoning. He himself would go even further and say that such sterol-poisoning was responsible for the entire degenerative process of senescence in man and the other mammals. What nobody had done hitherto was to look into the part played by fatty alcohols in the life of such animals as carp. That was the work he had been doing for the last year. His researches had convinced him of two or three things : first, that the fatty alcohols in carp did not accumulate in excessive quantity; second, that they did not undergo transformation into the more poisonous sterols; and third, that both these immunities were due to the peculiar nature of the carp's intestinal flora. What a flora! Dr. Obispo cried enthusiastically. So rich, so wonderfully varied! He had not yet succeeded in isolating the organism responsible for the carp's immunity to old age, nor did he fully understand the nature of the chemical mechanisms involved. Nevertheless, the main fact was certain. In one way or another, in combination or in isolation, these organisms contrived to keep the fish's sterols from turning into poisons. That was why a carp could live a couple of hundred years and show no signs of senility.

Could the intestinal flora of a carp be transferred to the gut of a mammal ? And, if transferable, would it achieve the same chemical and biological results ? That was what he had been trying, for the past few months, to discover. With no success, to begin with. Recently, however, they had experimented with a new technique—a technique that protected the flora from the process of digestion, gave it time to adapt itself to the unfamiliar conditions. It had taken root. The effect on the mice had been immediate and significant. Senescence had been halted, even reversed. Physiologically, the animals were younger than they had been for at least eighteen months—younger at the equivalent of a hundred than they had been at the equivalent of sixty.

Outside in the corridor an electric bell began to ring. It was lunch-time. The two men left the room and walked towards the elevator. Dr. Obispo went on talking. Mice, he said, were apt to be a bit deceptive. He had now begun to try the thing out on larger animals. If it worked all right on dogs and baboons, it ought to work on Uncle Jo.

Chapter Six

IN the small dining-room, most of the furnishings came from the Pavilion at Brighton. Four gilded dragons supported the red lacquered table, and two more served as caryatids on either side of a chimney-piece in the same material. It was the Regency's dream of the Gorgeous East. The kind of thing, Jeremy reflected, as he sat down on his scarlet and gold chair, the kind of thing that the word 'Cathay' would have conjured up in Keats's mind, for example, or Shelley's, or Lord Byron's—just as that charming 'Leda' by Etty, over there, next to the Fra Angelico's 'Annunciation,' was an accurate embodiment of their fancies on the subject of pagan mythology; was an authentic illustration (he chuckled inwardly at the thought) to the Odes to Psyche and the Grecian Urn, to *Endymion* and *Prometheus Unbound*. An age's habits of thought and feeling and imagination are shared by all who live and work within that age—by all, from the journeyman up to the genius. Regency is always Regency, whether you take your sample from the top of the basket or from the bottom. In 1820, the man who shut his eyes and tried to visualize magic casements opening on the foam of faery seas would see—what? The turrets of Brighton Pavilion. At the thought, Jeremy smiled to himself with pleasure. Etty and Keats, Brighton and Percy Bysshe Shelley—what a delightful subject! Much better than carp and Ossian; better inasmuch as Nash and the Prince Regent were funnier than even the most aged fish. But for conversational purposes and at the luncheon-table, even the best of subjects is

68

worthless if there is nobody to discuss it with. And who was there, Jeremy asked himself, who was there in this room desirous or capable of talking with him on such a theme? Not Mr. Stoyte; not, certainly, Miss Maunciple, nor the two young women who had come over from Hollywood to have lunch with her; not Dr. Obispo, who cared more for mice than books; nor Peter Boone, who probably didn't even know that there were any books to care for. The only person who might conceivably be expected to take an interest in the manifestations of the later-Georgian time spirit was the individual who had been introduced to him as Dr. Herbert Mulge, Ph.D., D.D., Principal of Tarzana College. But at the moment Dr. Mulge was talking in a rich vein of something that sounded almost like pulpit eloquence about the new Auditorium which Mr. Stoyte had just presented to the College and which was shortly to be given its formal opening. Dr. Mulge was a large and handsome man with a voice to match—a voice at once sonorous and suave, unctuous and ringing. The flow of his language was slow, but steady and apparently stanchless. In phrases full of the audible equivalents of Capital Letters, he now went on to assure Mr. Stoyte and anyone else who cared to listen that it would be a Real Inspiration for the boys and girls of Tarzana to come together in the beautiful new building for their Community Activities. For Non-Denominational Worship, for example; for the Enjoyment of the Best in Drama and Music. Yes, what an inspiration! The name of Stoyte would be remembered with love and reverence by successive generations of the College's Alumni and Alumnae,—would be remembered, he might say, for ever; for the Auditorium was a *monumentum aere perennius*, a Footprint on the Sand of Time—definitely a Footprint. And now, Dr. Mulge continued, between the mouthfuls of creamed chicken, now Tarzana's Crying Need was for a new Art School. Because, after all, Art, as we were now discovering, was one of the most potent of educational forces. Art was the aspect under which, in this twentieth century of ours, the Religious Spirit most clearly manifested itself. Art was the means by which Personalities could best achieve Creative Self-Expression and . . .

'Cripes!' Jeremy said to himself; and then: 'Golly!' He smiled ruefully at the thought that he hoped to talk to this imbecile about the relation between Keats and Brighton Pavilion.

Peter Boone found himself separated from Virginia by the blonder of her two young friends from Hollywood, so that he could only look at her past a foreground of rouge and eyelashes, of golden curls and a thick, almost visible perfume of gardenias. To anyone else, this foreground might have seemed a bit distracting; but for Pete it was of no more significance than the equivalent amount of mud. He was interested only in what was beyond the foreground—in that exquisitely abbreviated upper lip, in the little nose that made you want to cry when you looked at it, it was so elegant and impertinent, so ridiculous and angelic; in that long Florentine bob of lustrous auburn hair; in those wide-set, widely opened eyes with their twinkling surface of humour and their dark blue depths of what he was sure was an infinite tenderness, a plumb-less feminine wisdom. He loved her so much that, where his heart should have been he could feel only an aching breathlessness, a cavity which she alone could fill.

Meanwhile, she was talking to the blonde Foreground about that new job which the Foreground had landed with the Cosmopolitan-Perlmutter Studio. The picture was called 'Say it with Stockings,' and the Foreground was to play the part of a rich débutante who runs away from home to make a career of her own, becomes a strip-tease dancer in a Western mining-camp and finally marries a cow-puncher, who turns out to be the son of a millionaire.

'Sounds like a swell story,' said Virginia. 'Don't you think so, Pete?'

Pete thought so; he was ready to think almost anything if she wanted him to.

'That reminds me of Spain,' Virginia announced. And while Jeremy, who had been eavesdropping on the conversation, frantically tried to imagine what train of associations had taken her from 'Say it with Stockings' to the civil war—whether it had been Cosmopolitan-Perlmutter, Anti-Semitism, Nazis, Franco; or débutante, class war, Moscow, Negrin; or strip-tease, modernity, radicalism, Republicans—while he was vainly speculating thus, Virginia went on to ask the young man to tell them about what he had done in Spain; and when he demurred, insisted—because it was so thrilling, because the Foreground had never heard about it, because, finally, she wanted him to.

Pete obeyed. Only half-articulately, in a vocabulary composed of slang and clichés, and adorned by expletives and grunts—the vocabulary, Jeremy reflected as he listened surreptitiously through the booming of Dr. Mulge's eloquence, the characteristically squalid and poverty-stricken vocabulary to which the fear of being thought unsocially different or undemocratically superior, or unsportingly highbrow, condemns most young Englishmen and Americans—he began to describe his experiences as a volunteer in the International Brigade during

the heroic days of 1937. It was a touching narrative.
Through the hopelessly inadequate language, Jeremy
could divine the young man's enthusiasm for liberty
and justice; his courage; his love for his comrades; his
nostalgia, even in the neighbourhood of that short upper
lip, even in the midst of an absorbing piece of scientific
research, for the life of men united in devotion to a cause,
made one in the face of hardship and shared danger and
impending death.

'Gee,' he kept repeating, 'they were swell guys.'

They were all swell—Knud, who had saved his life one
day, up there in Aragon; Anton and Mack and poor little
Dino, who had been killed; André, who had lost a leg;
Jan, who had a wife and two children; Fritz, who'd had
six months in a Nazi concentration camp; and all the
others—the finest bunch of boys in the world. And what
did he do, but go and get rheumatic fever on them, and
then myocarditis—which meant no more active service;
no more anything except sitting around. That was why
he was here, he explained apologetically. But, gee, it
had been good while it lasted! That time, for example,
when he and Knud had gone out at night and climbed a
precipice in the dark and taken a whole platoon of Moors
by surprise and killed half a dozen of them and come back
with a machine-gun and three prisoners. . . .

'And what is *your* opinion of Creative Work, Mr.
Pordage?'

Surprised in flagrant inattention, Jeremy started guiltily.
'Creative work?' he mumbled, trying to gain a little
time. 'Creative work? Well, of course one's all for it.
Definitely,' he insisted.

'I'm glad to hear you say so,' said Dr. Mulge. 'Because
that's what I want at Tarzana. Creative work—ever more
and more Creative. Shall I tell you what is my highest

ambition?' Neither Mr. Stoyte nor Jeremy made any
reply. But Dr. Mulge proceeded, nevertheless, to tell
them. 'It is to make of Tarzana the living Centre of the
New Civilization that is coming to blossom here in the
West.' He raised a large fleshy hand in solemn assevera-
tion. 'The Athens of the twentieth century is on the
point of emerging here, in the Los Angeles Metropolitan
Area. I want Tarzana to be its Parthenon and its Academe,
its Stoa and its Temple of the Muses. Religion, Art,
Philosophy, Science—I want them all to find their home
in Tarzana, to radiate their influence from our campus,
to . . .'

In the middle of his story about the Moors and the
precipice, Pete became aware that only the Foreground
was listening to him. Virginia's attention had wandered,
surreptitiously at first, then frankly and avowedly—had
wandered to where, on her left, the less blonde of her two
friends was having something almost whispered to her
by Dr. Obispo.

'What's that?' Virginia asked.

Dr. Obispo leaned towards her and began again. The
three heads, the oil-smooth black, the elaborately curly
brown, the lustrous auburn, were almost touching. By
the expression on their faces Pete could see that the doctor
was telling one of his dirty stories. Alleviated for a
moment by the smile she had given him when she asked
him to tell them about Spain, the anguish in that panting
void where his heart ought to have been came back with
redoubled intensity. It was a complicated pain, made up of
jealousy and a despairing sense of loss and personal un-
worthiness, of a fear that his angel was being corrupted
and another, deeper fear, which his conscious mind refused to formulate, a fear that there wasn't much further
corruption to be done, that the angel was not as angelic

as his love had made him assume. The flow of his narrative suddenly dried up. He was silent.

'Well, what happened then?' the Foreground enquired with an eagerness and an expression of hero-worshipping admiration that any other young man would have found delightfully flattering.

He shook his head. 'Oh, nothing much.'

'But those Moors . . .'

'Hell!' he said impatiently. 'What does it matter, anyhow?'

His words were drowned by a violent explosion of laughter that sent the three conspiratorial heads, the black, the brown, the lovely auburn, flying apart from one another. He looked up at Virginia and saw a face distorted with mirth. At what? he asked himself in agony, trying to measure the extent of her corruption; and a kind of telescoped and synthetic memory of all the schoolboy stories, all the jokes and limericks he had ever heard, rushed in upon him.

Was it at that one that she was laughing? Or at that? Or, God, perhaps at *that*? He hoped and prayed it wasn't at *that*; and the more he hoped and prayed, the more insanely sure he became that *that* was the one it had been.

'. . . above all,' Dr. Mulge was saying, 'Creative Work in the Arts. Hence the crying need for a new Art School, an Art School worthy of Tarzana, worthy of the highest traditions of . . .'

The girls' shrill laughter exploded with a force of hilarity proportionate to the strength of the surrounding social taboos. Mr. Stoyte turned sharply in the direction from which the noise had come.

'What's the joke?' he asked suspiciously. He wasn't going to have his Baby listen to smut. He disapproved of smut in mixed company almost as whole-heartedly as his grandmother, the Plymouth Sister, had done. 'What's all that noise about?'

It was Dr. Obispo who answered. He'd been telling them a funny story he'd heard over the radio, he explained with that suave politeness that was like a sarcasm. Something delightfully amusing. Perhaps Mr. Stoyte would like to have him repeat it.

Mr. Stoyte grunted ferociously and turned away.

A glance at his host's scowling face convinced Dr. Mulge that it would be better to postpone discussion of the Art School to another, more propitious occasion. It was disappointing; for it seemed to him that he had been making good progress. But, there! such things would happen. Dr. Mulge was a college president chronically in quest of endowments; he knew all about the rich. Knew, for example, that they were like gorillas, creatures not easily domesticated, deeply suspicious, alternately bored and bad-tempered. You had to approach them with caution, to handle them gently and with a boundless cunning. And even then they might suddenly turn savage on you and show their teeth. Half a lifetime of experience with bankers and steel-magnates and retired meat-packers had taught Dr. Mulge to take such little setbacks as to-day's with a truly philosophic patience. Brightly, with a smile on his large, imperial-Roman face, he turned to Jeremy. 'And what do you think of our Californian weather, Mr. Pordage?' he asked.

Meanwhile, Virginia had noticed the expression on Pete's face and immediately divined the causes of his misery. Poor Pete! But really, if he thought she had nothing better to do than always be listening to his talk about that silly old war in Spain—or if it wasn't Spain, it was the laboratory; and they did vivisection there, which was just awful; because, after all, when you were hunting, the animals had a chance of getting away, particularly if you were a bad shot, like she was; besides, hunting was full of thrills and you got such a kick from being up there in the mountains in the good air; whereas Pete cut them up underground in that cellar place. . . . No, if he thought she had nothing better to do than that, he made a big mistake. All the same, he was a nice boy; and talk about being in love! It was nice having people around who felt that way about you; made you feel kind of good. Though it could be rather a nuisance sometimes. Because they got to feel they had some claim on you; they figured they had a right to tell you things and interfere. Pete didn't do that in so many words; but he had a way of looking at you—like a dog would do if it suddenly started criticizing you for taking another cocktail. Saying it with eyes, like Hedy Lamarr—only it wasn't the same thing as Hedy was saying with *her* eyes; in fact, just the opposite. It was just the opposite now— and what had she done? Got bored with that silly old war and listened in to what Sig was saying to Mary Lou. Well, all she could say was that she wasn't going to have anyone interfering with the way she chose to live her own life. That was her business. Why, he was almost as bad, the way he looked at her, as Uncle Jo, or her mother, or Father O'Reilly. Only, of course, they didn't just look; they said things. Not that he meant badly, of course, poor Pete; he was just a kid, just unsophisticated and, on top of everything, in love the way a kid is—like the high-school boy in Deanna Durbin's last picture. Poor Pete, she thought again. It was tough luck on him; but the fact was she never had been attracted by that big, fair, Cary Grant sort of boy. They just didn't appeal to her; that was all there was to it. She liked him;

and she enjoyed his being in love with her.   But that was all.

Across the corner of the table she caught his eye, gave him a dazzling smile and invited him, if he had half an hour to spare after lunch, to come and teach her and the girls how to pitch horseshoes.

Chapter Seven

THE meal was over at last; the party broke up. Dr. Mulge had an appointment in Pasadena to see a rubber-goods manufacturer's widow, who might perhaps give thirty thousand dollars for a new girls' dormitory. Mr. Stoyte drove into Los Angeles for his regular Friday afternoon board meetings and business consultations. Dr. Obispo was going to operate on some rabbits and went down to the laboratory to prepare his instruments. Pete had a batch of scientific journals to look at, but gave himself, meanwhile, a few minutes of happiness in Virginia's company. And for Jeremy, of course, there were the Hauberk Papers. It was with a sense of almost physical relief, a feeling that he was going home to where he belonged, that he returned to his cellar. The afternoon slipped past—how delightfully, how profitably! Within three hours, another batch of letters from Molinos had turned up among the account books and the business correspondence. So had the third and fourth volumes of *Félicia*. So had an illustrated edition of *Le Portier des Carmes*; and, bound like a prayer-book, so had a copy of that rarest of all works of the Divine Marquis, *Les Cent-Vingt Jours de Sodome*. What a treasure! What unexpected fortune! Or perhaps, Jeremy reflected, not so unexpected if one remembered the history of the Hauberk family. For the date of the books made it likely that they had been the property of the Fifth Earl— the one who had held the title for more than half a century and died at more than ninety, under William IV, completely unregenerate. Given the character of that old gentleman, one had no reason to feel surprised at the finding of a store of pornography—one had every reason, indeed, to hope for more.

Jeremy's spirits mounted with each new discovery. Always, with him, a sure sign of happiness, he began to hum the tunes that had been popular during his childhood. Molinos evoked 'Tara-rara Boom-de-ay!' *Félicia* and the *Portier des Carmes* shared the romantic lilt of 'The Honeysuckle and the Bee.' As for the '*Cent-Vingt Jours*,' which he had never previously read or even seen a copy of—the finding of that delighted him so much that when, as a matter of bibliographical routine, he raised the ecclesiastical cover and, expecting the Anglican ritual, found instead the coldly elegant prose of the Marquis de Sade, he broke out into that rhyme from 'The Rose and the Ring,' the rhyme his mother had taught him to repeat when he was only three years old and which had remained with him as the symbol of childlike wonder and delight, as the only completely adequate reaction to any sudden blessing, any providentially happy surprise.

> *Oh, what fun to have a plum bun!*
> *How I wish it never was done!*

And fortunately it wasn't done, wasn't even begun; the book was still unread, the hours of entertainment and instruction still lay before him. Remembering that pang of jealousy he had felt up there, in the swimming-pool, he smiled indulgently. Let Mr. Stoyte have all the girls he wanted; a well-written piece of eighteenth-century pornography was better than any Maunciple. He closed the volume he was holding. The tooled morocco was austerely elegant; on the back, the words 'The Book of Common Prayer' were stamped in a gold which the years had hardly tarnished. He put it down with the other *curiosa* on a corner of the table. When he had finished for the afternoon, he would take the whole collection up to his bedroom.

'Oh, what fun to have a plum bun!' he chanted to himself, as he opened another bundle of papers, and then, 'On a summer's afternoon, where the honeysuckles bloom and all Nature seems at rest.' That Wordsworthian touch about Nature always gave him a special pleasure. The new batch of papers turned out to be a correspondence between the Fifth Earl and a number of prominent Whigs regarding the enclosure, for his benefit, of three thousand acres of common land in Nottinghamshire. Jeremy slipped them into a file, wrote a brief preliminary description of the contents on a card, put the file in a cupboard and the card in its cabinet, and, dipping again into the bran pie, reached down for another bundle. He cut the string. 'You are my honey, honey, honeysuckle, I am the bee.' What would Dr. Freud have thought of that, he wondered? Anonymous pamphlets against deism were a bore; he threw them aside. But here was a copy of Law's *Serious Call* with manuscript notes by Edward Gibbon; and here were some accounts rendered to the Fifth Earl by Mr. Rogers of Liverpool: accounts of the expenses and profits of three slave-trading expeditions which the Earl had helped finance. The second voyage, it appeared, had been particularly auspicious; less than a fifth of the cargo had perished on the way, and the prices realized at Savannah were gratifyingly high. Mr. Rogers begged to enclose his draft for seventeen thousand two hundred and twenty-four pounds eleven shillings and fourpence. Written from Venice, in Italian, another letter announced to the same Fifth Earl the appearance upon the market of a half-length 'Mary Magdalen' by Titian, at a price which the Italian correspondent described as derisory. Other offers had already been made; but out of respect for the not less learned than illustrious English *cognoscente*, the vendor would wait until a reply had been received from his lordship. In spite of which, his lordship would be well advised not to delay too long; for otherwise . . .

It was five o'clock; the sun was low in the sky. Dressed in white shoes and socks, white shorts, a yachting-cap and a pink silk sweater, Virginia had come to see the feeding of the baboons.

Its engine turned off, her rose-coloured motor-scooter stood parked at the side of the road thirty or forty feet above the cage. In company with Dr. Obispo and Pete, she had gone down to have a closer look at the animals.

Just opposite the point at which they were standing, on a shelf of artificial rock, sat a baboon mother, holding in her arms the withered and disintegrating corpse of the baby she would not abandon even though it had been dead for a fortnight. Every now and then, with an intense, automatic affection, she would lick the little cadaver. Tufts of greenish fur and even pieces of skin detached themselves under the vigorous action of her tongue. Delicately, with black fingers, she would pick the hairs out of her mouth, then begin again. Above her, at the mouth of a little cave, two young males suddenly got into a fight. The air was filled with screams and barks and the gnashing of teeth. Then one of the two combatants ran away and, in a moment, the other had forgotten all about the fight and was searching for pieces of dandruff on his chest. To the right, on another shelf of rock, a formidable old male, leather-snouted, with the grey bobbed hair of a seventeenth-

century Anglican divine, stood guard over his submissive
female. It was a vigilant watch; for if she ventured to
move without his leave, he turned and bit her; and
meanwhile the small black eyes, the staring nostrils at
the end of the truncated snout, kept glancing this way
and that with an unsleeping suspicion. From the basket
he was carrying, Pete threw a potato in his direction, then
a carrot and another potato. With a vivid flash of
magenta buttocks the old baboon darted down from his
perch on the artificial mountain, seized the carrot and,
while he was eating it, stuffed one potato into his left
cheek, the other into the right; then, still biting at the
carrot, advanced toward the wire and looked up for
more. The coast was clear. The young male who had
been looking for dandruff suddenly saw his opportunity.
Chattering with excitement, he bounded down to the
shelf on which, too frightened to follow her master, the
little female was still squatting. Within ten seconds they
had begun to copulate.

Virginia clapped her hands with pleasure. 'Aren't they
cute!' she cried. 'Aren't they *human*!'

Another burst of screaming and barking almost
drowned her words.

Pete interrupted his distribution of food to say that it
was a long while since he had seen Mr. Propter. Why
shouldn't they all go down the hill and pay a call on him.

'From the monkey cage to the Propter paddock,' said
Dr. Obispo, 'and from the Propter paddock back to the
Stoyte house and the Maunciple kennel. What do you
say, angel?'

Virginia was throwing potatoes to the old male—
throwing them in such a way as to induce him to turn,
to retrace his steps towards the shelf on which he had
left his female. Her hope was that, if she got him to go

back far enough, he'd see how the girl friend passed the time when he was away. 'Yes, let's go and see old Proppy,' she said, without turning round. She tossed another potato into the enclosure. With a flutter of grey bobbed hair the baboon pounced on it; but instead of looking up and catching Mrs. B. having her romance with the ice-man, the exasperating animal immediately turned round towards the wire, asking for more. 'Stupid old fool!' Virginia shouted, and this time threw the potato straight at him, it caught him on the nose. She laughed and turned towards the others. 'I like old Proppy,' she said. 'He scares me a bit; but I like him.'

'All right then,' said Dr. Obispo, 'let's go and rout out Mr. Pordage while we're about it.'

'Yes, let's go and fetch old Ivory,' Virginia agreed, patting her own auburn curls in reference to Jeremy's baldness. 'He's kind of cute, don't you think?'

Leaving Pete to go on with the feeding of the baboons, they climbed back to the road and up a flight of steps on the further side, leading directly to the rock-cut windows of Jeremy's room. Virginia pushed open the glass door. 'Ivory,' she called, 'we've come to disturb you.'

Jeremy began to murmur something humorously gallant; then broke off in the middle of a sentence. He had suddenly remembered that pile of curious literature on the corner of the table. To get up and put the books into a cupboard would be to invite attention to them; he had no newspaper with which to cover them, no other books to mix them up with. There was nothing to be done. Nothing, except to hope for the best. Fervently he hoped for it; and almost immediately the worst happened. Idly, out of the need to perform some muscular action, however pointless, Virginia picked up a volume of Nerciat, opened it at one of its conscientiously detailed engravings, looked, then with wider eyes looked again and let out a whoop of startled excitement. Dr. Obispo glanced and yelled in turn; then both broke out into enormous laughter.

Jeremy sat in a misery of embarrassment, sicklily smiling, while they asked him if *that* was how he spent his time, if *this* was the sort of thing he was studying. If only people weren't so wearisome, he was thinking, so deplorably unsubtle!

Virginia turned over the pages until she found another illustration. Once more there was an outcry of delight, astonishment and, this time, incredulity. Was it possible? Could it really be done? She spelled out the caption under the engraving: '*La volupté frappait à toutes les portes*'; then petulantly shook her head. It was no good; she couldn't understand it. Those French lessons at High School—just lousy; that was all you could say about them. They hadn't taught her anything except a lot of nonsense about *le crayon de mon oncle* and *savez-vous planter le chou*. She'd always said that studying was mostly a waste of time; this proved it. And why did they have to print this stuff in French anyhow? At the thought that the deficiencies in the educational system of the State of Oregon might for ever prevent her from reading André de Nerciat, the tears came into Virginia's eyes. It was really *too* bad!

A brilliant idea occurred to Jeremy. Why shouldn't he offer to translate the book for her—*viva voce* and sentence by sentence, like an interpreter at a Council Meeting of the League of Nations? Yes, why not? The more he thought of it, the better the idea seemed to him to be. His decision was made and he had begun to consider how most felicitously to phrase his offer, when Dr. Obispo quietly took the volume Virginia was holding, picked up the three companion volumes from the table, along with *Le Portier des Carmes* and the *Cent-Vingt Jours de Sodome*, and slipped the entire collection into the side-pocket of his jacket.

'Don't worry,' he said to Virginia. 'I'll translate them for you. And now let's go back to the baboons. Pete'll be wondering what's happened to us. Come on, Mr. Pordage.'

In silence, but boiling inwardly with self-reproach for his own inefficiency and indignation at the doctor's impudence, Jeremy followed them out of the french window and down the steps.

Pete had emptied his basket and was leaning against the wire, intently following with his eyes the movements of the animals within. At their approach he turned towards them. His pleasant young face was bright with excitement.

'Do you know, doc,' he said, 'I believe it's working.'

'What's working?' asked Virginia.

Pete's answering smile was beautiful with happiness. For, oh, how happy he was! Doubly and trebly happy. By the sweetness of her subsequent behaviour, Virginia had more than made up for the pain she had inflicted by turning away to listen to that smutty story. And after all it probably wasn't a smutty story; he had been maligning her, thinking gratuitous evil of her. No, it certainly hadn't been a smutty story—not smutty because, when she turned back to him, her face had looked like the face of that child in the illustrated Bible at home, that child who was gazing so innocently and cutely while Jesus said, 'Of such is the Kingdom of Heaven.' And that was not the only reason for his happiness. He was happy, too, because it looked as though those cultures of the carp's intestinal flora were really having an effect on the baboons they had tried them on.

'I believe they're livelier,' he explained. 'And their fur—it's kind of glossier.'

The fact gave him almost as great a satisfaction as did Virginia's presence here in the transfiguring richness of the evening sunlight, as did the memory of her sweetness, the uplifting conviction of her essential innocence. Indeed, in some obscure way, the rejuvenation of the baboons and Virginia's adorableness seemed to him to have a profound connection—a connection not only with one another, but also and at the same time with Loyalist Spain and anti-fascism. Three separate things, and yet one thing. . . There was a bit of poetry he had been made to learn at school—how did it go ?

> *I could not love thee, dear, so much,*
> *Loved I not something or other* (he could not at the
>   moment remember what) *more.*

He did not love anything *more* than Virginia. But the fact that he cared so enormously much for science and justice, for this research and the boys back in Spain, did something to make his love for her more profound and, though it seemed a paradox, more whole-hearted.

'Well, what about moving on ?' he suggested at last.

Dr. Obispo looked at his wrist-watch. 'I'd forgotten,' he said. 'I've got some letters I ought to write before dinner. Guess I'll have to see Mr. Propter some other time.'

'That's too bad !' Pete did his best to impart to his tone and expression the cordiality of regret he did not feel. In fact, he was delighted. He admired Dr. Obispo, thought him a remarkable research worker—but not the sort of person a young innocent girl like Virginia ought to associate with. He dreaded for her the influence of so much cynicism and hardboiledness. Besides, so far as his own relations to Virginia were concerned, Dr. Obispo was always in the way. 'That's too bad!' he repeated, and the intensity of his pleasure was such that he fairly ran up the steps leading from the baboon-enclosure to the drive—ran so fast that his heart began palpitating and missing beats. Damn that rheumatic fever!

Dr. Obispo stepped back to allow Virginia to pass and, as he did so, gave a little tap to the pocket containing *Les Cent-Vingt Jours de Sodome* and tipped her a wink. Virginia winked back and followed Pete up the steps.

A few moments later, Dr. Obispo was walking up the drive, the others down. Or, to be more exact, Pete and Jeremy were walking, while Virginia, to whom the idea of using one's legs to get from anywhere to anywhere else was practically unthinkable, sat on her strawberry-and-cream coloured scooter and, with one hand affectionately laid on Pete's shoulder, allowed herself to be carried down by the force of gravity.

The noise of the baboons faded behind them, and at the next turn of the road there was Giambologna's nymph, still indefatigably spouting from her polished breasts. Virginia suddenly interrupted a conversation about Clark Gable to say, in the righteously indignant tone of a vice crusader, 'I just can't figure why Uncle Jo allows that thing to stand there. It's disgusting!'

'Disgusting?' Jeremy echoed in astonishment.

'Disgusting!' she repeated emphatically.

'Do you object to her not having any clothes on?' he asked, remembering, as he did so, those two little satin asymptotes to nudity which she herself had worn up there, in the swimming-pool.

She shook her head impatiently. 'It's the way the water comes out.' She made the grimace of one who had tasted something revolting. 'I think it's horrible.'

'But why?' Jeremy insisted.

'Because it's horrible,' was all the explanation she could give. A child of her age, which was the age, in this context, of bottle-feeding and contraception, she felt herself outraged by this monstrous piece of indelicacy from an earlier time. It was just horrible; that was all that could be said about it. Turning back to Pete, she went on talking about Clark Gable.

Opposite the entrance to the Grotto, Virginia parked her scooter. The masons had finished their work on the tomb and were gone; the place was empty. Virginia straightened her rakishly tilted yachting-cap as a sign of respect; then ran up the steps, paused on the threshold to cross herself and, entering, knelt for a few moments before the image. The others waited silently, in the roadway.

'Our Lady was so wonderful to me when I had sinus trouble last summer,' Virginia explained to Jeremy when she emerged again. 'That's why I got Uncle Jo to make this grotto for her. Wasn't it gorgeous when the Archbishop came for the consecration?' she added, turning to Pete.

Pete nodded affirmatively.

'I haven't even had a cold since She's been here,' Virginia went on, as she took her seat on the scooter. Her face fairly shone with triumph; every victory for the Queen of Heaven was also a personal success for Virginia Maunciple. Then abruptly and without warning, as though she were doing a screen test and had received the order to register fatigue and self-pity, she passed a hand across her forehead, sighed profoundly and, in a tone of utter dejection and discouragement, said, 'All the same, I'm feeling pretty tired this evening. Guess I was in the sun too much right after lunch. Maybe I'd better go and lie down a bit.' And affectionately but very firmly rejecting Pete's offer to go back with her to the castle, she wheeled her scooter round, so that it faced up-hill, gave the young man a last, particularly charming, almost amorous smile and look, said, 'Good-bye, Pete darling,' and, opening the throttle of the engine, shot off with gathering momentum and an accelerating roll of explosions up the steep curving road, out of sight. Five minutes later she was in her boudoir, fixing a chocolate-and-banana split at the soda-fountain. Seated in a gilded armchair upholstered in satin *couleur fesse de nymphe*, Dr. Obispo was reading aloud and translating as he went along from the first volume of *Les Cent-Vingt Jours*.

Chapter Eight

MR. PROPTER was sitting on a bench under the largest of his eucalyptus trees. To the west the mountains were already a flat silhouette against the evening sky, but in front of him, to the north, the upper slopes were still alive with light and shadow, with rosy gold and depths of indigo. In the foreground, the castle had put on a garment of utterly improbable splendour and romance. Mr. Propter looked at it and at the hills and up through the motionless leaves of the eucalyptus at the pale sky; then closed his eyes and noiselessly repeated Cardinal Bérulle's answer to the question: 'What is man?' It was more than thirty years before, when he was writing his study of the Cardinal, that he had first read those words. They had impressed him even then by the splendour and precision of their eloquence. With the lapse of time and the growth of his experience they had come to seem more than eloquent, had come to take on ever richer connotations, ever profounder significances. 'What is man?' he whispered to himself. '*C'est un néant environné de Dieu, indigent de Dieu, capable de Dieu, et rempli de Dieu, s'il veut.*' 'A nothingness surrounded by God, indigent and capable of God, filled with God, if he so desires.' And what is this God of which men are capable? Mr. Propter answered with the definition given by John Tauler in the first paragraph of his *Following of Christ*: 'God is a being withdrawn from creatures, a free power, a pure working.' Man, then, is as nothingness surrounded by, and indigent of, a being withdrawn from creatures, a nothingness capable of free power, filled with a pure working if he so desires. *If* he so desires, Mr. Propter was distracted into reflecting with a sudden, rather bitter sadness. But how few men ever do desire or, desiring, ever know what to wish for or how to get it! Right knowledge is hardly less rare than the sustained good-will to act on it. Of those few who look for God, most find, through ignorance, only such reflections of their own self-will as the God of battles, the God of the chosen people, the Prayer-Answerer, the Saviour.

Having deviated thus far into negativity, Mr. Propter was led on, through a continuing failure of vigilance, into an even less profitable preoccupation with the concrete and particular miseries of the day. He remembered his interview that morning with Hansen, who was the agent for Jo Stoyte's estates in the valley. Hansen's treatment of the migrants who came to pick the fruit was worse even than the average. He had taken advantage of their number and their desperate need to force down wages. In the groves he managed, young children were being made to work all day in the sun at the rate of two or three cents an hour. And when the day's work was finished, the homes to which they returned were a row of verminous sties in the waste land beside the bed of the river. For these sties, Hansen was charging a rent of ten dollars a month. Ten dollars a month for the privilege of freezing or suffocating; of sleeping in a filthy promiscuity; of being eaten up by bed-bugs and lice; of picking up ophthalmia and perhaps hookworm and amoebic dysentery. And yet Hansen was a very decent, kindly man: one who would be shocked and indignant if he saw you hurting a dog; one who would fly to the protection of a maltreated woman or a crying child. When Mr. Propter drew this fact to his attention, Hansen had flushed darkly with anger.

'That's different,' he had said.

Mr. Propter had tried to find out why it was different.

It was his duty, Hansen had said.

But how could it be his duty to treat children worse than slaves and inoculate them with hookworm?

It was his duty to the estates. He wasn't doing anything for himself.

But why should doing wrong for someone else be different from doing wrong on your own behalf? The results were exactly the same in either case. The victims didn't suffer any less when you were doing what you called your duty than when you were acting in what you imagined might be your own interests.

This time the anger had exploded in violent abuse. It was the anger, Mr. Propter had perceived, of the well-meaning but stupid man who is compelled against his will to ask himself indiscreet questions about what he has been doing as a matter of course. He doesn't want to ask these questions, because he knows that if he does he will be forced either to go on with what he is doing, but with the cynic's awareness that he is doing wrong, or else, if he doesn't want to be a cynic, to change the entire pattern of his life so as to bring his desire to do right into harmony with the real facts as revealed in the course of self-interrogation. To most people any radical change is even more odious than cynicism. The only way between the horns of the dilemma is to persist at all costs in the ignorance which permits one to go on doing wrong in the comforting belief that by doing so one is accomplishing one's duty—one's duty to the company, to the shareholders, to the family, the city, the state, the fatherland, the church. For, of course, poor Hansen's case wasn't in any way unique; on a smaller scale, and therefore with less power to do evil, he was acting like all those civil servants and statesmen and prelates who go through life spreading misery and destruction in the name of their ideals and under orders from their categorical imperatives.

Well, he hadn't got very far with Hansen, Mr. Propter sadly concluded. He'd have to try again with Jo Stoyte. In the past, Jo had always refused to listen, on the ground that the estates were Hansen's business. The alibi was so convenient that it would be hard, he foresaw, to break it down.

From Hansen and Jo Stoyte his thoughts wandered to that newly arrived family of transients from Kansas, to whom he had given one of his cabins. The three undernourished children, with the teeth already rotting in their mouths; the woman, emaciated by God knew what complication of diseases, deep-sunken already in apathy and weakness; the husband, alternately resentful and self-pitying, violent and morose.

He had gone with the man to get some vegetables from the garden plots and a rabbit for the family supper. Sitting there, skinning the rabbit, he had had to listen to outbursts of incoherent complaint and indignation. Complaint and indignation against the wheat market, which had broken each time he had begun to do well. Against the banks he had borrowed money from and been unable to repay. Against the droughts and winds that had reduced his farm to a hundred and sixty acres of dust and wilderness. Against the luck that had always been against *him*. Against the folks who had treated him so meanly, everywhere, all his life.

Dismally familiar story! With inconsiderable variations, he had heard it a thousand times before. Sometimes they were share-croppers from further south, dispossessed by the owners in a desperate effort to make the farming pay. Sometimes, like this man, they had owned their own place and been dispossessed, not by financiers, but by the forces of nature—forces of nature which they themselves had made destructive by tearing up the grass and planting nothing but wheat. Sometimes they had been hired men, displaced by the tractors. All of them had come to California as to a promised land; and California had already reduced them to a condition of wandering peonage and was fast transforming them into Untouchables. Only a saint, Mr. Propter reflected, only a saint, could be a peon and a pariah with impunity, because only a saint would accept the position gladly and as though he had chosen it of his own free will. Poverty and suffering ennoble only when they are voluntary. By involuntary poverty and suffering men are made worse. It is easier for a camel to pass through the eye of a needle than for an involuntarily poor man to enter the kingdom of heaven. Here, for example, was this poor devil from Kansas. How had he reacted to involuntary poverty and suffering? So far as Mr. Propter could judge, he was compensating himself for his misfortunes by brutality to those weaker than himself. The way he yelled at the children. . . . It was an all too familiar symptom.

When the rabbit was skinned and gutted, Mr. Propter had interrupted his companion's monologue.

'Do you know which is the stupidest text in the Bible?' he had suddenly asked.

Startled, and evidently a bit shocked, the man from Kansas had shaken his head.

'It's this,' Mr. Propter had said, as he got up and handed him the carcase of the rabbit. '"They hated me without a cause."'

Under the eucalyptus tree, Mr. Propter wearily sighed.

Pointing out to unfortunate people that, in part at any rate, they were pretty certainly responsible for their own misfortunes; explaining to them that ignorance and stupidity are no less severely punished by the nature of things than deliberate malice—these were never agreeable tasks. Never agreeable, but, so far as he could see, always necessary. For what hope, he asked himself, what faintest glimmer of hope is there for a man who really believes that 'they hated me without a cause' and that he had no part in his own disasters? Obviously, no hope whatever. We see, as matter of brute fact, that disasters and hatreds are never without causes; we also see that some at least of those causes are generally under the control of the people who suffer the disasters or are the object of the hatred. In some measure they are directly or indirectly responsible. Directly, by the commission of stupid or malicious acts. Indirectly, by the omission to be as intelligent and compassionate as they might be. And if they make this omission, it is generally because they choose to conform unthinkingly to local standards, and the current way of living. Mr. Propter's thoughts returned to the poor fellow from Kansas. Self-righteous, no doubt disagreeable to the neighbours, an incompetent farmer; but that wasn't the whole story. His gravest offence had been to accept the world in which he found himself as normal, rational and right. Like all the others, he had allowed the advertisers to multiply his wants; he had learned to equate happiness with possessions, and prosperity with money to spend in a shop. Like all the others, he had abandoned any idea of subsistence farming to think exclusively in terms of a cash crop; and he had gone on thinking in those terms, even when the crop no longer gave him any cash. Then, like all the others, he had got into debt with the banks. And finally, like all the others, he had learned that what the experts had been saying for a generation was perfectly true : in a semi-arid country it is grass that holds down the soil; tear up the grass, the soil will go. In due course, it had gone.

The man from Kansas was now a peon and a pariah; and the experience was making a worse man of him.

St. Peter Claver was another of the historical personages to whom Mr. Propter had devoted a study. When the slave-ships came into the harbour of Cartagena, Peter Claver was the only white man to venture down into the holds. There, in the unspeakable stench and heat, in the vapours of pus and excrement, he tended the sick, he dressed the ulcers of those whom their manacles had wounded, he held in his arms the men who had given way to despair and spoke to them words of comfort and affection—and in the intervals talked to them about their sins. *Their* sins! The modern humanitarian would laugh, if he were not shocked. And yet—such was the conclusion to which Mr. Propter had gradually and reluctantly come—and yet St. Peter Claver was probably right. Not completely right, of course; for, acting on wrong knowledge, no man, however well-intentioned, can be more than partially right. But as nearly right, at any rate, as a good man with a counter-Reformation Catholic philosophy could expect to be. Right in insisting that, whatever the circumstances in which he finds himself, a human being always has omissions to make good, commissions whose effects must, if possible, be neutralized. Right in believing that it is well even for the most brutally sinned against to be reminded of their own shortcomings.

Peter Claver's conception of the world had the defect of being erroneous, but the merit of being simple and dramatic. Given a personal God, dispenser of forgiveness, given heaven and hell and the absolute reality of human personalities, given the meritoriousness of mere good intentions and of unquestioning faith in a set of incorrect opinions, given the one true church, the efficacy of priestly mediation, the magic of sacraments—given all these, it was really quite easy to convince even a newly imported slave of his sinfulness and to explain exactly what he ought to do about it. But if there is no single inspired book, no uniquely holy church, no mediating priesthood nor sacramental magic, if there is no personal God to be placated into forgiving offences, if there are, even in the moral world, only causes and effects and the enormous complexity of inter-relationships—then, clearly the task of telling people what to do about their shortcomings is much more difficult. For every individual is called upon to display not only unsleeping good-will but also unsleeping intelligence. And this is not all. For, if individuality is not absolute, if personalities are illusory figments of a self-will disastrously blind to the reality of a more-than-personal consciousness, of which it is the limitation and denial, then all of every human being's efforts must be directed, in the last resort, to the actualization of that more-than-personal consciousness. So that even intelligence is not sufficient as an adjunct to good-will; there must also be the recollection which seeks to transform and transcend intelligence. Many are called, but few are chosen—because few even know in what salvation consists. Consider again this man from Kansas. . . . Mr. Propter sadly shook his head. Everything was against the poor fellow—his fundamentalist orthodoxy, his wounded and inflamed egotism, his nervous irritability, his low intelligence. The first three disadvantages might perhaps be removed. But could anything be done about the fourth? The nature of things is implacable towards weakness. 'From him that hath not shall be taken away even that which he hath.' And what were those words of Spinoza's ? 'A man may be excusable and nevertheless be tormented in many ways. A horse is excusable for not being a man ; but nevertheless he must needs be a horse, and not a man.' All the same, there must surely be something to be done for people like the man from Kansas—something that didn't entail telling harmful untruths about the nature of things. The untruth, for example, that there is a person up aloft, or the other more modern untruth to the effect that human values are absolute and that God is the nation or the party or the human race as a whole. Surely, Mr. Propter insisted, surely there was something to be done for such people. The man from Kansas had begun by resenting what he had said about the chain of cause and effect, the network of relationships—resenting it as a personal insult. But afterwards, when he saw that he was not being blamed, that no attempt was being made to come it over him, he had begun to take an interest, to see that after all there was something in it. Little by little it might be possible to make him think a bit more realistically, at least about the world of everyday life, the outside world of appearances. And when he had done that, then it mightn't be so overwhelmingly difficult for him to think a bit more realistically about himself—to conceive of that all-important ego of his as a fiction, a kind of nightmare, a frantically agitated nothingness capable, when once its frenzy had been quieted, of being filled with God, with a God conceived and experienced as a more than personal consciousness, as a free power, a pure working, a being withdrawn. . . . Suddenly, as he thus returned to his starting-point, Mr. Propter became aware of the long, circuitous, unprofitable way he had travelled in order to reach it. He had come to this bench under the eucalyptus tree in order to recollect himself, in order to realize for a moment the existence of that other consciousness behind his private thoughts and feelings, that free, pure power greater than his own. He had come for this; but memories had slipped in while he was off his guard; speculations had started up, cloud upon cloud, like sea-birds rising from their nesting-place to darken and eclipse the sun. Bondage is the life of personality, and for bondage the personal self will fight with tireless resourcefulness and the most stubborn cunning. The price of freedom is eternal vigilance; and he had failed to be vigilant. It wasn't a case, he reflected ruefully, of the spirit being willing and the flesh weak. That was altogether the wrong antithesis. The spirit is always willing; but the person, who is a mind as well as a body, is always unwilling—and the person, incidentally, is not weak but extremely strong.

He looked again at the mountains, at the pale sky between the leaves, at the soft russet pinks and purples and greys of the eucalyptus trunks; then shut his eyes once more.

'A nothingness surrounded by God, indigent of God, capable of God and filled with God if man so desires. And what is God? A being withdrawn from creatures, a free power, a pure working.' His vigilance gradually ceased to be an act of the will, a deliberate thrusting back of irrelevant personal thoughts and wishes and feelings. For little by little these thoughts and wishes and feelings had settled like a muddy sediment in a jar of water, and as they settled, his vigilance was free to transform itself into a kind of effortless unattached awareness, at once intense and still, alert and passive—an awareness whose object was the words he had spoken and at the same time that which surrounded the words. But that which surrounded the words was the awareness itself; for this vigilance which was now an effortless awareness—what was it but an aspect, a partial expression, of that impersonal and untroubled consciousness into which the words had been dropped and through which they were slowly sinking? And as they sank they took a new significance for the awareness that was following them down into the depths of itself—a significance new not in respect to the entities connoted by the words, but rather in the mode of their comprehension, which, from being intellectual in character, had become intuitive and direct, so that the nature of man in his potentiality and of God in actuality were realized by an analogue of sensuous experience, by a kind of unmediated participation.

The busy nothingness of his being experienced itself as transcended in the felt capacity for peace and purity, for the withdrawal from revulsion and desires, for the blissful freedom from personality. . . .

The sound of approaching footsteps made him open his eyes. Peter Boone and that Englishman he had sat with in the car were advancing up the path towards his seat under the eucalyptus trees. Mr. Propter raised his hand in welcome and smiled. He was fond of young Pete. There was native intelligence there and native kindliness; there was sensitiveness, generosity, a spontaneous decency of impulse and reaction. Charming and beautiful qualities! The pity was that by themselves, and undirected as they were by a right knowledge of the nature of things, they should be so impotent for good, so inadequate to anything a reasonable man could call salvation. Fine gold, but still in the ore, unsmelted, unworked. Some day, perhaps, the boy would learn to use his gold. He would have to wish to learn first—and wish also to unlearn a lot of the things he now regarded as self-evident and right. It would be hard for him—as hard, but for other reasons, as it would be for that poor fellow from Kansas.

'Well, Pete,' he called, 'come and sit with me here. And you've brought Mr. Pordage; that's good.' He moved to the middle of the bench so that they could sit, one on either side of him. 'And did you meet the Ogre?' he said to Jeremy, pointing in the direction of the castle.

Jeremy made a grimace and nodded. 'I remembered the name you used to call him at school,' he said. 'That made it a little easier.'

'Poor Jo,' said Mr. Propter. 'Fat people are always supposed to be so happy. But who ever enjoyed being laughed at? That jolly manner they sometimes have, and the jokes they make at their own expense—it's just a case of alibis and prophylactics. They vaccinate themselves with their own ridicule so that they shan't react too violently to other people's.'

Jeremy smiled. He knew all about that. 'It's a good way out of an unpleasant predicament,' he said.

Mr. Propter nodded. 'But unfortunately,' he said, 'it didn't happen to be Jo's way. Jo was the kind of a fat boy who bluffs it out. The kind that fights. The kind that bullies or patronizes. The kind that boasts and shows off. The kind that buys popularity by treating the girls to ice-creams, even if he has to steal a dime from his grandmother's purse to do it. The kind that goes on stealing even if he's found out and gets beaten and believes it when they tell him he'll go to hell. Poor Jo, he's been that sort of fat boy all his life.' He pointed once again in the direction of the castle. 'That's his monument to a faulty pituitary. And talking of pituitaries,' he went on, turning to Pete, 'how's the work been going?'

Pete had been thinking gloomily of Virginia—wondering for the hundredth time why she had left them, whether he had done anything to offend her, whether she was really tired or if there might be some other reason. At Mr. Propter's mention of work he looked up, and his face brightened. 'It's going just fine,' he answered, and, in quick, eager phrases, strangely compounded of slang and technical terms, he told Mr. Propter about the results they had already got with their mice and were beginning to get, so it seemed, with the baboons and the dogs.

'And if you succeed,' Mr. Propter asked, 'what happens to your dogs?'

'Why, their life's prolonged,' Pete answered triumphantly.

'Yes, yes, I know that,' said the older man. 'What I meant to ask was something different. A dog's a wolf that hasn't fully developed. It's more like the foetus of a wolf than an adult wolf; isn't that so.'

Pete nodded.

'In other words,' Mr. Propter went on, 'it's a mild, tractable animal because it has never grown up into savagery. Isn't that supposed to be one of the mechanisms of evolutionary development?'

Pete nodded again. 'There's a kind of glandular equilibrium,' he explained. 'Then a mutation comes along and knocks it sideways. You get a new equilibrium that happens to retard the development rate. You grow up; but you do it so slowly that you're dead before you've stopped being like your great-great-grandfather's foetus.'

'Exactly,' said Mr. Propter. 'So what happens if you prolong the life of an animal that has evolved that way?'

Pete laughed and shrugged his shoulders. 'Guess we'll have to wait and see,' he said.

'It would be a bit disquieting,' said Mr. Propter, 'if your dogs grew back in the process of growing up.'

Pete laughed again delightedly. 'Think of the dowagers being chased by their own Pekingese,' he said.

Mr. Propter looked at him curiously and was silent for a moment, as though waiting to see whether Pete would make any further comment. The comment did not come. 'I'm glad you feel so happy about it,' he said. Then, turning to Jeremy, '"It is not," if I remember rightly, Mr. Pordage,' he went on, '"it is not growing like a tree in bulk doth make men better be."'

'"Or standing long an oak, three hundred years,"' said Jeremy, smiling with the pleasure which an apt quotation always gave him.

'What shall we all be doing at three hundred?' Mr. Propter speculated. 'Do you suppose you'd still be a scholar and a gentleman?'

Jeremy coughed and patted his bald head. 'One will certainly have stopped being a gentleman,' he answered. 'One's begun to stop even now, thank heaven.'

'But the scholar will stay the course?'

'There's a lot of books in the British Museum.'

'And you, Pete?' said Mr. Propter. 'Do you suppose you'll still be doing scientific research?'

'Why not? What's to prevent you from going on with it for ever?' the young man answered emphatically.

'For ever?' Mr. Propter repeated. 'You don't think you'd get a bit bored? One experiment after another. Or one book after another,' he added in an aside to Jeremy. 'In general, one damned thing after another. You don't think that would prey on your mind a bit?'

'I don't see why,' said Pete.

'Time doesn't bother you, then?'

Pete shook his head. 'Why should it?'

'Why shouldn't it?' said Mr. Propter, smiling at him with an amused affection. 'Time's a pretty bothersome thing, you know.'

'Not if you aren't scared of dying or growing old.'

'Yes, it is,' Mr. Propter insisted; 'even if you're not scared. It's nightmarish in itself—intrinsically nightmarish, if you see what I mean.'

'Intrinsically?' Pete looked at him perplexed. 'I don't get it,' he said. 'Intrinsically nightmarish . . .?'

'Nightmarish in the present tense, of course,' Jeremy put in. 'But if one takes it in the fossil state—in the form of the Hauberk Papers, for example . . .' He left the sentence unfinished.

'Oh, pleasant enough,' said Mr. Propter, agreeing with his implied conclusion. 'But, after all, history isn't the real thing. Past time is only evil at a distance; and, of course, the study of past time is itself a process in time. Cataloguing bits of fossil evil can never be more than an *Ersatz* for the experience of eternity.' He glanced curiously at Pete, wondering how the boy would respond to what he was saying. Plunging like this into the heart of the matter, beginning at the very core and centre of the mystery—it was risky; there was a danger of evoking nothing but bewilderment, or alternatively nothing but angry derision. Pete's, he could see, was more nearly the first reaction; but it was a bewilderment that seemed to be tempered by interest; he looked as though he wanted to find out what it was all about.

Meanwhile, Jeremy had begun to feel that this conversation was taking a most undesirable turn. 'What precisely are we supposed to be talking about?' he asked acidulously. 'The New Jerusalem?'

Mr. Propter smiled at him good-humouredly. 'It's all right,' he said. 'I won't say a word about harps or wings.'

'Well, that's something,' said Jeremy.

'I never could get much satisfaction out of meaningless discourse,' Mr. Propter continued. 'I like the words I use to bear some relation to facts. That's why I'm interested in eternity—psychological eternity. Because it's a fact.'

'For you, perhaps,' said Jeremy in a tone which implied that more civilized people didn't suffer from these hallucinations.

'For anyone who chooses to fulfil the conditions under which it can be experienced.'

'And why should anyone choose to fulfil them?'

'Why should anyone choose to go to Athens to see the Parthenon? Because it's worth the bother. And the same is true of eternity. The experience of timeless good is worth all the trouble it involved.'

'"Timeless good,"' Jeremy repeated with distaste. 'I don't know what the words mean.'

'Why should you?' said Mr. Propter. 'One doesn't know the full meaning of the word "Parthenon" until one has actually seen the thing.'

'Yes, but at least I've seen photographs of the Parthenon; I've read descriptions.'

'You've read descriptions of timeless good,' Mr. Propter answered. 'Dozens of them. In all the literatures of philosophy and religion. You've read them; but you've never bought your ticket for Athens.'

In a resentful silence, Jeremy had to admit to himself that this was true. The fact that it was true made him disapprove of the conversation even more profoundly than he had done before.

'As for time,' Mr. Propter was saying to Pete, 'what is it, in this particular context, but the medium in which evil propagates itself, the element in which evil lives and outside of which it dies? Indeed, it's more than the element of evil, more than merely its medium. If you carry your analysis far enough, you'll find that time is evil. One of the aspects of its essential substance.'

Jeremy listened with growing discomfort and a mounting irritation. His fears had been justified; the old boy was launching out into the worst kind of theology. Eternity, timeless experience of good, time as the substance of evil—it was bad enough, God knew, in books; but, fired at you like this, point-blank, by somebody who really took it seriously, why, it was really frightful. Why on earth couldn't people live their lives in a rational, civilized way? Why couldn't they take things as they came? Breakfast at nine, lunch at one-thirty, tea at five. And conversation. And the daily walk with Mr. Gladstone, the Yorkshire terrier. And the library; the Works of Voltaire in eighty-three volumes; the inexhaustible treasure of Horace Walpole; and for a change the *Divine Comedy*; and then, in case you might be tempted to take the Middle Ages too seriously, Salimbene's autobiography and the Miller's Tale. And sometimes calls in the afternoon—the Rector, Lady Fredegond with her ear-trumpet, Mr. Veal. And political discussions—except that in these last months, since the *Anschluss* and Munich, one had found that political discussion was one of the unpleasant things it was wise to avoid. And the weekly journey to London, with lunch at the Reform, and always dinner with old Thripp of the British Museum; and a chat with one's poor brother Tom at the Foreign Office (only that too was rapidly becoming one of the things to be avoided). And then, of course, the London library; and Vespers at

Westminster Cathedral, if they happened to be singing Palestrina; and every alternate week, between five and six-thirty, an hour and a half with Mae or Doris in their flat in Maida Vale. Infinite squalor in a little room, as he liked to call it; abysmally delightful. Those were the things that came; why couldn't they take them, quietly and sensibly? But no, they had to gibber about eternity and all the rest. That sort of stuff always made Jeremy want to be blasphemous—to ask whether God had a *boyau rectum*, to protest, like the Japanese in the anecdote, that he was altogether flummoxed and perplexed by position of Honourable Bird. But, unfortunately, the present was one of those peculiarly exasperating cases where such reactions were out of place. For, after all, old Propter had written *Short Studies*; what he said couldn't just be dismissed as the vapourings of a deficient mind. Besides, he hadn't talked Christianity, so that jokes about anthropomorphism were beside the point. It was really too exasperating! He assumed an expression of haughty detachment and even started to hum 'The Honeysuckle and the Bee.' The impression he wanted to give was that of a superior being who really couldn't be expected to waste his time listening to stuff like this.

A comic spectacle, Mr. Propter reflected as he looked at him; except, of course, that it was so extremely depressing.

Chapter Nine

'TIME and craving,' said Mr. Propter, 'craving and time—two aspects of the same thing; and that thing is the raw material of evil. So you see, Pete,' he added in another tone, 'you see what a queer sort of present you'll be making us, if you're successful in your work. Another century or so of time and craving. A couple of extra lifetimes of potential evil.'

'*And* potential good,' the young man insisted with a note of protest in his voice.

'*And* potential good,' Mr. Propter agreed. 'But only at a far remove from that extra time you're giving us.'

'Why do you say that?' Pete asked.

'Because potential evil is *in* time; potential good isn't. The longer you live, the more evil you automatically come into contact with. Nobody comes automatically into contact with good. Men don't find more good by merely existing longer. It's curious,' he went on reflectively, 'that people should always have concentrated on the problem of evil. Exclusively. As though the nature of good were something self-evident. But it isn't self-evident. There's a problem of good at least as difficult as the problem of evil.'

'And what's the solution?' Pete asked.

'The solution is very simple and profoundly unacceptable. Actual good is outside time.'

'Outside time? But then how . . . ?'

'I told you it was unacceptable,' said Mr. Propter.

'But if it's outside time, then . . .'

'. . . then nothing within time can be actual good. Time

is potential evil, and craving converts the potentiality into actual evil. Whereas a temporal act can never be more than potentially good, with a potentiality, what's more, that can't be actualized except out of time.'

'But inside time, here—you know, just doing the ordinary things—hell ! we do sometimes do right. What acts *are* good ?'

'Strictly speaking, none,' Mr. Propter answered. 'But, in practice, I think one's justified in applying the word to certain acts. Any act that contributes towards the liberation of those concerned in it—I'd call it a good act.'

'Liberation ?' the young man repeated dubiously. The words, in his mind, carried only economic and revolutionary connotations. But it was evident that Mr. Propter wasn't talking about the necessity for getting rid of capitalism. 'Liberation from what ?'

Mr. Propter hesitated before replying. Should he go on with this ? he wondered. The Englishman was hostile; the time short; the boy himself entirely ignorant. But it was an ignorance evidently mitigated by good-will and a touching nostalgia for perfection. He decided to take a chance and go on.

'Liberation from time,' he said. 'Liberation from craving and revulsions. Liberation from personality.'

'But heck,' said Pete, 'you're always talking about democracy. Doesn't that mean respecting personality ?'

'Of course,' Mr. Propter agreed. 'Respecting it in order that it may be able to transcend itself. Slavery and fanaticism intensify the obsession with time and evil and the self. Hence the value of democratic institutions and a sceptical attitude of mind. The more you respect a personality, the better its chance of discovering that all personality is a prison. Potential good is anything that helps you to get out of prison. Actualized good lies outside the prison, in timelessness, in the state of pure, dis-interested consciousness.'

'I'm not much good at abstractions,' said the young man. 'Let's take some concrete examples. What about science, for instance? Is that good?'

'Good, bad and indifferent, according to how it's pursued and what it's used for. Good, bad and indifferent, first of all, for the scientists themselves—just as art and scholarship may be good, bad or indifferent for artists and scholars. Good if it facilitates liberation; indifferent if it neither helps nor hinders; bad if it makes liberation more difficult by intensifying the obsession with personality. And, remember, the apparent selflessness of the scientist, or the artist, is not necessarily a genuine freedom from the bondage of personality. Scientists and artists are men devoted to what we vaguely call an ideal. But what is an ideal? An ideal is merely the projection, on an enormously enlarged scale, of some aspect of personality.'

'Say that again,' Pete requested, while even Jeremy so far forgot his pose of superior detachment to lend his most careful attention.

Mr. Propter said it again. 'And that's true,' he went on, 'of every ideal except the highest, which is the ideal of liberation—liberation from personality, liberation from time and craving, liberation into union with God, if you don't object to the word, Mr. Pordage. Many people do,' he added. 'It's one of the words that the Mrs. Grundys of the intellect find peculiarly shocking. I always try to spare their sensibilities, if I can. Well, to return to our idealist,' he continued, glad to see that Jeremy had been constrained, in spite of himself, to smile. 'If he serves any ideal except the highest—whether it's the artist's ideal of beauty, or the scientist's ideal of truth, or the humanitarian's ideal of what currently passes for goodness—he's not serving God; he's serving a magnified aspect of himself. He may be completely devoted; but in the last analysis his devotion turns out to be directed towards an aspect of his own personality. His apparent selflessness is really not a liberation from his ego, but merely another form of bondage. This means that science may be bad for scientists, even when it appears to be a deliverer. And the same holds good of art, of scholarship, of humanitarianism.'

Jeremy thought nostalgically of his library at The Araucarias. Why couldn't this old madman be content to take things as they came?

'And what about other people?' Pete was saying. 'People who aren't scientists. Hasn't it helped to set them free?'

Mr. Propter nodded. 'And it has also helped to tie them more closely to themselves. And what's more, I should guess that it has increased bondage more than it has diminished it—and will tend to go on increasing it, progressively.'

'How do you figure that out?'

'Through its applications,' Mr. Propter answered. 'Applications to warfare, first of all. Better planes, better explosives, better guns and gases—every improvement increases the sum of fear and hatred, widens the incidence of nationalistic hysteria. In other words, every improvement in armaments makes it more difficult for people to escape from their egos, more difficult to forget those horrible projections of themselves they call their ideals of patriotism, heroism, glory and all the rest. And even the less destructive applications of science aren't really much more satisfactory. For what do such applications result in? The multiplication of possessable objects; the invention of new instruments of stimulation; the disseminations of new wants through propaganda aimed at equating possession with well-being and incessant stimulation with happiness.

'But incessant stimulation from without is a source of bondage; and so is the preoccupation with possessions. And now you're threatening to prolong our lives, so that we can go on being stimulated, go on desiring possessions, go on waving flags and hating our enemies and being afraid of air attack—go on and on, generation after generation, sinking deeper and deeper into the stinking slough of our personality.' He shook his head. 'No, I can't quite share your optimism about science.'

There was a silence while Pete debated with himself whether to ask Mr. Propter about love. In the end he decided he wouldn't. Virginia was too sacred. (But why, why had she turned back at the Grotto? What could he have said or done to offend her? As much to prevent himself from brooding over these problems as because he wanted to know the old man's opinions on the last of the three things that seemed to him supremely valuable, he looked up at Mr. Propter and asked, 'What about social justice? I mean, take the French Revolution. Or Russia. And what about this Spanish business— fighting for liberty and democracy against fascist aggression?' He had tried to remain perfectly calm and scientific about the whole thing; but his voice trembled a little as he spoke the last words. In spite of their familiarity (perhaps because of their familiarity), phrases like 'fascist aggression' still had power to move him to the depths.

'Napoleon came out of the French Revolution,' said Mr. Propter, after a moment's silence. 'German nationalism came out of Napoleon. The war of 1870 came out of German nationalism. The war of 1914 came out of

the war of 1870. Hitler came out of the war of 1914.
Those are the bad results of the French Revolution. The
good results were the enfranchisement of the French
peasants and the spread of political democracy. Put the
good results in one scale of your balance and the bad ones
in the other, and try which set is the heavier. Then perform the same operation with Russia. Put the abolition
of tsardom and capitalism in one scale ; and in the other
put Stalin, put the secret police, put the famines, put
twenty years of hardship for a hundred and fifty million
people, put the liquidation of intellectuals and kulaks and
old bolsheviks, put the hordes of slaves in prison camps ;
put the military conscription of everybody, male and
female, from childhood to old age, put the revolutionary
propaganda which spurred the bourgeoisie to invent
fascism.' Mr. Propter shook his head. 'Or take the
fight for democracy in Spain,' he went on. 'There was a
fight for democracy all over Europe not so long ago.
Rational prognosis can only be based on past experience.
Look at the results of 1914 and then ask yourself what
chance the loyalists ever had of establishing a liberal
régime at the end of a long war. The others are winning ;
so we shall never have the opportunity of seeing what
circumstances and their own passions would have driven
those well-intentioned liberals to become.'

'But, hell !' Pete broke out, 'what do you expect people
to do when they're attacked by the fascists ? Sit down
and let their throats be cut ?'

'Of course not,' said Mr. Propter. 'I *expect* them to
fight. And the expectation is based on my previous
knowledge of human behaviour. But the fact that people
generally do react to that kind of situation in that kind of
way doesn't prove that it's the best way of reacting.
Experience makes me expect that they'll behave like that.

But experience also makes me expect that, if they do behave like that, the results will be disastrous.'

'Well, how do you want us to act? Do you want us to sit still and do nothing?'

'Not nothing,' said Mr. Propter. 'Merely something appropriate.'

'But what is appropriate?'

'Not war, anyhow. Nor violent revolution. Nor yet politics, to any considerable extent, I should guess.'

'Then what?'

'That's what we've got to discover. The main lines are clear enough. But there's still a lot of work to be done on the practical details.'

Pete was not listening. His mind had gone back to that time in Aragon when life had seemed supremely significant. 'But those boys, back there in Spain,' he burst out. 'You didn't know them, Mr. Propter. They were wonderful, really they were. Never mean to you, and brave, and loyal and . . . and everything.' He wrestled with the inadequacies of his vocabulary, with the fear of making an exhibition of himself by talking big, like a highbrow. 'They weren't living for themselves, I can tell you that, Mr. Propter.' He looked into the old man's face almost supplicatingly, as though imploring him to believe. 'They were living for something much bigger than themselves—like what you were talking about just now; you know, something more than just personal.'

'And what about Hitler's boys?' Mr. Propter asked. 'What about Mussolini's boys? What about Stalin's boys? Do you suppose they're not just as brave, just as kind to one another, just as loyal to their cause and just as firmly convinced that it's the cause of justice, truth, freedom, right and honour?' He looked at Pete enquiringly; but Pete said nothing. 'The fact that people have a lot of virtues,' Mr. Propter went on, 'doesn't prove anything about the goodness of their actions. You can have all the virtues—that's to say, all except the two that really matter, understanding and compassion—you can have all the others, I say, and be a thoroughly bad man. Indeed, you can't be really bad unless you *do* have most of the virtues. Look at Milton's Satan for example. Brave, strong, generous, loyal, prudent, temperate, self-sacrificing. And let's give the dictators the credit that's due to them; some of them are nearly as virtuous as Satan. Not quite, I admit, but nearly. That's why they can achieve so much evil.'

His elbows on his knees, Pete sat in silence, frowning. 'But that feeling,' he said at last. 'That feeling there was between us. You know—the friendship; only it was more than just ordinary friendship. And the feeling of being there all together—fighting for the same thing—and the thing being worth while—and then the danger, and the rain, and that awful cold at nights, and the heat in summer, and being thirsty, and even those lice and the dirt—share and share alike in everything bad or good—and knowing that to-morrow it might be your turn, or one of the other boys—your turn for the field hospital (and the chances were they wouldn't have enough anaesthetics, except maybe for an amputation or something like that), or your turn for the burial-party. All those feelings, Mr. Propter—I just can't believe they didn't mean something.'

'They meant themselves,' said Mr. Propter.

Jeremy saw the opportunity for a counter-attack and, with a promptitude unusual in him, immediately took it. 'Doesn't the same thing apply to your feelings about eternity, or whatever it is ?' he asked.

'Of course it does,' said Mr. Propter.

'Well, in that case, how can you claim any validity for it? The feeling means itself, and that's all there is to it.'

'It means itself,' Mr. Propter agreed. 'But what precisely is this "itself"? In other words, what is the nature of the feeling?'

'Don't ask me,' said Jeremy with a shake of the head and a comically puzzled lift of the eyebrows. 'I really don't know.'

Mr. Propter smiled. 'I know you don't want to know,' he said. 'And I won't ask you. I'll just state the facts. The feeling in question is a non-personal experience of timeless peace. Accordingly, non-personality, timelessness and peace are what it means. Now let's consider the feeling that Pete had been talking about. These are all personal feelings, evoked by temporal situations, and characterized by a sense of excitement. Intensification of the ego within the world of time and craving—that's what these feelings meant.'

'But you can't call self-sacrifice an intensification of the ego,' said Pete.

'I can and I do,' Mr. Propter insisted. 'For the good reason that it generally is. Self-sacrifice to any but the highest cause is sacrifice to an ideal, which is simply a projection of the ego. What is commonly called self-sacrifice is the sacrifice of one part of the ego to another part, one set of personal feelings and passions for another set—as when the feelings connected with money or sex are sacrificed in order that the ego may have the feelings of superiority, solidarity and hatred which are associated with patriotism, or any kind of political or religious fanaticism.'

Pete shook his head. 'Sometimes,' he said, with a smile

of rueful perplexity, 'sometimes you almost talk like Dr. Obispo. You know—cynically.'

Mr. Propter laughed. 'It's good to be cynical,' he said. 'That is, if you know when to stop. Most of the things that we're all taught to respect and reverence—they don't deserve anything but cynicism. Take your own case. You've been taught to worship ideals like patriotism, social justice, science, romantic love. You've been told that such virtues as loyalty, temperance, courage and prudence are good in themselves, in any circumstances. You've been assured that self-sacrifice is always splendid and fine feelings invariably good. And it's all nonsense, all a pack of lies that people have made up in order to justify themselves in continuing to deny God and wallow in their own egotism. Unless you're steadily and un-flaggingly cynical about the solemn twaddle that's talked by bishops and bankers and professors and politicians and all the rest of them, you're lost. Utterly lost. Doomed to perpetual imprisonment in your ego—doomed to be a personality in a world of personalities; and a world of personalities is *this* world, the world of greed and fear and hatred, of war and capitalism and dictatorship and slavery. Yes, you've got to be cynical, Pete. Specially cynical about all the actions and feelings you've been taught to suppose were good. Most of them are not good. They're merely evils which happen to be regarded as creditable. But, unfortunately, creditable evil is just as bad as discreditable evil. Scribes and Pharisees aren't any better, in the last analysis, than publicans and sinners. Indeed, they're often much worse. For several reasons. Being well thought of by others, they think well of them-selves; and nothing so confirms an egotism as thinking well of oneself. In the next place, publicans and sinners are generally just human animals, without enough energy or self-control to do much harm. Whereas the Scribes and Pharisees have all the virtues, except the only two which count, and enough intelligence to understand everything except the real nature of the world. Publicans and sinners merely fornicate and overeat, and get drunk. The people who make wars, the people who reduce their fellows to slavery, the people who kill and torture and tell lies in the name of their sacred causes, the really evil people, in a word—these are never the publicans and the sinners. No, they're the virtuous, respectable men, who have the finest feelings, the best brains, the noblest ideals.'

'So what it all boils down to,' Pete concluded in a tone of angry despair, 'is that there just isn't anything you can do. Is that it?'

'Yes and no,' said Mr. Propter, in his quiet judicial way. 'On the strictly human level, the level of time and craving, I should say that it's quite true: in the last resort, there isn't anything you can do.'

'But that's just defeatism!' Pete protested.

'Why is it defeatism to be realistic?'

'There *must* be something to do!'

'I see no "must" about it.'

'Then what about the reformers and all those people? If you're right, they're just wasting their time.'

'It depends what they think they're doing,' said Mr. Propter. 'If they think they're just temporarily palliating particular distresses, if they see themselves as people engaged in laboriously deflecting evil from old channels into new and slightly different channels, then they can justifiably claim to be successful. But if they think they're making good appear where evil was before, why, then, all history clearly shows that they *are* wasting their time.'

'But why can't they make good appear where evil was before?'

'Why do we fall when we jump out of a tenth-story window? Because the nature of things happens to be such that we do fall. And the nature of things is such that, on the strictly human level of time and craving, you can't achieve anything but evil. If you choose to work exclusively on that level, and exclusively for the ideals and causes that are characteristic of it, then you're insane if you expect to transform evil into good. You're insane, because experience should have shown you that, on that level, there doesn't happen to be any good. There are only different degrees and different kinds of evil.'

'Then what do you want people to *do*?'

'Don't talk as though it were all my fault,' said Mr. Propter. 'I didn't invent the universe.'

'What ought they to do, then?'

'Well, if they want fresh varieties of evil, let them go on with what they're doing now. But if they want good, they'll have to change their tactics. And the encouraging thing,' Mr. Propter added in another tone, 'the encouraging thing is that there *are* tactics which will produce good. We've seen that there's nothing to be done on the strictly human level—or rather there are millions of things to be done, only none of them will achieve any good. But there *is* something effective to be done on the levels where good actually exists. So you see, Pete, I'm not a defeatist. I'm a strategist. I believe that if a battle is to be fought, it had better be fought under conditions in which there's at least some chance of winning. I believe that, if you want the golden fleece, it's more sensible to go to the place where it exists than to rush round performing prodigies of valour in a country where all the fleeces happen to be coal-black.'

'Then where ought we to fight for good?'

'Where good is.'

'But where is it?'

'On the level below the human and on the level above. On the animal level and on the level . . . well, you can take your choice of names: the level of eternity; the level, if you don't object, of God; the level of the spirit—only that happens to be about the most ambiguous word in the language. On the lower level, good exists as the proper functioning of the organism in accordance with the laws of its own being. On the higher level, it exists in the form of a knowledge of the world without desire or aversion; it exists as the experience of eternity, as the transcendence of personality, the extension of consciousness beyond the limits imposed by the ego. Strictly human activities are activities that prevent the manifestation of good on the other two levels. For, in so far as we're human, we're obsessed with time, we're passionately concerned with our personalities and with those magnified projections of our personalities which we call our policies, our ideals, our religions. And what are the results? Being obsessed with time and our egos, we are for ever craving and worrying. But nothing impairs the normal functioning of the organism like craving and revulsion, like greed and fear and worry. Directly or indirectly, most of our physical ailments and disabilities are due to worry and craving. We worry and crave ourselves into high blood-pressure, heart disease, tuberculosis, peptic ulcer, low resistance to infection, neurasthenia, sexual aberrations, insanity, suicide. Not to mention all the rest.' Mr. Propter waved his hand comprehensively. 'Craving even prevents us from seeing properly,' he went on. 'The harder we try to see, the graver our error of accommodation. And it's the same with bodily posture: the more we worry about doing the thing immediately ahead of us in time, the more we interfere with our correct body posture and the worse, in consequence, becomes the functioning of the entire organism. In a word, in so far as we're human beings, we prevent ourselves from realizing the physiological and instinctive good that we're capable of as animals. And, *mutatis mutandis*, the same thing is true in regard to the sphere above. In so far as we're human beings, we prevent ourselves from realizing the spiritual and timeless good that we're capable of as potential inhabitants of eternity, as potential enjoyers of the beatific vision. We worry and crave ourselves out of the very possibility of transcending personality and knowing, intellectually at first and then by direct experience, the true nature of the world.'

Mr. Propter was silent for a moment; then, with a sudden smile, 'Luckily,' he went on, 'most of us don't manage to behave like human beings all the time. We forget our wretched little egos and those horrible great projections of our egos in the ideal world—forget them and relapse for a while into harmless animality. The organism gets a chance to function according to its own laws; in other words, it gets a chance to realize such good as it's capable of. That's why we're as healthy and sane as we are. Even in great cities, as many as four persons out of five manage to go through life without having to be treated in a lunatic asylum. If we were consistently human, the percentage of mental cases would rise from twenty to a hundred. But fortunately most of us are incapable of consistency—the animal always resuming its rights. And to some people fairly frequently, perhaps occasionally to all, there come little flashes of illumination —momentary glimpses into the nature of the world as it is for a consciousness liberated from appetite and time, of the world as it might be if we didn't choose to deny God by being our personal selves. Those flashes come to us when we're off our guards; then craving and worry come rushing back and the light is eclipsed once more by our personality and its lunatic ideals, its criminal policies and plans.'

There was silence. The sun had gone. Behind the mountains to the west, a pale yellow light faded through green into a blue that deepened as it climbed. At the zenith, it was all night.

Pete sat quite still, staring into the dark, but still transparent sky above the northern peaks. That voice, so calm at first and then at the end so powerfully resonant, those words, now mercilessly critical of all the things to which he had given his allegiance, now charged with the half-comprehended promise of things incommensurably worthier of loyalty, had left him profoundly moved and at the same time perplexed and at a loss. Everything, he saw, would have to be thought out again, from the beginning—science, politics, perhaps even love, even Virginia. He was appalled by the prospect and yet, in another part of his being, attracted; he felt resentful at the thought of Mr. Propter, but at the same time loved the disquieting old man; loved him for what he did and, above all, for what he so admirably and, in Pete's own experience, uniquely was—disinterestedly friendly, at once serene and powerful, gentle and strong, self-effacing and yet intensely *there*, more present, so to speak, radiating more life than anyone else.

Jeremy Pordage had also found himself taking an interest in what the old man said, had even, like Pete, experienced the stirrings of a certain disquiet—a disquiet none the less disquieting for having stirred in him before. The substance of what Mr. Propter had said was familiar to him. For, of course, he had read all the significant books on the subject—would have thought himself bar-

barously uneducated if he hadn't—had read Sankara and
Eckhart, the Pali texts and John of the Cross, Charles de
Condran and the Bardo, and Patanjali and the Pseudo-
Dionysius. He had read them and been moved by them
into wondering whether he oughtn't to do something
about them; and, because he had been moved in this
way, he had taken the most elaborate pains to make fun
of them, not only to other people, but also and above all
to himself. 'You've never bought your ticket to Athens,'
the man had said—damn his eyes! Why did he want to
go putting these things over on one? All one asked was
to be left in peace, to take things as they came. Things
as they came—one's books, one's little articles, and Lady
Fredegond's ear-trumpet, and Palestrina, and steak-and-
kidney pudding at the Reform, and Mae and Doris.
Which reminded him that to-day was Friday; if he were
in England it would be his afternoon at the flat in Maida
Vale. Deliberately he turned his attention away from
Mr. Propter and thought instead of those alternate Friday
afternoons; of the pink lampshades; the smell of talcum
powder and perspiration; the Trojan women, as he called
them because they worked so hard, in their kimonos from
Marks and Spencer's; the framed reproductions of pictures by Poynter and Alma Tadema (delicious irony, that
works which the Victorians had regarded as art should
have come to serve, a generation later, as pornography
in a trollop's bedroom!); and, finally, the erotic routine,
so matter-of-factly sordid, so conscientiously and pro-
fessionally low, with a lowness and a sordidness that con-
stituted, for Jeremy, their greatest charm, that he prized
more highly than any amount of moonlight and romance,
any number of lyrics and *Liebestods*. Infinite squalor in
a little room! It was the apotheosis of refinement, the
logical conclusion of good taste.

Chapter Ten

THIS Friday, Mr. Stoyte's afternoon in town had been exceptionally uneventful. Nothing untoward had occurred during the preceding week. In the course of his various meetings and interviews nobody had said or done anything to make him lose his temper. The reports on business conditions had been very satisfactory. The Japs had bought another hundred thousand barrels of oil. Copper was up two cents. The demand for bentonite was definitely increasing. True, applications for bank credit had been rather disappointing; but the influenza epidemic had raised the weekly turnover of the Pantheon to a figure well above the average.

Things went so smoothly that Mr. Stoyte was through with all his business more than an hour before he had expected. Finding himself with time to spare, he stopped on the way home at his agent's, to find out what was happening on the estate. The interview lasted only a few minutes—long enough, however, to put Mr. Stoyte in a fury that sent him rushing out to the car.

'Drive to Mr. Propter's,' he ordered with a peremptory ferocity as he slammed the door.

What the hell did Bill Propter think he was doing? he kept indignantly asking himself. Shoving his nose into other people's business. And all on account of those lousy bums who had come to pick the oranges! All for those tramps, those stinking, filthy hobos! Mr. Stoyte had a peculiar hatred for the ragged hordes of transients on whom he depended for the harvesting of his crops, a hatred that was more than the rich man's ordinary dislike of the poor. Not that he didn't experience that complex mixture of fear and physical disgust, of stifled compassion and shame transformed by repression into chronic exasperation. He did. But over and above this common and generic dislike for poor people, he was moved by other hatreds of his own. Mr. Stoyte was a rich man who had been poor. In the six years between the time when he ran away from his father and grandmother in Nashville and the time when he had been adopted by the black sheep of the family, his Uncle Tom, in California, Jo Stoyte had learned, as he imagined, everything there was to be known about being poor. Those years had left him with an ineradicable hatred for the circumstances of poverty and at the same time an ineradicable contempt for all those who had been too stupid, or too weak, or too unlucky, to climb out of the hell into which they had fallen or been born. The poor were odious to him, not only because they were potentially a menace to his position in society, not only because their misfortunes demanded a sympathy he did not wish to give, but also because they reminded him of what he himself had suffered in the past, and at the same time because the fact that they were still poor was a sufficient proof of their contemptibleness and his own superiority. And since he had suffered what they were now suffering, it was only right that they should go on suffering what he had suffered. Also, since their continued poverty proved them contemptible, it was proper that he, who was now rich, should treat them in every way as the contemptible creatures they had shown themselves to be. Such was the logic of Mr. Stoyte's emotions. And here was Bill Propter, running counter to this logic by telling the agent that they oughtn't to take advantage of the glut of transient labour to force down wages; that they ought, on the contrary, to raise them—raise them,

if you please, at a time when these bums were swarming
over the State like a plague of Mormon crickets! And
not only that; they ought to build accommodation for
them—cabins, like the ones that crazy fool Bill had built
for them himself; two-roomed cabins at six or seven
hundred dollars apiece—for bums like that, and their
women, and those disgusting children who were so filthy
dirty he wouldn't have them in his hospital; not unless
they were really dying of appendicitis or something—you
couldn't refuse them then, of course. But meanwhile,
what the hell did Bill Propter think he was doing? And
it wasn't the first time either that he'd tried to interfere.
Gliding through the twilight of the orange groves, Mr.
Stoyte kept striking the palm of his left hand with his
clenched right fist.

'I'll let him have it,' he whispered to himself. 'I'll let
him have it.'

Fifty years before, Bill Propter had been the only boy
in the school who, even though he was the older and
stronger, didn't make fun of him for being fat. They had
met again when Bill was teaching at Berkeley and he himself had made good in the real estate game and had just
gone into oil. Partly in gratitude for the way Bill
Propter had acted when they were boys, partly also in
order to display his power, to redress the balance of
superiority in his own favour, Jo Stoyte had wanted to
do something handsome for the young assistant professor. But in spite of his modest salary and the two or
three miserable thousand dollars a year his father had left
him, Bill Propter hadn't wanted anything done for him.
He had seemed genuinely grateful, he had been perfectly
courteous and friendly; but he just didn't want to come
in on the ground floor of Consol Oil—didn't want to
because, as he kept explaining, he had all he needed and

preferred not to have anything more. Jo's effort to redress the balance of superiority had failed. Failed disastrously, because, by refusing his offer, Bill had done something which, though he called him a fool for doing it, compelled Jo Stoyte secretly to admire him more than ever. Extorted against his will, this admiration bred a corresponding resentment towards its object. Jo Stoyte felt aggrieved that Bill had given him so many reasons for liking him. He would have preferred to like him without a reason, in spite of his shortcomings. But Bill had few shortcomings and many merits, merits which Jo himself did not have and whose presence in Bill he therefore regarded as an affront. Thus it was that all the reasons for liking Bill Propter were also, in Jo's eyes, equally valid reasons for disliking him. He continued to call Bill a fool; but he felt him as a standing reproach. And yet the nature of this standing reproach was such that he liked to be in Bill's company. It was because Bill had settled down on a ten-acre patch of land in this part of the valley that Mr. Stoyte had decided to build his castle on the site where it now stood. He wanted to be near Bill Propter, even though, in practice, there was almost nothing that Bill could do or say that didn't annoy him. To-day, this chronic exasperation had been fanned by Mr. Stoyte's hatred of the transients into a passion of fury.

'I'll let him have it,' he repeated again and again.

The car came to a halt, and before the chaffeur could open the door for him, Mr. Stoyte had darted out and was hurrying in his determined way, looking neither to right nor left, up the path that led from the road to his old friend's bungalow.

'Hullo, Jo,' a familiar voice called from the shadow under the eucalyptus trees.

Mr. Stoyte turned, peered through the twilight, then,

without a word, hurried towards the bench on which the three men were sitting. There was a chorus of 'Good evenings,' and, as he approached, Pete rose politely and offered him his place. Ignoring his gesture and his very presence, Mr. Stoyte addressed himself immediately to Bill Propter.

'Why the hell can't you leave my man alone?' he almost shouted.

Mr. Propter looked at him with only a moderate astonishment. He was used to these outbursts from poor Jo; he had long since divined their fundamental cause and knew by experience how to deal with them.

'Which man, Jo?' he asked.

'Bob Hansen, of course. What do you mean by going to him behind my back?'

'When I went to you,' said Mr. Propter, 'you told me it was Hansen's business. So I went to Hansen.'

This was so infuriatingly true that Mr. Stoyte could only resort to roaring. He roared. 'Interfering with him in his work! What's the idea?'

'Pete's offering you a seat,' Mr. Propter put in. 'Or, if you prefer it, there's an iron chair behind you. You'd better sit down, Jo.'

'I'm not going to sit down,' Mr. Stoyte bellowed. 'And I want an answer. What's the idea?'

'The idea?' Mr. Propter repeated in his slow quiet way. 'Well, it's quite an old one, you know. I didn't invent it.'

'Can't you answer me?'

'It's the idea that men and women are human beings. Not vermin.'

'Those bums of yours!'

Mr. Propter turned to Pete. 'You may as well sit down again,' he said.

'Those lousy bums! I tell you I won't stand it.'

'Besides,' Mr. Propter went on, 'I'm a practical man. You're not.'

'Me not practical?' Mr. Stoyte echoed with indignant amazement. 'Not *practical*? Well, look at the place I live in and then look at this dump of yours.'

'Exactly. That proves the point. You're hopelessly romantic, Jo; so romantic, you think people can work when they haven't had enough to eat.'

'You're trying to make communists of them.' The word 'communist' renewed Mr. Stoyte's passion and at the same time justified it; his indignation ceased to be merely personal and became righteous. 'You're nothing but a communist agitator.' His voice trembled, Mr. Propter sadly noticed, just as Pete's had trembled half an hour before at the words 'fascist aggression.' He wondered if the boy had noticed or, having noticed, would take the hint. 'Nothing but a communist agitator,' Mr. Stoyte repeated with a crusader's zeal.

'I thought we were talking about eating,' said Mr. Propter.

'You're stalling!'

'Eating and working—wasn't that it?'

'I've put up with you all these years,' Mr. Stoyte went on. 'For old times' sake. But now I'm through. I'm sick of you. Talking communism to those bums! Making the place dangerous for decent people to live in.'

'Decent?' Mr. Propter echoed, and was tempted to laugh, but immediately checked the impulse. Being laughed at in the presence of Pete and Mr. Pordage might goad the poor fellow into doing something irreparably stupid.

'I'll have you run out of the valley,' Mr. Stoyte was roaring. 'I'll see that you're . . .' He broke off in the middle of the sentence and stood there for a few seconds in silence, his mouth still open and working, his eyes staring. That drumming in the ears, that tingling heat in the face—they had suddenly reminded him of his blood-pressure, of Dr. Obispo, of death. Death and that flame-coloured text in his bedroom at home. Terrible to fall into the hands of the living God—not Prudence's God, of course; the other one, the *real* one, the God of his father and his grandmother.

Mr. Stoyte drew a deep breath, pulled out his hand-kerchief, wiped his face and neck, then, without uttering another word, turned and began to walk away.

Mr. Propter got up, hurried after him and, in spite of the other's angry motion of recoil, took Mr. Stoyte's arm and walked along beside him.

'I want to show you something, Jo,' he said. 'Something that'll interest you, I think.'

'I don't want to see it,' said Mr. Stoyte between his false teeth.

Mr. Propter paid no attention, but continued to lead him towards the back of the house. 'It's a gadget that Abbot of the Smithsonian has been working on for some time,' he continued. 'A thing for making use of solar energy.' He interrupted himself for a moment to call back to the others to follow him; then turned again to Mr. Stoyte and resumed the conversation. 'Much more compact than anything of the kind that's ever been made before,' he said. 'Much more efficient, too.' And he went on to describe the system of trough-shaped re-flectors, the tubes of oil heated to a temperature of four or five hundred degrees Fahrenheit; the boiler for raising steam, if you wanted to run a low-pressure engine; the cooking-range and water-heater, if you were using it only for domestic purposes. 'Pity the sun's down,' he said, as they stood in front of the machine. 'I'd have liked to show you the way it works the engine. I've had two horse-power, eight hours a day, ever since I got the thing working last week. Not bad considering we're still in January. We'll have her working overtime all summer.'

Mr. Stoyte had intended to persist in his silence—just to show Bill that he was still angry, that he hadn't forgiven him; but his interest in the machine and, above all, his exasperated concern with Bill's idiotic, crackpot notions were too much for him. 'What the hell do you want with two horse-power, eight hours a day?' he asked.

'To run my electric generator.'

'But what do you want with an electric generator? Haven't you got your current wired in from the city?'

'Of course. And I'm trying to see how far I can be independent of the city.'

'But what for?'

Mr. Propter uttered a little laugh. 'Because I believe in Jeffersonian democracy.'

'What the hell has Jeffersonian democracy got to do with it?' said Mr. Stoyte with mounting irritation. 'Can't you believe in Jefferson and have your current wired in from the city?'

'That's exactly it,' said Mr. Propter; 'you almost certainly can't.'

'What do you mean?'

'What I say,' Mr. Propter answered mildly.

'*I* believe in democracy too,' Mr. Stoyte announced with a look of defiance.

'I know you do. And you also believe in being the undisputed boss in all your businesses.'

'I should hope so!'

'There's another name for an undisputed boss,' said Mr. Propter. '"Dictator."'

'What are you trying to get at?'

'Merely at the facts. You believe in democracy; but you're at the head of businesses which have to be run dictatorially. And your subordinates have to accept your dictatorship because they're dependent on you for their living. In Russia they'd depend on government officials for their living. Perhaps you think that's an improvement,' he added, turning to Pete.

Pete nodded. 'I'm all for the public ownership of the means of production,' he said. It was the first time he had openly confessed his faith in the presence of his employer; he felt happy at having dared to be a Daniel.

'"Public ownership of the means of production,"' Mr. Propter repeated. 'But unfortunately governments have a way of regarding the individual producers as being parts of the means. Frankly, I'd rather have Jo Stoyte as my boss than Jo Stalin. This Jo' (he laid his hand on Mr. Stoyte's shoulder), 'this Jo can't have you executed; he can't send you to the Arctic; he can't prevent you from getting a job under another boss. Whereas the other Jo . . .' he shook his head. 'Not that,' he added, 'I'm exactly longing to have even this Jo as my boss.'

'You'd be fired pretty quick,' growled Mr. Stoyte.

'I don't want any boss,' Mr. Propter went on. 'The more bosses, the less democracy. But unless people can support themselves, they've got to have a boss who'll undertake to do it for them. So the less self-support, the less democracy. In Jefferson's day, a great many Americans did support themselves. They were economically independent. Independent of government and independent of big business. Hence the Constitution.'

'We've still got the Constitution,' said Mr. Stoyte.

'No doubt,' Mr. Propter agreed. 'But if we had to make a new Constitution to-day, what would it be like? A Constitution to fit the facts of New York and Chicago and Detroit; of United States Steel and the Public Utilities and General Motors and the C.I.O. and the government departments. What on earth would it be like?' he repeated. 'We respect our old Constitution, but in fact we live under a new one. And if we want to live under the first, we've got to re-create something like the conditions under which the first was made. That's why I'm interested in this gadget.' He patted the frame of the machine. 'Because it may help to give independence to anyone who desires independence. Not that many do desire it,' he added parenthetically. 'The propaganda in favour of dependence is too strong. They've come to believe that you can't be happy unless you're entirely dependent on government or centralized business. But for the few who do care about democracy, who really want to be free in the Jeffersonian sense, this thing may be a help. If it makes them independent of fuel and power, that's already a great deal.'

Mr. Stoyte looked anxious. 'Do you really think it'll do that?'

'Why not?' said Mr. Propter. 'There's a lot of sunshine running to waste in this part of the country.'

Mr. Stoyte thought of his presidency of the Consol Oil Company. 'It won't be good for the oil business,' he said.

'I should hate it to be good for the oil business,' Mr. Propter answered cheerfully.

'And what about coal?' He had an interest in a group of West Virginia mines. 'And the railroads?' There was that big block of Union Pacific shares that had belonged to Prudence. 'The railroads can't get on without long hauls. And steel,' he added disinterestedly; for his holdings in Bethlehem Steel were almost negligible. 'What happens to steel if you hurt the railroads and cut down trucking? You're going against progress,' he burst out in another access of righteous indignation. 'You're turning back the clock.'

'Don't worry, Jo,' said Mr. Propter. 'It won't affect your dividends for quite a long while. There'll be plenty of time to adjust to the new conditions.'

With an admirable effort, Mr. Stoyte controlled his temper. 'You seem to figure I can't think of anything but money,' he said with dignity. 'Well, it may interest you to know that I've decided to give Dr. Mulge another thirty thousand dollars for his Art School.' (The decision had been made there and then, for the sole purpose of serving as a weapon in the perennial battle with Bill Propter.) 'And if you think,' he added as an afterthought, 'if you think I'm only concerned with my own interests, read the special World's Fair number of the *New York Times*. Read that,' he insisted with the solemnity of a fundamentalist recommending the Book of Revelation. 'You'll see that the most forward-looking men in the country think as I do.' He spoke with unaccustomed and incongruous unction, in the phraseology of after-dinner eloquence. 'The way of progress is the way of better organization, more service from business, more goods for the consumer!' Then, incoherently, 'Look at the way a housewife goes to her grocer,' he added, 'and buys a package of some nationally advertised cereal or something. *That's* progress. Not your crackpot idea of doing everything at home with this idiotic contraption.' Mr. Stoyte had reverted completely to his ordinary style. 'You always were a fool, Bill, and I guess you always will be. And remember what I told you about interfering with Bob Hansen. I won't stand for it.' In dramatic silence he walked away; but after taking a few steps he halted and called back over his shoulder, 'Come up to dinner, if you feel like it.'

'Thanks,' said Mr. Propter. 'I will.'

Mr. Stoyte walked briskly towards his car. He had forgotten about high blood-pressure and the living God and felt all of a sudden unaccountably and unreasonably happy. It was not that he had scored any notable success in his battle with Bill Propter. He hadn't; and, what was more, in the process of not scoring a success he had made, and was even half aware that he had made, a bit of a fool of himself. The source of his happiness was elsewhere. He was happy, though he would never have admitted the fact, because, in spite of everything, Bill seemed to like him.

In the car, as he drove back to the castle, he whistled to himself.

Entering (with his hat on, as usual; for even after all these years he still derived a childish pleasure from the contrast between the palace in which he lived and the proletarian manners he affected), Mr. Stoyte crossed the great hall, stepped into the elevator and, from the elevator, walked directly into Virginia's boudoir.

When he opened the door, the two were sitting at least fifteen feet apart. Virginia was at the soda-counter, pensively eating a chocolate-and-banana split; seated in an elegant pose on one of the pink satin armchairs, Dr. Obispo was in process of lighting a cigarette.

On Mr. Stoyte the impact of suspicion and jealousy was like the blow of a fist directed (for the shock was physical and localized in the midriff) straight to the solar plexus. His face contracted as though with pain. And yet he had seen nothing; there was no apparent cause for jealousy, no visible reason, in their attitudes, their actions, their expressions, for suspicion. Dr. Obispo's manner was perfectly easy and natural; and the Baby's smile of startled and delighted welcome was angelic in its candour.

'Uncle Jo!' She ran to meet him and threw her arms round his neck.' 'Uncle Jo!'

The warmth of her tone, the softness of her lips, had a magnified effect on Mr. Stoyte. Moved to a point at which he was using the word to the limit of its double connotation, he murmured, 'My Baby!' with a lingering emphasis. The fact that he should have felt suspicious, even for a moment, of this pure and adorable, this deliciously warm, resilient and perfumed child, filled him with shame. And even Dr. Obispo now heaped coals of fire on his head.

'I was a bit worried,' he said, as he got up from his chair, 'by the way you coughed after lunch. That's why I came up here, to make sure of catching you the moment you got in.' He put a hand in his pocket and, after half drawing out and immediately replacing a little leather-bound volume, like a prayer-book, extracted a stethoscope. 'Prevention's better than cure,' he went on. 'I'm not going to let you get influenza if I can help it.'

Remembering what a good week they had had at the Beverly Pantheon on account of the epidemic, Mr. Stoyte felt alarmed. 'I don't *feel* bad,' he said. 'I guess that cough wasn't anything. Only my old—you know: the chronic bronchitis.'

'Maybe it was only that. But all the same, I'd like to listen in.' Briskly professional, Dr. Obispo hung the stethoscope round his neck.

'He's right, Uncle Jo,' said the Baby.

Touched by so much solicitude, and at the same time rather disturbed by the thought that it might perhaps be influenza, Mr. Stoyte took off his coat and waistcoat and began to undo his tie. A moment later he was standing stripped to the waist under the crystals of the chandelier. Modestly, Virginia retired again to her soda-fountain. Dr. Obispo slipped the ends of the curved nickel tubes of the stethoscope into his ears. 'Take a deep breath,' he said as he pressed the muzzle against Mr. Stoyte's chest. 'Again,' he ordered. 'Now cough.' Looking past that thick barrel of hairy flesh, he could see, on the wall behind the inhabitants of Watteau's mournful paradise as they prepared to set sail for some other paradise, doubtless yet more heartbreaking.

'Say ninety-nine,' Dr. Obispo commanded, returning from the embarkation for Cythera to a near view of Mr. Stoyte's thorax and abdomen.

'Ninety-nine,' said Mr. Stoyte. 'Ninety-nine. Ninety-nine.'

With professional thoroughness, Dr. Obispo shifted the muzzle of his stethoscope from point to point on the curving barrel of flesh before him. There was nothing wrong, of course, with the old buzzard. Just the familiar set of râles and wheezes he always had. Perhaps it would make things a bit more realistic if he were to take the creature down to his office and stick him up in front of the fluoroscope. But, no; he really couldn't be bothered. And, besides, this farce would be quite enough.

'Cough again,' he said, planting his instrument among the grey hairs on Mr. Stoyte's left pap. And among other things, he went on to reflect, while Mr. Stoyte forced out a succession of artificial coughs, among other things, these old sacks of guts didn't smell too good. How any young girl could stand it, even for money, he really couldn't imagine. And yet the fact remained that there were thousands of them who not only stood it, but actually

enjoyed it. Or, perhaps, 'enjoy' was the wrong word.
Because in most cases there probably wasn't any question
of enjoyment in the proper, physiological sense of the
word. It all happened in the mind, not in the body.
They loved their old gut-sacks with their heads; loved
them because they admired them, because they were impressed by the gut-sack's position in the world, or his
knowledge, or his celebrity. What they slept with wasn't
the man; it was a reputation, it was the embodiment of a
function. And then, of course, some of the girls were
future models for Mother's Day advertisements; some
were little Florence Nightingales, on the look-out for a
Crimean War. In those cases, the very infirmities of their
gut-sacks were added attractions. They had the satisfaction of sleeping not only with a reputation or a stock
of wisdom, not only with a federal judgeship, for example, or the presidency of a chamber of commerce, but
also and simultaneously with a wounded soldier, with an
imbecile child, with a lovely stinking little baby who still
made messes in its bed. Even this cutie (Dr. Obispo shot
a sideways glance in the direction of the soda-fountain),
even this one had something of the Florence Nightingale
in her, something of the Gold Star Mother. (And that
in spite of the fact that, with her conscious mind, she felt
a kind of physical horror of physical maternity.) Jo
Stoyte was a little bit her baby and her patient; and at
the same time, of course, he was a great deal her own
private Abraham Lincoln. Incidentally, he also happened
to be the man with the cheque-book. Which was a consideration, of course. But if he were only that, Virginia
wouldn't have been so nearly happy as she obviously was.
The cheque-book was made more attractive by being in
the hands of a demi-god who had to have a nanny to
change his diapers.

'Turn round, please.'

Mr. Stoyte obeyed. The back, Dr. Obispo reflected, was perceptibly less revolting than the front. Perhaps because it was less personal.

'Take a deep breath,' he said; for he was going to play the farce all over again on this new stage. 'Another.'

Mr. Stoyte breathed enormously, like a cetacean.

'And another,' said Dr. Obispo. '*And* again,' said Dr. Obispo, reflecting as the old man snorted that his own chief asset was a refreshing unlikeness to this smelly old gut-sack. She would take him, and take him, what was more, on his own terms. No Romeo-and-Juliet acts, no nonsense about Love with a large L, none of that popular-song claptrap with its skies of blue, dreams come true, heaven with you. Just sensuality for its own sake. The real, essential concrete thing; no less, it went without saying, but also (and this most certainly didn't go without saying; for the bitches were always trying to get you to stick them on pedestals, or be their soul-mates), also no more. No more, to begin with, out of respect for scientific truth. He believed in scientific truth. Facts were facts; accept them as such. It was a fact, for example, that young girls in the pay of rich old men could be seduced without much difficulty. It was also a fact that rich old men, however successful at business, were generally so frightened, ignorant and stupid that they could be bamboozled by any intelligent person who chose to try.

'Say ninety-nine again,' he said aloud.

'Ninety-nine. Ninety-nine.'

Ninety-nine chances out of a hundred that they would never find out anything. That was the fact about old men. The fact about love was that it consisted essentially of tumescence and detumescence. So why embroider the fact with unnecessary fictions? Why not be realistic? why not treat the whole business scientifically?

'Ninety-nine,' Mr. Stoyte went on repeating, 'Ninety-nine.'

And then, Dr. Obispo went on to reflect, as he listened without interest to the whisperings and crepitations inside the warm, smelly barrel before him, then there were the more personal reasons for preferring to take love unadorned, in the chemically pure condition. Personal reasons that were also, of course, a fact that had to be accepted. For it was a fact that he personally found an added pleasure in the imposition of his will upon the partner he had chosen. To be pleasurable, this imposition of will must never be too easy, too much a matter of course. Which ruled out all professionals. The partner had to be an amateur and, like all amateurs, committed to the thesis that tumescence and detumescence should always be associated with LOVE, PASSION, SOUL-MATING—all in upper-case letters. In imposing his will, he imposed the contradictory doctrine, the doctrine of tumescence and detumescence for tumescence's and detumescence's sake. All he asked was that a partner should give the thesis a practical try-out—however reluctantly, however experimentally, for just this once only; he didn't care. Just a single try-out. After that it was up to him. If he couldn't make a permanent and enthusiastic convert of her, at any rate so far as he was concerned, then the fault was his.

'Ninety-nine, ninety-nine,' said Mr. Stoyte with exemplary patience.

'You can stop now,' Dr. Obispo told him graciously.

Just one try-out; he could practically guarantee himself success. It was a branch of applied physiology; he was an expert, a specialist. The Claude Bernard of the

subject. And talk of imposing one's will! You began
by forcing the girl to accept a thesis that was in flat con-
tradiction to all the ideas she had been brought up with,
all the dreams-come-true rigmarole of popular ideology.
Quite a pleasant little victory, to be sure. But it was
only when you got down to the applied physiology that
the series of really satisfying triumphs began. You took
an ordinarily rational human being, a good hundred-per-
cent. American with a background, a position in society,
a set of conventions, a code of ethics, a religion (Catholic
in the present instance, Dr. Obispo remembered parenthetically); you took this good citizen, with rights fully
and formally guaranteed by the Constitution, you took
her (and perhaps she had come to the place of assignation
in her husband's Packard limousine and direct from a
banquet, with speeches in honour, say, of Dr. Nicholas
Murray Butler or the retiring Archbishop of Indian-
apolis), you took her and you proceeded, systematically
and scientifically, to reduce this unique personality to a
mere epileptic body, moaning and gibbering under the
excruciations of a pleasure for which you, the Claude
Bernard of the subject, were responsible and of which
you remained the enjoying, but always detached, always
ironically amused, spectator.

'Just a few more deep breaths, if you don't mind.'

Wheezily Mr. Stoyte inhaled, then with a snorting
sigh emptied his lungs.

Chapter Eleven

THERE was silence after Mr. Stoyte's departure. A long silence, while each of the three men thought his own private thoughts. It was Pete who spoke first.

'Things like that,' he said gloomily, 'they get me kind of wondering if I ought to go on taking his money. What would you do, Mr. Propter, if you were me?'

'What would I do?' Mr. Propter reflected for a moment. 'I'd go on working in Jo's laboratory,' he said. 'But only so long as I felt fairly certain that what I was doing wouldn't cause more harm than good. One has to be a utilitarian in these matters. A utilitarian with a difference,' he qualified. 'Bentham crossed with Eckhart, say, or Nagarjuna.'

'Poor Bentham!' said Jeremy, horrified by the thought of what was being done to his namesake.

Mr. Propter smiled. 'Poor Bentham, indeed! Such a good, sweet, absurd, intelligent man! So nearly right; but so enormously wrong! Deluding himself with the notion that the greatest happiness of the greatest number could be achieved on the strictly human level—the level of time and evil, the level of the absence of God. Poor Bentham!' he repeated. 'What a great man he would have been if only he could have grasped that good can't be had except where it exists!'

'That sort of utilitarian you're talking about,' said Pete, 'what would he feel about the job I'm doing now?'

'I don't know,' Mr. Propter answered. 'I haven't thought about it enough to guess what he'd say. And, anyhow, we haven't yet got the empirical material on which a reasonable judgment could be based. All I know is that if I were in on this I'd be cautious. Infinitely cautious,' he insisted.

'And what about the money ?' Pete went on. 'Seeing where it comes from and who it belongs to, do you think I ought to take it ?'

'All money's pretty dirty,' said Mr. Propter. 'I don't know that poor Jo's is appreciably dirtier than anyone else's. You may think it is; but that's only because, for the first time, you're seeing money at its source—its personal, human source. You're like one of these city children who have been used to getting their milk in sterilized bottles from a shiny white delivery wagon. When they go into the country and see it being pumped out of a big, fat, smelly old animal, they're horrified, they're disgusted. It's the same with money. You've been used to getting it from behind a bronze grating in a magnificent marble bank. Now you've come out into the country and are living in the cowshed with the animal that actually secretes the stuff. And the process doesn't strike you as very savoury or hygienic. But the same process was going on, even when you didn't know about it. And if you weren't working for Jo Stoyte, you'd probably be working for some college or university. But where do colleges and universities get their money from ? From rich men. In other words, from people like Jo Stoyte. Again it's dirt served out in sterile containers—by a gentleman in a cap and gown this time.'

'So you figure it's all right for me to go on like I am now ?' said Pete.

'All right,' Mr. Propter answered, 'in the sense that it's not conspicuously worse than anything else.' Suddenly smiling, 'I was glad to hear that Dr. Mulge had got his

Art School,' he said in another, lighter tone. 'Immediately after the Auditorium, too. It's a lot of money. But I suppose the prestige of being a patron of learning is worth it. And, of course, there's an enormous social pressure on the rich to make them become patrons of learning. They're being pushed by shame as well as pulled by the longing to believe they're the benefactors of humanity. And, happily, with Dr. Mulge a rich man can have his kudos with safety. No amount of art schools at Tarzana will ever disturb the *status quo*. Whereas if I were to ask Jo for fifty thousand dollars to finance research into the technique of democracy, he'd turn me down flat. Why? Because he knows that sort of thing is dangerous. He likes speeches about democracy. (Incidentally, Dr. Mulge is really terrific on the subject.) But he doesn't approve of the coarse materialists who try to find out how to put those ideals into practice. You saw how angry he got about my poor little sun-machine. Because, in its tiny way, it's a menace to the sort of big business he makes his money from. And it's the same with these other little gadgets that I've talked to him about from time to time. Come and look, if it doesn't bore you.'

He took them into the house. Here was the little electric mill, hardly larger than a coffee-machine, in which he ground his own flour as he needed it. Here was the loom at which he had learnt and was now teaching others to weave. Next he took them out to the shed in which, with a few hundred dollars' worth of electrically operated tools, he was equipped to do any kind of carpentry and even some light metal-work. Beyond the shed were the still unfinished greenhouses; for the vegetable plots weren't adequate to supply the demands of his transients. There they were, he added, pointing through the increasing darkness to the lights of a row of cabins. He could put up only a few of them; the rest had to live in a sort of garbage-heap down in the dry bed of the river—paying rent to Jo Stoyte for the privilege. Not the best material to work with, of course. But such misery as theirs left one no choice. They simply had to be attended to. A few had come through undemoralized; and, of these, a few could see what had to be done, what you had to aim at. Two or three were working with him here; and he had been able to raise money to settle two or three more on some land near Santa Suzanna. Mere beginning—unsatisfactory at that. Because, obviously, you could not even start experimenting properly until you had a full-fledged community working under the new conditions. But to set a community on its feet would require money. A lot of money. But rich men wouldn't touch the work; they preferred art schools at Tarzana. The people who were interested had no money; that was one of the reasons why they were interested. Borrowing at the current commercial rates was dangerous. Except in very favourable circumstances, the chances were that you'd merely be selling yourself into slavery to a bank.

'It isn't easy,' said Mr. Propter, as they walked back to the house. 'But the great point is that, easy or not easy, it's there, waiting to be done. Because, after all, Pete, there *is* something to do.'

Mr. Propter went into the bungalow for a moment to turn out the lights, then emerged again on to the porch. Together, the three men walked down the path to the road. Before them the castle was a vast black silhouette punctured by occasional lights.

'There *is* something you can do,' Mr. Propter resumed; 'but only on condition that you know what the nature of the world happens to be. If you know that the strictly human level is the level of evil, you won't waste your time trying to produce good on that level. Good manifests itself only on the animal level and on the level of eternity. Knowing that, you'll realize that the best you can do on the human level is preventive. You can see that purely human activities don't interfere too much with the manifestation of good on the other levels. That's all. But politicians don't know the nature of reality. If they did, they wouldn't be politicians. Reactionary or revolutionary, they're all humanists, all romantics. They live in a world of illusion, a world that's a mere projection of their own human personalities. They act in ways which would be appropriate if such a world as they think they live in really existed. But, unfortunately, it doesn't exist except in their imaginations. Hence nothing that they do is appropriate to the real world. All their actions are the actions of lunatics, and all, as history is there to demonstrate, are more or less completely disastrous. So much for the romantics. The realists, who have studied the nature of the world, know that an exclusively humanistic attitude towards life is always fatal, and that all strictly human activities must therefore be made instrumental to animal and spiritual good. They know, in other words, that men's business is to make the human world safe for animals and spirits. Or perhaps,' he added, turning to Jeremy, 'perhaps, as an Englishman, you prefer Lloyd George's phrase to Wilson's: "A home fit for heroes to live in"—wasn't that it? A home fit for animals and spirits, for physiology and disinterested consciousness. At present, I'm afraid, it's profoundly unfit. The world we've made for ourselves is a world of sick bodies and insane or criminal personalities. How shall we make this world safe for ourselves as animals and as spirits ? If we can answer that question, we've discovered what to do.'

Mr. Propter halted at what appeared to be a wayside shrine, opened a small steel door with a key he carried in his pocket, and, lifting the receiver of the telephone within, announced their presence to an invisible porter, somewhere on the other side of the moat. They walked on.

'What are the things that make the world unsafe for animals and spirits ?' Mr. Propter continued. 'Obviously greed and fear, lust for power, hatred, anger . . .'

At this moment, a dazzling light struck them full in the face and was almost immediately turned out.

'What in heaven's name . . . ?' Jeremy began.

'Don't worry,' said Peter. 'They only want to make sure it's us, not a set of gangsters. It's just the searchlight.'

'Just our old friend Jo expressing his personality,' said Mr. Propter, taking Jeremy's arm. 'In other words, proclaiming to the world that he's afraid because he's been greedy and domineering. And he's been greedy and domineering, among other reasons, because the present system puts a premium on those qualities. Our problem is to find a system that will give the fewest possible opportunities for unfortunate people, like Jo Stoyte, to realize their potentialities.'

The bridge had swung down as they approached the moat, and now the boards rang hollow under their feet.

'You'd like socialism, Pete,' Mr. Propter continued. 'But socialism seems to be fatally committed to centralization and standardized urban mass production all round. Besides, I see too many occasions for bullying there—too many opportunities for bossy people to display their bossiness, for sluggish people to sit back and be slaves.'

The portcullis rose, the gates slid back to receive them.

'If you want to make the world safe for animals and spirits, you must have a system that reduces the amount of fear and greed and hatred and domineering to their minimum. Which means that you must have enough economic security to get rid at least of that source of worry. Enough personal responsibility to prevent people from wallowing in sloth. Enough property to protect them from being bullied by the rich, but not enough to permit them to bully. And the same thing with political rights and authority—enough of the first for the protection of the many, too little of the second for domination by the few.'

'Sounds like peasants to me,' said Pete dubiously.

'Peasants plus small machines and power. Which means that they're no longer peasants, except in so far as they're largely self-sufficient.'

'And who makes the machines? More peasants?"

'No; the same sort of people as make them now. What can't be made satisfactorily except by mass-production methods, obviously has to go on being made that way. About a third of all production—that's what it seems to amount to. The other two-thirds are more economically produced at home or in a small workshop. The immediate, practical problem is to work out the technique of that small-scale production. At present, all the research is going to the discovery of new fields for mass production.'

In the Grotto a row of twenty-five-feet electric candles burned in perpetual adoration before the Virgin. Above, on the tennis-court, the second butler, two maids and the head electrician were playing mixed doubles by the light of arc lamps.

'And do you figure people will want to leave the cities and live the way you're telling us, on little farms?'

'Ah, now you're talking, Pete!' said Mr. Propter approvingly. 'Frankly, then, I don't expect them to leave the cities, any more than I expect them to stop having wars and revolutions. All I expect is that, if I do my work and it's reasonably good, there'll be a few people who will want to collaborate with me. That's all.'

'But if you're not going to get more than just a few, what's the point. Why not try to do something with the cities and the factories, seeing that that's where most people are going to stay? Wouldn't that be more practical?'

'It depends how one defines the word,' said Mr. Propter. 'For example, *you* seem to think that it's practical to help a great many people to pursue a policy which is known to be fatal; but that it isn't practical to help a very few people to pursue a policy which there is every reason to regard as sound. I don't agree with you.'

'But the many are there. You've got to do something about them.'

'You've got to do something about them,' Mr. Propter agreed. 'But at the same time there are circumstances when you can't do anything. You can't do anything effective about anyone if he doesn't choose or isn't able to collaborate with you in doing the right thing. For example, you've *got* to help people who are being killed off by malaria. But in practice you can't help them if they refuse to screen their windows and insist on taking walks near stagnant water in the twilight. It's exactly the same with the diseases of the body politic. You've got to help people if they're faced by war or ruin or enslavement, if they're under the menace of sudden revolution or slow degeneration. You've got to help. But the fact remains, nevertheless, that you can't help if they persist in the course of behaviour which originally got them into their trouble. For example, you can't preserve people from the horrors of war if they won't give up the pleasures of nationalism. You can't save them from slumps and depressions so long as they go on thinking exclusively in terms of money and regarding money as the supreme good. You can't avert revolution and enslavement if they *will* identify progress with the increase of centralization and prosperity with the intensifying of mass production. You can't preserve them from collective madness and suicide if they persist in paying divine honours to ideals which are merely projections of their own personalities—in other words, if they persist in worshipping themselves rather than God. So much for conditional clauses. Now let's consider the actual facts of the present situation. For our purposes, the most significant facts are these : the inhabitants of every civilized country are menaced; all desire passionately to be saved from impending disaster; the overwhelming majority refuse to change the habits of thought, feeling and action which are directly responsible for their present plight. In other words, they can't be helped, because they are not prepared to collaborate with any helper who proposes a rational and realistic course of action. In these circumstances, what ought the would-be helper to do?'

'He's got to do *something*,' said Pete.

'Even if he thereby accelerates the process of destruction?' Mr. Propter smiled sadly. 'Doing for doing's sake,' he went on. 'I prefer Oscar Wilde. Bad art can't do so much harm as ill-considered political action. Doing good on any but the tiniest scale requires more intelligence than most people possess. They ought to be content with keeping out of mischief; it's easier and it doesn't have such frightful results as trying to do good in the wrong way. Twiddling the thumbs and having good manners are much more helpful, in most cases, than rushing about with good intentions, *doing* things.'

Floodlighted, Giambologna's nymph was still indefatigably spouting away against the velvet background of the darkness. Electricity and sculpture, Jeremy was thinking as he looked at her—predestined partners. The things that old Bernini could have done with a battery of projectors! The startling lights, the rich fantastic shadows! The female mystics in orgasm, the conglobulated angels, the skeletons whizzing up out of papal tombs like sky-rockets, the saints in their private hurricane of flapping draperies and wind-blown marble curls! What fun! What splendour! What self-parodying emphasis! What staggering beauty! What enormous bad taste! And what a shame that the man should have had to be content with mere daylight and tallow candles!

'No,' Mr. Propter was saying in answer to a protesting question from the young man, 'no, I certainly wouldn't advise their abandonment. I'd advise the constant reiteration of the truths they've been told again and again during the past three thousand years. And, in the intervals, I'd do active work on the technics of a better system, and active collaboration with the few who understand what the system is and are ready to pay the price demanded for its realization. Incidentally, the price, measured in human terms, is enormously high. Though, of course, much lower than the price demanded by the nature of things from those who persist in behaving in the standard human way. Much lower than the price of war, for example—particularly war with contemporary weapons. Much lower than the price of economic depression and political enslavement.'

'And what happens,' Jeremy asked in a fluting voice, 'what happens when you've had your war? Will the few be any better off than the many?'

'Oddly enough,' Mr. Propter answered, 'there's just a chance they may be. For this reason. If they've learnt the technique of self-sufficiency they'll find it easier to survive a time of anarchy than the people who depend for their livelihood on a highly centralized and specialized organization. You can't work for the good without incidentally preparing yourself for the worst.'

He stopped speaking, and they walked on through a silence broken only by the sound, from somewhere high overhead in the castle, of two radios tuned to different stations. The baboons, on the contrary, were already asleep.

Chapter Twelve

IN the columned Lady Chapel, with its hat-racks and its Magnascos, its Brancusi and its Etruscan sarcophagus used as an umbrella-stand, Jeremy Pordage began, all of a sudden, to feel himself more cheerful and at home.

'It's as though one were walking into the mind of a lunatic,' he said, smiling happily, as he hung up his hat and followed the others into the great hall. 'Or, rather, an idiot,' he qualified. 'Because I suppose a lunatic's a person with a one-track mind. Whereas this . . .'—he made a circular gesture—'this is a no-track mind. No-track because infinity-track. It's the mind of an idiot of genius. Positively stuffed with the best that has been thought and said.' He pronounced the phrase with a kind of old-maidish precision that made it sound entirely ludicrous. 'Greece, Mexico, backsides, crucifixions, machinery, George IV, Amida Buddha, science, Christian Science, Turkish baths—anything you like to mention. And every item is perfectly irrelevant to every other item.' He rubbed his hands together, he twinkled delightedly through his bifocals. 'Disquieting at first. But, do you know? I'm beginning to enjoy it. I find I really rather like living inside an idiot.'

'I don't doubt it,' said Mr. Propter, matter-of-factly. 'It's a common taste.'

Jeremy was offended. 'One wouldn't have thought this sort of thing was very common,' he said, nodding in the direction of the Greco.

'It isn't,' Mr. Propter agreed. 'But you can live in an idiot-universe without going to the expense of actually constructing it out of ferro-concrete and filling it with works of art.'

There was a pause while they entered the lift.

'You can live inside a cultural idiot,' Mr. Propter went on. 'Inside a patchwork of mutually irrelevant words and bits of information. Or, if you're a lowbrow, you can live in the idiot world of the *homme moyen sensuel*— the world where the irrelevances consist of newspapers and baseball, of sex and worry, of advertising and money and halitosis and keeping up with the Joneses. There's a hierarchy of idiocies. Naturally, you and I prefer the classiest variety.'

The elevator came to a halt. Pete opened the gate, and they stepped out into the whitewashed corridor of the sub-sub-basement.

'Nothing like an idiot-universe if you want a quiet irresponsible life. That is, provided you can stand the idiocy,' Mr. Propter added. 'A lot of people can't. After a time, they get tired of their no-track world. They feel the need of being concentrated and directed. They want their lives to have some sense. That's when they go communist, or join the Church of Rome, or take up with the Oxford Group. Anything, provided it will make them one-trackers. And, of course, in the overwhelming majority of cases they choose the wrong track. Inevitably. Because there are a million wrong tracks and only one right—a million ideals, a million projections of personality, and only one God and one beatific vision. From no-track idiocy most of them pass on to some one-track lunacy, generally criminal. It makes them feel better, of course; but, pragmatically, the last state is always worse than the first. If you don't want the only thing worth having, my advice is: Stick to idiocy.—Is this where you work?' he went on in another tone, as Jeremy opened the door of his vaulted study. 'And those are the Hauberk Papers, I take it. Plenty of them. The title's extinct, isn't it?'

Jeremy nodded. 'And so's the family—or very nearly. Nothing left but two old maids in a haunted house without any money.' He twinkled, uttered his little preparatory cough and, patting his bald crown, said with an exaggerated precision: 'Decayed gentlewomen.' Exquisite locution! It was one of his favourites. 'And the decay must have gone pretty far,' he added. 'Otherwise they wouldn't have sold the papers. They've refused all previous offers.'

'How fortunate one is, not to belong to an ancient family!' said Mr. Propter. 'All those inherited loyalties to bricks and mortar, all those obligations to tombstones and bits of paper and painted canvases!' He shook his head. 'What a dismal form of compulsory idolatry.'

Jeremy, meanwhile, had crossed the room, opened a drawer and returned with a file of papers which he handed to Mr. Propter. 'Look at these.'

Mr. Propter looked. 'From Molinos!' he said in surprise.

'I thought that would be your cup of tea,' said Jeremy, deriving a sly pleasure from talking about mysticism in the most absurdly inappropriate language.

Mr. Propter smiled. 'My cup of tea,' he repeated. 'But not my favourite blend. There was something not quite right about poor Molinos. A strain of—how shall I put it?—of negative sensuality. He enjoyed suffering. Mental suffering, the dark night of the soul—he really wallowed in it. No doubt, poor fellow, he sincerely believed he was destroying self-will; but, without his being aware of it, he was always turning the process of destruction into another affirmation of self-will. Which

F

was a pity,' Mr. Propter added, taking the letters to the light, to look at them more closely. 'Because he certainly did have some first-hand experience of reality. Which only shows that you're never certain of getting there, even when you've come near enough to see what sort of thing you're going to. Here's a fine sentence,' he put in parenthetically. '"*Ame a Dios*,"' he read aloud, '"*como es en sí y no como se lo dice y forma su imaginación*."'

Jeremy almost laughed. The coincidence that Mr. Propter should have picked on the same passage as had caught Dr. Obispo's eye that morning gave him a peculiar satisfaction. 'Pity he couldn't have read a little Kant,' he said. '*Dios en sí* seems to be much the same as *Ding an sich*. Unknowable by the human mind.'

'Unknowable by the *personal* human mind,' Mr. Propter agreed, 'because personality is self-will, and self-will is the negation of reality, the denial of God. So far as the ordinary human personality is concerned, Kant is perfectly right in saying that the thing in itself is unknowable. *Dios en sí* can't be comprehended by a consciousness dominated by an ego. But now suppose there were some way of eliminating the ego from consciousness. If you could do this, you'd get close to reality, you'd be in a position to comprehend *Dios en sí*. Now, the interesting thing is that, as a matter of brute fact, this thing can be done, has been done again and again. Kant's blind alley is for people who choose to remain on the human level. If you choose to climb on to the level of eternity, the *impasse* no longer exists.'

There was a silence. Mr. Propter turned over the sheets, pausing every now and then to decipher a line or two of the fine calligraphy. '"*Tres maneras hay de silencio*,"' he read aloud after a moment. '"*El primero es de palabras, el segundo de deseos y el tercero de pensamientos*."'

He writes nicely, don't you think? Probably that had a lot to do with his extraordinary success. How disastrous when a man knows how to say the wrong things in the right way! Incidentally,' he added, looking up with a smile into Jeremy's face, 'how few great stylists have ever said any of the right things. That's one of the troubles about education in the humanities. The best that has been thought and said. Very nice. But best in which way? Alas, only in form. The content is generally deplorable.' He turned back to the letters. After a moment, another passage caught his attention. '"*Oirá y leera el hombre racional estas espirituales materias, pero no llegera, dice San Pablo, a comprenderlas: Animalis homo non percipit ea quae sunt spiritus.*" And not merely *animalis homo*,' Mr. Propter commented. 'Also *humanus homo*. Indeed, above all *humanus homo*. And you might even add that *humanus homo non percipit ea quae sunt animalis.* In so far as we think as strictly human beings, we fail to understand what is below us no less than what is above. And then there's a further trouble. Suppose we stop thinking in a strictly human fashion; suppose we make it possible for ourselves to have direct intuitions of the non-human realities in which, so to speak, we're imbedded. Well and good. But what happens when we try to pass on the knowledge so acquired? We're floored. The only vocabulary at our disposal is a vocabulary primarily intended for thinking strictly human thoughts about strictly human concerns. But the things *we* want to talk about are non-human realities and non-human ways of thinking. Hence the radical inadequacy of all statements about our animal nature and, even more, of all statements about God or spirit, or eternity.'

Jeremy uttered a little cough. 'I can think of some pretty adequate statements about . . .' he paused, beamed, caressed his polished scalp; 'well, about the more *intime* aspects of our animal nature,' he concluded demurely. His face suddenly clouded; he had remembered his treasure-trove and Dr. Obispo's impudent theft.

'But what does their adequacy depend on?' Mr. Propter asked. 'Not so much on the writer's skill as the reader's response. The direct, animal intuitions aren't rendered by words; the words merely remind you of your memories of similar experiences. *Notus calor* is what Virgil says when he's talking about the sensations experienced by Vulcan in the embrace of Venus. Familiar heat. No attempt at description or analysis; no effort to get any kind of verbal equivalence to the facts. Just a reminder. But that reminder is enough to make the passage one of the most voluptuous affairs in Latin poetry. Virgil left the work to his readers. And, by and large, that's what most erotic writers are content to do. The few who try to do the work themselves have to flounder about with metaphors and similes and analogies. You know the sort of stuff: fire, whirlwinds, heaven, darts.'

'"The vale of lilies,"' Jeremy quoted. '"And the bower of bliss."'

'Not to mention the expense of spirit in a waste of shame,' said Mr. Propter; 'and all the other figures of speech. An endless variety, with only one feature in common—they're all composed of words which don't connote any aspect of the subject they're supposed to describe.'

'Saying one thing in order to mean another,' Jeremy put in. 'Isn't that one of the possible definitions of imaginative literature?'

'Maybe,' Mr. Propter answered. 'But what chiefly interests me at the moment is the fact that our immediate animal intuitions have never been given any but the most summary and inadequate labels. We say "red," for example, or "pleasant," and just leave it at that, without trying to find verbal equivalents for the various aspects of perceiving redness or experiencing pleasure.'

'Well, isn't that because you can't go beyond "red" or "pleasant"?' said Pete. 'They're just facts, ultimate facts.'

'Like giraffes,' Jeremy added. '"There ain't no such animal" is what the rationalist says, when he's shown its portrait. And then in it walks, neck and all!'

'You're right,' said Mr. Propter. 'A giraffe is an ultimate fact. You've got to accept it, whether you like it or not. But accepting the giraffe doesn't prevent you from studying and describing it. And the same applies to redness or pleasure or *notus calor*. They can be analysed, and the results of the analysis can be described by means of suitable words. But as a matter of historical fact, this hasn't been done.'

Pete nodded slowly. 'Why do you figure that should be?' he asked.

'Well,' said Mr. Propter, 'I should say it's because men have always been more interested in doing and feeling than in understanding. Always too busy making good and having thrills and doing what's "done" and worshipping the local idols—too busy with all this even to feel any desire to have an adequate verbal instrument for elucidating their experiences. Look at the languages we've inherited—incomparably effective in rousing violent and exciting emotions; an ever-present help for those who want to get on in the world; worse than useless for anyone who aspires to disinterested understanding. Hence, even on the strictly human level, the need for special impersonal languages like mathematics and technical vocabularies of the various sciences. Wherever men have felt the wish to understand, they've given up the traditional language and substituted for it another special language, more precise and, above all, less contaminated with self-interest. Now, here's a very significant fact. Imaginative literature deals mainly with the everyday life of men and women; and the everyday life of men and women consists, to a large extent, of immediate animal experiences. But the makers of imaginative literature have never forged an impersonal, uncontaminated language for the elucidation of immediate experiences. They're content to use the bare, unanalysed names of experiences as mere aids to their own and their reader's memory. Every direct intuition is *notus calor*, with the connotation of the words left open, so to speak, for each individual reader to supply according to the nature of his or her particular experiences in the past. Simple, but not exactly scientific. But then people don't read literature in order to understand; they read it because they want to re-live the feelings and sensations which they found exciting in the past. Art can be a lot of things; but in actual practice most of it is merely the mental equivalent of alcohol and cantharides.'

Mr. Propter looked down again at the close-set lines of Molinos's epistle. "*Oirá y leerá el hombre racional estas espirituales materias,*" he read out once more. "*Pero non llegerá a comprenderlas.*" He'll hear and read these things, but he won't succeed in understanding them. And he won't succeed,' said Mr. Propter, closing the file and handing it back to Jeremy, 'he won't succeed for one of two excellent reasons. Either he has never seen the giraffes in question, and so, being an *hombre racional*, knows quite well that there ain't no such animal. Or else he has had glimpses of the creatures, or has some other reason for believing in their existence, but can't understand what

the experts say about them; can't understand because of
the inadequacy of the language in which the fauna of the
spiritual world is ordinarily described. In other words,
he either hasn't had the immediate experience of eternity
and so has no reason to believe that eternity exists; or
else he *does* believe that eternity exists, but can't make head
or tail of the language in which it's talked about by those
who have had experience of it. Furthermore, when he
wants to talk about eternity himself—and he may wish
to do so, either in order to communicate his own experiences to others or to understand them better, from
the human point of view, himself—he finds himself on
the horns of a dilemma. For either he recognizes that the
existing language is unsuitable—in which case he has only
two rational choices: to say nothing at all, or to invent
a new and better technical language of his own, a calculus
of eternity, so to speak, a special algebra of spiritual experience—and if he does invent it, nobody who hasn't
learnt it will know what he's talking about. So much for
the first horn of the dilemma. The second horn is reserved for those who don't recognize the inadequacy of
the existing language; or else who do recognize it, but
are irrationally hopeful enough to take a chance with an
instrument which they know to be worthless. These
people will write in the existing language, and their writing will be, in consequence, more or less completely mis-
understood by most of their readers. Inevitably, because
the words they use don't correspond to the things they're
talking about. Most of them are words taken from the
language of everyday life. . . . But the language of everyday life refers almost exclusively to strictly human affairs.
What happens when you apply words derived from that
language to experiences on the plane of the spirit, the
plane of timeless experience? Obviously, you create a

misunderstanding; you say what you didn't mean to say.'

Pete interrupted him. 'I'd like an example, Mr. Propter,' he said.

'All right,' the other answered. 'Let's take the commonest word in all religious literature: "love." Love on the human level means—what? Practically everything from Mother to the Marquis de Sade.'

The name reminded Jeremy yet again of what had happened to the *Cent-Vingt Jours de Sodome*. Really it was too insufferable! the impudence of it . . . !

'We don't even make the simple Greek distinction between *erao* and *philo*, *eros* and *agape*. With us everything is just love, whether it's self-sacrificing or possessive, whether it's friendship or lust or homicidal lunacy. It's all just love,' he repeated. 'Idiotic word! Even on the human level it's hopelessly ambiguous. And when you begin using it in relation to experiences on the level of eternity—well, it's simply disastrous. "The love of God." "God's love for us." "The saint's love for his fellows." What does the word stand for in such phrases? And in what way is this related to what it stands for when it's applied to a young mother suckling her baby? or to Romeo climbing into Juliet's bedroom? or to Othello as he strangles Desdemona? or to the research worker who loves his science? or to the patriot who's ready to die for his country—to die and, in the meantime, to kill, steal, lie, swindle and torture for it? Is there really anything in common between what the word stands for in these contexts and what it stands for when one talks, let us say, of the Buddha's love for all sentient beings? Obviously, the answer is: No, there isn't. On the human level, the word stands for a great many different states of mind and ways of behaving. Dissimilar in many respects, but alike at least in this : they're all accompanied by emotional excitement and they all contain an element of craving. Whereas the most characteristic features of the enlightened person's experience are serenity and disinterestedness. In other words, the absence of excitement and the absence of craving.'

'"The absence of excitement and the absence of craving,"' Pete said to himself, while the image of Virginia in her yachting-cap, riding her pink scooter, kneeling in her shorts under the arch of the grotto, swam before his inward eye.

'Distinctions in fact ought to be represented by distinctions in language,' Mr. Propter was saying. 'If they're not, you can't expect to talk sense. In spite of which, we insist on using one word to connote entirely different things. "God is love," we say. The word's the same as the one we use when we talk about "being in love," or "loving one's children," or "being inspired by love of country." Consequently we tend to think that the thing we're talking about must be more or less the same. We imagine in a vague, reverential way, that God is composed of a kind of immensely magnified yearning.' Mr. Propter shook his head. 'Creating God in our own image. It flatters our vanity, and of course we prefer vanity to understanding. Hence those confusions of language. If we wanted to understand the word, if we wanted to think about it realistically, we should say that we were in love, but that God was x-love. In this way, people who had never had any first-hand experience on the level of eternity would at least be given a chance of knowing intellectually that what happens on that level is not the same as what happens on the strictly human level. They'd know, because they'd seen it in print, that there was some kind of difference between love and x-love.

Consequently, they'd have less excuse than people have to-day for imagining that God was like themselves, only a bit more so on the side of respectability and a bit less so, of course, on the other side. And, naturally, what applies to the word "love," applies to all the other words taken over from the language of everyday life and used to describe spiritual experience. Words like "knowledge," "wisdom," "power," "mind," "peace," "joy," "freedom," "good." They stand for certain things on the human level. But the things that writers force them to stand for when they describe events on the level of eternity are quite different. Hence the use of them merely confuses the issue. They just make it all but impossible for anyone to know what's being talked about. And, meanwhile, you must remember that these words from the language of everyday life aren't the only trouble-makers. People who write about experiences on the level of eternity also make use of technical phrases borrowed from various systems of philosophy.'

'Isn't that your algebra of spiritual experience?' said Pete. 'Isn't that the special, scientific language you've been talking about?'

'It's an attempt at such an algebra,' Mr. Propter answered. 'But, unfortunately, a very unsuccessful attempt. Unsuccessful because this particular algebra is derived from the language of metaphysics—bad metaphysics, incidentally. The people who use it are committing themselves, whether they like it or no, to an explanation of the facts as well as a description. An explanation of actual experiences in terms of metaphysical entities, whose existence is purely hypothetical and can't be demonstrated. In other words, they're describing the facts in terms of figments of the imagination; they're explaining the known in terms of the unknown. Take a few examples. Here's one: "ecstasy." It's a technical term that refers to the soul's ability to stand outside the body—and of course it carries the further implication that we know what the soul is and how it's related to the body and the rest of the universe. Or take another instance, a technical term that is essential to the Catholic theory of mysticism: "infused contemplation." Here the implication is that there's somebody outside us who pours a certain kind of psychological experience into our minds. The further implication is that we know who that somebody is. Or consider even "union with God." What it means depends on the upbringing of the speaker. It may mean "union with the Jehovah of the Old Testament." Or it may mean "union with the personal deity of orthodox Christianity." It may mean what it probably would have meant, say, to Eckhart, "union with the impersonal Godhead of which the God of orthodoxy is an aspect and a particular limitation." Similarly, if you were an Indian, it may mean "union with Isvara" or "union with Brahman." In every case, the term implies a previous knowledge about the nature of things which are either completely unknowable, or at best only to be inferred from the nature of the experiences which the term is supposed to describe. So there,' Mr. Propter concluded, 'you have the second horn of the dilemma—the horn on which all those who use the current religious vocabulary to describe their experiences on the level of eternity inevitably impale themselves.'

'And the way between the horns?' Jeremy questioned. 'Isn't it the way of the professional psychologists who have written about mysticism? They've evolved a pretty sensible language. You haven't mentioned them.'

'I haven't mentioned them,' said Mr. Propter, 'for the same reason as in talking about beauty I shouldn't mention professional aestheticians who had never been inside a picture gallery.'

'You mean, they don't know what they're talking about?'

Mr. Propter smiled. 'I'd put it another way,' he said. 'They talk about what they know. But what they know isn't worth talking about. For what they know is only the literature of mysticism—not the experience.'

'Then there's *no* way between the horns,' Jeremy concluded. His eyes twinkled behind his spectacles; he smiled like a child, taking a sly triumph in some small consummation of naughtiness. 'What fun it is when there isn't a way between!' he went on. 'It makes the world seem so deliciously cosy, when all the issues are barred and there's nowhere to go to with all your brass bands and shining armour. Onward, Christian soldiers! Forward, the Light Brigade! Excelsior! And all the time you're just going round and round—head to tail, follow-my-fuehrer—like Fabre's caterpillars. That really gives me a *great* deal of pleasure!'

This time Mr. Propter laughed outright. 'I'm sorry to have to disappoint you,' he said. 'But unfortunately there is a way between the horns. The practical way. You can go and find out what it means for yourself, by first-hand experience. Just as you can find out what El Greco's "Crucifixion of St. Peter" looks like by taking the elevator and going up to the hall. Only, in this case, I'm afraid, there isn't any elevator. You have to go up on your own legs. And make no mistakes,' he added, turning to Pete, 'there's an awful lot of stairs.'

Dr. Obispo straightened himself up, took the tubes of the stethoscope out of his ears and stowed the instrument away in his pocket along with the *Cent-Vingt Jours de Sodome.*

'Anything bad?' Mr. Stoyte asked anxiously.

Dr. Obispo shook his head and gave him a smile of reassurance. No influenza anyhow,' he said. 'Just a slight intensification of the bronchial condition. I'll give you something for it to-night before you go to bed.'

Mr. Stoyte's face relaxed into cheerfulness. 'Glad it was only a false alarm,' he said, and turned away to get his clothes, which were lying in a heap on the sofa, under the Watteau.

From her seat at the soda-counter, Virginia let out a whoop of triumph. 'Isn't that just swell!' she cried. Then, in another, graver tone: 'You know, Uncle Jo,' she added, 'he'd got me panicked about that cough of yours. Panicked,' she repeated.

Uncle Jo grinned triumphantly and slapped his chest so hard that its hairy, almost female accumulations of flesh shivered like jellies under the blow. Nothing wrong with *me*,' he boasted.

Virginia watched him over the top of her glass, as he got into his shirt and knotted his tie. The expression on her innocent young face was one of perfect serenity. But behind those limpid blue eyes her mind was simmering with activity. 'Was that a close call!' she kept saying to herself. 'Gee, was it close!' At the recollection of that sudden violent start at the sound of the elevator gate being opened, of that wild scramble as the footsteps approached along the corridor, she felt herself tingling with a delicious mixture of fear and amusement, of apprehension and triumph. It was the sensation she used to have as a child, playing hide-and-seek in the dark. A close call! And hadn't Sig been wonderful! What presence of mind! And that stethoscope thing he pulled out of his pocket—what a brain-wave! That had saved the situation. Because, without the stethoscope, Uncle Jo would have put on one of his jealousy acts. Though what right he had to be jealous, Virginia went on to reflect, with a strong sense of injury, she really didn't know. Seeing that nothing had happened except just a little reading aloud. And, anyhow, why shouldn't a girl be allowed to read that sort of thing if she wanted to? Especially as it was in French. And, besides, who was Uncle Jo to be prudish, she'd like to know? Getting mad with people only for telling you a funny story, when just look what he himself was *doing* all the time—and then expecting you to talk like Louisa M. Alcott, and thinking you ought to be protected from hearing so much as a dirty word! And the way he simply wouldn't allow her to tell the truth about herself, even if she had wanted to. Making a build-up of her as somebody quite different from what she really was. Acting almost as though she were Daisy Mae in the comic strip and he a sort of Little Abner rescuing her in the nick of time. Though, of course, she had to admit that it had happened at least once before he came along, because if it hadn't, there'd have been no excuse for *him*. It had happened, but quite un-willingly—you know, practically a rape—or else some fellow taking advantage of her being so dumb and innocent—at Congo Club with nothing on but a G-string and some talcum powder. And naturally she was always supposed to have hated it; crying her eyes out all the time until Uncle Jo came along; and then everything was different. But in that case, it now suddenly occurred to Virginia, if that was the way he thought about her, what the hell did he mean by coming home like this at seven-fifteen, when he'd told her he wouldn't be back till eight? The old double-crosser! Was he trying to spy on her? Because, if so, she wasn't going to stand for it; if so, then it just served him right that that was what Sig had been reading to her. He was just getting what he deserved for snooping around, trying to catch her doing something that wasn't right. Well, if *that* was how he was going to act, she'd tell Sig to come every day and read another chapter. Though how on earth the man who wrote the book was going to keep it up for a hundred and twenty days she really couldn't imagine. Considering what had happened already in the first week— and here was she, figuring that there wasn't anything she didn't know! Well, one lived and learned. Though there was some of it she really hadn't in the least wanted to learn. Things that made you feel sick to your stomach. Horrible! As bad as having babies! (She shuddered.) Not that there weren't a lot of funny things in the book too. The piece she had made Sig read over again—that was grand, that had given her a real kick. And that other bit where the girl . . .

'Well, Baby,' said Mr. Stoyte, as he did up the last button of his waistcoat. 'You're not saying much, are you? A penny for your thoughts.'

Virginia raised that childishly short upper lip in a smile that made his heart melt with tenderness and desire. 'I was thinking about you, Uncle Jo,' she said.

Chapter Thirteen

If thou appear untouch'd by solemn thought,
Thy nature is not therefore less divine;
Thou liest in Abraham's bosom all the year;
And worship'st at the Temple's inner shrine,
God being with thee when we know it not.

'AND very nice too,' Jeremy said aloud. *Transparent* was the word, he reflected. The meaning was there like a fly in amber. Or, rather, there was no fly; there was only the amber; and the amber was the meaning. He looked at his watch. Three minutes to midnight. He closed his Wordsworth—and to think, he went on bitterly to remind himself, to think that he might have been refreshing his memory of *Félicia*!—laid the volume down on the table beside his bed and took off his glasses. Deprived of their six and a half diopters of correction, his eyes were instantly reduced to a state of physiological despair. Curved crystal had become their element; unspectacled, they were like a pair of jellied sea-creatures suddenly taken out of water. Then the light went out; and it was as though the poor things had been mercifully dropped, for safe keeping, into an aquarium.

Jeremy stretched under the bedclothes and yawned. What a day! But now, thank God, the paradise of bed. The Blessed Damozel leaned out from the gold bed of heaven. But these sheets were cotton ones, not linen; which was really a bit discreditable in a house like this! A house full of Rubenses and Grecos—and your sheets were cotton! But that 'Crucifixion of St. Peter'—what a really staggering machine! At least as good as the

'Assumption' at Toledo. Which had probably been blown up by this time, incidentally. Just to demonstrate what happened when people took things too seriously. Not but that, he went on to reflect, there wasn't something rather impressive about that old Propter-Object. (For that was what he had decided to call the man in his own mind and when he wrote to his mother : the Propter-Object.) A bit of an Ancient Mariner, perhaps. The wedding guest, he beat his breast on occasions; ought perhaps to have beaten it more often than he had done, seeing what a frightful subversion of all the common decencies and, *a fortioro*, the common indecencies (such as *Félicia*, such as every other Friday afternoon in Maida Vale) the creature was inculcating. Not without a considerable persuasiveness, damn his glittering eyes! For this particular Mariner not only held you with that eye of his; he was also and simultaneously the loud bassoon you wanted to hear. One listened without reluctance—though, of course, one had no intention of permitting one's own particular little structures of decencies and indecencies to be subverted. One was not going to allow religion (of all things!) to invade the sanctities of private life. An Englishman's home is his castle; and, curiously enough, an American's castle, as he had discovered after the first shock began to wear off, was turning out to be this particular Englishman's home. His spiritual home. Because it was the embodiment of an imbecile's no-track mind. Because there were no issues and nothing led anywhere and the dilemmas had an infinity of horns and you went round and round, like Fabre's caterpillars, in a closed universe of utter cosiness—round and round among the Hauberk Papers, from St. Peter to La Petite Morphil to Giambologna to the gilded Bodhisattvas in the cellar to the baboons to the Marquis de Sade to St. François de

Sales to Félicia and round again in due course to St. Peter. Round and round, like caterpillars inside the mind of an imbecile; round and round in an infinite cosiness of issueless thoughts and feelings and actions, of hermetically bottled art and learning, of culture for its own sake, of self-sufficient little decencies and indecencies, of impassable dilemmas and moral questions sufficiently answered by the circumambient idiocy.

Round and round, round and round, from Peter's feet to Morphil's little buttocks to the baboon's, from the beautiful Chinese spiral of the folds in the Buddha's robe to the humming-bird drinking in mid-air to Peter's feet again with the nails in them . . . His drowsiness darkened into sleep.

In another room on the same floor of the donjon Pete Boone was not even trying to get to sleep; he was trying, on the contrary, to figure things out. To figure out science and Mr. Propter, social justice and eternity and Virginia and anti-fascism. It wasn't easy. Because, if Mr. Propter was right, then you'd have to start thinking quite differently about almost everything. 'Disinterested quest for truth'—that was what you said (if you were ever forced to say anything so embarrassing about why you were a biologist). And in the case of socialism it was 'humanity,' it was 'the greatest happiness of the greatest number,' it was 'progress'—and, of course, that linked up with biology again: happiness and progress through science as well as socialism. And while happiness and progress were on the way there was loyalty to the cause. He remembered a piece about loyalty by Josiah Royce, a piece he had had to read in his sophomore year at college. Something about all loyal people grasping in their own way some form of religious truth—winning some kind of genuine religious insight. It had made a big impression on him at the time. He had just lost his faith in that old Blood-of-the-Lamb business he'd been brought up in, and this had come as a kind of re-assurance, had made him feel that, after all, he *was* re-ligious even if he didn't go to church any more—religious because he was loyal. Loyal to causes, loyal to friends. He had been religious, it had always seemed to him, over there in Spain. Religious, again, when he felt that way about Virginia. And yet, if Mr. Propter was right, old Royce's ideas about loyalty were all wrong. Being loyal didn't of itself give you religious insight. On the con-trary, it might prevent you from having insight—indeed, was absolutely certain to prevent you, if you gave your loyalty to anything less than the highest cause of all; and the highest cause of all (if Mr. Propter was right) was almost terrible in its farness and strangeness. Almost terrible; and yet the more he thought about it, the more dubious he felt about everything else. Perhaps it really was the highest. But if it was, then socialism wasn't enough. And it wasn't enough, because humanity wasn't enough. Because the greatest happiness didn't happen to be in the place where people had thought it was, because you couldn't make it come by doing things in the sort of fields you worked in if you were a social reformer. The best you could do in those fields was to make it easier for people to go on to where the greatest happiness could be had. And, of course, what applied to socialism would apply to biology or any other science, if you thought of it as a means to progress. Because, if Mr. Propter was right, then what people called progress wasn't progress. That is, it wouldn't be progress unless it had made it easier for people to go on to where the greatest happiness actually was. Easier, in other words, to be loyal to the highest cause of all. And, obviously, if that was your standard, you had to think twice about using progress as a justification for science. And then there was that disinterested quest for truth. But again, if Mr. Propter was right, biology and the rest were the disinterested quest for only one aspect of truth. But a half-truth was a falsehood, and it remained a falsehood even when you'd told it in the belief that it was the whole truth. So it looked as though *that* justification wouldn't do either— or at any rate as though it wouldn't do unless you were at the same time disinterestedly trying to discover the other aspect of truth, the aspect you were looking for when you gave your loyalty to the highest cause of all. And meanwhile what about Virginia, he asked himself in mounting anguish, what about Virginia? For, if Mr. Propter were right, then even Virginia wasn't enough, even Virginia might actually be an obstacle to prevent him from giving his loyalty to the highest cause of all. Even those eyes and her innocence and that utterly adorable mouth; even what he felt about her; even love itself, even the best kind of love (for he could honestly say that he hated the other kind—that dreadful brothel in Barcelona, for example, and here, at home, those huggings after the third or fourth cocktail, those gropings by the roadside in a parked car)—yes, even the best kind of love might be inadequate, might actually be worse than inadequate. 'I could not love thee, dear, so much, loved I not something or other more.' Hitherto, something or other had been his biology, his socialism. But now these had turned out to be inadequate, or even, taken as ends in themselves, worse than inadequate. No loyalty was good in itself, or brought religious insight except loyalty to the highest cause of all. 'I could not love thee, dear, so much, loved I not the highest cause of all more.' But the question, the agonizing question, was this : Could you love the highest cause of all and go on feeling as you did about Virginia ? The worst love was obviously incompatible with loyalty to the highest cause of all. Obviously so ; because the worst love was just being loyal to your own physiology, whereas, if Mr. Propter was right, you couldn't be loyal to the highest cause of all without denying such loyalties to yourself. But was the best love so fundamentally different, after all, from the worst ? The worst was being loyal to your physiology. It was hateful to admit it ; but so too was the best : being loyal to your physiology and at the same time (which was its distinguishing mark) loyal also to your higher feelings—to that empty ache of longing, to that infinity of tenderness, to that adoration, that happiness, those pains, that sense of solitude, that longing for identity. You were loyal to these, and being loyal to these was the definition of the best kind of love, of what people called romance and praised as the most wonderful thing in life. But being loyal to these was being loyal to yourself ; and you couldn't be loyal to yourself and loyal at the same time to the highest cause of all. The practical conclusion was obvious. But Pete refused to draw it. Those eyes were blue and limpid, that mouth adorable in its innocence. And then, how sweet she was, how beautifully thoughtful ! He remembered the conversation they had had on the way into dinner. He had asked her how her headache was. 'Don't talk about it,' she had whispered ; 'it might upset Uncle Jo. Doc's been going over him with his stethoscope ; doesn't think he's so good this evening. I don't want to have him worrying about *me*. And anyhow, what is a headache ?' Not only beautiful, not only innocent and sweet, but brave too, and unselfish. And how adorable she had been to him all the evening, asking him about his work, telling him about her home in Oregon, making him talk about his home down in El Paso. In the end, Mr. Stoyte had come and sat down beside them—in silence, and his face black as thunder. Pete had glanced enquiringly at Virginia, and she had given him a look that said, 'Please go,' and another when he rose to say good-night, so pleadingly apologetic, so full of gratitude, so understanding, so sweet and affectionate, that the recollection of it was enough to bring the tears into his eyes. Lying there in the darkness, he cried with happiness.

That niche in the wall between the windows in Virginia's bedroom had been intended, no doubt, for a bookshelf. But Virginia was not very keen on books; the recess had been fitted up, instead, as a little shrine. You drew back a pair of short white velvet curtains (everything in the room was white), and there, in a bower of artificial flowers, dressed in real silk clothes, with the cutest little gold crown on her head and six strings of seed pearls round her neck, stood Our Lady, brilliantly illuminated by an ingenious system of concealed electric bulbs. Barefooted and in white satin pyjamas, Virginia was kneeling before this sacred doll's house, saying her evening prayers. Our Lady, it seemed to her, was looking particularly sweet and kind to-night. To-morrow, she decided, while her lips pronounced the formulas of praise and supplications, to-morrow morning, first thing, she'd go right down to the sewing-room and get one of the girls to help her make a new mantle for Our Lady out of that lovely piece of blue brocade she had bought last week at the junk shop in Glendale. A blue brocade mantle, fastened in front with a gold button—or, better still, with a little gold cord that you could tie in a bow, with the ends hanging down, almost to Our Lady's feet. Oh, that would be just gorgeous! She wished it were morning so that she could start right away.

The last prayer had been said; Virginia crossed herself and rose from her knees. Happening to look down as she did so, she saw to her horror that some of the cyclamen-coloured varnish had scaled off the nails of the second and third toes of her left foot. A minute later she was squatting on the floor beside the bed, the right leg outstretched, the other foot drawn across it, making ready to repair the damage. An open bottle stood beside her; she held a small paint-brush in her hand, and a horribly industrial aura of acetone had enveloped the Schiaparelli 'Shocking' with which her body was impregnated. She started to work, and as she bent forward, two strands of auburn hair broke loose from their curly pattern and fell across her forehead. Under frowning brows, the large blue eyes intently stared. To aid concentration, the tip of a pink tongue was held between the teeth. 'Hell!' she suddenly said aloud, as the little brush made a false stroke. Then, immediately, the teeth clamped down again.

Interrupting her work to allow the first coat of varnish to dry, she shifted her scrutiny from the toes to the calf and shin of her left leg. The hairs were beginning to grow again, she noticed with annoyance; it would soon be time for another of those wax treatments. Still pensively caressing the leg, she let her mind travel back over the events of the day. The memory of that close call with Uncle Jo still gave her shivers of apprehensive excitement. Then she thought of Sig with his stethoscope, and the upper lip lifted ravishingly in a smile of amusement. And then there was that book, which it served Uncle Jo right that she should have had Sig read to her. And Sig getting fresh with her between the chapters and making passes: that also served Uncle Jo right for trying to spy on her.

She remembered how mad she had got at Sig. Not so
much for what he actually did; for besides serving Uncle
Jo right (of course it was only *afterwards* that she discovered quite how right it served him), what he actually
did had been rather thrilling than otherwise; because,
after all, Sig was terribly attractive and in those ways
Uncle Jo didn't hardly count—in fact, you might almost
say that he counted the other way; in the red, so to
speak; counted less than nobody, so that anybody else
who *was* attractive seemed still more attractive when
Uncle Jo had been around. No, it wasn't what he
actually did that had made her mad at him. It was the
way he did it. Laughing at her, like that. She didn't
mind a bit of kidding at ordinary times. But kidding
while he was actually making passes—that was treating
her like she was a tart on Main Street. No romance, or
anything; just that sniggering sort of laugh and a lot of
dirty cracks. Maybe it was sophisticated; but she didn't
like it. And didn't he see that it was just plain dumb to
act that way? Because, after all, when you'd been reading that book with someone so attractive as Sig—well,
you felt you'd like a bit of romance. Real romance, like
in the pictures, with moonlight, and swing music, or
perhaps a torch singer (because it was nice to feel sad
when you were happy), and a boy saying lovely things
to you, and a lot of kissing, and at the end of it, almost
without your knowing it, almost as if it weren't happening to you, so that you never felt there was anything
wrong, anything that Our Lady would really mind . . .
Virginia sighed deeply and shut her eyes; her face took
on an expression of seraphic tranquillity. Then she
sighed again, shook her head and frowned. Instead of
that, she was thinking angrily, instead of that, Sig had
to go and spoil it all by acting hard-boiled and sophisti-

cated. It just shot all the romance to pieces and made you feel mad at him. And what was the sense in that? Virginia concluded resentfully. What was the sense in that, either from his point of view or from hers?

The first coat of varnish seemed to be dry. Bending over her foot, she blew on her toes for a little, then started to apply the second coat. Behind her, all of a sudden, the door of the bedroom was opened and as gently closed again.

'Uncle Jo?' she said enquiringly and with a note of surprise in her voice, but without looking up from her enamelling.

There was no answer, only the sound of an approach across the room.

'Uncle Jo?' she repeated and, this time, interrupted the painting of her toes to turn round.

Dr. Obispo was standing over her. 'Sig!' Her voice dropped to a whisper. 'What *are* you doing?'

Dr. Obispo smiled his smile of ironic admiration, of intense and at the same time amused and mocking concupiscence. 'I thought we might go on with our French lesson,' he said.

'You're crazy!' She looked apprehensively towards the door. 'He's just across the hall. He might come in. . . .'

Dr. Obispo's smile broadened to a grin. 'Don't worry about Uncle Jo,' he said.

'He'd kill you if he found you here.'

'He won't find me here,' Dr. Obispo answered. 'I gave him a capsule of Nembutal before he went to bed. He'll sleep through the Last Trump.'

'I think you're awful!' said Virginia emphatically; but she couldn't help laughing, partly out of relief and partly because it really was rather funny to think of Uncle Jo snoring away next door while Sig read her that stuff.

Dr. Obispo pulled the Book of Common Prayer out of his pocket. 'Don't let me interrupt your labours,' he said with the parody of chivalrous politeness. '"A woman's work is never done." Just go on as though I weren't there. I'll find the place and start reading.' Smiling at her with imperturbable impudence, he sat down on the edge of the rococo bed and turned over the pages of the book.

Virginia opened her mouth to speak; then, catching hold of her left foot, closed it again under the compulsion of a need even more urgent than that of telling him exactly where he got off. The varnish was drying in lumps; her toes would look just awful if she didn't go on with them at once. Hastily dipping her little brush in the bottle of acetone enamel, she started painting again with the focussed intensity of a Van Eyck at work on the microscopic details of the 'Adoration of the Lamb.'

Dr. Obispo looked up from the book. 'I admired the way you acted with Pete this evening,' he said. 'Flirting with him all through dinner, so that you got the old man hopping jealous of him. That was masterly. Or should one say mistressly?'

Virginia released her tongue to say emphatically, 'Pete's a nice boy.'

'But dumb,' Dr. Obispo qualified, as he sprawled with conscious elegance and a maddeningly insolent assumption of being at home across the bed.

'Otherwise he wouldn't be in love with you the way he is.' He uttered a snort of laughter. 'The poor chump thinks you're an angel, a heavenly little angel, complete with wings, harp and genuine eighteen-carat, fully jewelled, Swiss-made virginity. Well, if that isn't being dumb . . .'

'You just wait till I get time for you,' said Virginia

menacingly, but without looking up; for she had reached a critical phase in the execution of her work of art.

Dr. Obispo ignored the remark. 'I used to underestimate the value of an education in the humanities,' he said after a little silence. 'Now, I make that mistake no longer.' In a tone of deep solemnity, a tone, one might imagine, like Whittier's in a reading from his own works. 'The lessons of great literature!' he went on. 'The deep truths! The gems of wisdom!'

'Oh, shut up!' said Virginia.

'When I think what I owe Dante and Goethe,' said Dr. Obispo in the same prophetic style. 'Take the case of Paolo reading aloud to Francesca. With the most fruitful results, if you remember. "*Noi leggevamo un giorno, per diletto, di Lancilotto, come amor lo strinse. Soli eravamo e senz' alcun sospetto. Senz' alcun sospetto,*"' Dr. Obispo repeated with emphasis, looking, as he did so, at one of the engravings in the *Cent-Vingt Jours*. 'Not the smallest suspicion, mark you, of what was going to happen.'

'Hell!' said Virginia, who had made another slip.

'No, not even a suspicion of hell,' Dr. Obispo insisted. 'Though, of course, they ought to have been on the lookout for it. They ought to have had the elementary prudence to guard against being sent there by the accident of sudden death. A few simple precautions, and they could have made the best of both worlds. Could have had their fun while the brother was out of the way and, when the time for having fun was over, could have repented and died in the odour of sanctity. But then it must be admitted that they hadn't the advantage of reading Goethe's *Faust*. They hadn't learnt that inconvenient relatives could be given sleeping-draughts. And even if they had learnt, they wouldn't have been able to go to the drug-store and buy a bottle of Nembutal. Which shows that education in the humanities isn't enough; there must also be education in science. Dante and Goethe to teach you what to do. And the professor of pharmacology to show you how to put the old buzzard into a coma with a pinch of barbiturate.'

The toes were finished. Still holding her left foot, so as to keep it from any damaging contact until the varnish should be entirely dry, Virginia turned on her visitor. 'I won't have you calling him an old buzzard,' she said hotly.

'Well, shall we say "bastard"?' Dr. Obispo suggested.

'He's a better man than you'll ever be!' Virginia cried; and her voice had the ring of sincerity. 'I think he's wonderful.'

'You think he's wonderful,' Dr. Obispo repeated. 'But all the same, in about fifteen minutes you'll be sleeping with me.' He laughed as he spoke and, leaning forward from his place on the bed, caught her two arms from behind, a little below the shoulders. 'Look out for your toes,' he said, as Virginia cried out and tried to wrench herself away from him.

The fear of ruining her masterpiece made her check the movement before it was more than barely initiated. Dr. Obispo took advantage of her hesitation to stoop down, through the aura of acetone towards the nape of that delicious neck, towards the perfume of 'Shocking,' towards a firm warmth against the mouth, a touch of hair like silk upon the cheeks. Swearing, Virginia furiously jerked her head away. But a fine tingling of agreeable sensation was running parallel, so to speak, with her indignation, was incorporating itself in it.

This time, Dr. Obispo kissed her behind the ear. 'Shall I tell you,' he whispered, 'what I'm going to do to you?' She answered by calling him a lousy ape-man. But he told her all the same, in considerable detail.

Less than fifteen minutes had elapsed when Virginia opened her eyes and, across the now darkened room, caught sight of Our Lady smiling benignantly from among the flowers of her illuminated doll's house. With a cry of dismay she jumped up and, without waiting to put on any clothes, ran to the shrine and drew the curtains. The lights went out automatically. Stretching out her hands in the thick darkness, she groped her way cautiously back to bed.

PART TWO

Chapter One

'AGAIN, no dearth of news,' Jeremy wrote to his mother three weeks later. 'News of every kind and from all the centuries. Here's a bit of news, to begin with, about the Second Earl. In the intervals of losing battles for Charles I, the Second Earl was a poet. A bad poet, of course (for the chances are always several thousands to one against any given poet being good), but with occasional involuntary deviations into charm. What about this, for example, which I found in manuscript only yesterday?

> One taper burns, but 'tis too much ;
> Our loves demand complete eclipse.
> Let sight give place to amorous touch,
> And candle-light to limbs and lips !

Rather pretty, don't you think? But, alas, almost the only nugget so far unearthed from the alluvium. If only the rest were silence! But that's the trouble with poets, good no less than bad. They will not keep their traps shut, as we say in the Western hemisphere. What joy if the rest of Wordsworth had been silence, the rest of Coleridge, the rest of Shelley!

'Meanwhile, the Fifth Earl sprang a surprise on me yesterday in the form of a notebook full of miscellaneous jottings. I have only just started on them (for I mustn't spend all my time on any one item till I have the whole collection unpacked and roughly catalogued); but the fragments I've read are decidedly appetizing. I found this on the first page: "Lord Chesterfield writes to his

Son that a Gentleman never speaks to his footman, nor even the beggar in the street, *d'un ton brusque*, but 'corrects the one coolly and refuses the other with humanity. . . .' His lordship should have added that there is an Art by which such coolness may be rendered no less formidable than Anger and such humanity more wounding than Insult.

'"Furthermore, footmen and beggars are not the only objects on whom this Art may be exercised. His lordship has been ungallant enough in this instance to forget the Sex, for there is also an Art of coolly outraging a devoted female, and of abusing her Person, with all the *bienséance* befitting the most accomplished Gentleman."

'Not a bad beginning! I will keep you posted of any subsequent discoveries in this field.

'Meanwhile, contemporary news is odd, confused and a bit disagreeable. To begin with, Uncle Jo is chronically glum and ill-tempered these days. I suspect the green-eyed monster; for the blue-eyed monster (in other words, Miss Maunciple, the Baby) has been rolling them, for some time now, in the direction of young Pete. Whether she rolls more than the eyes, I don't know; but suspect the fact; for she has that inward, dreamy look, that far-away sleep-walker's expression, which one often remarks on the faces of young ladies who have been doing a lot of strenuous love-making. You know the expression I mean: exquisitely spiritual and pre-Raphaelitish. One has only to look at such a face to *know* that God Exists. The one incongruous feature in the present instance is the costume. A pre-Raphaelite expression demands pre-Raphaelite clothes: long sleeves, square yokes, yards and yards of Liberty velveteen. When you see it, as I did to-day, in combination with white shorts, a bandana and a cowboy hat, you're disturbed, you're all put out.

Meanwhile, in defence of Baby's Honour, I must insist that all this is mere hypothesis and guess-work. It may be, of course, that this new, spiritual expression of hers is not the result of amorous fatigue. For all I know to the contrary, Baby may have been converted by the teachings of the Propter-Object and is now walking about in a state of perpetual *samadhi*. On the other hand, I *do* see her giving the glad eye to Pete. What's more, Uncle Jo exhibits all the symptoms of being suspicious of them and extremely cross with everybody else. With me among others, of course. Perhaps even more with me than with others, because I happen to have read more books than the rest and am therefore more of a symbol of Culture. And Culture, of course, is a thing for which he has positively a Tartar's hatred. Only, unlike the Tartars, he doesn't want to burn the monuments of Culture, he wants to buy them up. He expresses his superiority to talent and education by means of possession rather than destruction; by hiring and then insulting the talented and educated rather than by killing them. (Though perhaps he would kill them if he had the Tartar's opportunities and power.) All this means that, when I am not in bed or safely underground with the Hauberks, I spend most of my time grinning and bearing, thinking of Jelly-Belly and my nice salary, in order not to think too much of Uncle Jo's bad manners. It's all very unpleasant; but fortunately not unbearable—and the Hauberks are an immense consolation and compensation.

'So much for the erotic and cultural fronts. On the scientific front, the news is that we're all perceptibly nearer to living as long as crocodiles. At the time of writing, I haven't decided whether I really want to live as long as a crocodile.' (With the penning of the second 'crocodile,' Jeremy was seized by a sudden qualm. His mother would be seventy-seven in August. Under that urbanity of hers, under the crackled glaze of the admirable conversation, there was a passionate greed for life. She would talk matter-of-factly enough about her own approaching extinction; she would make little jokes about her death and funeral. But behind the talk and the little jokes there lurked, as Jeremy knew, a fierce determination to hold on to what was left, to go on doing what she had always done, in the teeth of death, in defiance of old age. This talk of crocodiles might give pain; this expression of doubt as to the desirability of prolonging life might be interpreted as an unfavourable criticism. Jeremy took a new sheet of paper and started the paragraph afresh.)

'So much for the erotic and cultural fronts,' he wrote. 'On the scientific front, *rien de nouveau*, except that the Obispo is being more bumptious than ever; which isn't news, because he's always more bumptious than ever. Not one of my favourite characters, I'm afraid: though not unamusing when one feels inclined for a few moments of ribaldry. Longevity, it appears, is making headway. Old Parr and the Countess of Desmond are on the march.

'And what of the religious front? Well, our Propter-Object has given up his attempts at edification, at any rate so far as I'm concerned. Thank heaven! for when he dismounts from his hobby-horse, what excellent company he is! A mind full of all kinds of oddments; and the oddments are pigeon-holed in apple-pie order. One rather envies him his intellectual coherence; but consoles oneself by thinking that, if one had them, they'd spoil one's own particular little trick. When one has a gift for standing gracefully on one's head, one is foolish and ungrateful to envy the Marathon-runner. A funny little literary article in the hand is worth at least three Critiques of Pure Reason in the bush.

'My final item is from the home front and refers to your last letter from Grasse. What a feast! Your account of Mme de Villemomble was really Proustian. And as for the description of your drive to Cap d'Ail and your day with what remains of the Princess and *ce pauvre Hunyadi*—well, all I can say is that it was worthy of Murasaki: the essence of all tragedy refined to a couple of tablespoonfuls of amber-coloured tea in a porcelain cup no bigger than a magnolia flower. What an admirable lesson in the art of literary chastity! My own tendencies—only in the world of letters, I am thankful to say—are towards a certain exhibitionism. This vestal prose of yours puts me to shame.

'Well, there is nothing more to say, as I used to write when I was at school—very large, do you remember? in an effort to make the words fill up half a page of notepaper. There is nothing more to say, except, of course, the unsayable, which I leave unsaid because you know it already.'

Jeremy sealed up his letter, addressed it—to The Araucarias, for his mother would be back from Grasse by the time it had crossed the Atlantic—and slipped the envelope into his pocket. All around him the Hauberk Papers clamoured for his attention; but for some time he remained idle. His elbow on the desk, in an attitude of prayer, he meditatively scratched his head; scratched it with both hands where little spots had formed the dry scabs at the roots of the hair that still remained to him, scabs which it was an exquisite pleasure to prise up with the finger-nails and carefully detach. He was thinking of his mother and how curious it was, after all, that one should have read all the Freudian literature about the

Oedipus business, all the novels, from *Sons and Lovers* downwards, about the dangers of too much filial devotion, the menace of excessive maternal love—that one should have read them all, and still, with one's eyes open, go on being what one was: the victim of a greedy, possessive mother. And perhaps even odder was the fact that this possessive mother had also read all the relevant literature and was also perfectly aware of what she was and what she had done to her son. And yet she too went on being and doing what she had always been and done, just as he did, and with eyes no less open than his own. (There! the scab under the right hand had come loose. He pulled it out through the thick tufted hair above his ears and, as he looked at the tiny desiccated shred of tissue, was suddenly reminded of the baboons. But, after all, why not? The most certain and abiding pleasures are the tiniest, the simplest, the rudimentarily animal— the pleasure of lying in a hot bath, for example, or under the bedclothes, between waking and sleeping, in the morning; the pleasure of answering the calls of nature, the pleasure of being rubbed by a good masseur, the pleasure finally of scratching when one itched. Why be ashamed? He dropped the scab into the waste-paper basket and continued to scratch with the left hand.)

Nothing like self-knowledge, he reflected. To know why you do a thing that is wrong or stupid is to have an excuse for going on doing it. Justification by psychoanalysis—the modern substitute for justification by faith. You know the distant causes which made you a sadist or a money-grubber, a mother-worshipper or a son-cannibal; therefore you are completely justified in continuing to be a son-cannibal, mother-worshipper, money-grubber or sadist. No wonder if whole generations had risen up to bless the name of Freud! Well, that was how he and his mother managed things. 'We blood-sucking matriarchs!' Mrs. Pordage used to say of herself—in the presence of the Rector, what was more. Or else it was into Lady Fredegond's ear-trumpet that she proclaimed her innocence. 'Old Jocastas like me, with a middle-aged son in the house,' she would shout. And Jeremy would play up to her by coming across the room and bellowing into that tomb of intelligent conversation some feeble waggery about his being an old maid, for example, or about erudition as a substitute for embroidery; any rot would do. And the old harridan would utter that deep gangster's laugh of hers and wag her head till the stuffed sea-gulls, or the artificial petunias, or whatever it was that she happened to be wearing in her always extra-ordinary hat, nodded like the plumes of a horse in a French *pompe funèbre* of the first class. Yes, how curious it was, he said to himself again; but how sensible, con-sidering that they both, his mother and he, desired nothing better than to go on being just what they were. Her reasons for wanting to go on being a matriarch were ob-vious enough; it's fun to be a queen, it's delightful to receive homage and have a faithful subject. Less obvious, perhaps, at any rate to an outsider, were his own reasons for preferring the *status quo*. But, looked into, they turned out to be cogent enough. There was affection to begin with; for, under a certain superficial irony and airiness, he was deeply attached to his mother. Then there was habit—habit so long standing that his mother had come to be for him almost like an organ of his own body, hardly less dispensable than his pancreas or his liver. There was even a feeling of gratitude towards her for having done to him the things which, at the time she did them, had seemed the most cruelly unjustifiable. He had fallen in love when he was thirty; he had wanted to marry. Without making a single scene, without being anything but sympathetically loving towards himself and charming in all her dealings with dear little Eileen, Mrs. Pordage had set to work to undermine the relationship between the two young people; and had succeeded so well that, in the end, the relationship just fell in on itself, like a house sapped from beneath. He had been very unhappy at the time, and with a part of himself he had hated his mother for what she had done. But as the years passed he had felt less and less bitterly about the whole business, until now he was positively grateful to her for having delivered him from the horrors of responsibility, of a family, of regular and remunerative labour, of a wife who would probably have turned out to be a worse tyrant than his mother—indeed, who would certainly have turned out to be a worse tyrant; for the bulging, bustling matron into whom Eileen had by degrees transformed herself was one of the most disastrous females of his acquaintance: a creature passionately conventional, proud of her obtuseness, ant-like in her efficiency, tyrannically benevolent. In short, a monster. But for his mother's strategy he would now be the unfortunate Mr. Welkin who was Eileen's husband and the father of no less than four little Welkins as dreadful even in childhood and adolescence as Eileen had become in her middle age. His mother was doubtless speaking the truth when she jokingly called herself an old Jocasta, a blood-sucking matriarch; and doubtless, too, his brother Tom was right when he called him, Jeremy, a Peter Pan, and talked contemptuously of apron-strings. But the fact remained that he had had the opportunity to read what he liked and write his little articles; and that his mother saw to all the practical aspects of life, demanded in return an amount of devotion which it really wasn't very difficult to give, and left him free, on alternate Friday afternoons, to savour the refined pleasures of an infinite squalor in Maida Vale. Meanwhile, look what had happened to poor Tom! Second Secretary at Tokyo; First Secretary at Oslo; Counsellor at La Paz; and now back, more or less for good, in the Foreign Office, climbing slowly up the hierarchy, towards posts of greater responsibility and tasks of increasing turpitude. And as the salary rose and the morality of what he was called upon to do correspondingly sank, the poor fellow's uneasiness had increased, until at last, with the row over Abyssinia, he just hadn't been able to stand it any longer. On the brink of resignation or a nervous breakdown, he had managed, in the nick of time, to get himself converted to Catholicism. Thenceforward, he had been able to pack up the moral responsibility for his share in the general iniquity, take it to Farm Street and leave it there, in camphor, so to speak, with the Jesuit Fathers. Admirable arrangement! It had made a new man of him. After fourteen years of childlessness, his wife had suddenly had a baby—conceived, Jeremy had calculated, on the very night that the Spanish civil war began. Then, two days after the sack of Nanking, Tom had published a volume of comic verses. (Curious how many English Catholics take to comic versifying.) Meanwhile, he was steadily gaining weight; between the *Anschluss* and Munich he had put on eleven pounds. Another year or two of Farm Street and power-politics, and Tom would turn the scale at fourteen stone and have written the libretto of a musical comedy. No! Jeremy said to himself with decision. No! it simply wasn't admissible. Better Peter Pan and apron-strings and infinite squalor in a little room. Better a thousand times. Better to begin with, aesthetically; for this getting fat on *Realpolitik*, this scribbling of comic verses on the margins of an engraving of the Crucifixion—really, it was too inelegant. And that wasn't all: it was better even ethically; for, of course, the old Propter-Object was right: if you can't be sure of doing positive good, at least keep out of mischief. And there was poor old Tom, as busy as a beaver and, now that he was a Papist, as happy as a lark, working away at the precise spot where he could do the maximum amount of harm to the greatest possible number of people.

(The other scab came loose. Jeremy sighed and leaned back in his chair.)

One scratched like a baboon, he concluded; one lived, at fifty-four, in the security of one's mother's shadow; one's sexual life was simultaneously infantile and corrupt; by no stretch of the imagination could one's work be described as useful or important. But when one compared oneself with other people, with Tom, for example, or even with the eminent and august, with cabinet ministers and steel-magnates and bishops and celebrated novelists—well, really, one didn't come out so badly after all. Judged by the negative criterion of harmlessness, one even came out extremely well. So that, taking all things into consideration, there was really no reason why one should do anything much about anything. Having decided which, it was time to get back to the Hauberks.

Chapter Two

VIRGINIA did not wake up that morning till nearly ten; and even after having had her bath and eaten her breakfast she remained in bed for another hour or more, her eyes closed, leaning back motionless against the heaped-up pillows, like a beautiful young convalescent newly emerged from the valley of the shadow.

The valley of the shadow of death; of the greater deaths and all the little deaths. Through deaths come transfigurations. He who would save his life must lose it. Men and women are continually trying to lose their lives, the stale, unprofitable, senseless lives of their ordinary personalities. For ever trying to get rid of them, and in a thousand different ways. In the frenzies of gambling and revivalism; in the monomanias of avarice and perversion, of research and sectarianism and ambition; in the compensatory lunacies of alcohol, of reading, of daydreaming, of morphia; in the hallucinations of opium and the cinema and ritual; in the wild epilepsies of political enthusiasm and erotic pleasure; in the stupors of veronal and exhaustion. To escape; to forget one's own, old, wearisome identity; to become someone else or, better, some other *thing*—a mere body, strangely numbed or more than ordinarily sentient; or else just a state of impersonal mind, a mode of unindividualized consciousness. What happiness, what a blissful alleviation! Even for such as were not previously aware that there was anything in their condition that needed to be alleviated. Virginia had been one of those, happy in limitation, not sufficiently conscious of her personal self to realize its ugliness and inadequacy, or the fundamental wretchedness of the human state. And yet, when Dr. Obispo had scientifically engineered her escape into an erotic epilepsy more excruciatingly intense than anything she had known before or even imagined possible, Virginia had realized that, after all, there was something in her existence that required alleviating, and that this headlong plunge through an intenser, utterly alien consciousness into the darkness of a total oblivion was precisely the alleviation it required.

But, like all the other addictions, whether to drugs or books, to power or applause, the addiction to pleasure tends to aggravate the condition it temporarily alleviates. The addict goes down into the valley of the shadow of his own particular little death—down indefatigably, desperately down in search of something else, something not himself, something other and better than the life he miserably lives as a human person in the hideous world of human persons. He goes down and, either violently or in delicious inertia, he dies and is transfigured; but dies only for a little while, is transfigured only momentarily. After the little death is a little resurrection, a resurrection out of unconsciousness, out of self-annihilating excitement, back into the misery of knowing oneself alone and weak and worthless, back into a completer separateness, an acuter sense of personality. And the acuter the sense of separate personality, the more urgent the demand for yet another experience of assuaging death and transfiguration. The addiction alleviates, but in doing so increases the pains demanding alleviation.

Lying there, propped up against her pillows, Virginia was suffering her daily resurrection from the valley of the shadow of her nocturnal deaths. From having been epileptically something else, she was becoming her own self again—a self, it was true, still somewhat numbed and bewildered by fatigue, still haunted by the memory of strange scenes and overpowering sensations, but none the less recognizably the old Virginia; the Virginia who admired Uncle Jo for his success and was grateful to him for having given her such a wonderful time, the Virginia who had always laughed and thought life grand and never bothered about things, the Virginia who had made Uncle Jo build the Grotto and had loved Our Lady ever since she was a kid. And now this Virginia was double-crossing her poor old, admired Uncle Jo—not just telling a few little fibs, which might happen to anyone, but deliberately and systematically double-crossing him. And not only him; she was also double-crossing poor Pete. Talking to him all the time; giving him the glad eye (as glad an eye, at any rate, as she was capable of giving in the circumstances); practically making love to him in public, so that Uncle Jo wouldn't suspect Sig. Not that she wouldn't be glad in some ways if Uncle Jo did suspect him. She'd love to see him getting a punch on the jaw and being thrown out. Just love it! But meanwhile she was doing everything she could to cover him up; and in the process making that poor, idiot boy imagine she was stuck on him. A double-crosser—that was all she was. A double-crosser. The knowledge of this worried her, it made her feel unhappy and ashamed; it prevented her laughing at things the way she used to; it kept her thinking, and feeling bad about what she was doing, and re-solving not to do it again; resolving, but not being able to prevent herself doing it again, even though she really hated herself for doing it and hated Sig for making her and, above all, for telling her, in that horrible, hard-boiled, cynical way, just how he made her and why she couldn't resist it. And one of the reasons why she had to do it again was that it stopped her feeling bad about having done it before. But then, afterwards, she felt bad again. Felt so bad, indeed, that she had been ashamed to look Our Lady in the face. For more than a week now the white velvet curtains across the front of the sacred doll's house had remained drawn. She simply didn't dare to open them, because she knew that if she did, and if she made a promise there, on her knees, to Our Lady, it just wouldn't be any good. When that awful Sig came along again, she'd just go all funny inside, like her bones had all turned into rubber, and the strength would go out of her and, before she knew where she was, it would all be happening again. And that would be much worse than the other times, because she'd made a promise about it to Our Lady. So that it was better not to make any promise at all—not now, at any rate; not until there seemed to be some chance of keeping it. Because it just couldn't last this way for ever; she simply refused to believe she'd always have that awful rubber feeling in her bones. Some day she'd feel strong enough to tell Sig to go to hell. And when she did, she'd make that promise. Till then, better not.

Virginia opened her eyes, and looked with a nostalgic expression at the niche between the windows and the drawn white curtains that concealed the treasure within —the cunning little crown, the seed pearls, the mantle of blue silk, the benignant face, the adorable little hands. Virginia sighed profoundly and, closing her eyes again, tried, by a simulation of sleep, to recapture the happy oblivion from which the light of morning had forced her unwillingly to emerge.

Chapter Three

Mr. STOYTE had spent his morning at the Beverly Pantheon. Very reluctantly; for he had a horror of cemeteries, even his own. But the claims of money-making were sacred; business was a duty to which all merely personal considerations had to be sacrificed. And talk of business! The Beverly Pantheon was the finest real estate proposition in the country. The land had been bought during the War at five hundred dollars an acre, improved (with roads, Tiny Tajes, Columbariums and statuary) to the tune of about ten thousand an acre, and was now selling, in grave-sites, at the rate of a hundred and sixty thousand an acre—selling so fast that the entire capital outlay had already been amortized, so that everything from now on would be pure jam. And, of course, as the population of Los Angeles increased, the jam would become correspondingly more copious. And the population *was* increasing, at the rate of nearly ten per cent. per annum—and, what was more, the main accessions consisted of elderly retired people from other States of the Union; the very people who would bring the greatest immediate profit to the Pantheon. And so, when Charlie Habakkuk sent that urgent call for him to come over and discuss the latest plans of improvements and extensions, Mr. Stoyte had found it morally impossible to refuse. Repressing his antipathies, he had done his duty. All that morning the two men had sat with their cigars in Charlie's office at the top of the Tower of Resurrection; and Charlie had waved those hands of his, and spouted cigar-smoke from his nostrils, and talked—God, how he had talked! As though he were one of those men in a red fez trying to make you buy an Oriental carpet—and incidentally, Mr. Stoyte reflected morosely, that was what Charlie looked like; only he was better fed than most of those carpet boys, and therefore greasier.

'Cut the sales talk,' he growled out loud. 'You seem to forget I own the place.'

Charlie looked at him with an expression of pained surprise. Sales talk? But this wasn't sales talk. This was real, this was earnest. The Pantheon was his baby; for all practical purposes he had invented the place. It was he who had thought up the Tiny Taj and the Church of the Bard; he who, on his own initiative, had bought that bargain lot of statues at Genoa; he who had first clearly formulated the policy of injecting sex-appeal into death; he who had resolutely resisted every attempt to introduce into the cemetery any representation of grief or age, any symbol of mortality, any image of the suffer-ings of Jesus. He had had to fight for his ideas, he had had to listen to a lot of criticism; but the results had proved him right. Anyone who complained that there was no Crucifixion in the place could be referred to the published accounts. And here was Mr. Stoyte talking sarcastically about sales talk. Sales talk, indeed, when the demand for space in the Pantheon was so great that exist-ing accommodation would soon be inadequate. There would have to be enlargements. More space, more buildings, more amenities. Bigger and better; progress; service.

In the top of the Tower of Resurrection, Charlie Habakkuk unfolded his plans. The new extension was to have a Poets' Corner, open to any bona fide writer—though he was afraid they'd have to draw the line at the authors of advertising copy, which was a pity, because a lot of them made good money and might be persuaded to pay extra for the prestige of being buried with the moving-picture people. But that cut both ways—because the scenario writers wouldn't feel that the Poets' Corner was exclusive enough if you let in the advertising boys. And seeing that the moving-picture fellows made so much more than the others . . . well, it stood to reason, Charlie had concluded, it stood to reason. And, of course, they'd have to have a replica of Westminster Abbey in the Poets' Corner. Wee Westminster—it would sound kind of cute. And as they needed a couple of extra mortuary furnaces anyhow, they'd have them installed there in the Dean's Yard. And they'd put a new automatic record-player in the crypt, so that there'd be more variety in the music. Not that people didn't appreciate the Perpetual Wurlitzer; they did. But all the same it got a bit monotonous. So he'd thought they might have some recordings of a choir singing hymns and things, and perhaps, every now and then, just for a change, some preacher giving an inspirational message, so that you'd be able to sit in the Garden of Contemplation, for example, and listen to the Wurlitzer for a few minutes, and then the choir singing 'Abide with Me,' and then a nice sort of Barrymore voice saying some piece, like the Gettysburg Address, or 'Laugh and the World Laughs with You,' or maybe some nice juicy bit by Mrs. Eddy or Ralph Waldo Trine—anything would do so long as it was inspirational enough. And then there was his idea of the Catacombs. And, boy, it was the best idea he'd ever had. Leading Mr. Stoyte to the south-eastern window, he had pointed across an intervening valley of tombs and cypresses and the miniature monuments of bogus antiquity, to where the land sloped up again to a serrated ridge on the further side. There, he had shouted excitedly, there, in that hump in the middle; they'd tunnel down into that. Hundreds of yards of catacombs. Lined with reinforced concrete to make them earthquake-proof. The only class-A catacombs in the world. And little chapels, like the ones in Rome. And a lot of phoney-looking murals, looking like they were real old. You could get them done cheap by one of those W.P.A. art projects. Not that those guys knew how to paint, of course; but that was quite O.K. seeing that the murals had to look phoney anyhow. And they wouldn't have anything but candles and little lamps for people to carry around—no electric light at all, except right at the very end of all those winding passages and stairs, where there'd be a great big sort of underground church, with one of those big nude statues that were going up at the San Francisco Fair and that they'd be glad to sell for a thousand bucks or even less when the show was over—one of those modernistic broads with muscles on them—and they'd have her standing right in the middle there, with maybe some fountain spouting all around her and concealed pink lighting in the water so she'd look kind of real. Why, the tourists would come a thousand miles to see it. Because there was nothing people liked so much as caves. Look at those Carlsbad Caverns, for example; and all those caves in Virginia. And those were just common-or-garden natural caves, without murals or anything. Whereas these would be catacombs. Yes, sir; real catacombs, like the things the Christian Martyrs lived in—and, by gum, that was another idea! Martyrs! Why wouldn't they have a Chapel of the Martyrs with a nice plaster group of some girls with no clothes on, just going to be eaten by a lion? People wouldn't stand for the Crucifixion; but they'd get a real thrill out of that.

Mr. Stoyte had listened wearily and with repugnance. He loathed his Pantheon and everything to do with it. Loathed it because in spite of statues and Wurlitzer, it spoke to him of nothing but disease and death and corruption and final judgment; because it was here, in the Pantheon, that they would bury him—at the foot of the pedestal of Rodin's *Le Baiser*.' (An assistant manager had once inadvisedly pointed out the spot to him and been immediately fired; but there was no dismissing the memory of his offence.) Charlie's enthusiasm for catacombs and Wee Westminsters elicited no answering warmth; only occasional grunts and a final sullen O.K. for everything except the Chapel of the Martyrs. Not that the Chapel of the Martyrs seemed to Mr. Stoyte a bad idea; on the contrary, he was convinced that the public would go crazy over it. If he rejected it, it was merely on principle—because it would never do to allow Charlie Habakkuk to think he was always right.

'Get plans and estimates for everything else,' he ordered in a tone so gruff that he might have been delivering a reprimand. 'But no martyrs. I won't have any martyrs.'

Almost in tears, Charlie pleaded for just one lion, just one Early Christian Virgin with her hands tied behind her back—because people got such a kick out of anything to do with ropes or handcuffs. Two or three Virgins would have been much better, of course; but he'd be content with one. 'Just one, Mr. Stoyte,' he implored, clasping his eloquent hands. 'Only one.'

Obstinately deaf to all his entreaties, Mr. Stoyte shook his head. 'No martyrs here,' he said. 'That's final.' And to show that it was final, he threw away the butt of his cigar and got up to go.

Five minutes later, Charlie Habakkuk was letting off steam to his secretary. The ingratitude of people! The stupidity! He'd a good mind to resign, just to show the old buzzard that they couldn't get on without him. Not for five minutes. Who was it that had made the place what it was: the uniquest cemetery in the world? Absolutely the uniquest. Who? (Charlie slapped himself on the chest.) And who made all the money? Jo Stoyte. And what had *he* done to make the place a success? Absolutely nothing at all. It was enough to make you want to be a communist. And the old devil wasn't grateful or even decently polite. Pushing you around as though you were a bum off the streets! Well, there was one comfort: Old Jo hadn't been looking any too good this morning. One of these days, maybe, they'd have the pleasure of burying him. Down there in the vestibule of the Columbarium, eight foot underground. And serve him right!

It was not only that he didn't look too good; leaning back in the car which was taking him down to Beverly Hills on his way to see Clancy, Mr. Stoyte was thinking, as he had thought so often during these last two or three weeks, that he didn't feel too good. He'd wake up in the morning feeling kind of sluggish and heavy; and his mind didn't seem to be as clear as it was. Obispo called it suppressed influenza and made him take those pills every night; but they didn't seem to do him any good. He went on feeling that way just the same. And, on top of everything else, he was worrying himself sick about Virginia. The Baby was acting strange, like someone that wasn't really there; so quiet, and not noticing anything, and starting when you spoke to her and asking what you said. Acting for all the world like one of those advertisements for Sal Hepatica or California Syrup of Figs; and that was what he'd have thought it was, if it hadn't been for the way she went on with that Peter

Boone fellow. Always talking to him at meals; and asking him to come and have a swim; and wanting to take a squint down his microscope—and what sort of a damn did *she* give for microscopes, he'd like to know? Throwing herself at him—that was what it had looked like on the surface. And that kind of syrup-of-figs way of acting (like people at those Quaker Meetings that Prudence used to make him go to before she took up with Christian Science)—that all fitted in. You'd say she was kind of stuck on the fellow. But then why should it have happened so suddenly? Because she'd never shown any signs of being stuck on him before. Always treated him like you'd treat a great big dog—friendly and all that, but not taking him too seriously; just a pat on the head and then, when he'd wagged his tail, thinking of something else. No, he couldn't understand it; he just couldn't figure it out. It looked like she was stuck on him; but then, at the same time, it looked like she just didn't notice if he was a boy or a dog. Because that was how she was acting even now. She paid a lot of attention to him—only the way you'd pay attention to a nice big retriever. And that was what had thrown him out. If she'd been stuck on Pete in the ordinary way, then he'd have got mad, and raised hell, and thrown the boy out of the house. But how could you raise hell over a dog? How could you get mad with a girl for telling a retriever she'd like to have a squint down his microscope? You couldn't even if you tried; because getting mad didn't make any sense. All he'd been able to do was just worry, trying to figure things out and not being able to. There was only one thing that was clear, and that was that the Baby meant more to him than he had thought, more than he had ever believed it possible that anyone should mean to him. It had begun by his just wanting

her—wanting her to touch, to hold, to handle, to eat;
wanting her because she was warm and smelt good;
wanting her because she was young and he was old, because she was so innocent and he too tired for anything
not innocence to excite. That was how it had begun;
but almost immediately something else had happened.
That youth of hers, that innocence and sweetness—they
were more than just exciting. She was so cute and lovely
and childish, he almost felt like crying over her, even
while he wanted to hold and handle and devour. She
did the strangest things to him—made him feel good,
like you felt when you'd tanked up a bit on Scotch, and
at the same time made him feel *good*, like you felt when
you were at church, or listening to William Jennings
Bryan, or making some poor kid happy by giving him
a doll or something. And Virginia wasn't just anybody's
kid, like the ones at the hospital; she was *his* kid, his
very own. Prudence wasn't able to have children; and
at the time he'd been sore about it. But now he was
glad. Because if he'd had a row of kids, they'd be standing in the way of the Baby. And Virginia meant more
to him than any daughter could mean. Because even if
she were *only* a daughter, which she wasn't, she was
probably a lot nicer than his own flesh-and-blood daughter
would have been—seeing that, after all, the Stoytes were
all a pretty sour-faced lot and Prudence had been kind of
dumb even if she was a good woman, which she certainly
was—maybe a bit too good. Whereas with the Baby
everything was just right, just perfect. He had been
happier since he'd known her than he'd ever been in
years. With her around, things had seemed worth doing
again. You didn't have to go through life asking 'Why?'
The reason for everything was there in front of you,
wearing that cunning little yachting-cap, maybe, or all

dressed up with her emeralds and everything for some party with the moving-picture crowd.

And now something had happened. The reason for carrying on was being taken away from him. The Baby had changed; she was fading away from him; she had gone somewhere else. Where had she gone? And why? Why did she want to leave him? To leave him all alone. Absolutely alone, and he was an old man, and the white slab was there in the vestibule of the Columbarium, waiting for him.

'What's the matter, Baby?' he had asked. Time and again he had asked, with anguish in his heart, too miserable to be angry, too much afraid of being left alone to care about his dignity, or his rights, about anything except keeping her, at whatever cost: 'What's the matter, Baby?'

And all she ever did was to look at him as though she were looking at him from some place a million miles away—to look at him like that and say: Nothing; she was feeling fine; she hadn't got anything on her mind; and, no, there wasn't anything he could do for her, because he'd given her everything already, and she was perfectly happy.

And if he mentioned Pete (kind of casually, so she shouldn't think he suspected anything) she wouldn't even bat an eyelid; just say: Yes, she liked Pete; he was a nice boy, but unsophisticated—and that made her laugh; and she liked laughing.

'But, Baby, you're different,' he would say; and it was difficult for him to keep his voice from breaking, he was so unhappy. 'You don't act like you used to, Baby.'

And all she'd answer was, that that was funny because she felt just the same.

'You don't feel the same about me,' he would say.

And she'd say she did. And he'd say no. And she'd say it wasn't true. Because what reasons did he have for saying she felt different about him? And of course she was quite right; there weren't any reasons you could lay your finger on. He couldn't honestly say she acted less affectionate, or didn't want to let him kiss her, or anything like that. She was different because of something you couldn't put a name to. Something in the way she looked and moved and sat around. He couldn't describe it except by saying it was like she wasn't really there where you thought you were looking at her, but some place else; some place where you couldn't touch her, or talk to her, or even really see her. That was how it was. But whenever he had tried to explain it to her, she had just laughed at him and said he must be having some of those feminine intuitions you read about in stories—only his feminine intuitions were all wrong.

And so there he'd be, back where he started from, trying to figure it out and not being able to, and worrying himself sick. Yes, worrying himself sick. Because when he'd got over feeling sluggish and heavy, like he always did in the mornings now, he felt so worried about the Baby that he'd start bawling at the servants and being rude to that god-damned Englishman and getting mad with Obispo. And the next thing that happened was that he couldn't digest his meals. He was getting heartburn and sour stomach; and one day he had such a pain that he'd thought it was appendicitis. But Obispo had said it was just gas; because of his suppressed influenza. And then he'd got mad and told the fellow he must be a lousy doctor if he couldn't cure a little thing like that. Which must have put the fear of God into Obispo, because he'd said, 'Just give me two or three days more. That's all I need to complete the treatment.' And he'd said that suppressed influenza was a funny thing; didn't seem to be anything, but poisoned the whole system, so you couldn't think straight any more; and you'd get to imagining things that weren't really there, and worrying about them.

Which might be true in a general way; but in this case he just knew it wasn't all imagination. The Baby *was* different; he had a reason for being worried.

Sunk in his mood of perplexed and agitated gloom, Mr. Stoyte was carried down the windings of the mountain road, through the bowery oasis of Beverly Hills, and eastward (for Clancy lived in Hollywood) along Santa Monica Boulevard. Over the telephone, that morning, Clancy had put on one of his melodramatic conspirator acts. From the rigmarole of hints and dark allusions and altered names, Mr. Stoyte had gathered that the news was good. Clancy and his boys had evidently succeeded in buying up most of the best land in the San Felipe Valley. At another time, Mr. Stoyte would have exulted in his triumph; to-day, even the prospect of making a million or two of easy money gave him no sort of pleasure. In the world he had been reduced to inhabiting, millions were irrelevant. For what could millions do to allay his miseries? The miseries of an old, tired, empty man; of a man who had no end in life but himself, no philosophy, no knowledge but of his own interests, no appreciations, not even any friends—only a daughter-mistress, a concubine-child, frantically desired, cherished to the point of idolatry. And now this being, on whom he had relied to give significance to his life, had begun to fail him. He had come to doubt her fidelity—but to doubt without tangible reasons, to doubt in such a way that none of the ordinary satisfying reactions, of rage, of violence, of recrimination, was appropriate. The sense was going out of his life and he could do nothing; for he was in a situation with which he did not know how to deal, hopelessly bewildered. And always, in the background of his mind, there floated an image of that circular marble room, with Rodin's image of desire at the centre, and that white slab in the pavement at its base—the slab that would some day have his name engraved upon it: Joseph Panton Stoyte, and the dates of his birth and death. And along with that inscription went another, in orange letters on a coal-black ground: 'It is a terrible thing to fall into the hands of the living God.' And meanwhile here was Clancy, conspiratorially announcing victory. Good news! Good news! A year or two from now he would be richer by another million. But the millions were in one world and the old, unhappy, frightened man was in another, and there was no communication between the two.

Chapter Four

JEREMY worked for a couple of hours, unpacking, examining, provisionally cataloguing, filing. There were no finds this morning—merely accounts and legal documents and business letters. Stuff for Coulton and Tawney and the Hammonds; not at all his cup of tea.

By half-past twelve the weight of boredom had become too much for him. He broke off and, in search of a little spiritual refreshment, turned to the Fifth Earl's vellum-bound notebook.

'July 1780,' he read. 'Sensuality is close allied with Sorrow, and it sometimes happens that, on account of the very sincerity of her Grief, the weeping Widow is betrayed by her own Feelings and finds herself unable to resist the importunities of the funeral Guest, who knows the Art of passing imperceptibly from Condolence to Familiarity. I myself have posthumously cuckolded a Duke and two Viscounts (one of them no later than last night) upon the very Beds from which, but a few hours before, they had been borne in Pomp to the ancestral Sepulchre.'

That was something for his mother, Jeremy reflected. The sort of thing she really adored! He had a good mind, if it wasn't too horribly expensive, to cable it to her in a night letter.

He returned to the notebook.

'One of the Livings in my Gift having unexpectedly fallen vacant, my Sister sent to me to-day a young Divine whom she commends, and I believe her, for his singular Virtue. I will have no Parsons around me but such as drink deep, ride to Hounds and caress the Wives and daughters of their Parishioners. A Virtuous Parson does nothing to test or exercise the Faith of his Flock; but as I have written to my Sister, it is by Faith that we come to Salvation.'

The next entry was dated March 1784.

'In old Tombs newly opened a kind of ropy Slime depends from the roof and coats the walls. It is the condensation of decay.'

'January 1786. Half a dozen pensées in as many years. If I am to fill a volume at this rate, I must outlast the patriarchs. I regret my sloth, but console myself with the thought that my fellow men are too contemptible for me to waste my time instructing or entertaining them.'

Jeremy hurried over three pages of reflections on politics and economics. Under the date of March 12th, 1787, he found a more interesting entry:

'Dying is almost the least spiritual of our acts, more strictly carnal even than the act of love. There are Death Agonies that are like the strainings of the Costive at stool. To-day I saw M. B. die.'

'January 11th, 1788. This day fifty years ago I was born. From solitude in the Womb, we emerge into solitude among our Fellows, and return again to solitude within the Grave. We pass our lives in the attempt to mitigate that solitude. But Propinquity is never fusion. The most populous City is but an agglomeration of wildernesses. We exchange Words, but exchange them from prison to prison, and without hope that they will signify to others what they mean to ourselves. We marry, and there are two solitudes in the house instead of one; we beget children, and there are many solitudes. We reiterate the act of love; but again propinquity is never fusion. The most intimate contact is only of Surfaces, and we couple, as I have seen the condemned Prisoners at Newgate coupling with their Trulls, between the bars of our cages. Pleasure cannot be shared; like Pain, it can only be experienced or inflicted, and when we give Pleasure to our Lovers or bestow Charity upon the Needy, we do so, not to gratify the object of our Benevolence, but only ourselves. For the Truth is that we are kind for the same reason as we are cruel, in order that we may enhance the sense of our own Power; and this we are for ever trying to do, despite the fact that by doing it we cause ourselves to feel more solitary than ever. The reality of Solitude is the same in all men, there being no mitigation of it, except in Forgetfulness, Stupidity or Illusion; but a man's sense of Solitude is proportionate to the sense and fact of his Power. In any set of circumstances, the more Power we have, the more intensely do we feel our solitude. I have enjoyed much Power in my life.'

'June 1788. Captain Pavey came to pay his respects to-day, a round, jovial, low man, whom even his awe of me could not entirely prevent from breaking out into the vulgar Mirth which is native to him. I questioned him concerning his last Voyage, and he very minutely described for me the mode of packing the Slaves in the holds; the chains used to secure them; the feeding of them and, in calm weather, the exercising on deck, though always with Nets about the bulwarks, to prevent the more desperate from casting themselves into the sea; the Punishments for the refractory; the schools of hungry sharks accompanying the vessel; the scurvy and other diseases, the wearing away of the negroes' Skin by the hardness of the planks on which they lie and the continual Motion of the waves; the Stench so horrible that even the hardiest seaman will turn pale and swoon away, if he ventures into the hold; the frequent Deaths and almost incredibly rapid Putrefaction, especially in damp Weather near the Line. When he took his leave, I made him a present of a gold snuff box. Anticipating no such favour, he was so coarsely loud in his expression of thanks and future devotion to my Interests, that I was forced to cut him short. The snuff box cost me sixty guineas; Captain Pavey's last three Voyages have brought me upwards of forty thousand. Power and wealth increase in direct proportion to a man's distance from the material objects from which wealth and power are ultimately derived. For every risk taken by the General Officer, the private soldier takes a hundred; and for every guinea earned by the latter the General earns a hundred. So with myself and Pavey and the Slaves. The Slaves labour in the Plantation for nothing but blows and their diet; Captain Pavey undergoes the hardships and dangers of the Sea and lives not so well as a Haberdasher or Vintner; I put my hands to nothing more material than a Banker's draft, and a shower of gold descends upon me for my pains. In a world such as ours, a man is given but three choices. In the first place, he may do as the multitude have always done and, too stupid to be wholly a knave, mitigate his native baseness with a no less native folly. Second, he may imitate those more consummate fools who painfully deny their native Baseness in order to practise Virtue. Third, he may choose to be a man of sense—one who, knowing his native Baseness, thereby learns to make use of it and, by the act of knowledge, rises superior to it and to his more foolish Fellows. For myself, I have chosen to be a man of sense.'

'March 1789. Reason promises happiness; Feeling protests that it is Happiness; Sense alone gives Happiness. And Happiness itself is like dust in the mouth.'

'July 1789. If Men and Women took their Pleasures as noisily as the Cats, what Londoner could ever hope to sleep of nights?'

'July 1789. The Bastille is fallen. Long live the Bastille!'

The next few pages were devoted to the Revolution. Jeremy skipped them. In 1794 the Fifth Earl's interest in the Revolution gave place to interest in his own health.

'To those who visit me,' he had written, 'I say that I have been sick and am now well again. The words are quite untrue; for it was not I who lay at Death's door, nor is it I who am recovered. The first was a special creation of Fever, an embodiment of Pain and Lassitude; the second is not I, but an old man, weak, shrunken and without desires. My name and some memories are all that remain to me of the Being I once was. It is as if a Man had died and willed to some surviving Friend a handful of worthless trinkets to remember him by.'

'1794. A sick, rich Man is like one who lies wounded and alone in the deserts of Egypt; the Vultures hover lower and lower above his head and the Jackals and Hyenas prowl in ever-narrowing circles about the place where he lies. Not even a rich Man's Heirs could be more unsleepingly attentive. When I look into my Nephew's face and read there, behind the mask of Solicitude, his impatient longing for my Death and his disappointment that I am not already gone, I feel an influx of new Life and Strength. If for no other reason, I will live on to rob Him of the Happiness which he still believes (for he is confident of my Relapse) to be within his Grasp.'

'1794. The World is a Mirror, reflecting his image to the Beholder.'

'January 1795. I have tried King David's remedy

against old age and found it wanting. Warmth cannot be imparted, but only evoked; and where no lingering spark persists, even tinder will not raise a flame.

'It may be as the Parsons say, that we are saved by another's vicarious suffering; but I can vouch for the fact that vicarious pleasure is without efficacity, except only to enhance the sentiments of Superiority and Power in him who inflicts it.'

'1795. As the Satisfactions of Sense decay, we compensate ourselves for their loss by cultivating the sentiments of Pride and Vanity. The love of Domination is independent of the bodily faculties and therefore, when the body loses its powers, may easily take the place of vanished Pleasure. For myself, I was never without the love of Dominion even when in the Throes of Pleasure. Since my late Death, the Phantom that remains of me is forced to content itself with the first, less substantial and, above all, less harmless of these two Satisfactions.'

'July 1796. The fishponds at Gonister were dug in the Ages of Superstition by the monks of the Abbey upon whose foundations the present House is built. Under King Charles I, my great-great-grandfather caused a number of leaden Disks engraved with his cypher and the date, to be attached by silver rings to the tails of fifty well-grown carp. Not less than twenty of these fish are alive to-day, as one may count whenever the bell is rung that calls the Creatures to be fed. With them come others even larger than they—survivors, it may be, from the monkish times before King Henry's Dissolution of the Religious Houses. Watching them through the pellucid Water, I marvel at the strength and unimpaired agility of these great Fishes, of which the oldest were perhaps alive when the Utopia was written, while the youngest are co-eval with the author of Paradise Lost. The latter attempted to justify God's ways to Man. He would have done a more useful Work in undertaking to explain the ways of God to Fish. Philosophers have wasted their own and their readers' time in speculations upon the Immortality of the Soul; the Alchemists have pored for centuries over their crucibles in the vain hope of discovering the Elixir or the Stone. Meanwhile, in every pond and river, one may find Carps that have outlived three Platos and half a dozen Paracelsuses. The Secret of eternal Life is not to be found in old Books, nor in liquid Gold, nor even in Heaven; it is to be found in the Mud and only awaits a skilful Angler.'

Outside the corridor the bell rang for lunch. Jeremy rose, put the Fifth Earl's notebook away and walked towards the lift, smiling to himself at the thought of the pleasure he would derive from telling that bumptious ass, Obispo, that all his best ideas about longevity had been anticipated in the eighteenth century.

Chapter Five

LUNCHEON, in the absence of Mr. Stoyte, was a very cheerful meal. The servants went about their business unreprimanded. Jeremy could talk without the risk of being snubbed or insulted. Dr. Obispo was able to tell the story about the chimney-sweep who applied for life-insurance after going on his honeymoon, and, from the far-away depths of that almost trance-like state of fatigue —that state which she deliberately fostered, so as not to have to think too much and feel too badly about what was happening—Virginia was at liberty to laugh at it as loudly as she liked. And though with one part of herself she would have liked not to laugh at all, because she didn't want to make Sig think she was encouraging him in any way, with another part she wanted to laugh, indeed couldn't help laughing, because, after all, the story was really very funny. Besides, it was such a relief not to have to put on that act with Pete for the benefit of uncle Jo. No double-crossing. For once, she could be herself. The only fly in the ointment was that this self she was being was such a miserable specimen : a self with bones that would go like rubber whenever that horrible Sig chose to come along ; a self without the strength to keep a promise even to Our Lady. Her laughter abruptly ceased.

Only Pete was consistently unhappy—about the chimney-sweep, of course, and Virginia's burst of merriment; but also because Barcelona had fallen and, with it, all his hopes of a speedy victory over fascism, all prospect of ever seeing any of his old comrades again. And that wasn't all. Laughing at the story of the chimney-sweep was only a single painful incident among many. Virginia had allowed the first two courses of the meal to come and go without once paying any attention to him. But why, why? His distress was aggravated by bitter bewilderment. Why? In the light of what had been happening during the past three weeks it was inexplicable. Ever since the evening of the day she had turned back at the Grotto, Virginia had been simply wonderful to him— going out of her way to talk to him, inviting him to tell her things about Spain and even about biology. Why, she had actually asked to look at something under the microscope. Trembling with happiness, so that he could hardly adjust the slide, he had focussed the instrument on a preparation of the carp's intestinal flora. Then she had sat down in his place, and as she bent over the eyepiece her auburn curls had swung down on either side of the microscope and, above the edge of her pink sweater, the nape of her neck had been uncovered, so white, so tangibly inviting, that the enormous effort he had had to make to prevent himself from kissing it had left him feeling almost faint.

There had been times during the ensuing days when he wished that he hadn't made that effort. But then his better self would reassert its rule and he was glad again that he had. Because, of course, it wouldn't have been right. For, though he had long since given up the family belief in that Blood-of-the-Lamb business, he still remembered what his pious and conventional mother had said about kissing anyone you weren't engaged to; he was still at heart the earnest adolescent whom Reverend Schlitz's eloquence had fired during the perplexities of puberty with a passionate determination to be continent, a conviction of the Sacredness of Love, an enthusiasm for something wonderful called Christian marriage. But at the moment, unfortunately, he wasn't earning enough to feel justified in asking Virginia to accept his sacred love and enter into Christian marriage with him. And there was the added complication that on his side the Christian marriage wouldn't be Christian except in substance, whereas Virginia was attached to the institution which Reverend Schlitz sometimes called the Whore of Babylon and the Marxists regarded as pre-eminently detestable. An institution, moreover, that would think as poorly of him as he thought of it—though he thought rather less poorly of it now that Hitler was persecuting it in Germany and since he had been looked after by those Sisters of Mercy in Spain. And even if those religious and financial difficulties could somehow be miraculously smoothed away, there remained the dreadful fact of Mr. Stoyte. He *knew*, of course, that Mr. Stoyte was nothing more than a father to Virginia, or at most an uncle—but knew it with that excessive certainty that is born of desire; knew it in the same way as Don Quixote knew that the pasteboard vizor of his helmet was as strong as steel. It was the kind of knowledge about which it is prudent to make no enquiries; and of course, if he asked Virginia to marry him, such enquiries, or the information such enquiries might be expected to elicit, would almost inevitably be forced upon him.

Yet another complicating factor in the situation was Mr. Propter. For if Mr. Propter was right, as Pete was coming to feel more and more certain that he was, then it was obviously unwise to do something that would make more difficult the passage from the human level to the level of eternity. And though he loved Virginia, he found it difficult to believe that marriage to her would be anything but an obstacle to the enlightenment of everybody concerned.

Or rather, he *had* thought this; but in the course of the last week or two his opinion had changed. Or, to be more exact, he no longer had an opinion; he was just uncertain and bewildered. For Virginia's character seemed almost suddenly to have changed. From being childlike, loud and extraverted, her innocence had become quiet and inscrutable. In the past, she had treated him with the jocular and casual friendliness of mere good-fellowship; but recently there had been a strange altera-tion. The jokes had stopped and a kind of earnest solici-tude had taken their place. She had been simply wonder-ful to him—but not in the way a girl is wonderful to a man she wants to fall in love with her. No, Virginia had been wonderful like a sister—and not an ordi-nary sister, either: almost a Sister of Mercy. Not just any Sister of Mercy: that particular Sister who had nursed him when he was in hospital at Gerona; the young Sister with the big eyes and the pale oval face, like the face of the Virgin Mary in a picture; the one who always seemed to be secretly happy, not because of any-thing that was going on around her, but because of some-thing inside, something extraordinary and beautiful be-hind her eyes that she could look in at; and when she'd looked at it, there was no reason any more why she should feel scared by an air-raid, for example, or upset by an amputation. She evidently saw things from what Mr. Propter called the level of eternity; they didn't affect her in the way they'd affect a person living on the human level. On the human level you were scared and angry; or, if you were calm, you made yourself calm by an effort of will. But the Sister was calm without making an effort of will. At the time, he had admired without comprehension. Now, thanks to Mr. Propter, he could begin to understand as well as admire.

Well, that was the face that Virginia's had reminded
him of during the past weeks. There had been a kind of
sudden conversion from the outward-looking life to the
inward, from open responsiveness to secret and mysterious abstraction. The cause of this conversion was
beyond his comprehension; but the fact was manifest,
and he had respected it. Respected it by not kissing her
neck as she bent over the microscope; by never even
touching her arm or taking her hand; by not saying to
her one word of all he felt about her. In the strange,
inexplicable circumstances of her transformation, such
actions, he had felt, would have been inappropriate to the
point positively of sacrilege. It was as a sister that she
had chosen to be wonderful to him; it was therefore as
a brother that he had responded. And now, for no
known reason, she seemed suddenly to have become
unaware of his existence.

The sister had forgotten her brother; and the Sister of
Mercy had forgotten herself—forgotten herself so far as
to listen to Dr. Obispo's ignoble anecdote about the
chimney-sweep, even to laugh at it. And yet, Pete
noticed in bewilderment, the moment she stopped laughing, her face resumed its expression of inwardness and
secrecy and detachment. The Sister of Mercy remembered herself as promptly as she had forgotten. It was
beyond him; he simply couldn't figure it out.

With the arrival of the coffee, Dr. Obispo announced
that he proposed to take the afternoon off and, as there
was nothing that urgently needed doing in the laboratory,
he advised Pete to do the same. Pete thanked him and,
pretending to be in a hurry (for he didn't want to go
through the humiliation of being ignored when Virginia
discussed her plans for the afternoon), swallowed his
coffee and, mumbling excuses, left the room. A little

later he was out in the sunshine, walking down towards the plain.

As he went, he thought of some of the things Mr. Propter had said to him in the course of his recent visits.

Of what he had said about the silliest text in the Bible and the most sensible. 'They hated me without a cause' and 'God is not mocked; as a man sows, so shall he reap.'

Of what he had said about nobody ever getting something for nothing—so that a man would pay for too much money, for example, or too much power, or too much sex, by being shut up more tightly inside his own ego; so that a country that moved too quickly and violently would fall under a tyranny, like Napoleon's, or Stalin's, or Hitler's; and a people that was prosperous and internally peaceful would pay for it by being smug and self-satisfied and conservative, like the English.

The baboons were gibbering as he passed. Pete recalled some of Mr. Propter's remarks about literature. About the wearisomeness, to an adult mind, of all those merely descriptive plays and novels which critics expected one to admire. All the innumerable, interminable anecdotes and romances and character-studies, but no general theory of anecdotes, no explanatory hypothesis of romance or character. Just a huge collection of facts about lust and greed, fear and ambition, duty and affection; just facts, and imaginary facts at that, with no co-ordinating philosophy superior to common sense and the local system of conventions, no principle of arrangement more rational than simple aesthetic expediency. And then the astonishing nonsense talked by those who undertake to elucidate and explain this hodge-podge of prettily patterned facts and fancies! All that solemn tosh, for example, about Regional Literature—as though there were some special and outstanding merit in recording un-co-ordinated facts about the lusts, greeds and duties of people who happen to live in the country and speak in dialect! Or else the facts were about the urban poor and there was an effort to co-ordinate them in terms of some post-Marxian theory that might be partly true, but was always inadequate. And in that case it was the great Proletarian Novel. Or else somebody wrote yet another book proclaiming that Life is Holy; by which he always meant that anything people do in the way of fornicating, or getting drunk, or losing their tempers, or feeling maudlin, is entirely O.K. with God and should therefore be regarded as permissible and even virtuous. In which case it was up to the critics to talk about the author's ripe humanity, his deep and tender wisdom, his affinities with the great Goethe, and his obligations to William Blake.

Pete smiled as he remembered, but with a certain ruefulness as well as amusement; for he too had taken this sort of thing with the seriousness its verbiage seemed to demand.

Misplaced seriousness—the source of some of our most fatal errors. One should be serious, Mr. Propter had said, only about what deserves to be taken seriously. And, on the strictly human level, there was nothing that deserved to be taken seriously except the suffering men inflicted upon themselves by their crimes and follies. But, in the last analysis, most of these crimes and follies arose from taking too seriously things which did not deserve it. And that, Mr. Propter had continued, was another of the enormous defects of so-called good literature; it accepted the conventional scale of values; it respected power and position; it admired success; it treated as though they were reasonable the mainly lunatic preoccupations of statesmen, lovers, business men, social climbers, parents. In a word, it took seriously the causes of suffering as well as the suffering. It helped to perpetuate misery by explicitly or implicitly approving the thoughts and feelings and practices which could not fail to result in misery. And this approval was bestowed in the most magnificent and persuasive language. So that even when a tragedy ended badly, the reader was hypnotized by the eloquence of the piece into imagining that it was all somehow noble and worth while. Which of course it wasn't. Because, if you considered them dispassionately, nothing could be more silly and squalid than the themes of *Phèdre*, or *Othello*, or *Wuthering Heights*, or the *Agamemnon*. But the treatment of these themes had been in the highest degree sublime and thrilling, so that the reader or the spectator was left with the conviction that, in spite of the catastrophe, all was really well with the world, the all too human world, which had produced it. No, a good satire was much more deeply truthful and, of course, much more profitable than a good tragedy. The trouble was that so few good satires existed, because so few satirists were prepared to carry their criticism of human values far enough. *Candide*, for example, was admirable as far as it went; but it went no further than debunking the principal human activities in the name of the ideal of harmlessness. Now, it was perfectly true that harmlessness was the highest ideal most people could aspire to; for, though few had the power to do much positive good, there was nobody who could not refrain, if he so desired, from evil. Nevertheless, mere harmlessness, however excellent, most certainly didn't represent the highest possible ideal. *Il faut cultiver notre jardin* was not the last word in human wisdom; at the best it was only the last but one.

The sun was in such a position that, as he walked down the hill, Pete saw two little rainbows spouting from the nipples of Giambologna's nymph. Thoughts of Noah immediately arose in conjunction with thoughts of Virginia in her white satin bathing-costume. He tried to repress the latter as incompatible with the new thoughts he was trying to cultivate about the Sister of Mercy; and since Noah was not a subject that would bear much thinking about, he proceeded instead to concentrate on that talk he had had with Mr. Propter about sex. It had begun with his own puzzled questionings as to what sort of sexual behaviour was normal—not statistically normal, of course, but normal in that absolute sense in which perfect vision or unimpaired digestion may be called normal. What sort of sexual behaviour was normal in that sense of the word? And Mr. Propter had answered: None. But there must be, he had protested. If good could be manifested on the animal level, then there must be some kind of sexual behaviour that was absolutely normal and natural, just as there was an absolutely normal and natural sort of digestive activity. But man's sexual behaviour, Mr. Propter had answered, wasn't on the same level as digestion. A rat's love-making—yes, that *was* on the same level as digestion; for the entire process was instinctive; in other words, was controlled by the physiological intelligence of the body—the same physiological intelligence as correlated the actions of heart and lungs and kidneys, as regulated temperature, as nourished the muscles and made them do the work demanded of them by the central nervous system. Men's bodily activities were controlled by the same physiological intelligence; and it was that intelligence which, on the animal level, manifested good. In human beings, sexual behaviour was almost completely outside the jurisdiction of this physiological intelligence. It controlled only the cellular activities which made sexual behaviour possible. All the rest was non-instinctive and took place on the strictly human level of self-consciousness. Even when men thought that they were being most exclusively animal in their sexuality, they were still on the human level. Which meant that they were still self-conscious, still dominated by words—and where there were words, there, of necessity, were memories and wishes, judgments and imaginations. There, inevitably, were the past and the future, the actual and the fantastic; regret and anticipation; good and evil; the creditable and the discreditable; the beautiful and the ugly. Among men and women, even the most apparently bestial acts of eroticism were associated with some or all of these non-animal factors—factors which were injected into every human situation by the existence of language. This meant that there was no one type of human sexuality that could be called 'normal' in the sense in which one could say that there was a normality of vision or digestion. In *that* sense, all kinds of human sexuality were strictly abnormal. The different kinds of sexual behaviour could not be judged by referring them to an absolute natural norm. They could only be judged in reference to the ultimate aims of each individual and the results observed in each case. Thus, if an individual wanted to be well thought of in any given society, he or she could safely regard as 'normal' the type of sexual behaviour currently tolerated by that local religion and approved by the 'best people.' But there were some individuals who cared little for the judgment of an angry God or even of the best people. Their principal desire was for intense and reiterated stimulation of their senses and their feelings. For these, it was obvious, 'normality' in sexual behaviour would be quite different from what it was for the more social-minded. Then there would be all the kinds of sexuality 'normal' to those desirous of making the best of both worlds—the personal world of sensations and emotions, and the social world of moral and religious conventions. The 'normalities' of Tartuffe and Pecksniff; of the clergymen who can't keep away from schoolgirls, the cabinet ministers with a secret mania for handsome youths. And, finally, there were those who were concerned neither to get on in society, nor to placate the local deity, nor to enjoy repeated emotional and sensuous stimulations, but whose chief preoccupation was with enlightenment and liberation, with the problem of transcending personality, of passing from the human level to the level of eternity. Their conceptions of 'normality' in sexual behaviour would not resemble those of the men and women in any of the other categories.

From the concrete tennis-court the children of the Chinese cook were flying kites in the shape of birds and equipped with little whistlcs, so that they warbled plaintively in the wind. The cheerful quacking sound of Cantonese drifted down to Pete's ears. Across the Pacific, he reflected, millions upon millions of such children had died already or were dying. Below them, in the Sacred Grotto, stood the plaster figure of Our Lady. Pete thought of Virginia kneeling in white shorts and a yachting-cap, of the abusive eloquence of Reverend Schlitz, of Dr. Obispo's jokes, of Alexis Carrel on the subject of Lourdes, of Lee's *History of the Inquisition*, of Tawney on the relationship between Protestantism and Capitalism, of Niemöller and John Knox and Torquemada and that Sister of Mercy and again of Virginia, and finally of Mr. Propter as the only person he knew who could make some sense out of the absurd, insane, diabolical confusion of it all.

Chapter Six

SOMEWHAT to Jeremy's disappointment, Dr. Obispo was not at all mortified by the information that his ideas had been anticipated in the eighteenth century.

'I'd like to hear some more about your Fifth Earl,' he said, as they glided down into the cellars with the Vermeer. 'You say he lived to ninety?'

'More than ninety,' Jeremy answered. 'Ninety-six or seven, I forget which. And died in the middle of a scandal, what's more.'

'What sort of a scandal?'

Jeremy coughed and patted the top of his head. 'The usual sort,' he fluted.

'You mean, the old bozo was still at it?' Dr. Obispo asked incredulously.

'Still at it,' Jeremy repeated. 'There's a passage about the affair in the unpublished papers of Greville. He died just in time. They were actually on the point of arresting him.'

'What for?'

Jeremy twinkled again and coughed. 'Well,' he said slowly and in his most Cranford-like manner, 'it seems that he had a tendency to take his pleasures rather homicidally.'

'You mean, he'd killed someone.'

'Not actually killed,' Jeremy answered: 'just damaged.'

Dr. Obispo was rather disappointed, but consoled himself almost immediately by the reflection that, at ninety-six, even damage was pretty creditable. 'I'd like to look into this a little further,' he added.

'Well, the notebook's at your disposal,' said Jeremy politely.

Dr. Obispo thanked him. Together they walked towards Jeremy's work-room.

'The handwriting's rather difficult,' said Jeremy as they entered. 'I think it might be easier if I read it aloud to you.'

Dr. Obispo protested that he didn't want to waste Jeremy's time; but as the other was anxious to find an excuse for putting off to another occasion the wearisome task of sorting papers that didn't interest him, the protest was out-protested. Jeremy insisted on being altruistic. Dr. Obispo thanked him and settled down to listen. Jeremy took his eyes out of their native element for long enough to polish his spectacles, then began to re-read aloud the passage he had been reading that morning when the bell rang for lunch.

'"It is to be found in the Mud,"' he concluded, '"and only awaits a skilful Angler."'

Dr. Obispo chuckled. 'You might almost use it as a definition of science,' he said. 'What is science? Science is angling in the mud—angling for immortality and for anything else that may happen to turn up.' He laughed again and added that he liked the old bastard.

Jeremy went on reading.

'"August 1796. To-day my gabbling niece Caroline reproached me with what she called the Inconsistency of my Conduct. A man who is humane with the Horses in his stables, the Deer in his park and the Carp in his fishponds should show his Consistency by being more sociable than I am, more tolerant of the company of Fools, more charitable towards the poor and humble. To which I answered by remarking that the word, Man, is the general Name applied to successions of inconsistent Conduct, having their source within a two-legged and

featherless Body, and that such words as Caroline, John
and the like are the proper names applied to particular
successions of inconsistent Conduct within particular
Bodies. The only Consistency exhibited by the mass of
Mankind is a Consistency of Inconsistency. In other
words, the nature of any particular succession of inconsistent Conduct depends upon the history of the individual
and his ancestors. Each succession of Inconsistencies is
determined and obeys the Laws imposed upon it by its
own antecedent Circumstances. A Character may be
said to be consistent in the sense that its Inconsistencies
are predestined and cannot pass beyond the boundaries
ordained for it. The Consistency demanded by such
Fools as Caroline is of quite another kind. These reproach us because our successive Acts are not consistent
with some arbitrarily selected set of Prejudices, or ridiculous code of rules, such as the Hebrew, the Gentleman-
like, the Iroquois or the Christian. Such Consistency
is not to be achieved, and the attempt to achieve it
results only in Imbecility or Hypocrisy. Consider, I said
to Caroline, your own Conduct. What Consistency,
pray, do you find between your conversations with the
Dean upon Redemption and your Draconian birchings
of the younger Maids ? between your conspicuous chari-
ties and the setting of man-traps on your estates ? between
your appearances at Court and your *chaise percée* ? or
between divine service on Sunday morning and the
pleasures enjoyed on Saturday night with your husband
and on Friday or Thursday, as all the world suspects,
with a certain Baronet who shall be nameless ? But before
I had concluded my final question, Caroline had left
the room."'

'Poor Caroline,' said Dr. Obispo, with a laugh. 'Still,
she got what she asked for.'

Jeremy read out the next entry.

'"December 1796. After this second attack of pulmonary congestion, Convalescence has come more slowly than before and advanced less far. I hang here suspended above the pit as though by a single thread, and the substance of that thread is Misery."'

With an elegantly bent little finger, Dr. Obispo flicked the ash of his cigarette on to the floor.

'One of those pharmaceutical tragedies,' he commented. 'With a course of thiamin chloride and some testosterone I could have made him as happy as a sand-boy. Has it ever struck you,' he added, 'what a lot of the finest romantic literature is the result of bad doctoring?

> *I could lie down like a tired child*
> *And weep away this life of care.*

Lovely! But if they'd known how to clear up poor Shelley's chronic tuberculous pleurisy it would never have been written. Lying down like a tired child and weeping life away happens to be one of the most characteristic symptoms of chronic tuberculous pleurisy. And most of the other *Weltschmerz* boys were either sick men or alcoholics or dope addicts. I could have prevented every one of them from writing as he did.' Dr. Obispo looked at Jeremy with a wolfish smile that was almost childlike in the candour of its triumphant cynicism. 'Well, let's hear how the old boy gets over his troubles.'

'"December, 1796,"' Jeremy read out. '"The prowlings of my attendant hyaenas became so intolerable to me that yesterday I resolved to put an end to them. When I asked them to leave me alone in the future, Caroline and John protested their more than filial Affection. In the end I was forced to say that, unless they were gone by noon to-day, I would order my Steward to bring a score of men and eject them from my House. This morning, from my window, I watched them take their departure."'

The next note was dated January 11th, 1797. '"This year the anniversary of my birth calls up Thoughts more gloomy than ever before. I am too weary to record them. The day being fine and remarkably warm for the Season, I had myself carried in my chair to the fish-ponds. The bell was rung, and the Carp at once came hurrying to be fed. The spectacle of the brute Creation provides me with almost my sole remaining pleasure. The stupidity of the Brutes is without pretensions and their malignity depends on Appetite and is therefore only intermittent. Men are systematically and continuously cruel, while their Follies are justified in the names of Religion and Politics, and their Ignorance is muffled up in the pompous garments of Philosophy.

'"Meanwhile, as I watched the fishes pushing and jostling for their dinner, like a crowd of Divines in search of Preferment, my Thoughts returned to the perplexing Question upon which I have so often speculated in the past. Why should a man die at three-score years and ten, when a Fish can retain its Youth for two or three centuries? I have debated with myself a number of possible answers. There was a time, for example, when I thought that the longer life of Carp and Pike might be due to the superiority of their Watery Element over our Air. But the lives of some subaqueous Creatures are short, while those of certain Birds exceed the human span.

'"Again, I have asked myself if the Fish's longer years might not be due to its peculiar mode of begetting and bearing its young. But again I am met by fatal Objections. The Males of Parrots and Ravens do not onanize,

but copulate; the females of Elephants do not lay eggs
but bear their young, if we are to believe M. de Buffon,
for a period of not less than four and twenty months.
But Parrots, Ravens and Elephants are long-lived Creatures; from which we must conclude that the Brevity of
human Life is due to other Causes than the manner in
which Men beget and Females reproduce their Kind.

'"The only Hypotheses to which I can see no manifest
Objections are these: the Diet of such fish as Carp and
Pike contains some substance which preserves their Bodies
from the Decay which overtakes the greater number of
Creatures even while they are alive; alternatively the
substance which prevents Decay is to be found within the
Body of the Fish, especially, it would be reasonable to
guess, in the Stomach, Liver, Bowels and other Organs
of Concoction and Assimilation. In the short-lived animals, such as Man, the Substances preventive of Decay
must be presumed to be lacking. The question then
arises whether these Substances can be introduced into the
human Body from that of the Fish. History does not
record any remarkable instances of longevity among the
Ichthyophagi, nor have I ever observed that the Inhabitants
of sea ports and other places where there is an abundance
of Fish were specially long-lived. But we need not conclude from this that the Substance preventive of Decay
can never be conveyed from Fish to Man. For Man
cooks his Food before eating it, and we know by a
thousand instances that the application of Heat profoundly modifies the nature of many Substances; moreover, he throws away, as unfit for his Consumption,
precisely those Organs of the Fish in which it is most
reasonable to assume that the Substance preventive of
Decay is contained."'

'Christ!' said Dr. Obispo, unable to contain himself

any longer. 'Don't tell me that the old buzzard is going to eat raw fish-guts!'

Bright behind their bifocals, Jeremy's eyes had darted down to the bottom of the page and were already at the top of the next. 'That's exactly what he is doing,' he cried delightedly. 'Listen to this: "My first three attempts provoked an uncontrollable retching; at the fourth I contrived to swallow what I had placed in my mouth, but within two or three minutes my triumph was cut short by an access of vomiting. It was only after the ninth or tenth essay that I was able to swallow and retain even a few spoonfuls of the nauseating mince meat."'

'Talk of courage!' said Dr. Obispo. 'I'd rather go through an air-raid than that.'

Jeremy, meanwhile, had not so much as raised his eyes from the book.

'"It is now a month,"' he read, '"since I began to test the truth of my Hypothesis, and I am now ingesting each day not less than six ounces of the raw, triturated Viscera of freshly opened Carp."'

'And the fish,' said Dr. Obispo, slowly shaking his head, 'has a greater variety of parasitic worms than any other animal. It makes my blood run cold even to hear about it.'

'You needn't worry,' said Jeremy, who had gone on reading. 'His Lordship does nothing but get better and better. Here's a "singular accession of Strength and Vigour during the month of March." Not to mention "Revival of appetite and Improved memory and powers of ratiocination." I like that ratiocination,' Jeremy put in appreciatively. 'Such a nice period piece, don't you think? A real Chippendale word!' He went on reading to himself, and after a little silence announced triumphantly: 'By April he's riding again "an hour on the bay gelding every afternoon." And the dose of what he calls his "visceral and stercoraceous pap" has been raised to ten ounces a day.'

Dr. Obispo jumped up from his chair and began to walk excitedly up and down the room. 'Damn it all!' he shouted. 'This is more than a joke. This is serious. Raw fish-guts; intestinal flora; prevention of sterol poisoning; and rejuvenation. Rejuvenation!' he repeated.

'The Earl's more cautious than you are,' said Jeremy. 'Listen to this. "Whether I owe my recovery to the Carp, to the Return of Spring, or to the *Vis medicatrix Naturæ*, I am not yet able to determine."'

Dr. Obispo nodded approvingly. 'That's the right spirit,' he said.

'"Time,"' Jeremy continued, '"will show; that is, if I can force it to show, which I intend to do by persisting in my present Regimen. For I take it that my Hypothesis will be substantiated if, after persisting in it for some time longer, I shall have recovered not only my former state of Health, but a measure of Vigour not enjoyed since the passing of Youth."'

'Good for him!' Dr. Obispo exclaimed. 'I only wish old Uncle Jo could look at things in that scientific way. Or, maybe,' he added, suddenly remembering the Nembutal and Mr. Stoyte's childlike faith in his medical omniscience, 'maybe I don't wish it. It might have its inconveniences.' He chuckled to himself over his private joke. 'Well, let's go on with our case history,' he added.

'In September he can ride for three hours at a stretch without fatigue,' said Jeremy. 'And he's renewing his acquaintance with Greek literature, and thinks very poorly of Plato, I notice. After which we have no entry till 1799.'

'No entry till 1799!' Dr. Obispo repeated indignantly. 'The old bastard! Just when his case is getting really interesting, he goes and leaves us in the dark.'

Jeremy looked up from the notebook, smiling. 'Not entirely in the dark,' he said. 'I'll read you his first entry after the two years of silence, and you can draw your own conclusions about the state of his intestinal flora.' He uttered a little cough and began to read in his Mrs. Gaskell manner. '"May 1799. The most promiscuously abandoned Females, especially among Women of Quality, are often those to whom an unkind Nature has denied the ordinary Reason and Excuse for Gallantry. Cut off by a constitutional Frigidity from the enjoyments of Pleasure, they are in everlasting rebellion against their Fate. The power which drives them on to multiply the number of their Gallantries is not Sensuality, but Hope; not the wish to reiterate the experience of a familiar Bliss, but rather the aspiration towards a common and much vaunted Felicity which they themselves have had the misfortune never to know. To the Voluptuary, the woman of easy Virtue is often no less obnoxious, though for other reasons, than she seems to the severe Moralist. God preserve me in Future from any such Conquests as that which I made this Spring at Bath!"' Jeremy put down the book. 'Do you still feel that you've been left in the dark?' he asked.

Chapter Seven

WITH a deafening shriek the electric smoothing-tool whirled its band of sandpaper against the rough surface of the wood. Bent over the carpenter's bench, Mr. Propter did not hear the sound of Pete's entrance and approach. For a long half-minute the young man stood in silence, watching him while he moved the smoothing-tool back and forth over the board before him. There was sawdust, Pete noticed, in the shaggy eyebrows, and on the sunburnt forehead a black smear where he had touched his face with oily fingers.

Pete felt a sudden twinge of compunction. It wasn't right to spy on a man if he didn't know you were there. It was underhand: you might be seeing something he didn't want you to see. He called Mr. Propter's name.

The old man looked up, smiled, and stopped the motor of his little machine.

'Well, Pete,' he said. 'You're just the man I want. That is, if you'll do some work for me. Will you? But I'd forgotten,' he added, interrupting Pete's affirmative answer, 'I'd forgotten about that heart of yours. These miserable rheumatic fevers! Do you think you ought to?'

Pete blushed a little; for he had not yet had time to live down a certain sense of shame in regard to his disability. 'You're not going to make me run the quarter-mile, are you?'

Mr. Propter ignored the jocular question. 'You're sure it's all right?' he insisted, looking with an affectionate earnestness into the young man's face.

'Quite sure, if it's only this sort of thing.' Pete waved his hand in the direction of the carpenter's bench.

'Honest?'

Pete was touched and warmed by the other's solicitude. 'Honest!' he affirmed.

'Very well then,' said Mr. Propter, reassured. 'You're hired. Or rather you're not *hired*, because you'll be lucky if you get as much as a Coca-Cola for your work. You're conscribed.'

All the other people round the place, he went on to explain, were busy. He had been left to run the entire furniture factory single-handed. And the trouble was that it had to be run under pressure; three of the migrant families down at the cabins were still without any chairs or tables.

'Here are the measurements,' he said, pointing to a typewritten sheet of paper pinned to the wall. 'And there's the lumber. Now, I'll tell you what I'd like you to do first,' he added, as he picked up a board and laid it on the bench.

The two men worked for some time without trying to speak against the noise of their electric tools. Then there was an interim of less noisy activity. Too shy to embark directly upon the subject of his own perplexities, Pete started to talk about Professor Pearl's new book on population. Forty inhabitants to the square mile for the entire land area of the planet. Sixteen acres per head. Take away at least half for unproductive land, and you were left with eight acres. And with average agri-cultural methods a human being could be supported on the produce of two and a half acres. With five and a half acres to spare for every person, why should a third of the world be hungry?

'I should have thought you'd have discovered the

answer in Spain,' said Mr. Propter. 'They're hungry because man cannot live by bread alone.'

'What has that got to do with it?'

'Everything,' Mr. Propter answered. 'Men can't live by bread alone, because they need to feel that their life has a point. That's why they take to idealism. But it's a matter of experience and observation that most idealism leads to war, persecution and mass insanity. Man cannot live by bread alone; but if he chooses to nourish his mind on the wrong kind of spiritual food, he won't even get bread. He won't even get bread, because he'll be so busy killing or preparing to kill his neighbours in the name of God, or Country, or Social Justice, that he won't be able to cultivate his fields. Nothing could be simpler or more obvious. But at the same time,' Mr. Propter concluded, 'nothing is unfortunately more certain than that most people will go on choosing the wrong spiritual food and thereby indirectly choosing their own destruction.'

He turned on the current, and once more the smoothing-tool set up its rasping shriek. There was another cessation of talk.

'In a climate like this,' said Mr. Propter, in the next interval of silence, 'and with all the water that'll be available when the Colorado River aqueduct starts running next year, you could do practically anything you liked.' He unplugged the smoothing-tool and went to fetch a drill. 'Take a township of a thousand inhabitants; give it three or four thousand acres of land and a good system of producers' and consumers' co-operatives: it could feed itself completely; it could supply about two-thirds of its other needs on the spot; and it could produce a surplus to exchange for such things as it couldn't produce itself. You could cover the State with such townships. That is,' he added, smiling rather mournfully, 'that is, if you could get the permission from the banks and a supply of people intelligent and virtuous enough to run a genuine democracy.'

'You certainly wouldn't get the banks to agree,' said Pete.

'And you probably couldn't find more than quite a few of the right people,' Mr. Propter added. 'And of course nothing's more disastrous than starting a social experiment with the wrong people. Look at all the efforts to start communities in this country. Robert Owen, for example, and the Fourierists and the rest of them. Dozens of social experiments and they all failed. Why? Because the men in charge didn't choose their people. There was no entrance examination and no novitiate. They accepted anyone who came along. That's what comes of being unduly optimistic about human beings.'

He started the drill and Pete took his turn with the smoothing-tool.

'Do you think one oughtn't to be optimistic?' the young man asked.

Mr. Propter smiled. 'What a curious question!' he answered. 'What would you say about a man who installed a vacuum pump in a fifty-foot well? Would you call him an optimist?'

'I'd call him a fool.'

'So would I,' said Mr. Propter. 'And that's the answer to your question; a man's a fool if he's optimistic about any situation in which experience has shown that there's no justification for optimism. When Robert Owen took in a crowd of defectives and incompetents and habitual crooks, and expected them to organize themselves into a new and better sort of human society, he was just a damned fool.'

There was silence for a time while Pete did some sawing.

'I suppose I've been too optimistic,' the young man said reflectively, when it was over.

Mr. Propter nodded. 'Too optimistic in certain directions,' he agreed. 'And at the same time too pessimistic in others.'

'For instance ?' Pete questioned.

'Well, to begin with,' said Mr. Propter, 'too optimistic about social reforms. Imagining that good can be fabricated by mass-production methods. But, unfortunately, good doesn't happen to be that sort of commodity. Good is a matter of moral craftsmanship. It can't be produced except by individuals. And, of course, if individuals don't know what good consists in, or don't wish to work for it, then it won't be manifested, however perfect the social machinery. There!' he added, in another tone, and blew the sawdust out of the hole he had been drilling. 'Now for these chair-legs and battens.' He crossed the room and began to adjust the lathe.

'And what do you think I've been too pessimistic about ?' Pete asked.

Mr. Propter answered, without looking up from his work : 'About human nature.'

Pete was surprised. 'I'd have expected you to say I was too optimistic about human nature,' he said.

'Well, of course, in certain respects that's true,' Mr. Propter agreed. 'Like most people nowadays, you're insanely optimistic about people as they are, people living exclusively on the human level. You seem to imagine that people can remain as they are and yet be the inhabitants of a world conspicuously better than the world we live in. But the world we live in is a consequence of what men have been and a projection of what they are now. If men continue to be like what they are now and have been in the past, it's obvious that the world they live in can't become better. If you imagine it can, you're wildly optimistic about human nature. But, on the other hand, you're wildly pessimistic if you imagine that men and women are condemned by their nature to pass their whole lives on the strictly human level. Thank God,' he said emphatically, 'they're not. They have it in their power to climb out and up, on to the level of eternity. No human society can become conspicuously better than it is now, unless it contains a fair proportion of individuals who know that their humanity isn't the last word and who consciously attempt to transcend it. That's why one should be profoundly pessimistic about the things most people are optimistic about—such as applied science, and social reform, and human nature as it is in the average man or woman. And that's also why one should be profoundly optimistic about the thing they're so pessimistic about that they don't even know it exists—I mean, the possibility of transforming and transcending human nature. Not by evolutionary growth, not in some remote future, but at any time—here and now, if you like —by the use of properly directed intelligence and goodwill.'

Tentatively he started the lathe, then stopped it again for further adjustments.

'It's the kind of pessimism and the kind of optimism you find in all the great religions,' he added. 'Pessimism about the world at large and human nature as it displays itself in the majority of men and women. Optimism about the things that can be achieved by anyone who wants to and knows how.' He started the lathe again and, this time, kept it going.

'You know the pessimism of the New Testament,' he went on through the noise of the machine. 'Pessimism about the mass of mankind : many are called, few chosen.

Pessimism about weakness and ignorance : from those
that have not shall be taken away even that which they
have. Pessimism about life as lived on the ordinary
human level; for that life must be lost if the other eternal
life is to be gained. Pessimism about even the highest
forms of worldly morality : there's no access to the kingdom of heaven for anyone whose righteousness fails to
exceed that of the Scribes and Pharisees. But who are
the Scribes and Pharisees ? Simply the best citizens; the
pillars of society; all right-thinking men. In spite of
which, or rather because of which, Jesus calls them a
generation of vipers. Poor dear Dr. Mulge!' he added
parenthetically. 'How pained he'd be if he ever had the
misfortune to meet his Saviour !' Mr. Propter smiled to
himself over his work. 'Well, that's the pessimistic side
of the Gospel teaching,' he went on. 'And, more systematically and philosophically, you'll find the same things
set forth in the Buddhist and Hindu scriptures. The
world as it is and people on the strictly human level—
they're beyond hope : that's the universal verdict. Hope
begins only when human beings start to realize that the
kingdom of heaven, or whatever other name you care to
give it, is within and can be experienced by anybody
who's prepared to take the necessary trouble. That's
the optimistic side of Christianity and the other-world
religions.'

Mr. Propter stopped the lathe, took out the chair-leg
he had been turning and put another in its place.

'It isn't the sort of optimism they teach you in the
liberal churches,' said Pete, thinking of his transition
period between Reverend Schlitz and militant anti-
fascism.

'No, it isn't,' Mr. Propter agreed. 'What they teach
you in liberal churches hasn't got anything to do with

Christianity or any other realistic religion. It's mainly drivel.'

'Drivel!'

'Drivel,' Mr. Propter repeated. 'Early twentieth-century humanism seasoned with nineteenth-century evangelicalism. What a combination! Humanism affirms that good can be achieved on a level where it doesn't exist and denies the fact of eternity. Evangelicalism denies the relationship between causes and effects by affirming the existence of a personal deity who forgives offences. They're like Jack Spratt and his wife : between the two of them, they lick the platter clean of all sense whatsoever. No, I'm wrong,' Mr. Propter added, through the buzz of the machine, 'not *all* sense. The humanists don't talk of more than one race, and the evangelicals only worship one God. It's left to the patriots to polish off that last shred of sense. The patriots and the political sectarians. A hundred mutually exclusive idolatries. "There are many gods and the local bosses are their respective prophets." The amiable silliness of the liberal churches is good enough for quiet times; but note that it's always supplemented by the ferocious lunacies of nationalism for use in times of crisis. And those are the philosophies young people are brought up on. The philosophies your optimistic elders expect you to reform the world with.' Mr. Propter paused for a moment, then added, '"As a man sows, so shall he reap. God is not mocked." Not mocked,' he repeated. 'But people simply refuse to believe it. They go on thinking they can cock a snook at the nature of things and get away with it. I've sometimes thought of writing a little treatise, like a cook-book, "One Hundred Ways of Mocking God" I'd call it. And I'd take a hundred examples from history and contemporary life, illustrating what happens when people undertake to do things without paying regard to the nature of reality. And the book would be divided into sections, such as "Mocking God in Agriculture," "Mocking God in Politics," "Mocking God in Education," "Mocking God in Philosophy," "Mocking God in Economics." It would be an instructive little book. But a bit depressing,' Mr. Propter added.

Chapter Eight

THE news that the Fifth Earl had had three illegitimate children at the age of eighty-one was announced in the notebook with a truly aristocratic understatement. No boasting, no self-congratulation. Just a brief, quiet statement of the facts between the record of a conversation with the Duke of Wellington and a note on the music of Mozart. One hundred and twenty years after the event, Dr. Obispo, who was not an English gentleman, exulted noisily, as though the achievement had been his own.

'Three of them,' he shouted in his proletarian enthusiasm. '*Three!* What do you think of that?'

Brought up in the same tradition as the Fifth Earl, Jeremy thought that it wasn't bad, and went on reading.

In 1820 the Earl had been ill again, but not severely; and a three months' course of raw carps' entrails had restored him to his normal health, 'the health,' as he put it, 'of a man in the flower of his age.'

A year later, for the first time in a quarter of a century, he visited his nephew and niece, and was delighted to find that Caroline had become a shrew, that John was already bald and asthmatic, and that their eldest daughter was so monstrously fat that nobody would marry her.

On the news of the death of Bonaparte he had written philosophically that a man must be a great fool if he could not satisfy his desire for glory, power and excitement except by undergoing the hardships of war and the tedium of civil government. '"The language of polite conversation," he concluded, "reveals with a sufficient clarity that such exploits as those of Alexander and Bonaparte have their peaceful and domestic equivalents. We speak of amorous *Adventures*, of the *Conquest* of a desired Female and the *Possession* of her Person. For the Man of sense, such tropes are eloquent indeed. Considering their significance, he perceives that war and the pursuit of Empire are wrong because foolish, foolish because unnecessary, and unnecessary because the satisfactions derivable from Victory and Dominion may be obtained with vastly less trouble, pain and ennui behind the silken curtains of the Duchess's Alcove or on the straw Pallet of the Dairy Maid. And if at any time such simple Pleasures should prove insipid, if, like the antique Hero, he should find himself crying for new Worlds to conquer, then by the offer of a supplementary guinea, or in very many instances, as I have found, gratuitously, by the mere elicitation of a latent Desire for Humiliation and even Pain, a man may enjoy the privilege of using the Birch, the Manacles, the Cage and any such other Emblems of absolute Power as the Fancy of the Conqueror may suggest and the hired Patience of the Conquered will tolerate or her consenting Taste approve. I recall a remark by Dr. Johnson to the effect that a man is seldom more innocently employed than when making Money. Making Love is an even more innocent employment than making Money. If Bonaparte had had the Wisdom to vent his Desire for Domination in the Saloons and Bed Chambers of his native Corsica, he would have expired in Freedom among his own people, and many hundreds of thousands of men now dead or maimed or blind would be alive and enjoying the use of their faculties. True, they would doubtless be employing their Eyes, Limbs and Lives as foolishly and malignantly as those whom Bonaparte did not murder are employing them to-day. But though a Superior Being might applaud the one-time Emperor for having removed so great a quantity of Vermin from the Earth, the Vermin themselves will always be of another Opinion. As a mere Man of Sense, and not a Superior Being, I am on the side of the Vermin."'

'Have you ever noticed,' said Dr. Obispo reflectively, 'the way even the most hard-boiled people always try to make out they're really good. Even this old buzzard—you'd think *he* wouldn't care how he rated, so long as he got his fun. But no; he has to write a long screed proving what a much better man he is than Napoleon. Which, of course, he is by any reasonable standard. But you wouldn't expect him to go out of his way to say so.'

'Well, nobody else was likely to say so,' Jeremy put in.

'So he had to do it himself,' Dr. Obispo concluded. 'Which just proves my point. Iagos don't exist. People will do everything Iago did; but they'll never say they're villains. They'll construct a beautiful verbal world in which all their villainies are right and reasonable. I'd hoped that old carp-guts would be an exception. But he isn't. It's really rather a disappointment.'

Jeremy giggled with a certain patronizing disdain. 'You'd have liked him to do the Don-Juan-in-hell-act. The *calme héros courbé sur sa rapière.* You're more romantic than I thought.' He turned back to the notebook and, after a pause, announced that in 1823 the Fifth Earl had spent some hours with Coleridge and found his conversation deep, but singularly muddy—"characteristics," he had added, "which are admirable in Fish Ponds, but deplorable in rational Discourse, which should be pellucid and always shallow enough for a man to wade through without risk of drowning himself in an abyss of nonsense." Jeremy beamed with pleasure. Coleridge was not a favourite of his. 'When I think of the rot people are still talking about the rubbish that old dope-addict wrote . . .'

Dr. Obispo cut him short. 'Let's hear some more about the Earl,' he said.

Jeremy returned to the notebook.

In 1824 the old gentleman was lamenting the passage of the Bill which assimilated the transportation of slaves to piracy and so made the trade a capital offence. Henceforward, he would be a matter of eight or nine thousand a year the poorer. But he consoled himself by thinking of Horace living in philosophic tranquillity on his Sabine farm.

In 1826 he was deriving his keenest pleasure from a re-perusal of Theocritus and the company of a young female, called Kate, whom he had made his housekeeper. In the same year, despite the curtailment of his income, he had been unable to resist the temptation of purchasing an exquisite 'Assumption of the Virgin' by Murillo.

1827 had been a year of financial reverses; reverses that were connected, apparently, with the death, following an abortion, of a very young maid employed by the housekeeper as her personal attendant. The entry in the notebook was brief and obscure; but it seemed to imply that the girl's parents had had to be paid a very substantial sum.

A little later, he was unwell again and wrote a long and minute description of the successive stages of decay in the human corpse, with special reference to the eyes and lips. A short course of triturated carp restored him to a more cheerful frame of mind, and in 1828 he made a voyage to Athens, Constantinople and Egypt.

In 1831 he was in negotiations for the purchase of a house near Farnham.

'That must be Selford,' Jeremy put in. 'The house

where these things came from.' He indicated the twenty-seven packing-cases. 'Where the two old ladies are living.' He continued his reading. '"The house is old, dark and inconvenient, but stands in sufficiently extensive Grounds upon an Eminence above the River Wey, whose southern bank at this point rises almost perpendicularly in a Cliff of yellow sandstone, to the height of perhaps one hundred and twenty feet. The Stone is soft and easily worked, a Circumstance which accounts for the existence beneath the house of very extensive Cellars which were dug, it would seem, about a Century ago, when the Vaults were used for the storage of smuggled Spirits and other goods on their way from the coasts of Hampshire and Sussex to the Metropolis. To allay the fears of his Wife, who dreads to lose a child in their subterranean meanders, the Farmer who now owns the House has walled off the greater part of his Cellarage; but even that which remains presents the appearance of a veritable Catacomb. In Vaults such as these a man could be assured of all the Privacy required for the satisfaction of even the most eccentric Tastes."' Jeremy looked up over the top of his book. 'That sounds a bit sinister, don't you think ?'

Dr. Obispo shrugged his shoulders. 'Nobody can have enough privacy,' he said emphatically. 'When I think of all the trouble I've had for want of some nice cellars like the ones you've been reading about . . .' He left the sentence unfinished, and a shadow crossed his face: he was thinking that he couldn't go on giving Jo Stoyte those Nembutal capsules indefinitely, damn him !

'Well, he buys the house,' said Jeremy, who had been reading to himself. 'And he has repairs and additions made in the Gothic manner. And an apartment is fitted up in the cellars, forty-five feet underground and at the end of a long passage. And, to his delight, he finds that there's a subterranean well, and another shaft that goes down to a great depth and can be used as a privy. And the place is perfectly dry and has an ample supply of air, and . . .'

'But what does he do down there ?' Dr. Obispo asked impatiently.

'How should I know ?' Jeremy answered. He ran his eyes down the page. 'At the moment,' he went on, 'the old boy's making a speech to the House of Lords in favour of the Reform Bill.'

'In favour of it ?' said Obispo in surprise.

'"In the first days of the French Revolution,"' Jeremy read out, '"I infuriated the adherents of every political Party by saying: 'The Bastille is fallen; long live the Bastille.' Forty-three years have elapsed since the occurrence of that singularly futile Event, and the correctness of my Prognostications has been demonstrated by the rise of new Tyrannies and the restoration of old ones. It is therefore with perfect Confidence that I now say: 'Privilege is dead; long live Privilege.' The masses of mankind are incapable of Emancipation and too inept to direct their own Destinies. Government must always be by Tyrants or Oligarchs. My opinion of the Peerage and the landed Gentry is exceedingly low; but their own opinion of themselves must be even lower than mine. *They* believe that the Ballot will rob them of their Power and Privileges, whereas *I* am sure that, by the exercise of even such little Prudence and Cunning as parsimonious Nature has endowed them with, they can with ease maintain themselves in their present pre-eminence. This being so, let the Rabble amuse itself by voting. An Election is no more than a gratuitous Punch and Judy Show, offered by the Rulers in order to distract the attention of the Ruled."'

'How he'd have enjoyed a modern communist or fascist election !' said Dr. Obispo. 'By the way, how old was he when he made this speech ?'

'Let me see.' Jeremy paused for a moment to make the calculation, then answered : 'Ninety-four.'

'Ninety-four !' Dr. Obispo repeated. 'Well, if it wasn't those fish-guts, I don't know what it was.'

Jeremy turned back to the notebook. 'At the beginning of 1833 he sees his nephew and niece again, on the occasion of Caroline's sixty-fifth birthday. Caroline now wears a red wig, her eldest daughter is dead of cancer, the younger is unhappy with her husband and is addicted to piety, the son, who is now a Colonel, has gambling debts which he expects his parents to pay. Altogether, as the Earl remarks, "a most enjoyable evening."'

'Nothing about those cellars ?' Dr. Obispo complained.

'No ; but his housekeeper, Kate, has been ill and he's giving her the carp diet.'

Dr. Obispo showed a renewal of interest. 'And what happens ?' he asked.

Jeremy shook his head. 'The next entry's about Milton,' he said.

'Milton ?' exclaimed Dr. Obispo in a tone of indignant disgust.

'He says that Milton's writings prove that religion depends for its existence upon the picturesque use of intemperate language.'

'He may be right,' said Dr. Obispo irritably. 'But what I want to know is what happened to that housekeeper.'

'She's evidently alive,' said Jeremy. 'Because here's a little note in which he complains about the tediousness of too much female devotion.'

'Tedious !' Dr. Obispo repeated. 'That's putting it mildly. I've known women who were like fly-paper.'

'He doesn't seem to have objected to an occasional infidelity. There's a reference here to a young mulatto girl.' He paused; then, smiling, 'Delicious creature,' he said. '"She combines the brutish imbecility of the Hottentot with the malice and cupidity of the European." After which the old gentleman goes out to dinner at Farnham Castle with the Bishop of Winchester and finds his claret poor, his port execrable and his intellectual powers beneath contempt.'

'Nothing about Kate's health?' Dr. Obispo persisted.

'Why should he talk about it? He takes it for granted.'

'I'd hoped he was a man of science,' said Dr. Obispo almost plaintively.

Jeremy laughed. 'You must have very odd ideas about fifth earls and eleventh barons. Why on earth should they be men of science?' Dr. Obispo was unable to answer. There was a silence, while Jeremy started a new page. 'Well, I'm damned!' he broke out. 'He's been reading James Mill's *Analysis of the Human Mind*. At ninety-five. I think that's even more remarkable than having a rejuvenated housekeeper and a mulatto. "The Common Fool is merely stupid and ignorant. To be a Great Fool a man must have much learning and high abilities. To the everlasting credit of Mr. Bentham and his Lieutenants it must be said that *their* Folly has always been upon the grandest scale. Mr. Mill's *Analysis* is a veritable Coliseum of silliness." And the next note is about the Marquis de Sade. By the way,' Jeremy interpolated, looking up at Dr. Obispo, 'when are you going to return me my books?'

Dr. Obispo shrugged his shoulders. 'Whenever you like,' he answered. 'I'm through with them.'

Jeremy tried not to show his delight and, with a cough, returned to the notebook. '"The Marquis de Sade,"' he read aloud, '"was a man of powerful genius, unhappily deranged. In my opinion, an Author would achieve Perfection if he combined the qualities of the Marquis with those of Bishop Butler and Sterne."' Jeremy paused. 'The Marquis, Bishop Butler and Sterne,' he repeated slowly. 'My word, you'd have a pretty remarkable book!' He went on reading. '"October 1833. To degrade oneself is pleasurable in proportion to the height of the worldly and intellectual Eminence from which one descends and to which one returns when the act of Degradation is concluded." That's pretty good,' he commented, thinking of the Trojan Women and alternate Friday afternoons in Maida Vale. 'Yes, that's pretty good. Let me see, where are we? Oh yes. "The Christians talk much of Pain, but nothing of what they say is to the point. For the most remarkable Characteristics of Pain are these: the Disproportion between the enormity of physical suffering and its often trifling causes; and the manner in which, by annihilating every faculty and reducing the body to helplessness, it defeats the Object for which it was apparently devised by Nature: viz. to warn the sufferer of the approach of Danger, whether from within or without. In relation to Pain, that empty word, Infinity, comes near to having a meaning. This is not the case with Pleasure; for Pleasure is strictly finite and any attempt to extend its boundaries results in its transformation into Pain. For this reason, the infliction of Pleasure can never be so delightful to the aspiring Mind as the infliction of Pain. To give a finite quantity of Pleasure is a merely human act; the infliction of the Infinity we call Pain is truly god-like and divine."'

'The old bastard's going mystical in his old age,' Dr. Obispo complained. 'Almost reminds me of Mr. Propter.' He lit a cigarette. There was a silence.

'Listen to this,' Jeremy suddenly cried in a tone of excitement. '"March 11th, 1834. By the criminal negligence of Kate, Priscilla has been allowed to escape from the subterranean place of confinement. Bearing as she does upon her Person the evidence that she has been for some weeks past the subject of my Investigations, she holds in her hands my Reputation and perhaps even my Liberty and Life."'

'I suppose this is what you were talking about before we started reading,' said Dr. Obispo. 'The final scandal. What happened?'

'Well, I suppose the girl must have told her story,' Jeremy answered, without looking up from the page before him. 'Otherwise how do you account for the presence of this "hostile Rabble" he's suddenly started talking about? "The Humanity of men and women is inversely proportional to their Numbers. A Crowd is no more human than an Avalanche or a Whirlwind. A rabble of men and women stands lower in the scale of moral and intellectual being than a herd of Swine or of Jackals."'

Dr. Obispo threw back his head and uttered a peal of his surprisingly loud, metallic laughter. 'That's exquisite!' he said. 'Exquisite! You couldn't have a better example of typically human behaviour. *Homo* conducting himself like *sub-homo* and then being *sapiens* in order to prove that he's really *super-homo*.' He rubbed his hands together. 'This is really heavenly!' he said; then added: 'Let's hear what happens now.'

'Well, as far as I can make out,' said Jeremy, 'they have to send a company of militia from Guildford to protect the house from the rabble. And a magistrate has issued a warrant for his arrest; but they're not doing anything for the time being, on account of his age and position and the scandal of a public trial. Oh, and now they've sent for John and Caroline. Which makes the old gentleman wildly angry. But he's helpless. So they arrive at Selford; "Caroline in her orange wig, and John, at seventy-two, looking at least twenty years older than I, who was already twenty-four when my Brother, then scarcely of age, had the imprudence to marry an attorney's Daughter and the richly merited misfortune to beget this Attorney's Grandson whom I have always treated with the Contempt which his low origin and feeble Intellect deserve, but to whom the negligence of a Strumpet has now given the Power to impose his Will upon me."'

'One of those delightful family reunions,' said Dr. Obispo. 'But I suppose he doesn't give us any of the details?'

Jeremy shook his head. 'No details,' he said. 'Just an outline of the negotiations. On March the seventeenth they tell him that he can avoid prosecution if he makes over his unentailed property by deed of gift, assigns them the revenues of the entailed estates, and consents to enter a private asylum.'

'Pretty stiff conditions!'

'Which he refuses,' Jeremy continued, 'on the morning of the eighteenth.'

'Good for him!'

'"Private madhouses,"' Jeremy read out, '"are private prisons in which, uncontrolled by Parliament or Judiciary, subject to no inspection by the Police and closed even to the humanitarian visitations of Philanthropists, hired Torturers and Gaolers execute the dark designs of family Vengeance and personal Spite."'

Dr. Obispo clapped his hands with delight. 'There's another beautiful human touch!' he cried. 'Those humanitarian visitations of philanthropists!' he laughed

aloud. 'And hired torturers! It's like a speech by one
of the Foundling Fathers. Magnificent! And then one
thinks of those slave-ships and little Miss Priscilla. It's
almost as good as Field-Marshal Goering denouncing un-
kindness to animals. Hired torturers and gaolers,' he
repeated with relish, as though the phrase were a delicious
sweetmeat, slowly melting upon the palate. 'What's the
next move?' he asked.

'They tell him he'll be tried, condemned and trans-
ported. To which he answers that he prefers transportation to a private asylum. "At this it was evident that
my precious nephew and niece were nonplussed. They
swore that my treatment in the Madhouse should be
humane. I answered that I would not accept their word.
John talked of his honour. I said, An Attorney's honour,
no doubt, and spoke of the manner in which a lawyer
sells his convictions for a Fee. They then implored me
for the good name of the Family to accept their offers.
I answered that the good name of the Family was indifferent to me, but that I had no desire to undergo the
Humiliations of a Public Trial or the pains and discom-
forts of Transportation. I was ready, I said, to accept any
reasonable alternative to Trial and Transportation; but
I would regard no Alternative as reasonable which did
not in some sort guarantee my proper treatment at their
hands. Their word of honour I did not regard as such a
Guarantee; nor could I accept to be placed in an Institution where I should be entrusted to the care of Doctors
and Keepers in the pay of those whose Interest it was
that I should perish with all possible Celerity. I therefore
refused to subscribe to any Arrangement which left me
at their Mercy without placing them to a corresponding
extent at mine."'

'The principles of diplomacy in a nutshell!' said Dr.

Obispo. 'If only Chamberlain had understood them a little better before he went to Munich! Not that it would have made much difference in the long run,' he added. 'Because, after all, it doesn't really matter what the politicians do: nationalism will always produce at least one war each generation. It has done in the past, and I suppose we can rely on it to do the same in the future. But how does the old gentleman propose to put his principles into practice? He's at their mercy all right. How's he going to put them at his?'

'I don't know yet,' Jeremy answered from the depths of the recorded past. 'He's gone off on one of his philosophizing jaunts again.'

'Now?' said Dr. Obispo in astonishment. 'When he's got a warrant out against him?'

'"There was a time,"' Jeremy read, '"when I believed that all the Efforts of Humanity were directed towards a Point located approximately at the Centre of the female Person. To-day I am inclined to think that Vanity and Avarice play a more considerable part even than Lust in shaping the course of men's Actions and determining the nature of their Thoughts." And so on. Where the devil does he get back to the point again? Perhaps he never does; it would be just like him. No, here's something: "March 20th. To-day, Robert Parsons, my Factor, returned from London bringing with him in the Coach, three strong boxes containing Gold coin and Bank Notes to the value of two hundred and eighteen thousand pounds, the product of the sale of my Securities and such Jewels, Plate and works of Art as it was possible to dispose of at such short notice and for cash. With more time I could have realized at least three hundred and fifty thousand pounds. This loss I can bear philosophically; for the sum I have in hand is amply sufficient for my purposes."'

'What purposes?' asked Dr. Obispo.

Jeremy did not answer for a little while. Then he shook his head in bewilderment. 'What on earth is happening now?' he said. 'Listen to this: "My funeral will be conducted with all the Pomp befitting my exalted Rank and the eminence of my Virtues. John and Caroline were miserly and ungrateful enough to object to the expense; but I have insisted that my Obsequies shall cost not a penny less than Four Thousand Pounds. My only Regret is that I shall be unable to leave my subterranean Retreat to see the Pageantry of Woe and to study the expression of grief upon the withered faces of the new Earl and his Countess. To-night I shall go down with Kate to our Quarters in the Cellarage; and to-morrow morning the World will hear the news of my death. The body of an aged Pauper has already been conveyed hither in Secret from Haslemere, and will take my place in the Coffin. After the Interment the New Earl and Countess will proceed at once to Gonister, where they will take up their Residence, leaving this house untenanted except for Parsons, who will serve as Caretaker and provide for our material wants. The Gold and Bank Notes brought by Parsons from London are already bestowed in a subterranean hiding-place known only to myself, and it has been arranged that, every First of June, so long as I live, five thousand pounds in cash shall be handed over by myself to John, or to Caroline, or, in the event of their predeceasing me, to their Heir, or to some duly authorized Representative of the Family. By this arrangement, I flatter myself, I fill the Place left vacant by the Affection they most certainly do not feel." And that's all,' said Jeremy, looking up. 'There's nothing else. Just two more blank pages, and that's the end of the book. Not another word of writing.'

There was a long silence. Once more Dr. Obispo got up and began to walk about the room.

'And nobody knows how long the old buzzard lived on?' he said at last.

Jeremy shook his head. 'Not outside the family. Perhaps those two old ladies . . .'

Dr. Obispo halted in front of him, and banged the table with his fist. 'I'm taking the next boat to England,' he announced dramatically.

Chapter Nine

TO-DAY, even the Children's Hospital brought Mr. Stoyte no consolations. The nurses had welcomed him with their friendliest smiles. The young house physician encountered in the corridor was flatteringly deferential. The convalescents shouted 'Uncle Jo!' with all their customary enthusiasm, and, as he paused beside their beds, the faces of the sick were momentarily illuminated with pleasure. His gifts of toys were received as usual, sometimes with noisy rapture, sometimes (more touchingly) in the silence of a happiness speechless with amazement and incredulity. On his round of the various wards, he saw, as on other days, the pitiful succession of small bodies distorted by scrofula and paralysis, of small emaciated faces resigned to suffering, of little angels dying, and martyred innocents and snub-faced imps of mischief tortured into a reluctant stillness.

Ordinarily it all made him feel good—like he wanted to cry, but at the same time like he wanted to shout and be proud : proud of just being human, because these kids were human and you'd never seen anything so brave as they were ; and proud that he had done this thing for them, given them the finest hospital in the State, and all the best that money could buy. But to-day his visit brought none of the customary reactions. He had no impulsion either to cry or to shout. He felt neither pride, nor the anguish of sympathy, nor the exquisite happiness that resulted from their combination. He felt nothing—nothing except the dull, gnawing misery which had been with him all that day, at the Pantheon, with Clancy, in his down-town office. Driving out from the city, he had looked forward to his visit to the hospital as an asthma patient might look forward to a dose of adrenalin or an opium-smoker to a long-postponed pipe. But the looked-for relief had not come. The kids had let him down.

Taking his cue from what had happened at the end of previous visits, the porter smiled at Mr. Stoyte as he left the hospital and said something about it being the finest bunch of great little kids he ever knew. Mr. Stoyte looked at him blankly, nodded without speaking, and passed on.

The porter watched him go. 'Jeepers Creepers!' he said to himself, remembering the expression on Mr. Stoyte's face.

Mr. Stoyte drove back to the castle feeling as unhappy as he had felt when he left it in the morning. He went up with the Vermeer to the fourteenth floor; Virginia was not in her boudoir. He went down to the tenth; but she was not in the billiard-room. He dropped to the second; but she was being neither manicured nor massaged. In a sudden access of suspicion he descended to the sub-sub-basement and almost ran to see if she were in the laboratory with Pete; the laboratory was empty. A mouse squeaked in its cage, and behind the glass of the aquarium one of the aged carp glided slowly from shadow into light and from light once more into green shadow. Mr. Stoyte hurried back to the elevator, shut himself in with the Dutchman's dream of everyday life mysteriously raised to the pitch of mathematical perfection, and pressed the topmost of the twenty-three buttons.

Arrived at his destination, Mr. Stoyte slid back the gate of the elevator and looked out through the glass panel in the second door.

The water of the swimming-pool was perfectly still. Between the battlements, the mountains had taken on their evening richness of golden light and indigo shadow. The sky was cloudless and transparently blue. A tray with bottles and glasses had been set on the iron table at the further side of the pool, and behind the table stood one of the low couches on which Mr. Stoyte was accustomed to take his sun-baths. Virginia was lying on this couch, as though anaesthetized, her lips parted, her eyes closed, one arm dropped limply and its hand lying palm upwards on the floor, like a flower carelessly thrown aside and forgotten. Half concealed by the table, Dr. Obispo, the Claude Bernard of his subject, was looking down into her face with an expression of slightly amused scientific curiosity.

In its first irrepressible uprush, Mr. Stoyte's fury came near to defeating its own homicidal object. With a great effort, he checked the impulse to shout, to charge headlong out of the elevator, waving his fists and foaming at the mouth. Trembling under the internal pressure of pent-up rage and hatred, he groped in the pocket of his jacket. Except for a child's rattle and two packets of chewing-gum left over from his distribution of gifts at the hospital, it was empty. For the first time in months he had forgotten his automatic.

For a few seconds Mr. Stoyte stood hesitating, undecided what to do. Should he rush out, as he had first been moved to do, and kill the man with his bare hands ? Or should he go down and fetch his gun ? In the end, he decided to get the gun. He pressed the button, and the lift dropped silently down its shaft. Unseeing, Mr. Stoyte glared at the Vermeer; and from her universe of perfected geometrical beauty the young lady in blue satin turned her head from the open harpsichord and looked out, past the draped curtain, over the black-and-white tessellated floor—out through the window of the picture-frame into that other universe in which Mr. Stoyte and his fellow-creatures had their ugly and untidy being.

Mr. Stoyte ran to his bedroom, opened the drawer in which his handkerchiefs were kept, rummaged furiously among the silks and cambrics, and found nothing. Then he remembered. Yesterday morning he had worn no jacket. The gun had been in his hip-pocket. Then Pedersen had come to give him his Swedish exercises. But a gun in the hip-pocket was uncomfortable if you did things on your back, on the floor. He had taken it out and put it away in the writing-desk in his study.

Mr. Stoyte ran back to the elevator, went down four floors and ran to the study. The gun was in the top left-hand drawer of the writing-table; he remembered exactly.

The top left-hand drawer of the writing-table was locked. So were all the other drawers.

'God damn that old bitch!' Mr. Stoyte shouted as he tugged at the handles.

Thoughtful and conscientious in every detail, Miss Grogram, his secretary, always locked up everything before she went home.

Still cursing Miss Grogram, whom he hated at the moment almost as bitterly as he hated that swine there on the roof, Mr. Stoyte hurried back to the elevator. The gate was locked. During his absence in the study, some-body must have pressed the recall button on some other floor. Through the closed door he could hear the faint hum of the machinery. The elevator was in use. God only knew how long he would have to wait.

Mr. Stoyte let out an inarticulate bellow, rushed along the corridor, turned to the right, opened a swing-door, turned to the right again and was at the gate of the service lift. He seized the handle and pulled. It was locked. He pressed the recall button. Nothing happened. The service elevator was also in use.

Mr. Stoyte ran back along the corridor, through the swing-door, then through another swing-door. Spiral round a central well that went down two hundred feet into the depth of the cellars, the staircase mounted and descended. Mr. Stoyte started to climb. Breathless after only two floors, he ran back to the elevators. The service elevator was still in use; but the other responded to the call of the button. Dropping from somewhere overhead, it came to a halt in front of him. The locked door unlocked itself. He pulled it open and stepped in. The young lady in satin still occupied her position of equilibrium in a perfectly calculated universe. The distance of her left eye from the left side of the picture was to its distance from the right side as one is to the square root of two minus one; and the distance of the same eye from the bottom of the picture was equal to its distance from the left side. As for the knot of ribbons on her right shoulder—that was precisely at the corner of an imaginary square with the sides equal to the longer of the two golden sections into which the base of the picture was divisible. A deep fold in the satin skirt indicated the position of the right side of this square, and the lid of the harpsichord marked the top. The tapestry in the upper right-hand corner stretched exactly one-third of the way across the picture and had its lower edge at a height equal to the base. Pushed forward by the browns and dusky ochres of the background, the blue satin encountered the black-and-white marble slabs of the floor and was pushed back, to be held suspended in mid picture-space, like a piece of steel between two magnets of opposite sign. Within the frame nothing could have been different; the stillness of that world was not the mere immobility of old paint and canvas; it was also the spirited repose of consummated perfection.

'The old bitch!' Mr. Stoyte kept growling to himself, and then, turning in memory from his secretary to Dr. Obispo, 'The swine!'

The elevator came to a stop. Mr. Stoyte darted out and hurried along the corridor to Miss Grogram's empty office. He thought he knew where she kept the keys; but it turned out that he was wrong. They were somewhere else. But where? where? where? Frustration churned up his rage into a foam of frenzy. He opened drawers and flung their contents on the floor, he scattered the neatly filed papers about the room, he overturned the dictaphone, he even went to the trouble of emptying the bookshelves and upsetting the potted cyclamen and the bowl of Japanese goldfish which Miss Grogram kept on the window-sill. Red scales flashed among the broken glass and the reference-books. One gauzy tail was black with spilt ink. Mr. Stoyte picked up a bottle of glue and, with all his might, threw it down among the dying fish.

'Bitch!' he shouted. 'Bitch!'

Then suddenly he saw the keys, hanging in a neat little bunch on a hook near the mantelpiece, where, he suddenly remembered, he had seen them a thousand times before.

'Bitch!' he shouted with redoubled fury as he seized them. He hurried towards the door, pausing only to push the typewriter off its table. It fell with a crash into the chaos of torn paper and glue and goldfish. That would serve the old bitch right, Mr. Stoyte reflected with a kind of maniacal glee as he ran towards the elevator.

Chapter Ten

Barcelona had fallen.

But even if it had not fallen, even if it had never been besieged, what then?

Like every other community, Barcelona was part machine, part sub-human organism, part nightmare-huge projection and embodiment of men's passions and insanities—their avarice, their pride, their lust for power, their obsession with meaningless words, their worship of lunatic ideals.

Captured or uncaptured, every city and nation has its being on the plane of the absence of God. Has its being on the plane of the absence of God, and is therefore foredoomed to perpetual self-stultification, to endlessly reiterated attempts at self-destruction.

Barcelona had fallen. But even the prosperity of human societies is a continual process of gradual or catastrophic falling. Those who build up the structures of civilization are the same as those who undermine the structures of civilization. Men are their own termites, and must remain their own termites for just so long as they persist in being only men.

The towers rise, the palaces, the temples, the dwellings, the workshops; but the heart of every beam is gnawed to dust even as it is laid, the joists are riddled, the floors eaten away under the feet.

What poetry, what statues—but on the brink of the Peloponnesian War! And now the Vatican is painted—just in time for the sack of Rome. And the Eroica is composed—but for a hero who turns out to be just

another bandit. And the nature of the atom is elucidated
—by the same physicists as volunteer in war-time to
improve the arts of murder.

On the plane of the absence of God, men can do nothing else except destroy what they have built—destroy
even while they build—build with the elements of destruction.

Madness consists in not recognizing the facts; in making wishes the fathers of thoughts; in conceiving things
to be other than they really are; in trying to realize
desired ends by means which countless previous experiments have shown to be inappropriate.

Madness consists, for example, in thinking of oneself as
a soul, a coherent and enduring human entity. But,
between the animal below and the spirit above there is
nothing on the human level except a swarm of con-
stellated impulses and sentiments and notions; a swarm
brought together by the accidents of heredity and language; a swarm of incongruous and often contradictory
thoughts and desires. Memory and the slowly changing
body constitute a kind of spatio-temporal cage, within
which the swarm is enclosed. To talk of it as though
it were a coherent and enduring 'soul' is madness. On
the strictly human level there is no such thing as a
soul.

Thought-constellations, feeling-arrangements, desire-
patterns. Each of these has been built up and is strictly
conditioned by the nature of its fortuitous origin. Our
'souls' are so little 'us' that we cannot even form the
remotest conception how 'we' should react to the universe, if we were ignorant of language in general, or even
of our own particular language. The nature of our
'souls' and of the world they inhabit would be entirely
different from what it is, if we had never learnt to talk,

or if we had learnt to talk Eskimo instead of English. Madness consists, among other things, in imagining that our 'soul' exists apart from the language our nurses happen to have taught us.

Every psychological pattern is determined; and, within the cage of flesh and memory, the total swarm of such patterns is no more free than any of its members. To talk of freedom in connection with acts which in reality are determined is madness. On the strictly human level no acts are free. By their insane refusal to recognize facts as they are, men and women condemn themselves to have their desires stultified and their lives distorted or extinguished. No less than the cities and nations of which they are members, men and women are for ever falling, for ever destroying what they have built and are building. But whereas cities and nations obey the laws that come into play whenever large numbers are involved, individuals do not. Or rather need not; for though in actual fact most individuals allow themselves to be subjected to these laws, they are under no necessity to do so. For they are under no necessity to remain exclusively on the human level of existence. It is in their power to pass from the level of the absence of God to that of God's presence. Each member of the psychological swarm is determined; and so is the conduct of the total swarm. But beyond the swarm, and yet containing and interpenetrating it, lies eternity, ready and waiting to experience itself. But if eternity is to experience itself within the temporal and spatial cage of any individual human being, the swarm we call the 'soul' must voluntarily renounce the frenzy of its activity, must make room, as it were, for the other timeless consciousness, must be silent to render possible the emergence of profounder silence. God is completely present only in the complete absence of what we call our

humanity. No iron necessity condemns the individual
to the futile torment of being merely human. Even the
swarm we call the soul has it in its power temporarily to
inhibit its insane activity, to absent itself, if only for a
moment, in order that, if only for a moment, God may
be present. But let eternity experience itself, let God be
sufficiently often present in the absence of human desires
and feelings and preoccupations: the result will be a
transformation of the life which must be lived, in the
intervals, on the human level. Even the swarm of our
passions and opinions is susceptible to the beauty of
eternity; and, being susceptible, becomes dissatisfied with
its own ugliness; and, being dissatisfied, undertakes to
change itself. Chaos gives place to order—not the arbi-
trary, purely human order that comes from the sub-
ordination of the swarm to some lunatic 'ideal,' but an
order that reflects the real order of the world. Bondage
gives place to liberty—for choices are no longer dictated
by the chance occurrences of earlier history, but are made
teleologically and in the light of a direct insight into the
nature of things. Violence and mere inertia give place to
peace—for violence is the manic, and inertia the de-
pressive, phase of that cyclic insanity, which consists in
regarding the ego or its social projections as real entities.
Peace is the serene activity which springs from the knowledge that our 'souls' are illusory and their creations
insane, that all beings are potentially united in eternity.
Compassion is an aspect of peace and a result of the same
act of knowledge.

Walking at sunset up the castle hill, Pete kept thinking
with a kind of tranquil exultation of all the things Mr.
Propter had said to him. Barcelona had fallen. Spain,
England, France, Germany, America—all were falling;
falling even at such times as they seemed to be rising;

destroying what they built in the very act of building. But any individual has it in his power to refrain from falling, to stop destroying himself. The solidarity with evil is optional, not compulsory.

On their way out of the carpenter's shop Pete had brought himself to ask Mr. Propter if he would tell him what he ought to do.

Mr. Propter had looked at him intently. 'If you want it,' he had said, 'I mean, if you *really* want it . . .'

Pete had nodded without speaking.

The sun had set; and now the twilight was like the embodiment of peace—the peace of God, Pete said to himself, as he looked across the plain to the distant mountains, the peace that passes all understanding. To part with such loveliness was unbearable. Entering the castle, he went straight to the elevator, recalled the cage from somewhere up aloft, shut himself up with the Vermeer and pressed the highest of the buttons. Up there, at the top of the keep, he would be at the very heart of this celestial peace.

The elevator came to a halt. He opened the gates and stepped out. The swimming-pool reflected a luminous tranquillity. He turned his eyes from the water to the sky, and from the sky to the mountains; then walked round the pool in order to look down over the battlements on the further side.

'Go away!' a muffled voice suddenly said.

Pete started violently, turned and saw Virginia lying in the shadow almost at his feet.

'Go away,' the voice repeated. 'I hate you.'

'I'm sorry,' he stammered. 'I didn't know . . .'

'Oh, it's you.' She opened her eyes, and in the dim light he was able to see that she had been crying. 'I thought it was Sig. He went to get a comb for my hair.'

She was silent for a little; then suddenly she burst out, 'I'm so unhappy, Pete.'

'Unhappy?' The word and her tone had utterly shattered the peace of God. In an anguish of love and anxiety he sat down beside her on the couch. (Under her bath-robe, he couldn't help noticing, she didn't seem to be wearing anything at all.) 'Unhappy?'

Virginia covered her face with her hands and began to sob. 'Not even Our Lady,' she gasped in an incoherency of grief. 'I can't even tell *her*. I feel so mean . . .'

'Darling!' he said in a voice of entreaty, as though imploring her to be happy. He began to stroke her hair. 'My darling!'

Suddenly there was a violent commotion on the further side of the pool; a crash as the elevator gates were flung back; a rush of feet; an inarticulate yell of rage. Pete turned his head and was in time to see Mr. Stoyte rushing towards them, holding something in his hand, something that might almost have been an automatic pistol.

He had half risen to his feet, when Mr. Stoyte fired.

Arriving two or three minutes later with the comb for Virginia's hair, Dr. Obispo found the old man on his knees, trying, with a pocket-handkerchief, to stanch the blood that was still pouring out of the two wounds, one clean and small, the other cavernous, which the bullet had made as it passed through Pete's head.

Crouching in the shadow of the battlements, the Baby was praying. 'Holy-Mary-Mother- of-God-pray-for-us sinners-now-and-in-the-hour- of-our-death-Amen,' she repeated, again and again, as fast as her sobs would permit her. Every now and then she would be seized and shaken by an access of nausea, and the praying would be interrupted for a moment. Then it began again where she had left off '. . . us-sinners-now- and-in-the-hour-of-our-death-Amen-Holy-Mary-Mother-of-God . . .'

Dr. Obispo opened his mouth to make an exclamation, then closed it again, whispered, 'Christ!' and walked quickly and silently round the pool. Before making his presence known, he took the precaution of picking up the pistol and slipping it into his pocket. One never knew. Then he called Mr. Stoyte's name. The old man started, and a hideous expression of terror appeared on his face. Fear gave place to relief as he turned round and saw who it was that had spoken to him.

'Thank God it's you,' he said; then suddenly remembered that this was the man he had meant to kill. But all that had been a million years ago, a million miles away. The near, immediate, urgent fact was not the Baby, not love or anger; it was fear and this thing that lay here on the ground.

'You got to save him,' he said in a hoarse whisper. 'We can say it was an accident. I'll pay him anything he likes. Anything in reason,' an old reflex impelled him to add. 'But you got to save him.' Laboriously he heaved himself to his feet and motioned Dr. Obispo to his vacated place.

The only movement Dr. Obispo made was one of withdrawal. The old man was covered with blood, and he had no wish to spoil a ninety-five-dollar suit. 'Save him?' he repeated. 'You're mad. Look at all the brain lying there on the floor.'

From the shadows behind him, Virginia interrupted the sobbing mutter of her prayers to scream. 'On the floor,' she kept wailing. 'On the floor.'

Dr. Obispo turned on her savagely. 'Shut up, do you hear?'

The screams abruptly ceased; but a few seconds later there was a sound of violent retching; then 'Holy-Mary-

Mother-of-God-pray-for-us-sinners-now-and-in-the-
hour-of-our-death-Amen-Holy-Mary-Mother-of-God-
pray-for-us- sinners . . .'

'If we're going to try and save anybody,' Dr. Obispo
went on, 'it had better be you. And believe me,' he
added emphatically, throwing all his weight on his left
leg and using the toe of his right shoe to point at the body,
'you need some saving. It's either the gas chamber or
St. Quentin for life.'

'But it was an accident.' Mr. Stoyte began to protest
with a breathless eagerness. 'I mean, it was all a mistake.
I never wanted to shoot him. I meant to . . .' He broke
off and stood in silence, his mouth working, as though
he were trying to swallow some unspoken words.

'You meant to kill me,' said Dr. Obispo, completing
the sentence for him and smiling, as he did so, with the
expression of wolfish good-humour which was characteristic of him in any situation where the joke was at all
embarrassing or painful. Secure in the knowledge that
the old buzzard was much too scared to be angry, and
that anyhow the gun was in his own pocket, he prolonged
the joke by saying, 'Well,' sententiously, 'that's what
comes of snooping.'

'. . . now-and-in-the-hour-of-our-death-Amen,' Virginia gabbled in the ensuing silence. 'Holy-Mary-
Mother . . .'

'I never meant it,' Mr. Stoyte reiterated. 'I just got
mad. Guess I didn't really figure out what I was
doing. . . .'

'Tell that to the jury,' said Dr. Obispo sarcastically.

'But I swear it: I didn't really know,' Mr. Stoyte protested. His harsh voice broke grotesquely into a squeak.
His face was white with fear.

The doctor shrugged his shoulders. 'Maybe,' he said.

'But not knowing doesn't make any difference to that.'
He stood on one leg again to point an elegantly shod foot
in the direction of the body.

'But what shall I *do*?' Mr. Stoyte almost screamed in
the anguish of his terror.

'Don't ask me.'

Mr. Stoyte initiated the gesture of laying his hand im-
ploringly on the other's sleeve; but Dr. Obispo quickly
drew back. 'No, don't touch me,' he said. 'Just look at
your hands.'

Mr. Stoyte looked. The thick, carrot-like fingers were
red; under the horny nails the blood was already caked
and dry, like clay. 'God!' he whispered. 'Oh my God!'

'. . . and-at-the-hour- of-our-death-Amen-Holy-
Mary . . .'

At the word 'death' the old man started as though he
had been struck with a whip. 'Obispo,' he began again,
breathless with apprehension, 'Obispo! Listen here—
you got to help me out of this. You got to help me,' he
entreated.

'After you did your best to do *that* to me?' The
white-and-tan shoe shot out again.

'You wouldn't let them get me?' Mr. Stoyte wheedled,
abject in his terror.

'Why wouldn't I?'

'But you can't,' he almost shouted. 'You can't.'

Dr. Obispo bent down to make quite sure, in the fading
light, that there was no blood on the couch; then, pulling
up his fawn-coloured trousers, sat down. 'One gets tired
of standing,' he said in a pleasant conversational tone.

Mr. Stoyte went on pleading. 'I'll make it worth your
while,' he said. 'You can have anything you care to ask
for. Anything,' he repeated without any qualifying
reference, this time, to reason.

'Ah,' said Dr. Obispo, 'now you're talking turkey.'

'... Mother-of-God,' muttered the Baby, 'pray-for-us-sinners-now-and-in-the-hour-of-our-death-Amen-Holy-Mary-Mother-of-God-pray-for-us-sinners-now...'

'You're talking turkey,' Dr. Obispo repeated.

PART THREE

Chapter One

THERE was a tap at the door of Jeremy's work-room; it was Mr. Propter who entered. He was wearing, Jeremy noticed, the same dark-grey suit and black tie as he had worn at Pete's funeral. The urban costume diminished him; he seemed smaller than in his working clothes, and at the same time less himself. That weather-beaten, emphatically featured face of his—that face of a statue high up on the west front of a cathedral—looked curiously incongruous above a starched collar.

'You've not forgotten?' he said, when they had shaken hands.

For all reply, Jeremy pointed to his own black jacket and sponge-bag trousers. They were expected at Tarzana for the ceremonial opening of the new Stoyte Auditorium.

Mr. Propter looked at his watch. 'We've got another few minutes before we need think of starting.' He sat down. 'What's the news?'

'Couldn't be better,' Jeremy answered.

Mr. Propter nodded. 'Now that poor Jo and the others have gone, it must be quite agreeable here.'

'All alone with twelve million dollars' worth of bric-à-brac,' said Jeremy. 'I have the most enormous fun.'

'How little fun you'd be having,' said Mr. Propter meditatively, 'if you'd been left in company with the people who actually made the bric-à-brac. With Greco, and Rubens, and Turner, and Fra Angelico.'

'God preserve us!' said Jeremy, throwing up his hands.

'That's the charm of art,' Mr. Propter went on. 'It

K   283 represents only the most amiable aspects of the most talented human beings. That's why I've never been able to believe that the art of any period threw much light on the life of that period. Take a Martian; show him a representative collection of Botticellis, Peruginos and Raphaels. Could he infer from them the conditions described by Machiavelli?'

'No, he couldn't,' Jeremy agreed. 'But meanwhile, here's another question. The conditions described by Machiavelli—were they the real conditions? Not that Machiavelli didn't tell the truth. The things he described really happened. But did contemporaries think them as awful as they seem to us when we read about them now? *We* think they ought to have been miserable about what was happening. But were they?'

'Were they?' Mr. Propter repeated. 'We ask the historians; and of course they can't answer—because obviously there's no way of compiling statistics about the sum of happiness, nor any way of comparing the feelings of people living under one set of conditions with the feelings of people living under another and quite different set. The real conditions at any given moment are the subjective conditions of the people then alive. And the historian has no way of finding out what those conditions were.'

'No way except through looking at works of art,' said Jeremy. 'I'd say they do throw light on the subjective conditions. Take one of your examples. Perugino's a contemporary of Machiavelli. That means that at least one person contrived to be cheerful all through an unpleasant period. And if one could be, why not many?' He cleared the way for a quotation with a little cough. '"The state of the country never put a man off his dinner."'

'Massive wisdom!' said Mr. Propter. 'But remember that the state of Dr. Johnson's England was excellent, even at its worst. What about the state of a country like China, say, or Spain—a country where a man can't be put off his dinner, for the simple reason that there isn't any dinner? And conversely, what about all the losses of appetite at times when everything's going well?' He paused, smiled enquiringly at Jeremy, then shook his head. 'Sometimes there's a lot of cheerfulness as well as a lot of misery; sometimes there seems to be almost nothing but misery. That's all the historian can say in so far as he's a historian. In so far as he's a theologian, of course, or a metaphysician, he can maunder on indefinitely, like Marx or St. Augustine or Spengler.' Mr. Propter made a little grimace of distaste. 'God, what a lot of bosh we've managed to talk in the last few thousand years!' he said.

'But it has its charm,' Jeremy insisted. 'Really *good* bosh . . .'

'I'm barbarous enough to prefer sense,' said Mr. Propter. 'That's why, if I want a philosophy of history, I go to the psychologist.'

'"Totem and Taboo?"' Jeremy questioned in some astonishment.

'No, no,' said Mr. Propter with a certain impatience. 'Not *that* kind of psychologist. I mean the religious psychologist; the one who knows by direct experience that men are capable of liberation and enlightenment. He's the only philosopher of history whose hypothesis has been experimentally verified; therefore the only one who can make a generalization that covers the facts.'

'And what are his generalizations?' said Jeremy. 'Just the usual thing?'

Mr. Propter laughed. 'Just the usual thing,' he answered: 'the old, boring, unescapable truths. On the human level.

men live in ignorance, craving and fear. Ignorance, craving and fear result in some temporary pleasures, in many lasting miseries, in final frustration. The nature of the cure is obvious; the difficulties in the way of its achieving it, almost insuperable. We have to choose between almost insuperable difficulties on the one hand and absolutely certain misery and frustration on the other. Meanwhile, the general hypothesis remains as the intellectual key to history. Only the religious psychologist can make any sense of Perugino and Machiavelli, for example; or of all this.' He pointed towards the Hauberk Papers.

Jeremy twinkled behind his glasses and patted his bald patch. 'Your true scholar,' he fluted, 'doesn't even *want* to make sense of it.'

'Yes, I always tend to forget that,' said Mr. Propter rather sadly.

Jeremy coughed. '"Gave us the doctrine of the enclitic *De*,"' he quoted from the 'Grammarian's Funeral.'

'Gave it for his own sake,' said Mr. Propter, getting out of his chair. 'Gave it regardless of the fact that the grammar he was studying was hopelessly unscientific, riddled with concealed metaphysics, utterly provincial and antiquated. Well,' he added, 'that's what one would expect, I suppose.' He took Jeremy's arm, and they walked together towards the elevator. 'What a curious figure old Browning is!' he continued, his mind harking back to the Grammarian. 'Such a first-rate intelligence, and at the same time *such* a fool. All that preposterous stuff about romantic love! Bringing God into it, putting it into heaven, talking as though marriage and the higher forms of adultery were identical with the beatific vision. The silliness of it! But, again, that's what one has to expect.' He sighed. 'I don't know why,' he added after a pause, 'I often find myself remembering that rhyme of his—I can't even recall which poem it comes from—the one that goes: "one night he kissed My soul out in a burning mist." My soul out in a burning mist, indeed!' he repeated. 'Really, how much I prefer Chaucer on the subject. Do you remember? "Thus swivèd is this carpenterès wife." So beautifully objective and unemphatic and free of verbiage! Browning was always rambling on about God; but I suspect he was much further away from reality than Chaucer was, even though Chaucer never thought about God if he could possibly help it. Chaucer had nothing between himself and eternity but his appetites. Browning had his appetites, plus a great barrage of nonsense—nonsense, what's more, with a purpose. For, of course, that bogus mysticism wasn't merely gratuitous bosh. It had an object. It existed in order that Browning might be able to persuade himself that his appetites were identical with God. "Thus swivèd is this carpenterès wife,"' he repeated, as they entered the elevator and went up with Vermeer to the great hall. '"My soul out in a burning mist!" It's extraordinary the way the whole quality of our existence can be changed by altering the words in which we think and talk about it. We float in language like icebergs—four-fifths under the surface and only one-fifth of us projecting into the open air of immediate, non-linguistic experience.'

They crossed the hall. Mr. Propter's car was standing outside the front door. He took the wheel; Jeremy got in beside him. They drove off, down the curving road, past the baboons, past Giambologna's nymph, past the Grotto, under the portcullis and across the drawbridge.

'I so often think of that poor boy,' said Mr. Propter, breaking a long silence. 'Dying so suddenly.'

'I'd no idea his heart was as bad as that,' said Jeremy.

'In a certain sense,' Mr. Propter went on, 'I feel responsible for what happened. I asked him to help me in the carpenter's shop. Made him work too hard, I guess—though he insisted it was all right for him. I ought to have realized that he had his pride—that he was young enough to feel ashamed of admitting he couldn't take it. One's punished for being insensitive and unaware. And so are the people one's insensitive about.'

They drove past the hospital and through the orange groves in silence. 'There's a kind of pointlessness about sudden and premature death,' said Jeremy at last. 'A kind of specially acute irrelevance . . .'

'Specially acute?' Mr. Propter questioned. 'No, I shouldn't say so. It's no more irrelevant than any other human event. If it seems more irrelevant, that's only because, of all possible events, premature death is the most glaringly out of harmony with what we imagine ourselves to be.'

'What do you mean?' Jeremy asked.

Mr. Propter smiled. 'I mean what I presume *you* mean,' he answered. 'If a thing seems irrelevant, there must be something it's irrelevant to. In this case, that something is our conception of what we are. We think of ourselves as free, purposive beings. But every now and then things happen to us that are incompatible with this conception. We speak of them as accidents; we call them pointless and irrelevant. But what's the criterion by which we judge? The criterion is the picture we paint of ourselves in our own fancy—the highly flattering portrait of the free soul making creative choices and being the master of its fate. Unfortunately, the picture bears no resemblance to ordinary human reality. It's the picture of what we'd like to be, of what, indeed, we might become if we took the trouble. To a being who is in fact

the slave of circumstance there's nothing specially irrelevant about premature death. It's the sort of event
that's characteristic of the universe in which he actually
lives—though not, of course, of the universe he foolishly
imagines he lives in. An accident is the collision of a
train of events on the level of determinism with another
train of events on the level of freedom. We imagine that
our life is full of accidents, because we imagine that our
human existence is lived on the level of freedom. In fact,
it isn't. Most of us live on the mechanical level, where
events happen in accordance with the laws of large numbers. The things we call accidental and irrelevant belong
to the very essence of the world in which we elect to
live.'

Annoyed at having, by an unconsidered word, landed
himself in a position which Mr. Propter could show to be
unwarrantably 'idealistic,' Jeremy was silent. They drove
on for a time without speaking.

'That funeral!' Jeremy said at last; for his chronically
anecdotal mind had wandered back to what was concrete,
particular and odd in the situation under discussion. 'Like
something out of Ronald Firbank!' He giggled. 'I told
Mr. Habakkuk he ought to put steam heat into the statues.
They're dreadfully unlifelike to the *touch*.' He moved
his cupped hand over an imaginary marble protuber-
ance.

Mr. Propter, who had been thinking about liberation,
nodded and politely smiled.

'And Dr. Mulge's reading of the service!' Jeremy went
on. 'Talk of unction! It couldn't have been oilier even
in an English cathedral. Like vaseline with a flavour of
port wine. And the way he said, "I am the resurrection
and the life"—as though he really meant it, as though he,
Mulge, could personally guarantee it, in writing, on a

money-back basis : the entire cost of the funeral refunded if the next world fails to give complete satisfaction.'

'He probably even believes it,' said Mr. Propter meditatively. 'In some curious Pickwickian way, of course. You know : it's true, but you consistently act as though it weren't; it's the most important fact in the universe, but you never think about it if you can possibly avoid it.'

'And how do *you* believe in it ?' Jeremy asked. 'Pickwickianly or unPickwickianly ?' And when Mr. Propter answered that he didn't believe in that sort of resurrection and life : 'Oho !' he went on in the tone of an indulgent father who has caught his son kissing the housemaid, 'Oho ! So there's also a Pickwickian resurrection ?'

Mr. Propter laughed. 'I think there may be,' he said.

'In which case, what has become of poor Pete ?'

'Well, to start with,' said Mr. Propter slowly, 'I should say that Pete, *qua* Pete, doesn't exist any longer.'

'Super-Pickwickian !' Jeremy interjected.

'But Pete's ignorance,' Mr. Propter went on, 'Pete's fears and cravings—well, I think it's quite possible that they're still somehow making trouble in the world. Making trouble for everything and everyone, especially for themselves. Themselves in whatever form they happen to be taking.'

'And if by any chance Pete hadn't been ignorant and concupiscent, what then ?'

'Well, obviously,' said Mr. Propter, 'there wouldn't be anything to make further trouble.' After a moment's silence, he quoted Tauler's definition of God. '"God is a being withdrawn from creatures, a free power, a pure working."'

He turned the car off the main road, into the avenue of pepper trees that wound across the green lawns of the

Tarzana Campus. The new Auditorium loomed up, austerely romanesque. Mr. Propter parked his old Ford among the lustrous Cadillacs and Chryslers and Packards already lined up in front of it, and they entered. The press photographers at the entrance looked them over, saw at a glance that they were neither bankers, nor movie stars, nor corporation lawyers, nor dignitaries of any church, nor senators, and turned away contemptuously.

The students were already in their places. Under their stares, Jeremy and Mr. Propter were ushered down the aisle to the rows of seats reserved for distinguished guests. And what distinction! There, in the front row, was Sol R. Katzenblum, the President of Abraham Lincoln Pictures Incorporated and a pillar of Moral Re-Armament; there, beside him, was the Bishop of Santa Monica; there too was Mr. Pescecagniolo, of the Bank of the Far West. The Grand Duchess Eulalie was sitting next to Senator Bardolph; and in the next row were two of the Engels Brothers and Gloria Bossom, who was chatting with Rear-Admiral Shotoverk. The orange robe and permanently waved beard belonged to Swami Yogalinga, founder of the School of Personality. Beside him sat the Vice-President of Consol Oil and Mrs. Wagner . . .

Suddenly the organ burst out, full blast, into the Tarzana Anthem. The academic procession filed in. Two by two, in their gowns and hoods and tasselled mortarboards, the Doctors of Divinity, of Philosophy, of Science, of Law, of Letters, of Music, shuffled down the aisle and up the steps on to the platform, where their seats had been prepared for them in a wide arc close to the back drop. At the centre of the stage stood a reading-desk, and at the reading-desk stood Dr. Mulge. Not that he did any reading, of course; for Dr. Mulge prided himself on being able to speak almost indefinitely without a note.

The reading-desk was there to be intimately leant over, to be caught hold of and passionately leant back from, to be struck emphatically with the palm of the hand, to be dramatically walked away from and returned to.

The organ was silent. Dr. Mulge began his address—began it with a reference, of course, to Mr. Stoyte. Mr. Stoyte whose generosity ... The realization of a Dream ... This embodiment of an ideal in Stone ... The Man of Vision. Without Vision the people perish ... But this Man had had Vision ... The Vision of what Tarzana was destined to become ... The centre, the focus, the torch-bearer ... California ... New Culture, richer science, higher spirituality ... (Dr. Mulge's voice modulated from bassoon to trumpet. From vaseline with a mere flavour of port wine to undiluted fatty alcohol.) But, alas (and here the voice subsided pathetically into saxophone and lanoline), alas ... Unable to be with us to-day ... A sudden distressing event ... Carried off on the threshold of life ... A young collaborator in those scientific fields which he ventured to say were as close to Mr. Stoyte's heart as the fields of social service and culture ... The shock ... The exquisitely sensitive heart under the sometimes rough exterior ... His physician had ordered a complete and immediate change of scene ... But in spite of physical absence, his spirit ... We feel it among us to-day ... An inspiration to all, young and old alike ... The torch of Culture ... The Future ... The Ideal ... The Spirit of Man ... Great things already accomplished ... God had walked in power through this campus ... Strengthened and guided ... Forward ... Onward ... Upward ... Faith and Hope ... Democracy ... Freedom ... The imperishable heritage of Washington and Lincoln ... The glory that was Greece reborn beside the waters of the Pacific ... The flag ... The mission . . . The manifest destiny . . . The will of God . . . Tarzana . . .

It was over at last. The organ played. The academic procession filed back up the aisle. The distinguished guests straggled after it.

Outside, in the sunshine, Mr. Propter was button-holed by Mrs. Pescecagniolo.

'I thought that was a wonderfully inspirational address,' she said with enthusiasm.

Mr. Propter nodded. 'Almost the most inspirational address I ever listened to. And God knows,' he said, 'I've heard a lot of them in the course of my life.'

Chapter Two

Even in London there was a little diluted sunshine—sunshine that brightened and grew stronger as they drove through the diminishing smoke of the outer suburbs, until at last, somewhere near Esher, they had travelled into the most brilliant of early spring mornings.

Under a fur rug, Mr. Stoyte sprawled diagonally across the rear seat of the car. More for his own good, this time, than for his physician's, he was back again on sedatives, and found it hard, before lunch, to keep awake. With a fitful stertorousness he had dozed almost from the moment they drove away from the Ritz.

Pale and with sad eyes, silently ruminating an unhappiness which five days of rain on the Atlantic and three more of London gloom had done nothing to alleviate, Virginia sat aloof in the front seat.

At the wheel (for he had thought it best to take no chauffeur on this expedition) Dr. Obispo whistled to himself and, occasionally, even sang aloud—sang, '*Stretti, stretti, nell' estasí d' amor*'; sang, 'Do you think a l-ittle drink'll do us any harm ?'; sang, 'I dreamt I dwelt in marble halls.' It was partly the fine weather that made him so cheerful—spring-time, he said to himself, the only merry ring-time, not to mention the lesser celandines, the windflowers, whatever they might be, the primroses in the copse. And should he ever forget his bewilderment when English people had started talking about cops in the singular and in contexts where policemen seemed deliriously out of place ? 'Let's go and pick some primroses in the cops.' Surprising intestinal flora ! Better even than the

294

carp's. Which brought him to the second reason for his satisfaction with life. They were on their way to see the two old Hauberk ladies—on their way, perhaps, to finding something interesting about the Fifth Earl, something significant about the relationship between senility and sterols and the intestinal flora of the carp.

With mock-operatic emphasis he burst again into song.

'I drea-heamt I dwe-helt in mar-harble halls,' he proclaimed, 'with vass-als and serfs at my si-hi-hide. And of all who assembled with-hin those walls, that I was the hope and the pri-hi-hide.'

Virginia, who had been sitting beside him, stony with misery, turned round in sudden exasperation. 'Oh, for heaven's sake!' she almost screamed, breaking a silence that had lasted all the way from Kingston-on-Thames. 'Can't you be quiet?'

Dr. Obispo ignored her protests. 'I had riches,' he sang on (and reflected, with an inward chuckle of satisfaction as he did so, that the statement now happened to be true), 'I had riches too grea-heat to cou-hount.' No; that was an exaggeration. Not at all too great to count. Just a nice little competence. Enough to give him security and the means to continue his researches without having to waste his time on a lot of sick people who ought to be dead. Two hundred thousand dollars in cash and forty-five hundred acres of land in the San Felipe Valley—land that Uncle Jo had positively sworn was just on the point of getting its irrigation water. (And if it didn't get it, God! how he'd twist the old buzzard's tail for him!) 'Heart failure due to myocarditis of rheumatic origin.' He could have asked a lot more than two hundred thousand for that death-certificate. Particularly as it hadn't been his only service. No, sir! There had been all the mess to clear up. (The ninety-five-dollar fawn-coloured suit was ruined after all.) There had been the servants to keep away; the Baby to put to bed with a big shot of morphia; the permission to cremate the body to be obtained from the next of kin, who was a sister, living, thank God, in straitened circumstances, and at Pensacola, Florida, so that she fortunately couldn't afford to come out to California for the funeral. And then (most ticklish of all) there had been the search for a dishonest undertaker; the discovery of a possible crook; the interview, with its veiled hints of an unfortunate accident to be hushed up, of money that was, practically speaking, no object; then, when the fellow had fired off his sanctimonious little speech about its being a duty to help a leading citizen to avoid unpleasant publicity, the abrupt change of manner, the business-like statement of the unavoidable facts and the necessary fictions, the negotiations as to price. In the end, Mr. Pengo had agreed not to notice the holes in Pete's skull for as little as twenty-five thousand dollars.

'I had riches too gre-heat to cou-hount, could boast of a hi-yish ancestral name.' Yes, decidedly, Dr. Obispo reflected, as he sang, decidedly he could have asked for a great deal more. But what would have been the point? He was a reasonable man; almost, you might say, a philosopher; modest in his ambitions, uninterested in worldly success, and with tastes so simple that the most besetting of them, outside the sphere of scientific research, could be satisfied in the great majority of cases at practically no expense whatsoever, sometimes even with a net profit, as when Mrs. Bojanus had given him that solid gold cigarette-case as a token of her esteem—and then there were Josephine's pearl studs, and the green enamel cuff-links with his monogram in diamonds from little what's-her-name . . .

'But I a-halso drea-heamt which plea-heased me most,' he sang, raising his voice for this final affirmation and putting in a passionate tremolo, 'that you lo-hoved me sti-hill the same, that you lo-hoved me sti-hill the same, that you loved me,' he repeated, turning away for a moment from the Portsmouth road to peer with raised eyebrows and a look of amused, ironical enquiry into Virginia's averted face, 'you lo-hoved me sti-hill the same,' and, for the fourth time with tremendous emphasis and pathos, 'that you lo-ho-ho-hoved me sti-hi-hill the same.'

He shot another glance at Virginia. She was staring straight in front of her, holding her lower lip between her teeth, as though she were in pain but determined not to cry out.

'Did I dream correctly?' His smile was wolfish.

The Baby did not answer. From the back seat Mr. Stoyte snored like a bulldog.

'Do you lo-ho-hove sti-hi-hill the same?' he insisted, making the car swerve to the right as he spoke, and putting on speed to pass a row of Army lorries.

The Baby released her lip and said, 'I could kill you.'

'Of course you could,' Dr. Obispo agreed. 'But you won't. Because you lo-ho-ho-hove me too much. Or rather,' he added, and his smile became more gleefully canine with every word, 'you don't lo-ho-ho-hove *me*; you lo-ho-ho-hove . . .' he paused for an instant: 'Well, let's put it in a more poetical way—because one can never have too much poetry, don't you agree? you're in lo-ho-hove with Lo-ho-ho-hove, so much in lo-ho-ho-hove that, when it came to the point, you simply couldn't bring yourself to bump me off. Because, whatever you may feel about me, I'm the boy that produces the lo-ho-ho-hoves.' He began to sing again: 'I dre-heamt I kihilled the goo-hoo-hoo-hoose that laid-haid the go-holden e-he-heggs.'

Virginia covered her ears with her hands in an effort to shut out the sound of his voice—the hideous sound of the truth. Because, of course, it was true. Even after Pete's death, even after she had promised Our Lady that it would never, never happen again—well, it had happened again.

Dr. Obispo continued his improvisation. 'And that thu-hus I'd lo-host my so-hole excuse for showing the skin of my le-he-hegs.'

Virginia pressed her fingers more tightly over her ears. It had happened again, even though she'd said no, even though she'd got mad at him, fought with him, scratched him; but he'd only laughed and gone on; and then suddenly she was just too tired to fight any more. Too tired and too miserable. He got what he wanted; and the awful thing was that it seemed to be what she wanted —or, rather, what her unhappiness wanted; for the misery had been relieved for a time; she had been able to forget the blood; she had been able to sleep. The next morning she had despised and hated herself more than ever.

'I had grottoes and candles and doodahs galore,' Dr. Obispo sang on; then relapsed into speech; 'not to mention fetishes, relics, mantras, prayer-wheels, gibberish, vestments. But I also dreamt which pleased me most —or rather more, seeing that we have to rhyme with galore' (he opened his mouth and let out his richest and most tremulous notes), 'that you lo-hoved me sti-hill the same, that you lo-ho-ho-ho-ho-ho-ho-ho-ho-ho-ho-ho-ho-ho-hoved me . . .'

'Stop!' Virginia shouted at the top of her voice.

Uncle Jo woke up with a start. 'What's the matter?' he asked.

'She objects to my singing,' Dr. Obispo called back to him. 'Goodness knows why. I have a charming voice. Particularly well adapted to a small auditorium, like this car.' He laughed with whole-hearted merriment. The Baby's antics, as she vacillated between Priapus and the Sacred Grotto, gave him the most exquisite amusement. Along with the fine weather, the primroses in the cops and the prospect of learning something decisive about sterols and senility, they accounted for the ebullience of his good-humour.

It was about half-past eleven when they reached their destination. The lodge was untenanted; Dr. Obispo had to get out and open the gates himself.

Within, grass was growing over the drive and the park had sunk back towards the squalor of unmodified nature. Uprooted by past storms, dead trees lay rotting where they had fallen. On the boles of the living, great funguses grew like pale buns. The ornamental plantations had turned into little jungles, impenetrable with brambles. Perched on its knoll above the drive, the Grecian gazebo was in ruins. They rounded a curve, and there was the house, Jacobean at one end, with strange accretions of nineteenth-century Gothic at the other. The yew hedges had grown up into high walls of shaggy greenery. The position of what had once been formal flower-beds was marked by rich green circles of docks, oblongs and crescents of sow-thistles and nettles. From the tufted grass of a long untended lawn emerged the tops of rusty croquet hoops.

Dr. Obispo stopped the car at the foot of the front steps and got out. As he did so, a little girl, perhaps eight or nine years old, darted out of a tunnel in the yew hedge. At the sight of the car and its occupants the child halted, made a movement of retreat, then, reassured by a second glance, came forward.

'Look what I got,' she said in sub-standard Southern English, and held out, snout downwards, a gas-mask half filled with primroses and dog's-mercury.

Gleefully, Dr. Obispo laughed. 'The cops!' he cried. 'You picked them in the cops!' He patted the child's tow-coloured head. 'What's your name?'

'Millie,' the little girl answered; and then added, with a note of pride in her voice: 'I 'aven't been somewhere for five days now.'

'Five days?'

Millie nodded triumphantly. 'Granny says she'll 'ave to take me to the doctor.' She nodded again, and smiled up at him with the expression of one who has just announced his forthcoming trip to Bali.

'Well, I think your Granny's entirely right,' said Dr. Obispo. 'Does your Granny live here?'

The child nodded affirmatively. 'She's in the kitchen,' she answered; and added irrelevantly, 'she's deaf.'

'And what about Lady Jane Hauberk?' Dr. Obispo went on. 'Does *she* live here? And the other one— Lady Anne, isn't that it?'

Again the child nodded. Then an expression of sly mischief appeared on her face. 'Do you know what Lady Anne does?' she asked.

'What does she do?'

Millie beckoned to him to bend down so that she could put her mouth to his ear. 'She makes noises in 'er stomick,' she whispered.

'You don't say so!'

'Like birds singing,' the child added poetically. 'She does it after lunch.'

Dr. Obispo patted the tow-coloured head again and said, 'We'd like to see Lady Anne and Lady Jane.'

'See them?' the little girl repeated in a tone almost of alarm.

'Do you think you could go and ask your Granny to show us in?'

Millie shook her head. 'She wouldn't do it. Granny won't let nobody come in. Some people came about these things.' She held up the gas-mask. 'Lady Jane, she got so angry I was frightened. But then she broke one of the lamps with her stick—you know, by mistake: bang! and the glass was all in bits, all over the floor. That made me laugh.'

'Good for you,' said Dr. Obispo. 'Why shouldn't we make you laugh again?'

The child looked at him suspiciously. 'What do you mean?'

Dr. Obispo assumed a conspiratorial expression and dropped his voice to a whisper. 'I mean, you might let us in by one of the side-doors, and we'd all walk on tip-toes, like this'; he gave a demonstration across the gravel. 'And then we'd pop into the room where they're sitting and give them a surprise. And then maybe Lady Jane will smash another lamp, and we'll all laugh and laugh and laugh. What do you say to that?'

'Granny'd be awfully cross,' the child said dubiously.

'We won't tell her you did it.'

'She'd find out.'

'No, she wouldn't,' said Dr. Obispo confidently. Then changing his tone, 'Do you like candies?' he added.

The child looked at him blankly.

'Lovely candies?' he repeated voluptuously; then suddenly remembered that, in this damned country, candies weren't called candies. What the hell did they call them? He remembered. 'Lovely sweets!' He darted back to the car and returned with the expensive-looking box of chocolates that had been bought in case Virginia should feel hungry by the way. He opened the lid, let the child take one sniff, then closed it again. 'Let us in,' he said, 'and you can have them all.'

Five minutes later they were squeezing their way through an ogival french window at the nineteenth-century end of the house. Within, there was a twilight that smelt of dust and dry-rot and moth-balls. Gradually, as the eyes became accustomed to the gloom, a draped billiard-table emerged into view, a mantelpiece with a gilt clock, a bookshelf containing the Waverley Novels in crimson leather, and the eighth edition of the *Encyclopaedia Britannica*, a large brown painting representing the baptism of the future Edward VII, the heads of five or six stags. Hanging on the wall near the door was a map of the Crimea; little flags on pins marked the position of Sevastopol and the Alma.

Still carrying the flower-filled gas-mask in one hand, and with the forefinger of the other pressed to her lips, Millie led the way on tiptoes along a corridor, across a darkened drawing-room, through a lobby, down another passage. Then she halted and, waiting for Dr. Obispo to come up with her, pointed.

'That's the door,' she whispered. 'They're in there.'

Without a word, Dr. Obispo handed her the box of chocolates; the child snatched it and, like an animal with a stolen tit-bit, slipped past Virginia and Mr. Stoyte, and hurried away down the dark passage to enjoy her prize in safety. Dr. Obispo watched her go, then turned to his companions.

There was a whispered consultation, and in the end it was agreed that Dr. Obispo should go on alone.

He walked forward, quietly opened the door, slipped through and closed it behind him.

Outside, in the corridor, the Baby and Uncle Jo waited for what seemed to them hours. Then, all at once, there was a crescendo of confused noise which culminated in the sudden emergence of Dr. Obispo. He slammed the door, pushed a key into the lock and turned it.

An instant later, from within, the door-handle was violently rattled, a shrill old voice cried, 'How dare you?' Then an ebony cane delivered a series of peremptory raps and the voice almost screamed, 'Give me back those keys. Give them back at once.'

Dr. Obispo put the key of the door in his pocket and came down the corridor, beaming with satisfaction.

'The two god-damnest-looking old hags you ever saw,' he said. 'One on each side of the fire, like Queen Victoria and Queen Victoria.'

A second voice joined the first; the rattling and the rapping were redoubled.

'Bang away!' Dr. Obispo shouted derisively; then, pushing Mr. Stoyte with one hand and with the other giving the Baby a familiar little slap on the buttocks, 'Come on,' he said. 'Come on.'

'Come on where?' Mr. Stoyte asked in a tone of resentful bewilderment. He'd never been able to figure out what this damn fool expedition across the Atlantic was for—except, of course, to get away from the castle. Oh, yes, they'd had to get away from the castle. No question about that; in fact, the only question was whether they'd ever be able to go back to it, after what happened—whether they'd ever be able to bathe in that pool again, for example. Christ! when he thought of it . . .

But, then, why go to England? At this season? Why not Florida or Hawaii? But no; Obispo had insisted it must be England. Because of his work, because there might be something important to be found out there. Well, he couldn't say no to Obispo—not now, not yet. And besides, he couldn't do without the man. His nerves, his digestion—all shot to pieces. And he couldn't sleep without dope; he couldn't pass a cop on the street without his heart missing a beat or two. And you could say, 'God is love. There is no death,' till you were blue in the face; but it didn't make any difference. He was old, he was sick; death was coming closer and closer, and unless Obispo did something quick, unless he found out something soon . . .

In the dim corridor Mr. Stoyte suddenly halted. 'Obispo,' he said anxiously, while the Hauberk ladies hammered with ebony on the door of their prison, 'Obispo, are you absolutely certain there's no such thing as hell ? Can you prove it ?'

Dr. Obispo laughed. 'Can you prove that the back side of the moon isn't inhabited by green elephants ?' he asked.

'No, but seriously . . .' Mr. Stoyte insisted, in anguish.

'Seriously,' Dr. Obispo gaily answered, 'I can't prove anything about any assertion that can't be verified.' Mr. Stoyte and he had had this sort of conversation before. There was something, to his mind, exquisitely comic about chopping logic with the old man's unreasoning terror.

The Baby listened in silence. She *knew* about hell; she *knew* what happened if you committed mortal sins— sins like letting it happen again, after you'd promised Our Lady that it wouldn't. But Our Lady was so kind and so wonderful. And, after all, it had really been all that beast Sig's fault. Her own intentions had been absolutely pure; and then Sig had come along and just made her break her word. Our Lady would understand. The awful thing was that it had happened again, when he hadn't forced her. But even then it hadn't *really* been her fault—because, after all, she'd been through that terrible experience; she wasn't well; she . . .

'But do you think hell's possible?' Mr. Stoyte began again.

'Everything is possible,' said Dr. Obispo cheerfully. He cocked an ear to listen to what the old hags were yelling back there behind the door.

'Do you think there's one chance in a thousand it may be true? Or one in a million?'

Grinning, Dr. Obispo shrugged his shoulders. Ask Pascal,' he suggested.

'Who's Pascal?' Mr. Stoyte enquired, clutching despairingly at any and every straw.

'He's dead,' Dr. Obispo positively shouted in his glee. 'Dead as a door-nail. And now, for God's sake!' He seized Uncle Jo by the arm and fairly dragged him along the passage.

The terrible word reverberated through Mr. Stoyte's imagination. 'But I want to be certain,' he protested.

'Certain about what you can't know!'

'There *must* be a way.'

'There isn't. No way except dying and then seeing what happens. Where the hell is that child?' he added in another tone, and called, 'Millie!'

Her face smeared with chocolate, the little girl popped up from behind an umbrella-stand in the lobby. 'Did you see 'em?' she asked with her mouth full.

Dr. Obispo nodded. 'They thought I was the Air Raid Precautions.'

'That's it!' the child cried excitedly. 'That was the one that made her break the lamp.'

'Come here, Millie,' Dr. Obispo commanded. The child came. 'Where's the door to the cellar?'

An expression of fear passed over Millie's face. 'It's locked,' she answered.

Dr. Obispo nodded. 'I know it,' he said. 'But Lady Jane gave me the keys.' He pulled out of his pocket a ring on which were suspended three large keys.

'There's bogies down there,' the child whispered.

'We don't worry about bogies.'

'Granny says they're awful,' Millie went on. 'She says they're something chronic.' Her voice broke into a whimper. 'She says if I don't go somewhere more regular-like, the bogies will come after me. But I can't 'elp it.' The tears began to flow. 'It isn't my fault.'

'Of course it isn't,' said Dr. Obispo impatiently. 'Nothing is ever anybody's fault. Even constipation. But now I want you to show us the door of the cellar.'

Still in tears, Millie shook her head. 'I'm frightened.'

'But you won't have to go down into the cellar. Just show us where the door is, that's all.'

'I don't want to.'

'Won't you be a nice little girl,' Dr. Obispo wheedled, 'and take us to the door?'

Stubborn with fear, Millie continued to shake her head.

Dr. Obispo's hand shot out and snatched the box of chocolates out of the child's grasp. 'If you don't tell me, you won't have any candies,' he said, and added irritably, 'sweets, I mean.'

Millie let out a scream of anguish and tried to get back at the box; but he held it high up, beyond her reach. 'Only when you show us the door of the cellar,' he said; and, to show that he was in earnest, he opened the box, took a handful of chocolates and popped them one after another into his mouth. 'Aren't they good!' he said as he munched. 'Aren't they just wonderful! Do you know, I'm glad you won't show us the door, because then I can eat them all.' He took another bite, made a grimace of ecstasy. 'Ooh, goody, goody!' He smacked his lips. 'Poor little Millie! She isn't going to get any more of them.' He helped himself again.

'Oh, don't, don't!' the child entreated each time she saw one of the brown nuggets of bliss disappearing between Dr. Obispo's jaws. Then a moment came when greed was stronger than fear. 'I'll show you where it is,' she screamed, like a victim succumbing to torture and promising to confess.

The effect was magical. Dr. Obispo replaced in the box the three chocolates he was still holding and closed the lid. 'Come on,' he said, and held out his hand for the child to take.

'Give me the box,' she demanded.

Dr. Obispo, who understood the principles of diplomacy, shook his head. 'Not till you've taken us to the door,' he said.

Millie hesitated for a moment; then, resigned to the hard necessity of keeping to her side of the bargain, took his hand.

Followed by Uncle Jo and the Baby, they made their way out of the lobby, back through the drawing-room, along the passage, past the map of the Crimea and across the billiard-room, along another passage and into a large library. The red plush curtains were drawn; but a little light filtered between them. All round the room the brown and blue and crimson strata of classic literature ran up to within three feet of the high ceiling, and at regular intervals along the mahogany cornice stood busts of the illustrious dead. Millie pointed to Dante. 'That's Lady Jane,' she whispered confidentially.

'For Christ's sake!' Mr. Stoyte broke out startlingly.

'What's the big idea? What the hell do you figure we're doing?'

Dr. Obispo ignored him. 'Where's the door?' he asked.

The child pointed.

'What do you mean?' he started angrily to shout. Then he saw that what he had taken for just another section of the book-filled shelves was in fact a mere false front of wood and leather simulating thirty-three volumes of the Collected Sermons of Archbishop Stilling-fleet and (he recognized the Fifth Earl's touch) the Complete Works, in seventy-seven volumes, of Donatien Alphonse François, Marquis de Sade. A keyhole revealed itself to a closer scrutiny.

'Give me my sweets,' the child demanded.

But Dr. Obispo was taking no risks. 'Not till we see if the key fits.'

He tried and, at the second attempt, succeeded. 'There you are.' He handed Millie her chocolates and at the same time opened the door. The child uttered a scream of terror and rushed away.

'What's the big idea?' Mr. Stoyte repeated uneasily.

'The big idea,' said Dr. Obispo, as he looked down the flight of steps that descended, after a few feet, into an impenetrable darkness, 'the big idea is that you may not have to find out whether there's such a place as hell. Not yet awhile, that's to say; not for a very long time maybe. Ah, thank God!' he added. 'We shall have some light.'

Two old-fashioned bull's-eye lanterns were standing on a shelf just inside the door. Dr. Obispo picked one of them up, shook it, held it to his nose. There was oil in it. He lit them both, handed one to Mr. Stoyte and, taking the other himself, led the way cautiously down the stairs.

A long descent; then a circular chamber cut out of the

yellow sandstone. There were four doorways. They chose one of them and passed, along a narrow corridor, into a second chamber with two more doorways. A blind alley first; then another flight of steps leading to a cave full of ancient refuse. There was no second issue; laboriously, with two wrong turnings on the way, they retraced their steps to the circular chamber from which they had started, and made trial of its second doorway. A flight of descending steps; a succession of small rooms. One of these had been plastered, and upon its walls early eighteenth-century hands had scratched obscene *graffiti*. They hurried on, down another short flight of steps, into a large square room with an air-shaft leading at an angle through the rock to a tiny, far-away ellipse of white light. That was all. They turned back again. Mr. Stoyte began to swear; but the doctor insisted on going on. They tried the third doorway. A passage, a suite of three rooms. Two outlets from the last, one mounting, but walled up with masonry after a little way; the other descending to a corridor on a lower level. Thirty or forty feet brought them to an opening on the left. Dr. Obispo turned his lantern into it, and the light revealed a vaulted recess, at the end of which, on a stuccoed pedestal, stood a replica in marble of the Medici Venus.

'Well, I'm damned!' said Mr. Stoyte, and then, on second thoughts, was seized with a kind of panic. 'How the hell did *that* get here, Obispo?' he said, running to catch up the doctor.

Dr. Obispo did not answer, but hurried impatiently forward.

'It's crazy,' Mr. Stoyte went on apprehensively, as he trotted behind the doctor. 'It's downright crazy. I tell you, I don't like it.'

Dr. Obispo broke his silence. 'We might see if we can

get her for the Beverly Pantheon,' he said with a wolfish joviality. 'Hullo, what's this?' he added.

They emerged from the tunnel into a fair-sized room. At the centre of the room was a circular drum of masonry, with two iron uprights rising from either side of it, and a cross-piece, from which hung a pulley.

'The well!' said Dr. Obispo, remembering a passage in the Fifth Earl's notebook.

He almost ran towards the tunnel on the further side of the room. Ten feet from the entrance, his progress was barred by a heavy, nail-studded oak door. Dr. Obispo took out his bunch of keys, chose at random and opened the door at the first trial. They were on the threshold of a small oblong chamber. His bull's-eye revealed a second door on the opposite wall. He started at once towards it.

'Canned beef!' said Mr. Stoyte in astonishment, as he ran the beam of his lantern over the rows of tins and jars on the shelves of a tall dresser that occupied almost the whole of one of the sides of the room. 'Biloxi Shrimps. Sliced Pineapple. Boston Baked Beans,' he read out, then turned towards Dr. Obispo. 'I tell you, Obispo, I don't like it.'

The Baby had taken out a handkerchief saturated in 'Shocking' and was holding it to her nose. 'The smell!' she said indistinctly through its folds, and shuddered with disgust. 'The smell!'

Dr. Obispo, meanwhile, was trying his keys on the lock of the other door. It opened at last. A draught of warm air flowed in, and at once the little room was filled with an intolerable stench. 'Christ!' said Mr. Stoyte, and behind her handkerchief the Baby let out a scream of nauseated horror.

Dr. Obispo made a grimace and advanced along the

stream of foul air. At the end of a short corridor was a third door, of iron bars this time, like the door (Dr. Obispo reflected) of a death-cell in a prison. He flashed his lantern between the bars, into the foetid darkness beyond.

From the little room Mr. Stoyte and the Baby suddenly heard an astonished exclamation and then, after a moment's silence, a violent, explosive guffaw, succeeded by peal after peal of Dr. Obispo's ferocious, metallic laughter. Paroxysm upon uncontrollable paroxysm, the noise reverberated back and forth in the confined space. The hot, stinking air vibrated with a deafening and almost maniacal merriment.

Followed by Virginia, Mr. Stoyte crossed the room and hastened through the open door into the narrow tunnel beyond. Dr. Obispo's laughter was getting on his nerves. 'What the hell . . . ?' he shouted angrily as he advanced; then broke off in the middle of the sentence. 'What's that?' he whispered.

'A foetal ape,' Dr. Obispo began; but was cut short by another explosion of hilarity, that doubled him up as though with a blow in the solar plexus.

'Holy Mary,' the Baby began behind her handkerchief.

Beyond the bars, the light of the lanterns had scooped out of the darkness a narrow world of forms and colours. On the edge of a low bed, at the centre of this world, a man was sitting, staring, as though fascinated, into the light. His legs, thickly covered with coarse reddish hair, were bare. The shirt, which was his only garment, was torn and filthy. Knotted diagonally across the powerful chest was a broad silk ribbon that had evidently once been blue. From a piece of string tied round his neck was suspended a little image of St. George and the Dragon

in gold and enamel. He sat hunched up, his head thrust
forward and at the same time sunk between his shoulders.
With one of his huge and strangely clumsy hands he was
scratching a sore place that showed red between the hairs
of his left calf.

'A foetal ape that's had time to grow up,' Dr. Obispo
managed at last to say. 'It's *too* good!' Laughter over-
took him again. 'Just look at his face!' he gasped, and
pointed through the bars. Above the matted hair that
concealed the jaws and cheeks, blue eyes stared out of
cavernous sockets. There were no eyebrows; but under
the dirty, wrinkled skin of the forehead a great ridge of
bone projected like a shelf.

Suddenly, out of the black darkness, another simian
face emerged into the beam of the lantern—a face only
lightly hairy, so that it was possible to see, not only the
ridge above the eyes, but also the curious distortions of the
lower jaws, the accretions of bone in front of the ears.
Clothed in an old check ulster and some glass beads, a
body followed the face into the light.

'It's a woman,' said Virginia, almost sick with the
horrified disgust she felt at the sight of those pendulous
and withered dugs.

The doctor exploded into even noisier merriment.

Mr. Stoyte seized him by the shoulder and violently
shook him. 'Who are they?' he demanded.

Dr. Obispo wiped his eyes and drew a deep breath;
the storm of his laughter was flattened to a heaving calm.
As he opened his mouth to answer Mr. Stoyte's question,
the creature in the shirt suddenly turned upon the creature
in the ulster and hit out at her head. The palm of the
enormous hand struck the side of the face. The creature
in the ulster uttered a scream of pain and rage, and shrank
back out of the light. From the shadow came a shrill,

furious gibbering that seemed perpetually to tremble on the verge of articulate blasphemy.

'The one with the Order of the Garter,' said Dr. Obispo, raising his voice against the tumult, 'he's the Fifth Earl of Gonister. The other's his housekeeper.'

'But what's happened to them ?'

'Just time,' said Dr. Obispo airily.

'Time ?'

'I don't know how old the female is,' Dr. Obispo went on. 'But the Earl there—let me see, he was two hundred and one last January.'

From the shadows the shrill voice continued to scream its all but articulate abuse. Impassibly the Fifth Earl scratched the sore on his leg and stared at the light.

Dr. Obispo went on talking. Slowing up of development rates . . . one of the mechanisms of evolution . . . the older an anthropoid, the stupider . . . senility and sterol poisoning . . . the intestinal flora of the carp . . . the Fifth Earl had anticipated his own discovery . . . no sterol poisoning, no senility . . . no death, perhaps, except through an accident . . . but meanwhile the foetal anthropoid was able to come to maturity . . . It was the finest joke he had ever known.

Without moving from where he was sitting, the Fifth Earl urinated on the floor. A shriller chattering arose from the darkness. He turned in the direction from which it came and bellowed the guttural distortions of almost forgotten obscenities.

'No need of any further experiment,' Dr. Obispo was saying. 'We know it works. You can start taking the stuff at once. At once,' he repeated with sarcastic emphasis.

Mr. Stoyte said nothing.

On the other side of the bars, the Fifth Earl rose to his

feet, stretched, scratched, yawned, then turned and took a couple of steps towards the boundary that separated the light from the darkness. His housekeeper's chattering became more agitated and rapid. Affecting to pay no attention, the Earl halted, smoothed the broad ribbon of his order with the palm of his hand, then fingered the jewel at his neck, making as he did so a curious humming noise that was like a simian memory of the serenade in *Don Giovanni*. The creature in the ulster whimpered apprehensively, and her voice seemed to retreat further into the shadows. Suddenly, with a ferocious yell, the Fifth Earl sprang forward, out of the narrow universe of lantern light into the darkness beyond. There was a rush of footsteps, a succession of yelps; then a scream and the sound of blows and more screams; then no more screams, but only a stertorous growling in the dark and little cries.

Mr. Stoyte broke the silence. 'How long do you figure it would take before a person went like that?' he said in a slow, hesitating voice. 'I mean, it wouldn't happen at once . . . there'd be a long time while a person . . . well, you know; while he wouldn't change any. And once you get over the first shock—well, they look like they were having a pretty good time. I mean in their own way, of course. Don't you think so, Obispo?' he insisted.

Dr. Obispo went on looking at him in silence; then threw back his head and started to laugh again.

THE HISTORY OF VINTAGE

The famous American publisher Alfred A. Knopf (1892–1984) founded Vintage Books in the United States in 1954 as a paperback home for the authors published by his company. Vintage was launched in the United Kingdom in 1990 and works independently from the American imprint although both are part of the international publishing group, Random House.

Vintage in the United Kingdom was initially created to publish paperback editions of books bought by the prestigious literary hardback imprints in the Random House Group such as Jonathan Cape, Chatto & Windus, Hutchinson and later William Heinemann, Secker & Warburg and The Harvill Press. There are many Booker and Nobel Prize-winning authors on the Vintage list and the imprint publishes a huge variety of fiction and non-fiction. Over the years Vintage has expanded and the list now includes great authors of the past – who are published under the Vintage Classics imprint – as well as many of the most influential authors of the present. In 2012 Vintage Children's Classics was launched to include the much-loved authors of our youth.

For a full list of the books Vintage publishes, please visit our website
www.vintage-books.co.uk

For book details and other information about the classic authors we publish, please visit the Vintage Classics website
www.vintage-classics.info

www.vintage-classics.info

Visit www.worldofstories.co.uk for all your
favourite children's classics